1984

THE FALL OF A TITAN

THE FALL

OF A

TITAN

IGOR GOUZENKO

Translated from the Russian by Mervyn Black

NEW YORK

W·W·NORTON & COMPANY·INC·

CONTENTS

▼

CONTENTS

BOOK I

PART ONE

CHAPTER 1

AT LAST they met. First a woman with a child in her arms interrupted them. She sat down on the bench where Drozd was waiting for Professor Feodor Novikov. Drozd rose from the bench, covertly giving Novikov a signal to follow him. Then two young students from Rostov University caught sight of the professor and engaged him in conversation. Drozd waited for him patiently at some distance, pretending to read a paper until the professor was able to get rid of the students.

Eventually they left and Novikov followed Drozd in the direction of the river Don, trying not to lose sight of him. Drozd led the way beyond the wharves and came out at Nakhichevan on the outskirts of Rostov, continuing along the lonely shore where only seagulls could see them. When he came to a shallow gully, well screened by bushes, Drozd signaled the professor to come up.

"The place selected was most unsuitable," he said with a trace of annoyance.

"Yes, that's true. Too many people know me there," agreed Novikov as he studied Drozd's face. It was just as he had expected—dry, serious, without any trace of humor, except, perhaps, for the slightly sarcastic set of the strong, sharply carved lips.

Drozd was middle-aged, with hair graying at the temples, and his fairly full face just missed being fleshy. He was of medium height. His manner was tense; his greenish eyes looked hard and sullenly calm. Like all people who worked in the Party or Government departments he affected a semimilitary style of dress: a light green shirt with pockets and a turned-down collar, a leather military belt girding his waist. The ends of his breeches were tucked into the tops of highly polished boots. He could be placed as a Party worker of average rank. But to the expression of official hardness on his face, which is peculiar to such people, was also added an aura of power—not the ordinary kind. One felt that this man was used to giving orders and did not like arguments.

Without wasting any time Drozd came at once to the reason for summoning Professor Novikov to this secret meeting. "I came here straight from the station. There is just one man besides yourself whom I intend to see here. After that I shall return tomorrow to Moscow. What we are about to discuss now will be known only to you and to me. Do you understand?"

Novikov nodded. He noticed that Drozd spoke with the precise, clipped phrases of a military officer. He kept both hands on his belt and did not gesticulate when he was talking.

Taking a silver cigarette case from his pocket, he offered it to Novikov. "Do you smoke?" Novikov took a cigarette and noticed with annoyance that his fingers were trembling a little. "Take more," invited Drozd. "These are Moscow cigarettes. You won't get any like that here."

Novikov took several, put all but one in his pocket, and thanked Drozd. From the avidity with which Novikov inhaled Drozd guessed at the man's inner emotion. Now the calm face which Novikov had tried to preserve did not appear so placid.

Lighting a cigarette, Drozd continued: "Your work will be exceptionally complicated and responsible. I know that you are not a greenhorn and that you have worked with us before. But what you have done so far was child's play compared to this task. You will be dealing with no ordinary man."

"Who is this man?" asked Novikov.

"The writer Mikhail Gorin," replied Drozd, watching with interest the effect this name produced on Novikov.

"The writer Mikhail Gorin! What has happened to Gorin?" Novikov exclaimed in amazement. He knew from experience that if he, Novikov, was needed, something must have happened to Gorin. He was genuinely surprised. The great Russian writer, whom the Party called the father of Soviet literature, whose works had been translated into all the languages of the world! A whole generation of revolutionaries in Russia and abroad had been brought up on his books. Everybody knew that he was a great friend of Lenin, and then Stalin—at least all the

4

Soviet almanacs described him as such. Impossible! This was probably some kind of joke.

But the expression on Drozd's face showed clearly that he was not joking. "It has become known to the Politburo that Gorin is on the point of blowing up. From the time that the Party decided to adopt harsh measures in putting through collectivization, Gorin has on several occasions expressed his displeasure and even indignation among his close friends. The Party can't disregard incidents of that kind. It's one thing for the small fry to try to make a noise—they can be kept quiet; but when a titan like Gorin makes a noise, the Government must take notice and do something about it.

"In short, the Politburo wants to see Gorin on its side—where he has been up to now. During these strained times his voice, supporting the policy of the Party, is of exceptional value not only inside the country but abroad as well. Gorin is well known for his humanitarianism. We need the word of a humanitarian now as much as we need air. There is your task—to make him speak this word!" Drozd gave the last phrase special emphasis, as though it were not his own but that of some very highly placed person. Novikov actually trembled from the unexpectedness of it all.

"How can you be sure that I will be able to cope with such a task?" he cried in great agitation. "Why! it's hard even to say such a thing—to *make* Gorin speak! To *change* Gorin!"

Drozd looked at him quietly for a minute, then said: "It is our opinion that no one but you can accomplish this task."

This was said forcibly: too forcibly for Novikov.

"But I'm not even acquainted with Gorin," he protested.

"Therein lies your greatest advantage. A new man—new ideas. Old acquaintances would be useless for our purpose."

When Novikov seemed about to offer some other objection Drozd added quickly: "I know, I know. You wonder how you are to become acquainted with Gorin. That has already been arranged. One of Gorin's friends is also our good friend." Here Drozd smirked. "He will introduce you into Gorin's house. From that moment you will have to use your own judgment."

Novikov turned toward the river as though he wished to tear himself away from the persistent gaze of Drozd, which prevented him from thinking independently.

While Novikov sought counsel in the boundless expanse of the Don, Drozd studied him with a sidewise glance. He saw a man somewhat taller than himself and younger. Drozd knew that Novikov was only thirty. Rather thin of face, he was well built, with broad shoulders; and his thinness of face, with the skin drawn tightly over his prominent cheek bones, was not unhealthy; on the contrary it gave him a strong, energetic look. His light flaxen hair, long and thick, lay gracefully over the broad skull. The wide straight mouth gave to his rather large face a pleasant and kind expression. But the main thing that struck Drozd was the high forehead and below it the deeply set steel-gray eyes. They sparkled with intelligence. Their gaze was steady, direct, and honest.

"This one will do," thought Drozd, convinced of the wisdom of the choice. "The fellow is clever, but modest. Daring, but not rash. He is just the kind to make a success of it."

As if answering his thoughts, Novikov said: "All right! I will do my best, but I do not guarantee success."

Thereupon Drozd spoke slowly and impressively: "It must be a success. It will be better for you that way. Remember that the Polit-buro, and Comrade Stalin personally, expect success. This is a doubly secret Government task." And already smiling, he added: "If you are successful I will envy you."

"And if I fail?" Novikov wanted to ask, but refrained. He knew the answer himself.

CHAPTER 2

THIS WAS a hard time for the Russian people. Against their wishes Stalin was imposing collectivization on the country. The horror, the sorrow, the humiliation for millions of peasants and workers which this policy wrought exceeded in awfulness all the calamities that history had ever seen. This period will remain everlastingly the darkest blot on the human conscience. For millions of wholly innocent persons this policy meant death from starvation, the firing squad, torture, and exile to concentration camps.

During this time, on the orders of the Soviet Government, the new Soviet intelligentsia was diligently engaged in painting these hideous crimes in rainbow colors. All kinds of justification were put forward for the cruelties perpetrated. In the name of the peasants and workers, bloated from hunger, words of gratitude were written to Stalin for his supposed care for their welfare.

In this mad rush of servility, fawning and dancing under the whip of the Government, one voice was conspicuously absent—the voice of

6

the writer Mikhail Gorin. His silence reduced the whole value of the thousand-voice chorus of the other writers.

Gorin occupied a special position among Soviet writers. Unlike them he owed the Soviet Government nothing for his success. On the contrary, the Soviet Government was very much in his debt. Gorin earned his reputation as a great writer before the revolution. Lenin considered it an honor to be counted as one of his friends. Stalin, following his example, did everything possible to spread the impression that he also was a friend of Gorin. His meetings with Gorin were photographed and publicized by the Soviet propaganda machine as evidence of their close friendship. When the masters of propaganda ran out of photographs all kinds of pictures were drawn and painted showing Stalin and Gorin together, invariably shaking hands, invariably looking trustfully into each other's eyes. The painting by the artist Pcholin —"Comrades Stalin and Voroshilov listening to Gorin reading one of his poems"—seemed to be particularly valuable. By special order of Stalin it was hung in the Tretyakov Gallery, while reproductions of it were distributed all over the country by the millions.

It was not difficult to understand why all this was done. The name of Gorin had become the symbol of humanism. To the tyrant Stalin the friendship of the humanist Gorin was as necessary as rouge to an ugly woman.

Until recently Gorin had not shunned Stalin's friendship. He sincerely believed that Stalin was doing everything for the best. Such information as reached his ears concerning brutalities or injustices he brushed aside as the panicky outcry of the frightened intellectuals who were blind to the great historical transformation, and were incapable of looking at things objectively. Stalin did everything in his power to encourage that idea.

There came a time, for instance, when Gorin expressed the desire to visit one of the concentration camps. He was tired of listening to rumors about monstrous brutalities: he wished to investigate these rumors himself. With Stalin's personal permission it was arranged that Gorin should visit one of the camps in the north, where the White Sea canal was being built.

The entrance to the camp was decorated with fresh fir branches and placards, the largest of which bore one of Gorin's famous sayings: "There is nothing on earth more precious than man."

The paths and roads in the camp had been spread with fresh sand, the barrack huts whitewashed and painted. Going into the first barrack, Gorin and the people accompanying him, including Voroshilov, saw a number of surprisingly well-fed, contented-looking men sitting around a table playing chess or reading books. So gullible was Gorin that it did not surprise him to see that the clothes worn by the "convicts" were spotlessly clean, nor that the books looked as if they had been purchased the day before.

In honor of the important guests the "convicts" put on a concert, which wound up with a general dance. An excellent male chorus sang Gorin's favorite song—"The Volga Boatmen." The organizers of this farce were so carried away that they wanted to make Gorin "an honorary convict," but Voroshilov dampened their enthusiasm in time.

Gorin was thoroughly taken in. On his return from the canal he wrote an article about the great educational role of the labor camps and earned Stalin's personal gratitude for this.

But something must have happened, and Gorin began to see things more clearly. Now his objective point of view did not seem to him to be so objective. Either he had to forget everything he had written before the revolution, or he had to make a revaluation of it.

But to forget was impossible. That would mean to forget his very being. A revaluation? His conscience protested against that. He was proud of his fame: Mikhail Gorin—great humanitarian, fighter against baseness, meanness, brutality, all that was dark and evil in life. To be unfaithful to his fame—that he could not do.

And so he pondered—and remained silent. The truth, as it was unveiled before his eyes, was too terrible. It stupefied him, fettered his will. He—a fearless man before the revolution, flinging out proud words about freedom, about human dignity—now failed to find within himself the strength to throw the accusing words again in the face of the tyrant, to protest. He could only remain silent.

And this, in the eyes of the Politburo, was in itself a crime. They needed his voice, his authority. The people must see that the great writer was supporting Stalin and the Politburo. To them Gorin's silence had become blasphemy, brazen defiance, insolent revolt. On Stalin's instructions the Politburo made a decision: to look into the matter, to correct the situation, to take measures—Gorin must be placed in the general chorus of the praisers of the Soviet regime.

But how to do that? How to control the soul and will of that man? The point was that Gorin was a man and not a slave. But it was not the first time that the Politburo had run up against the problem of turning a man into a slave. The branch of science that deals with such problems had reached a high state of efficiency; the use of it had become a fine art. The most able, the most experienced people were engaged in it.

Thus, at Stalin's nod, Drozd and Novikov appear on the scene.

With cold calculation, like surgeons undertaking a complicated operation, they weigh their chances of success, select the means for accomplishing their task. Like good surgeons they have a wealth of experience to draw upon, a thorough knowledge of their business—to them the deeper secrets of their profession are well known. They are proud of their trade. There are no doubts in their hearts, their hands never waver. They are overflowing with the desire to perform their task well, to justify the trust of their all-powerful master.

Their patient knows nothing of this, he suspects nothing. He suffers, is racked by doubts and keeps silent. Meanwhile the cold fingers of the surgeons are ready to touch his ailing soul. . . .

CHAPTER 3

THEY HAD been talking for over an hour. The sun, rising above the river, was gathering strength. A slight breeze ruffled the surface of the water and the broad expanse of the Don burned with a blinding glitter. Tender light clouds, like swansdown, floated in the pale blue sky. All was silent. Only the dull noise of the far-off city was borne to them in an uneven rumble.

Drozd sat with his back against the trunk of a tree. Novikov, on a stone beside it, was drawing patterns in the sand with the toe of his shoe while he listened to him. Now that the main points had been settled and they had agreed on everything, Drozd became more approachable, less official. He was relaxing.

"Well," he said, "I imagine that is all we have to discuss. Today, at his apartment, you will meet the man who will introduce you to Gorin. His name is Glushak, Academician Pyotr Glushak. I have given you his address. As I have already told you, do not discuss your task with him. He has been told nothing about this affair. His role is ended when he introduces you to Gorin. . . . Now, is there anything else? Oh, yes. Gorin does not like people with obtrusive manners. So you must take that into account. Well, that seems to be all."

Novikov was silent. He was thinking how nice it would be to bathe in the river and to forget, even for a minute, this entire conversation,

9

this whole burden so suddenly dropped in his lap. He recalled his childhood, how he used to go to the river and spend whole days there. That was a happy time! There was no Drozd, no worry, no responsibility. Everything was gay and bright, like the Don just now.

It seemed almost as though Drozd were reading his thoughts, for he said: "It's as hot as hell. How about a swim in the river to cool off a bit? Some questions may come to your mind while you're in the water."

Without waiting for Novikov's answer he began to pull off his boots. Novikov followed his example. They stripped to the skin. Naked, Drozd did not appear so well built as when he was dressed. His stomach stuck out a little.

He ran down the bank and threw himself into the water, squealing like a boy. A flock of seagulls flew into the air. Novikov laughed and ran into the water after him.

Finishing their swim, they lay around lazily on the warm sand, talking idly.

"How do you live?" asked Drozd.

"Not badly," Feodor replied evasively.

Drozd noted the evasion and commented in a conciliatory voice: "Yes, times are pretty hard right now. The collectivization is just like a second revolution: one can't avoid sacrifices. But that will pass. The food situation here must be pretty bad? Eh?"

"Yes," Feodor nodded. "It's bad. People are dying from hunger."

"That's all right. There'll be plenty left for breeding."

Novikov said nothing.

"How are you getting along at the University?" asked Drozd. "I heard that you have become famous through your work on the ancient Slavs."

"Oh, I don't think that I merit such praise," Feodor remarked humbly. However, he was pleased that Drozd knew of his success and had mentioned it.

After they had talked in this aimless fashion for about half an hour, they dressed.

"I think it better that we part now." Drozd extended his hand to Feodor. "I wish you success."

Drozd's hand was plump and strong. Novikov suddenly became aware of his fast-beating heart. Only then did he feel the full force of the responsible, serious, and difficult task ahead of him.

He waited until Drozd had gone some distance and was hidden from view by a clump of low bushes; then, slowly, he set off in the direction of the town.

CHAPTER 4

ALTHOUGH NOVIKOV had a long way to go he did not want to take a street car. He was loath to ride with the crowds of jostling, hungry, and irritable people, to breathe the sweaty odor of dirty human bodies after his swim in the clear waters of the Don. Besides, he wanted to think over everything that had happened this morning. It seemed to him that it was best to do this during a long walk. So instead of turning toward Nakhichevan and taking a street car, he walked along the bank of the river. There were no wharves here, but many rowboats lay lazily on their sides along the shore. Nets, hung up to dry on long oars, cast spidery shadows on the ground.

Near one of the bushes he saw several men and women, obviously a family. They were sitting in front of a small fire over which water boiled in a tin kettle. Before them, on a cloth, were spread onions, dried fish, and a piece of black bread. They ate in silence, looking at the sparkling river. As he passed them, they followed him with their eyes without stopping their chewing.

Soon he came to the wharves. They were littered with a disorder of barrels, boats turned upside down, bales of goods. A watchman stood at nearly every warehouse, yawning from the heat and boredom. From the ships to the wharf and back again on the swaying gangplanks the stevedores scurried: ragged, half naked, with hungry faces.

Novikov noticed one of the stevedores stealthily making a hole in the sack he was carrying on his shoulder, trying to get his hand inside. A sharp blow on the back from a stick—and the stevedore's hand was jerked out in fear.

"Look out there! What the hell are you after?" the overseer with drink-sodden face shouted threateningly. He was raising his stick for a second blow, but the stevedore increased his pace and the body of the man following him obstructed the overseer, who was too lazy to stir from his place. He merely swore foully and at length.

Narrow, steep, and crooked lanes led from the port to the city. Here were the workers' districts of Rostov. Novikov walked past the squalid one-story houses. Here was no grass, no clean air. It did not seem possible that the Don—with its spaciousness, its clear air and green banks—lay not more than a mile or two away.

Here everything was smothered in grease and machine oil. Instead

11

of grass—slag; instead of clean water—fetid slops; instead of fresh air and the free breezes—clouds of coal dust, the foul breath of the factories. A fine, choking dust hung in the air. It penetrated everything: clothes, eyes, teeth. One saw few men or women: they were at work. But there were many children. They dug in the refuse heaps, fighting each other over some scrap with the ferocity of homeless dogs. A rare passer-by walked on the clammy stones of the sidewalks. No laughter was heard among them, nor happy chatter; there were no flashing smiles. Two kings reigned here: hunger and dirt. Hunger corroded the people from the inside, dirt from the outside.

The window panes, intended to allow the rays of the sun to shine in, were so small and dirty that only pitiful fragments of sunshine could reach the people. The windows were opened hopefully for more light. But through the open windows the stench of the factories and clouds of flies from the refuse heaps burst into the rooms.

Through these open windows Novikov saw the gloomy interiors, the dull gray walls, the peeling plaster, the wretched warped furniture, the rusty iron rods of the bedsteads, the dirty rags for bedclothes. Every room was the same: two or three beds placed around the walls, a rough table in the center. There were few chairs—and very seldom, wardrobes.

Novikov was used to these sights and through habit had come to accept them, as inevitable, as night and day. Only one thought struck him: "They are starving now. What are they going to do during the winter?"

The faces of the passers-by gave one frightful answer: "We'll be dying."

Always when Novikov saw this poverty it shocked him. But it did not evoke anger, or indignation—only fear. He was afraid of falling, himself, into such poverty through some turn of an unlucky fate. At times he shuddered at the thought. It forced him to be always alert, goaded him into redoubling his efforts and energies, advancing still another step higher—farther and farther from that horrible abyss. With this thought always in his mind he had shaped his career. He was practical and he was proud of the fact.

On the corner of one block a new wing to the jail was being built, a massive and gloomy structure. A high brick wall surrounded it. Well-fed bull-necked guards, in blue caps, paced the walk outside the walls. The small barred windows of the jail were daubed with white paint.

"Who knows what goes on inside there? Nothing can penetrate these thick walls and barred windows," thought Novikov. Unconsciously he increased his pace. Buildings of that kind always left him with an unpleasant feeling.

At the corner of the side street and the main street of Rostov, Engels Avenue, a small park was spread out. This was the only bright spot in the dull streets with their gray houses and rickety board fences and dark porches.

Here Novikov turned onto the main street. It was a broad thoroughfare with street-car lines running down the middle and policemen in white gloves regulating traffic. Buses, street cars, automobiles, and horse-drawn vehicles—all moved up and down in a continuous stream, with a rumble and a clanging, and tooting of horns and cries of drivers.

It was the lunch hour and the street was crowded. The paving stones and the walls of the buildings reflected the heat of the sun. The air was stifling. Like many others, Novikov sought the shady side of the street.

He looked at the passing crowd absent-mindedly, thinking, with something akin to envy, that those people led only one life. It might be a difficult one, complicated and not happy, but it was still only one life. He was leading two: one as a professor at the University of Rostov, the other as a secret agent of the Government among the intellectuals. Both his lives were complicated and entailed much responsibility; both demanded all his energy and all his attention. And the worst of it was that each interfered with the other; they were continually tangling in the most unexpected way, leading to all kinds of paradoxical situations, creating inner tension.

Of course the second, the secret life, brought him material happiness that he could hardly attain through straightforward means. Without the secret life he would not be what everybody thought he was: a professor, the Dean of Russian History at Rostov University, and that while still a young man.

However, Novikov recognized also that in the tense times through which he was living all his material welfare could disappear into a bottomless pit in the space of a moment: everything could be reduced to dust and, if God willed, he might at best remain alive. How many such instances he had seen with his own eyes among his colleagues and acquaintances! And for him, with his double life, the chances for such a mishap were twice as great. No, a single life is more than enough for any man.

"Who are you shoving? Are you blind, or what?" Suddenly he heard an angry voice beside him. Novikov turned around at the shout and met inflamed eyes in a thin, nervous face. The man into whom he had un-

13

intentionally bumped stopped for a moment to curse at him and then went about his business.

"Probably some clerk. The people are hungry, tired, and their nerves are raw," Novikov remarked to himself.

The little episode was so common that he did not bother to answer the harsh shout, and within a minute had completely forgotten it. He had his own worries. As always when he received a new task, the thought "how best to begin?" occupied him fully. This was something he had to think about and decide entirely alone—he dared not share his thoughts even with his best friends.

Inside he had complete confidence in himself, but never before had he to tackle anything like this task. First, he must learn all he could about Gorin's character before he met him, so that he would not commit some irreparable error right at the start. But how to do this? From his books and writings? Ah! Books are one thing, but the author in real life is another. He was fully aware of this. Of course, it would do no harm to read some of his books again. But that was of secondary importance.

Novikov knew from experience that an idea would come of itself, like a bolt from the blue: unexpectedly, like today's meeting with Drozd.

He turned his thoughts again to his lot. He was seeking a better life for himself. It could not be said that he had reached the goal of his youthful dreams. But he had lived long enough to be able to recall his rainbow fancies with a tolerant smile. Besides, he found some consolation in the knowledge that the lives of many of those whom he had known from childhood had been cast in a mold much worse than his. Very much worse.

CHAPTER 5

FROM THE WINDOWS of the second story of the large building Novikov was passing came the smell of soup, the rattle of dishes, and the talk of many people. Novikov at once felt hungry and remembered that it was lunch time. He increased his pace and soon came to the gates of the University, whose buildings occupied a whole block on Engels Avenue.

The dining hall was in the basement, and the entrance to it from the campus. Novikov joined a queue of students, lecturers, and University employees who were still waiting to get in. The queue moved ahead slowly because the old disabled soldier who was checking the passes was completely blind in one eye and could open the other one only with difficulty. He squinted a long time over each pass and wasted still more time swearing at the impatient clamor of the hungry queue.

A plywood partition divided the large basement into two unequal parts. The large part, to the right, was reserved for the students; the smaller, to the left, for the lecturers. Novikov turned to the left.

The Director and the Secretary of the Party Committee ate in a small room on the second floor. What kind of meals were served there no one knew exactly. But sometimes the cooks would blab and divulge these weighty secrets to the ordinary mortals. Then the mouths of the ordinary mortals would water.

Entering the dining hall, Novikov found his brother Nikolai waiting for him. Nikolai was five years his junior, and beside Novikov's tall figure he looked much smaller and stouter. Even a casual glance showed him to be more artless than his elder brother; he was, indeed, of a different type altogether. He was quick to laugh, gay, talkative, and vivacious. Although he was not so handsome as Feodor the general impression he made was pleasant. His eyes did not reflect the cleverness of Feodor; on the other hand, their frank good nature and a kind of pleasant unconcern gained him many friends.

He was attending the Medical Faculty of the University and, as a student, should have eaten in the large dining hall. But thanks to the efforts of his elder brother he had a lecturer's pass. In order to obtain this, Feodor had got him appointed a kind of third assistant to the Librarian in his Faculty of History. This was obviously a trumped-up job, and useful to nobody except Nikolai. His work in the library took up one or two hours in the evening and earned him only a few rubles a month. But the main thing—and much more important than any kind of money—was that it placed him on a level with the lecturers and opened the doors of their mess to him. Nikolai had a very poor opinion of the students' mess and called it the bread-and-water cell. He treasured his position in the Library very much and, as it depended on his brother Feodor's good will, he never forgot to emphasize his love and loyalty to him.

At the moment he was impatiently waiting for Feodor so that they could sit at the same table. He was hoping that his brother would leave some of his food on his plate, so that he could benefit by it. This did not happen very often, but Nikolai never passed up such chances.

They took a table in a far corner of the room. The walls of the mess were painted dark green. Two banners, left from the last Mayday celebration, draped the walls and bore the slogans:

THE KULAKS MUST BE LIQUIDATED AS A CLASS!
and
LET US UPROOT THE REMNANTS OF
BOURGEOIS SURVIVALS FROM THE LIFE
AND CONSCIOUSNESS OF THE PEOPLE!

The entire appearance of the mess did nothing to induce appetite, but nobody worried about that. The customers ate whatever was placed before them. Only people with political or stomach troubles lost their appetites.

Nikolai was expecting his brother to tell him where he had spent the forenoon. He knew that Feodor had no lectures that day and he had not seen him at the University. But Feodor was silent and pre-occupied. At last Nikolai could restrain his curiosity no longer and asked him in his point-blank way.

Feodor replied evasively: "I went to Nakhichevan for a swim. I decided to relax a little."

"You seem very thoughtful. You haven't lost your appetite, have you?" Nikolai asked, thinking hopefully of the coming meal.

"On the contrary, I am as hungry as a wolf," the other replied, a barely concealed contempt in his voice. Nikolai paid no heed to his brother's mood: he was used to his aloof manner.

A rosy-cheeked young waitress approached them and asked for the coupons. In handing her his own and his brother's coupons Nikolai could not refrain from pinching her plump, well-rounded arms. "How do you do, Nadya? How are you?"

"I'm all right, thank you."

"You're looking better every day."

"And why shouldn't I?" she asked, smiling with the familiarity of intimate acquaintance. Her simple peasant face was pleasing. The small eyes looked out kindly on the world, and rather stupidly.

"If I come to see you tonight, will you feed me?" Nikolai whispered.

"A lot I care! Why should I look for trouble?" she replied, but her tone held so much promise that Nikolai fairly squirmed in his seat.

When she had finished brushing the crumbs from the table and gone for their food, Nikolai leaned over the table and said confidentially to Feodor: "She's a nice girl. We're great friends. Generally speaking, you know, it's crazy not to be friendly with the kitchen staff. I know one student—a historian. One of the cooks keeps him. Actually, she's

16

as ugly as hell. But this, brother, is no joke: every evening complete extra dinners. My student has swollen—like this!" Here Nikolai blew out his cheeks to show how the fortunate one had filled out. Enviously he added: "It's easy for him, of course. He's a good-looking chap. Just winks an eye—and there's his dinner. He takes everything else philosophically. 'That,' he says, 'is why they cram our heads full of learning here: so that our bellies may be full.' Quite a philosopher, eh?"

The first course was served. Nadya placed two small pieces of bread and two plates of soup on the table—pea soup with little lumps of fat. Feodor noticed that there were more lumps in Nikolai's plate than in his. "H'm," he thought, "it appears that friendship with the kitchen does pay."

But Nikolai stirred the soup with his spoon fastidiously, grumbling the while: "It looks to me as if you were becoming stingy, Nadya. There's absolutely no fat in this stuff. Is that all you think of your friends?"

But Nadya had already left the table, bumping into chairs with her broad hips.

Nikolai ate hungrily, but managed to tell all that he'd heard in the way of gossip during the day: "You know the new assistant in the Library? Yesterday I came up to her, you know, just for a little chat. She gave me such a cold look and said through her nose like some noble lady: 'Go away, Nikolai! I despise you!' Just imagine! She despises me! But she'll change her tune in a week. I'll still get what I want from her."

"You'd better leave her alone. Aren't there enough girls in your class for you? And listen, dear brother, these affairs of yours with girls will lead to a bad end," Feodor grumbled. But he didn't expect to change him.

"Aha! Feodor! Have I by chance been playing in your back yard?" Nikolai's eyes twinkled.

"Oh! what's the use? It's impossible to talk to you seriously." In vexation Feodor even pushed his plate away. But he corrected his mistake in time.

The second course arrived. It was a meat ball with more bread in it than meat. Beside it lay a couple of leaves of boiled cabbage and a small spoonful of mashed potatoes. Everything was on a minute scale.

When Nadya served them she placed an extra meat ball stealthily on Nikolai's plate. "Eat it up quickly before somebody sees," she whispered hurriedly, trying to screen their table with her broad behind.

17

Nikolai at once cut the meat ball in two, giving half to Feodor. They both ate with the speed of expert jugglers, in complete silence and in the most serious manner. From a casual glance one would not have thought that Professor Novikov and his brother were munching a stolen meat ball but rather that they were discussing the question of the ancient Slavs.

When Nadya saw that the meat ball had disappeared safely, she left the table reassured, bumping Nikolai accidentally, as it were, with her plump elbow.

"Thank you, Nadya," he had time to say.

Feodor didn't reproach his brother with flippancy this time. He merely asked: "Are you the only one she takes compassion on?"

"Ha! She has compassion enough for a dozen. Just look how she's bursting from the food she gets in the kitchen!"

After he had finished his meat ball Feodor lit a cigarette. Remembering suddenly that it came from Moscow, he tried to hide it, but it was already too late. Nikolai sniffed at the smoke and exclaimed: "I say, brother! Where did you get such fine cigarettes?"

Obviously irritated, Feodor replied: "Oh! this one has been lying around since the Director gave me some on his return from Moscow."

Nikolai looked at him suspiciously: "Well, you might leave the butt for me anyway."

"I still have one left. I'll give it to you. But don't go around boasting about it."

CHAPTER 6

AFTER LUNCH the brothers parted. Feodor went home, Nikolai to a lecture.

Feodor lived on Budenny Avenue, one of the main traffic arteries of the city, broad and noisy. From the wharf the avenue rose so steeply that instead of going straight up the hill, the drivers zig-zagged from one side of the street to the other, creating constant collisions, bottlenecks and traffic jams. Motor trucks ran into horse-drawn wagons, the street cars were unable to move because some worn-out nag had stalled on the tracks; trucks and automobiles, their wheels locked, blocked the traffic. The most deafening shouts and swearing filled the air.

The two rooms that Novikov rented were in a house that had been built long before the revolution of 1917. The last repairs had been made

18

by the owner before it passed into the possession of the people. The word "people" is very resonant but also impersonal and vague. So this house, like all other houses in Rostov, was neglected and dirty, and simply cried out for repairs.

By a lucky turn of fate the former owner of the house, instead of being shot and buried in his own back yard, as befits all exploiters and parasites, lived in a small room in the basement.

The other apartments in the two-story building were occupied by a motley assortment of people, whose numbers Novikov had never been able to estimate.

The former landlord had grown shabby and old, and had begun to look like his own house—pitiful and dirty. He was registered as the janitor—a nonessential occupation—and so received the lowest category of rations. Since the energy provided by this ration was only enough for a man to sit and spit on the floor, that was just what the former landlord did. From morning till night he sat on the front doorstep looking at the passers-by and spitting under their feet.

There had been a time, in the early days after the revolution, when from habit he had cleaned up the house and tried to make repairs wherever possible. He hated to see the house in a state of disrepair. But nobody appreciated his work. Some of the people even began to look on him with suspicion, called his care of the house a survival of the spirit of private ownership and almost a hostile gesture on his part.

Once the janitor from the neighboring house, who had a special reason for being annoyed, came over and said to him very impressively: "Look here, Ivan. You'd better give up your landlordish habits. This is no longer the Tsar's time. The house isn't yours now, but belongs to the Soviet, and you are no longer the landlord. You'd better look out or we'll put you up against a wall—and out goes your bourgeois soul!" And he left, his mustache bristling.

After this conversation Ivan gave up everything and just sat on the doorstep; he had been sitting thus for about ten years. He had stopped thinking of the house as his own for a long time now; and the condition of the house, the street, and himself had become a matter of supreme indifference to him.

When Novikov came to the door the janitor, sitting in his accustomed place, didn't move to allow him to pass; he almost had to step over the old man to open the door and go up the stairs. It was so dark inside that he had to strike a match to keep from breaking his neck. The filthy staircase smelled of kerosene, unwashed clothes, mice, and cats' dung.

On the landing, Novikov unlocked one of the three doors facing him. Through the other two came the cries of children, the hissing of primus stoves, and the scolding of women.

Novikov occupied the two best rooms in the house. By Rostov standards that was great luxury. Some of the occupants considered themselves lucky to have one room for the whole family. Usually they lived on the communal principle, several people, regardless of family ties, occupying one room.

It was not surprising that everybody envied Novikov. Of course, the inevitable informer had appeared on the scene. To drive Novikov out of the house he wrote a trumped-up story about him. However, it was so foolishly and clumsily composed that even the officers of the secret police, the NKVD, usually willing and anxious to believe everything, merely laughed at it.

The informer assured the police that nearly every night strikes took place in Novikov's rooms. Obviously, the informer didn't know the meaning of the word "strikes." He had only heard that it was something for which people were shot, and it had seemed to him the most efficient way of getting rid of the "damned bourgeois," as they called Professor Novikov at the house on Budenny Avenue.

The informer would have been greatly surprised had he known that Novikov had his own secret ties with the NKVD, and that it was with their help that he occupied those two rooms.

The first room, which opened onto the landing, served Novikov as a study, dining room, sitting room, and at times as kitchen. Rarely as the latter, however, as he ate usually in the University mess. In one corner of the room stood a primus stove, on which Novikov prepared his tea. Novikov didn't like it because he had to air the room for several hours after using it.

A table with a colored tablecloth occupied the center of the room, and four chairs were drawn up to it. A divan stretched along one wall and a bookcase took up nearly the entire space of the opposite wall. A smaller table with a writing set stood in front of the window.

In the second room, which was smaller, was a narrow single bed and a trunk with Novikov's clothes. Each room had one window, looking into the courtyard with its garbage heaps and clotheslines. The everlasting noise of crying and squalling children rose from there. Three latrines which served the entire house could also be seen from Novikov's windows. Every morning before the three doors there was a line-up of people fidgeting with impatience.

There was no running water in the apartment and Novikov washed himself over a pail by pouring water from a jug that he hooked on the wall. He kept his rooms very clean and tidy by not allowing anything useless to lie around. Only the bare necessities were in sight.

All in all, Novikov was very proud of his apartment and was particularly glad of one thing—that it gave him privacy, a thing almost unheard of in Rostov.

After glancing over the room he swept it and straightened the tablecloth. He noticed that the pail in the corner was full. Picking it up, he went downstairs, stepped over the old janitor, and turned into the gloomy entrance to the back yard. There he swilled out his pail into the garbage heap and returned to his rooms.

Glancing at his watch, he saw that it was three o'clock. At five o'clock he had a seminar for a group of students who were preparing papers on themes dealing with the period of Peter the Great.

CHAPTER 7

WHILE AWAITING the arrival of the students, Novikov took one of Gorin's books from the bookcase. It happened to be *Father;* and stretching out on the divan, he opened it at random.

Gorin had written the book in 1905. Novikov knew it well, for he had studied it while attending the Institute. The thought came to him that from this day on he would be seeing and hearing Gorin everywhere. As he read, he tried to picture the author in his mind. Through the text the face of the writer appeared thoughtful, with sad, penetrating eyes. Yet one could sense in him considerable hatred and a sort of hidden scorn of the people.

His reading was interrupted by the arrival of the students. Three young men and four girls greeted him, admired his apartment, laughing and talking, and eventually disposed themselves about the room.

Novikov liked the students, their high-spirited youth, gay and light-hearted, that ignored misfortune. His colleagues, the professors and lecturers, with their everlasting talk about queues, rations, starving families, although they roused his sympathy, unconsciously repelled him. He was single, young, and had no family. Not so long ago he himself had been a student like these young people and actually he felt more akin to them than to his colleagues—such clever and such terribly boring old men.

On their part the students repaid him with respect and love. To his

21

lectures—stimulating and outspoken—came students from other faculties. He was famous not only within the walls of the University of Rostov but far beyond its confines.

One of the girls, dressed in a gray blouse and red skirt, the latter obviously made from an old curtain, picked up the book which Novikov had left on the divan and asked: "Professor Novikov, are you reading this book?"

"Yes. It turned up handy in an idle moment and I decided to read it again."

The idea came to Novikov to turn the conversation cautiously onto Gorin. He wanted to know what they thought of him. He liked the idea so much that he decided to put it into effect at once.

"I found a lot in it that is helpful, not only from the literary point of view, but from the historical standpoint. The period preceding the revolution of 1905 is shown exceptionally clearly and vividly. No doubt you have all read this book?"

"Yes, of course," came the reply in chorus.

"Tell me," Novikov continued, trying to make his question sound as casual as possible, "how did the author himself, Gorin, appear to you while you were reading his book?"

Although the question was unexpected, it was greeted with pleasure by everyone. The first to answer was a student whose weak blue eyes peered through steel-rimmed glasses: "Whenever I read his books Gorin appears to me as very clever, noble, and sincere; the kind of man who places service to the people above his own personal interests."

"He displays a great knowledge of life, the rough side as well as the finer, the simple life as well as the complex," said the girl in the curtain skirt. "He has been everywhere—he has traveled the length and breadth of Russia. He knows the people probably better than any other Russian writer. But most important—he loves the people."

A third student added: "When I read Gorin's books he strikes me as being very wise."

"But to me it appears. . . . No, I am even convinced of this, that Gorin is very crafty, sarcastic, covetous, and quite cunning," said a girl who was sitting beside the table.

They all raised their eyebrows in surprise that almost amounted to horror. Novikov was just as much taken aback as the others. A student sitting at the opposite side of the table exclaimed: "Oh, Lida! You're always coming out with some eccentric remark like that!" It looked, indeed, as if he were apologizing to Novikov for the girl's outburst.

"No! that's true!" Lida protested hotly. "At first I thought that

22

Gorin was an unselfish man, that he loved the people. That's how I used to think when I read his books for the first time. But now they don't appear to me like that at all. Now they breathe coldness to me, and there appears to be little sincerity in them. And that's all!" she finished abruptly.

But seeing the bewilderment on the faces of her fellow students, she hastened to add: "Now, when I read his books, the face of the author appears to me as sarcastic and bitter. He does not sympathize with the people whose sufferings he describes in such a masterly way. More than that—he sneers at them. You remember how he describes Cheprok in the novel *Logovo?* How foolishly he ended his life? That ending alone breathes of the evil mockery of the author. Read Gorin again, bearing my words in mind, and you will see that I am right."

Lida stopped to catch her breath. Novikov looked at her with interest. Her face was flushed from excitement and had become alive and attractive. Now, on that dark and mobile face, almost the face of a child, the eyes, small and slightly slanted, shone with such radiance that they lit up her entire face, making it surprisingly beautiful. The first impression of plainness, which was imparted by her somewhat sallow complexion, disappeared and there remained only a pleasing warm feeling. Everybody was soon smiling broadly. When one looked at her, her slanderous words somehow no longer seemed so terrible.

Novikov was smiling also. He noticed that she was dressed better than the other girls, her clothes were of finer quality. But the thing that amazed him most was that her appraisal of Gorin coincided almost exactly with the conclusions he had drawn while reading Gorin before the arrival of the students. He also had noticed that hidden sarcasm. True, his feeling was slightly different from Lida's, and milder, judging by her blunt words. Nevertheless, the similarity of the deductions was there. However, Novikov considered this feeling too vague, too ill-defined, and too personal to be shared with his students.

Therefore, addressing Lida, he said, as gently as possible: "I have read *Logovo,* but it did not impress me in the way you have just mentioned. I agree that Cheprok's end is very strange. Most probably it is one of the artifices used by the author for the better expression of his thoughts, rather than a hidden sarcasm. The whole story arouses sympathy for the working people and hatred against their oppressors."

Lida blushed to the ears.

"She's just a child," Novikov thought. He was used to seeing such confusion among the girls who attended his lectures. Many of them, he knew, harbored tender feelings for him.

"Maybe I'm wrong," Lida said humbly. "Maybe I have formed this opinion, which appears to you so strange, because I have seen Gorin. It is quite possible that if I didn't see him so often I would think about him exactly as you do."

The girl's last words made Novikov prick up his ears. "You mean to say that you are acquainted with Gorin?" he asked, trying to keep his voice calm.

"Yes. His daughter and I are good friends and I often visit at his house."

"And that is the opinion you have formed of him?"

"It came out against my will . . ." Lida apparently already regretted that she had become heated in the argument.

Novikov noticed her confusion, and to help her out of the embarrassing situation said, looking at his watch: "I would gladly continue discussing Gorin with you but unfortunately our time is limited and we should be getting on with our seminar."

He had decided, however, that come what may, he must have a talk with Lida alone. He felt that she would tell him something about Gorin that would be interesting and useful to him. Aloud he said: "Tell me, Lida . . . Lida . . ."

"Sidorov."

"Oh, yes. Sidorov. Tell me, Lida Sidorov, what you think about the reforms of Peter the Great. Let us see if you are as well acquainted with him as you are with Gorin."

Everybody laughed and the seminar began.

The students remained with Novikov about two hours. After bidding them farewell he changed his clothes, putting on a white shirt and tie, and left his apartment. It was only a few blocks to Glushak's place. Novikov had plenty of time before keeping his appointment, so he did not hurry.

Dusk had not yet fallen but the heat had begun to abate. Going to a little park that had been laid out around a statue of Lenin, Novikov sat down on a bench, opened up his newspaper and began to read. He scarcely understood what he was reading. His thoughts wandered from the present to the distant past. At times they went over all the details of today's meeting with Drozd; at others they embraced whole years of his life.

24

CHAPTER 8

HIS CHILDHOOD flashed before him—peaceful, bright, and happy. It always seemed to him as if filled with sunshine, like a beautiful spring day. He saw his home, his mother—a kind woman, affectionate and amazingly gentle. His father's face was quite different—stern, with clever gray eyes and a bristling mustache. But when looking on his children he always smiled, and they knew that he also was kind.

Pavel Novikov was a railway builder. They lived luxuriously in a large house with an impressive entrance and garden, had servants and a governess, kept horses and a shining carriage. Everybody in town respected Pavel Novikov and there were some who feared him. He was away from home most of the time. But his every arrival was an event in itself. There were presents for all the family. Rushing into the hall, he embraced everybody in sight, lifting his wife and the children into the air, kissing them and tickling their happy faces with his rough mustache.

Gay times would begin. His father did not like to sit still, was always thinking up new amusements—sometimes they went for a drive into the country, or for a row on the Don, at others they went visiting their friends or received them in their own house. Then, along with the grown-ups, their children would arrive and there began something like a fairy tale: scampering around with girls in the garden, intercepting their glances, sly and funny, the first secret kisses in dark corners, the terribly solemn vows of love and friendship, tearful reproaches of faithlessness, and pouting lips at parting.

Feodor was still studying at the Gymnasium and was but a boy when war broke out in 1914. It meant very little change for him. If anything, life became gayer than ever and time flew more quickly. He used to go with the other pupils from the school to the Rostov station to look at the Russian soldiers, the Don and Kuban Cossacks, and the natives from Kabarda and Ingushia embarking for the front with their horses, guns, and field kitchens. A call, and he would have followed them at once.

At that time his dreams were filled with smart soldiers, toy guns, beautiful battles. The guns fired, and the white puffs from the explosions, on the background of the blue sky, looked delicate and innocent as spring clouds.

25

It seemed only a short time later when one Sunday Feodor and his friends were awaiting as usual the arrival from the east of the military train with recruits, to greet them and cheer them. A train pulled in from the west, somehow unobserved, and stopped at the most distant platform. No triumphal delegation with flowers and flags was on the platform to welcome it—only a few station employees.

Suddenly Feodor saw them unloading stretchers with men over whom gray blankets and greatcoats had been thrown. "Wounded— they have brought the wounded from the front," the rumor began to spread in the crowd. Along with the others Feodor ran to the end of the platform, jumping across the tracks.

He stopped, struck dumb, beside a row of stretchers. What he saw shattered his childish picture of gay soldiers and beautiful battles. On the stretchers lay soldiers in shabby shirts, with gray wasted faces. Some had their heads bound up; others had bandaged arms, legs. All wore the same expression of pain, their dulled eyes looking beyond the crowd. They moaned: some loudly, with strain; some piteously; others whimpered quietly like hurt dogs.

That day Feodor left the station without waiting for the arrival of the recruit train.

Feodor began to notice that his father's face was growing more serious and anxious. He seldom smiled now at the sight of the children. Uneasy days set in. People spoke of bad news from the fronts, of disorders in the capital, of the increasing cost of living, even of starvation. Vague and frightening rumors crept out of Petrograd and Moscow. The word "revolution" was more often on the lips of Rostov's inhabitants.

Life had changed noticeably. The Novikovs got rid of their servants, keeping only one general maid; all but one of the horses were sold. His father no longer built railroads. Sitting at home doing nothing, he grew morose and irritable. His friends used to come to talk with him, sometimes in whispers, sometimes loudly with wild gesticulations; and yet again, they would sit silently by the window, watching the autumn rain beat a monotonous tattoo against the panes.

CHAPTER 9

AT THIS TIME, when Russia was approaching the fateful October of 1917, an incident occurred in the life of Feodor that had a profound influence on the formation of his character.

It happened when his Gymnasium was closed and the building turned into a military hospital. Feodor was in his last year. Hurried examinations were held for the seniors so that they could leave with a formal diploma. No wounded had as yet been brought into the building; only the hospital workers bustled about, cleaning rooms, arranging hospital cots and fixing up the operating rooms and the doctors' offices. The school desks were piled up in the playground. The examinations were held in one of the classrooms not yet taken over by the hospital.

Once, when Feodor was walking alone down the corridor, he saw a young girl in the uniform of a nurse, with a large red cross on her headband. Two braids of chestnut hair fell over her shoulders.

Feodor saw her and unconsciously stopped. He did not even notice that she was not alone, but was walking beside an elderly doctor in a white smock. All that Feodor saw was her face, the beauty of it. She was about twenty years of age, fairly tall, with a shapely, fully developed figure.

Feodor stood in their path, as if he had forgotten where he was and what he was doing. He was unaware that the doctor, mumbling some kind of apology, had to pass around him. He only saw that the girl, slowing her step, raised her heavy eyelashes and looked at him with some surprise. Something must have struck her as amusing about the lanky Gymnasium student with his wide adoring eyes, for she shrugged her shoulders and turned away.

As she passed, her white dress brushed against his hand. She and the doctor were already some distance down the corridor, and still Feodor stood as though stunned by some unexpected blow. He saw how the girl walked along the corridor, swaying her body slightly, and suddenly Feodor noticed with dismay that her every movement seemed to send a stab into his heart. His mouth became dry.

From that moment the image of the nurse haunted him wherever he went. Possibly if he had met her later in life he would have passed her without being so dazzled by her beauty. But he was only sixteen; the world was full of fantasy for him, and maidens' glances or sneers could turn his head like a sudden hurricane. He had fallen in love with the nurse with all his ardent young soul. He saw nothing except her proud beauty and the commanding glance of her dark blue eyes. He no longer noticed the worried looks of his father, nor listened to the conversation of the grown-ups; nor did he see the enormous changes that were taking place right before his wide-open but unseeing eyes. For him the whole world consisted only of the girl in the white uniform and the headdress with the red cross.

He found out all he could about her at once. But it was not much. She had only recently come to Rostov and few people there knew her. Her name, it appeared, was Irina Tropinin and she had lived with her wealthy parents in Moscow before the turbulent times had forced them to move to Pyatigorsk in the Caucasus. There she became a nurse and she had come to Rostov to work in the new hospital. She rented a one-room annex in the courtyard of an old house.

Feodor began to follow Irina Tropinin around like a shadow and even volunteered to help the hospital staff in establishing itself in the new premises, just to have a better chance of seeing and hearing Irina. At first she was amused by the passionate glances of the Gymnasium student who was many years younger than she. Later, finding him everlastingly in her path irked her to nausea and she tried to avoid him. But the cooler Irina was, the more inflamed Feodor became. He deified her name and trembled at sight of her. He even began to compose poetry. It was a poor imitation of the Symbolists—very popular at that time. In these poems Irina was no longer a nurse, but a never-fading star, while he was a wandering comet burning up with passion . . . In short, he was afire.

At last he decided to tell her all. He wandered around the town all day, choosing the words for his confession. After repeating the fateful phrase aloud a hundred times, he finally went to her home.

It was quite late in the evening. A fog from the Don had fallen over the town. The streets were dimly lit by the light from the lamps and the windows of the houses. Over the stone pavement the wind drove the tattered decrees of the Provisional Government, which had just been constituted in Petrograd.

Going into the yard Feodor noticed that the blinds of both windows were down, but narrow strips of light shone at the edges of the blinds. So she was at home.

He imagined the whole scene—also in a somewhat Symbolist spirit. Rushing into the room, he would declare his love while she, so innocent and pure, would understand and appreciate the depth of his feelings, take his outstretched hands in hers, and, laying her proud head on his shoulder, begin to cry softly from happiness. Beyond that his imagination did not go. In order to conquer the last traces of hesitation, he practically flew up the steps and pulled the door wide open. He did not notice that the door was locked and with his sudden jerk he tore off the flimsy hook.

The bright light in the room blinded him. When, the next second, he

28

opened his eyes, he saw a sight which no longer blinded him, but nearly killed him. His Irina, his dream and happiness, to whose image he prayed, was sitting in the lap of a husky hussar. The hussar wore only his undershirt and crimson breeches which fitted tightly over his muscular thighs. His tunic and high boots lay on the floor beside the armchair on which they were sitting.

The hussar was very hairy; the curly growth on his chest thrust itself through his shirt. Irina was stroking his hair with one hand, while the other . . .

"What is the meaning of this?" A harsh shout interrupted Feodor's observations. The hussar had recovered himself first. "Get out of here! Get out, you Gymnasium rat!"

Feodor, however, had time to notice that on the little table beside the armchair there were bottles and wine glasses. Irina looked around with a vacant expression in her eyes. His unfading star was very drunk and did not seem to understand what was going on. In the meantime, the hussar, pushing the goddess off his knees roughly, lifted one of his spurred boots from the floor and threw it at Feodor. The boot hit him in the chest. Feodor stumbled back toward the door and nearly tripped over the sill. As he rushed out of the room into the darkness the second boot followed him, striking the back of his neck sharply. Running down the steps he heard Irina's drunken voice telling the hussar: "He's some kind of psychopath, crazy. Follows me around all the time; I can't get rid of him."

The hussar, bellowing something incoherent, slammed the door shut.

When Feodor had recovered a little on the street, it was not the pain from the blows that he felt, but an aching anguish in his heart. Weaving from side to side like a drunken man, looking blankly around him, he walked on aimlessly. The picture of the dark hussar with the tipsy Irina on his knees stood vividly before his eyes.

Feodor stopped under a street lamp. A woman approached him out of the fog.

"What a nice-looking boy, and lonely! Come along with me and I'll make you happy."

Feodor looked at the prostitute with a blank stare. Suddenly he laughed. Everything in his immediate past, all his youthful dreams and feelings, his night invasion of Irina's room, the unexpected scene with the hussar—everything struck him in one revealing flash as being so foolish and funny that he burst out laughing.

He laughed in the prostitute's face. Surprised, she looked at the lanky lad in the uniform of a Gymnasium student, roaring with laughter at God knew what, and didn't know whether she was supposed to laugh with him or to be offended.

"Ha, ha, ha!" Tears appeared in his eyes. The prostitute became offended, spiteful.

"If you don't want to you don't need to. But why laugh? And a student . . ." she said, leaving Feodor. The tapping of her heels on the stone pavement was heard long after her slatternly figure had disappeared into the fog.

"That's what I needed," Feodor said aloud. "That's just what I needed. Dreaming away like some calf! Enough of such foolishness!"

In later years Novikov always recalled with gratitude the prostitute, the mere sight of whom had sobered him. And for him this passage from youthful fancy to conscious living, which no one can escape, had been not too painful.

"Good thing it happened when I was sixteen," he used to think later. "The earlier the better."

This incident shook him deeply and awakened him. When he recovered he saw that his daydreaming life had ended, his illusions had dissipated, his fantasies were dispelled, and a new conscious life had begun, which was farther from pure happiness than his dreams. But this, on the other hand, was real life. And besides, his dreams now looked childish to him. He had grown up.

When Novikov returned home that night he found his father in a state of unusual alarm. "Where have you been?" he asked Feodor roughly. "We have been looking for you all over the place. There is bad news from Petrograd. The Bolsheviks have driven out the Provisional Government by force and have taken over. At any moment they may conquer the whole of Russia!"

Feodor looked at his father with surprise. He did not understand why he should be so upset because some Bolsheviks had driven out the Provisional Government that he himself had said was useless anyway.

In his room, while undressing, Feodor thought: "I've had enough of surprises. Nothing can astonish me now. The Bolsheviks will conquer Russia. Ha! Today I have conquered my own heart. That is more important."

In his sleep Feodor saw the prostitute. She held out her painted lips to him—lured him. It was disgusting, repulsive. Feodor ground his teeth in his sleep.

CHAPTER 10

VAINLY, FEODOR thought that his young soul was so tempered that it could withstand any trials without wavering. The trials had only begun. The whole country was tossing about in wild delirium. Age-old principles, settled life, cracked and crumbled apart. In the mad whirlwind of revolution characters much stronger than Feodor's were swept aside and destroyed.

The revolution had only just begun, but already the country was unrecognizable. Next morning Feodor awoke to a new world.

His father, pale, his eyes wide, woke him up. Feodor had never seen him like that before.

"Get up quickly, Feodor. The revolution is in the city!"

"What revolution?"

"The soldiers and sailors have seized the railway station, the telegraph, the power stations, and the arsenal. Arrests and shootings are going on all over the town. They may come here any minute now. We must get out before they do. Dress as quickly as you can. Hurry!"

Feodor threw on his clothes and went into the sitting room. His mother, almost worn out, was stupidly running around picking up things that were of no use to anyone and stuffing them into bundles. The maid was sitting motionless, staring dully in front of her. For no apparent reason she held a little teapot in her hand. Nikolai and their sister Olga huddled together from the chill of the morning, understanding little of what was going on. His father was carrying bundles and suitcases into the yard. Feodor began to help him. When he came out onto the porch he looked around: heavy clouds were creeping across the gray morning sky. A drizzling rain fell, it was cold. In the yard stood a dripping horse, hitched to a britchka.

Feodor stood and listened. Their house was situated far from the center of the city, in a quiet boulevard of lindens. To his ear there came a strange rumble from the direction of the city, unusual at this early hour. Somewhere near-by a heavy truck roared. Above the noise he heard men's voices—shouting something; it was impossible to hear what. After the truck had gone there was quiet again; only the menacing rumble from the city remained.

"Where are we going, Father?"

"I don't know myself. It seems to me better to go up the Don, to the

Cossack district. When things have settled down we can return to Rostov."

Suddenly through the open gate a rider dashed into the yard. The horse was all in a lather, snorting, stamping its hoofs. From its open mouth white foam dropped to the ground.

The rider, in the uniform of an officer, jumped from the horse, ran up to Pavel Novikov. Feodor hardly recognized the officer as one of his father's friends.

"Thank God you are here, Pavel," he said in breathless haste. "I was afraid that I would miss you. Give me some civilian clothes—please, quick. I must change right away. In an officer's uniform they will shoot me like a dog."

"At once, at once. Feodor, run into the house and bring out one of your suits and a coat. Your clothes will fit him perfectly."

Feodor ran off. Returning in a moment with the clothes, he handed them to the officer. The latter tore off his uniform with feverish haste and changed quickly into Feodor's suit.

"If you only knew what is going on in town! Before my very eyes the soldiers shot down officers. I barely escaped with my life. Jumped on my horse—and away! They fired at me, but missed. Hurry! Soon all the roads out of town will be closed by the Red Guards."

The officer looked at the britchka with the bundles and suitcases piled up. "Pavel, have you gone out of your mind? Why are you losing precious time with all that trash? Take only what you can stuff into your pockets. If the Red Guards don't take it from you the bandits around town will, and they will probably beat you up because of it. Lose no time! Run while you still can!"

The officer leaped onto his horse. "Good-bye, Pavel. Thanks for the clothes. It may be that we shall not see each other any more! . . ."

"Where are you going?"

"To Novocherkask. General Kaledin is there. Alas! Now Mother Russia has really tied herself into a knot! How will it all end?" And the officer galloped into the street.

Pavel Novikov scurried about. "Finish loading. Call everybody! It's time to go."

Feodor called his mother, the children, and the maid from the house. As they started out his father impulsively threw a couple of bundles from the cart onto the mud, but the load was eased very little by this.

The farther they drove along the street the more frequently they met vehicles like their own loaded with chattels, bundles, and trunks.

32

Near the highway leading out of the city the stream of traffic was continuous. Soon they had to stop.

"They say the Red Guards have closed the road. They're not allowing anyone to pass."

"Perhaps some other roads are still open."

"Oh, yes! Certainly! They would be sure to leave them open especially for you!"

Along the road, on the sidewalk, two sailors rode past the traffic. Their horses pranced; the pedestrians sprang aside. Two machine-gun cartridge belts were drawn criss-cross over their sailor's tunics. One, with prominent cheek bones, pockmarked, shouted at the people in the carriages: "Turn back, you unharvested bourgeoisie! Turn back, you ———! Nobody leaves the town anyway—we'll make soap out of you yet. Turn around! Or we'll tear you into ribbons with our grenades. The power is ours now!"

His companion laughed, baring his teeth. Both were drunk and happy. Both had red faces, radiant from vodka and the exultant feeling of unbridled power.

The people on the vehicles quieted down. One by one they turned about and headed back toward the city. The Novikovs, squeezing through the throng with difficulty, reached their home about two hours later.

Feodor, snatching a hasty snack, ran into the city. He was tortured by curiosity. Unlike his father, he felt no fear. A kind of excitement oppressed him; he could not sit at home; he wanted to be in the crowd, among the people where big events were taking place. He heard much that was new, much that was surprising that day. The nearer he came to the center the more lively were the streets. Many, like himself, driven by curiosity, were running to the main square. A crowd had gathered at the corner of Sennaya and Sadovaya Streets. In the crowd men were pulling off their caps and crossing themselves. At their feet lay a lifeless body—shirt bathed in blood.

"Just look at his massive arms, may God rest his soul."

"They are no use to him now."

Feodor ran on. He saw several more abandoned corpses. They had been lying around since morning, like sacks that were no longer useful. Crowds of the curious gathered around each corpse. Feodor looked at them all, listened to everything.

Two well-dressed elderly men walked past him, leaving strange words in their wake: "He treated us to cheese from women's milk and then showed us a cow."

"A Holstein?"

There was an immense crowd of people on the main square. Two armed sailors of the Black Sea Fleet stood on guard in front of the former Governor's palace. A grenade hung from the belt of each. One carried a rifle with fixed bayonet on his shoulder, while the other had a huge Mauser strapped to his waist. Both wore red armbands. They were checking the passes of people going into the building. Another two sailors of the Black Sea Fleet, with a machine gun between them, stood guard at the gate leading into the courtyard of the palace. The barrel of the machine gun looked bluntly at the crowd.

The Military Revolutionary Committee of the City of Rostov had established itself in the palace.

A large truck drove up to the gate with a roar and in a cloud of smoke. A dozen or so officers, with two old generals among them, were huddled together in the truck. They were prisoners. Some of the crowd whistled shrilly, others shouted "Hurrah!" while still others crossed themselves. The truck drove into the yard, the gates were closed. And again the blunt nose of the machine gun looked at the crowd.

"Now I suppose they'll shoot the poor sinners."

"What did you expect? This is revolution!"

Suddenly the French doors leading onto a balcony on the second story of the building were thrown open and a tall stranger in a leather jacket stepped out. His dark unruly hair stuck out from under his cap. He raised his arms and the crowd became silent.

"Comrades!" he shouted, and waited for complete quiet. "Comrades! I congratulate you upon the victory of the revolution!"

"The same to you, comrade!" a voice called from the crowd.

"Ha, ha, ha!" roared the crowd.

"Hey, uncle! Shut up and let the man speak!"

"Comrades!" the tall man on the balcony repeated. "I congratulate you upon the victory of the revolution. The power is now yours, the people's power. The land now belongs to the peasants, and the factories to the workers. But the counterrevolutionary scum doesn't want you to have such a life. It wants to strangle revolutionary Rostov with the bloody hands of General Kaledin. That will never happen! As one man we rise to the defense of Rostov and bravely save it!"

The crowd around Feodor roared like a tempest. He was crushed and squeezed from all sides. Now the orator thumped his huge fist on the railing of the balcony; the railing shook while he, flushed and sweating, cursed Kaledin, Kornilov, and Kerensky in the lowest language. He made it clear that but for these bloodthirsty monsters every-

34

body would by now be living in the palaces with their families, drinking vodka and leading a heavenly life.

Feodor stood in the growing crowd, unconsciously subjecting himself to someone's will. At that moment he was one of the mob, ready to believe everything. Forgetting himself, he shouted "Hurrah!" as one orator after another came onto the balcony and damned the souls of the native and world bourgeoisie. Like all the others, he did not consider the meaning of the words. Logic and reason were not important. The important thing was the passion and wrath with which the words were spoken.

The picture of one of the orators in particular remained long in Feodor's memory—a woman in a soldier's shirt with a red kerchief tied about her head. At the height of the enthusiasm she pulled out a huge Mauser and, brandishing it over the crowd, shouted, distorting her face and straining the veins in her neck: "For Kaledin—a bullet in the head! For Kornilov—a bullet in the head! We will shoot all the reptiles and castrate them . . ." ending up with a dozen words of the filthiest language.

And these half-crazed ravings were received with a roar of approval.

But everything comes to an end, even the oratory of commissars. After a dozen or so orators had followed each other, some broad-chested and lusty, others thin with consumptive faces, the meeting was closed. At once the gate of the courtyard was swung wide and a company of Red Guards marched in orderly formation into the square. Deliberately, without show of haste, they pressed the crowd back. The square was cleared with an efficiency that would have filled a Cossack regiment with envy.

"Does that mean," Feodor thought, "that while the orators were inflaming the mob, someone on the Revolutionary Committee did not forget to plan and to put this measure into effect? Was it possible, therefore, that all these passionate speeches were the result, not of spontaneous and sincere enthusiasm, but rather of cold and clear calculation?"

Feodor recalled last night's conversation with his father.

"Yes, probably he knew a lot more than I did. It will not be so easy to drive out these Bolsheviks. They are tenacious."

The crowd also gradually came down to earth after its first intoxication. Feodor noticed some confused looks and embarrassed smiles.

"Look how they're pushing us around! The devils, as if we were a bunch of cattle!"

"And what did you expect? Honey cake?"

35

"Bah! Get your ginger-bread, uncle! A rifle butt in the teeth!"

They began to laugh, but somehow it sounded false.

Twilight was changing into darkness when Feodor arrived home. He found his father entirely composed and seemingly resigned to whatever the future held in Rostov.

"Do you know, Feodor, I am glad that we didn't leave. When all's said and done, we are in our own home, surrounded by our own things. Otherwise we would have had to roam around among the Cossacks. They would hardly have received us with open arms."

CHAPTER 11

A STRANGE, anxious time set in. Life became tense and uncertain.

During these days Feodor often thought of Irina Tropinin. A vague feeling of anxiety bothered him. He could not stay at home. Every day he wandered around the city, looking into suspicious and gloomy faces. The people seemed to be waiting for something to happen, something unknown, yet frightful.

Feodor himself was only hazily aware of what he sought. He would sit on a bench in the park watching the trees silently shed their last yellow leaves. Then he would be seized by such a longing for Irina that he was ready to forgive her everything, even the hussar, if only he could see her again, look into her deep blue eyes and hear her voice. But when he remembered the hussar he was overcome by a furious jealousy. He would bite his lips, beat his fists on the bench, get up—cursing Irina, the hussar, and himself aloud. But the next minute he forgave her everything. Thus the days passed.

By night the city slept an uneasy sleep. The dark figures of Red Guards flitted among the shadows of the streets. There were many of them. They took possession of the large empty houses abandoned by owners who had managed to leave the city. There, amidst unheard-of luxury, they drank vodka, stoked the stoves with the furniture, and fought over women. When the swansdown quilts and mattresses made them feel stuffy, they sallied forth into the parks and continued their orgies under the dark autumn sky. The frightened residents looked from behind their shutters at the figures of the new masters wandering about the park like phantoms, pulling up the skirts of their women, smashing the glass of the street lights, embracing each other in maudlin drunkenness, carousing, relieving themselves disgustingly. Terrified by these scenes, the residents closed their shutters more tightly to keep out the cries of the bandits and the squeals of their women.

The Red Guards, like the rest of the Russians, were nervous, unbalanced. When in the dead of night they robbed passers-by of their coats and watches, they either brandished their revolvers threateningly, ready to kill without mercy, or hiccupping drunkenly, would try to kiss their victims amid a flood of remorseful tears. They were strangers, even to themselves.

But mankind can adapt itself to anything. Very little time passed after the revolution before the absurd, unnatural state of things began to be accepted as commonplace, the chaos and confusion as normal. The people were engaged in something much more vital than drawing conclusions about what is normal and what is not. They were searching for food. The problem of how to live through the day and go to bed with a full stomach became the main concern in life for the townspeople of Rostov. There was simply no time left for philosophical deliberations.

Pavel Novikov and Feodor spent whole days in the market bartering things for vegetables and meat. The mother and the younger children did the housework. The maid had slipped away to live with relatives in her native village where, compared with the famine-stricken city, there was a heavenly abundance.

Pavel Novikov was planning an expedition into the country. He figured that the Red Guards' watch on the city would relax in time and that he would be able to leave with Feodor in search of food. The prospect of a hungry winter filled him with fear. He and his wife had already begun to select things which they considered would be most in demand by the peasants, to barter for flour, lard, potatoes.

Just as the Novikovs were ready to set out on their risky expedition an unforeseen incident upset all their plans.

One clear morning Feodor was standing in the yard watching the dreamy smile of the tired autumn sun, when four armed riders came through the gate and pulled up in front of him. By their red armbands he knew them to be Red Guards. One of them, a thin, muscular, gloomy-looking fellow, drew a little ahead of the others. He seemed to be the leader. The other three crowded behind him, looking at Feodor with a rather animal-like curiosity.

The leader addressed Feodor: "Is this the home of engineer Pavel Novikov?"

"Yes."

"Call everybody out into the yard. We'll have a little chat with them."

Feodor ran into the house and a minute later came back with the whole frightened family. The Red Guards still sat on their horses. For a few moments they looked over the Novikovs as if they were studying them for some purpose known only to themselves. Finally the leader broke the silence:

"Citizen Novikov, your house and all your property are confiscated. Listen to the decree of the Revolutionary Committee of the City of Rostov dealing with this."

The Novikovs looked at him blankly, not seeming to understand the meaning of his words. Meantime, the leader pulled a folded paper from the deep cuff of his cavalry greatcoat, opened it up and began to read:

"By special decree of the Military Revolutionary Committee of the City of Rostov the house of engineer Pavel Novikov is confiscated for the needs of the revolution. All the furniture and contents of the house are henceforth regarded as the property of the Proletarian State. Any encroachment on this property will be stopped short by death without trial.

"Citizen Novikov is not to be regarded as a parasite and exploiter, but as an Intellectual, confused by bourgeois culture, and is therefore not subject to arrest. Instead, he and all able-bodied members of his family are to be mobilized for manual labor at the disposition of the Revolutionary Committee.

"The present order must be fulfilled without question under penalty of death.—Chairman of the Military Revolutionary Committee, NIKO-LAI CHUBAREV."

Pavel Novikov, pale and trembling, felt numb all over, as though he had just looked at certain death. The thought that at that very moment they were losing everything they had worked for all their lives was so monstrous and absurd that he felt neither horror nor fear, only a cold sinking feeling—complete ruin, the end.

"What shall we do now?" the mother whispered. The children nestled closer to their parents, as though looking for protection. "Where shall we go now?"

"That's not our business," the leader answered.

The father recovered himself to ask: "Could we occupy the stables?"

The riders glanced at each other. After a moment's thought the leader waved his hand in a generous gesture: "You can occupy the stables. The order says nothing about that. But don't forget! Tomorrow morning you must go to the Revolutionary Committee to get your ration cards and shovels. You will begin to work tomorrow, digging trenches."

Suddenly the mother turned and ran into the house.

"Where are you going?" Raising his whip, the leader cried: "Stop! You old devil!" He nodded to one of the Red Guards, who dismounted and started after her. But she had already come out. In her trembling hands she carried an ikon.

"You have no need of an ikon anyway. You don't believe in God!" she cried in a sharp voice to the Red Guards and ran straight to the stables.

The leader shrugged his shoulders. "Take it. Kiss it if you like. We wouldn't take it as a gift."

The Red Guards laughed together.

"Well, I suppose that's all. Akimov," the leader addressed the dismounted man, "you will remain here until further orders. You may issue the laborers Novikov the necessary bedclothes and winter garments, so they won't freeze. But don't forget to get a receipt from them for these things."

"I will, Comrade Commander!" replied Akimov. "What about food, Comrade Commander?"

"It belongs to them. Don't touch it. However, I understand they are not selfish people and will probably share with you. Isn't that so?" he turned to Pavel Novikov. An evil smile played on his lips. "Silence is a sign of consent. They will share with you. Well, let's go. Who's next on the list? I think it's Arbouzov . . ." And the three Red Guards rode out of the yard leaving the Novikovs with Akimov in charge.

CHAPTER 12

THE FAMILY stood in the dark stable, not knowing what to do. Their new position was so unexpected and unbelievable that it completely stunned them. Everything was like an absurd dream. The father was the first to rally: "Well, let's do something about it. Even if we stay here only for a week we'll have to fix ourselves more comfortably. Why not begin by cleaning the place up a bit?"

They all set about tidying up the stable. Feodor noticed how his mother would suddenly drop her hands in despair and stare steadily before her. Then, as if aroused, she would take hold of her broom again. An hour and a half later the stable looked cleaner and somehow much brighter. They sat down to rest.

Suddenly the Red Guard Akimov appeared in the doorway.

"Well, bourgeois," he said good-naturedly, "how's the world using you?" He had already been sampling some of Novikov's wines. His broad high-cheekboned face was red and he smiled pleasantly. Feodor noticed that Akimov was wearing a pair of his father's new trousers and a shirt. Receiving no answer, he continued to lean against the door jamb, not the least bit disconcerted. His tall figure filled a good half of the wide door. Turning his smiling eyes from one to the other of the Novikovs, he continued to talk:

"I'm surprised at you. How can you become so upset over that trash? All right—you have lost your house. So what? Why should you grieve? The main thing is that you are still alive. As to the house—bah! Today you have it, tomorrow—phuy! It's gone up in smoke. And quite simply too. All it needs is a match, and it's all over. Somebody asks: how did it catch fire? Just so! the Novikovs set fire to it. And, of course, that means the Novikovs against the wall. . . . But don't be afraid. I'm just talking, giving an example to show you what I mean. I have no ill feeling toward you."

Feodor looked with interest at the talkative Red Guard. His words showed unshakable conviction, a sort of naïve consciousness of his own rightness.

Akimov continued: "On the other hand, probably you are offended at me. How is it, you ask, that he has put on our trousers and our shirt? But why be offended? Surely we are all Russians, people of one kin! We must live in peace, share and share alike just like brothers."

"And that is how you understand equality and fraternity?" sneered Pavel Novikov.

"Equality and fraternity?" repeated Akimov thoughtfully. "These are sacred words. Nobody understands their true meaning. Man can harbor them only deep in his soul."

"But you seem to have understood them very well," Pavel retorted bitterly, glancing at his trousers, filled to bursting by the muscular legs of the Red Guard philosopher. The latter, paying no attention to the gibe, continued: "If the soul is shallow these words mean nothing to it. A shallow soul cannot withstand revolution. For revolution the soul must be ready to forget everything—everything but the main idea. That's how it is! Only Russians have the capacity for revolution."

"Why is that?" asked Pavel, mildly interested.

40

"Because the Russian people are damned. Their soul is like a bottomless barrel—it will hold everything, but still remain empty! For example: here am I, talking with you as with a friend and I'm glad to see you and I'm even ready to give my life for you, you're so dear to me just now. But suppose they say to me tomorrow: 'Akimov, shoot the Novikovs in the name of the revolution!' I would shoot you and have less pity for you than a fly. I have no pity for myself, let alone for others."

"That's not the Russian people," the mother interjected heatedly, "but simply you. You don't believe in God, that's why you are running amuck. You have taken our house from us, you have taken Rostov from the people, and you will go on doing this to the whole of Russia."

"Alas! dear mother! You say Russia. Why! Russia is only the beginning! For the Russian, half the world is too little!"

"What the devil does he need the whole world for?" Pavel Novikov cried out in exasperation. "Surely he is not overcrowded in Russia. Russia is a huge country."

"It is not the country that matters, but that the Russian nation must save the world, humanity. That was written by fate at its birth."

Akimov's brow was sweating. He left the place by the door and walked slowly into the stable. His eyes were no longer smiling.

Pavel Novikov got up to meet him. Akimov's words had evidently irritated him. "And what if the other peoples don't want you to save them? What if they feel quite satisfied without your so-called—eh—what you might call . . . your mystic mission?"

"They don't want it just because they don't know."

"And how do you expect to teach them?"

"By force!"

The father was flabbergasted.

"Well, now, that is a little too much. Aren't you overstepping yourselves? You might burst your pants, Comrade Akimov!" and Novikov emphasized the word "comrade" with a sneer. "It would be much better if you got down to business and cleared up the chaos in your own country instead of intruding on other people and teaching them."

"Of course, you wouldn't understand that," Akimov replied pointedly. "You hang on to the old order. And in general, Citizen Novikov," he added—stressing the "citizen" as Novikov had emphasized the "comrade"—"we had better not quarrel: we might get excited and end up in a fight. I came to you on business. I need your son for a moment. I have to make an inventory of the property. He can help me."

41

"All right, take him. Perhaps he will be able to understand you better than I."

"Who knows? Maybe he will." And Akimov left the stable, followed by Feodor.

During the entire conversation Feodor had not taken his eyes off Akimov. In some strange way the man attracted him. Not only his words astounded him, but his unshakable conviction.

"So that is the kind of people they are, these Bolsheviks," he thought.

It was the first time he had heard of the wild mixture of Russian nationalism with the revolutionary program. The effect was stunning. And if Akimov's idea seemed illogical, it was still very forceful—a breathtaking idea.

"Who knows?" he thought, as he followed Akimov, "maybe this strange man, probably a former village school teacher, actually bears the seeds of some unknown purpose, mysterious and frightening in its immensity. 'For the Russian, half the world is too little,' " he recalled Akimov's words. "At least, he isn't petty," Feodor thought, looking at Akimov's broad back and unconsciously straightening his own shoulders.

At that moment the loss of his father's house and property, even the welfare of his family, appeared to him of little consequence. "Of what importance is our home when the whole nation has been uprooted by people like this Akimov?"

Feodor was impressionable. The seeds sown by the crafty Akimov, as it were by chance, had fallen on fertile ground.

Akimov noticed the sparkle in Feodor's eyes. Striding through the deserted rooms of the house, he droned in his deep bass: "You should leave the old folks. You can't hang on to your mother's skirts forever, you know. They have lived their lives, while all your life is ahead of you. You've got to live now or never!"

"Yes, but how to live?"

"To live means to burn, to fight!"

"But can't one live in peace?"

"Peace? No, brother, peace is not for us. You and I will never see peace in our time. This is an age of strife!"

The crystal chandeliers tinkled from Akimov's heavy tread; his deep bass voice resounded, insistent and overwhelming, while Feodor's heart was heavy with anxiety—as if a precipice were opening before him. It lured and yet frightened him.

The bass voice droned on in his ears, preventing him from collecting himself. "We are the future. Therefore, youth must be with us. You, I see, have some doubts. Throw them overboard. Cut yourself off from the past, as with a knife. All this warmth, comfort, peace, and quietness have gone and will never return. You have no need of it now. Throw everything over and come with us!"

They spent the whole day going over the house. Akimov dictated, enumerating the various items, while Feodor wrote them down in a notebook.

In the evening, when Feodor went into the garden after supper, he saw Akimov grooming his horse. He was rubbing it so hard that the animal turned and looked at him reproachfully. It was sunset, and a blood-red streak flamed in the western sky.

When he caught sight of Feodor the Red Guard smiled: "You're admiring the sunset? It's beautiful, without a doubt. Look how red it is: as if all the blood shed by the people were being reflected in the sky. Red has always been the color of passion and sin, of hate and revenge. Now it has become the color of the revolution. Here—you see? I have a red band on my arm. That means blood!"

"What has made him so bitter?" Feodor asked himself. "Perhaps such is the grim law of life. Perhaps it is impossible to fight to the end, tear the throat of the enemy, and still retain the gentle heart of a child."

As if he had read Feodor's thoughts, Akimov said: "We bear hatred toward people within us—for their own good. I love the people, although they are basically trash. Their weaknesses must be destroyed by fire and the sword."

CHAPTER 13

IN THE MORNING the whole family went to the office of the Military Revolutionary Committee. The place was crowded with people who had come for their ration cards and shovels, and to register for work with the new authority. Young Red Guards marshaled the newcomers into queues. A man was calling out names through a wicket in the wall.

Ahead of Feodor stood the lawyer Arbouzov, a smallish man about fifty years of age. Shaking his gray head, he said to his neighbor: "We asked for it! Everybody was shouting: 'Freedom! Freedom! Down with the Tsar!' I myself hung a red ribbon across my chest. And now I am free indeed—like a bird—I have neither house nor home."

"They kill each other as they please," his neighbor commented. "That's freedom for you!"

A middle-aged man, probably an artisan, looking confused, beat his chest and cried: "Let me perish, let my talent perish! But the people! Why should the people be destroyed? I pity them! They've become like the beasts of the forest—they crave human blood and are still not sated."

A teacher of literature known to Feodor, with pince-nez and a goatee, responded in his shrill tenor: "Wasn't I right, Piotr Lukich, when I told you that the time was coming about which it is written: 'The living will envy the dead!' "

"Right! Right!"

At last came the Novikovs' turn. Pavel Novikov was handed a ration card for the family and then they were all sent into the yard for shovels. They were given only three. Nikolai and Olga were sent home—they were too young.

"Fall in!" resounded the command.

They fell in slowly and raggedly. With the help of kicks and buffetings by the Red Guards, something like a formation took shape. They stood in four ranks facing the building: a most motley crowd, people of the most varied conditions and professions—tradesmen, engineers, teachers, merchants, lawyers, civil servants. In their utter helplessness they presented a pitiful and comic appearance. The Red Guards crowded in groups before the squad, stared at them, bared their teeth, cracked jokes.

"All right, awkward squad! You've sat around on your backsides long enough. Now you're going to do some work!"

Suddenly all the laughter and joking of the Red Guards stopped. They drew themselves up stiffly, turned their heads toward the gate. Three horsemen rode onto the square. Feodor at once recognized the dark one in the leather jacket as the orator who had congratulated the people of Rostov on their revolutionary victory. There was no mistaking his position; he was the leader. The other two lined up on either side of him.

The rider in the leather jacket looked over the uneven ranks slowly and smiled slightly. Turning to the comrade on his right he whispered something. The latter moved his horse a few paces to one side and shouted:

"Labor battalion! Atten—shun!" The shuffle of feet was heard from the squad—then everything was quiet. "Listen to the speech of Com-

44

rade Chubarev, Chairman of the Rostov Military Revolutionary Committee!"

"So that's who Chubarev is," thought Feodor. "That's the man who has the power to confiscate property, and to shoot people without trial!"

A deathly silence reigned on the square. The man in the leather jacket held the gaze of everyone there. Feodor noticed how his short fingers jerked slightly on the reins. On his weather-beaten face the deep lines of a strong will stood out noticeably. "Most likely a military man," thought Feodor: "probably from some Cossack regiment."

Chubarev's horse pricked up its ears, rolled its eyes at the mare beside it, and snorted loudly.

"Citizen Intellectuals!" Chubarev began. "You have been mobilized by the revolution for the construction of defense works. You will dig trenches around the city of Rostov. Take care and work well; do not be lazy. I know you have been pampered in the past and you are soft. But we'll beat that foolishness out of you. Those who work badly will go without their lunch.

"And don't try to be smart! You Intellectuals like to blabber. We Bolsheviks go against your grain. I would advise you to keep a tight rein on your tongues, otherwise we might be tempted to cut them off along with your heads."

Here Chubarev laughed so heartily that a chill ran down the spines of the "pampered Intellectuals." Raising in his right hand the crop with a piece of lead braided in at one end, he threatened the squad with it.

"I warn you to put all thoughts of trying to escape from work, or from the city, out of your minds. I have no doubt that there are many among you who would like to slip away and get under the tail of that dog Kaledin. But you won't get anywhere: I have personally given orders that anyone trying to leave the city is to be shot on the spot. And now—to the field! We can't lose any more time. I will inspect your work personally."

After this short but impressive speech, the people in the squad lost heart completely. Everyone felt at once that he was without rights, defenseless, as if he had been condemned to death. To the shouts of the Red Guards, the column moved toward the southern outskirts of the city. They marched out of step, looking wearily at the ground, rarely exchanging words.

Outside the city they found that the first line of trenches was already

45

being dug. About a thousand of their fellows, mobilized like themselves, were working under the supervision of armed Red Guard cavalry. The Novikovs' battalion was halted about a mile farther on and ordered to extend the formation and begin digging. Barbed-wire entanglements were placed in front of the trenches, which stretched for miles, their flanks abutting on the Don. The authorities evidently intended to encircle the city with several lines of defense.

Pavel and Feodor worked hard. The mother, however, had to stop frequently to catch her breath.

At midday they were given lunch. They stood in line while the Red Guards ladled hot borshch from the field kitchens into mess tins. All ate hungrily, without talking. Feodor stood in line awaiting his turn impatiently. While he was looking around idly his glance fell on a man in a shabby coat standing with his back toward him, about ten paces ahead. There was something vaguely familiar about the figure. Feodor strained his memory, but could not recall him.

Then the man turned, as if he had felt the impact of Feodor's gaze on him. Feodor nearly cried out. The hussar! Of course, the hussar! The same officer whom he had caught in Irina's apartment on that ill-fated night.

The hussar looked at Feodor and suddenly turned pale. For a second he looked lost, then he turned away and never glanced in Feodor's direction again.

A fit of jealousy seized Feodor. Again he felt a sharp pain in his heart, as when he ran from Irina's apartment.

"Apparently he wasn't able to escape that night. He has changed into civilian clothes and is probably posing as a teacher or bookkeeper or something," thought Feodor, and suddenly it dawned on him that he held the hussar's life in his hands. "That's why he turned pale when he saw me."

When, after lunch, they all went again to the trenches, Feodor noticed that the hussar passed by him twice, watching him. His eyes were dry, unblinking, dreadful. Then he jumped into the trench. Feodor shrank back. From the nearness of the man whom he hated with all his soul, his heart began to beat wildly; his hands turned cold.

Throwing out the earth in front of him, the hussar was silent. Several times he squinted sidewise at Feodor, as if he were hesitating whether to say something or not. Finally, without stopping his work, and looking straight before him, he said in a low voice, so that only Feodor could hear him: "You must keep silent. If you tell anybody who I am I will kill you on the spot."

46

Feodor made no answer. He kept his eyes on the damp earth turning off his shovel.

"Well?"

"Don't be afraid. I won't give you away." And then Feodor surprised himself by asking, "Have you known Irina for a long time?"

The hussar did not answer at once.

"That is of no importance now. The important thing is that you forget about me and keep silent. Do you understand?"

Then, after a moment's thought he added: "As for Tropinin, anybody in Moscow who was not too lazy could have her."

"You lie!" Feodor shouted, flaring up.

"What was that?" asked his father, who was working on his other side.

"Nothing. Something came into my head. That's all," Feodor replied.

The hussar jumped back when Feodor shouted and the look in his wicked eyes slashed Feodor as with a knife: "Look out now! Be careful!"

CHAPTER 14

DURING THE EVENING roll call, Feodor watched to see when the hussar would step out and answer to his name.

"Novikov, Pavel!"

His father took one step forward and answered: "Here!"

"Novikov, Feodor!"

"Here!"

"Novikov, Maria!"

"Here!"

The roll call went on, but there was no sign of the hussar officer. Only toward the end the name of "Bourjak, Ivan" was called and the hussar stepped out of the ranks.

"I wonder where he got that name?" Feodor asked himself.

Everybody expected that they would be dismissed when the roll call ended. Instead, they were kept standing in formation for a long time, with no explanation. A strong wind was blowing. Low dark clouds raced over the steppes, above the heads of the tired people.

At last three horsemen rode up to the battalion. These were the Chairman, Chubarev, and his aides.

47

Sitting at ease on his restless horse, Chubarev shouted gaily: "Well, Intelligentsia! Did you work well? It's good to feel your bones a little, isn't it? The doctors recommend . . ."

Suddenly he knit his brows: "The following will take ten paces forward: Komarov, Piotre; Lebedev, Sidor; Rudak, Zachary!"

Three men stepped out with measured tread: ". . . eight, nine, ten. Halt!"

The called-out men stood motionless. It seemed that, like the rest, they did not know why they were wanted by Chubarev. He turned to the first one:

"Komarov! What is your real name?"

There was dead silence. The far-away hoot of a steamer on the Don came faintly over the air.

"What do you mean—real?" the man asked in a voice that trembled from apprehension. "I am Komarov."

"You lie! Your name is Nikolai Vasiltsev—Lieutenant Colonel Nikolai Vasiltsev! What have you to say about that?"

"That's not true! It's absolutely not true. My name is Komarov."

"Shut up, you snake!" Harsh oaths rent the air. "You shouldn't learn to lie on the threshold of death. That won't help!"

Chubarev's face became purple. Turning to the battalion, he shouted hoarsely: "We have found three officers among you. These enemies of the people will be shot right now."

These words, not fully comprehended at first, took the people's breath away. Somewhere a woman sighed audibly. Chubarev, satisfied with the effect produced, continued: "No doubt there are many more birds of that breed among you. However, we will catch up with them all in time and wring their necks."

One of the aides rode up to Chubarev and said something in a low voice. Chubarev shook his head and answered, so that his words could be heard by everybody: "Why in the ravine? We can shoot them right here. It will be a good lesson for the Intelligentsia. They may as well know that we don't stand on ceremony with our enemies."

Feodor couldn't take his eyes off the three condemned men. They had somehow unconsciously drawn close together and stood as a group against the background of the gray sky.

Suddenly Komarov ran several steps in Chubarev's direction and fell on his knees. Extending his hands beseechingly, he spoke hurriedly and passionately: "Don't kill me! Have mercy! I have a wife and children in Voronezh. Do not kill me. For the sake of my children, have mercy!" There was already no hope in his voice, only unspeakable yearning, a consciousness that there was no escape.

Chubarev's face twitched as he looked at the abject man on his knees before him. The short stubby fingers unfastened the flap of his holster.

"Get up, you scoundrel!"

One of the doomed men ran to the side of his craven comrade and tried to lift him to his feet.

"Shame on you! Komarov! Get up!" he cried. But Komarov tore himself free and ran over to Chubarev, catching hold of his boot with trembling hands. Chubarev freed his boot roughly and kicked him. Komarov fell to the ground. Continuing to look at him, Chubarev drew his revolver. At sight of the revolver Komarov's lips twisted crookedly, began to quiver.

"Why?" he cried. "Don't! I don't want to . . ."

Chubarev aimed the revolver at his face.

"A-a-a-ay!" Komarov screamed, piercingly.

A shot resounded. Feodor saw how the revolver jumped in Chubarev's hand. The screaming stopped.

Instinctively Feodor pressed closer to his father. He felt sick.

"What are they doing? What are they doing?" his father was repeating.

The next moment Feodor saw Komarov's lifeless body lying close to the beautiful legs of Chubarev's horse. Somebody's hollow voice, as though coming from far away, said: "Remove the carrion. Shoot the other two in the ravine. The show is over!"

Feodor did not recognize, only sensed, that it was Chubarev's voice. Then he lost consciousness.

CHAPTER 15

WHEN HE CAME TO, he saw his mother's face bent over him, her eyes full of tears. "Fedya dear! You have recovered! Pavlusha! He's all right now!"

Feodor raised his head. He saw the people crossing the field toward the city in straggling groups. His father was standing at his side, anxiously watching him.

"Was I out long?"

"Only for a couple of minutes."

Feodor got up. He felt a strange weakness all over his body.

"You aren't the only one who felt badly," his father remarked.

"I wonder what the hussar is thinking now?" thought Feodor, and suddenly it seemed to him that a strange voice whispered: "Take care, Feodor! Be careful!" So clearly did he hear the words that he even turned around. But there was no one near, except the Red Guard cavalry patrolling the trenches. He told himself: "Nonsense—there's nothing to be afraid of."

But the next instant he suddenly thought of the extraordinary danger of his own position. "After today's scene the hussar, in sheer desperation, is capable of going to any lengths to escape the fate of the three officers whose end he witnessed. Of course, he will do anything. He doesn't trust me. He knows that I hate him and he is afraid that I will give him up at any moment. Therefore . . ."

"Come along," Feodor urged his parents, "let's go home quickly. I feel all right now."

The sun was already setting. The sunset that evening was the same as yesterday's, perhaps brighter and more colorful. Dark clouds emphasized and set off the blood-red band flaming in the west. Looking at the sunset, Feodor remembered Akimov. "All right, Bolshevik! We'll see what you have to say when I tell you about today's brutality."

It was quite dark when the Novikovs reached their own street. All was quiet here, almost desolate. Here and there a feather of light shone through the cracks of the closed shutters, and the street lamps that had not yet been broken by hoodlums shed a dim light on the pavement. The gathering clouds in the sky made the autumn night darker.

The Novikovs walked slowly, because the mother had to rest frequently. She walked leaning on the arm of her husband. Two or three pedestrians overtook them. And now the steps of the last one were swallowed in the stillness ahead. They were alone.

All at once it seemed to Feodor that someone was following them. He stopped to listen, but couldn't hear a sound. Then suddenly and quite close by, he heard quick steps, as if someone were trying to catch up with them. Involuntarily Feodor shuddered. He strained his sight, peered into the darkness. A frightful suspicion filled him. The back of his neck grew cold.

His father noticed his nervousness. "Why are you continually looking back, Feodor?"

Feodor touched his arm: "Doesn't it seem to you that someone is following us?"

50

His parents stopped to listen.

"No, I can't see or hear anything," Pavel Novikov said at last, while his wife shook her head wearily.

But Feodor was certain that his fears were well founded. He hoped that someone from a neighboring house would come out. But nobody came. The street was completely deserted. Only somewhere far ahead, probably on the next street, could be heard the steps and voices of some belated couple.

"Let's knock at somebody's door," Feodor suggested in a shaky voice.

"Why?" his father asked in surprise.

"I'm certain that we are being followed."

"Nonsense. You're simply imagining things. Who would want to follow us? It's merely your nerves playing tricks with you after today's experience. And I don't blame you."

"No, Papa, it's not my nerves."

At that very moment, not only Feodor but his father and mother also saw a man jump across the lighted spot on the sidewalk and disappear into the darkness. Everything happened in a few seconds, but Feodor managed to recognize the man.

"The hussar! The hussar!" Feodor cried out as fear struck at his heart. "Run! Run! Hide somewhere! It's the hussar!"

"What hussar? What are you talking about?" his parents exclaimed together. But this time they looked apprehensively behind them.

The hussar must have heard their cries. His steps became loud and sharp. He was no longer hiding. The Novikovs ran. They had only half a block to go to reach their own house, not more than five lots away.

Suddenly Feodor noticed that in their anxiety to reach safety they were running straight into the circle of light shed by the next street lamp.

"Run to the side," he shouted, "get into the shadows," and he pulled at his father's arm with all his strength.

The latter caught hold of his wife, and dashed after him. But it was too late. A shot was heard, hard by. Feodor could hear the whine of the bullet. He threw himself on the ground, a second shot sounded and at the same time he saw his father stumble and fall, dragging Maria with him.

"O-o-o-oh . . ." he groaned.

Ignoring danger, Feodor crawled over to his father's side. Doors banged in the near-by houses and gates swung open; the cries of running people were heard.

Feodor saw a dark figure break from the shadow of a house, cross the street, and disappear down a lane between two houses.

"Catch him! Catch the hussar!" he shouted at the top of his voice, pointing to the lane. Two men ran after the hussar.

"Dear Pavlusha! Speak to me," begged his mother. She bent over her husband, unbuttoned his coat. Blood was oozing through the thin cloth of his shirt on the left side.

Feodor saw how one tremor after another passed through his father's body. He did not groan. The tremors became fewer and weaker. "He's still alive," said one of the onlookers. "Run for a doctor quickly."

The surrounding crowd was growing.

"Why! That's Novikov!" a familiar voice rang out.

Feodor raised his eyes. Akimov pushed his way through the crowd. Like all the others, he had run when he had heard the shots and cries. At once he began to give orders. He felt the pulse. "He's still alive, but it's touch and go. Here! Feodor! Take off your shirt and we'll make a temporary bandage until the doctor comes."

Feodor tore off his shirt and handed it to Akimov, who ripped it into strips. Bending over Novikov, he bandaged his chest tightly. A bright red stain appeared on the bandage at once.

"We'll have to carry him into the house," said Akimov. "There's no need for him to be wallowing in the dirt here. All right, children!" He turned to the crowd: "Come now, help me. Take his feet, someone. And you, there! Take his head, but be careful. Go easy!"

Three of them raised Pavel Novikov carefully and carried him into the house. Supporting his mother, Feodor followed behind. Without turning his head, Akimov addressed Feodor: "Nikolai and Olga had supper with me. They're asleep now. Who shot him? Bandits, or what?"

One of the men answered for Feodor: "Some kind of a hussar. The young lad here kept shouting: 'The hussar! The hussar! Catch the hussar!' Ivan here and I ran after him, but in the dark what can you expect?"

"The hussar? Aha!" Akimov asked no more questions.

Very gently they laid Pavel Novikov on the bed in his own bedroom. Akimov himself had told them to carry him there. The people crowded in. Men, women, and children looked gravely at the motionless Novikov.

The doctor came. They made way for him. He looked closely at Novikov's face, felt his pulse, placed a mirror to his mouth, and shook his head.

"He is dead."

A sharp, terrible cry broke from the mother. Horror was reflected in her fixed eyes. She shook her head and sank down beside her husband. Seeing her, Nikolai and Olga began to cry. They had been awakened by the noise, and stood close to each other amid the crowd of strangers.

"No! No!" the mother whispered between her sobs. "It can't be. It can't be."

Feodor looked at his father's face, which appeared yellow in the feeble lamplight. His open eyes looked somewhere above, into the unattainable. They seemed to be seeing something unexpected and not at all appalling, so clearly had a kind of quiet wonder frozen in them.

A desperate pain seized Feodor's throat. He went outside. In the darkness he cried bitterly, without restraint. He forgot time, his own existence—and was full only of thoughts about his father, his death and his murderer. An all-consuming rage choked him. "All right, hussar," he thought. "You won't get away this time."

A heavy hand settled on his shoulder. He did not turn. He knew it was Akimov. Keeping his hand on Feodor's heaving shoulder, Akimov stood for a time without speaking; then, very simply and sincerely, he asked: "And what are you going to do now, Feodor?"

"A lot you care," Feodor replied with bitterness, between sobs.

"Whether I care or not is a matter of tenth-rate importance. Now you're the head of the Novikov family. You won't recognize your mother any more. She's dead with grief now, and she'll never be the same again. So—you have to think for them all."

Feodor was silent. He didn't need Akimov to tell him that the old life was gone forever, that from now on a new, different life would begin. But what kind of life? He didn't know.

"Why did the hussar shoot your father?" Akimov asked.

"He was shooting at me," Feodor replied. "He's an officer; he was afraid that I would give him up."

"Well, and now what? Would you give him up?"

Feodor shook with anger. "I'll choke the life out of him with my bare hands, let alone give him up!"

"Oho!" Akimov remarked approvingly. "I see that you have plenty of fury. That's good. Nowadays one can't live without fury."

Feodor was silent.

"Fine: just stay here a little while and cry. The more you cry the better—it will ease your soul. And remember—you are crying for the last time."

"Why?" asked Feodor, taken by surprise.

"Because you have grown up," the other replied. "Your childhood is speaking to you for the last time. Grown-ups cry, of course, but without tears. And that, my brother, is harder to bear." Leaving Feodor, he went into the house.

CHAPTER 16

THEY BURIED Feodor's father the next day. Akimov knocked the coffin together from rough boards. He had gone to the Revolutionary Committee to report the incident and returned with a written order: "To attend the funeral of the former Intellectual Pavel Novikov, his wife Maria and son Feodor are excused from work for twenty-four hours."

Very few people followed engineer Pavel Novikov to his last resting place: only his wife, the children, Akimov, and some curious urchins. All his old friends had either escaped from Rostov or were working— digging trenches. Maria Novikov had wanted to find a priest, but it was as if the priests had disappeared into the ground. Those who remained alive were in hiding.

At the cemetery Akimov took off his gray forage cap and delivered a speech at the open grave: "And so Citizen Pavel Nikolayevitch Novikov is dead. He did not die his own death. He was smitten by a damned officer's bullet. But who knows? Maybe that is all for the best. He was not created to go through these hard times. I knew him only slightly—just for a few hours. But he struck me as being a good man. It's a pity he died so soon. I hadn't time to argue with him at length, but he seemed to be heated in argument—very heated. We might even have come to blows . . . Well—sleep peacefully, Citizen Novikov— we'll do all the worrying for you. Amen!"

To the accompaniment of such a strange speech Pavel Novikov, engineer, was buried in the late fall of 1917. Perhaps the Red Guard Akimov was right. Perhaps he was not created for these new times. The old world, in which Novikov had felt at home, was destroyed without the least hope of its ever returning. The new world had received him in an unfriendly manner.

After finishing his speech, Akimov spat on his hands, and grabbing a shovel, began to fill the grave. Feodor trembled when the first clods of earth dropped with the sound of finality on the lid of the coffin, but he did not cry. He merely clenched his fists and swore, beneath his breath, to avenge his father's death.

When the grave was filled, Akimov dug up a small birch sapling and transplanted it in the loose earth. "Maybe the little weeping birch will bring forth leaves in the spring," he remarked sentimentally.

On their return home from the cemetery, Akimov drew Feodor aside. "We'll have to go to the Revolutionary Committee. There's a man who wants to see you there."

"All right," Feodor replied indifferently. He guessed why he was being called.

But Feodor could not guess that when he stepped over the threshold of the Revolutionary Committee office he would have taken the most important step in his life. It was exactly at that moment that he cut himself off from his past—sharply and finally, as with a knife. But that was not enough. He was required, not only to forget his past, but to stamp out the conception of life that he had imbibed with his mother's milk: his understanding of honor, conscience, human dignity.

He entered the corridor of the Revolutionary Committee office without any emotion or fear, without any foreboding. There was only a great emptiness in his heart. It seemed to him that he had looked at the world through the eyes of another man, and he saw that it was not the same world—it was strange and unfamiliar. He did not recognize even himself: rage, rage only, filled him.

Akimov stopped in front of a door in the long corridor. It bore no inscription. "Here we are," he said, and knocked gently. The door opened, and they entered to meet a thin, middle-aged man. It was cold in the room and the man had thrown a greatcoat over his shoulders. A blue haze of tobacco smoke hung in the air.

"Comrade Potapov," Akimov addressed the man, saluting smartly, "permit me to report. This is Feodor Novikov, the young fellow I told you about."

"Good. You may go now, Comrade Akimov."

Potapov sat down at his desk, motioning Feodor to take a chair opposite him.

"Today," he began, leaning back in his chair and bringing the tips of his fingers together, "you buried your father. You have my full sympathy. I understand your condition and won't keep you long. I heard a lot about your father quite some time ago. He was a big man— the kind that keep the world going around. And to think that it was some swine of an officer that killed him. That is fate for you!"

Potapov looked into Feodor's eyes and said sharply: "We'll find that officer. He won't get away from us!" Then in his former quiet voice, he asked: "Didn't he call himself Bourjak?"

"Yes," Feodor nodded in agreement. "I heard him answer to that name at roll call."

"Of course, that isn't his name. He took the documents of a murdered civil servant. It's quite possible that he killed him himself. Quite possible. We have thoroughly frightened these officers. They have really gone crazy. And now he is hiding somewhere, but he won't be able to keep under cover very long. Hunger will force him to crawl out. He will have to go to the market to barter something for food, for bread. That's all to the good, as long as somebody isn't hiding him. Have you any idea who might be taking care of him?"

The question came unexpectedly. Feodor trembled. The name of Irina Tropinin flashed through his head. But his heart rebelled against dragging her into the story. He shook his head: "No, I don't know."

Potapov looked at him searchingly.

"Tell me, how did you become acquainted with him?"

"Several months ago," began Feodor, hoping that his voice didn't betray him as he lied, "I was returning by train from Kuban to Rostov. I had sold one of our prize horses there. In the train I met this hussar, who had somehow learned the reason for my trip to Kuban and decided, probably, that I had quite a sum of money on me. He invited me to play cards. I consented. He lost heavily, but had no intention of paying up. He tried to treat the whole thing as a joke. I insisted on payment. Then he got mad, threatened to pull my ears and throw me off the train if I didn't keep quiet. I replied just as roughly. Afterwards I forgot all about him. But when he met me yesterday in the field he recognized me and became frightened. He thought that I would give him up on account of the debt he owed me."

Potapov listened attentively. It was impossible to tell by his face whether he believed Feodor or not. Feodor already congratulated himself on having thought up a plausible tale. He had, as a matter of fact, made a trip to one of the Cossack villages in the Kuban the previous August and had sold one of his father's horses there.

"So you don't know where he might be hiding now?" Potapov asked.

"No, I don't know," Feodor replied. "I have no idea."

"That's bad. You see, outside of yourself, nobody can recognize him. We have no photographs of him. But we must catch him. Not one officer must remain alive in Rostov. Kaledin is preparing his attack and we must be on the alert. And, of course, your father is calling for vengeance." Potapov remained silent for a few moments, as if he expected Feodor to make some comment. But Feodor said nothing. Potapov went on: "I think we must join forces. We must make use of you. You will have to go with one of our men and hang around the market, stroll about the streets. Who knows? You may run into the hussar. You don't mind helping us, do you?"

Before Feodor could reply, Potapov continued: "You will be released from work and your ration cards will be continued. And incidentally, we shall be occupying your house one of these days so that you will have to move out. We shall give you an apartment of two or three rooms in the city. That will be much better than living in the stables. And you can take whatever you need from the house. I'll speak to the right person about this." Potapov looked at Feodor, as much as to say: "Don't you think that I'm a kind and considerate person?"

He got up and, stretching out his hand to Feodor, said: "I wish you success. If you find the hussar, I promise you we will release your mother from work. She's too old to be handling a shovel."

Feodor wasn't sure that he liked this unexpected turn in his affairs. However, he dared not think of refusing. Everything seemed to have arranged itself without effort, and so quickly that Feodor had not had time to gather his thoughts. Potapov spoke in a soft insinuating voice. What he asked was a trifle, a small favor. Besides, he spoke as if all this was of more advantage to Feodor than to him.

CHAPTER 17

OF COURSE they caught the hussar. The snow was falling in heavy, wet flakes. A raw wintry day had wearied the people to death. Feodor and his Red Guard companion, disguised as a couple of laborers, were standing in the market place watching the faces of the jostling crowd. The shivering people were bartering all kinds of trash in exchange for bread or potatoes.

Suddenly Feodor saw him. The hussar was in threadbare rags and almost barefooted. In his outstretched hands he was holding a pair of boots—they looked like the ones he had thrown at Feodor that fateful night—offering them right and left. He did not speak, but almost whispered through his frozen lips: "Here you are. A pair of leather boots. You can have them for five pounds of bread."

Thin and dirty almost beyond recognition, he was a pitiful sight.

Feodor's heart wavered, but he overcame the fleeting feeling of pity for the murderer of his father. He jabbed the Red Guard with his elbow: "There he is!"

The hussar caught sight of them, recognized Feodor, and hurled himself in fear into the crowd. But he did not escape. He was caught and led away. What they did with him afterward Feodor did not know.

His mother was released from work immediately, as Potapov had promised, but he demanded that Feodor write a report about the capture of the hussar. Only then did Feodor realize the trend of events. But it was too late to retreat.

One day Akimov met him on the street.

"Well, Feodor, so now you are with us?"

"Yes, I suppose so."

"What do you mean, 'I suppose so'? Hasn't everything been settled?"

"I hadn't expected to come to you in that way," Feodor rejoined sadly.

"Aha," Akimov nodded. "I understand. That, my brother, is quite important. The enemy is crafty and full of guile. He can't be taken without cunning. We must have people with heads on their shoulders, people like you: educated people with brains. Stop grieving. If you've got to make a clean cut, make it."

Feodor thought to himself: "Why, indeed, should I go on grieving and feeling sad? Didn't I listen to this same Akimov and his arguments about the Russian and his mysterious mission in the world? Now go ahead and discover the mystery. No, it is impossible to be just an observer. One must be either on one side or the other. Here, everything is new. There, the old and outworn ideas. Here, a great deal of brutality, coarseness—that's quite true. But, on the other hand—what ideas!"

Aloud he said to Akimov: "You know, Akimov, you have the knack of inflaming people. I will tell you truly: I am with you wholeheartedly. Just answer me one question, however: I have wanted to ask you this for some time. You remember the day my father died, Chubarev shot a defenseless man before our eyes with his own hand. That was terrible! Now tell me, was that necessary?"

Akimov did not reply at once. Then he said, weighing his words: "That's a difficult question. Lenin says that it is better for two-thirds of humanity to perish, as long as the remaining third lives better. You know, when you begin to think about them, these are terrible words. For me, Lenin is everything. But to hear such words, even from him, makes you tremble. You must become like a stone, kill your soul, as it were, before you can believe such words. Therefore Chubarev understood them deeply, otherwise he could not have done what he did."

"And what about yourself?" Feodor asked.

"As I told you before," Akimov replied simply, as if he were a mere pawn in the game, "I am a soldier of the revolution. If I am told to do so, I will shoot anyone. You know the saying: 'Death is defied by death.' That is, nothing is possible without death."

"You mean that there is no other way?"

"None. That is clear."

"And," Feodor went on, "it is necessary to kill innocent, defenseless people? Simply because they think differently from you?"

"Yes. Even the innocent. That is, they become guilty when they think differently. You see, this is a war of ideas. Ideas are in the head. Therefore, aim for the head, cut off the head. I must tell you, though, that all these questions are coming into your head because you have never been in battle, you have never seen death on a large scale. But as soon as you have fought a little, everything will become clear to you, and you will understand what Lenin meant. And, I may as well tell you, there won't be much delay on that count."

Akimov was right. A week hadn't passed before the news spread like wildfire: "Kaledin has begun his offensive!"

In the morning of December 8, 1917, Feodor heard the far-off booming of cannon. Kaledin's troops were storming the first outworks of the Rostov fortifications. General Kaledin had been able to muster a much larger force than the Revolutionary Committee had thought possible. But they were even more surprised when they saw with what ferocity these troops fought.

Under their assault, the lines of defense so painstakingly constructed by the Revolutionary Committee crumbled and were broken through. Artillery of every conceivable kind laid a continual barrage on the trenches and barbed-wire entanglements. Through the fresh breaches, wave after wave, Kaledin's units flowed.

The Red Guards fought back desperately but could not hold out. One after another the lines of trenches were giving up. The battle was transferred to the City itself. They fought for every building. The railway station changed hands several times. But slowly, foot by foot, Kaledin's army advanced. Finally, on the seventh day of the battle, the last remnants of the Red Guards were driven out of Rostov. They retreated toward the north, in the direction of Voronezh. Feodor Novikov was not among them.

On the third day of the fighting, when it was clear that the Reds could not hold the city, Potapov had summoned him to his office.

The first thing that Feodor saw when he entered the room was the thin, sharp profile of Potapov bent over the large marble fireplace. He was burning documents, stirring the charred sheets with a poker. The flames from the fireplace lit up his bent figure with a flickering light. Like the last time, a greatcoat was thrown carelessly over his shoulders. He was smoking a pipe.

"Ah," he exclaimed, turning to look at Feodor without interrupting his work. "So you have come. That's good."

With some surprise, Feodor noticed that Potapov showed not the least sign of excitement, as if, indeed, the fate of the Revolutionary Committee were not being decided just outside the windows. The air vibrated to the continual rumble of the artillery fire. When a shell burst nearby, the former Governor's palace shook and the window panes rattled.

"I must congratulate you on your baptism of fire. I am glad on your account. It has been reported to me that you have fought like a true Red Guardsman!" Potapov glanced at Feodor's tall figure, ragged, dirt-stained from the filth of the trenches. "And so, Comrade Novikov . . . you will allow me to call you 'comrade'?"

"Please," Feodor replied, "as you wish."

"Well then, I suppose that it is quite clear to you that we must retreat from the city. Of course, that retreat will be only temporary. In a month or two we will drive Kaledin out of Rostov. The point is, however, that you must remain behind."

"What?" Feodor shouted in surprise.

Potapov smiled. He knocked out his pipe on the marble fireplace. "I thought you would have guessed as much yourself. Surely it is obvious. We will retire, but we shall need eyes and ears here. You will be contacted by one of our comrades. He will show you what you have to do. I must warn you, however, there must be no tricks. Don't forget that your report on the catching of the hussar is in our hands. But even without that you wouldn't get away from us. If necessary, we would get you from under the very ground. But I am sure that we won't have to adopt such measures. I trust you."

Potapov chose his words carefully and spoke very gently, but to Feodor at that moment his whole figure, outlined by the light from the fireplace, looked sinister and frightening. His face, thin, ascetic, with the skin drawn tightly over the cheekbones, was grim. His eyes, in deep shadow, looked out sternly and steadily. Feodor began to feel uncomfortable.

"Comrade Potapov," he said, "will you allow me rather to remain with the regiment? I don't want to become a spy. Before God! I don't like the idea."

Potapov frowned.

"Spy? Who said anything about a spy? We have no spies. We have only self-denying people who risk their lives. These are the workers in one of the most important branches of warfare—reconnaissance." Feodor felt a note of resentment in his voice. "You are young, Comrade Novikov. You are full of all kinds of bourgeois prejudices, and that is why you are talking such nonsense. You have to be a little romantic, you must look for adventure instead of shunning it. You happen to fit into the picture better than anyone else. Nobody will suspect you, Feodor Novikov—the son of Pavel Novikov, well-known engineer."

"That is true," Feodor replied, "but I feel that nothing will come of it. It would be much better for me to remain on the firing line."

"No. We have enough fighting men without you. Your desire to remain on the firing line is very praiseworthy. I like to hear that sort of thing, particularly from one of your origin. I must tell you frankly that the fact that you took up arms voluntarily and fought along with us has influenced me greatly in my decision to give you this task." Potapov looked at him searchingly, then added, lowering his voice a little: "I could, of course, simply order you and you would be bound to obey. Do you want that, or not? It seems to me much better to arrange it in a friendly manner, without orders."

Feodor dropped into a chair and said dully: "Yes, it's much better without an order."

CHAPTER 18

FEODOR LEARNED later that the branch of which Potapov was the head in the Rostov Revolutionary Committee was part of the most secret organ of the Bolshevik Party, formed long before the 1917 revolution. It had been organized on Lenin's initiative after the first unsuccessful revolution of 1905. The wave of defeatist feeling that followed the failure, and the dejection among the members of the

61

underground, suggested to Lenin the idea of creating organizations within the party whose function would be to check on the members and to trail them when necessary.

From the first days of the revolution of 1917 these organizations developed and grew, becoming part of the military revolutionary committees all over Russia. They carried on espionage and counterespionage against the troops of Kornilov, Kaledin, and other generals. In December 1917, Lenin created the notorious All-Russian Extraordinary Commission, which was given unlimited powers in putting into effect the policy of War Communism, that is to say, of the red terror. It was headed by a man who became one of the sinister figures in the history of Soviet power—Felix Dzerzhinsky, a man with the face of a Don Quixote and the heart of the butcher Nero.

The Commission was called, for short, the Cheka. Several years later its name was changed to GPU, then NKVD, and still later it became the MVD, the Ministry of Internal Affairs. But whatever name it adopted, the idea remained the same. It was the main whip in the hands of the Politburo, with the help of which the slightest opposition was destroyed; it carried out such monstrous measures as collectivization, the purges, the transplanting of whole untrustworthy republics, the building of canals and war plants with slave labor, the forced population of the north.

The methods remained the same as in the time of War Communism: torture, exile, the firing squad. The only notable difference was that with the years the administrators became rich in experience, more refined in their cruelty. It was into their hands that Feodor fell in his youth. He was not the first, nor would he be the last, to fall an easy prey of such clever people as Potapov. Late, much too late, they realized where they had landed, after finding themselves enmeshed, hand and foot, as helpless as flies in a spider's web.

The relationship between Feodor and the well-known engineer Pavel Novikov, his education and upbringing, had exceptional value in the eyes of Potapov. Many years later, if Potapov had remained alive, he would have remembered his selection with pride, for Feodor Novikov developed into one of the outstanding secret agents of the Politburo.

But in 1917 he was a bit of a puzzle to Potapov. And even Feodor himself did not yet know where his heart lay. True, he had taken a rifle and fought in the ranks of the Red Guards. But that was the result of spontaneous impulse rather than of deep conviction. In his desperate search for a way out of the blind alley into which Potapov had led him through the hussar, the idea of fighting in the ranks of the Red Guards seemed to him, in some strange way, the only honorable solution to his problem. It was better to fight in the open than to be a spy. Furthermore, Feodor continually felt Akimov's influence over him, although that was not the main reason.

"I see that you are hesitating," Potapov said. "You are young, but I have decided to take the risk. Let us call this a scientific experiment."

A shell burst just outside the building. The window panes were strewn all over the room, and a breath of hot air brushed Feodor's face. He jumped up from the chair. Potapov hurriedly threw a whole bundle of papers into the fire.

"See how they're hitting us!" he said. "The devils know what to aim at. We'll have to slip away. Well, good-bye! Go and live in your own house. Our man will visit you there when it becomes necessary. Wait! Leave me your rifle—you won't need it any more."

Taking the rifle from Feodor, he smiled a broad open smile. Feodor shuddered, so terrible did this smile appear to him: terrible, precisely because it was too gay and too confident.

Feodor remained in Rostov. He thought very little about his own position. To what end, since the circle was closed?

He worried about his mother's health. Since the death of her husband it was difficult to recognize Maria Novikov: now she was a diffident, pale woman, broken by sorrow, aged, bent, and absentminded. Every feature of her thin face touched Feodor's heart with pain.

The arrival of the Whites cheered her up a little, but not for long. Hunger remained the same as under the Reds. The peasants from the near-by villages supplied the city badly with food, as they were afraid of the bandits who had become very active in the whole district; there were also the periodic raids by small detachments of Red Guards.

Feodor and his mother bartered nearly all their personal belongings for food. From standing long hours in the cold on the market-place his mother's legs and back began to ache. She caught cold easily, and often coughed during the night.

One evening, on her return from market, she complained of a pain in her chest, and asked Feodor to prepare his own dinner. She went to bed, and never left it again. In a week she was dead.

Just before her death, she beckoned her children to her side with a weak gesture of her hand. Approaching the bed, Feodor raised her thin hand. It was cold. His mother's face seemed drawn, the features had become sharper. Already the shadow of death lay on it. His heart quailed.

She raised her eyes to his, without moving her head:

"Dear son, Fedya," she whispered with difficulty, "do not neglect Kolya and little Olga. Be to them as a fath . . . fath . . ."—and suddenly she sighed, without finishing the word. Her head rolled to one side of the pillow and jerked strangely. A small, lonely tear rolled out of her open, motionless eye and down her wrinkled cheek.

"Mama!" Olga cried wildly.

Feodor pressed the lifeless hand of his mother, then laid it gently on the blanket. His lips were trembling.

He walked over to the window and stood there, senselessly looking at the beautiful, delicate designs so cleverly woven on the pane by the frost. The joyful rays of the sun played on them, undisturbed by the near presence of death. Bright and gay, they spoke to the depressed Feodor about the triumph of nature and of life eternal. His mother's last words suddenly acquired a simple and deep meaning. He shook his head, turned toward the weeping Nikolai and Olga, and embraced them with the same tenderness with which his father used to embrace the three of them.

CHAPTER 19

ON FEBRUARY 19, 1918, the Reds reoccupied Rostov. They were not the same regiments that had been driven out of Rostov two months before by General Kaledin. They even called themselves by another name—the Red Army.

Feodor served through the Civil War in a cavalry regiment of the Red Army—or, to be more accurate, in the Cheka branch of the regiment, but that was a secret known to very few. He experienced everything: long, exhausting marches in the saddle, attacks, retreats, the filth and stench of military hospitals, hunger and cold.

In this way four stormy years passed; years too significant to leave Feodor unchanged. It was difficult to recognize him. He had broadened in the shoulders, grown up. No trace was left of the young Gymnasium student who had composed poetry in the spirit of the Symbolists, and who had loved with an unworldly love. He had become hardened, secretive, reserved, experienced in life—and in love.

He met Irina Tropinin again, but under vastly different circumstances from their first encounter. It happened in Odessa, that beautiful city on the shores of the Black Sea. At that time, the staff of the volunteer White army under General Denikin was stationed there. Feodor walked about the wide, straight streets of the city in the uniform of a lieutenant, jingling his spurs, twirling his newly developed mustache. Nobody would have guessed, looking at the young well-built officer with the calm face, that he was risking his life every minute.

He knew perfectly well that the Whites did not stand on ceremony with spies, and particularly with Cheka agents. However, he felt comparatively safe. In the pocket of his uniform he carried reliable documents, taken from a killed White lieutenant. On all these documents the name of the original owner had been skillfully changed to his own. He had insisted on this precaution, as he felt that he was bound to meet some of his acquaintances in Odessa.

Life in Odessa at this time was a strange, hectic experience. Celebrities of all kinds from Petrograd, Moscow, Rostov—from all parts of Russia—had rushed in fear of the Bolsheviks to the port city in incredible numbers, and they seemed to have eclipsed the local residents entirely. Well-known members of the Duma and Senators rubbed shoulders with no less famous writers. There were so many generals that nobody paid them any attention.

The superficial feverish activity of these transient denizens of the overcrowded city was astounding in its gaiety, its disorderly confusion, and its heedlessness. An experienced observer would have noticed an undercurrent of unease, a sense of yearning expectation, in these people. They were, of course, waiting for the answer to the cursed questions: How would all this end? Where was Russia going? The more their hearts fretted, the more lively and carefree they appeared.

Officers coming from the front were quick to catch the general atmosphere and tried to outdo those in the rear. They were hilarious, they drank, they lived for the moment. The Odessa Theatre, a beautiful building, an exact copy of the famous Vienna Theatre, was open. Well-known Moscow and Petrograd artists gave nightly performances. A great many restaurants and cafes opened up. In the evenings a military band played in the park which stretched along the picturesque shore.

The moonlight glitter on the waters of the Black Sea, the pungent smell of the cypress, the soft music, the intoxicating Caucasian wine, and the heavy perfumes of the beautiful women—all blended into a wonderland of forgetfulness. The war was forgotten, the faces of those at the front, distorted by hate, disappeared into the golden mist. There

65

was only a desire to think about what made life beautiful: women, love, happiness . . .

Men and women fell into easy flirtations. Meetings in this strange unreal atmosphere seemed exceptionally romantic, the faces of the women fantastically beautiful, their smiles full of promise. The fact that danger hung over them all, and death lurked in the offing, merely increased the desire to enjoy every minute of life while it lasted. The elderly recalled their youth; those who had just begun to live hurried, eager to try everything.

Feodor, who was more an observer than a participant in the Odessa life unfolding before him, gradually became infected with the common sickness. In him it expressed itself in the form of grief, but he did not want to grieve alone. He wandered about the boulevards, ate and drank in restaurants and cafes—feeling himself drawn to places where there were many people, seeking he knew not what or whom.

Once, in his wanderings, he entered a small cafe called the Sea Rooster, which an enterprising Greek had built on the very shore of the sea. From the open veranda one could hear, above the lapping of the waves, the whispering of lovers in the bushes surrounding the place. Feodor was drinking a sour Georgian wine, lazily turning his glance from the sea to the faces of the women seated at the tables, restlessly yearning for happiness.

He had accomplished, in the main, the task the Reds had sent him to perform in Odessa. He still had to find out some names, some details about Denikin's staff. But that was easy. Now he could afford to relax a little. The happiness which he contemplated took the form of a woman. His imagination, bewitched by the magic of the moonlight, conjured up for him a beautiful and tender profile, but it was not the profile of Irina Tropinin. He had almost forgotten her. Since he had last seen her a lot of water had flowed under the bridge—stormy water and murky. It had washed out and taken with it his first boyish love.

Now he merely wanted to hear a gentle girlish voice calling his name; he wanted to have a girl beside him on this fairylike night—almost any girl, as long as she was affectionate and possessed of the same desire he had: to love and be loved.

When suddenly Irina Tropinin appeared on the veranda, extraordinarily beautiful and graceful, more desirable than in his most daring thoughts, Feodor lost his head.

Irina's entrance was quite unusual. Suddenly the lights in the cafe went out, leaving only the candles, stuck into shells on the tables. The breeze wafted the flames, throwing weird flickering shadows on the

66

walls and the balustrade of the veranda. An invisible guitar began to play. Some hand seemed to be picking hesitantly at the strings for several minutes, as if an errant soul, laden with grief, were searching for a theme and unable to find it. In hopeless anguish the chords sounded: sometimes loud, calling passionately, then soft and entreating.

Then all at once the theme became clearer, the chords more confident. A shaft of light fell on the low platform at the end of the veranda and Feodor saw Irina. He rubbed his eyes, but she didn't disappear. How different she looked now from that drunken Irina whom he had last seen sitting on the knees of the hussar. This was his own Irina again, proud in her beauty, the unapproachable Irina who had captivated his boyish imagination in the Gymnasium. His old dream came to life. But now she seemed even more dazzling, more lovely.

A dress of black silk sheathed her graceful figure. Her low-cut bodice emphasized her round shoulders and her firm breasts. Her shapely white arms were bare, and in her hands she held a gossamer scarf.

She stood motionless. The fresh breeze from the sea fluttered the hem of her dress and unfurled the scarf in her hands, and her eyes, between half-lowered lashes, sparkled.

Feodor's heart beat fast. The unexpected appearance of Irina and the manner of her entry were almost like an omen, whether for good or ill he was not sure.

"Irina! Irina!" he whispered. "It's really you? And how does it happen that you are here?"

An elderly man sitting at the next table remarked: "Of course it's Irina. Who but Irina has such a heavenly figure? But wait until she sings! That is really charming! And she isn't a Gypsy either, but Russian."

Feodor drained his glass in one gulp and paid no more attention to his neighbor. Irina began to sing. It was an old Gypsy song: "Quietly like a shadow, wherever you go I follow, always there . . ."

What can a Gypsy song speak about if not love, jealousy, and revenge? And what did Feodor and the people around him want to hear about if not love, a broken life, the past lost forever, and the dark, uncertain future? But it was not the words of the song that struck Feodor so much as Irina's voice and the way she sang. She began her song somewhat hesitantly, lazily, as if she were just rambling. Her eyes were still shaded by their heavy lashes. They fluttered slightly. To Feodor they seemed not eyelashes, but two dark butterflies quivering above her eyes, screening Irina from the audience, whose boring faces prevented her from enjoying the naïve but moving song. As Feodor sat and listened he was filled with wildly mixed emotions in which there was everything: joy at the meeting, melancholy for his past innocent dreams, present desire for passionate love.

When she began the second verse she raised her eyes and it seemed to Feodor that the cafe was lit up. She stepped down from the low platform and moved slowly among the tables, stopping a moment at each one. Two or three paces behind her the guitar player followed, dressed in an embroidered Russian shirt, baggy pantaloons of velveteen, and polished top boots. All eyes followed Irina's every movement. The air was hushed; only an occasional deep sigh or the faint tinkle of glass was heard. The people drank in sadness, without inward enjoyment, as if this song mixed bitterness into each drop of wine.

A stout, red-cheeked colonel, forgetting himself, stretched out his hands toward Irina as she came to his table. With a slow but strong movement she brushed away his hand and passed on to the next table.

With baited breath Feodor waited for Irina to come to him. The nearer she came the more inflamed became his desire to get up, and—right there before all the people—to press her to his body until it hurt; to kiss her proud lips, to look into the bottomless depths of her deep blue eyes, to remind this unapproachable girl of his existence. Let everything else go to pieces and vanish after that; everything except this one moment . . .

By now Irina's voice was firm and even threatening. Her dark brows were drawn together. She was the incarnation of a jealous woman thirsting for vengeance. And when she stamped her foot angrily she sang: "Your burning eyes will become dim, your lips silent forever . . ." Feodor felt a chill run up and down his spine.

She was there—at his table. His eyes sought hers. Their glances met. A tremor seemed to flit across her face for an instant. It could have been the flickering candle light throwing deceptive shadows on her pale excited face. The next moment she had left his table with her swaying gait so familiar to Feodor, and so inflaming to his desire to possess her.

"Darling Irina!" he burst out involuntarily. "Don't you remember me, Irina?" But he was not the only one calling her. Everybody on the veranda had come under her spell. The lips of one officer, drunk, with bleary eyes, suddenly became distorted and a wine glass trembled in his hand.

"Irina! Go and die! Oh! What is life, what is life?" he repeated senselessly.

68

Suddenly the song ended. Irina cut it off in the middle of a line. At the same instant, before the audience had time to recover, there was a loud strumming of guitars. A Gypsy chorus appeared on the platform. A gay dance tune burst out. Now Irina cried out shrilly and eagerly:

"Oh! How lonely I am! How sad I feel!"

The Gypsies caught up the tune at once: ". . . I have no one to love, no one to play with."

A tremor passed over Irina's shoulders, then dropped to her firm breasts which quivered under the tightly fitting dress. She spun into a Gypsy dance.

The sudden change from the melancholy song to the furious dance took everybody by surprise. From all sides hysterical yells resounded, joyful, tearful: "Faster, Irina! Faster, faster! Give it all you've got!"

The drunken officer who, a minute ago, had been ready to die from melancholy, was now clapping his hands joyfully like a child and shouting louder than anyone else: "This is life! This is what I love!"

Like everyone else, Feodor had been astounded by the sudden change. His throat felt tight. "Friend! My joy!" he shouted, beside himself. "I had no idea you were like this."

Nobody paid any attention to his outburst. All looked as if they were going out of their minds. They jumped onto chairs, stamped their feet on the floor. The floor shook, the dishes tinkled. The Gypsies bellowed in wild whoops and whistles. Breezes crisscrossed the cafe.

One of the Gypsies, bald but dashing and agile, leaped out from the chorus and began to whirl in front of Irina like a devil. With his hands he beat time to the music—on the soles of his boots, on the floor, on his bald head and even on his pursed lips.

Irina floated in the whirling vortex, tapping her heels, calling out couplets. Sometimes she retreated from the Gypsy, as if she were luring him on: in feigned fright she opened her eyes wide, smiling roguishly. Then she knit her brows and rushed at him, and so fiercely, that everybody held his breath. Angrily tapping her heels, she impudently slapped the Gypsy with the hem of her skirt as he whirled before her on the floor. At such times Feodor caught a glimpse of the white lace of her petticoat and her shapely legs in their silk stockings.

He was already jealous—jealous of everybody: of the bald Gypsy with the boldly sparkling eyes, of the stout red-cheeked colonel familiarly feeling Irina with his oily ogling, of his drunken neighbor to the left, sensually smacking his lips and almost drooling—he was jealous of all these half-drunk, half-in-love men.

When the colonel, unable to restrain himself any longer, jumped up from his chair, pushed the Gypsy aside roughly, and then began to stamp awkwardly in front of Irina, his heavy buttocks and flabby belly shaking like pudding, Feodor could not remember how he came to be in the middle of the floor, face to face with him. The colonel had just caught Irina around the waist.

"Take your hands off her, you son of a bitch!" he shouted, and turned pale with rage. One blow on the jaw toppled the colonel, whose legs were none too steady. Before anyone recovered Feodor lifted Irina in his arms and rushed toward the exit. Behind him the Gypsies shouted, women screamed, somebody fired a shot, somebody smashed dishes—but he heard nothing. "This will be my night! Even if it costs me my life!" was the one thought in his mind.

Irina struggled in his arms, beat her fists on his chest, scratched his face. But Feodor, happy, sweating, drunk—not so much from wine as from excitement—smiled broadly as he looked into her angry eyes.

"Let me go! Now I know you—you're that Gymnasium student from Rostov."

"I was a student, but not now. Now I'm a lieutenant and no worse than the hussar!"

Irina ground her teeth in helpless fury. She began to beat his chest more vigorously. But what were her blows to him? He was exultant, choked by the nearness of her warm, beautiful body.

When he got out of the cafe Feodor looked around quickly. Some distance along the embankment he saw a carriage, the drowsing driver sitting on the box. Feodor ran along the moonlit path, bearing his precious burden.

"Hey! Ivan!" he ordered. "Get a move on! Quick!"

"I'm not Ivan, I'm Pyotr."

"Never mind. Hurry! I'll give you a big tip."

Feodor placed Irina on the seat without letting go of her, then jumped in beside her. The driver rose, whipped up the horse: "Now then, dear one! Wake up!"

The horse dashed off along the embankment, just as the people were rushing out of the cafe, shouting and waving their arms. A voice with a Greek accent came wailing from the veranda: "Rinye! Rinye! Where are you?"

"Let me go! Can't you hear? The manager is calling me! Let me go!" Irina pleaded. "You've had your fun; now let me go. You're drunk. Go home and sleep it off."

"Sleep on such a night? You're joking, Irina. Besides what have you lost there? They're the drunk ones, not me. I am sober." And as if to prove his words Feodor kissed her hard on the lips.

CHAPTER 20

THERE WAS no pursuit. Gradually the carriage slowed down and the horse trotted along the seashore at an even pace. The bright moonlight made every detail visible. Feodor noticed how a small vein in Irina's neck throbbed gently. She resisted no longer. When Feodor tore himself away from her lips to catch his breath she said, almost without a trace of anger: "At least you might let my hands go, you devil. Just look how you've bruised my wrists. They'll be black and blue. Let go, I tell you! I won't run away."

Feodor didn't want to move, nor to lose contact with her body. A happy smile hovered around his lips. For the first time Irina looked directly and with more interest into his eyes. Then she began to laugh —a little nervously, as if she were shivering from cold.

"What are you laughing at?" Feodor asked.

"I just remembered how you hit the colonel," she replied. "The fat-bellied fool fell so funnily, like a bolster of feathers. You could be hanged for that, you know."

"That's all right. They won't hang me."

"Are you brave?"

"And are you faint-hearted?"

"Me? No."

"Then why are you trembling?"

"It's a little chilly, that's all."

"Wait a minute. I'll throw my jacket over your shoulders. So! Is that better?"

"Much better. Still, you are a scoundrel."

"That's quite true, Irina."

In the half light of the moon Feodor wasn't sure whether she was smiling, or frowning to hide her smile. She shrank under his jacket, stroking her right wrist, which hurt from his rough handling.

"I scratched your cheek. It's sore, isn't it?" she said.

"That's nothing," Feodor replied gallantly. "Bruises and scratches become men's faces."

"You are from the front, of course?" asked Irina.

71

"Yes, but why are you so sure of that?"

"All the men who come from the front act crazy. All of them are in a hurry to live; they do foolish things, are terribly rough, terribly sentimental—and in general, very lovable."

"An excellent description," Feodor said, and immediately added, with a touch of jealousy: "You know a lot of them, I suppose."

Irina's eyes sparkled with mischief. "And what if I do? Are you going to throw me out of the carriage on that account?"

Feodor caught her arm, so frightened was he by this proposal. "No! Irina! I'm sorry! Forgive me. Tell me rather, how did you happen to come here?"

"I fled from Rostov the first night of the revolution."

"And the hussar?"

"He remained. He was too drunk to move."

"The hussar could have meant nothing to her, if she can talk about him so casually," thought Feodor to himself, with a sense of relief. Aloud he said: "I didn't know you could sing and dance."

"I didn't know it myself. But hunger is a good teacher."

"So you have had a hard time?"

"It isn't easy for anybody here," she said bitterly. "All this gaiety, these sprees, all that—it's affected, anything to drown the melancholy. Actually they all hate it. One hope alone sustains them."

"Hope?"

"Yes," Irina replied. "We are all waiting for Denikin's victory."

"Ah, yes, of course . . ."

"Tell me," Irina asked anxiously. "When, in the end, will the Reds be defeated? When will the old life return?"

"Soon, darling, soon . . ."

"Soon? Everybody says soon, but the years go by and there is no end to the horror. All Odessa is living in the past." Irina stared into the distance. Her gaze was intent and sad, as if she, like Odessa, were living at present through something far distant in time, but close to her heart.

"Even now you are thinking of the past, aren't you?" Feodor asked sympathetically. His voice seemed to be asking: "Can't you be happy with me now?"

Irina smiled at him. "Yes, I was remembering one of my childhood dreams. While I was quite small and going to the Gymnasium in Moscow, all the girls were in love with our literature teacher, a dark, long-legged fellow. But I hated him. He reminded me of one of my uncles, who always had something wrong with his stomach; it was always rumbling. The teacher seemed to me to be the same kind of prosy and boring man. Secretly I dreamt of something unusual, like a bandit running away with me. . . . And so, tonight, when you unexpectedly rushed in . . ."

"And rescued you from the fat colonel?" Feodor laughed.

"Don't laugh. At first I was ready to kill you, I was so angry. And then I recalled my dream, and everything began to be interesting. Funny, foolish—yes—but pleasant. I forgave you only because of that stupid dream."

"Well, thanks anyway. And you are right: dreams come true. I have proved that today."

It seemed to Feodor that Irina herself had moved closer to him. The jacket had fallen off her sloping shoulders. He felt the warmth of her body. His heart began to beat quickly and heavily. It became unbearable. Irina saw his agitation.

"Lieutenant, have patience. You began so well . . . I will help you to finish," and raising her eyes to the moon, she added softly—"to finish my dream."

Then Feodor seized her awkwardly and roughly by the shoulders, turning her toward him, and began kissing her cheeks, lips, her eyes . . .

She tore herself out of his embrace and spoke to the driver: "Coachman, drive to Richelieu 15."

"Who lives there?" Feodor asked, without thinking.

"That is my apartment," Irina replied. "There we shall be together, the three of us. You, me, and my dream."

It seemed only a minute before the driver stopped his horse in front of a modest entrance. The hall smelled of perfume. In the semidarkness Feodor lifted Irina in his arms and carried her into the first room. The burning lips close to his ear whispered: "The bedroom is to the right, Lieutenant."

The rest was like living in a mist. The night was full of ecstasy, almost of madness. Everything vanished. There remained only lips pressed to his and the passionately yearning look in her eyes . . .

Feodor spent three days with Irina before leaving Odessa. These three days he lived as if he were drunk with happiness. They parted friends. Each was grateful to the other: Irina because he had brought back the past to her, Feodor because she had given him unforgettable moments of the present. The sweet sorrow of this meeting remained with him throughout his life. He came to know other women—the easy ones and the hard, the simple ones and the complex, but none took Irina's place in his memories.

CHAPTER 21

TIME PASSED. The Civil War ended. With great difficulty Feodor managed to wheedle a permit from his chief to attend the University. This had been his dream throughout the whole Civil War.

Handing him his credentials for study, the chief said: "Remember, Comrade Novikov, wherever you are, be ready to fulfill your duty. With regard to your studies, we will help you. We are sending you to the best in the country—to Moscow University. We will still need people with clear heads."

But Feodor had his own ideas. Secretly he hoped to escape from the circle into which he had fallen in Rostov. He began to study zealously in self-oblivion.

It was his ambition to advance in scholarship, to make the Cheka forget about him. But it was not possible. Soon after he entered the University the Cheka established contact with him. He was given a task—to keep the students under observation.

Lecturers and students respected his intelligence, but he made no close friends. Many did not like him, and some even feared this clever fellow with the quiet voice, the welcoming smile, and the searching look.

Feodor joined the Party while he was at the University. He submitted his application on the day of Lenin's death when, at the "Call of Lenin," the doors of the Party were swung wide open to thousands and thousands of new members.

After Lenin's death a dog fight between Trotzky and Stalin developed. The name of Trotzky thundered all over the country. He was at the height of his fame. Some students did not even know of Stalin; Trotzky was popular among them, and many spoke freely at Party meetings in his support.

The Party felt the absence of its master. Confusion set in; a peculiar kind of democracy developed. Members of the Party could speak at meetings without fear of arrest. Many did, if for no other reason than to make a noise. The illusory feeling of freedom went to the heads of some, especially the young ones. It was a new and interesting experi-

74

ence to be able to argue at a meeting, then when it was over to slap your opponent on the back and joke and laugh with him.

However, a few years later, there were not many who laughed. Smiles disappeared; jokes were forgotten. The hot-heads learned, but too late, that their oratory had been noted down by Stalin's people. For many, their speeches were not to be romantic memories of their carefree student days but rather their death sentences—admission to the torture chamber.

Novikov was not among the victims. He was too experienced to be carried away by the apparent freedom. He sat quietly by, refusing to make public speeches on the ground that he was too busy with his studies. He made no special friends either among the Trotzkyites or among the Stalinists. The students were surprised at his political inertness, and among themselves regarded him as somewhat queer. Meanwhile, he examined the situation carefully, weighing the forces of the opponents. The Trotzkyites were the more readily carried away by speeches—they inflamed the people with the fire of phrases. The Stalinists also talked a lot, but they worked more quietly in the background. Secretly they were building up a group of merciless people, in love with power, drunk at the sight of blood.

Feodor had been through the Civil War and he knew that beautiful speeches not backed by force were as effective as blank shells: a lot of noise, but no danger. Also he thought it was more than a mere accident that his chief in the secret work was a Stalinist. Long before others, he sensed the unseen though menacing power of Stalin.

A year after Lenin's death he saw the situation clearly: Stalin would win. Only then did Novikov begin to show himself quietly, and, naturally, on the side of the victorious faction. Instead of falling into disgrace at the end of the struggle, he became one of the thousands of small but necessary bolts in the complicated machine which made Stalin undisputed dictator of the Party and of Russia.

After brilliantly completing his course in the Faculty of History, Novikov was sent to the University in his own town of Rostov, to do postgraduate work as a lecturer. Feodor went to work with redoubled zeal, cherishing anew the old hope of breaking away from secret work. He thought that now his chances were greater. But again, at a secret meeting, he was given to understand what was required of him.

"All these old Intellectuals are untrustworthy," he was told. "We must keep a sharp eye on them. That will be your task. You must become a good postgraduate and, who knows, you may go a long way.

Do your best, and it won't be our fault if you don't rise—we will help you."

Feodor understood then that to become simply a scholar was not for him. He accepted his defeat and decided not only to resign himself to it, but to squeeze the most out of the situation. He did his very best.

In 1932 Novikov became a professor. He attained this spectacular step up in his career by using his talents and his peculiar position. He wrote an original work on the ancient Slavs. He felt, before anybody else, where the trend in Party policy was leading in the sphere of history. The indications were minor and not yet clear, but he came to one definite conclusion: the trend was in the direction of Russian nationalism.

At that time Novikov had no idea how sweeping this policy would be. He merely felt the stirring of a faint breeze and decided to move with it. Only several years later did it become the all-embracing idea of propaganda for everything Russian—not only in the sphere of history, but in all fields of knowledge without exception: science, industry, agriculture, art, everything.

While all the historians around him were still beating the old drum, Novikov suddenly introduced a new and startling rhythm. His success exceeded his own expectations.

The fact that he had always cherished this idea of Russian nationalism may have contributed to his success. It had become his second nature. But now he did not approach the subject like a boy—in exaltation; nor as he had felt when listening to the wild speeches of Akimov about the mystic role of the Russian people. That had passed. Now he meditated on the theme with cold calculation, knowing exactly where he stood. It was no longer important to him whether he believed what he wrote or not, whether it was true or not. There was only one all-important test: would his work find favor in the eyes of the Politburo? His great boldness lay in taking a new step at a time when there was no official Party doctrine in that field.

He took the chance. He won. His work, *On the Sources and Origin of Ancient Slav Culture,* received the highest blessing of the Party.

An enthusiastic review was published in *Pravda* as a feature article in six columns. That was all that was needed. *Pravda* and Politburo were synonymous, and the law for everybody. Novikov knew perfectly well that all that remained for the critics, no matter what they may have thought about his work, was to repeat *Pravda* in chorus. Any original, independent appraisal of his work could go no further than the addition of a few laudatory epithets not yet used by *Pravda*.

Thus, with one stroke, Feodor cut through to a smooth road leading to his cherished dream—the title of Professor.

The chief innovation in his work lay in the complete rejection of the centuries-old concept that the first Russian Empire and Russian culture were conceived in the south of Russia, in the Kiev District, by the Varangians coming down from the northwest. Novikov simply discarded as a myth what had been accepted by all historians without exception, confirmed by ancient chronicles, regarded as established fact beyond the least doubt. Novikov boldly announced that these were fairy tales invented by historians fawning before western culture. He repudiated any influence from the west on the formation of the first Russian Empire and thereby gained the favor of the Politburo.

One part of his work, quoted in *Pravda,* embodied the core of his idea: "The genesis of Russian national culture lies in the deep, many-centuries-old historical process of the independent development of the Slavic peoples, beginning with the Antesian Slavs. The genesis of the Kiev Empire, as well as the further form of Russian statism, must be reckoned, not from the western Varangian princes Rurik and Oleg, but from the Antesian princes Bozh, Mizamir, and Andragast, from the campaign of the Slavs against Byzantium in the sixth century."

As is usual in such cases, all the chief newspapers and journals adopted the tone set by *Pravda*. Novikov's work at once acquired political importance. Most newspapers reprinted the *Pravda* review in full. Only a few wrote their own comments, following, of course, the spirit of *Pravda*. The Rostov paper *Molot* preferred the easy way. After reprinting the *Pravda* article, it went on to present Novikov to its readers as "the well known professor of Russian History at Rostov University," although he was as yet only a postgraduate lecturer and his reputation had been confined to the walls of the University.

Exactly half an hour after receiving his copy of *Pravda* the Director called Novikov to his office. Novikov hardly recognized him. The usually cold and aloof Director had changed suddenly into an amiable and cordial man. He fawned on Novikov.

"Allow me to congratulate you," he beamed, coming forward with outstretched hand as Novikov entered the room. "From the bottom of my heart I congratulate you on your success. Your achievement brings honor to the whole University. I am calling the Academic Council together today and I am certain that all the members will consider it an honor to award you the title of Professor. We should have done it before."

"Really, really!" Novikov protested with mock humility. "Surely I am not worthy of such an honor!"

The Director was delighted. He threw up his hands.

"Ah! Such modesty! Such modesty! Real, genuine Bolshevik modesty! We must take a leaf out of your book, Comrade Novikov."

Novikov smiled to himself. "You old goat," he thought, "why don't you ask me how my work became known to *Pravda* and, consequently, must have been approved in advance by the Central Committee without your knowledge? You dare not ask such a question now."

Indeed, the Director dared not ask any questions. He knew that Novikov had stolen a march on the Academic Council. But it was too late now to do anything about it. Whatever earns the approval of *Pravda* becomes sacred: it must not be touched; it may only be praised.

Novikov had, indeed, resorted to a trick. He knew perfectly well that to write a scholarly work was one thing: to achieve its success was another. He had worked as quietly as possible, telling nobody about his undertaking. He had been in no hurry to submit it to the Academic Council of the University, as postgraduates usually do. From the experience of others he knew that even if his work had pleased the Council and had been placed to his credit, that would have been only one small step ahead on the long, hard road to his goal of professorship.

Furthermore, if the members of the Council scented something new in the work and wanted to make a success of it, Novikov would gain nothing thereby. Knowing the rabbit hearts of the Director and members of the Academic Council, who feared anything new, anything outside the decrees received from Moscow, Novikov could not expect such initiative from them.

Even supposing the unexpected happened and the Academic Council decided to give it publicity—even then all the credit would go to the Director and the prominent professors, leaving the real author in the shade. This would be accomplished very simply. They would praise his work and say something like this: "It's not badly written, Comrade Novikov; indeed, not at all badly written. However, it contains a great number of immature thoughts, unclear passages. You will be credited with this, of course, and we hope that in your next work you will be able to avoid these mistakes." Amen!

Then, after a month or two, there would appear a scholarly work under the signature of a dozen venerable professors, with another title and slightly changed content. You would not be able to find

78

Novikov's name if you searched every page with a microscope. He had known all this, and so decided to proceed differently.

CHAPTER 22

AT ONE of his secret meetings with the chief of undercover work he appeared with his treatise. "Do you remember, Comrade Loginov" (this was long before the appearance of Drozd; Novikov was accustomed to frequent replacements in his chiefs), "you promised to help me? You advised me to do my best and that if I did not make progress it would not be your fault . . . Well, I am forced to ask your help."

"All right," Loginov said impatiently, "speak out. I'm listening."

"You would like to see me holding the title of Professor, wouldn't you?"

"Of course I would," agreed his chief. "But wait a minute! That can't be done all at once. You'll have to work well for about ten years, and in time you will be awarded a title. We will help you in that, of course. But the road from lecturer to professor is long. In fact, some people remain lecturers all their lives."

"The others," said Feodor. "Let's leave them in peace. Just tell me one thing. Would you like to see me a professor, not after ten years, but now?"

Loginov frowned. "Listen, you crazy chump! I already told you that's impossible. You have just barely begun to work as a lecturer. And furthermore, it would be much too obvious. People would begin to wonder."

"You don't understand," Feodor persisted. "I am merely asking you—would you like to see me as a professor or not?"

"All right, we would; of course we would! Our work would only gain from that, as you would then be mixing with the highest circles of the Intellectuals. But, I repeat, that is just one of your fantastic dreams . . ."

"That's all I wanted to hear," Novikov interrupted him. "And as for dreams, here in this parcel lies the key to their fulfillment." He held out the parcel, wrapped in newspaper, to Loginov. It was, indeed, a fairly voluminous typescript.

Loginov didn't take the parcel, but hid his hands behind his back. "What is this? Aladdin's lamp?"

"Please don't joke. I ask you to do only one thing. Give this work to someone in the Central Committee of the Party in Moscow, in the department of propaganda. To someone with influence and weight. Do you understand?"

"And then what?"

"Nothing more. That is all I ask."

"But what kind of a work is this?" Loginov asked with a little more interest.

"It's about the ancient Slavs. An old theme, but written from an entirely new point of view."

"Ah! I understand. You want to take the risk!"

"Yes, I'll risk it."

"And if you fail?" Loginov asked. "I suppose you will again ask us to help you?"

"Why should I? If you need me you will help me. If not—that is my risk."

"Has your Academic Council seen this work?"

"Of course it has," Feodor lied easily.

"Well? What was the result?"

"The usual one. You know: 'It is a good piece of work, well written,' and then they filed it away. You know these birds."

Loginov took the parcel with a resolute movement of his hand.

"All right," he said, "I'll do what you ask. But watch yourself. It's your venture. I don't know a thing about the ancient Slavs, but I do know something about contemporary people on the Central Committee. You may bump into something that won't make you happy afterwards. I am agreeing to your request only because I know that you are fairly level headed. I will send off the work to the right place. Are you satisfied?"

"Perfectly," replied Feodor with relief. "Thank you."

Six months later Feodor received a newspaper clipping of the article from *Pravda* by mail, addressed to his house. In the right-hand corner there was a note in Loginov's handwriting: "You have won. Congratulations."

The Director knew nothing of this. All he knew was that somehow Novikov's work had got into the hands of the high and mighty in Moscow—over his head. There they praised it. That was enough; he knew now what was required of him.

When Novikov came before the Academic Council that evening, the Director and members of the Council pretended that they had been acquainted with his work for a long time and that the whole incident, including the appearance of the article in *Pravda,* had been done with their knowledge. Novikov likewise played his part well. In his speech he purposely emphasized the following words: "I would not have been able to create this work, on which *Pravda* has commented so warmly, without the sincere help and support of the entire personnel of Rostov University, and in the first instance of the members of the Academic Council and the Comrade Director."

The Director merely screwed up his eyes, as though to say: "What a fraud! First he fools us, then sings like a nightingale."

Novikov was awarded the title of Professor unanimously. In his concluding speech, the Director said: "Today's award of the learned title to Comrade Novikov is a great and happy event for Rostov University. It is pleasant to see how the new Soviet Intelligentsia is growing, how the best sons of the Soviet people are grasping at knowledge. Before us we have a brilliant example: a former warrior of the Red Army, who took part in the Civil War and defended the young Soviet State bravely. After finishing his education under the Soviet regime, he became a lecturer in our University. And now, thanks solely to his talent, he has advanced into the front ranks of Soviet scholarship and has become a pioneer and pathfinder. Only in our Soviet regime, only under the tireless care for its scholars by the genius of humanity, the coryphaeus of scholars, the great Comrade Stalin, are such brilliant achievements possible—witnesses of which we are now. Where would Comrade Novikov have been at this moment if it had not been for the Soviet regime—where would he have been, I ask you? He would have been a mere hireling, wallowing in poverty somewhere, living from hand to mouth, working for some parasitic exploiter. Isn't that the case, Comrade Novikov?" Novikov, who had so luckily escaped the fate of a hireling, nodded his head in agreement, looking very serious. "You see? And now who is he? Now he is a Professor. Now the Soviet regime has untied his hands and made everything possible for him. All that is needed is work, effort—there is no limit to boldness, no obstacles for the most daring innovators!

"I wish you, Professor Novikov, new successes in your work for the good of our great motherland, to the glory of our dear and beloved Comrade Stalin!"

All the members of the Academic Council stood up and applauded. That was the usual rule: to applaud at the mention of Stalin's name. Novikov also stood up. He also applauded: but he was not thinking of Stalin. With an exulting heart ready to burst out of his chest in triumph, he was applauding Feodor Novikov, innovator Novikov, Novikov who could surmount all obstacles, Novikov who had fooled the Academic Council, dearly beloved Professor Novikov.

Within six months, and without special effort on his part, he was appointed chairman of the department of Russian History. During that half year his position and authority were strengthened greatly. The People's Commissariat of Education confirmed his treatise as a textbook for higher educational institutions. His theory became a dogma. This happened very soon after the Central Committee of the Party passed a resolution "On the mistakes in the teaching of Russian History," and sharply rejected Rurik and Oleg and the western Varangians, officially expressing its complete approval of the theory advanced by Novikov.

Immediately a whole band of professors, academicians, and just plain writers—like a pack of hungry dogs unleashed—snapped at the bone thus thrown by the Central Committee. The newspapers and journals were bespattered with historical articles. The question of the ancient Slavs and the damned Varangians acquired as much priority as the fulfillment of the five-year plan and events in Germany. Dozens of chefs with learned titles began to cook new works like pancakes, new "discoveries," new "interpretations" of old chronicles, all manner of "research." Reading these exercises of the venerable savants, Professor Novikov merely smiled. The important thing was precedence, and that indisputably belonged to him.

He decided he must do everything possible to consolidate the successes and prepare the ground for new achievements. By becoming a professor he had jumped far ahead. That was true. But the race was long and the course intricate. Although the title of Professor was important it did not alter to any appreciable degree his material position. Even the chairmanship, with several older professors and a dozen lecturers under him, and with a salary twice as large as before, did not satisfy him.

What was the use of money if he still had to eat in the mess hall for lecturers, where he got the same kind of rotten food as the least penniless lecturer? What importance did money have, even if he got it in sackfuls, if the stores where he could spend it had nothing to sell except volumes of Karl Marx and chessboards? If you wanted to trade on the black market, you needed money by the carload, not by the sackful.

82

It was not surprising that Novikov's imagination was constantly disturbed by the mysterious dining room upstairs, where the Director and the Secretary of the Party Committee of the University had their meals. He must become Director. That would open the door into a new world for him as an equal of the few favorites of fortune. Besides the dining room, the Directorship would give him a free four-room apartment attached to the University; the special stores now closed to him, where only directors of plants, the chiefs of trusts, the secretaries of Party Committees went, would open their doors to him. These were the bold dreams of Feodor Novikov. Why not? Everything was possible. He was a member of the Party, a professor well known from one end of the Soviet Union to the other. Indeed, why not?

Just when Novikov was planning how best to undermine the Director and accomplish his downfall, along came Drozd with his task. With his whole being, Novikov felt that his time had come. Fate itself, in the form of Drozd, had handed him the key to success. Now, or never, he would realize his audacious dream. If he fulfilled the task of the Government he would attain the Directorship. Didn't Drozd say that in case of success he would envy him? And what if he did not fulfill the task? What then? But Novikov rejected the possibility of failure. He had always been lucky. He must succeed now.

He raised his eyes and only then noticed that while he had been meditating, considerable time had passed. It was already late. The statue of Lenin with its outstretched hand, in front of which he sat on the bench, stood out as a silhouette against the background of the gray sky. Suddenly above his head music began to play. Three loudspeakers were arranged fanwise on the roof of a corner building. A military march was being played. Then the music stopped, and a thick voice began to announce the latest news: "Citizens! Check your clocks. It is eight-thirty. I repeat—eight-thirty. Here is the latest news:

"The kolkhoz shock workers, meeting in a district conference in Rostov, have sent a letter to the great Stalin. In their letter they thank Comrade Stalin for their happy and joyous life.

"The shock brigade of comrade Pyotr Rybalko at Plant Number Seven in Rostov has fulfilled the quarterly plan of production by a hundred and three per cent before the time limit. The portrait of Comrade Rybalko has been hung on the honor board of the plant. 'In the name of the great Stalin we have worked,' Comrade Rybalko announced. 'In the name of the great Stalin we have succeeded!'

"Today a delegation of Young Pioneers visited the great Soviet writer Mikhail Gorin. The children tied a red Pioneer tie around the neck of the writer and appointed him honorary leader of their group. They promised him they would grow up as real Stalinists . . ."

Feodor rose. "Enough of reminiscences," he thought. "It's time to go to Glushak's."

PART TWO

CHAPTER 1

USUALLY one trouble in a morning is enough to ruin the whole day. On this ill-starred morning, Academician Pyotr Glushak was visited by two troubles, one worse than the other.

As he entered his study in the Rostov branch of the Academy of Sciences, of which he was the president, his technical assistant, a thin young girl with a flat-chested figure and boyish haircut, reported to him that the Secretary of the Party Committee wished to see him immediately. In telling him this she emphasized the word "immediately" and it seemed to Glushak that her colorless eyes sparkled with malicious joy.

Trying not to betray his uneasiness, Glushak ordered her dryly: "While I go down to Comrade Mirzoyan, you will prepare the materials on the languages of the people of the Northern Caucasus. Today a group of linguists will make a report."

Glushak found Comrade Mirzoyan, Secretary of the Party Committee, at his usual occupation: rolling his customary cigarette from a piece of newspaper. Mirzoyan had the bad habit of smoking the cheapest and most evil-smelling tobacco. As Secretary of the Party Committee he had every opportunity to indulge in Moscow cigarettes, but he preferred makhorka; its common quality emphasized his simple nature. Mirzoyan never forgot to remind the savants of the historic significance of his mission. "I was sent to the Academy by Moscow to get things into order and to inspire you old-fashioned scientists with the new, healthy Bolshevik spirit."

In Mirzoyan this Bolshevik spirit reeked strongly of rank tobacco. In everything else the Secretary tried to adhere to the habits and manners affected in the highest Party circles. Although he himself did not belong to these circles he nevertheless considered himself a person of importance and was not inclined to yield in anything to the powerful of this world.

Like the Secretary of the Northern Caucasus Province Committee of the Party, Comrade Larin, he regularly manicured the nails on his thick fingers, yellow-stained from tobacco. In accordance with the practice introduced by the other Province Secretary, every morning a barber came to Mirzoyan's office and shaved him. He shaved not only his chin, but his entire head. From constant shaving, his round skull shone like a well-polished samovar. Mirzoyan ate well, had grown fat, had allowed his stomach to expand, walked slowly and importantly— exactly as he had seen members of the Politburo walking in the films. Under his official Party uniform, cut from coarse wool, Mirzoyan wore silk underwear. Imitating the fashion adopted in the highest circles, he used perfume liberally; and entirely on his own, imitating no one, he sweated like a hard-driven donkey. His large office, covered with carpets (Mirzoyan, like many Armenians, had a liking for oriental rugs), constantly stank of a strange mixture of perspiration, cheap tobacco, and the strong cloying smell of expensive perfumes.

The Secretary met Glushak with his usual greeting: "Come in, come in—don't be afraid. I see you have grown soft on good cigarettes and turn your nose aside from our workingman's tobacco. But that's all right, you'll become used to it. Only harmful insects are afraid of strong tobacco." And Mirzoyan laughed loudly, terribly pleased with his own joke.

Glushak had heard this joke a dozen times, but as always, he answered the Secretary with a shallow laugh, although he did not want to laugh at all, and his eyes were watering from the acrid tobacco smoke.

The Secretary stopped laughing abruptly, noisily inhaled smoke into his lungs, and assumed a serious expression.

"Comrade Glushak, the Party Bureau is entrusting you with a responsible task," he began. Mirzoyan never spoke in his own name. No matter how insignificant the business, he always presented it in the name of the Party Bureau. This Bureau was rather mysterious. Officially, it should have met once a week to decide Party questions. But, as everything was decided above, and Mirzoyan alone was quite capable of handing down ready-made orders, the Bureau was as useful to him as a fifth leg to a dog. Nevertheless Mirzoyan knew from experience that it never did any harm to give Party democracy its due—in words.

Glushak was a member of the Bureau and knew perfectly well that it had not met since the last Mayday celebration. Nevertheless, without blinking an eye, he swallowed Mirzoyan's fiction.

The other continued: "The Party Bureau has decided that you should prepare and read a report at the ceremonial opening of the Rostov Affiliate of the Marx-Engels Institute. The opening will take place day after tomorrow. And—this is a secret, but I can tell you—some very important persons from Moscow will be present. So, you understand, keep on the alert; don't mess things up." Mirzoyan pulled out a large handkerchief, wiped the beads of perspiration from his shaven head, and sighed deeply: "You know, if anything goes wrong, I'll be responsible." Here he rolled his eyes with the air of a martyr.

"Damn your smoked soul!" thought Glushak. "Of course, you'll put the blame on me if you need to."

Mirzoyan noticed his sour expression and hastened to add: "But don't be afraid. You won't spoil the game, I'm sure of that. The theme of the report is 'Marxism-Leninism—the Guiding Star of Soviet Science!' Bring out as many local examples as possible, cases from the experience of the Rostov scientists. Do you understand?"

Glushak understood. He also understood that after the Secretary's words the whole day was spoiled. To write a report, and especially for important visitors from Moscow, was the last thing he would wish. In order to earn for themselves the reputation of being merciless and deeply principled champions of Marxist truth they were always ready to sink people even more buoyant than some Academician Glushak.

"You sly Armenian! You have made me your scapegoat again," thought Glushak bitterly. "Actually, infamous wretch, it's you who should deliver the report." But he did not attempt to refuse the task. He knew that all his protests or entreaties would fall on the heart of the fat Secretary as on a down quilt. He decided only to write the report as safely as possible, working it up with general phrases and accepted situations. "I'm too old to show off and take chances," he thought.

While Glushak was returning along the corridor to his office, the polite and abject smile which he wore in the presence of the Secretary gradually left his face. Glushak was a nimble-minded old man who had seen a lot and knew how to act. At first glance he gave the impression of being quiet and restrained, crowned with hoary hairs and the experience of sixty years. The shock of gray, forcing itself from under the black academic cap, gave him the stately and stern appearance of a man of science. But under these gray hairs, the alert observer would notice that his red, smooth-shaven face with the small nose and small lips was rather agitated. There was an expression of vague expectancy in his light, narrow eyes, which evaded any direct look. Glushak walked with a careful, noiseless step: not as if the soft carpets of the Academy were under his feet, but an invisible rope stretched over a chasm.

In his office Glushak stamped to his desk and, trying not to meet the questioning glance of his assistant, ordered her abruptly: "Comrade Pankratov, prepare me some quotations from Lenin and Stalin dealing with science. As many as possible."

"What about the linguistic group, Comrade President?" the girl asked respectfully, indicating with her hand the files which she had just placed on his desk.

Glushak blew up: "You heard me! I said to prepare the quotations! Must I repeat myself every time?" and Glushak impatiently pushed aside the stack of folders. "Put this away."

Suddenly he twitched his nose.

"Comrade Pankratov, again you stink of some kind of trash! If you can't get perfume, don't use scent at all. Why spray yourself with men's eau de Cologne? After all, this is the Academy—not a barber shop!" Glushak completely forgot that a minute ago he had been smelling the wild odors of Mirzoyan, resignedly, even with a smile.

As usual his bad mood expressed itself in badgering his subordinate. Pankratov's exaggerated politeness, her smug look, irritated him. Glushak was secretly afraid of her. But the more he feared her the more readily he tormented her and made her life miserable.

"Now, what are you standing there for?" he shouted at her.

"I beg your pardon," the girl murmured, "but I thought . . ."

"The gobbler thought on the turkey hen! Go away! Don't allow anyone to disturb me."

The girl flushed crimson, quickly took the folders and, almost at a run, left the office. In the next room she gazed out of the window. The leaves of the trees rustled invitingly, but instead of the trees she saw the face of Glushak, distorted with anger, and thought sadly: "Should I write a complaint, or not?"

But she hated and feared Mirzoyan more than Glushak and there was nobody, besides Mirzoyan, to whom she could write. After grieving a little and waiting until her ears cooled down, she sighed deeply and began to select the quotations from Lenin and Stalin on the importance to Soviet scientists of the study of Marxism.

CHAPTER 2

GLUSHAK HATED to put things off, particularly unpleasant ones. Immediately after his assistant left, he started writing the report. The work demanded attention and accuracy, and his thoughts kept wandering. He was sorry for himself. It was disgusting to think that he, a highly esteemed scientist, a gray-haired elderly man, should have to humiliate himself before this ass Mirzoyan, smile with him, laugh at his foolish jokes.

". . . but there's no other way. Everybody does the same. It's no use kicking."

Glushak recalled how Mirzoyan, immediately after his arrival at the Academy, established order. He made a rule: every morning before beginning work all the intellectuals must do gymnastics. In the big hall the Academicians, professors, and technical colleagues fell in, drew in their stomachs, stuck out their backsides. Mirzoyan inspected the company importantly, looked at them sternly, checked the line-up, where necessary slapped a stomach—"pull it in!"

Then briskly he gave the command: "Ready! One—two! one—two!"

On the command the intellectuals jerked their arms and legs, wheezed and panted, while Mirzoyan beat time with the palms of his hands, repeating: "In a healthy body—a healthy mind!"

After this a rumor went around that before his appointment to the Academy, Mirzoyan had been commandant of a concentration camp. For his good work on the bodies, he was promoted—to keep an eye on the minds of the Academicians. But it was difficult to confirm the rumor. Possibly evil tongues were wagging.

Mirzoyan soon dropped the gymnastic exercises—they bored him. Besides his belly had begun to grow noticeably.

Then he established a new rule: when the Academicians met him, they must draw up to attention, click their heels and report briskly: "Comrade Mirzoyan, Academician So-and-so!"

On the command "At ease!" the man of science could continue on his journey.

Soon this novelty bored Mirzoyan. He thought up another one. At the end of each week all the Academicians must take a test on political literacy. Each one was given Stalin's book, *Problems of Leninism,* with the command: "For the week, five pages—to be learned thoroughly!" At the end of the week Mirzoyan received the Academicians in his office one by one. While they recited, he checked with the book. One word wrong—failure! "Learn it again!"

A whole month had passed since Mirzoyan had called anyone, which meant that this idea bored him too.

"What will he think up now?" reflected Glushak, working over his report. "Dances, called to political slogans? They say that's the fashion now."

Finally Glushak managed to squeeze out several introductory phrases. He was just going to read them over when his telephone rang. An unknown voice gave the password. The password was simple and, indeed, a little poetic: "Was it you who ordered the flowers?" And, as always when he heard the password, Glushak's heart sank and his hands grew cold. The password meant a secret meeting, and a secret meeting could bring anything.

The voice in the black receiver ordered: "We shall meet at the corner of Sennaya and Budenny Streets at two o'clock."

"All right!" Glushak replied, and did not recognize his own voice. Frowning, he went to the meeting.

The news, that he had been entrusted with making Professor Novikov acquainted with Gorin, stunned him. The mission was given to him by Drozd in a very terse form, without any explanation. One could only guess at its significance.

On the way back to the Academy Glushak went over in his mind every word Drozd had spoken, fixed in his memory the least change of expression on his face. What he remembered was not comforting. Drozd had been cold, businesslike, even contemptuous.

Suddenly Glushak stopped. A terrible suspicion dawned on him: "They want to replace me with Novikov! . . . Yes, yes, of course, that's it! I read in the paper about this Novikov, this upstart. They are boosting him as the best example of a young Soviet scholar. How do you like that! I didn't know that he was tied up with the NKVD. Now everything is clear—all this ballyhoo was just a build-up for him! Now they'll introduce him to Gorin with my help, and then . . . then . . . they will discharge me. They'll send me as far away from Gorin as possible. What is to be done now? What? . . ."

Glushak squirmed like a worm under a boot. This secret work, his friendship with Gorin, which the police were using for their own ends, was his only prop. It alone gave him support in life's adversities.

His head began to spin at the thought. "How have I failed? Did I not try hard enough? Did I not do everything they demanded of me? Why do they no longer need me? Is that how they pay for so many years of blameless accomplishments? For my doglike devotion?"

Glushak walked on, the houses and streets of Rostov passing dimly before his eyes. Somebody greeted him, somebody called him by name—he replied mechanically to the greetings, not recognizing anyone.

"What should I do now? Go and complain? But to whom? Ask Drozd? Ridiculous. No, I've become old, that's what. . . . I'm simply a rag, a useless rag."

In the reception room of his office he met again the cold expectant eyes of Pankratov. He shuddered in spite of himself. At that moment her glance personified the entire hostile world, ready to fall upon him.

"Why! This is the first step, the first step toward my downfall. After this everything will go. I won't be able to hold out a month as president. I must do something, must take some step. But what?"

He found himself behind his desk. In front of him lay the unfinished report. "I must forget myself, even for a little while," he thought, and dipped his pen into the ink.

Glushak knew from experience that in moments of agitation nothing soothes and diverts the mind like work. During the rest of the working hours he managed to write the draft of the report and, what was more important, to compose himself. The first wave of desperate fear passed.

"Maybe I'm imagining all this. Maybe I shouldn't worry. At least I'll see this Novikov tonight and find out what's in the wind. He will know the whole story. He'll tell me," Glushak comforted himself, but doubts lay on his heart like a heavy weight.

He returned home at six o'clock in the evening, exhausted, his face as gray as dust. As soon as he saw his wife he embraced her with unusual tenderness.

"What's wrong with you, Petya?" she exclaimed, glancing into his face. "You don't look yourself. Trouble at work again, darling?"

"It's nothing, Olga. I'm just tired. It'll pass," he replied, kissing her forehead, while to himself he thought: "This day will bring misfortune to me and to you."

"Well, if you're just tired—that can be cured. Rest a while, and you'll

91

feel better." His wife felt reassured at once. She was one of those fortunate people who become upset only when there is trouble, not before it comes.

Glushak's wife was a small, active woman. Younger than he by fifteen years, she still preserved traces of her former beauty. A kind of tender and soft strength was suggested by her face with its broad features and turned-up nose. Compared to Glushak, who often gave way to melancholy and gloomy forebodings, she was always in good spirits, looked at life through cheerful eyes. But beneath her good nature and outright light-heartedness lay a sound, practical mind and a native astuteness.

They had no children. In her heart she grieved deeply over this. Maybe it was on that account that she so dearly loved her husband, as if he were a big child requiring attention.

Glushak, putting his arm around her waist, went into the dining room with her.

"Olga, tonight Professor Novikov of Rostov University is coming for supper," he said quietly, looking away. He did not want Olga to connect his bad mood with the coming of Novikov.

"Is he the one who wrote something about the ancient Slavs?"

"Yes, the same."

"How interesting!" exclaimed Olga. "I shall certainly ask him— surely he doesn't believe his own rubbish?"

Startled, Glushak gave her a sharp look.

"Please, Olga, be careful in your conversation with him," he began to warn her in an agitated voice: "Don't talk without thinking. He is, as you know, one of the young scholars . . . what is it they call them? —the new Soviet type."

Olga interrupted him: "Petya, you're always getting worked up about nothing. Young people babble a lot more than their elders."

"Nevertheless, be careful. I don't know him well yet."

"All right, all right, I'll be careful," Olga replied, appeasingly, stroking his hand. "For supper, I'll prepare a snack, with vodka. We still have some herring and a bottle of Moscow vodka. Does he drink?"

"I don't know. But prepare everything properly," said Glushak wearily. "You see, he will be a frequent guest."

"Has he been appointed to the Academy?"

"No, but . . . but I'll be seeing him often. Please don't ask me any more."

"You're tired, Petya. Go and lie down before supper. Rest. Seriously,

92

you look ill. Here, I'll help you." Olga began to unbutton his shirt. Glushak gently pushed her aside.

"Unfortunately, I can't rest. I must prepare a report. That son of a devil, Mirzoyan, has foisted some new work onto me."

"My God! Do they never give a man a rest? Why doesn't he make the report himself?"

"And why should he when there is Glushak?" he said bitterly.

CHAPTER 3

GLUSHAK DECIDED to rehearse the report before supper. He went into the bedroom, where there was a wardrobe with a mirror. When he saw his own reflection he hardly recognized himself. "Surely I don't look like that?" he whispered.

His usually narrow eyes were wide open, the pupils fixed. His bloodless lips were twisted into a pitiful grimace.

"That is the face of fear," Glushak thought. He rubbed his cheeks, his forehead, his eyes, with the palm of his hand, as if he were trying to rub the terrible mask off his face. "That is the face I saw in 1920, when I returned from prison. It is the face of horror, of physical pain; an inhuman face."

Wave after wave of fear for himself and his wife flooded Glushak's heart. It grew and became oppressing. He wanted to share his apprehensions with her. "She is such a cheerful, spirited woman," he thought of her with gratitude, "she knows so well how to comfort."

Glushak stretched out his arm imposingly, as if he were addressing an unseen audience, and began to speak in a loud voice, suited for a large hall: "Comrades! Today's solemn opening of the affiliate of the Marx-Engels Institute in our city betokens . . ."

"No," he thought, "I won't tell her. She might betray her agitation in the presence of Novikov. That can't be permitted. I'll tell her after he has gone, when everything is clearer." And Glushak finished the phrase: ". . . betokens an event of historical importance."

From the hall came the sound of an opening door and someone's steps.

"It's too early for Novikov. It must be Alexei," Glushak thought.

Alexei, his wife's younger brother, lived in their apartment. Four years previously, on arriving in Rostov, he asked if he could spend the night with them until he could find living accommodation for himself.

He was still spending the night there. He was studying literature and worked all day in the library, and at night slept on a mattress spread out on the dining-room floor. During the day the mattress was hidden behind the sofa.

Glushak lived in what was regarded as style. As an Academician he was lodged in the House of Scientists, one of the best buildings in the city. As president, he occupied the best apartment in the building— three rooms: bedroom, dining room and kitchen. Besides, he kept a maid—a young peasant girl, Fyokla by name. Fyokla left the house early in the morning and spent the whole day standing in queues for bread, kerosene, groceries, and clothing. At night she slept on the kitchen floor. Olga had to clean the apartment and cook the meals herself.

From the bedroom, Glushak heard the quiet voice of his wife giving Alexei some orders: "Please go to the neighbor's, to Academician Vatrushev, and borrow some jam. Get plenty—get a saucerful. Tell them that we are having a visitor today and that we'll give it back to them as soon as the coupons are announced."

"Do you think they'll give it?" Alexei asked in a doubtful voice.

"They ought to. When they were celebrating his birthday I gave them a whole half pound of sugar and waited almost a month before they paid me back. They'll be swine if they don't give it."

"Oh. That's different. In that case I won't ask, I'll just demand," replied Alexei, and left.

"How like Olga he is," thought Glushak, continuing to gesticulate in front of the mirror and read his report. "The same cheerful eyes. And like her—never downhearted."

In half an hour Alexei returned, with Fyokla. They were laughing at something.

"Olga Nikolyaevna," Fyokla began quickly in an unusually shrill voice. "I got nothing today. They promised to issue overshoes, but didn't." And she threw the empty shopping bag into the corner in disgust.

"What were you laughing at just now?" Olga asked, surprised.

Fyokla became confused. "Oh, nothing. Alexei was telling me all kinds of foolishness on the stairs."

"How many times have I told you that my brother is not Alexei to you, but Alexei Nikolayevitch? What familiarity!"

"I'm not offended," Alexei interceded for Fyokla.

"All right. It doesn't matter about the overshoes. It's a long time till winter. Did you bring the jam?" Olga turned to Alexei.

94

"I did. Here you are," and he handed her a saucer with raspberry jam. "I had a talk with Academician Vatrushev himself. He doubts that we will give it back."

"He has no business doubting," Olga grumbled.

"What shall I do now?" asked Fyokla.

"Go clean the herring and the potatoes. And you, Alexei, go and help her."

"With pleasure," replied Alexei and followed the girl into the kitchen.

Alexei and Fyokla were great friends. Several times Glushak, waking in the night, had found Alexei's mattress empty, and heard furtive noises in the kitchen. Once he spoke about this to his wife. She merely smiled. "I know. I'm not blind. So what? It's an affair of youth. Thank God that he didn't bring a wife into the house. Where would we have put them? Under the table?"

"The point is, it's dangerous. What if she becomes pregnant?"

"I have talked to her . . . She's no fool."

"You think of everything!" said Glushak in surprise. And completely satisfied with his wife's reply, he never mentioned her brother's night adventures again.

Glushak recalled the first days of his acquaintance with his wife. What a beautiful time that was! He—a well-known professor of whom the students were afraid, was shy and blushed in front of Olga. She—a young student—fell in love with him, passionately and tenderly, with her first maiden love.

That was long before the revolution, long before the war of 1914. He was giving a course in applied mechanics at the Technical Institute in St. Petersburg. He met Olga first at the lectures and could not forget the merry girl with the turned-up nose. He began to seek meetings with her. They became friends. They went walking on Nevsky Prospect, rowing on the river Neva. They admired the white nights, dreamed of the future. And it was very easy for them to dream. Pyotr Glushak's career was established. She wanted only one thing—to be his wife. Like all bachelors, Glushak led a disordered life, took little care of himself. Olga decided to change all that.

"How funny you are! Is that any way to live? Sloppy room, meals any old time! . . . That's impossible!" she said, throwing up her pretty hands. Glushak smiled guiltily, kissed the dimples in her cheeks, and said nothing. What was there to say when his heart was so full? She took his apartment, his meals, his whole life into her loving hands, and suddenly his life became unrecognizable. Only then did he appreci-

95

ate what he had been missing. Comfort, an orderly life, the warm caresses of a loved friend—that was what his heart had been yearning for secretly. He introduced her to his brother Vladimir, also a scientist, and equally famous. He presented her to his friends, to the writer Gorin, and to the scientists Grigoryev and Perventsov.

"What friends you have—all great people!" said Olga, her eyes sparkling with delight. "But for me—you yourself are the greatest, the greatest genius!"

It was like a dream. Pyotr's marriage didn't lessen his devotion to his work; on the contrary, it heightened it. He was not vain, yet it pleased him to see the joy his success brought to Olga.

Pyotr was a physicist, Vladimir a biologist. Both were proud of their fame but careless and imprudent with it. Like his brother, Pyotr was interested in nothing except science. Questions of politics interested them little. They considered the revolution an occupation for madmen.

"Forget politics," Glushak told his students at a time when everything breathed of revolution and nearly every one of his listeners dreamed of becoming a Robespierre. "Do not think of what is useless. Politics will destroy you; only knowledge will save you."

The brothers spoke freely, afraid of nothing. They were surprised how others could be scared. When Pyotr was cautioned about being indiscreet, he replied in the words of the poet: "Perfect love banishes fear," and added proudly: "I love knowledge; that is sufficient to make me above fear."

Yes, those were different times. . . .

"And now there is not the least bit of pride in me," thought Glushak bitterly. "I'm afraid of everything, even of myself."

When did it begin? It began when someone hissed like a snake against his brother Vladimir. Without suspecting it the brothers had many enemies. Somebody overheard Vladimir's bold statements, and reported him to the Cheka. Vladimir Glushak—politically dangerous. Knowledge, reputation, title did not help: Vladimir disappeared just as easily and unnoticed as if he had been an unwanted cretin.

When they arrested Vladimir, Pyotr protested loudly; then they arrested him. An official of the Cheka came and searched the apartment, calling him "darling" all the time, and took him away to jail in a cab.

They threw him into a dark, stinking cell. Glushak was not long in jail, only a week. But every day seemed an eternity. During the day he listened to steps in the corridor, the slamming of iron doors, the grating of locks. At night, he slept badly. In his dreams someone's iron hands were choking his throat.

One night heavy steps and the grating of the rusty bolt of the next cell raised him from his straw mattress. A group of people burst in on his neighbor. Glushak already knew it was Vladimir, his brother. Rough voices were heard. Whoever had gone in was demanding something. Glushak pressed his ear to the cold wall. The wall was thick; he couldn't hear what his brother replied. Suddenly the sound of a blow was heard . . . another one . . . a third . . . his brother groaned.

"He has begun to talk!" a hoarse voice cried out triumphantly. "Beat him harder!"

There was a sharp blow; then suddenly a howl, a horrible, inhuman howl pierced the thick stone wall as if it had been paper.

Glushak jumped away from the wall, rushed around the cell, tried to hide in a corner. He could not see Vladimir, but he imagined clearly his face lying against the floor, distorted by pain, his eyes rolled up, the veins in his neck distended—and the twisted, howling mouth. There is nothing more terrible than a human howling! But the most terrible thing was to hear his brother howling. Pyotr himself was howling. Contracting his body into a ball, trying to dissolve in the darkness, to disappear in the weblike cracks of the wall, Glushak yelled. After each blow behind the wall, he let out a wailing, whining sound.

"A . . . a . . . a . . . ay."

In the cell there was no longer the proud scientist Pyotr Glushak. There was a pitiful, hurt dog, suffering pain, pain, pain . . .

Many years had passed since then, but still Glushak remembered that feeling of horror. These blows behind the wall had beat out of his soul all faith in himself, in people, in everything breathing. He shrank. His mind, which nearly left him on that ominous night, demanded but one thing: to escape, to escape at any price!

A savior appeared in the person of a commissar of the Cheka, wearing riding breeches with red piping. He smiled in a friendly way and looked him over. It was the glance of a trader in life. Was Glushak ready or not? Glushak was ready. That was clear at the first glance.

The commissar smiled and set the conditions: "We will free you if you work for us."

Without hesitation Glushak agreed. To get away, only to get away from these damp walls, from these horrible, inhuman groans and howls, from these terrible dreams and that still more terrible vigil.

"Not a word to anyone that you have been our guest," the commissar reminded him.

When Glushak left the jail he fell to the ground and kissed the earth. He looked at the sun. For the first time, after a week of darkness, it shone on him and he laughed at it, as a child laughs at the smile of its mother. Unrestrained happiness swelled his chest. He laughed like a madman and tears gushed from his narrow eyes.

He left the jail in a strange condition. He was not the same Glushak. He was only the ruins of Glushak. The wasted body was healed in a fortnight, but the soul—never. His condition could be compared to the rotting oak: outside it looks majestic and mighty, but inside— emptiness, decay. Fear built itself a nest in his heart.

Of the existence of this inner Glushak almost no one knew. Even Olga, his wife, knowing everything he had gone through, thought that he had forgotten the week in jail. At times Glushak himself was deceived. There were happy hours, even days, when the memories faded in his brain, became groundless as a dim dream. Then Glushak, relieved, would sigh: "An end to torment, and forever!"

But "forever" lasted only a day, and such days were not many.

Glushak was an old and close friend of Gorin. A shrewd writer, liking and able to analyze the hidden workings of human souls, Gorin nevertheless noticed no change in his friend. Glushak remained for him a keen scientist, proud and fearless, a member of the Pleiad of giants to which he himself belonged. Gorin treasured friendship with such people, particularly since he noticed that proud and fearless people were becoming scarcer and scarcer in Russia. . . .

CHAPTER 4

THE MAID met Novikov. He had not expected such luxury and felt a little embarrassed at first. The neat appearance of the hall and the good quality of the furnishings impressed him.

Novikov had never seen Academician Glushak, although he had heard much about him and often pictured him in his imagination. He knew that he was an old and respected scientist, famous not only in Russia but abroad as well. He knew that his brother, Vladimir Glushak, also an Academician, had disappeared somewhere. Some said that he had been exiled to Siberia to a concentration camp, and had died there. Others declared that he had been sent as one of a scientific delegation abroad, where he deserted, and now was blasting the Soviet Union and his own brother from exile.

All this had surrounded the name of Academician Glushak with mystery and aroused Novikov's respect. "He must, indeed, be a valued scientist, if in spite of his brother, they not only did not put him in jail, but made him president." So Novikov had thought. Now, when he learned from Drozd that Glushak had contact with the NKVD, a feeling of scorn rose in him against his will, as if he had unexpectedly found a counterfeit coin in his pocket. Glushak was an esteemed scientist—yes. But, like Novikov, he was also an informer, an agent—that meant that his high position as president, his pleasant apartment and this maid, had been earned not through his scientific labors alone, but in some secret and not altogether honorable way, about which people usually prefer to remain silent. Novikov could excuse himself, but not somebody else.

While waiting to be announced, he heard a loud voice in the distance: "Under the banner of Lenin-Stalin the Soviet scientists advance . . ."

"Why have they turned on the radio so loudly?" he thought, surprised. But suddenly the words were cut off, and in a minute a thick-set gray-haired old man came into the hall.

"Professor Novikov, I am very glad to see you. I am Pyotr Glushak," and the old man stretched out a pudgy hand to Novikov.

"What an imposing old fellow he is," flashed through Novikov's head. He wanted to have a better look into Glushak's eyes, but could not. The old man's glance was evasive.

"May I make you acquainted? My wife, Olga. Professor Novikov." Glushak introduced his wife, who had come into the hall behind him. The small strong hand shook Novikov's.

When they entered the dining room a lanky young man rose from a chair.

"My wife's brother, Alexei Nikolayevitch Dorogov," explained Glushak. "And now, comrades, I think we are all acquainted. Please come to the table." And in the Russian way, they immediately sat down at the table.

The table had a stylish, but hungry, appearance. It was covered with an old-fashioned, expensive tablecloth, apparently preserved from pre-revolutionary days as was nearly everything in Glushak's apartment. A small silver samovar gleamed on the table, cosily whistling its tender melody. The silver, good dishes, napkins, and wine glasses were placed correctly for four persons. But amid all this luxury Novikov noticed

99

only one plate with a salt herring, several pieces of black bread, and a bottle of vodka.

"Well—the supper isn't very good," thought Novikov, disappointed. "We'll have to wash down the vodka with tea, I suppose."

After pouring the vodka for everybody, Glushak raised his glass, squinting through it at the light: "Well—here's to a pleasant acquaintance!"

"Between scholars," added Alexei. He emptied his glass and nibbled at a piece of herring. "Olga and I, as ordinary mortals, will drink to the honor of sitting at the same table as the great ones and eating fish with them."

Glushak frowned. "When people drink vodka they are all equal."

"Especially if they are under the table," Novikov interjected jokingly.

They all laughed.

"Are you married, Professor?" Olga turned to Novikov.

"Not yet."

"So, you are a bachelor, like my brother Alexei. That shows your good sense."

"Why?" asked Novikov, surprised.

"These days the young people get married early, without any money, with nothing behind them—like birds. No doubt it is very romantic. But life demands the practical. In our time men married when they were sure that they could not only kiss their wives under the bushes, but live under a roof."

Novikov smiled. "I haven't married yet mainly because I haven't found a suitable girl. Besides, I'm very busy."

"Don't listen to her, Professor," Alexei put in. "She's delivering a lecture on good sense for my ears. My far-sighted sister is afraid that I will complicate her apartment situation."

"You're being coarse," Olga reproved him simply. "However, you are right. For you to get married now would be the height of indiscretion. Pass me the bread, please."

Novikov looked at Olga with interest. "It's she who sets the tone in this family," he thought, watching her smiling lively face. "Apparently an outspoken woman. And her little brother also belongs to the smart ones."

"Tell me, Comrade Dorogov, where do you work?" he asked Alexei.

"He is our literary man," Glushak replied for him.

"Literary man?" Novikov repeated. He didn't like literary people,

100

and always tried to avoid conversations with them. He knew one at the University only too well. It was impossible to talk with him. He would get excited, wave his arms, sputter saliva and quotations from Shakespeare or Pushkin, deafen his listener with other people's thoughts. Finally, reaching a state of frenzy, he would suddenly jump up and rush away to the lavatory. Literature affected him, apparently, like a laxative.

So Novikov, hearing that Alexei was a literary man, looked him over cautiously: What if he suddenly became hysterical?

But Alexei sat quietly, chewing his fish.

Novikov asked him: "Have you any published works?"

Alexei shook his head: "No, and there won't be."

Novikov was astonished: "But a literary man . . ."

"He is a refugee," Olga explained.

Novikov's eyebrows jumped higher. "What?"

"He ran away into translation. To you, as a professor, a colleague of my husband, I may say: he ran away from the storms of current politics," said Olga with a barely noticeable sneer. "Alexei found himself a private haven in the pursuit of literary translation. In this little field he is required to decide nothing, nor to think for himself: the material for translation is selected, read and approved by a government official. No responsibility. Very simple."

Novikov looked questioningly at the "refugee" Alexei. The latter nodded his head: "That's true. I did write a book, but I stopped in time. Too many published men are engaged at present in physical labor in the north. The climate there is bad for me."

"So—he's foxy!" thought Novikov.

Glushak sat on pins and needles. Nervously drumming with his thick fingers on the table, he listened sullenly to Olga and Alexei. "No. I should have warned Olga more thoroughly," he thought with irritation. "Now try and stop them! And what an idea! . . . 'as a colleague of my husband.' They'd bite their tongues off if they found out that this 'colleague' had met Drozd this morning."

To end the ticklish conversation Glushak said to Novikov: "As you know, I am a physicist and not a historian. I read your work on the ancient Slavs, however, with interest. You have, indeed, brought about a revolution in Russian history."

Novikov was about to thank Glushak for his compliment, but Alexei opened his mouth first: "I always thought that historians described revolutions but did not make them."

101

Glushak nearly dropped his fork. Even Olga looked disapprovingly at her brother, on whose face an insolent smile hovered. Novikov, however, merely shrugged his shoulders.

"Yes, you're right. The task of historians is to write about facts of the past, and not to imagine them," he said, giving Alexei a cold look. "Unfortunately, instead of that, they merely repeat each other. As you know, frequent repetition is still not evidence of truth. Particularly when the disclosure of new historical facts——"

"Have you uncovered such facts?" Alexei asked him outright. Red spots suddenly appeared on his cheeks, possibly from vodka, possibly from excitement.

"Alexei! Don't interrupt!" shouted Glushak irritably.

Novikov continued: "Yes, some facts have been uncovered. But most of them were known long ago. Only they were concealed or presented in a distorted form. No, I haven't made any revolution. I have simply re-examined the facts. It's just not my nature to repeat another's ideas." Novikov sighed, and added: "I doubt if I would make a good translator."

"Excellent!" Glushak exclaimed.

"Not badly put," responded Alexei. "But not strongly enough to spoil my appetite." And laughing good-naturedly, he helped himself to a piece of herring.

In spite of themselves everybody smiled, and Olga said: "I doubt if anything could spoil your appetite." Then she turned to Novikov: "I don't want to argue, Professor, but I always thought that the Russian Empire began with the Ruriks," and she hastened to add: "We were taught that."

A naïve, disarming smile appeared on her face. Novikov, fearing that the conversation might take a too serious trend, replied reassuringly: "You don't need to worry about that. You're not at school. This is more for the new generation."

"Still, it's strange. All your life they teach you about Ruriks and Olegs and then, in your old age, you find out that it's all not true. Everything is changed so drastically . . ."

"For me it's all the same, Ruriks or Mizamirs," exclaimed Alexei, "as long as I remain Alexei."

"That's a small consolation. Now they even change people," Novikov replied. It was difficult to know whether he was speaking seriously or joking.

"How is that?" Glushak asked, looking at him guardedly.

"Look at our Rostov Academician Bogoraz—the surgeon. He

changes the appearance of people. He will, on demand, graft on noses of any dimensions, lips, and . . ."—here Novikov hesitated a little and looked towards Olga—". . . and anything else."

To his amazement, Olga neither pretended lack of understanding nor showed embarrassment, but said very simply: "I know what you mean. That's very funny. *Pravda* writes about it fairly often."

Alexei waved his hand in contempt: "Ha! What a fuss they make of these Bogoraz operations! Let any foreigner come to Rostov, and immediately they hurry him off to see Bogoraz: 'Let's show you our operations!' When all's said and done, it's quite clear that if they can graft on a nose, they can graft on anything else," Alexei spoke bluntly and poured himself some vodka.

Glushak frowned: "Nothing is clear. If it were clear, *Pravda* would not be writing about it. . . . And in general, it's not for us to judge." Alexei completely exasperated him. "What made him burst out like that?" he wondered. "He meets Novikov for the first time, doesn't know who he is, why he came, but argues, tries to be smart, speaks freely in front of him as if he were his blood brother. He must have drunk too much." And Glushak, to be on the safe side, moved the bottle of vodka further out of Alexei's reach.

Olga defended her brother: "And if we are not to judge, then who is? You must agree, Petya, this is very interesting."

"There are many interesting things about which it is best to keep quiet," mumbled Glushak.

"It's better to speak about the weather," said Alexei contemptuously.

"Yes, even the weather."

"What are you getting angry about?" Olga asked her husband jokingly. "Why! I haven't sent you yet to Bogoraz for repairs."

Alexei laughed loudly and winked at Novikov. Novikov smiled. Glushak only wheezed.

"She is definitely a smart woman," thought Novikov. "But what is Glushak so excited about?"

CHAPTER 5

AFTER SUPPER the Academician invited his guest into the bedroom.

"This is the bedroom and my study. I will shut the door and nobody will interrupt us while we talk."

In the little room, crowded with the bed, the bookcase, the desk, and the chairs, Glushak lit the table lamp and pushed a chair toward Novikov.

They sat down and were silent for a minute. One half of Novikov's face was in the lamplight, the other half in shadow. He looked straight into Glushak's bitter face, with its lowered eyes contemplating his plump hands lying on his knees. Glushak was the first to speak:

"Comrade Drozd asked me to make you acquainted with Gorin."

Novikov thought: "Drozd never asks—he orders." He observed Glushak with interest. His bitter look, the not altogether sincere first words, the evasive glance—all reflected the tangled labyrinth of his inner world. Novikov at once became alert. "Something is preventing Glushak from being himself," he thought. "Why is he posing in front of me, like a girl before her sweetheart?"

To encourage Glushak Novikov said as simply as possible: "I'm not familiar with the circumstances. Can you tell me what kind of man this Gorin is? I believe you have known him for a long time."

Glushak became more free in his manner. He lit a cigarette, leaned back in his chair, and began to talk like an expert: "Gorin is a complex character. He is many sided. He has, like the Hindu divinity Brahma, many faces. And each one of them would be sufficient for a complete human character . . ."

"You mean, he is changeable?"

"Not at all."

"Isn't that a paradox?"

"By no means. Don't forget that he is a great creative soul, difficult to understand, but sensitive and alive. You know Gorin, as the press writes about him: a man of keen mind, great heart, strong passion, and brilliant talent. True. But there is something more: firmness of principle. Yes, yes. In spite of all this diversity he is firm. Many people even reproach him for such firmness, finding in it the signs of pride and lack of feeling."

"For example, the student Lida Sidorov," thought Novikov. Her strange outburst at today's seminar now became clearer to him. However, he didn't interrupt Glushak. The latter continued: "It is impossible to measure people like Gorin with the common yardstick. The paradox appears only at first sight. On close examination it isn't there. On the contrary, there is the unity of a rich creative nature. All this apparent diversity, all these contradictions are explained by one constant characteristic: his passionate search for truth. His literary work is merely one of the manifestations of this passion. That is what has

104

given to his writing such extraordinary purposefulness, such deep meaning, making him one of the greatest writers of our time. It is well known that literature which is not inspired by passion has a short life. Gorin is continually searching for all-embracing truth, as the scientist Einstein searches for an all-embracing formula to explain the universe. Only Gorin's universe is the human soul. It would be difficult to say which is the more complex and vast. Is that not so?"

"Yes. Many people have broken their hearts over that question," replied Novikov.

"Exactly. Gorin, however, has not broken his heart. This passion of his, this constant craving to find the universal truth, makes him seem changeable. Each event, each human being, Gorin looks upon as a touchstone for his formula.

"He works like a chemist using one reagent after another. Depending on how he approaches a person, he appears different. Sometimes he is the rigid moralist, at others the all-forgiving humanist; again he is irritable, brusque, or gently tolerant of human weaknesses. Or like a fisherman: he throws out different kinds of bait, to see what kind of a fish will bite—or human soul. His favorite expression is: 'Let's see what he will say to that.' "

"What would you say?" Novikov interrupted Glushak. "How should I approach him so that my relationship with him will be lasting?"

"It is very difficult to give you an accurate answer. The trouble is that once Gorin has formed an opinion of a person he seldom changes it. It would need a very serious reason to make him change. So your first meeting with him, your first conversation, will be decisive. Generally speaking it is very difficult to make friends with Gorin. He uses his age as a shield to avoid people who do not interest him. Gorin carries this shield with him all the time. If he loses interest in a person, he confounds him with: 'I'm an old man, you are young. We cannot understand each other.' He has spoken—and the conversation is finished."

Glushak talked on, trying to provoke as much comment as possible from Novikov, so that he could find the answer to the tormenting question: Why are they making Novikov acquainted with Gorin, and what effect will that acquaintance have on his personal fortunes? Novikov, however, said little, dropping only an occasional remark, which showed his desire to learn as much as possible about Gorin. That was all. To his unspoken question Glushak received no answer. It was clear that Novikov did not intend to be frank. Unable to guess his thoughts, Glushak felt depressed like a boy before a stern schoolteacher.

Novikov was equally surprised that Glushak spoke so confusingly and tried to detect the concealed train of thought behind his flow of words. But he failed to find it. Eventually this game of cat and mouse began to bore him.

"Don't you think that we are wandering too far afield?" he remarked.

Glushak replied evasively: "Sometimes, in order to see things better, it is necessary to step back instead of drawing nearer."

Novikov smiled crookedly: "Unfortunately, my problem is to draw near."

"Yes, yes, of course . . ." Glushak caught himself up quickly.

Novikov realized that Glushak was simply trying to scare him with difficulties. He decided to speak plainly. "I should tell you that I am not afraid of difficulties. On the contrary, they attract me."

"So that's the kind he is," thought Glushak. Novikov looked very menacing: something evil, something dangerous appeared in his face —appeared and vanished. Novikov again sat in front of him, smooth, calm, only a little more tired than before.

"What's wrong with him?" thought Novikov in the meantime. He half started to rise.

Glushak caught the movement and turned hurriedly from the table to bring out a bottle of vodka and two glasses from the little cupboard. "I'm afraid I've wearied you with my conversation, Professor. Let's down one to revive our strength." He laughed, handing Novikov a full glass.

Although Novikov was surprised by the unexpected appearance of the vodka, he accepted the glass. "And when shall we meet Gorin?" he asked.

"The day after tomorrow a great banquet will be held at the opening of the Marx-Engels Institute. He has been invited."

"Will he go?"

"I don't know. He doesn't particularly like to attend meetings of that kind. But I believe it would be wise for you to be there. I am to deliver a report and can easily get you an invitation."

"I already have one."

"Excellent! I'll introduce you there to Gorin. Everything will come off very naturally. Before that I'll talk to him about you, get him interested. Drozd and I decided that we should proceed warily in this affair."

"That's bad," thought Novikov. "Very bad indeed. This Glushak is doing his best to preserve his independence, to emphasize his importance. What makes him so scared, and why is he wriggling like that in front of me? He's twice my age. What's he afraid of? I think I'm beginning to understand Drozd and his contempt for Academicians."

The prospect of being in contact with such a man, of being friendly with him—even for appearances—did not appeal to Novikov.

Meanwhile, Glushak was hesitating about putting his plaguing question. His face became strangely tense and his blue eyes flickered. Eventually he could not restrain himself. Hoping that a glass of vodka would have loosened Novikov's tongue, he asked him straight out: "Tell me, Professor Novikov, why are they making you acquainted with Gorin?" And waiting for the answer, Glushak leaned forward, looking into his companion's face. For the first time during the entire evening Novikov caught his glance. It was unpleasant, like that of a clever, wheedling dog.

Novikov, feeling complete contempt for Glushak's name and gray hairs, said roughly, looking mockingly into his flickering eyes: "Don't you and Drozd know that?"

CHAPTER 6

LIDA SIDOROV was puzzled. Andrei Demin had behaved very strangely today. All day he had been sitting dejected, not even glancing at her during recess. Usually, as soon as the bell sounded and the professor left the auditorium, he was the first to jump up. He would come over and place both hands on her shoulders. She would shake them off and run out into the corridor, knowing that he was following. In the corridor it was dark—Andrei would twist her arms behind her back so Lida couldn't help but lift her pointed little breasts toward him. Her blouse would strain at its buttons; she would blush in excitement. Andrei would make fierce eyes, threaten to kiss her. She would struggle, call him a devil, hope for the kiss . . .

But Andrei would merely whisper: "How beautiful you are, Lida . . ."

Lida would open her eyes wider, wishing he were bolder. But the awkward lad with the bright affectionate gaze and the freckled face was not born to make love boldly. He had kissed her only once, and that by accident—another student, passing them, had bumped their heads together for mischief. The kiss was accidental, but Lida remembered it well. They were unable to try another—the bell rang for assembly, Andrei dropped her hands and, breathless and blushing, they returned to the auditorium. She liked that game. It became almost a custom with them.

But today something had happened to Andrei. Lida watched him closely. If he had looked at her he would have seen the perplexity and silent reproach on her face. But Andrei noticed nothing. He sat sorrowful, looking out of the window lost in thought.

Lida interpreted all this in her own way. "He'll wait a long while! I will certainly not go to him!"

She rose, proudly tossed her thick braid of hair and went over to a group of students gathered around the lecturer's desk. The students were talking about the forthcoming examinations and the mean tricks of strict professors. Lida was going to join in the conversation when a hand was suddenly laid on her shoulder. Beaming, she turned around quickly, then frowned.

"Oh! It's you!" she exclaimed, more disappointed than surprised. Behind her stood Oleg Durov.

"Weren't you expecting that?" he asked blankly, enveloping her in an odor of tobacco and vodka. Lida puckered her face in distaste, but did not shake off his hand. More than ever, she wanted to make Andrei angry.

Oleg had just come into the auditorium. He still had his cap on, cocked dashingly on the back of his head. A thick tuft of red hair hung over his insolent, protuberant eyes. They were gleaming strangely.

"He has hatched something up," thought Lida.

A muscular, lanky young fellow, Oleg Durov was one of those celebrities no Soviet town can escape. He adorned Rostov as a boil adorns a sick man's face. Oleg, however, did not consider himself a boil. His insolent, defiant pose showed clearly that he felt himself superior. Hook-nosed, he looked like a bird of prey. His unhealthy thin face was the very incarnation of overbearing arrogance. He never removed his cap or his jacket, although it was forbidden to enter the auditorium in outer clothing. He smoked openly, against the rules of the University. Yet nobody reproved him.

Who on earth was he? A student, but with this difference: his father was the head of the NKVD of Rostov Province.

Oleg Durov was an exact copy of another celebrity—Stalin's son Yakov, whose exploits resounded all over Russia, notwithstanding all the efforts of the police to smother the gossip. Although Oleg's domain was not so extensive, his activity was no less feverish than that of the Moscow celebrity. The son of the terrible Durov could allow himself many liberties. And he was not idle. No week passed

108

in Rostov without a scandal, wild drinking orgies, fights, rape, with Oleg as the leading actor.

Oleg was enrolled as a student in the University. Papa Durov apparently wanted to make a man of his son. But the only subject that interested Oleg at the University was girls, of whom he was a passionate hunter. He appeared seldom at lectures, came to the University mostly during recesses, and to various classes. During the past week he had been a frequent visitor at the Faculty of History. The reason for his sudden interest in history was not hard to guess. Better than anyone else, Lida Sidorov knew it. The attentions of the Rostov grandee oppressed her. But it was as difficult to get rid of him as of a cold in the head.

With the appearance of Oleg, the conversation of the students stopped; all involuntarily turned their attention to him. Against a background of poorly dressed students he presented a bright picture. Everything on him gleamed: his oiled hair, the new yellow leather jacket thrown carelessly over his shoulders, the blouse embroidered with red cockerels, the pressed blue pants tucked into the tops of his boots, Cossack style. Under his jacket a Finnish knife, in its sheath, hung on a short chain.

Pleased that all eyes were trained on him, Oleg flauntingly pulled at his shirt and with a show of ownership, drew Lida closer to him. Lida noticed that his thin, clutching hand was shaking slightly.

One of the students envied his rich clothes. "What a jacket! I'll bet it's imported!"

"Hey! Oleg! Did you dress up like that for the exams?" another one asked, half seriously, half in fun. Everybody laughed.

"Look! He's wearing a Finnish knife—to frighten the professors!" someone at the back called out.

"Ha! Ha! Ha!"

Oleg frowned.

"Shut up!" he muttered between clenched teeth. "The professors are all my friends. I don't need to frighten them. And incidentally, I myself have come to examine one of you," and on his thin lips a malicious smile began to play.

All pricked up their ears. Oleg looked around the auditorium, as if searching for someone. His eyes were yellow and catlike, affectionately rapacious. They stopped on Andrei Demin who was still sitting alone at the back of the auditorium, looking out of the window.

Nodding toward Andrei, Oleg asked Lida: "What's wrong with your admirer over there? Why is he so down in the mouth today?"

"How should I know?" replied Lida, and there was resentment in her voice. "Maybe he's sick."

"Sick, you say? Well, well . . ." Letting go of her shoulder, he slouched over to Andrei. His boots squeaked with every step.

To Lida there was something evil in Oleg's words.

"Leave him alone, please," she begged. But Oleg paid no attention. He stopped in front of Andrei, spreading his legs wide.

"He's sick, eh?" Mockingly, he placed his hand on Andrei's brow, as if he were going to feel his temperature. A shadow flitted across Andrei's face. He pushed Oleg's hand away and stood up face to face with him.

Everyone in the auditorium unconsciously compared them. Andrei was short, broad shouldered, a rather clumsy, large-headed figure. He suggested something amusingly bearish that was pleasing. He always looked at the world frankly; friendliness and intelligence shone in his mild blue eyes. One of the most able students, he was at the same time surprisingly modest. Since he was the son of a school teacher and therefore one of the poorest in the class, it was his lot always to wear torn shoes, patched pants and shirt. But even these patches fitted him, as no one else. Thanks to his quiet temperament, his amusing shyness, and his brilliant abilities, he was a general favorite.

Now—standing by the window in front of the lanky figure of the brazen Oleg, and in the golden sunlight, from the patches on his knees to his light flaxen hair—he obviously gained by the comparison. The sympathies of the students were on his side. Evidently Oleg felt this. He inhaled the last of his cigarette, spat out the chewed butt through his moist lips, and expelled the smoke in a slow stream into Andrei's face. This was an insult. It would either enrage Andrei or humiliate him. But the smoke thinned and Andrei stood as before—calm, quiet. Only his face, gentle until now, became grim. He cast a contemptuous, brief glance over Oleg, as dumb people do when they want to call someone a fool. And like a dumb person, he remained silent.

"Good man!" thought each one of the students. "He didn't let himself be provoked."

Andrei was going to walk past Oleg, but the latter barred his way. "Wait a minute, sick one! Where are you hurrying? Answer me one question. Tell me, when did your father kiss you last?" The question was unexpected, absurd, but concealing some kind of sinister hint. Everybody felt this at once.

Andrei suddenly paled and Oleg laughed insolently. "Why are you

110

silent? Why don't you tell how they came last night and took your father where he should be? Eh?"

There was a sudden strange quiet in the auditorium. Lida's heart tensed with unspeakable pain. "So, that's why Andrei was so sad today. So that's why he didn't come to me . . ."

Andrei rushed at Oleg, caught his arm. "You know where my father is! Tell me, what's happened to him? I beg you, tell me!"

Andrei had forgotten that he was facing the lowest kind of rascal and scoundrel, with neither feeling nor heart. He saw only a man who knew the fate of his father. Holding his breath, Andrei awaited his answer.

Oleg pulled away his arm and laughed triumphantly.

Andrei trembled. Empty-eyed as a lunatic, he stared into the laughing face. "Where is he?" he shouted in a voice not his own. "What have they done with my father?"

"Aha! It looks as if you were beginning to get better!" said Oleg, and suddenly hissed into Andrei's face: "Your father is so sick that no doctor will be able to help him." He was going to say more, but the expression on Andrei's face stopped him.

Andrei was unrecognizable. His lips were trembling, spasms twisted his face, his eyes blazed. "Hangman! And your father's a hangman!" he screamed like a maniac. His voice rose, and Oleg jumped back.

"All right now, don't yell!" he said threateningly. "Have you forgotten what I can do with you? Look out, or they'll break your bones too, like your father's——"

He hadn't time to finish the phrase. Andrei, half screaming, half sobbing, threw himself on his tormentor. With his first blow he almost knocked the lanky Oleg off his feet. They clinched and fell on the floor. The cap fell off Oleg's head, his leather jacket lay under them. Two students tried to separate them.

"He's got a knife! He'll kill Andrei!" Lida cried out.

But the knife was already gleaming. There was a strange crunching noise, a wild scream. Blood flowed over Andrei's face.

The students tore the panting Oleg away. One of them knocked the blood-covered knife out of his hand.

"Go to hell!" snarled Oleg, breaking out of their grasp. Covered with sweat, purple with rage, Oleg tried to recover his breath. He glared at Andrei on the floor before him, as though seeing him for the first time: with both hands pressed to his face, Andrei was writhing and moaning.

"Look! He's wounded him in the eye!"

Suddenly everybody was quiet.

"My God!" Lida cried, cold with horror. Someone added a loud curse.

Three students separated themselves from the group and moved on Oleg, silent, frowning, their fists clenched. Oleg shrank back. His hands were trembling, his wet lower lip hung loosely. "You, you . . . what's this?" he stammered, backing toward the wall.

All at once the class monitor, Frolov, appeared between the students and Oleg.

"What's wrong with you? Have you gone crazy?" he shouted fiercely at the students, blocking their way. "Hurt him, and Durov would take us apart, bone from bone! If you're not worried about your own hides, think about mine! I'd get it first. I'm responsible for the whole class." The others, coming to their senses, moved away.

Casting an insolent look over the cowed students, Oleg picked up his leather jacket and cap. A kind of dazed smirk wandered over his lips.

They carried the maimed and groaning Andrei out of the auditorium. The students poured out behind. Oleg remained in the room alone. He searched for his knife, but could not find it.

CHAPTER 7

PROFESSOR NOVIKOV was hurrying to his lecture when he met the crowd of students in the corridor, carrying Andrei.

"What happened?" Novikov asked, looking into the blood-covered face. "Who did that to him?"

At that moment Oleg came out of the auditorium door. Frolov pointed at him. "He stabbed him with a knife, Comrade Professor."

Oleg shuffled away, rubbing a bruise under his eye. His hands were still covered with blood. Everybody shunned him.

Novikov, at a loss, looked at the wounded Andrei, at the lad with the bloody hands, at the submissive students. Nothing in the whole scene made sense.

"What are you standing there for?" he shouted at them. "Take him to the militia!"

The students looked at each other in confusion, but made no move.

112

In front of Novikov, frightened, the monitor Frolov was making warning gestures.

"Cowards!" thought Novikov, feeling his anger begin to boil against these sheep. Not waiting for them, he started to seize the bully himself.

But at that moment someone caught him by the sleeve. Novikov turned around, ready to blurt out a curse. In front of him stood the Director, holding the blood-covered knife one of the students had handed him. Without letting go of Novikov's sleeve, the Director said quietly, but distinctly: "Professor Novikov, don't hurry. That is Oleg, the son of Durov."

Novikov looked at him blankly, not understanding. Then he said: "You mean, the son of that Durov?"

"Yes, of that one," answered the Director, grinning wryly. Satisfied that Novikov understood, he let him go.

Novikov said nothing. Knitting his brows, he went into the classroom. Durov passed, looking at him insolently. The confused smirk had left his face and was replaced by the usual arrogance. Novikov was no longer surprised. Everything made sense.

He was at the door of the auditorium when he heard the Director's voice. "Comrade Durov, I must apologize for this incident. Rest assured, we shall call this hooligan Demin to order. The necessary steps will be taken and he will not be able to repeat such unheard-of indecency. You have not hurt yourself, I hope? Perhaps I should call a doctor?"

Novikov turned aside, unable to believe his ears. The Director was standing in front of Oleg. His pose, his gestures, his whole short, fat figure were slavishly servile. He wiped the blood from Oleg's Finnish knife with his own handkerchief.

"Please, here is your penknife; you dropped it. If you lose such a good thing—your father won't be pleased. Hee—hee—hee!" he laughed shallowly, handing the knife to Durov by the handle.

Silently Oleg took it, placed it in its leather sheath and, without thanking the Director, passed him, stepping straight and firmly like an Olympian god.

The Director turned to the students: "Well, why are you standing there? Didn't you hear the bell? Everyone to his place!"

Novikov entered the auditorium. It was empty and bare there. He sat down at the desk and waited for the students. His glance wandered aimlessly around from one object to another. Suddenly it stopped at a dark stain on the floor.

"Blood," he thought with sudden alarm. For some reason he remembered Gorin and shuddered. "Nonsense," he muttered. "Gorin and my task have no relation to blood."

One after another the students came into the class.

CHAPTER 8

THE SQUARE roared like the ocean in a storm. The uneven thousand-voiced clamor, the shrill music of the military bands, the metallic bellowing of the radio, the piercing calls of command—all these noises, hurled over the crowd, were rushing tumultuously in all directions with a wild force, seeking, but not finding, an outlet. The great square suddenly became cramped. The noises beat against the walls of the surrounding buildings and, like warriors before an impregnable fortress, were thrown back again: disordered, maimed, angered. Retreating, they ran into new waves of crazy sound, perished under them, blended with them, creating a tempestuous cacophony, an absurd hymn to chaos. The air vibrated from the roar and the hubbub. Above the crowd, in the dust made golden from the rays of the hot June sun, fluttered innumerable banners, swaying in heavy folds of red velvet.

Above this agitated sea of humanity the platform rose like a cliff. The platform was festive: it was draped in red, in foliage and flowers. A dozen men stood there, but the crowd saw only one.

"Gorin! Gorin!" shouted the crowd, drowning out the blare of the music.

The tall, stooped, elderly man on the platform raised his broad-brimmed hat. For an instant his bristly hair, in its odd French cut, was silver-tinged by the sun. His greeting called forth a renewed outburst of enthusiasm.

"Long live the great writer, Gorin!"

Rostov was having an unprecedented celebration. Even Mayday paled before what was taking place on the square now. The entire population of the city, old and young, was crammed there. One after another the delegations from the kolkhozes of the Northern Caucasus Province arrived. To the right of the platform, representatives from Moscow, Leningrad, and other large cities of Russia had been standing from early morning. The shirts of the representatives were soaked in perspiration; on their heads were handkerchiefs and newspapers; they were afraid of sunstroke.

114

A dozen newsreel men zealously cranked the handles of their cameras, and about fifty reporters were scratching with their pens. The authorities wanted to preserve every smallest detail of the celebration for history.

There was an expectant feeling in the air.

Nikolai Novikov, deafened and rumpled, with difficulty managed to make his way through the crowd. In front of him, his brother Feodor worked zealously with his elbows. In his left hand, above his head, he held a pass to the reserved area. Their pass for two was their only salvation from the crush. The crowd was nervous, angry, and noisy. Nikolai fended people off with his fists and elbows, covered them with obscene oaths, pushed the broad-shouldered Feodor ahead like a ram. He lost his cap. His ruffled hair was wet. From the unbearably hot and dusty air, from the sour-smelling clothes and the perspiration of dirty human bodies, his breathing grew tight.

"Push harder, Feodor!" he shouted to his brother. "One more minute in this stinking crowd and I'll choke!"

Feodor made a last effort and they squeezed through to a line of NKVD soldiers who were holding back the people. Feodor showed his pass, and they were allowed through. Here was plenty of room. The brothers recovered their breath.

The spectators' places were set apart, to the left of the platform, for the "best people"—outstanding members of the Party, trusted scientists, writers, intellectuals. Feodor Novikov, as a famous professor, was trusted to fifteen paces from the platform. "Not bad," he said to himself with satisfaction. "On the last Mayday I stood thirty paces off."

Nikolai quickly made himself at home. He looked around in all directions, waved his hand at the newsreel camera, made faces. "To think of all this fuss," he shouted in surprise, "only to open a new building!"

"This isn't an ordinary building. The opening of the Marx-Engels Institute is of great political importance," said Feodor authoritatively.

To tell the truth, he himself was confused. He was prepared for an ordinary meeting of an average size, something like last year's unveiling of the monument to Pavel Morozov, the Pioneer who betrayed his father to the police as an enemy of the people. "Looks as if Moscow wants this event to thunder all over the country. Possibly they may be tying some new campaign in with it. Perhaps the education of Party cadres," he tried to explain the riddle to himself.

115

One of the newsreel men, flashy in his checked riding breeches and yellow boots, disheveled, his face covered with sweat, ran up to the Novikovs:

"Hey! You!" he shouted to Feodor. "You with the thin face—get over to one side."

Novikov was not offended. The newsreel men, particularly those from Moscow, felt themselves in full control. This was their show. If his face did not satisfy their ideal of a healthy, happy Soviet man, then it was best to get out of the way. Feodor stood behind the plumper Nikolai. The latter blew out his cheeks, began to pull faces.

"Look at the building! Admire it! I want to take a close-up!" the newsreel man shouted to him.

Nikolai raised his head, stared, scratched the back of his neck as if a dozen fleas had bitten him.

"That's good! Now you've seen a friend in the crowd! Wave to him!" ordered the newsreel man.

Nikolai pulled out a handkerchief, not of the first freshness, and waved it to a solid-looking old man. Feodor recognized Academician Glushak. The latter, his face twitching nervously, turned away.

"He's probably thinking I put Nikolai up to that," thought Feodor with annoyance. He wanted to kick his brother to quiet him.

"Excellent! Once more!" shouted the operator.

The crowd roared and grew ever more dense. From the steps of the granite stairway, Novikov was able to survey the whole square. The crowd, it seemed, had one common face—exhausted, red-eyed—and one common breath—unhealthy, sour. When the wind blew in Novikov's direction he, like all the "best people of the town," covered his nose with a handkerchief.

"That's Rostov breathing," he thought, screwing up his face.

Shoulder to shoulder, facing the crowd, stood a double row of NKVD men, young and vigorous. They had an air of being the select few whom all these gray people must obey. For complete safety, machine guns had been placed on the roofs of the surrounding buildings. Novikov saw the blue caps of the machine-gunners popping up from time to time among the chimneys. He was used to these machine guns. They had become part and parcel of every holiday, like the potted flowers on the platform.

All Rostov, the whole tremendous mass of poorly dressed people, stood in front of the tall building, which stretched up toward the sun with its white marble columns, cold and clean like morning on the

116

river. To the broad granite steps these people had been driven from the working districts where the sun, seen only through a veil of dust, appears as a dim, strange planet; where the dusty leaves hang on the trees as if they were made of dirty paper.

History knows how to speak in the language of stone. We are reminded of thousands of years of slavery by the savage stone monuments of the past. Architectural styles change. Temples turn into ruins. But the slave brand remains. It outlives the ages. Now, in Rostov, this building had been built by slave labor. Openly, for a whole year, thousands of convicts were driven there under guard every day from the neighboring concentration camp. The local newspaper *Molot* enthusiastically called this monument the "embodiment of the shining ideas of communism." The convicts were yesterday's peasants, workers, intellectuals. Every day the inhabitants of Rostov—people like Novikov and Glushak—passed the new construction. They saw the exhausted and ragged apparitions moving in the stone dust, and thought with a shudder that they could become like them. They well knew the price of the shining ideas of communism.

After the convicts had done their job and were no longer needed, they were taken away. The broad, ceremonial stairway was swept clean. Its glistening granite no longer brought to mind slave labor. Today, instead of hungry convicts, there on the clean, bright platform, rising in the middle of the stairway and decorated with live flowers, stood well-fed, contented, important people. Varying in height, build, color of hair, they all had one face—the face of authority, stern, official, inscrutable.

Only Mikhail Gorin did not look like them; he appeared as a strange curiosity, as a visitor from an entirely different world.

Here in the world of authority, there can be nothing humorous, nothing that might hint at irony, even at kindly irony. People of power must have no weaknesses. But the whole of Gorin's figure called forth a smile. The mushroomlike broad hat seemed to be pushing comically over his ears. The big gray mustache hanging downward, the prominent cheek bones, the deep-set eyes peering sadly and mildly out from under the overhanging thick eyebrows, made him look very like a kindly walrus. Against the background of the representatives of authority, with their movements like mechanical dolls, the amusing figure of Gorin appeared as the only thing human. Perhaps that was the reason the crowd so eagerly shouted his name, the reason he was their favorite.

Novikov watched every movement of the people on the platform.

The center of his attention was, of course, Mikhail Gorin. His tall thin figure rose beside the fat Larin, First Secretary of the Party and virtual master of the Province. Everybody called him "the Rostov Stalin."

If the crowd recognized only Gorin, the "best people of the town" surrounding the platform saw only Larin. They looked on him as on their future. To them he was a vivid example of a brilliantly achieved career. He was their ideal. Even his outward appearance conformed to such an ideal. Larin was fat, pompous, deliberate. His narrow high-bridged nose, puffy cheeks, and firmly outlined lips revealed his domineering, haughty, and cruel character. In his searching look of an experienced master of the people, their uncertain fate was reflected as in a mirror. He made them happy if he looked kindly, drove them into a cold sweat when he was stern. They, on the other hand, responded with one look—devoted and submissive.

Gorin was talking to a thick-set elderly man standing on the other side of him, dressed, like all the others, in a white Party tunic. Novikov noticed to his surprise that he wore a black bow tie. Not so much by his face as by this detail, Novikov recognized him as Academician Shchusev, the architect and builder of the new building.

"No Party boss would stick that old-fashioned tie on," Novikov decided. "So it must be him."

That morning the papers had announced that Shchusev was given the Order of Lenin for the successful completion of the building. Novikov had heard that Shchusev built houses well, but that he built his own career even better.

His success during the Soviet regime began with the death of Lenin. The Government commissioned him to build the mausoleum on Red Square in Moscow. Shchusev fulfilled the task. Lenin was stuffed with straw and placed in the mausoleum, while Shchusev received the honorary title of people's artist and a very paying position—court architect of the Politburo. Not a single villa on the Black Sea nor any palace near Moscow was erected for its exacting members without the magic touch of his imagination and his grasping hand.

"What is the symbol on the sleeve of that one with the gloomy face?" Nikolai asked Feodor. He was looking at the platform also.

"Why! Don't you know, man? That's Durov: the chief of the NKVD," Feodor replied. "That's a gold circle with a sword across it on his sleeve—the drawn sword of revolution."

"What a mug he's got. It's simply asking for a brick to be thrown at it," Nikolai said in a low voice.

"You can say that to me. I wouldn't advise you to say it to others."

Indeed, Durov made a strong impression. He was the incarnation of crude force, raw, untouched either by surface culture or inner human feelings. This was primitive force, arrogantly striking the eye like a huge boulder in the middle of a field. And, like a boulder, it was in its own way expressive.

Durov's face was coarse, with high cheek bones and a low forehead, very prominent arched eyebrows and narrow eyes that looked out wickedly. But what caught the eye first were the unusually long and powerful hands. His large palms on the rail of the platform, Durov clasped and unclasped his fingers. He did this repeatedly, with an evil suggestion: slowly he clenched his fingers into a fist, held them that way for a minute or two, as if he were clutching someone by the throat, then unclenched them quickly, to clench them again slowly.

"I wouldn't like to fall into his clutches," Nikolai whispered to his brother in genuine awe. "Look at that huge hand! He's like a gorilla, except that he smokes and drinks vodka."

"Shut up! Look and admire!" Feodor interrupted him abruptly.

Novikov knew that in the NKVD, particularly where it was necessary to seize, torture, and shoot without consideration, the most coarsely built massive types, men with huge fists and small skulls, were selected. As a finishing touch they were given specially selected names, loud-sounding, harsh, which spoke for themselves: "Mountain," "Fist," "Grab."

Squeezed into the very corner of the platform by Durov stood Kashirin, the Commanding Officer of the Rostov Military District. His face, affectedly stern and too martial, was red from the heat, the tight uniform, and self-satisfaction. A tragic fate awaited this self-confident man. This was the same Kashirin who later was one of the extraordinary commission, headed by Voroshilov, which shot the Commander-in-Chief of the Armed Forces, Marshal Tukhachevsky. A few months after the liquidation of Tukhachevsky all the members of that commission, with the exception of Voroshilov, were in their turn liquidated.

But it is doubtful if he felt any premonition at that moment. He zealously expanded his chest, glittering dazzlingly with orders of the Government's trust, before the lenses of the newsreel cameras; he saluted; he gazed afar as if he were on a battlefield; all in all, he was

119

occupied with himself. And being so, he did not forget to elbow some third secretary of the Party, also burning with a passion to leave his physiognomy to posterity, who was pressing against him from behind. That rough gesture may have cost Kashirin his life later.

CHAPTER 9

SOMEONE behind Novikov mentioned Veria's name. "Veria—he's a fox. Don't put your finger into his mouth—he'll bite it off."

His pince-nez sparkling in the sun, Veria reminded one not of a fox but of a chameleon. The shortest of those on the platform, he had a small round bald head, a big mouth, and large protruding ears. The normal-sized pince-nez which he wore looked like two saucers. The appearance of the man aroused a kind of squeamish feeling.

Veria was a relatively new man in the Province. He had arrived in Rostov only a year and a half before to occupy the place of the Second Secretary of the Party, who had died suddenly during one of the routine purges. Right after their first look at the new chief, everybody decided that he would not last even a month in Rostov. "No simpleton can be Second Secretary of the Province," the Party officials reasoned among themselves gravely. "His voice is squeaky, his figure insignificant. That kind can't instil fear. They'll bring him to his knees and lay him in his coffin."

However, Veria turned out to be a hard nut. Nobody brought him to his knees, the coffin remained empty. His squeaky voice was able to drive hearts into the pits of stomachs just as well as the rough bass of Durov.

Veria had not patterned his career along traditional lines. His small head was always stirring with wicked, cunning, and slippery ideas. Not everyone understood them at once. But when they did understand, they gaped. Anyone else in his position would have destroyed himself long ago.

"Either he's as clever as the devil or as lucky as the fool in the fairy tale," thought the embarrassed officials. But it was very clear that Moscow supported Veria, and his influence there was almost equal to Larin's.

Novikov placed him among the Party workers of the new school, more artful and diverse in their methods than those of the stereotyped school of Larin. However, all differences ended there. Both were true servants of the Politburo.

Veria knew how to advance and retreat when necessary. But the more craftily he yielded in small things, the more fiercely he defended the interest of the Politburo in important matters. Novikov appreciated this, particularly after one episode which he himself witnessed.

Rostov University was "patron" of a factory, Aksai Plant. A "patronage committee," of which Novikov was a member, arranged regular lectures on political subjects for the workers. Used though he was to everything, Novikov was astounded to see the conditions in which the workers worked and lived. There was no end, it seemed, to their endurance. Once, however, it broke. Driven to desperation, they wrote a complaint. They did not deliver it to the chairman of the trade-union committee. They knew that he would simply hand it over to the NKVD agent. He could do this quite conveniently, being simultaneously chairman and agent. They asked the patrons to submit the complaint to the Province Committee of the Party.

The complaint fell into Veria's hands. He decided to investigate it personally, ordering the patrons also to come to the plant. On the following day, at the head of a brilliant cavalcade of his assistants and bodyguards, Veria drove in his automobile into the great yard of the plant. The workers' barracks were located in the same yard. Beside the plant gate stood a two-story house. On the ground floor the administrative offices were located, on the second the apartment of the director of the plant.

"Well, what has been going on here?" Veria asked the workers who had come out to meet the important guests. At sight of the shining automobile, the gleaming boots and belts, the holsters with revolvers, the workers sulked and kept silent. They were expecting retaliation. "Don't be afraid! We are all one family," Veria said, acting the "hail-fellow-well-met" role. "Oh, don't take any notice of them." He waved a hand at his suite. "They're just like French poodles, for ornament."

The "French poodles" neighed like horses at their chief's joke.

"You, there!" Veria poked a manicured finger at the chest of the nearest worker. "What are you complaining about?"

Then they all began to speak at once, hurrying and interrupting each other. The women, many with children in arms, pushed the men aside, chattering loudly and shrilly. They blurted out everything that had been oppressing their hearts and souls.

121

"We have only three washtubs in the whole barracks, Comrade Commissar!" one shouted. "We have to wash our clothes and bathe our children in them. Is that right?"

"Everything is filthy!" another cried. "There are more than a hundred of us here, and about half have families!"

"The floor is rotting, and we have begun to rot! Rats are all over the place. Just yesterday the Fedyukins' three-months-old baby was bitten to death. They run over us when we're asleep!"

"There aren't enough beds. Many of us are sleeping on the floor."

"Cattle are better housed than we!"

Veria was an experienced demagogue. He listened attentively to the workers, didn't interrupt, from time to time even encouraged them. Then, turning to the beefy director, he looked at him sternly and questioningly.

What could the director say? A month before, the same Veria had sent around a secret order to all directors of plants to list all moneys spent on Party and propaganda work under the item: "Expenses for housing and improving living conditions." For the actual living needs of the workers not a kopek was released. The director knew this; Veria knew this; only the workers knew nothing. They felt the effects only too well on their hides.

So the director merely shrugged his shoulders. "My workers, as you see, want to live in palaces, Comrade Veria," he said sarcastically, and added ominously: "Probably they need another climate also."

Suddenly Veria became unrecognizable. He turned purple, his eyes bloodshot. Novikov thought he was going to have an apoplectic fit. Flashing his pince-nez threateningly, he screamed at the director: "Why! You son of a bitch! Laughing at the needs of the workers, eh? I'll bet you drive your wife around in the car. I'll bet you've bought her a fox coat! But you don't worry one bit about the workers! You wouldn't even buy a plain chair for their backsides!"

"That's true! That's true!" shouted the encouraged workers. The dumbfounded director just blinked. He thought that Veria had gone off his head.

But the latter continued to attack him: "You have forgotten that the power is the people's, the worker-peasants'! Have you forgotten what Comrade Stalin teaches? That all of us, you and I, are merely servants of the people, servants of these very workers that you are making fun of! You have forgotten that care for the workers is the first duty of communists! You forgot, eh? Well, we'll remind you of it!"

122

"Boys!" he turned suddenly to the workers. "Run into the director's apartment, take everything he has! The furniture, dishes, everything! Bring it all out here. Don't stand on ceremony!"

The workers stood open-mouthed, thunderstruck by his words. The director turned pale.

"Well, what are you gaping at? Didn't you hear what I said?" Veria raised his voice. "Take the director's things, I tell you! Take them all into the barracks." Veria turned to his suite: "And you, too, get a move on—help the comrade workers!"

The bodyguards were the first to run into the director's house; next a group of workers—the bolder ones. Soon the director's wife, screaming like a stuck pig, ran out of the house, followed by a train of sofas, upholstered armchairs, tables, chairs. Veria himself helped with a sofa, pushing it through the door of the barracks. This evoked a loud burst of approval.

"Hurrah for Veria!" one old worker began to bawl like a drunk.

They arranged the furniture somehow between the cots, not noticing how it crowded the room. They stroked the fabrics, sat on the cushioned armchairs, got up and sat down again, pushed each other off the sofas, pulled up their legs, roared with laughter, enjoyed themselves like children.

Veria showed a surprise equal to theirs, as if he were seeing such furniture for the first time in his life. "Look!" he said shaking his head. "Now you are real aristocrats. Regular dukes, out-and-out dukes. Well, boys! I'll bet it wouldn't be a great sin if you worked extra after such a reward. Am I right?"

"Right! Right!" the workers responded, more interested in the furniture than in his words. "If people care about us, we won't remain in their debt. Of course we'll work! What's work to us!"

"Fine! That's good!" said Veria. "Comrade Director, you take note of that. Meet the wishes of the workers. They're talking business! Pay attention to them." After chatting a little more, Veria got into his car, waved his hand, and departed.

The following day the director, only too willing to meet the wishes of the workers, increased the working day by an hour and a half.

A month later, Novikov saw new and better furniture in the director's apartment. In the yard, near the workers' barracks, the director's old table and sofa stood in the rain. The workers had put them there: it was crowded enough in the barracks without them. In time all the furniture joined the rubbish in the yard, but this happened gradually and was somehow unnoticed. On the other hand everybody recalled Veria's magnificent gesture very well, and talk about him spread all over Rostov. His name became popular.

"Veria—he's one of us! He isn't slow in defending the common people!" was heard frequently among the workers.

"Yes, he's crafty," thought Novikov. "In his place, Larin would have sent Durov to the complaining workers. Durov would have shot two or three as an example, and sent another ten to a concentration camp. The rest would have been silenced, nursing hatred and thirst for vengeance in their hearts. But Veria, pretending to be the simple man, understanding the needs of the workers, made a dramatic, memorable gesture which actually didn't improve their position, but made them work more than they had before. Not everybody can put over a trick like that."

Novikov liked to analyze and theorize. This crafty tactic of Veria's he called "the scapegoat policy." The director of the Aksai Plant had been the temporary scapegoat.

Novikov looked at the slight figure of Veria on the platform with particular respect. He heard the same voice still talking behind him: "This Veria will go far, believe me."

"He probably will," Novikov thought. "Such people are needed by the Party no less than the Durovs."

Beside Veria stood a young man with a pale, haughty face. He was dressed like all the others, in a white Party tunic.

"Do you know who that is?" Feodor asked Nikolai.

"I don't know," replied Nikolai, "but I can ask around." After a few minutes he reported in a mysterious whisper what he had found out. "That's the son of the new member of the Politburo, Shcherbakov. He arrived yesterday with Yudin, the director of the Marx-Engels Institute in Moscow."

"Oh-ho!" said Feodor, screwing up his gray eyes. "No doubt he's here as his father's proxy."

"That's it, something like that."

As for Yudin, Novikov knew him from his student days in Moscow. He used to deliver lectures on Marxism in the Moscow University. "How he has gone ahead!" thought Novikov with surprise. "He has become one of the biggest propagandists of the Party."

The director of the important Moscow Institute, Yudin, was a man of fifty with a shock of tousled black hair. He combed it frequently with his fingers. His watchful black eyes looked at people coldly and mockingly. While he was talking he licked his red lips from time to

124

time with his thick tongue. It looked as if his tongue were too large for his mouth and continually crawling out.

Academician Glushak, like everybody else, watched the platform. There, beside Yudin, he saw Mirzoyan. But Glushak was not surprised. There had been great changes these past days for his hated chief. Fortune was smiling on him: he was appointed Director of the new Institute. Yudin personally had brought this order from Moscow. Mirzoyan, in his new capacity as Director of the Institute, would open the meeting. He beamed like a new samovar. He felt as if it were his birthday, as though his dreams had come true, that he had already entered the higher world of the Larins, the Verias, the Yudins. It was not for nothing that he had manicured his nails, developed a stomach, and smoked makhorka. "You'll have to replace makhorka with good cigarettes now," he reflected. "You're in the highest sphere now, not just in some Academy . . ."

Mirzoyan tightened his belt so as not to intrude on his chiefs. But that didn't improve him: now, instead of one belly, he showed two, like a thick sausage tied in the middle with string.

Looking at the double belly, Glushak rejoiced over his recent chief's promotion. "Maybe the new Party secretary at the Academy will be better than this smoked ham," he hoped.

The crowd filled the whole square and the streets adjoining it. Larin looked it over once more with a lazy glance, then gave the signal to begin the meeting. First, the radio was silenced. Then, one after another, the bands stopped playing. Little by little the square became silent, like a cooling volcano.

Mirzoyan cleared his throat, trying the microphone. "Comrades," he said, "I pronounce this solemn meeting, dedicated to the opening of the Marx-Engels Institute, open. The opening speech will be delivered by the Second Secretary of the Northern Caucasus Province Committee of the Communist Party, Comrade Veria!"

"Why doesn't Larin himself speak?" thought Novikov in surprise. Thousands of others were asking themselves the same question.

CHAPTER 10

WHEN MIRZOYAN made his simple announcement, Larin started. He knew that Veria was to deliver the speech. But still he started. It happened unexpectedly, against his will. At the same time he felt, almost physically, the state of perplexity which seized the crowd. In thousands of heads flashed the same thought. Thousands of eyes were fixed on him questioningly. They awaited his reaction. Larin's face became a cold, impenetrable mask.

All day he had been in a tense state. As before a storm, there was a depression that could find no release. Outwardly all was calm. Larin's face was a good screen. But behind the stolid screen the most unpleasant feelings were romping around like mice. And the forthcoming speech of Veria was to blame for everything.

A month ago, he had hardly given the Institute a thought. He was completely indifferent as to who should deliver the oration: Veria or one of the third secretaries.

But the nearer the day for opening the Institute approached, the more convinced Larin became that Moscow for some reason was giving this event extraordinary significance. Indeed, when he learned that representatives from the large cities were coming to Rostov, that practically the entire Moscow press would be there, that the radio was to broadcast the celebration all over the country, Larin made a quick decision: he himself would deliver the speech. The event had taken on too great proportions to entrust the speech to a subordinate person. Everybody thought the same: everybody, except Veria. He announced one day, quite insistently, his desire to deliver the speech. Larin refused him rudely.

But two days later the order came from Moscow. The order was signed by the new member of the Politburo, Shcherbakov. Now his son had arrived in Rostov, sticking out like an eyesore to Larin. Shcherbakov wrote in an indifferent tone: "Inasmuch as Comrade Veria was responsible for the building of the Institute, he will deliver the opening speech." But the indifferent tone didn't deceive Larin. He became wary. It was no longer his wounded pride that was aroused, but something much more serious. Strange things were brewing behind his back. He felt, but could neither see nor control them. Accustomed to power, Larin found himself set aside.

"What's wrong with you, Larin?" he asked himself with alarm. "Have your teeth become blunt? You are no longer able to bite into life and tear it apart, as you used to do."

And he felt himself falling into self-pity and melancholy foreboding.

Shcherbakov was right. The building of the Institute was Veria's brain child. Larin remembered how, a year and a half ago, soon after

126

his arrival in Rostov, Veria had suggested the construction of an Institute for the training of Party cadres. Everybody thought this idea absurd. To think of opening a Party Institute in Rostov was flippancy, when cities of more importance had nothing of the kind. To dream of a new building was sheer foolishness when even for the simple repair of essential offices Moscow did not release a kopek.

Veria introduced his proposal at an enlarged conference of the Party Committee, where all the top Party officials of the Province met. At that time Larin did not know his assistant well. Like many others, he considered him an empty vessel, an eccentric.

Larin remembered that occasion vividly. Veria had come from behind the table of the Presidium and stood up on the platform. As usual, he began in a roundabout way. He never spoke straightforwardly. He liked to set riddles for his audience. His pince-nez sparkling like saucers, Veria looked over the hall with his small, sharp eyes.

"Who among you knows the word 'empiriocriticism'?" he had asked unexpectedly.

The hall was silent. If anyone knew, he kept quiet. From Veria's tone it was clear that he did not expect an answer.

"Nobody!" shouted Veria triumphantly. "I thought so! That is very bad. The members of the Party must understand thoroughly the weapons with which its founder, the great Lenin, fought. Do you realize that with this word 'empiriocriticism,' and with others like it, Lenin broke the heads of the enemies of the Party who were hiding behind the screen of scientific objectivity? Do you know that for a member of the Party, particularly for its commanders, the ability to say the right word in the right place is just as important as to stop the mouths of the Party's enemies in time?

"Comrades! Our country is going through a difficult period. A fierce class war is in progress. We are living in hell, comrades. But we must sing heavenly songs. And we haven't learned how to sing heavenly songs yet. The voice is hoarse, breaks too often, is off key. We must learn this clever art at any price. Here in Rostov we need an institution where trusted members of the Party may acquire it. I speak allegorically, but you understand me, comrades. We need a higher Party school. We need a school for the re-education of the old Party leaders and for the training of new ones. I propose that the construction of such an institution be begun at once!"

Veria's squeaky voice, his small figure, the thin fingers gripping the reading stand, together produced the impression of an angry monkey. He looked insignificant. But he was the Second Secretary of the

127

Province. The hall was silent. The hall awaited the word of Larin. Larin slowly turned his stolid head toward Veria.

"Comrade Veria," he began in a serious tone, so as not to hurt the insignificant Veria whose idea could not, of course, provoke anything but mirth. "Your proposal for the construction of a Party school has been duly noted. The present conference suggests that you put your idea into more detailed form, including the financial estimate. The detailed plan will be examined by the Party Committee in due course. Now, next question."

Veria, apparently satisfied, left the platform, sat down beside the fat Larin, and polished his pince-nez.

"Fool," thought the hall.

"Fool," thought Larin. "A few more such senseless proposals and they'll send that monkey to the zoo."

From his first appearance in Rostov, Larin treated Veria with secret enmity. He was confident that the arrival of Veria meant the beginning of a new struggle for power in Rostov. In this rapacious world it could not be otherwise. Before Veria, during Larin's tenure of office, the Second Secretary of the Party had been changed five times. Each one had tried to push Larin out. But each one had broken his own neck. Larin was an old and experienced animal. He knew well the laws of the Party lair.

Larin kept an eye on Veria. He didn't seem a dangerous rival, and Larin decided not to hinder him: "It's better to leave people like that alone. They will ruin themselves quicker without outside help."

A week later Veria presented the estimate for the building. When Larin looked at it he nearly jumped with joy. The whole project was a wild delirium, a page from a fantastic novel whose author was a lunatic. Veria was proposing a multimillion-ruble building, faced on the outside with granite and marble and finished inside with hardwood and semiprecious stones. In front of the building he planned a tremendous square, capable of holding several thousand people. For this it would be necessary to demolish at least ten blocks of houses. "And all this under Rostov conditions, where people live like herrings in a barrel," sneered Larin to himself.

He rubbed his hands. Veria had put the noose around his own neck. It remained only for Larin to pull the rope. "Marvelous," he said aloud. "I suggest that you, as the author, send the project to Moscow in your name."

Veria apparently expected this. The fool actually did everything that Larin advised. The project was sent to Moscow.

128

And the project was accepted by Moscow.

Larin didn't believe his eyes when he received the reply. Moscow introduced some changes, but Larin saw clearly that each one would cost several million rubles more. Even the fantastic Martian square was confirmed. The desperate wails of Larin, that the cost of construction would swallow up the better half of the city budget, did not help. Nor did his long report, deploring the senseless destruction of space in Rostov was worth its weight in gold. For the first time Larin defended the interests of his fellow citizens. And not without reason: his whole prestige was in jeopardy. But nothing helped. Moscow did several blocks of houses at a time when every square meter of living not heed Larin's tears; its decision remained unchanged.

Soon a resolution of the Central Committee of the Party appeared in *Pravda:* "Meeting the wishes of the toilers of the City of Rostov, the Central Committee of the All-Union Communist Party resolves: to authorize the construction of the Marx-Engels Institute in Rostov."

That sealed the verdict. Veria began the construction. Dust rose in Rostov. One after another the demolished buildings fell with a crash. Thousands of families had to be resettled in barracks on the outskirts of the city.

Only then did Larin really see Veria. "That monkey has a long invisible tail. It reaches right to Moscow and there somebody jerks it all the time," Larin decided belatedly.

With wariness came hate. Hate for Veria's protruding ears, his little round head, his mouth twisted into a lying smile. With what satisfaction Larin would have strangled him, if only to hear his squeaky voice no more, never again to see his slippery piercing glance. And now he had to stand beside him on the platform, feel the warmth of his repulsive little body. It was torture.

Larin no longer doubted that Veria had been sent to Rostov specially with the idea of building the Institute. Why? That remained a riddle. Larin had a foreboding, however, that Veria's speech would clear things up. He froze in tense expectation. That was why, unconsciously, as happens in a dream, he had started at Mirzoyan's words.

For the first time Larin faced the unknown. For the first time this overbearing man, who inspired fear, felt himself helpless and pitiful.

If Larin could hardly conceal his fear, it cost Veria much more effort to hide his joy. He was suffocating from it. Like a bird, it was singing in his breast. It hid cleverly behind his pince-nez, awaiting the moment to jump out. His whole fate would be decided this day. No one else suspected it as yet, but this event, this whole celebration was to be the most critical moment in his life.

Larin feared that Veria was engaged in a crafty intrigue to occupy his place. But if he had been able at that moment to look into Veria's soul, he would have laughed at his own naïveté. He would have recoiled from the monstrous audacity and boundless ambition of the little Veria. This dwarf was not aiming at his position. His dreams ascended higher, to the inaccessible, to the Politburo.

The speech which he had to give now seemed to Veria like the driving force of his fantastic flight. Larin would have been still more surprised if he had known that Veria was not dreaming vainly.

"Comrades!" began Veria. "Today we are opening a building in which the best sons of the Soviet people will study, the future leaders of our Party. It is not by chance that the Party attached such tremendous importance to this opening. The task of educating the masses of the toilers in the Bolshevik spirit, the task of bringing up the new Soviet man, is the foremost task of the Communist Party. This the great Stalin teaches us . . ."

Larin listened attentively. In the flow of Veria's words he tried to find the key to his own terrible riddle. The flow became ever more fluent, ever quicker. Larin's ears caught no hints. "Surely my premonition didn't deceive me?" wondered Larin. "Surely I wasn't mistaken?" But his former self-possession was slowly returning.

Veria was by now not speaking but shouting, often beating the hot air with his small fists: "We must perfect the Soviet man to a point where he will have no defects, until his moral and political character correspond to the pure ideals of our Party and of Comrade Stalin. Our enemies are trying to frighten us, proclaiming that we shall produce a mechanical man, a man without a face. No! a thousand times no! The result will be a beautiful man, full of vital, vivid personal life . . ."

The beautiful words flew lightly out of Veria's breast, where, like the wind on the steppes, joy made merry. "Yes, yes. I will have a vivid personal life," he thought, enjoying the delightful, intoxicating wine of his dreams. His blood became heady and boiled. "I shall live in palaces, with a swimming pool, servants . . . I'll send my old woman to hell. Then I'll get a nice little ballerina from the Bolshoi Theatre, better than that old grouch Kalinin has. Am I any worse than he! Veria will yet show himself!"

His voice rang out and broke on the most unexpected high notes: "Only in the Soviet state have individual human personalities, those

130

of millions of simple people, fused into one whole with the State—which, for the first time, has begun to serve the great principles of freedom, humanism, education, the entire life of each individual man. For the first time the people have the opportunity of enjoying and admiring the might and greatness of the State, without feeling strangeness or enmity from it, but on the contrary, feeling it as their own strength, friendly to the happiness and joy of every honest Soviet man."

"Veria certainly knows how to sing heavenly songs," thought Larin, barely able to keep up with the flow of his words. "He looks like a plucked crow, but sings like a nightingale."

"Is he worked up!" thought the chief of the NKVD, Durov, in surprise. He looked to the left toward the irrepressible orator, but all he saw was Larin's big belly.

Durov understood little of what Veria was saying. However, the words "for the first time the people have the opportunity of enjoying and admiring the might and greatness of the State" pleased him very much. Durov always identified himself with his conception of the State. Veria's words made him unconsciously stick out his chest proudly, and his coarse features took on a dignified look. He glanced from under his dark brows at the people standing behind the solid ranks of the NKVD, looking for signs of the admiration of which Veria spoke. But the eyes of the people were dull, tired, even angry. Durov frowned.

"Veria is lying," he decided. "How much longer is he going to blabber? It's hot, God damn it, and my throat has dried up. It would be good to down a glass or two."

CHAPTER 11

"THAT'S an interesting thought," Mikhail Gorin reflected, listening attentively to Veria's words. "Delivered in a rather too grandiose style, but basically interesting: the identification of the State with the individual personality—the old problem that has always agitated the minds of philosophers."

Gorin thought of the telegram lying in his pocket from the French writer Romain Rouen. He had just arrived in the Soviet Union, was at present in Moscow. Rouen had requested an interview with him. "I will certainly touch on this question in my conversation with Romain

131

Rouen," decided Gorin. "These westerners shout a lot about human individuality. We shall see what he has to say about it."

Gorin listened to Veria with interest. It wasn't easy. Veria's words filled the air with an invisible but irritating pall. Like dust it filled the ears and even, it seemed, got into the eyes and throat. Gorin shook his head several times as if to rid himself of the unpleasant feeling, but the heavy pall remained. "Why does he speak so poorly?" Gorin was irritated. "It's very difficult to follow him."

Gorin's thoughts wandered from the speech. His glance rested on the main portal of the new building. In the white Ural marble and black Karelian granite the tremendous square was reflected as in a mirror.

"Where have I seen a portal like that?" he tried to remember. "Ah, yes, in the ruins of Rome. White columns, bright sunshine. The depressing solemnity of the temples of the pagans. It's strange that there should be such a resemblance. After thousands of years! Although, actually, this building is also a temple. Here the pontiffs of the Party will be trained. Here mysteries will be performed."

Looking at the building, Gorin began to think about its architect. This man, with the narrow slits of mocking eyes, interested him. The severe portal, the clear bas-relief, each separate detail to the last door knob, were made from drawings of Shchusev. "He's an artful fellow, that Shchusev. How skillfully he catches the spirit of the times!"

But Shchusev was never a slave of fashion. His powerful talent invariably carried him to the head of each new architectural trend. The political weather changed—and Shchusev's style changed, lightly and simply, like a garment: without emotion, without twinges of conscience.

Gorin looked sidewise at Shchusev's sunlit profile. He knew that the slightly swollen eyes and the perpetual injured expression on Shchusev's face were merely the mask of a self-satisfied and cunning old man. Yes, sly Shchusev had left many stone landmarks behind him. From them, as from books, could be studied the stormy tempo of recent history.

Gorin recalled the time, before the First World War, when there was great enthusiasm in Russia over gaudy Russian architecture: bellied columns, like samovars, cockerel-like ornaments—a heavy, awkward style. Shchusev at that time designed and built the Kazan Station in Moscow. The station became the classical example of modern style, only it was neither awkward nor heavy. On the contrary Gorin liked it.

The war and the revolution accustomed the architects to carrot tea

132

and bold ideas. Around them were ruins. While people couldn't find enough boards to build outhouses in the yards, the architects were designing hundred-story buildings with rainpipes of pure gold. These delirious projects, conjured into life by hungry bellies and the breathtaking promises of the revolutionary slogans, became as characteristic of that period as the Mauser of the Chekist.

Shchusev, consigning the paunchy columns to history, made a design for the headquarters of the Comintern more extravagant than any of them. The many-storied building with rhomboid windows was divided into five circles: according to the number of continents. Each circle was to revolve at a different speed, depending on the successes of the revolution in the corresponding part of the world. No one was crazy enough to surpass this project, much less to build it. The Shchusev headquarters of the Comintern became the classic example of the paper architecture of War Communism.

The death of Lenin brought Shchusev a new problem. On the old Red Square a modern monument had to be built. It was not an easy task. But after the headquarters of the Comintern he was afraid of nothing. Any incongruity between ancient and modern architecture did not bother him as much as the problem of how to express correctly the spirit of the new times.

The spirit of the new times was unlimited dictatorship. Even the dead Lenin must serve the living dictator, strengthen his power and authority. Shchusev began looking for historical examples. The mausoleum of the Persian emperor Cyrus against the background of the tremendous monumental wall gave him an idea. He surrounded the body of the dictator Lenin with the stone casing of the Persian autocrat.

The members of the Politburo knew nothing about ancient architecture, but they liked very much the massive, severe lines of the mausoleum. Its platform became their favorite place from which to watch the demonstrations of their slaves and accept expressions of their adoration and fear. The mausoleum became the pedestal of the Politburo, affirming with its granite language their authority. It also made Shchusev the first architect of the Soviet regime.

Soon it became fashionable in Russia to talk about the new Soviet man, new Soviet science, new Soviet music. Architecture trudged along behind. It was easy to hang a label on music: It was enough for the composer to call his new symphony *Glory to the Great Stalin in D Major* and he could congratulate himself on a composition of socialist realism. Architecture was too graphic and tangible. New labels, like poorly prepared stucco, would not stick. The Soviet architects, vainly seeking a new style, rushed at times to the classic Palladio, at others to the modernist Le Corbusier. For a long time even Shchusev had no luck.

But now in Rostov, standing in front of his new masterpiece, Shchusev felt confident that he had created the new style. The building has pleased the Politburo, pleased Stalin. And was not that the most important indication of the new style? Shchusev squinted at the sun, put on an injured look, but in his heart he smirked with self-satisfaction: he was again ahead of everybody.

With the habit of a writer Gorin looked for a comparison to the building. "It's clear," he finally decided, "that the building is like the people on the platform. It has the face of a Party bureaucrat. The same severe, cold lines."

Gorin found more strength than beauty in the building. The dark granite of the portals, the light marble of the square columns rising to five stories in height, the five heavy beaten-brass doors glimmering dully in the shadow of the columns, the long, broad flight of steps— everything combined to give the building a solemn and official look. Especially the steps. Gorin imagined the feelings of a man ascending them: with each step he would become more and more filled with awe and even fear.

It was not thus that Gorin had visualized the building of the future when he had dreamed of the new world in 1912 on Capri. He had gone there from Imperial Russia, which seemed to him an oppressive and senseless despotism. Then, admiring the Bay of Naples, he dreamed of the new man, not afraid of buildings but entering them as an equal, moving in them freely. He dreamed of buildings full of sunshine and fresh air, where nothing would curb man's breathing or cramp his thoughts. But this building oppressed.

Maybe the architect had made a mistake. Maybe this building didn't reflect the modern idea. But Gorin knew Shchusev too well to admit such a thought. Who had such an extraordinary sense of reality as this sly rogue?

"Is it possible that this creation of his has caught the spirit of the times?" thought Gorin bitterly. "Is it possible that I am deceiving myself—that I am stubbornly refusing to accept the world as it is, and am looking for something that was never there nor ever will be?"

Irritated, Gorin whispered to Shchusev: "Your building is undoubtedly very sumptuous and expressive . . . in its own way. But I feel no warmth, no friendliness in it. It doesn't attract me."

134

Shchusev shrugged his shoulders.

"That building is a symbol. A serious political symbol," he replied quietly so as not to interrupt Veria. "A symbol can only remind one of a great idea, imbue respect for that idea, reflect its strength and invincibility. If such a building begins to attract, it ceases to be a symbol, it becomes a toy."

"What kind of idea is that?" asked Gorin angrily.

Shchusev brought his puffy face close to Gorin and, winking in Veria's direction, replied: "That is the idea of the magical merging of the individual with the State, Comrade Gorin."

Gorin understood Shchusev's sarcasm. "You mean rather that your building reflects the idea of the might of the State and the insignificance of the separate individual. Not the merging, but the oppression of the individual by the State? Is that true?"

Shchusev's small eyes began to smile slyly, but he didn't reply.

"The difference between us, it seems, is that he doesn't deceive himself," sighed Gorin. "This rogue is actually cleaner of soul than I."

There was one remaining possibility. Gorin leaned toward Shchusev: "Tell me, did you make this monument as it is now without any outside influence, from beginning to end?"

"I was given an order. I fulfilled it to the best of my ability," replied Shchusev. "To meet the wishes of my client is my rule, exactly as you write your articles—laudatory odes to the Government. You and I have the same client!"

Gorin frowned. A shadow lay on his high forehead. "That is not true. I have no client. I write according to my own will."

With a sarcastic smile Shchusev drew his lips together.

"That may be," he replied noncommittally. "That may be. I am so used to working for clients that I have stopped seeing anything degrading in it. It's not degrading, but difficult."

"I can imagine. It must be terribly difficult," responded Gorin.

Shchusev waved his hand. "If you only knew what foolishness I have run into," he said. "For example, I submitted the first design of the Institute to the Politburo. They didn't like it: they saw, if you please, a cross in the design. 'For a political building such a symbol is absolutely out of place.' I tried to calm them; I said nobody would see this cross except flyers and crows. I told them that the cross in the plan had no relation to religion, that cross-shaped buildings were built in Rome even before the appearance of Christianity, as the most suitable form for massive structure. No, they didn't want to listen. 'Throw the cross out of the plan,' they said. You know what it means to alter the

135

plans of a building? It means everything has to be done over again. All right, I did it over again. I brought them the new design. They were satisfied. Now, as you see, the building is like a five-pointed star."

Gorin began to laugh heartily. "That's a good joke," he exclaimed.

His homely face brightened. His recent anger and hidden annoyance had passed. Standing as before, slightly bent and placing his broad-molded hands on the handrail of the platform, he surveyed the square with laughing eyes.

"A hardy old man," thought Shchusev, admiring him. "But how difficult it is for him."

Larin turned at the sound of the laughter and glanced inquiringly at Gorin. In a few words Gorin, with a smile under his gray mustache, told him the story about the cross. Larin listened attentively but didn't understand a thing. In his ears rang the shrill voice of Veria.

"How can Gorin laugh at such a moment?" he thought. "There's a saintly soul! He is to be envied. No cares, no fears."

CHAPTER 12

SEIZED by the fire of oratory, confident of his own triumph, Veria was entirely transformed: his joy no longer hid behind his pince-nez. Now it shone in his eyes, rang in his voice, flashed in his brusque gestures, was reflected all over his small face, which had become suddenly overbearing and arrogant. Veria alone knew that soon a fateful phrase would resound over the square. After that everything would be different.

"I can imagine their faces," flashed through his mind. "Now it comes . . ."

"The fact that this building is being erected now in Rostov is not accidental, comrades. For here, in Rostov in 1907, Comrade Stalin, while in the revolutionary underground, wrote his historical work *Anarchism or Socialism*. In it, with great force, he . . ." Veria went on talking, but watched the effect.

The effect did not come at once. But it grew like a snowball. In a minute the entire square was stupefied. Nobody had ever heard of Stalin's *Anarchism or Socialism*. Nobody knew that Stalin had ever been in Rostov. They all realized that they were present at the remaking of history. The expressions on their faces became strange, not so much surprised as embarrassed, or perhaps wary.

136

Larin paled. He had expected anything but that. He realized at once that his end had come. After the remaking of history follows a purge. An old, experienced Party man, he knew this law. And he also knew that if they ignored him in this event, it meant that he was no longer needed. It had happened with others before; now it was happening to him. In one instant the whole square, the red banners, even the sun, seemed to turn black.

"Death," he thought.

All the "best people of the town," crowding around the platform, understood clearly that the rise of Veria meant the fall of Larin. On them all lay the shadow of disfavor of the new authority—the specter of a purge. Suddenly the right eye of the editor of the newspaper *Molot* twitched, and his stomach became weak; he was Larin's nephew. The legs of the chief of propaganda, a good friend of Larin's, gave under him. He was aghast to find himself sitting on the steps of the granite stairs. "Don't ruin yourself, get up!" cried his brain. But he couldn't get up. It was as if someone had poured lead into him. "I'm lost, lost . . ."

Academician Glushak nervously wiped beads of cold perspiration from his face. "What am I afraid of?" He was irritated with himself. "I seem to be in favor. They entrusted me with the report at the banquet. But can one be sure?"

The fat Mirzoyan was terribly jealous of Veria. He had known him before in the Caucasus, where they had both been small officials, messmates. "The bastard! How he has climbed up! Damn him!" he puffed and wheezed. "Thanks be, he didn't forget me. . . . But bastard anyhow!"

Novikov noticed Larin's sudden paleness. He himself was seriously alarmed by the implications of Veria's speech. "When they chop a tree, the chips fly." Novikov's imagination drew pictures of the onflowing events. "There will be a purge. Heads will fall. It looks as if Larin will be the first. I must be careful, or the axe may graze me too."

Feverishly he began to search his past for the least hint, for the smallest reason why he might be in the path of this remaking of history. But his whole career was concerned with ancient history; he had nothing to fear. He looked at Gorin with interest. "Will he swallow this lie like all the others?"

He noticed how Gorin looked with surprise at Shchusev; and the sly smirk at the corners of Shchusev's lips.

"That's who should be afraid," thought Novikov suddenly about

137

Gorin. "That's who is standing like a big clod in the path of this new enterprise of Stalin's."

All at once this thought made him shudder. He saw his own place in the oncoming events clearly and precisely. He felt something new and dark, something sinister in his role. Stalin's hatred of everything that could hinder the carrying out of his ambition knew no bounds. Would he violate the only great writer in Russia? Would he demand more from Novikov than merely the repairing of Gorin's soul? Novikov grew cold. Veria's speech could have the most serious consequences on his fate. In any case, his responsibility to fulfill Drozd's task had increased a hundred times.

Not everybody appreciated the importance of this moment. Durov didn't understand why Veria's words had produced such an effect on the people. "Well, they opened an archive with Stalin's work in it. So what? That's what they wanted . . ." He didn't think, at that moment, that soon, very soon, his powerful hands would be needed by Moscow, his stone heart, his unquenchable thirst for blood. A great work awaited him.

Unconsciously everything that was happening around him imprinted itself vividly on Larin's mind. He saw how the chief of propaganda flopped on his backside on the step and couldn't get up; how young Shcherbakov smiled maliciously and whispered something into Yudin's ear; how Yudin, licking his red lips with his thick tongue, nodded.

"About me," flashed into Larin's mind.

"Be courageous, be wise and careful. They are watching you closely," whispered Larin to himself. "Not everything is lost yet. It's not too late to jump on Veria's wagon." But deep inside him someone whispered in anguish: "It's useless, Larin. Your days are numbered. It doesn't matter what you do—you're through! You are too experienced not to know that."

Deathly silence reigned on the square. Only Veria's voice rang out insistently and boldly: ". . . It would be difficult to overestimate the importance of this work. In it Stalin defends and develops in a masterly way the theoretical principles of the Party, affirms and evolves dialectical and historical materialism, based on the tremendous wealth of ideas of Marx and Engels, generalizing the experience of the proletarian struggle in the epoch of imperialism, broadly drawing on the newest data of natural history, physics, and chemistry."

Gorin could not stand it; he leaned over and whispered to Larin: "Tell me," he said softly, "wasn't Comrade Stalin too busy in 1907 robbing banks in Tiflis for the material support of the Party to have time for developing its theoretical principles in Rostov?"

In Gorin's voice there was sincere perplexity. Larin raised empty, resigned eyes to him. "Comrade Stalin could write his work in spare moments in the evening after work," he replied, without noticing that he was talking nonsense.

Veria's voice rose even higher: "This work of Comrade Stalin is the summit of Marxist philosophical thought!"

"So that's the idea!" Novikov scoffed to himself. "Stalin wants to take precedence over Lenin. Even the dead Lenin gives him no peace. He wants to be the first theoretician of the Party also!" It wasn't by chance that Veria announced Stalin's alleged work as written in 1907 —two years before the appearance of Lenin's book *Materialism and Empiriocriticism!* That book is officially considered the exposition of the theoretical foundations of the Party. In Stalin's 'work' the thoughts of Lenin are repeated—but writing it two years before Lenin gives him precedence. History is being changed before my eyes."

Nikolai nudged him covertly with his elbow. Feodor turned and saw the completely carefree face of his brother, spreading in a broad smile. "What are you grinning at?" Feodor asked sharply.

"Listen," whispered Nikolai, barely able to keep from laughing. "That has your ancient Slavs beat!"

Now Novikov understood why they had built this building, this gigantic square, had chased the reporters here, and were broadcasting the celebration all over the Soviet Union. This was the build-up for the "discovery of Stalin's work in the archives." "Yes," he sighed, glancing over the building. "It's an expensive frame that Stalin has chosen for his 'work.' His vanity knows no bounds."

Veria was shouting into the microphone, the radio was carrying his words over the square, over the whole country. "Almost thirty years have passed, but how up-to-date and current this work sounds! *Anarchism or Socialism* enters into the treasure-house of ideas of our Party as an outstanding contribution to Marxist theory."

Novikov noticed Glushak slipping away from his place and hurrying to the exit. "Hurrying to rewrite his report for the banquet." Novikov twisted his thin lips sardonically. "He won't be alone today scratching with his pen, catching up with history."

Veria was finishing: "Hail! To our great teacher, leader, genius of humanity, coryphaeus of science, founder and theorist of our Party— our dear and beloved Comrade Stalin!"

"Hurrah-ah-ah!" Yudin was the first to shout. "To the great Stalin —hurrah!"

A roar rolled over the square.

Something incredible happened to Nikolai. A demon began to whirl his arms and legs. He jumped like a maniac, slapped his hands, spun around where he stood, shouted: "Hurrah! Hurrah!" But in his eyes Feodor saw mad laughter.

He was not surprised. "Probably many are expressing their scorn and contempt in the same way," he thought. "It's hard to see yourself made a fool of. It's better to join the bedlam, to purposely exaggerate the expressions of rapture. Nikolai is overdoing it, though. Someone might notice."

"Don't play the fool, Nikolai," he said to his brother sternly. "Take a grip on yourself."

Mirzoyan's voice roared: "Bands—*The International!*"

The brassy strains of *The International* ascended over the square. Everybody stood erect. The people on the platform brought their hands to the brims of their caps.

Larin stood turned to stone, looking straight ahead. Some power was drawing him to look to the left, where beside him stood the hated Veria. Unable to resist the strange feeling, he turned his head and a cold shiver ran up his spine.

Directly in front of him were Veria's eyes, staring at him. The eyes were observing him with a kind of cold, sharp curiosity. They looked into the very soul of Larin, caught by surprise, and understood everything.

Smiling, Veria said: "What a glorious day, Comrade Larin. Don't forget, you are to cut the ribbon."

His voice sounded unfamiliar and arrogant.

CHAPTER 13

FOR SOME TIME the observant Feodor had noticed a woman standing not far from him among the onlookers. Her behavior seemed strange to him. She apparently neither heard nor saw what was going on around her. Only when the crowd shouted "Hurrah" and applauded more loudly than usual, she would clap her hands mechanically without changing her tense and concentrated expression. Her eyes never left the platform and only Gorin seemed to interest her there. Even

140

when Veria pronounced his explosive phrase not a muscle moved in her thin, petrified face.

"Maybe she's deaf," thought Novikov.

But the woman didn't give the impression of being deaf. The words of others simply did not reach her. She was completely absorbed by some burdensome and important thought. Novikov noticed how, from time to time, her lips moved soundlessly.

He was struck by the unusual gauntness of the woman. Her sunken cheeks were a mass of fine wrinkles. Her staring eyes, encircled by dark unhealthy rings, looked inflamed and red, either from sleeplessness or from recent tears. Her lips, gathering in sorrowful lines, with difficulty concealed some inner mental suffering. Her thin knotted fingers were nervously twisting and untwisting the ends of her kerchief.

She was poorly clad: old shoes with worn heels, many patches and cracks, a coarse dark skirt, light blouse with frayed cuffs, obviously washed frequently, and a torn and faded kerchief on her head, distinguished her among the decently dressed people of Rostov, crowded into the observation places. Her appearance suggested that she belonged rather to those who stood in a dense crowd behind the double row of NKVD guards.

"Probably somebody's poor relative who got a pass by chance and now stands there embarrassed and uncomfortable," concluded Novikov.

Meanwhile the bands had finished playing *The International*. The time had come for the ceremony of cutting the ribbon. A red silk ribbon was stretched between two columns in front of the central door. The platform was at the foot of the triumphal steps. From the platform, a rich red carpet crept upward. Larin was the first to step onto the soft fabric; behind him poured all the others. Someone put a pair of scissors into his hand.

The master of the Province began to ascend the carpet slowly and importantly, stepping heavily, and rather awkwardly extending his right hand, with the scissors open, in front of him.

Behind him came the procession of fame and power: Gorin, Shchusev, Veria, Shcherbakov, Yudin, Durov, Kashirin, Mirzoyan, and several third secretaries of the Party. With the exception of Gorin, who was dressed in a light gray civilian suit, soft hat, black tie and shoes, all the others were dressed in exactly the same semimilitary summer uniform: Party tunic, pants, uniform cap of good white cloth, and black leather boots.

In spite of the simplicity of dress the procession presented a bright picture; the white cloth shone in the sun like snow, the new belts and boots mirrored the light in their high polish; Kashirin's chest, adorned with orders, blinded the eyes, and on Durov's sleeve sparkled the gold sword of revolution.

Novikov glanced again at the strange woman. Her appearance shocked him. With her whole body she pressed forward, as if the group on the steps were drawing her like a magnet. Novikov noticed a small piece of paper fall from her hand and drop at her feet. For some reason he was convinced that she had dropped the paper on purpose.

"Her pass," he thought.

Suddenly the woman broke from her place and began to run quickly toward the steps, where the carpet was spread. She tripped. She lost her kerchief. Her gray hair became tousled in the wind. She pushed people aside without seeing them. She passed the editor of *Molot,* who was still shivering as if caught in a chilly rain; she passed the chief of propaganda, who had recovered. Going up the steps before anyone could collect himself, she ran out onto the empty space where the all-powerful people were walking, with Larin at their head. These people noticed her and stopped, on the alert.

Several NKVD officers, pulling out their revolvers, rushed at the woman. But it was too late to shoot. She was approaching the group. Everyone held his breath. A hush fell.

"Surely not an assassination!" flashed into Novikov's head. He saw how Durov and Kashirin drew their Brownings and pointed them at the woman. But apparently the pitiful appearance of the woman, her empty hands stretched out in front of her, convinced them that she was harmless. They lowered their guns but did not put them back in their holsters. Larin, his eyes agoggle, looked blankly at the disturber, threateningly pointing the scissors at her.

The woman's gray hair streamed in the wind, her face quivered, and her eyes were wild.

"Crazy!" thought everybody.

Suddenly the woman fell to her knees, as if she had been mowed down. She took no notice of the revolvers, nor of the threatening gestures. She saw only Gorin. Throwing her head back, she crawled to the writer and beseechingly extended her hands to him. Gorin looked at her, embarrassed and, it seemed, even unfriendly. He saw how she was gasping for breath, how soundlessly her lips moved. She couldn't speak. But her eyes, full of mute entreaty, held his attention.

"Calm yourself. What's the matter with you?" Gorin asked in a shaking voice. His words were heard distinctly in the reigning quiet.

The best people in the town craned their necks. With keen curiosity they fixed their eyes on the tall figure of the writer and the woman bowed down before him. Feodor held his breath. He was stunned by such an unexpected event. Nikolai, on the other hand, was flushed with pleasure. To watch a scandal was one of his passions.

The officers of the NKVD who had run up and caught the woman by the elbows wanted to lead her away, but Gorin stopped them with a gesture. He wanted to hear what the woman had to say.

"You are an honest man . . . Mikhail Gorin . . . you are a great man . . . everybody listens to you . . . you have a heart . . . for God's sake, help . . . help me," at last she forced out.

"How? How can I help you?" asked Gorin promptly.

"My son . . . They took him yesterday. He has been beaten up. . . . he is wounded. . . . He needs care, maybe he is dying right now, but they won't allow me even to see him. . . . Where is justice, Gorin? Where, I ask you?" she cried in anguish.

From the side Novikov saw how the tears gushed from her eyes and began to roll down the etched wrinkles on her thin cheeks, sparkling in the sunlight. Her words came rushing, but excitement choked her: "They arrested my husband, and now they have taken everything that was left to me in life—my son. You yourself have said—the son is not responsible for the father. You wrote so beautifully about that! Now I ask you before all the people—save my son!" The force and passion of her prayer were capable of calling forth a miracle.

"Calm yourself, please," Gorin comforted her awkwardly, twisting his face in distress. "There must have been some misunderstanding. What is your name? What is your son's name?"

"Andrei Demin. . . . He's a student, one of the best. He was always quiet, bothered nobody. Oleg Durov tormented him, wounded him. He stuck a knife into his eye. . . ." She burst into sobs, her whole body trembled violently.

Larin scowled: the woman's cries got on his nerves.

Before Novikov's eyes the whole scene at the University reappeared vividly: the wounded Andrei, the insolent figure of Oleg Durov, the fawning face of the Director. "So the Director kept his promise. Got Andrei arrested!"

Abruptly Gorin turned to Durov, squinting with annoyance at his Browning. "Put that thing away, Durov," he said roughly. "Tell me, what was Andrei Demin arrested for? What charges have you against him?"

143

Durov's eyes glittered with restrained anger. "Andrei Demin was arrested yesterday for hooliganism, Comrade Gorin," he answered. "Judging by the mother, they're apples from the same tree." And Durov looked at the woman rapaciously.

Gorin angrily knit his brows. "For hooliganism, you say? I don't believe that, somehow. I know one rotten apple in Rostov: a certain Oleg. He should have been arrested long ago for hooliganism."

Hearing the name of his son, Durov grimaced. On his broad, bony face the pockmarks began to turn brown. But he answered nothing.

Rage seized Gorin. This happened very seldom with him. His gray eyes became darker, his voice hard. He placed his broad hand on the bony shoulder of the woman, looked into her face. "All right, Mrs. Demin. I will clear all this up myself. We aren't barbarians. Nobody will suffer without reason."

Shcherbakov and Yudin, whom this scene evidently bored, exchanged perplexed looks.

On hearing Gorin's words, so full of conviction, Mrs. Demin began to laugh, but her laughter was like sobs. "Thank you, dear one. All my life I'll never forget . . . thank you . . ."

The wind carried away the end of her phrase from Novikov's ears, but he heard how, suddenly and maliciously, Shcherbakov laughed. Mirzoyan responded with forced and servile laughter. He fawned in front of the young grandee, the son of the all-powerful Shcherbakov.

Veria took the woman by the arm. "Comrade Gorin, I will lead her into the shade. She needs a drink of water," he said to the writer.

Gorin turned to him quickly. "Please, Comrade Veria, look after her."

Veria led the woman into the shade of the columns.

The group resumed its journey. But the festive spirit had changed into vexation and irritation. For some unclear reason the dignitaries blamed the unpleasant incident not on the woman but on Gorin.

One of the newsreel operators threw his cap down in disgust. "I have spoiled an expensive film. The devil take the old woman and . . ." he hesitated. But everyone who heard him knew that he was going to say "Gorin."

Novikov remembered the pass which Mrs. Demin had dropped. He approached the place where the pass lay and, unnoticed, put his foot over it. When he was sure that nobody was looking, he stooped, as if to tie his shoelace, and covertly picked up the yellow sheet of paper. He read it through. The pass was in the name of Lida Sidorov. Novikov's eyebrows rose.

144

"So that's how it is! A little conspiracy," he smiled to himself and placed the pass in his pocket. "With this pass I can reach the very soul of this emotional girl."

In the meantime Veria and Andrei's mother were standing in the portal, behind one of the columns. She was leaning against it. The heavy thumping of her heart had shaken her whole being. Veria gave her a glass of water; she grew more calm, but her thin shoulders were shaking as if she had a chill. "Thank you, thank you! It's such a pity about my son, my darling. . . ."

Veria saw that she was becoming quiet. Then he asked her kindly and with a wheedling smile: "How did you get through the guard to the observation places? Unless you had a pass?"

The woman shuddered; at once the light died in her eyes. Veria's small figure suddenly took on the merciless appearance of a stone idol. She became frightened, she wanted to flee from his glance. "They let me through . . . I asked them and they let me through . . . one of the officers . . ."

"Ah! So that's how it was. They allowed you through. I see," Veria repeated in a strange voice, parading his pince-nez.

He called one of the officers of the NKVD. "Take this woman home. She needs a rest."

The officer clicked his heels, saluted. "At once, Comrade Veria." He turned to her: "Come along, mother." Slowly they moved away.

Veria rejoined the group. Larin had just cut the ribbon. Simultaneously came the discharge of guns and the bands struck up again.

Suddenly loud shouts were heard above the music: "Gorin! Gorin!" the name became clearer and clearer.

Soon the whole crowd chorused in rhythm: "Gorin! . . . Gorin!" The clamor drowned the bands.

Gorin stood between the two central columns. He turned to the crowd and raised his hat above his head. Now his homely but expressive face was clearly seen by the people on the square. A mesh of wrinkles like the bark of an oak, it was firm and energetic. His whole figure breathed of the dignity of age and the live warmth of the man with a kind and passionate heart.

It was obvious that the enthusiastic shouts of the crowd moved and embarrassed him. His eyes blinked; the drooping gray mustache twitched; on his face, instead of a smile, appeared a grimace of distress. He pressed his hat to his heart.

Durov, looking at him, bit his lips ill-naturedly. His fingers clenched and unclenched violently. Approaching Veria, he hissed: "There you

145

have the 'conscience of the people.' That's all he's good for, getting in the way."

Veria looked hard at him with his sharp eyes, bared his small teeth: "Have patience, Durov. Have patience."

PART THREE

⊓⊔

CHAPTER 1

HOW BEAUTIFUL is a June morning on the Don! The vast green expanse of the steppe stretches away into the distance, merges with the sky in a blue haze. In the clear, boundless heavens the clouds tower one above the other, sailing along full of life, bright sunlight, and joyous power.

Suddenly the steppe breaks off and falls toward the Don. The river, like the steppe itself, is broad and free. The sky, the sun, the birds are reflected in its clear, smooth surface. There seems to be no top or bottom to this immense vastness—only the smiling summer sun, the gay movements of the clouds, the raging of the wind. For a city dweller to stand on the steep bank of the Don is both pleasant and frightening.

One moment, and you no longer feel the ground under your feet— you seem to be flying along with the clouds in the air, borne on the rollicking wind into the blue, far-off distance. You become light, almost weightless, as if the steppe winds had blown all cares and sorrows away. You breathe more freely, reinvigorated, filled with robust strength.

It was such a flow of invigorating strength that Nina Gorin felt when she rode onto the drill square in the compact Cossack ranks. The vast training grounds on the river bank was enclosed by a low willow hedge and from her saddle Nina saw the blazing Don, the green steppe, and the scurrying clouds.

The lads to right and left of her were singing with wild shrieks and whoops, looking at the bright sky without blinking. The Don sun—

147

that celestial smith—tempered them with his rays, making them strong and resonant like iron bells. The song rang brassily and rasped the ears, but Nina enjoyed it.

The small company rode onto the square; the song was cut short. Over the snorting of the horses resounded the word of command: "Draw—sabers!"

A steel flash of blades flung upwards and froze to stillness, like the wing of a hawk in the sun.

"Cut—stakes! One at a time—march!"

"Rudoy, Ivan!"

"Lip, Pyotr!"

One after another, the riders rushed between the rows of stakes stuck into the ground, cut them down close to the bottom.

"Gorin, Nina!"

A rider with an amazingly small waist dashed out of the ranks, red hood fluttering in the wind.

"Well done, for a girl! Next!" exclaimed the bearded commander of the company.

The rider, making a half circle on the large square, was returning to the formation. Now they all saw the broadly smiling face of the girl. It was Nina's eighteenth summer. Her tanned cheeks still glowed with the bloom of youth. But the Cossack uniform was already tight for her firm breasts. The saber drill kindled her blood, rejoiced her heart.

She had started training with them a year after her arrival from Italy where, on the island of Capri, Mikhail Gorin had spent year after year following the revolution, studying his homeland, Russia, from afar. Their return to Russia made a strong impression on Nina. Only then did she understand what tremendous influence her father had on the Russian mind. Everywhere, even at the smallest stations, past which the train rushed without stopping, crowds of people met them with flowers, with placards, with portraits of Gorin. But what she saw at the Kursk Station in Moscow surpassed all her expectations. The great square was packed with people, although rain was falling and it was cold. Thousands upon thousands of people shouted Gorin's name, affectionately waving their hands. What she saw filled Nina's heart with warm love toward these gray shabby people, and with boundless pride in her father.

Gorin returned to Russia at the personal request of Stalin, who had kept up a regular correspondence with him since 1924—the year of Lenin's death. After living in Moscow two hectic months—crammed with receptions at the Kremlin, talks with endless delegations, and the

148

acceptance of awards—tired, dizzy, but rejuvenated in spirit, Gorin wished to go to Rostov to live near the Don where he had spent his tempestuous, roving youth.

The first year in Rostov passed like a strange dream. Russia, Russian life, was so unlike what Nina had left in Italy. They lived wonderfully, incomparably better than in Italy. They were given a huge palace in the country which, before the revolution, had belonged to the heirs of Count Zubov. The palace was full of spacious rooms, luxurious furniture, and servants. The palace was their world. In spite of its size, this world soon appeared limited to Nina. Indeed, she saw the outside world mostly through the windows of the palace, or from the car in which the chauffeur drove her every morning to the Conservatory, where she studied music. It seemed to her a poor world, strange but not terrifying, although she guessed that she saw only the outward aspect of events without understanding their true meaning. Russia remained a mystery to her.

Feeling this, she was surprised that her father was able to write with such an assured, even instructive tone about current life in Russia. He worked feverishly. From morning to night, shut up in his study, he wrote articles. He could write about everything: about the tasks of Soviet literature; about the lessons of history; about the greatness of Marxist ideas and the harmfulness of bourgeois philosophy; about the new kolkhozes—which he did not know thoroughly; about the new Soviet man—whom he seldom met. His every word was treasured by Moscow as though made of gold. All his articles appeared in *Pravda* and *Izvestia* and were broadcast over the radio.

"Surely my father can't have become familiar with everything so quickly after an absence of so many years from his native country. How can he be its first expert?" the perplexed Nina asked herself.

She began to feel lonely. The splendor of the rooms bored her, the huge palace seemed like a prison, and the obliging servants, following her every footstep, like guards. The few acquaintances with whom she found herself surrounded seemed artificial, boring.

Mikhail Gorin noticed her low spirits. Like all fathers, he ascribed this to the usual girlish foolishness which can be cured either by fresh air or by interesting young men. He didn't want to part with her. So there remained the fresh air, of which there was more than enough around Rostov.

"You are studying your music too hard," he said to her once. "You must have some recreation. How would you like me to show you some real Cossacks?"

149

Nina accepted with pleasure. They went to one of the Cossack villages where the Soviet Government had revived, as an experiment, the old Cossack traditions, forgotten after the revolution. At her first sight of the Cossacks, Nina's eyes lit up. She wanted to ride a horse herself.

Everything was possible for the daughter of Gorin. She was enrolled in a cavalry company, with the right to attend when she liked. The entire company nearly fell off their horses when she appeared in a white Cossack tunic, drawn tight by a belt around her waist, slender and willowy as a reed in the Don; she wore wide blue trousers, fine boots, and a Kuban hat of gray lamb. Instead of the rough Cossack forelock, a strand of fair hair stole out from under the jauntily cocked hat.

Looking at such a picture, the young lads immediately felt lonesome, and the commander of the company, already up in years, to cover up his own confusion, shouted at them more roughly than usual:

"To horse! You so-and-so!"

In this way her training began. She learned easily to guide a horse. "You are a born Cossack," laughed Mikhail Gorin. "Horses obey your musical fingers better than the piano."

Everything went well, except that the Cossacks, after their first shyness wore off, began to steal covetous glances at her. Those who were bolder would press their knees against hers while in formation or would spread their elbows wide—contrary to regulations—and brush them against her breasts.

It became necessary to engage a companion. The Chief of the NKVD of the Province, Durov, who was responsible for the safety of Gorin's family, found such a girl. In the routine of Komsomol discipline a student of the Rostov University, Lida Sidorov, was ordered to attend the cavalry company with Nina. Being the daughter of the director of an important war plant and therefore dressed better than the other students, Lida was more suited to the role of chaperone than anyone else. They soon became close friends.

The year of training passed like spring rain on the steppe—suddenly and quickly. Nina began to feel happier, more responsive to life. She wished life could always be like this.

CHAPTER 2

AFTER TWO hours of drill, Nina heard with regret the command: "At ease! Dismiss!"

From habit, her horse, jumping lightly over the hedge, dashed towards the steppe. The blue wind, playing in the field, seemed to be murmuring: "How wonderful! How wonderful is everything!"

There are moments in everyone's life when the wind and the sun, all nature, opens wide its embrace, filling his heart with pure joy. That was how Nina felt now. The clear Don, the gay clouds, the developing muscles of her healthy body, the intoxication of youth and swift motion . . . "Why do I feel so happy today?" she thought. "The day is like any other. But today everything seems different."

Suddenly she understood.

"Of course! I'm alone today. Lida is not with me." Nina blushed at this thought. "A nice friend I am! As soon as I'm left alone, I rejoice."

She was so used to having Lida with her that when she wasn't around she felt strange. But the strange feeling was pleasant, a feeling of release.

The sun's rays, mingling with the songs of the larks, poured from the sky onto the steppe which appeared now bright, now dark from the shadows of the clouds. The horse pricked its ears, snorted, went into an easy gallop, trembled when gophers ran across its path. There was a fragrance of mint and honey clover. The tall grasses bent, shadowy, swaying like waves, losing themselves in the sunny ripple. With this aroma the breeze seemed to Nina to waft a new feeling into her heart, sweet and tender, harbinger of thrilling experiences to come.

"Nina! Nina!" suddenly a loud shout sounded.

She turned around. A rider was overtaking her at full gallop.

She smiled happily yet anxiously, for it was Rudoy, a lively young Cossack, who had several times escorted her to the estate. But Lida had always been with them. She recalled how several times that morning she had caught his intent expectant glance on her.

"Hey! Hey!" With a wild whoop Rudoy galloped past her, waving his crop recklessly, eyes sparkling.

"He's a wild one!" thought Nina, following him with her eyes.

Rudoy tore over the steppe, circling Nina in a wide arc. She felt that this was for her benefit. His horse, a shapely bay mare, as if understanding what was required of her, proudly arching her neck, confident of her own beauty, bore Rudoy over the ground with playful grace. In the hot June sun the rider with the forelock and the bay mare seemed to be cast in one piece of bronze. "Wild—but handsome," she caught herself thinking.

Rudoy rode up. The collar of his red shirt was wide open; from his right wrist his crop hung loosely by a thong.

"What a beautiful day, Comrade Nina!" he greeted her, teeth flashing in his dark face.

"Very pleasant," she replied with studied coolness. But in her eyes shone laughter, on her cheeks played happy dimples. With difficulty she held in her stallion, a black Don beauty with a noble fire in its glowing eyes. It whinnied, pranced and, arching its neck, squinted at Rudoy's mare.

"It's a lovely day," continued Rudoy, "but you are still more lovely!"

"What will you say next!" laughed Nina.

"No—I'm telling you the truth—you are a picture!" Rudoy began to protest hotly. He seemed afraid that she wouldn't believe him. "Oh! What a pity I haven't any education! I can't find words. I can only say —there's nobody in the whole wide world more beautiful than you!"

"Don't tell me—no."

"No! Honest—no!"

Indeed, Nina was strikingly pretty with her refined face, tanned cheeks, large gray eyes encircled by dark lashes. She breathed of youth, energy, unconscious happiness. The Cossack uniform did not hide her girlish figure, but rather emphasized it. Rudoy's bold look stripped off her clothes to reveal the charm of her naked beauty, the fresh, untouched body of a girl, ripe for men's embraces and caresses. The sudden discovery provoked and frightened Rudoy.

Nina, as if on purpose, didn't sit quietly in the saddle: now she fixed her hair under the gray Kuban hat, now she leaned backward and rested her hand on the horse's crupper, laughing, narrowing her eyes against the wind. Under the Cossack tunic, her breasts stood out shamelessly—girlish, well molded. Rudoy stared, and a mischievous devil kept urging him: "Go ahead, fool! Embrace her! Kiss her right on the lips."

"Why are you looking at me so strangely? Like a mouse at a piece of cheese!" teased Nina.

"It's all right for you to laugh, Nina. If only you knew the feelings of a man's heart," said Rudoy seriously, and he sighed deeply.

Nina laughed aloud. "I suppose you say the very same thing to all the girls in the village."

"You won't believe me." She felt resentment in his voice. "I'm not the only one! Do you know what the boys in the company are saying about you?"

"What are they saying?"

"They say that they would chop off a finger just for one night with you."

"What!" Nina's face flushed crimson to the collar of her shirt. Tears appeared in her eyes. Gathering the reins, she said dryly to Rudoy, not looking at him: "It's time for you to go back to the village, Comrade Rudoy."

"You're mistaken. I have leave."

"Oh, I see! . . . Well, so long! I must go home." She put spurs to her stallion. He reared, ready to dash off. But Rudoy blocked the path with his own horse.

"Stop your fooling, Rudoy!"

Not understanding, he looked in perplexity into her furious eyes, more beautiful than ever. "Let me escort you. It's dangerous to be alone on the steppe. Something might happen——"

"I'm not afraid on the steppe," Nina interrupted curtly. "Get out of the way! Don't bother me!"

She tried to ride around Rudoy, but the latter leaned over and caught the horse's bridle. Before her eyes, his dusty cap, aslant, began to dance. "I didn't mean to be rude to you, Nina. Believe me——"

"I believe you."

"May I go with you?"

"No!"

In trying to avoid Rudoy's glance she raised her face toward the sky. In her angry gray eyes a delicate cloud was reflected. As he looked at this cloud, Rudoy's spirits fell completely.

"That's what it is to be uneducated! I didn't want to offend, and I offended," he said with unaffected bitterness. "When I overtook you I thought: now Nina is alone, without her shadow at last. Maybe I'll persuade her to go to the Don with me, to spend an hour or so on the beach. But it has turned out so stupidly."

Nina looked with interest at his coarse face, with its simple and open features. She felt sincerity and hurt in his voice. But her wariness did not leave her on that account. She merely said, more gently: "That's a nice horse, Rudoy."

"It's a good one, but it overreaches itself a little," replied Rudoy, and

153

looked at her with hope: had she really forgiven? Aloud he said: "Maybe you will go to the Don after all? It's the only place to get away from the heat."

Rudoy looked at her pleadingly, awaiting her answer. Nina's stallion neighed angrily, and all atremble from impatience, was prancing under her, stamping his thin legs.

"All right," said Nina. "Let's race to the beach. Do you want to?"

"Great! Let's go!" exclaimed Rudoy, beaming with joy.

He broke away first. After him, bent over her stallion's neck and pressing her knees to his warm flanks, flew Nina. Her mount let out his stride like a fleet wolfhound. The grass, the bushes, merged into a one-colored ribbon, fluffy dandelions bore down on them. A mad joy flowed into her from the swift ride. She shouted loudly and shrilly. It was the cry of irrepressible happiness. The wind whistled a happy refrain, bearing away the recent resentment. Thus they galloped, intoxicated by the speed. Nina's stallion was not a pure-bred racehorse for nothing. Soon she began to pull up on Rudoy. When she was even with him she turned her face towards him and, without knowing why, screwed up her eyes and stuck out her tongue. Rudoy shouted something to her, but she didn't catch what he said. She heard the rough breathing of his horse, saw how he beat her feverishly with his whip, but without avail—he dropped behind hopelessly. Then Nina began to wheel toward the steppe. "Good-bye, Rudoy!"

"Hey! Where are you going?"

"Home!"

"That's cheating!" But Nina wasn't even looking at him. Her red hood fluttering in the wind, she galloped away over the tall grass.

Stopping his horse at the very brink of the river, Rudoy looked long after the retreating girl. When she disappeared he said to his horse sadly, slapping her muscular withers: "You sure spoiled my chances, Swallow, letting her get ahead!" Swallow merely shook her head, dropping white foam onto the grass. Somewhat scared and agitated by the presence of the girl a few moments ago, Rudoy was now furious that she had dared to run away.

"All right," he thought, compressing his thin lips in a resentful smile. "All right, there'll be a holiday yet on our street."

This "holiday" had been a constant dream of Rudoy's since Nina had appeared in the company, and all the girls in the village now looked trashy in comparison to her. Rudoy had a taste for girls. He was a happy, sinewy fellow, of the breed to whom life never becomes dull; life means fun, love, caresses.

154

Rudoy, however, accepted his defeat stoically. "Maybe it's for the best that she ran away," he reflected, calming down a little. "Keep away from that kind of kitten! Why ask for trouble? She's not like village girls that you can push any time into a straw stack. What on earth made me blurt out such nonsense to her? . . . What a damn fool! . . . She may even complain to her father and I'll get it pretty hot. Very simple. They'll send me back to the kolkhoz to work. There wouldn't be any time for girls . . ."

Rudoy groaned at the thought of going back to the kolkhoz. From the time that the Cossack company had been organized and he was enrolled in it, he had lived well. He had filled out, his face was rounded, his cheeks had taken on color. To lose this well-fed life, and over a girl, would be terrible. Then he recalled how Nina had stuck out her tongue at him, and calmed down. In that gesture he sensed a disturbing promise.

CHAPTER 3

RUDOY SAT in his saddle not knowing what to do: whether to return to the village for the remaining hours of his leave, or to stay here and rest on the river bank alone.

The soft lapping of small waves caressed his ears, reminding him of the coolness of the river. He was about to jump from his saddle and stretch out on the grass when he heard a sharp clatter and Swallow neighed softly and nervously. Rudoy turned around. Nina rode up to him. He broke into a smile. "Nina! It's you! Well, that's good!"

Nina came to a halt beside him. In her eyes there was a willful, boyish look. A blue flower was stuck in her hair. It went well with her gray eyes and the gray Kuban hat.

"You thought that I was afraid of you and ran away?" she said in a slightly shaking voice. "You might as well know that I am afraid of no one, not even of you on the wide open steppe."

"Why should you be afraid of me? I'm a gentle sort of fellow."

"No, seriously. I simply don't know what to do with myself. I was lonely, and so I came. But don't go around boasting that you spent the day alone with me," she added. "The village girls will tear out my eyes."

"They wouldn't believe me in any case!" Rudoy replied simply.

Nina laughed. "Your sincerity deserves a reward."

"You're in a strange mood today, Nina," Rudoy remarked. "You're not like yourself."

"No! Today I am the real Nina, more so than ever before," she said; and then, looking at a flock of gulls, added with a touch of bitterness, "I am celebrating my release from Lida. It's wonderful!"

"That's understandable. We know that kind of friend. They pretend friendship, and then write against you," Rudoy concluded, following his own line of thought. "I have been politically literate from childhood."

"Oh! Not that, Rudoy—not that! I simply don't know myself, what I want, I'm lonely . . ."

"Well, you won't be lonely with me."

"I won't?"

"No!"

"You're a good fellow, Rudoy."

Rudoy, breathing deeply, cast a passionate glance over her. She was sitting in front of him in a halo of her light hair. The wind played caressingly with this golden cloud. From the river came a cool breeze, heavy with the smell of water.

"How beautiful the Don is!" exclaimed Nina. "Do you like it?"

"I haven't seen other rivers—I don't know."

"I've seen many rivers, but the Don affects me in a special way. In its quiet current you can feel a hidden strength."

The quiet Don was Nina's passion. Her lively, nervous character, inherited from her father and like him thirsting for impressions, was thrown into an unexplainable emotion at sight of this endless, everlasting, moving force. From such a simple thing as a river, its banks and the blue distance, somewhere inside her, restless, impatient feelings began to stir; it dawned on her suddenly that in life much was still unknown to her, mysterious, exciting . . .

"Kiss me, Rudoy . . ." she said softly, not looking at him, and suddenly blushed brightly, childishly ardent, near tears. Rudoy trembled from surprise; the blood rushed in a heavy wave to his heart. He looked at her but could barely see her. Her lips were curved stubbornly like an ancient Cossack bow, and like a drawn bow they trembled nervously. Only at the corners of her lips a sly smile lurked.

Rudoy clasped her impetuously and firmly and drew her to him. But, just as he was about to touch her inviting lips, Nina suddenly slashed his horse. Swallow jumped to one side. Leaning over in his passionate gesture, Rudoy nearly lost his balance.

156

"Damn you, Swallow, stop! Oh! It was you, Nina!"

She burst out laughing. "No, not I . . . Probably a groundhog frightened her."

Rudoy frowned. "This is some kind of a circus, and not love. My heart is bursting, while you are joking."

"Have patience, Cossack—and you'll be the ataman yet . . . All right then, come on and do your business, or I'll go home."

Feeling foolish, and having no faith in the girl, Rudoy again embraced her, but this time more firmly, and kissed her cheek. She tightened up inside as if she were under torture. From shame and anguish her eyes closed for an instant. But when she opened them she cried out in alarm: "Rudoy, we aren't alone! There are people!"

"I don't believe it. Another trick?"

"No, it's true. Look there, on the beach."

Without letting her go, Rudoy looked down reluctantly. There by the water's edge some people were moving around. The muffled sound of conversation was carried to them, the crunch of sand under the strangers' feet and the lapping of the water. Nina and Rudoy started back from one another. Four men and two women were getting into rowboats. They hurriedly loaded nets into them. Nina heard one of the men curse softly but fiercely.

Rudoy suddenly slapped his thigh.

"That must be some city folks who have a fancy to be fishermen. Well, I never!" he exclaimed in surprise and rather spitefully.

"So what?" asked Nina, not understanding his sudden excitement.

"What do you mean—what? They can be exiled for ten years for that! To catch fish in State waters is forbidden by law." Rudoy repeated the strange words as if by heart, and added with glee: "Well, I'll show them a fish or two! Just you watch! This'll be lots of fun." Before she had time to say anything, Rudoy drove his spurs into Swallow's flanks. Bunching her hind legs, the mare slithered down the steep bank. For an instant the bushes concealed the rider, but soon Nina saw Rudoy emerge onto the sand, waving his crop, and swoop down on the people. He began striking them right and left with his whip. They jumped out of the boats, tripped, fell into the water, shouted and wept. Above it all thundered Rudoy's voice: "I'll flog you to death! I'll flog you to death as class enemies!"

"How dare he? What's he doing? Why?" the astounded and frightened Nina cried aloud.

She saw how one of the men, his hands shaking with fear, covered his head, how Rudoy's whip slashed with a whine down the length of his back, how the man fell on his face in the boat. The gulls, excited and crying shrilly, soared above.

The color left Nina's face. Her beautiful eyes, a minute ago happy and loving, suddenly dimmed.

"Leave them alone!" she screamed in a voice not her own, her whole body trembling. "Leave them in peace, I tell you!"

But the raging Rudoy didn't hear her; he continued to rain merciless blows on the unfortunate poachers. "All right, then!" muttered Nina. And gathering up her reins, she dashed down to the beach.

She still did not understand what had taken place. Convulsively gripping the handle of her whip, seized by a mad fury that sees nothing and thinks of nothing, she descended on Rudoy.

"You scoundrel! How dare you touch them!" she cried, and without stopping, struck Rudoy's face a sharp blow with her whip. She was in a rage, and rage doubled her strength. A blood-red streak welled up on Rudoy's cheek. The sharp pain and her harsh words forced him to abandon his victims. Lowering his crop, he looked into Nina's blazing eyes, at her face twisted with fury, and simply didn't know what to do. The people also looked on in confusion, not understanding from where this unexpected protection came, this well-dressed, beautiful, furious girl.

Silent, timid, with eyes wide with fear, they already considered themselves lost. On all of them lay the terrible marks of want, of hunger, and of Rudoy's merciless crop. A thin man caught Nina's eye, apparently a worker, judging by the hands stained by machine oil. His shirt had been torn to shreds by Rudoy's whip, his raw-ribbed chest and hollow stomach were bared, his dirty toes stuck out of battered boots. Unshaven, with a long nose pinched like that of a corpse, he looked at Nina from sunken blue eyes. He was unable to utter a word; only with those eyes, in which tears glistened, did he thank her.

The people, dumbstruck in the first instant, groaned, then ran in all directions like frightened animals. Behind, trying to keep up with them, waddling heavily, ran a woman. Only now Nina noticed her high and ungainly belly. Nina's heart contracted painfully. Her rage filled her breast, choked her.

"You beast!" she shouted, and again swung at Rudoy. Raising his arms in defense, Rudoy recoiled backwards. Her blow landed on Swallow, who jumped to one side; Rudoy, losing his balance, fell into the water. Nina's stallion neighed threateningly, reared above the fallen

158

Cossack. "I'll never forgive you for this!" she cried, and in her exasperation threw her whip at the soaking Rudoy.

Shaking from excitement, from pity for the beaten-up, hungry people, and from hatred for Rudoy, she rode up the river bank. At the top she held in her stallion and looked back. Of the people there was nothing to be seen now; they had hidden themselves in the bushes. Rudoy alone, soaking wet, his wide trousers clinging to his legs, was trying to get into the stirrup, hopping on one foot in the water beside the excited Swallow. He looked pitiful.

"Oh! you low beast!" Nina said aloud to herself, somehow surprised, as though she saw something in Rudoy now that she had not seen before. The picture of the ragged oppressed people shook her to the depths of her soul. It destroyed the last of any feeling for Rudoy that had been there.

She turned toward home. On the way, fixing her Kuban hat, she felt the flower.

"To hell with it!" she cried out with unexpected anger, and jerking it out of her hair she threw it onto the dusty road. And suddenly, unable any longer to bear the tension that was exhausting her, she sobbed aloud, her shoulders shaking desperately.

"Damned Rudoy! . . . Damned country that makes such beasts! . . ."

The wind carried her sobs away into the steppe, even as it bore the gay, free clouds above her head.

CHAPTER 4

MIKHAIL GORIN returned home from the meeting about three in the afternoon. In the open car beside him sat the architect Shchusev.

Shchusev was in excellent humor, whistled softly to himself, blinked like a cat in the sun, but did not chatter with Gorin during the drive. He knew the writer was in a bad mood.

The car drove into a pine-shaded avenue which stretched a whole mile to the gates of the country house. It was dark and cool here. The tires crunched softly on the sand-sprinkled road. Then, beyond the graceful pines the palace showed white in the distance.

At the ornamental iron gates a sentry, eaten up with boredom, gladly shouldered his rifle, as if on parade, froze to a stiff pose, peered into the car. Without stopping, the chauffeur shouted the password to him.

159

Gorin frowned, said to Shchusev, as if he were apologizing: "I live like a general on a campaign, Viktor. Sentries, rifles, passwords! I can't get used to it. Really, who do they want to guard me from?"

Shchusev chuckled in reply: "Of course you're a general on the march. Didn't you yourself write: 'We are going through a great historical campaign against the old, the dying but still dangerous . . .'"

"That's true, I wrote that."

They drove around a flower bed, bright in red explosions of bloom, and stopped in front of a broad colonnade. In the pediment, over the portal, muses with broken fingers played on harps. The palace was old, but solidly and beautifully built. In the olden days it had belonged to the heirs of the famous Zubov, a stove tender in the palace of Catherine the Great. Because of his unusual virility he became a favorite of the Empress, who gave him a count's title and half of Rostov Province.

Looking at the expansive colonnade of the palace, architect Shchusev thought: "Long ago Count Zubov died, long ago his lusty flesh crumbled to dust, and his heirs have died or scampered away abroad. Now a new man has taken up residence here. And he also, if not with his body, then with his mind, delights the current ruler of Russia. What a strange fate for a building!"

A small lively old man with an imposing nose and roguish eyes opened the car door, outstripping a young servant lad: it was Cheprok, an old tramp, friend of Gorin, an inseparable part of his family. He greeted them, smiling radiantly. "Thanks be to God! At last you have arrived. We thought that you had stayed to lunch in the city. I'll bet you're tired from the meeting."

With a firm movement the old man took Gorin's arm, helped him out of the car. An agreeable whiff of wine and horseradish came from Cheprok. Wrinkling his nose, Gorin shook a finger at him: "You've been tipping the bottle again, old friend."

Cheprok had lived a turbulent life. In his youth there were times when, with the lanky Gorin, he had tramped along the Don, the Volga, walked all over Russia. Only jail parted them. There, with thieves and tramps like himself, Cheprok played a card game called "Noses." From this old jail sport Cheprok's nose had swollen and become red as an overripe tomato. Cheprok would surely have perished somewhere between a saloon and the jail, except that Gorin became a great writer, remembered his old friend, found him, and gave him shelter. Cheprok had lived with Gorin many years now, had become a sort of nurse to him, and never left his side. He went with him to Italy. There, under a strange sun, he taught the Capri fishermen to plait Russian sandals,

160

himself learned from them oaths as salty as sea water, and the ticklish art of eating spaghetti.

Gorin immortalized the old man by drawing him as the kind-hearted but tragically ending hero of the tale *Logovo*. In life, however, Cheprok had not the slightest intention of dying: gray, sinewy, dried by sun and wind, he merely bent with the years, but did not break.

"Well, old man, report what's new. Everybody home?"

"They're home, all right. Nina just arrived from her riding, but looking sad, even tears in her eyes. Your wife's with her now," and Cheprok added significantly: "You'd better go and find out what's wrong."

"No need to. Women's business; let them straighten it out themselves. And how is Pavel?"

The old man sighed, shook his head, and answered in a low voice, so that Shchusev wouldn't hear: "Bad. He's sitting alone, drinking . . . I tried to reason with him, but he only got mad, nearly killed me. Even made me drink a glass. 'Drink, you old fogy!' says he. 'Your soul will be cleaner.' What a calamity!"

"All right, I'll have a talk with him myself."

"Glushak's here too. He's sitting in the library, waiting for you. What got him into the habit of coming here?"

"Now that's none of your business," Gorin interrupted him. That Cheprok disliked Glushak he had known for a long time, although he had never been able to understand this enmity. "Take us to him," he ordered Cheprok.

The old man merely knit his brows, grumbling: "It's too bad you won't listen to me. I wouldn't let this Glushak near the gates. . . . Damn him and triple damn him!"

"Shut up, I tell you!" Gorin lost his temper and, dropping back a little, he took the arm of Shchusev, who was following behind. "I'll introduce you to Pyotr. He's a smart man, if ever there was one."

In the library Glushak met them with a pleasant smile, genially extended his hands. "Mikhail, at last you have come! I didn't wait for the end of the meeting and left early."

"You did right to leave," mumbled Gorin, pressing Glushak's puffy hand. "I saw you go. But allow me to introduce you: Academician Pyotr Glushak, Academician Viktor Shchusev."

"A pleasure to meet you." Glushak hurried to shake the architect's hand and smiled broadly, although he flushed from annoyance. He had wanted to talk with Gorin alone, and had not counted on the presence of a stranger.

Cheprok drew aside the heavy curtains on the six large windows, one after another. (For Glushak alone, he had not drawn them: "Let him sit in the dark, the fat owl.")

Filled with light, the library at once seemed to expand. The feathery fir trees scraped the very glass of the windows. The library, the largest room in the palace, had previously been the ballroom. Gorin had covered all the walls, from floor to ceiling, with shelves of books. In the center he placed a heavy oak table, around it arranged divans and armchairs. Here, shut away by himself, he loved to work.

"Cheprok, bring us something to drink before dinner," Gorin ordered.

When the old man left, Gorin winked at Glushak: "The old devil, for some reason or other he doesn't like you. Why?"

Glushak became confused, lowered his small eyes. "I don't think he likes anybody but you. . . ."

"He's probably jealous," Shchusev interjected, seating himself comfortably in an armchair. "Such people are like children. They become completely devoted and they hate just as completely. They have no middle course."

"And yet, he's an awfully good fellow," replied Gorin, an affectionate smile on his face. "Everybody respects him here. All the help, sharp-tongued as the lads are, are afraid of him. He's little, but prickly—don't touch him without gloves."

The prickly old man brought three glasses and Caucasian wine on a tray, poured it out, and left quietly.

"I like wine," said Gorin. "Wine and women. . . . For women I'm probably too old now, but wine—no. For wine you need no effort, it enters you itself, fires the blood."

Shchusev turned the glass in his hand, his crafty eyes good-naturedly half closed. "An old Georgian proverb says: 'Woman gives birth to children, wine to inspiration.'"

". . . but both demand moderation," interposed Glushak, assuming, as usual, an impressive expression.

Gorin frowned.

"I don't like that word 'moderation,'" he said. "It smacks of something restricted, of something timid. A man with a strong, live nature cannot be moderate, no matter in what: whether in creative effort, in habits, or in love. . . ." Emptying his glass at a gulp, Gorin got up, with long strides approached one of the windows and opened it. The fragrance of the garden burst into the room. "No, in nature there is

162

nothing stinted—nothing. Moderation was invented by people with timid souls."

The short-cut gray hair of the writer became dappled with sunshine. A deep wrinkle furrowed his brow. His pose reminded Glushak and Shchusev, both at the same time, of his famous portrait, painted by the artist Repin: the tall figure of Mikhail Gorin on the rocky shore of the Black Sea, the broad, open face of the writer turned to meet the fresh wind. "The likeness is striking," thought Shchusev, "although in the portrait Gorin is young, well built, with a big shock of light flaxen hair—not gray."

"Tell me, Viktor," Gorin turned to Shchusev suddenly, "what would you have done today, there on the square, if you had been in my place?"

"Did something happen?" asked Glushak eagerly.

Shchusev shrugged his shoulders, smiled. "Nothing special. Mikhail, having as you know, a heart of gold, decided to help Durov's latest victim."

Shchusev explained in a carefree tone. Gorin waved his hand impatiently, as though he wanted to stop him. He didn't like Shchusev's efforts to present the episode with the poor woman in such a bantering manner. But Glushak, who had already noticed Gorin's agitation, was consumed by curiosity. With Gorin, he awaited the answer.

"I'll tell you the truth," began Shchusev, "although I know that you will be displeased with my answer."

"Go ahead!" exclaimed Gorin.

"I would not have listened to that woman, and I would not have interfered with the NKVD in doing its work. Let them lead her away."

"Why?"

"I wouldn't like to say."

"Tell me. We are all our own people, we're old, there is no Judas among us. . . . Go ahead and talk!" Gorin insisted. He came close to Shchusev. The palm of his heavy hand fell onto the shoulder of the architect. He peered into his eyes.

Shchusev held his glance, answered quietly: "I'm not afraid of a Judas. . . . My words are not important. The chief judges me by what I build for him, not by my words. Several times I've said things straight to his face for which others would have lost their heads long ago. But for me, everything is forgiven."

"All right then, speak."

163

"But I don't want to speak, because it will certainly annoy you. Besides, today is a great day for me—the building was successfully opened, I'm in a good mood. Why spoil it?"

"Viktor, you must answer. I insist."

Shchusev shrugged his shoulders. "All right. . . . Mikhail, do you remember in 1902 the Academy of Sciences elected you an honorary member, but Tsar Nikolai—he didn't like you—deprived you of the honorary title . . ."

"Well?"

"And immediately, Anton Chekhov resigned from the Academy as a gesture of protest, and following him a dozen writers and scientists swarmed out? How the whole country flared up, how many noble, passionate and angry words were spoken and poured out on the pages of the papers."

"I remember; I remember. But what do you mean by that?"

Shchusev was silent. His wry face, illuminated by the light from the window, was diabolically wise.

"Mikhail," he said at last, "tell me, will there be even one word printed in the paper tomorrow about today's happening? Will anybody dare to describe your noble gesture?"

"You mean that there is no public opinion."

"Exactly."

"I don't believe that. . . . There is a public opinion. Only now it is not a confused chorus of papers who express it, but the Party and the Government. And if they consider that the attention of the people should be turned to more significant matters than the noble gestures of the writer Gorin, so it should be. . . . It is important to understand the spirit of the people. The Party has understood that spirit."

Shchusev snorted. "Why deceive yourself? When you have no pants and you can't cover your front, why cry out that you don't need pants, that spiritual clothing serves you better than solid cloth? . . . That's all right to dish out to foreigners, to lie to them, so as not to be shamed in front of them. To say black is white, and white black. Many of them ask for it themselves. Tell them the truth, and they'll be disappointed. But here, among ourselves, why confuse things? What isn't there . . . just isn't."

Gorin was silent. He filled the three glasses with wine, gestured his guests to drink.

"So, according to you, I made a fool of myself today," he said at last and sighed. "It is hard to admit this. Indeed, I hate to see that idiot

164

Durov getting away with his dirty work and nobody daring to say a word to him."

"If there is no way to help the thousands, is it worth while helping one man?" Shchusev asked. "Stop Durov from crippling the son of that woman today, and he will cripple a dozen others tomorrow. . . . And anyway, the trouble is not in Durov. It's much better, Mikhail, not to think, not to torture yourself. Take an example from me—when I'm designing a building, I don't think about the ugly fact that prisoners will build it. I think about its proportions. If you like, I think about socialist realism."

"But that is heartlessness!" Glushak exclaimed, and for some reason blushed.

Shchusev's sharp glance with its hidden mockery slid over the confused face of the Academician. "You mean to say that you think about much more exalted things than saving your skin?" he asked the scientist bitingly.

Glushak sank into the armchair. "What a coarse fellow," he thought. "How rude!" He waited for the next jab of the architect, but the latter said, smiling: "I hear that you are going to deliver a report this evening. Please, have pity on us, make it as short as possible."

". . . And without surprises, please," interjected Gorin. "What Veria handed us this morning was enough."

CHAPTER 5

THE CONVERSATION was interrupted. A servant, with frightened eyes, opened the door, approached Gorin on tiptoe and whispered something to him. The face of the writer became tense.

"All right, let him come in."

The servant departed. In a minute a stocky, military man in NKVD uniform entered. He cast a quick glance over the company, brought it to a halt on Gorin.

"Comrade Gorin, a personal letter from Comrade Veria." He clicked his heels, handed the letter to the writer: "Comrade Veria asked that you give your reply through me."

"All right. . . . Sit down, please."

Gorin opened the letter, ran his eyes over it.

"Dear Mikhail Alexeyevich," Veria wrote. "I am sorry that today's

165

incident caused you worry. Please don't fret about anything. I have personally taken all the necessary steps: the son of Citizen Demin has already been freed and sent to the best hospital in Rostov. I was successful in speaking by telephone with Professor Filatov—he is leaving Odessa today for the operation. We hope that the eye will be saved. (Incidentally, the professor asked me to give you his best wishes.)

"Those who are guilty of the unlawful arrest of the student will be punished. As it has now been found out, young Demin, after an ordinary student fight over a girl, was arrested on the instructions of the Director of the University. Apparently even men of learning can sometimes commit unpardonable foolishness.

"I have also ordered Comrade Durov to investigate the details of the arrest of the student's father and to report to me. I hope that all these measures will be satisfactory to you. We are all looking forward to seeing you at tonight's banquet.

"I have the following news. The French writer, Romain Rouen, will arrive tomorrow evening. He has already left Moscow. I heard that you intended to have him stay at your house. But as Academician Shchusev is already visiting you, would it not be better to accommodate the foreigner in one of the government summer houses? This, of course, is at your discretion. I merely ask you to give your decision on this point to the officer I have sent, in order that we may have time to make the necessary preparations.—Sincerely yours, L. VERIA."

"Excellent!" Gorin exclaimed, overjoyed. "Viktor, read this! This is a good answer to your words!"

Shchusev took the letter, quickly read it through and returned it to Gorin with a smile. "I congratulate you on your success, Mikhail. I'm very glad."

"My God! How naïve people are at times!" he thought to himself, looking at the suddenly transformed, happy face of Gorin. "How easily they fall for cheap sops, for affected sincerity, played by such archknaves as Veria! But he seems to fall much too easily. Probably Gorin understands the farce no less than I, but it's much easier for him to play the role of the conqueror . . . even in a farce. Well, so much the better for him."

"Excellent!" exclaimed Gorin again. "And in addition to everything else, Romain Rouen arrives tomorrow! There's plenty of room in the house. Let him stay with me. Tell Veria so!"

"Exactly, Comrade Gorin! May I leave?" Veria's messenger asked in military style.

"Yes, of course. . . . But wait a minute," said Gorin. "Stay to din-

166

ner with us. Now that there's no need for Veria to make any preparations to accommodate the Frenchman, you have plenty of time. Right, that's what we'll do!" and before the officer could answer, Gorin shouted: "Cheprok! Call everybody down—it's dinner time. Where's Luba? Nina?—Tell them to come to us."

Shortly afterwards, Gorin's wife, Luba, came in, and behind her Nina, very pale, with shadows under her eyes and swollen lips.

Noticing his daughter's paleness, Gorin frowned and looked questioningly at his wife. His momentary glance seemed to say: "I don't know anything about what has happened but I hope that everything has turned out all right." His wife likewise, with a look and by some unexplainable means which develops as a matter of course between husband and wife, replied: "All is well. I'll tell you afterwards."

Gorin calmed down, became cheerful again. He drew Nina to him with his arm. Kindly wrinkles appeared around his laughing eyes. Nina embraced him, bringing her cheek to his.

"My daughter, my daughter! Just look how she has grown up!" Gorin looked her over. "It seems not long ago that Cheprok used to carry her in his arms, bathed her in the salt water of Capri. She screamed like a piglet. And now—I'm afraid it's time for her to get married!"

"Has she a sweetheart?" asked Shchusev.

Gorin waved his arm. "You'd better ask her yourself. I haven't seen one yet."

"No, and there won't be!" Nina stubbornly bit her lower lip.

"Nonsense!" exclaimed Shchusev. "Such beauty and no sweetheart —that's a crime! If I were about thirty years younger, I wouldn't miss such a chance."

"Now you're talking!" remarked Gorin. "First-class goods and not without reason: I made it myself." He turned Nina around and patted her on the backside. "My masterpiece."

She flushed to her ears, broke away from him, sat down beside Glushak—as if she were looking to the staid scientist for protection.

She was no longer wearing the Cossack uniform. A silk dress to her knees made her more grown up, more womanly.

"Uncle Pyotr, who is the military man?" she asked Glushak in a whisper.

"Veria's messenger. Mikhail invited him to dinner." And Glushak shrugged his shoulders, as much as to say, "Isn't your father a queer fellow?"

Mikhail Gorin, noticing the questioning glances of his wife and

167

daughter, hurried to introduce the newcomer. The NKVD man drew himself up, clicked his heels, and announced proudly: "Major of the State Security, Second Rank, Semyonov." The new police titles had just been introduced by the Government. To avoid any misunderstanding, he added: "The title of major is the equivalent of a commander of an army brigade."

"Oh! That means that you are a general!" exclaimed Gorin. "Well, now, we'll call you General Semyonov—it's shorter and richer."

Everybody laughed; the major blushed.

"Tell me, Comrade Semyonov," asked Shchusev. "If it isn't a secret, what are they going to do now with the Director of Rostov University? You are, no doubt, in the know." Shchusev's question was asked in a tone of simple curiosity, but Gorin felt that the architect put this question for his benefit.

"At the very least he will be removed from his position," the major answered with assurance.

"You see, Mikhail, what you have done? Now the Director will suffer. And he is one of us, a scientist," Shchusev remarked half jokingly.

"Maybe he deserves it," mumbled Gorin.

"Absolutely right, Comrade Gorin," the major supported the writer. "This Director fully deserves punishment. He is not popular among the students. We've been thinking for a long time . . ." Here Semyonov stuttered a little. "I mean, the Department of Higher Education and the Party Committee have thought about his transfer to some other work for a long time."

Nina followed the confident major with attention, noticed his use of the word "we," thought, "Here are the rulers of this country. 'We thought,' 'We decided' . . . My God! with whom is my father mixed up!"

"Besides, the present Director isn't firm enough," continued the major. "And not sufficiently flexible. Handling five thousand students is no joking matter. Finally, and probably worse, he is old fashioned. Times change; new, fresh executives are needed!"

"Is there a candidate already for the duties of Director?" asked Glushak interestedly.

"Yes, there is. Two. One—a certain Livenko. The Moscow Department of Higher Education is proposing him. The other one—our Rostovian, Professor Feodor Novikov."

"Novikov!" shouted Glushak in spite of himself, and reddened suddenly.

168

"Yes, Novikov," repeated the major, not noticing the Academician's agitation. He added significantly: "Comrade Veria is backing him. My opinion is that more than likely Novikov will be the Director. No doubt you know him."

"Yes, I am acquainted with him—slightly, however . . ." Glushak replied.

"What do you think of him?" Gorin asked the Academician. "It seems to me he wrote a historical book on the Slavs."

"A very clever fellow . . . a resolute young man . . ." Glushak wrung the praise out of himself reluctantly. Oh, how he wanted to say now: "Novikov—an upstart, a shady character, a snake, a small-time crook, not worthy of attention." But just try to say these words when the two glassy eyes of the major are looking at you.

"You speak as if he was very young," remarked Gorin.

"He is very young," Glushak said eagerly. "Just imagine, he's not more than thirty."

"There you are! Look how quickly the new cadres grow." Gorin turned to Shchusev: "Now, you can see yourself, even here the affair has turned out for the best. Instead of that fool of a Director, there will be this clever fellow. That he is young is no misfortune, as long as there's a clear head on his shoulders."

"You have a light hand, Mikhail," commented the architect. "You're lucky."

Gorin turned to Glushak. "Pyotr, when there's a chance, don't forget to make me acquainted with Novikov."

What was there left for Glushak to do? He said: "As far as I know, Professor Novikov will be at the banquet this evening."

"That's fine! I will certainly have a talk with him."

Gorin's words were like a blow in Glushak's heart. "Well, it's begun . . ." he thought.

CHAPTER 6

THE ATTENTIVE glance of Luba Gorin did not miss Glushak's strange behavior. He seemed to be terribly excited, nervous and distracted. He replied to her words at random. She noticed how, from time to time, he cast an unhappy, almost a warning glance at Gorin, how he fidgeted in his armchair at every word of her husband. Clearly something was bothering him. But what?—Luba couldn't understand.

169

"When we sit down to the table I'll place him next to me," she thought. After deciding this, she began anxiously to wait for the servant to call them to dinner.

An unexpected event spoiled her plan. Behind the door a noise was suddenly heard; something fell with a crash; Cheprok's high-pitched voice bellowed: "I won't let you in! You can kill me, but I won't let you in!"

"Oh, no? You will!" howled someone. "Get to hell out of there, you old bastard!"

And at that very moment both halves of the door opened and into the room flew Cheprok, sprawled out full length on the floor. A tall man appeared in the doorway. His appearance was frightful; he breathed heavily, his face, swollen from drink, twitched; the glazed eyes looked dully at the stretched-out Cheprok.

"Pavel!" shouted Gorin. "What are you doing here! Didn't the doctor order you to stay in bed!" He rose.

That Pavel, Gorin's son by his first wife, was a drunkard was known to everyone present. They all pitied Pavel as they would pity a sick person and sympathized with the writer. Now, when he appeared before them in the flesh in all his ugliness, they shuddered involuntarily. Still young, but already with a bald spot in his thin hair, with bags under his red eyes and a pale, swollen face, he aroused only disgust. He was swaying. In his thin hand a sheet of paper shook.

"Father," he asked hoarsely, "do you want to hear my poem?" He noticed the military man. "Who is that? A new bodyguard? What do you want them for? What does he understand about poetry? . . . Where was I? Oh, yes . . . here is the poem." He stopped as if to collect his thoughts.

"I must first explain what it is about. Otherwise you won't understand. The affair takes place in Greece—two thousand years ago . . . or no—wait; yesterday. . . . But it doesn't matter——"

"Pavel, go and lie down. You must rest. After a good sleep you can read me your poem." Gorin put an arm about his son's shoulder, looked at the paper—the page was empty. "Well, there you see, you haven't written anything yet."

Pavel jerked his head, twisted his face into a drunken smile: "Father, I don't recognize you . . . I wrote . . . I didn't write . . . my poem is written in my heart . . . yes."

Pavel broke away from his father. Swaying, he approached the group. "The affair takes place in Greece. A leader of science, a certain Svintus, occupied the country . . . To glorify his victories he en-

170

gaged a court poet, a certain Poeticus. One of the daily duties of this poet was to lick the dirty backside of the leader. And so, my poem begins like this . . ."

Gorin's face darkened; a new, unpleasant expression appeared on it. He approached his son, grabbed him roughly, swung him around, and suddenly hit him on the cheek with the flat of his hand.

"Shut up!" he growled. "Don't dare to talk like that!"

"Father! What are you doing!" screamed Nina. She was going to get up but Glushak held her back: "Don't, Nina."

A red blotch grew on Pavel's cheek. He looked at his father with a long, heavy look and said, surprised: "Father, you hit me . . . What for? Surely you're not afraid of my words? And they call you the conscience of the people! It turns out that I am your conscience . . ." Suddenly he began to cry. The bags under his eyes shook; tears rolled down his cheeks.

Major Semyonov came up to Pavel and put his arm around his waist: "Come along, dear, come to bed. Come to bye-bye."

Something unexplainable happened to Nina. The blow struck by her father did not react on her heart like the simple touching of Pavel by the NKVD man. It was as if something had been torn loose inside her and had dropped, as happens only in an evil foreboding. She jumped up from her chair, approached her brother, and pushed Semyonov aside quite roughly. "I'd better help him."

Pavel smiled at her, a pitiful smile: "Ah, it's you, little sister . . . you're my best friend. Just say the word—I'll do anything for you."

"Come along then; let's go, Pavel."

Pavel obediently followed her.

Upstairs in his room Nina put Pavel to bed, wiped his cheek with a napkin. With an uncertain movement Pavel caught her hand, kissed it. Still sobbing, he repeated: "Nina, . . . there have been worse times, but never more odious," and sticking out his lip fiercely, he added: "No one dares touch me . . . yes." Then, breathing heavily, he fell asleep.

CHAPTER 7

AS NINA went downstairs the telephone rang. The excited, and it seemed to her exultant, voice of Lida Sidorov said: "Nina, I don't want to say much, but tell your father he's a wonderful man. I was mistaken about him before."

"That's excellent news, little idiot. But why, all of a sudden, such an admission?"

"Later—later I'll tell you. . . . I had a great sorrow, but it's better now. Only be sure and tell him what I said."

"All right, I'll tell him. . . . Will you be at the banquet tonight?"

"No. I don't think so . . . Well, good-bye! I'm in a hurry."

Nina shrugged her shoulders, replaced the receiver. She went into the library. "Father, you have a new admirer," she was going to say, but stopped. She felt that her words would be out of place.

"Major Semyonov," Gorin was saying, "I have changed my mind. Tell Veria that it will be better to accommodate the writer Romain Rouen in a Government summer house."

The major nodded his head understandingly. "All right, Comrade Gorin. In that case, I'd better go as quickly as possible. Excuse me, but I won't be able to stay for dinner."

Academician Glushak left with the major. The latter offered to drive him into town. In the car they were silent all the way, thinking their own thoughts.

Glushak's heart was heavy within him. He had gone to Gorin's with the firm resolve to warn him somehow about Novikov. But everything had happened contrariwise. Besides, Pavel had to stumble in, just when the NKVD man was there. And now a report must be written about the incident. An unpleasant, dirty business. Glushak sighed, sorry for himself: "Yes, like a loathsome reptile a traitor was put inside me . . . I hate to betray and betray."

CHAPTER 8

THERE WAS a knock at the door. Lida Sidorov tensed, but did not get up, just looked at the door, wrung her hands.

The knocking became louder. She rose from the sofa, murmured: "Now, keep a grip on yourself, Lida." Approaching the door, she asked with a quiver: "Who's there?"

"May I come in? I'm a student from the University."

Lida opened the door. In front of her stood a stocky young man with a smile on his broad face. "I'm Nikolai Novikov," he introduced himself. "Are you Lida Sidorov?"

"Yes."

172

Nikolai measured her from head to foot with an unceremonious look. His face showed obvious disappointment. "My God, what taste Feodor has!" he thought. "She's just a child. Almost no breasts. And legs . . ."

Lida waited. But Nikolai was in no hurry. Finishing with her, he leisurely looked over the hall: "You have expensive furniture."

"Why have you come? Speak up!"

"The point is, little sister," Nikolai suddenly changed to a whisper, "a certain person, well known to you, is waiting outside." Nikolai winked.

"I don't understand. Who is this person?"

"You'll see later. Come quickly."

"Why are you whispering?" Lida asked loudly.

Nikolai, his eyes popping in fear, suddenly covered her mouth with his hand. "Hush! The roomers will hear. This is a secret."

Pulling his hand away roughly, Lida cried: "There are no roomers here. Besides, I am alone now. What's the matter with you anyway?" By this time Lida was furious.

"You're alone? Why didn't you say so in the first place?" Nikolai suddenly became bold. Pushing Lida aside rudely, he went into the sitting room: "My! My! What a place! A sofa, armchairs, carved table, and expensive carpet! . . . I'm beginning to understand Feodor. No doubt your father is a commissar. Right?"

"Listen! If you don't tell me at once what is the matter, I'll call the militia."

Nikolai stood in front of her, raised her stubborn chin with two fingers and, looking into her angry face attentively, shook his head: "No, I don't understand a thing. Why has Feodor got mixed up with you? However, that's not my business. Listen: this is what we'll do. Why should you go out? Let him come in. It's very comfortable here." Without waiting for Lida's consent Nikolai went out onto the porch and shouted: "Feodor, come here! She's alone!"

Feodor emerged from behind a tree, came onto the porch with quick steps. "Professor Novikov!" exclaimed Lida in amazement, and laughed involuntarily. "What were you doing in the bushes?"

"Excuse the mystery," replied Novikov, "but I wanted to be sure that I would be able to talk with you alone."

Lida led them into the living room, with a gesture invited them to sit down. Nikolai was first to seat himself in an armchair, extended his legs. Looking around slyly and smiling, as though to encourage them, he was about to smoke.

"Ah-ah, Nikolai!" Feodor shook his head. "I said 'alone.' You'd better go out. See that nobody disturbs us."

As soon as they were alone Feodor took out a small sheet of paper, handed it to Lida. "Comrade Sidorov, do you recognize this pass?" he asked the girl point blank.

Lida got up, drew herself taut and said in a breaking voice: "Professor Novikov, I understand: you have come to arrest me. All right —I'm ready!" In her eyes, full of desperate resolution and pity for herself, tears appeared.

Feodor couldn't help laughing. "What nonsense! On the contrary, I want to warn you."

"Don't torture me! Tell me what has happened!" she demanded.

"Happened?" repeated Novikov. "Do you know that the woman to whom you gave this pass was nearly killed?"

Lida turned pale, sank into an armchair.

"But I wanted to help her," she said softly.

Feodor began to pity her. "Don't upset yourself, please. The woman spoke with Gorin. . . . Is that what you wanted?"

Lida became more cheerful. The broad, strong, face of the Professor inspired trust. "Yes, of course," she replied. "And Gorin? Tell me, did he do what she asked?"

"He promised. . . . But that isn't the point. You ran a great risk. Tell me, this Andrei Demin—is he your friend?" At Novikov's words it was as if a shadow spread over the room. Lida covered her eyes with her hands. "All right, I see he is a friend. But such a friend that you should risk your safety and your family's on his account?"

Lida was silent. Her heart sank. Each word hurt her.

"Who is your father, Lida? You live in a separate house—he must be a very important person."

"My father is the director of Plant Number Seven."

"That explains it," thought Novikov. "The director of one of the largest war plants in Russia." Officially it was called an agricultural implement plant. But in Rostov everyone knew that tanks were produced there.

"There, you see. Your father works hard, has attained a high position, and you with your thoughtlessness . . ."

"Surely it isn't thoughtlessness to help a friend in trouble?" Lida interrupted hotly.

Feodor shrugged his shoulders. "You are very young, Lida, and you don't know life. In life there is no objective understanding of honor and dignity: there are only different points of view. What at times ap-

174

pears to the individual as honorable the State may consider not merely thoughtlessness but crime. It is impossible to reconcile such contradictions—they can only be subordinated, one to the other. . . . And as a rule the State, the authority, wins. But let's leave that. If it isn't a secret, why did you select Gorin? Why did you send Demin's mother to him?"

Lida answered, but not at once. "It isn't a secret, of course. I'll tell you, because I trust you. But there's one thing that worries me: will anything good come of Gorin's promise? As you see, Professor," she added with a weak smile, "I am still holding to my personal point of view."

"Well, for Andrei—probably yes. At least temporarily."

"That's all I want to know." Lida rose. "Excuse me, Professor, I want to say a few words on the telephone to a friend." Lida went into the hall. She returned after a few minutes looking happy, excited. She sat down on the sofa beside Novikov, trustingly placed her hand on his sleeve. "I don't know why, but you seem to me a wonderful person, Professor Novikov. You are quite unlike the other professors. Who else would have come to me, warned me? They are all such cowards . . . without soul . . . while I, of course, am foolish and might have done a lot of harm."

Lida looked into his eyes and suddenly kissed his cheek. Feodor had not expected this. Now she appeared more childish than ever.

"Thank you for your faith, Lida," said he, blushing slightly. "You are, however, a very passionate girl, full of impulses."

There was a noise behind the window. Feodor got up, approached it, but Nikolai was already gone.

"Don't play the fool, Nikolai," shouted Feodor. "I know that you were peeping." Feodor shut the window.

"That's better. . . . Now Lida, if you trust me, tell me everything." He looked at her seriously, with the indulgent smile of a grown-up. Lida noticed for the first time that his eyes were light gray, with a dry luster.

"I didn't sleep all night; I was tired—forgive me if I don't speak connectedly," she replied, "but after what happened yesterday, after the brutality of Oleg Durov, how could anyone sleep? Why don't they arrest him? Why did they arrest Andrei instead? Mikhail Gorin—he has written so much about the just law of the country, that an honest man would never suffer, never perish in our country . . . I read and did not believe Gorin. I knew him too well to believe in his sincerity, but I could be mistaken. And so, this morning, I decided to help Andrei and at the same time test Gorin. 'The son is not responsible for the father.' This phrase of his is on everybody's lips. Let him show his sincerity in practice. Yes, let him!

"I never thought of the danger of my scheme. I only wanted to ease Andrei's sufferings. . . . I didn't go to the meeting. My father was furious. He is very scrupulous in such things as attending meetings or demonstrations. He threw my pass on the table: 'Maybe you'll change your mind and come along.' I took the pass, but instead of going to the meeting, I went to Andrei's mother. How poorly they live! In a damp basement in an old half-ruined monastery! It's a communal house now. When I arrived, his mother was half dead with grief. I explained my idea to her, gave her the pass. She agreed to do everything I instructed her to. Full of despair, she was ready to catch at the slightest hope. . . . When we parted she kissed me. 'Andrei has often spoken about you,' she said, and I saw that Andrei was everything to her, her very life. I wished her luck, returned home to wait for the storm. But instead of the storm—you came, and as a good friend . . ." Holding back her tears and unable to say more, Lida bent towards Feodor's hand and pressed her face to it. Then she cried like a little girl, her shoulders shaking.

"Still a child," thought Feodor, awkwardly comforting her: "Lida, Lida, everything will be all right."

Without noticing, he raised his arm and put it around her—she was so frail, so unhappy . . .

CHAPTER 9

IT WAS FOUR O'CLOCK when Sidorov and his wife returned from the meeting. The plant director was out of sorts. Veria's speech had upset his nerves, like those of many others.

Their car, an old Benz, was roaring monstrously, bumping from one side to the other—the road wasn't worth a damn, and like the car, unpleasant thoughts were jumping in Sidorov's head: "Here we are—start all over again. Barely recovered from last year's purge, and now there's a new one on the horizon. Do they never get fed up? When will we ever live quietly? You can scrape through one purge—well, at the outside, two—but when the devil brings them every year . . . and each worse than the last . . . one would need to be the devil himself to remain alive."

They were nearing their house. The birch grove parted, showing the

176

small blue balconies, the blue window frames, the blue roof . . . The sentimental color was not a favorite of the serious-minded Sidorov. He had inherited it from prerevolutionary days. A certain Ribin, a rich merchant, built his mistress a summer house in the grove—as far away as possible from his wife's eyes. He stuck on little balconies, porches, little pot-bellied columns, and to match the color of the lovely eyes of his heart's desire, he slapped on, wherever he could, the heavenly blue. Looking over the familiar features of the Ribin temple of love, Sidorov suddenly noticed a figure drawn up at a window of the house. There was no doubt: someone was peeping in.

"Stop, Ivan!" he commanded the chauffeur. "Stop, you devil!" The car came to a halt a little distance from the house.

"So, it's begun," thought Sidorov. "It's begun . . . I see Durov has already sent his spies. But why, damn him, does he want to watch me?"

Sidorov told his wife to sit still, to wait in the car; he got out, signed to the chauffeur to follow him. Quietly they crept up to the house, hid behind some bushes.

Nikolai, completely absorbed in his occupation—as ancient as life itself—did not notice them. When Lida kissed Feodor, he clicked his tongue approvingly. "Not bad! . . . Not bad at all, for a beginner!"

He had craned his neck to watch the couple better, when someone's strong hands covered his mouth and yanked him behind the bushes. "Lug him to the garage," whispered Sidorov, his face twitching in anger. "And be quiet about it—there may be someone else inside. Don't frighten them."

They brought the desperately kicking Nikolai to the frame garage. The chauffeur, Ivan, a tremendous fellow with a paw like a bear's and the kind-hearted face of a small child, pressed Nikolai politely against the wall. The latter's ribs cracked. Sidorov closed the door; it became dark in the garage. Nikolai's hair began to stir, his heart thumped like a mouse in a trap.

"All right, let him go," said Sidorov.

Ivan, smiling, released Nikolai's mouth. The latter began to gulp air fast.

"Well, chum, speak up. Why were you climbing in the window?" the plant director asked sweetly. He was a past master, knew how to interrogate.

Nikolai wanted to answer, but couldn't. His lips moved, but for some reason no sound came. "I'm done for," he thought. "They'll nail me——"

"Let your pants down!" suddenly ordered the director.

177

"Why—wh—why?" whispered Nikolai, breaking out in a cold sweat.

"Let 'em down, I tell you!" roared Sidorov. "Ivan, help him!"

Ivan helped. Of Nikolai's pants there remained only two torn rags. His bare knees rattled together.

"Bend him over!"

Ivan bent Nikolai's head over, squeezed it between his legs. The backside of the prisoner quivered nervously like a dog's.

"Not that end." Sidorov was angry. "Turn his head toward me. So— that's better. You, Ivan, take the hind end; I'll take the front. Now, who sent you here? Why were you spying?" asked the director, bending towards Nikolai's face.

"I wasn't spying."

"Ivan, smack him—hard."

The chauffeur let go with his belt on Nikolai's backside.

"Ivan, don't!" screamed Nikolai. "I'll tell everything. . . . My brother's there—Feodor. Professor Feodor Novikov." Nikolai pronounced the word "Professor" with as much dignity as a grown man without pants, squeezed between someone's knees, can display.

"What are you blabbering? Ivan, go ahead."

"No, it's the truth. They're kissing in there . . ."

"Kissing! Who's kissing?" shouted the director. "Speak plainer, stupid. Or I'll skin you!"

"Sidorov's daughter and Professor— Let me go, for God's sake," begged Nikolai. "What have I got to do with it? My brother's pawing the girl. Why skin me? Beat up my brother, if you want to!"

"We'll beat him up too," the plant director promised. "Wait, Ivan —take him along with us." He turned to Nikolai. "Pick up your pants. We'll see . . ."

Ivan raised Nikolai, warned him gently: "Just try to run away. Just try to."

With threatening stride Sidorov entered the porch of the house, jerked the door open. Behind him minced his wife. She was tired of sitting in the car; curiosity consumed her. Lida was sitting beside Feodor. His arm was still around her shoulder.

"What's going on here?" shouted Sidorov with such force that both of them jumped. "Daughter! Lidka! So that's why you didn't go to the meeting. . . . Amusing yourself with kisses! Fine!" He turned to Feodor. "And who are you?"

"Professor Feodor Novikov. Are you Lida's father?"

"Professor?" angrily repeated the director, not answering his ques-

178

tion. "And this, I suppose, is your learned colleague?" With his hand he indicated Nikolai, hanging on to his pants.

"That's my brother," replied Feodor, and smiled in spite of himself. Nikolai looked less pitiful than silly.

"Good! At last, thank God, we have all become acquainted," Sidorov announced sarcastically. "Maybe you will tell me now, Professor, what you are doing in my house with my daughter?"

"I came to help your daughter to analyze a historical problem," replied Novikov, and felt that his answer sounded as foolish as the torn pants looked on the embarrassed Nikolai.

"Well, well! And do you explain history with your arms?"

"Papa, don't be vulgar!" pleaded Lida.

"Shut up! There'll be a separate talk with you . . ."

But here his wife intervened. "Really, Leonid, what are you flying into a temper for? The teacher came, not grudging his own time, to help our daughter, and then you fall on him like a dragon." She turned to Novikov with a smile. "Don't pay any attention to him. He's always in a bad mood before dinner. You see, he thought that you were thieves. You should have seen what a fright he was in!"

"Like hell he was in a fright!" thought Nikolai, still shivering as from a chill.

"You needn't be alarmed, young man," Natalia Sidorov encouraged Nikolai. "We'll give you something to put on. My husband's pants will fit you and you'll get back to the city. They'd arrest you in that outfit. Might think you were a fugitive convict."

She returned in a few minutes with a pair of her husband's wide pants. Nikolai changed behind the door and came out looking like a Turkish sultan. Making a hasty farewell, the brothers departed.

As soon as the door closed behind them, Lida—with the words, "How coarse you are, Papa!"—ran off to her bedroom to cry.

CHAPTER 10

THE DIRECTOR and his wife were left alone. They were silent.

"Leonid," said his wife at last. "That was probably her sweetheart . . . and not so bad at that."

"What will you say next!"

"Who else! Of course, her sweetheart."

"Ah! Somehow I don't believe him—what sort of a professor is he?"

179

her husband challenged. "Did you notice how he flashed his eyes over me? Like steel. We've seen that kind before! People like him were in charge of firing squads in the Civil War. And his brother doesn't look like a brother at all. Different type altogether."

"Of course, everything always looks queer to you. Somewhere I have heard that name—Professor Novikov. Just imagine! Our quiet, mild daughter, but how clever . . ."

"In what way is she clever?" Her husband showed interest.

"Others in her place would be fooling around with boys like herself, but our daughter has charmed the heart of a man with a position."

"So; you've already settled it. No: I don't believe that everything's as simple as that. Call Lidka!"

Lida entered, eyes lowered.

"Well, daughter, they've caught up with you," her father greeted her. "But don't lie now; tell us the whole truth. Otherwise, in spite of your years, I'll thrash the hide off you."

Lida groaned, fell to her knees, her head in her mother's lap, and half in tears told everything.

With every word Sidorov's eyes opened wider and wider. "Gorin . . . Durov . . . a secret about a pass . . ." resounded in his head. "No, this is some kind of a nightmare. Just where is this fool girl getting my name involved?" When Lida had finished, he said chokingly, still not believing his ears:

"Well, little daughter, you've started something. Do you want to drive your own father into the noose, into the firing squad?" Suddenly his eyes rolled back, his obese body stiffened, his hands gripped the arms of the chair so hard they became white.

"Leonid, what's wrong with you?" cried his wife. She ran to her husband and raised his head. "Lidka—water!"

They brought the water. Sidorov drank, looked around the room with wandering eyes, met the frightened gaze of his wife. Suddenly throwing the water from the glass into her face, he croaked through clenched teeth:

"So he was a sweetheart! You fool!"

CHAPTER 11

PEOPLE GO to banquets for different reasons: the Frenchman to shock people with the low neckline of his lovely wife, the American to tell his neighbor a couple of spicy jokes, the Russian to prove to his comrades that he is not yet liquidated. But nobody ever attends a banquet to hear speeches.

Yet a banquet without a speech is not a banquet; a speech is as indispensable as a cork in a wine bottle. But after opening the bottle, one can delight in the sunny flow of the intoxicating liquid. After listening to a speech, one can eat and drink with a clear conscience: the taxpayers' money has not been spent in vain.

When Academician Glushak finished his report, everybody sighed with relief, applauded out of courtesy, and immediately, forgetting the man of science, began to discharge the next and much more pleasant duty: drinking toasts.

After the first toast, proposed by Mirzoyan to the master of science, the genius of humanity, the teacher and leader, Veria jumped up. Novikov noticed that Veria acted as if Larin weren't there.

"Comrades!" squeaked Veria loudly, flashing his glasses. "To the stormy petrel of the revolution, the father of Soviet literature, the old friend of the great Stalin, to our Rostovian—Mikhail Alexeyevich Gorin!"

The hall replied with the merry clink of glasses.

In the gigantic hall of the new political Institute more than five hundred people of the aristocracy of Rostov Province, with their wives and grown-up sons and daughters, had gathered. The snow-white rows of tables, like the outspread wings of fabulous swans, bore unheard-of luxury, food and wine. The light blue velvet of the chairs, the red carpet runners on the polished floor, the noiseless waiters, the frightening presence of the great ones, blinded the eyes and the brain, turning the world into a mirage and nearby objects into the unattainable, like the incandescent crystals of the chandeliers, floating under the ceiling.

They drank one toast after another. Tongues were loosed; through the growing din of male voices was heard the unrestrained laughter of women—the banquet was really under way.

Then Mirzoyan, flushed with wine and excitement, signaled to the waiters to bring in the main course.

Four youths, dressed as for a comic opera in red silk shirts, triumphantly carried in two roast wild boars on a tremendous platter. To loud shouts of "Hurrah!" they placed the burden on the center table. Mirzoyan, his olive eyes popping, watched every movement. The lads bowed respectfully to the guests—and suddenly, in the momentarily silent hall, was heard the rending of wood—as if the table

181

had collapsed. The hall responded with a burst of laughter and a new "Hurrah!" Mirzoyan sighed, relieved. The whole scene, with the comic opera youths and the crashing of the table (symbol of plenty!), had been rehearsed several times before the banquet.

Mirzoyan had decided to prepare a celebration with a flourish, with dash! This was his holiday. In order not to be shamed before Moscow guests, the whole evening had been copied, to the smallest details, from Kremlin dinners—even to the waiters. A hundred or so NKVD men with close-shaven heads had been selected. They were ordered to wash with particular care and for three days before the banquet not to smoke makhorka, so they wouldn't smell. Mirzoyan personally instructed them how to serve the important guests.

"Remember!" he shouted, "you're not on a search party in the workers' barracks, but at a State banquet. Don't stick your ugly mugs out, don't talk loudly. More meekness in your faces and bodies . . ." and, picking up a tray, Mirzoyan put on a servile face and waltzed between the tables with his fat belly. The men merely blinked, watching the mincing agility of the chief.

In the preparation of the dinner itself the happy Armenian had been guided by the natural instincts of a glutton. Where his culinary knowledge was short, he made up in lavish quantity.

On the tables there was such a mass of different kinds of food that it would probably have been enough to feed the whole of starving Rostov. But to Mirzoyan it was still not enough. Every now and then he jumped up, ran into the kitchen, scolded, waved his arms, hurried the dozen or so chefs working like devils in Hades. Then he ran out again, wiping the sweat from his round head. Behind him followed a train of immense dishes: pasties as thick as a man's arm, with ten kinds of filling; cabbage, meat, apples, salmon; veal roasts of the most tender cuts; geese practically floating in gravy.

Mirzoyan jealously watched the guests making away with these riches. Over there the chief of the Gigantic State Seed Farm, a thin but surprisingly gluttonous person, ate hurriedly, hardly chewing the food, as if he had starved for a week; there the chief of the Rostov Coal Trust just drank vodka; and yonder the director of the Red Aksai Plant waved a greasy goose wing in front of his neighbor, the Secretary of the Taganrog City Committee, arguing about something.

But most of all Mirzoyan was pleased with Durov. Pushing aside the plates, forks, glasses, all sorts of trifles, with his elbows on the delicate tablecloth, Durov was squaring up to a huge dish of a whole suckling pig. He ate raptly, without interruption, moving his swarthy jaws like

182

grindstones, only rarely looking wolfishly from under his dark eyebrows.

"Doesn't he eat viciously!" admired Mirzoyan. "Like a dog with a bone. Try to take it away—he'd tear you to pieces."

At the other end of the table, opposite her father, sat Nina Gorin. Turning her pretty face to young Shcherbakov, who was sitting next to her, she was discussing something with him and only from time to time did she take a small portion on her fork.

Mirzoyan scowled disgustedly. "A completely spoiled brat," he thought. "That's western culture for you: Italy and so on. . . . She can't even eat properly."

Novikov sat beside Sidorov. The latter had arranged it on purpose. Just before dinner, as soon as he saw Novikov in the crowd, he called the bustling Mirzoyan aside, whispered to him: "Do me a favor, friend—place Professor Novikov beside me."

Mirzoyan winked at him: "And your daughter—beside him?"

"What has my daughter got to do with it?" The director became angry. "You place Novikov. I must have a talk with him. As to who will be with my daughter—I don't care a damn."

"Just as you like," laughed Mirzoyan. "A young fellow has already asked me to place him beside her."

"Who is that?"

"You'll see."

During the dinner Sidorov saw. Right across from him, beside Lida, sat lanky Oleg Durov. Popping insolent eyes, he greeted him gaily: "How do you do, Daddy! Didn't you expect me?"

Sidorov merely squirmed in his seat. Angrily he thought: "If I only had you alone somewhere, I'd daddy you."

Trying to ignore the Durov son and heir, Sidorov devoted himself entirely to Novikov. The important director fairly fawned on him. He poured him vodka, slapped him familiarly on the shoulder, looked into his eyes. In these eyes was a smile, full of loving kindness.

"Damn it," thought Sidorov, "he's a hard nut to crack! Who the hell is he—Durov's spy or Lida's sweetheart?" Leaning toward the professor, he whispered, intentionally exaggerating his tipsiness: "You must forgive me . . . I didn't mean it—that is, to beat up your brother and shout at you. I thought thieves were breaking in. . . . But, of course, you're not thieves!"

"Not thieves? Not thieves!"

"So you've forgiven me? No ill feelings, eh?"

183

"Of course not! What an idea!"

Sidorov was silent for a little, then whispered anew: "And Lidka . . . I keep my daughter on a tight rein. Look, she's sitting and squirming, as if on needles. And her eyes are lowered. . . . That's because her backside's burning. After you left I whaled her."

"Really?" Novikov was amazed. "What for?"

"She wouldn't come to the banquet. And so she won't commit any more foolishness, like the pass . . ."

"Ah—that's different! She deserved a good lesson."

"Of course she deserved it. But now she's been punished and all is forgiven. Isn't that so?" Sidorov peered searchingly at him.

"What's it to me?" Novikov was surprised. "I merely tried to warn her in a friendly way."

"So it was all your own idea?"

"Of course! How else?"

The director became cheerful, slapped the professor on the back: "Come to our summer house some day when you're free. I have a yacht . . . with a wine cellar and so on. I live well, you'll be glad. Eh?"

"I'll come; I will certainly come."

"And bring your brother along. I'll apologize to him personally."

"I'll bring my brother along too."

"You're a good sport, Professor."

"And you're a good fellow too, Comrade Sidorov."

"Let's drink!"

"Let's drink!"

They drank and ate a little.

Sidorov poured more vodka into Novikov's glass and, leaning over quite close to his ear, whispered hotly: "As far as Lidka's concerned —why, I don't object. If you like her, take her. That's youth. Only, look out—don't fool. I won't let anybody ruin my daughter." And sticking out his jaw fiercely, he added: "If it's marriage—then get married."

Novikov immediately sobered.

"What do you mean, Comrade Sidorov? Ruin? Marriage? Sweetheart? Where did you get all this? My interest in your daughter is purely scholastic." Novikov giggled nervously: "Why, if you're worried about ruin, just look across the table . . ."

The plant director, his drunken eyes wide, stared across at Oleg and Lida. Suddenly he thumped the table so hard with his fist that the dishes jumped.

184

"Oleg!" he roared. "Take your paws away from Lida's thighs at once!"

Taken by surprise, Oleg choked on his vodka and withdrew his left hand quickly from under the table.

"Have you gone crazy, Comrade Sidorov?" he said rudely. "Nobody's pawing your Lidka. Why, she has nothing to paw, anyway . . ."

The neighboring diners, hushed for a moment, laughed loudly, and then continued their conversations.

Lida, flushing crimson all over, was afraid to raise her eyes to Novikov. The latter, to divert the enraged Sidorov, began to tell him about some incidents in the Civil War. He lied to make it more interesting.

The dinner was coming to an end. A Cossack chorus on the terrace outside the window struck up a marching song, whistling and whooping. Many of the guests began to hum, to beat time with their feet. Gorin was the first to start singing. Leaning back, and resting both hands on the table, he sang loudly and cheerfully with real pleasure.

Veria, already noticeably drunk, suddenly jumped up from the table, and running to the glass doors leading onto the balcony, opened both halves with a jerk. Here, not on the platform but among his own people, he was informal to the point of vulgarity.

"Come on, lads! Let's get into the hall!" he shouted to the chorus. "It'll be more fun! Boys! What a life!" And he slapped his thighs.

The young Cossacks, dressed in fresh uniforms as for a parade, pushed in a close-packed crowd into the hall, stood shyly, three deep against the wall. Then, clearing their throats for the start, they again whooped up their song.

At the back of the chorus, on the right, stood the tall Rudoy. With the swollen wale on his face powdered, he ripped out the song in furious rage, straining the sinews of his neck into cords.

He had already noticed Nina amidst the unaccustomed brilliance and luxury. The latter, dainty in a dress of some airy material that Rudoy hadn't seen even in the movies, beautiful and unattainable, sat as among her equals with Larin, Veria. . . . Tell the boys that you kissed her today on the steppe—they'd laugh at you.

Rudoy still could not understand Nina's sudden rage, why she had whipped him there on the shore. "How did I annoy her?" he thought with anguish. "Maybe I didn't kiss her right? And now she sits like some queen talking to her neighbor. What about? Complaining about me?"

When they finished singing, Veria shouted:

"Give the Cossacks a tumbler of vodka each!" and himself was first to carry one to a curly-headed lad with an accordion: "Drink, Cossack! Today is a great day!"

Lida, glad of the opportunity to be rid of the clinging Oleg, poured some wine into a glass and, getting up from the table, approached Rudoy from the side. "Hello, Rudoy! Here, have a drink . . ."

"How do you do, Lida?" greeted the other. "H—m—. Tastes pretty good. But not strong. What is it, champagne or something?"

"No, champagne is light and fizzy—this is red and sour. Would you like me to bring you some vodka?"

"Fine! Bring me some. But wait—let's talk. . . . Why weren't you riding today?"

"I couldn't come. . . . Rudoy! Where on earth did you decorate your face?"

"Scratched myself against a bush."

"Tell me, why did they select your chorus for the banquet? You don't sing very harmoniously."

"Some fat Armenian chose us."

"Mirzoyan?"

"I suppose so, yes. He liked us better than the other choirs. 'We,' says he, 'have to keep up a style. The Moscow guests like the exotic. There must be war and terror in your faces; but how you're going to sing—that's not important: everybody will be drunk anyway, they won't know the difference."

Lida laughed.

"Indeed, you all look fierce, and you more than the rest. Have you seen Nina? She's here. . . . Do you want me to call her?"

"No, don't."

"Afraid to show your face, monster?" Lida made fun of him.

"Yes, maybe . . ."

Lida was silent.

"Why are you so sad today, Lida?" asked Rudoy.

"I had a great trouble, Rudoy."

"What kind of trouble? Can you tell me?"

"Not here. When you finish singing, stay on the terrace. I'll come to you. I think I should have a talk with you."

"No chance that way. They'll kick us out of here as soon as we finish singing."

"Not necessarily. Everybody's drunk—they won't think about you."

186

Oleg appeared. In his hand he had a tumbler of vodka, in his eyes an evil gaiety.

Lida had only time to say to Rudoy: "Don't forget. I'll see you after . . ."

"All right, I'll try," replied Rudoy.

Catching Lida around the waist with his left hand, Oleg shouted to the Cossacks: "Why aren't you singing, fools? Did we give you the vodka for nothing?" And he turned to the girl. "Come on, Lida, the dancing's begun." And pulling her along, "There's a pair showing off a new rumba—you'll die laughing. The body motion is . . . just like in bed!"

CHAPTER 12

MIKHAIL GORIN did not forget his intention to meet Professor Novikov. As soon as dinner was over he reminded Glushak of it.

"Bring him into the club room. It's too noisy here." Rising from the table, he turned to Shchusev: "Viktor, if you don't mind, let's go together. We'll see what the future University Director is like."

Glushak looked around in search of Novikov. The latter was still carrying on a drunken conversation at the table with Sidorov. Which of them was the more drunk was hard to tell from a distance. "Not bad, a pretty good Director," thought Glushak with malicious pleasure, and strutted gaily toward the pair. "My God, my God, everything may turn out not so badly after all . . ."

But as soon as Glushak gave Gorin's invitation, the drunken smile, the cheery good nature left the professor's face. It became hard and businesslike.

"All right, Comrade Glushak, lead me to him," he said curtly to the Academician and patted his sloping shoulders: "Why aren't you happy?"

Glushak hastened to smile. But the smile was pathetic.

Sidorov merely blinked on seeing such a sharp change in his new friend. But, as he was by now really drunk, he pulled a tearful face, wagged his head several times, and dropped it accurately onto a plateful of gravy. His wife was not beside him; she had gone to dance.

Glushak wanted to move the plant director's head to the tablecloth, but Novikov stopped him. Twisting his thin lips in contempt, he said, "Don't! The fool will sober up quicker that way."

187

Feodor Novikov walked along the corridor, listening inattentively to Glushak, trying not to look at his rumpled face and nervous, twitching lips. Like a mirror this face reflected his soul, tortured by fear.

"I would ask you, Comrade Novikov," Glushak hastily begged, "to remind Comrade Drozd—when the opportunity occurs—about my earnest endeavors to help you. For example, the first meeting with Gorin, to which you are going now, has been arranged to the smallest detail by me. Everything has been thought out so well, that no possible suspicion . . ."

Novikov suddenly halted. His eyes became cold and cruel.

"Comrade Glushak," he said, looking the timid figure of the Academician up and down, "your efforts will be appraised to the full. As far as Drozd is concerned, he is now in Moscow polishing up a large Order of Lenin for you. . . . Satisfied? Now, shut up and let's go!"

Glushak wrinkled his brow as if in pain and said nothing.

In the large club room, paneled in mahogany, only the table lamps were lit, creating a subdued light. On the mottled Persian carpet stood several small tables, surrounded by armchairs and sofas. On the windows and doors hung expensive drapes. The room was decorated, if not with taste, at least with luxury: for the future leaders of the Party money wasn't spared. Novikov noticed that on the wall, opposite a dozen portraits of sullen members of the Politburo, there hung a charcoal sketch of Mikhail Gorin. It was an almost standard fixture of every club room in Russia.

Gorin and Shchusev were sitting in a far corner at a table, playing chess. Glushak introduced Novikov to them.

"Sit down beside me," Gorin said, indicating an empty armchair. "I play chess badly, but Viktor seems to have decided to play at 'loser wins.' "

"Don't crow before your victory, Mikhail," the architect said, and moved his knight. "How do you like the field of battle now?"

Novikov played chess rather well—he had been keen on it during his student days. He saw at once the weakness of Shchusev's move. As he expected, in six moves Gorin had the architect in checkmate.

Satisfied, Gorin rubbed his hands. "Get out of the armchair! You're not worthy to occupy it," he said to Shchusev. "Comrade Novikov, sit down. You play, of course?"

"Yes, I used to play at Moscow University."

"Well, that's not so long ago. You're still young."

Novikov, setting up the pieces on the board, raised his eyes. For an instant their glances met. It happened so unexpectedly that Novikov started. He felt an involuntary sense of fear, as if Gorin had unceremoniously pried open the door of the darkest compartment of his soul. But his confusion lasted only for an instant. Novikov turned his eyes away, slammed that door shut.

Gorin lit his pipe, smiled. "Well, let's begin . . ."

Novikov noted that Gorin began with the Capablanca opening, tiresome and dull at the beginning, but designed by its naïveté and simplicity to lull the vigilance of the opponent, only to bring him to lightning defeat with a dozen surprise moves.

"He wants to finish me quickly," thought Novikov. "It won't work, Comrade Gorin. No one has got rid of me quickly yet." Suddenly he knew that he must win, at all costs. The simple game of chess with Gorin became a symbol. Novikov was playing a satanic game with fate itself, and his stake was life.

"I like to sit on the sidelines and watch others play chess, more than to play myself," said Gorin. "Chess seems to me more exciting than boxing, and probably more merciless. I had the rare opportunity of watching the present world champion, Botvinnik, at play. He's an amazing personality. He has great endurance and composure. Do you know, you remind me of him?"

"Why, of course—history and chess are very much alike," said Novikov with a smile.

Gorin looked at him attentively through a thin haze of smoke.

"I should be afraid to compare history with chess," he said after a pause. "In chess nothing is known, there is only the brain and the will of two people, and the dumb figures on the board ready to obey the least impulse of the two brains. But in history— . . . I mean, of course, past history. Present history, as such, doesn't exist. There is the future, there is illusion, to which each new day brings merciless blows . . . In past history all the moves have been made, all the checkmates have been called long ago. The enjoyment of chess lies in the creative work, in the knowledge that one can alter its course. The game of history, unfortunately, one can only contemplate."

"I don't agree with you, Comrade Gorin," said Novikov, without raising his eyes from the board. "History is a science. And as a science it is always moving forward, developing, and each day drawing nearer to its goal—the highest objectivity. In this science creative work is necessary, as in any other branch of knowledge. It calls for more than mere contemplation."

"What about historical facts?" exclaimed Gorin, holding a white castle in the air. "What more can you do than contemplate them? Only

189

in fantastic novels can scientists alter the past by means of monstrous speed and the fourth dimension. In life people have not yet learned to do this."

"I wouldn't say that," Shchusev interjected, laughing. "For instance, today: Veria, without any fourth dimension, changed history to such an extent that many people had stomach trouble."

Gorin brushed this aside: "The petty efforts of a careerist don't mean anything . . . Professor, your move."

The conversation lapsed for a while. Novikov moved. Gorin leaned over the board, and Novikov studied his features. He had that strange feeling one gets on first seeing, close up, a face that is very familiar from portraits. He suddenly noticed that most important peculiarity which not one artist had been able to capture: the living quality of the flesh which manifested almost imperceptibly the working of the mind.

"My goodness, you've set me a difficult problem," mumbled Gorin, biting his mustache.

"Aha! You're beginning to give up," Shchusev remarked triumphantly. "With youth you don't win an easy victory."

"You, Viktor, are the devil of defeat! A temporary setback doesn't mean anything." At last Gorin moved.

"Now you think, and I'll bother you with my talk," he joked. "So, what do you mean by the highest objectivity in history, and what are we to do with historical facts?"

"I am used to giving lectures to students. I feel silly talking to you in an instructional tone. Indeed, you know better than I both history and what is required of it."

"Mikhail wants to check up on you," Shchusev smiled. "He checks up on everybody."

"No, that's not so," Gorin protested hotly. "I am curious to know how far I have lagged behind youth, behind contemporary life. The fear of being backward is my greatest dread."

"You're not backward, Mikhail. You've nothing to be afraid of," said Glushak. During the whole conversation he had not yet said a word, only tensely and attentively watched the hated Novikov.

Gorin turned to him quickly. "We're old men, Pyotr. Only youth can tell us whether we have fallen behind or not."

"But youth often runs ahead, goes to extremes," replied Glushak gloomily.

"So what is the highest objectivity?" Gorin repeated the question to Novikov, not listening to the old Academician.

Novikov raised his head. His face was serious, open, with a large

190

forehead. "Marxism, the Party," he replied precisely. "Marxism demands Partyism from the historian, to understand it as the highest form of objectivity, to repudiate the acceptance of apparent facts."

"So . . . and with regard to these facts?"

"Historical facts—they are no more than stones and bricks: only a well-trained Marxist can create of this material a graceful edifice."

"Therefore, according to you, historical facts are like the pawns on the board: they can be combined and moved around without end."

"That's putting it too simply, but near the truth," replied Novikov.

"There you are!" suddenly shouted Gorin and thumped his hand on the table. The pieces on the board jumped. Glushak started. "There you have an object lesson, Viktor, Pyotr." He cast a triumphant glance at the Academicians. "You and I think, conjecture, cudgel our brains, while youth already has all the answers. Everything precisely and clearly, no doubts whatever."

Novikov was disconcerted. He was unable to tell whether Gorin was speaking seriously or making fun of him. "He's probably laughing," he thought, looking at the strangely excited face of the writer.

But Gorin's eyes were not laughing. They were directed searchingly at Novikov. "Well, all right . . . but we writers, artists, what should we do?" he asked Novikov heatedly, as if much depended for him on the reply. "You see, we're not scientists. We create graceful works of art, not by the application of the laws of science, but by intuition. How should we stand before the face of the highest objectivity?"

"The intuition of the artist is sometimes worth the logic of the man of science," replied Novikov.

Gorin was silent.

It seemed to Novikov that he had stopped on purpose, fearing to overstep some invisible line. The writer was listening to him, if not trustfully at least attentively, but as if he were forcing himself to a conviction of something that he did not believe, although he wanted to believe it. Novikov tried to explain this enigma to himself. "It looks as if Gorin needs a prop. His revolt is the revolt of a blind man, thrashing around in the dark. Give him your hand—and he will go along submissively like a lamb. But one must convince everybody, and above all him, that he is going of his own accord, without any outside help. Well, that won't be hard to do . . ."

THEY CONTINUED the game in silence. Novikov could not but notice the hands of the writer. They were in front of his eyes the whole time, clearly outlined against the design of the chess board. Their movements were light and measured. But more than anything the shape of the hands amazed Novikov: large, strong, not in the least ungainly, but on the contrary full of an artistic grace and expression—sensitive hands, such as only people with great creative talent have. "I would not be surprised if Edison or Tolstoy had hands like those," thought Novikov. "Everything is possible for such hands: to plow the earth and to write a brilliant work."

Shchusev was about to break the silence. He had been looking more attentively at the young professor. "This fellow has some object," he thought, examining Novikov's energetic, broad face, between half-lowered eyelids. "A man of the new times. A hundred per cent type of Soviet man. Just a careerist. There is a saying about such: the architect of his own fate. But this architect is shaping his fate, not with his hands, but with his teeth . . . A dangerous animal. As University Director he will be very good, perfectly suited to the times. He'll take the students in hand; they'll be like silk. No wonder Veria is supporting him."

"You just spoke about intuition and precise facts," Shchusev addressed Novikov. "But that kind of approach will lead to a distortion of the past. One can imagine what would happen if artists with their intuition began to meddle—it wouldn't be history, but porridge."

Novikov squinted at him. He was already a little afraid of Shchusev, with his clever and crafty face. The architect watched the progress of the conversation attentively, only rarely interjecting an ironic remark. It was precisely this irony of his that Novikov feared more than anything. However, he replied firmly. "Historical works, the drama for example, of necessity distort the past in order to satisfy contemporary problems and interests."

"Bah!" answered Shchusev with distaste. "That's not drama, but politics turned upside down into the past!"

Novikov shrugged his shoulders.

"Actually, what I'm saying is not new," he replied. "Even Dostoyevsky noticed this peculiarity of the historical drama. He wrote that in imagining the past, events present themselves inevitably in their final form, that is, with the addition of all subsequent development which has not yet occurred at the moment the artist is trying to re-create through the personalities and actions of his drama. Therefore, the essential nature of the historical event cannot be presented by the artist exactly as it took place in reality."

"Dostoyevsky said that?" asked Shchusev.

"Yes, he said that."

"But he could have been mistaken?"

"In the present case he was not mistaken. . . . That is an ingenious remark," interjected Gorin. "Mistakes are, of course, unavoidable. But in drama, as distinct from the precise historical textbooks, details are not as important as the spirit of the time. The better the spirit is grasped, the better the writer."

"Absolutely right," endorsed Novikov.

"You should yourself write a historical drama, Mikhail," said Glushak, simply for the sake of saying something. From long silence his lips had stuck together.

To his surprise, Novikov seized on his words eagerly.

"A very good idea, Academician Glushak," said he. "Comrade Gorin, why don't you write a historical novel? Show all the young writers how to solve difficult problems!"

Gorin shook his head. "I've really never written on historical themes —didn't like them. My element is real life—I write from nature. Besides, all the themes of the past are already exhausted."

"How can you say so!" exclaimed Novikov. "What about Peter the Great's time? What could be more timely?"

"Alexei Tolstoy is engaged with Peter. Why take away another writer's bread?"

"Well then, Ivan the Terrible? . . . There is a mighty theme! No one, as yet, has mastered it."

"Many have written on that theme also, plays as well as books."

"Yes, but how they wrote!" exclaimed Novikov hotly. "They whined, they shed false tears, but they did not write. They frightened the timid intellectuals with the man's brutality, drove their hearts into their boots. They described to the minutest detail the color of the blood on the snow, the human hair on the merciless axe of Ivan the Terrible. They wrote about everything, but overlooked the main thing. They overlooked the fact that this same monstrous Ivan made that on which we are standing today: Russia, our native land!"

Gorin looked at the professor in amazement. Novikov spoke heatedly—and apparently quite sincerely.

As if he were musing over something, Gorin reclined against the back of his chair. "Ye—es!" he drawled at last, with a deep sigh. "That is really a powerful theme. It has scope, expanse . . . exactly what I like." But suddenly he shook his head regretfully: "No, nothing will come of that. One would have to dig into archives. Not for me! I don't like digging into the rotten past."

"That's a secondary matter," Novikov hastened to remark. "If you like, I will gladly dig up the necessary material for you. I have a friend in Moscow; he works in the State Archives. He'll arrange everything."

Gorin sat silent, thinking.

"You've got me stirred up," he said quietly. "It looks as if the itch is beginning—to write something big, serious, such as I used to dream about in my youth." He lifted a castle, squeezed it in his heavy fist: "There, it's as if all drama—Ivan the Terrible along with his axe—are squeezed in my fist." Noticing that Novikov was going to say something, he forestalled him, flashing his aroused eyes: "All right, let it be for now. . . . Make your move, Director."

Novikov raised his brows in amazement, not taking in the last word of the writer. "What's the Director got to do with it?" he thought. But he didn't meditate long. He exulted. "By the devil!" he thought. "Everything has come out of its own accord, exactly as I hoped: like a bolt from the blue. That coward Glushak, although he didn't want to, has helped me to get the whole thing started. A historical novel! That's where I'll keep the pressure on. That's where my strength is. What do I know better than Russian history? Why didn't I see that before? . . . Gorin's interest has already been awakened. Now my biggest worry is not to let it wane. I'll have to steer this ox along the right road . . . and hustle him. When he gets moving, he'll roar himself! He'll break fences—look out! 'The Time of the Terrible!' What can be better? Let him with his mighty talent justify that crazy bloody sadist. Let him adorn the shoulders of this ancient megalomaniac and despot with the mantle of the patriot, and his face, distorted by frenzy, with the noble mask of the thinker. . . . Let him do it! Why, for that, Stalin will make me not only Director, but will shower me with such rewards—perhaps beyond my very dreams . . ."

Exciting thoughts raced through Novikov's head, outrunning each other. The squares on the chessboard merged into a mottled design.

"Easy, Feodor, easy," he calmed himself mentally. "Now everything depends on your endurance, your coolness. Better forget the conversation for the time being. Concentrate on the chess game."

On the board only five pieces remained.

"Look here, the knight—that's Gorin," Novikov said to himself, pressing his thin lips to hide a smile. "And this castle in my hand—that is I, Novikov, and that bishop is Drozd and his task. Well, what of it, I will do this . . ." Engrossed in his thoughts, Novikov didn't notice that Gorin's wife Luba had entered the room. He didn't hear her, stopping at the door, say in a frightened voice: "Mikhail! Viktor! . . . You sit here and don't know anything. An awful thing has happened: Larin has shot himself!"

"Comrade Gorin, checkmate!" said Novikov loudly, joyfully raising his eyes.

Nobody answered him.

CHAPTER 14

LARIN'S LARGE HEAD lay on the glass top of the desk. Under the glass, covering the whole table, was a map of the Northern Caucasus Province. A large, important province, the sovereign master of which had been Larin. A province larger than Germany, with a population greater than Sweden. Larin liked to remind his subordinates about these geographical details. Now, over this province spread a sluggish pool of dark blood.

The frightened "best people of Rostov" stood in a group at the door of Mirzoyan's new office, stared at the remains of Larin, whom they had feared, envied, and imitated—from his leonine bearing to his habit of shaving in his office. They looked and could not believe their eyes: Mirzoyan, with pale sunken face; Durov, with twitching mouth; Kashirin, petrified and quite unmartial. All crowded each other, afraid to approach the corpse.

"There's a paper under his hand," someone in the crowd remarked.

"Looks like a telegram . . ."

"Let's see it——"

"Leave it! Better wait for Veria . . ."

"Look at the telegram!" somebody's excited, almost hysterical voice shouted. "We must know why he shot himself!"

"Read it, Durov!" Mirzoyan whispered between pale lips.

Durov went to the desk, raised the heavy hand clutching the burnished revolver in a death grip, took the telegram. He read it slowly, nodded his head understandingly: "A call to Moscow . . ."

Everything became clear.

Veria entered. He looked at the corpse, read the fatal message stained with blood, spat violently on the parquet floor.

"Carrion!" he said, and cursed long and filthily. "What a hero! A Soviet man must sleep with his wife and die—not when he himself wants to, but when Moscow says to. Take him away!"

He squeezed through the crowd into the corridor. It was still more crowded there. Glancing in contempt over the hundreds of faces frozen into a horrified question, he shouted shrilly: "What are you crowding for? Nothing special has happened. Some fool has just put a bullet into his forehead. Why has the music stopped? Get back to the hall and go on with the dance!"

Soon the disorderly sound of a rumba was heard from the orchestra; the frightened musicians were mixing up the notes.

Larin's body was carried past the Second Secretary. He didn't even look at the corpse; brandishing his pince-nez, he gave a brief order: "Comrade Durov, remain with me," and went into the office, closing the door behind him.

The crowd slowly dispersed. Here and there odd phrases were heard: "I can't understand it. At dinner he looked so cheerful."

"And he ate so well. I was watching him on purpose . . ."

During the dinner Larin certainly hadn't looked like a person on the brink of death. He had joked, smiled, and apparently had not noticed Veria's insolent conduct at all. He had managed to calm down, recover himself, and even accomplish a few things.

The first few minutes after the meeting had been terrible. There was confusion, alarm. He had been afraid to face people, but felt that to go home just then, and isolate himself from events, would be suicide. So, immediately after the meeting he went to the headquarters of the Provincial Committee of the Party, a large building on Engels Street. There was authority, there were the nerves of the Province, there was his salvation.

Passing through the reception room into his office he told the adjutant on duty: "Send Comrade Lebedev to me."

Now, as never before, it was necessary to hold onto trusted people, and Larin had no more trusted friend than Lebedev. Apart from him and his nephew—the editor of the Provincial paper *Molot*—he trusted nobody. He knew most of them would desert if fortune turned its back on him.

It had taken Larin many years and a great deal of work to surround himself with loyal people who depended on him body and soul. Craftily he had woven the web around himself, but the busy bee Veria had flown into it, threatening to destroy all his cunning work and touching even him with his deadly sting.

Larin sat in his office, pressing his temples, listening. Everything was quiet. But he knew in his heart that thousands of brains were working feverishly, that the packed Provincial Committee building was boiling with secret excitement. They would be whispering among themselves, looking with evil distrust at one another, wondering who would win the trial by combat. The two camps, Larin's and Veria's, were preparing for the last encounter. Larin picked up the telephone.

"Connect me with the editor's office."

Silence, then after a minute the answer: "Comrade Larin, the editor is not here. Do you want to speak with his assistant?"

"No, it's not necessary." He lowered the receiver.

"Hell! Lebedev's taking a long time to come. He only needs three minutes to drop from the fourth to the third floor."

Somebody was knocking gently on the second door leading directly into the corridor. This was a solid door, covered on the inside with felt and leather, always locked. "Lebedev," thought Larin. "But why doesn't the damn fool go through the reception room?"

Larin went to the door, opened it slowly. A thick-set man, solid as flint, jumped quickly inside. His head was completely bald. His eyes were hidden behind sly wrinkles.

"No one noticed. The corridor is empty," he remarked softly, glancing quickly around Larin's office.

"You've come at the wrong time," the First Secretary said angrily. "I'm waiting for Lebedev."

"You're waiting in vain, Comrade Larin. It's precisely about him that I want to say a couple of words to you."

The thick-set fellow's name was Prokhor—the eyes and ears of Larin. Larin had many like him. But Prokhor was the most valuable: he worked in Veria's secretariat. Larin trusted him to the limit, and not without reason: he knew that Prokhor's soul had been sold to him long ago.

Previously Prokhor had worked in the editorial office. He was not a bad assistant, but he had one failing: he liked to drink. He had

197

looked after reading proofs in the editor's absence and okayed them for the press. But once a disaster happened. Prokhor had lapped up too much and slipped. Some fool of a typesetter left a letter out of a slogan on the front page, right beside Stalin's name. The result was an indecent word, and the slogan became a political heresy. And so *Molot* astounded its readers the next morning. Prokhor was led off to the firing squad, but Larin saved him. He twisted the affair cleverly: blamed everything on the editor. Prokhor was only too happy to give up his place in front of the wall to his chief. Larin put his nephew Olgin on the paper to replace the late unfortunate.

After this incident, Prokhor had sobered up. He took life more seriously, and remembered even in his sleep that save for Larin he would not be among the living. Larin found him new work, also with a purpose, in the office of the Second Secretary. When Veria came to Rostov, Prokhor was already there, waiting for his new chief. In this new position Prokhor's talents showed themselves to the best advantage. He played his part cleverly: outwardly a simpleton, joker, tippler, but inside, crafty, brave, and merciless as a wild beast. Prokhor knew how to gain Veria's confidence, although he hated the Georgian with his whole heart. Only Veria's thoughts he was unable to read, otherwise he knew everything. Now he stood there, fidgety, sharp, looking at Larin impatiently, wrinkling his narrow eyes. It was obvious that he brought him important news.

Larin locked the door to the reception room. He said curtly, "Speak!"

Prokhor looked around, stepped closer to Larin, and whispered softly in excitement: "Olgin and Lebedev have just been with Veria."

Larin opened his eyes wide—dull, fierce eyes.

"Olgin, my nephew?"

"Yes . . ."

"You lie! That's impossible. . . . Look out! You know what'll happen if you lie!"

"Have I ever told you a lie? Of course, it's obvious, they want to make a deal . . . to suck up. They were scared stiff. While they were waiting in the outer office they smoked about a dozen cigarettes."

"So . . . and what then?"

"Then they came out looking very satisfied. Apparently Veria pumped them full of ideas, pepped them up. And they had time to spread a little talk here and there: it's your finish, they say. Some are beginning to follow their example."

Larin went to the window, stared outside with an empty look.

"Olgin, Lebedev," he thought, "the most loyal dogs, are deserting, saving their own skins. And my nephew—he got his nerve back in a hurry! What is this anyway? Surely the end hasn't come?"

"Things are bad," he said aloud. "Dogs, bastards. . . . I didn't expect . . . Well, let them—nothing can be done. . . . Thank you, Prokhor, but don't come to me any more . . . Take no risks. If everything blows over, I'll not forget you." And suddenly pressing his hand to his heart, Larin went over to the desk chair, lowered himself heavily into it.

Not understanding yet what was happening, Prokhor leaped to Larin's side, helped him to sit down. Prokhor had never seen him so depressed, so outspoken. He looked at him in silence; then, suddenly shaking his fat shoulder, he shouted: "Comrade Larin! Comrade Larin!" Prokhor couldn't say anything else. His face was twisted with excitement. A cold sweat broke out on his white baldness.

Prokhor's wail, terrible, almost beastlike, restored Larin's confidence with unexpected force. Like the steppe wind, courage raced into his soul. The gamble of life and death seized him.

He got up.

"Prokhor, hide yourself a minute. Behind those drapes there."

Seeing a sharp change in Larin, Prokhor shook his fist almost gaily, as much as to say "That's the stuff!" and he hid himself behind the heavy drapes at the window.

Larin, opening the door into the reception room, shouted to the orderly: "Bring me the personal files of Comrades Lebedev and Olgin."

"Right away!"

Larin sat down at the desk. His face was pale, but determined. "All right," he thought. "The stinking torment of treachery can still be stopped. It's only necessary to act quickly, more quickly . . . It's all a matter of minutes—if I don't act fast, I'll be left alone, without any support. One must show one's strength, let them know it's still dangerous to play with the lion, he has sharp fangs and claws!" Larin thumped the desk hard: crushed the traitors.

The orderly brought two files. He placed them on the desk in front of Larin. "Comrades Lebedev and Olgin have come. They are waiting in the reception room," he said respectfully.

"All right—I'll call them."

Larin opened Lebedev's file. On the first page was a photograph. Provincial chief of propaganda. The face of a toady. "Why didn't I see through him before? His tongue has always supported those who were the stronger. All right, just wait, you bastard!"

What Larin was looking for in the personal file had been marked with red pencil: compromising, the most intimate personal details which probably they had forgotten and which, possibly, were not true. "Fine, I'll remind them—and if need be, I'll invent facts."

Larin lifted the telephone receiver, said impatiently to the orderly: "Tell them both to come in."

Olgin and Lebedev came into the office cheerfully, confidently. They were used to the friendly reception of their patron. "Just take a look at them," thought Larin. "They've already forgotten how they fell on their backsides on the square."

Olgin, Larin's nephew, was particularly free and easy. He plumped himself into an armchair beside the desk without invitation, squinted at Larin's fat belly, and rattled like a magpie: "Comrade Larin, how do you like the brew Veria served? He overdid it, the wretch! Moscow will hardly be pleased."

"I think so too. Veria went too far." Lebedev supported Olgin and smiled to Larin innocently. "May I have a cigarette?"

"Of course, of course . . ." replied Larin, longing to wipe the smile from Lebedev's face, so hateful was it to him.

Editor Olgin continued to rattle along: "When all's said and done there's a limit to everything. For a dozen or so years we've been writing the same thing. Stalin's biography is as well known now to everybody as their own navels. And suddenly, a certain Veria brings forth a surprise . . ."

Larin waited until they had unburdened themselves fully. Then, with round, heavy eyes he looked at the pair and said very seriously: "That may be so, my friends. Only I called you on another matter. A very serious one. Comrade Veria has just asked me to investigate certain aspects of your personal life. He says some parents are complaining about you, about something you had done with their boys. To you, as to my friends, I may say, without giving away a secret: Comrade Veria intends to charge you both with a criminal offense. Personally, I am very disturbed on your account."

It was as if both visitors had swallowed their lying tongues. Without tearing their eyes away, they looked at Larin dumbfounded. "What kind of parents? What kind of boys? What kind of criminal acts?" whirled in their brains.

Larin spoke unhurriedly, with enjoyment. For the full effect he turned over the pages of their personal files with a thick manicured finger. He saw before him two people whose lives now lay in his well-groomed hands.

200

"You know that Kalinin's former deputy, Yenukidze, was shot for that kind of capers . . ." he continued.

"What on earth is this!" exclaimed the pale Olgin. "Why, we've just been talking to Veria and he didn't say a word on the subject. On the contrary, he very warmly——" He suddenly cut himself off.

"So, continue, continue . . ." Larin encouraged him kindly. "What were you talking about so very warmly with Veria?"

"No—no—nothing special."

At last Larin became tired of playing. He got up. He was the old Larin, tall, fleshy, whose glance drove his subordinates into a cold sweat.

"You're lying, you blackguards!" he said distinctly, face growing red. "You think you can plot behind my back and get away with it, play at conspiracies with Veria. You sons of bitches!" And, going around the desk, he came close to them, hissed in their faces: "Only, the game has ended for you. Tomorrow you will both put on wooden nighties . . ."

"W—what, w—what are you saying?" babbled the editor, turning pale. Both, as if at a command, jumped up from their seats.

"Prokhor!" ordered Larin. "Come out!"

CHAPTER 15

PROKHOR CAME from behind the drapes. Baring his large yellow teeth wickedly, he said: "Good day, dear comrades. It's a long time since we met."

Olgin and Lebedev both began to move backward from him, as from a ghost. The editor's jaw sagged.

"Comrade Prokhor, you—you're here?"

Now they understood what a dangerous game Larin was playing with them. The ominous fact that Larin did not hesitate to show them that Prokhor was with him meant that he was not afraid of them now, that he counted them as nothing, a complete blank. That meant . . .

Suddenly Olgin, screaming horribly, made a rush for the door. But Prokhor, flexing himself like a cat, jumped on him and with a powerful blow of his fist felled him to the carpet.

"O—oh!" groaned the editor. His long legs, in well-polished top boots, spread themselves on the floor like a pair of scissors. Prokhor kicked him in the head with his heavy boot. Blood began to trickle from his ears.

In the meantime Lebedev, his face gray, was cautiously stealing towards the window. Larin pulled out his revolver, aimed it at the crafty one. The heavy wrinkles on his face jerked nervously. "Now, now, you swine, no capers. Stand where you are!" he barked.

Prokhor prodded Lebedev in the back and pushed his nose against a map hanging on the wall, then hit him hard on the back of the head.

"Stand there! Don't move! Study your geography."

Then he and Larin carried the still groaning Olgin into a corner of the office, also turning his face to the wall.

"Comrade Larin," whispered Prokhor. "You'd better ring up Grab at the special branch. It's time for me to disappear."

"Major Semyonov is there. He may warn Veria."

"No, Semyonov went with a letter to Gorin. He won't be back for a couple of hours."

"That's fine. You watch them while I phone."

Larin lifted the receiver. "Give me the special branch. . . . Comrade Grab, is that you? Larin speaking. Come here at once. And bring a couple of the boys along, dependable ones. Only quietly. . . . Yes."

"Larin, you won't get away with this!" mumbled Lebedev nervously. "For unlawful violence you will answer in accordance with Party discipline."

Prokhor pushed his face roughly into the wall.

"Shut up, I tell you, or it'll be worse for you." Then he turned to Larin: "Glance into the corridor—is it empty?"

Larin cautiously opened the door, looked out.

"There's nobody. You can go."

"Well, so long. But be careful, Comrade Larin! Carry out the job to the end. You can't retreat now."

"I know, I know . . ."

"Good. Now all the sneaks will shy away from Veria's door as from the gates of hell," said Prokhor. And he winked, then disappeared into the shadows of the corridor.

While he was still closing the door Larin heard bold military steps in the corridor. That was Grab coming with his men. They thundered with their heavy boots into the reception room, past the adjutant, who jumped up in fright.

A tall military man in the uniform of the NKVD, his riding breeches with wings like a bat, entered the office. Grab's dark, pimply face was gloomy—there were red veins in his eyes: possibly from sleeplessness,

202

or maybe from vodka. Glancing at Lebedev standing with his face to the wall, Grab asked Larin: "What do you want done with him?"

"Comrade Grab!" shouted Lebedev, turning from the wall. "Arrest Larin! He unlawfully, along with . . ."

Lebedev was unable to finish. With a bound Grab hurried to him and hit him a terrific blow on the neck with the edge of his palm. Larin wrinkled his face. Lebedev's head dropped onto his chest. His body slid down the wall, pulling the map with it.

"What are your orders, Comrade Larin?"

"These two must be officially documented." Larin pointed also at Olgin in the corner. "Moral degeneration. Do you understand?"

"Precisely, Comrade Larin. Everything will be done."

Larin moved closer to Grab and said softly: "Did Semyonov see you?"

"No, he went away," replied Grab just as softly.

"Listen, my friend. Fix it so that there'll be nothing of them left in an hour. Not later. Do you understand? Bring their confessions not to me, but to Durov. Try to have Durov pass some kind of a resolution on them."

"That can always be done. He'll sign—I'll slip it in among other papers."

"That's it, that's it . . ." Larin smiled. "Now go ahead, don't lose any time."

Grab gave the signal to his three men. With practiced movements they caught the prisoners under the shoulders, dragged them through the reception room. The completely terrified adjutant looked aghast at the bloody, lifeless faces of Lebedev and Olgin.

In the doorway Larin smiled at him. "A slight faint. They recover quickly," he said, and added: "—in the other world."

Returning to his desk, he ordered: "Tell them to bring my lunch. I'll eat it here in my office."

Larin was tucking away a chicken heartily when the furious Veria burst in: "Comrade Larin, what's the matter? Why were Lebedev and Olgin arrested?"

Calmly, as if he were discussing the weather, Larin replied: "The Special Branch arrested them, for moral degeneration, I think. I have just received their testimony from Durov. . . . Here, feast your eyes on it." And Larin, so as not to soil the pages with his greasy fingers, pushed the papers toward Veria with his elbow. "Signed by themselves. It's awful! I would never have expected it!"

Veria turned the pages, threw them onto the table.

"This sort of thing must be very carefully investigated," he commented, and added, "I can't say anything—it's a serious crime: I think I'll talk with them myself."

Larin waved a chicken wing distressfully. "Unfortunately it's too late. They hanged themselves in the cells."

Silence.

"Both?"

"Both," replied Larin, zealously sucking a bone.

Veria threw a glance full of hate at Larin's fat face, smeared around the mouth with chicken grease. It breathed of good health, kindness, glistened in the light. Stalin looked down from the wall at them, smiling, with his eyes screwed up. It was difficult to tell which one he approved of most.

Veria suddenly got up, pushed back the chair with a crash.

"All right, Comrade Larin! . . . So long. I hope we'll meet at the banquet."

"Of course, of course. . . . If only I don't choke on a bone."

Veria slammed the door.

Larin followed him with his eyes and spat with relish onto the carpet. Veria's nervous outburst cheered him up. The news about the ruin of Lebedev and Olgin was already being passed around. Now people were afraid to approach Veria. The gossip and whisperings had stopped. Each one thought the other was an agent of Larin. In a word, the Party Committee was living a normal life. Larin was and remained the complete master of the Province. There were no volunteers to dispute it.

When the orderly came to take away the dishes, Larin, yawning, said to him: "I'll take a nap for an hour or so before the banquet. I'm not to be disturbed."

Lying down on the leather-covered divan, he thought: "Let Veria tear around in his office, like a puma in a cage. As for me, I'm going to sleep. There's nothing better than a well-earned rest."

At the banquet he immediately noticed a change for the better. People looked at him with respect, with fear. Larin became quite cheerful, smiled to right and left, made jokes.

When dancing began, a group of girls came to him and asked him to allow the forbidden rumba. Magnanimously Larin gave his consent.

"I'll permit it. The rumba is, of course, a poisonous belching of western culture—entertainment not fit for a communist. But everybody here is politically sound. Go ahead, poison yourselves!"

204

Larin's words were greeted with a loud "Hurrah!" and the delighted squeals of the girls. From sheer joy the musicians burst out with such a cacophony from the stage that Larin almost changed his decision.

"They've lapped it up, the non-Party devils."

It immediately became apparent that nobody knew the rumba. They all stood against the wall and looked at each other. There was only one expert—the chief engineer of Sidorov's plant. He had seen a French couple dancing at the Intourist restaurant in Moscow.

Like most of the men in the hall, the engineer was wearing boots and cavalry breeches. He approached a plumpish girl and, catching her suddenly with great force, as if she had been a bucking heifer, began to rumba with her in front of everybody, bending her in a most indecent manner. The girl blushed, lowered her eyes in embarrassment, but submitted, secretly enjoying the forbidden fruit.

Others poured out after the engineer. Awkwardly they picked up the rumba, stepped on each other's feet, even fell. The men snickered, winked, cursed delightedly—the girls merely squealed and sighed. It became really lively when Larin took into his lordly embrace a pretty little blonde and began to execute western pretzels in his elephantine boots.

And then suddenly:

"Comrade Larin, an urgent telegram for you."

Larin's eyes were blank, the charming curls of the blonde were still reflected in them.

The adjutant respectfully pranced nearby, waiting.

"Ah, a telegram. . . . Later, later! . . ."

"It's urgent, Comrade Larin."

Larin straightened, politely asked the fascinating blonde to excuse him, went puffing after the adjutant. "All right, let's have it. No, let's go into the corridor; it's too crowded here."

If Larin had glanced at Veria at that moment, he would have seen how maliciously he was smiling, flashing his gold teeth. He would not have liked that smile. But Larin noticed nothing. On his cheeks he still felt the tickle of the silken hair, and in his ears he heard the clear rhythm of the rumba. . . .

In the corridor he opened the envelope. In it lay the already deciphered telegram.

He glanced at it and suddenly his face paled. A burning, unbearable pain pierced his brain and his heart. The floor began to rock under his feet. His mouth suddenly opened wide, ready to scream for help, but he merely groaned. The adjutant looked at him cautiously.

"Will there be any answer, Comrade Larin?"

Larin waved his hand weakly without answering. Then, reeling, he wandered along the corridor.

There were many corridors, long, intricate, like a labyrinth, like a trap. Everywhere was the smell of fresh paint and wax. Larin walked heavily and, not knowing why, increased his step as if he were hurrying to some goal, vague, but very important.

Suddenly he heard footsteps behind him. He turned into a narrow dark corridor. The steps followed him. He began to run. They also began to run.

"They're watching me . . ."

Now the goal became clear. "I must run, run from these steps, from the unseen enemy. . . . Why didn't I think of this before?" His breathing became quicker; cold sweat poured down his back. "They want my blood, they want to hear me howl, the Sadist in Moscow wants to enjoy my death agony."

Larin ran into a dark room, hid behind a wooden object—probably a lecturer's reading stand. He held his breath. Suddenly he recalled how in his childhood he had held his breath like this while hiding behind a bush, when his mother was looking for him with a switch. . . . Sweet, lovely childhood. Larin smiled in the darkness.

Steps were heard at the door. Two persons passed. They were talking softly.

"He ran farther along . . ."

"Of course not! We've made a mistake. He certainly did not go into this corridor."

The pair cursed and turned back.

"Aha! I fooled them, fooled them!" murmured Larin joyfully, and stuck out his tongue at his enemies.

He came out of his hiding place, carefully closed the door and, finding a switch, turned on the light. He was standing in a well-furnished office, with a carpet, armchairs, and a sofa. The object behind which he had hidden was not a reading stand but a large writing desk, covered with glass. Under the glass was a map.

"Probably Mirzoyan's office."

Larin sat down in the desk chair.

"I must hurry. They may come again . . ."

With a nervous gesture he took a revolver from his pocket. He looked at it—it was a cold, black object. "But I must not hesitate. I must act . . . in it there is salvation. And why should I be afraid? I am not here. I am far away . . . a little boy, hiding behind the bushes. Here—here everybody is an enemy, a mortal enemy: Veria, Durov, the Sadist in Moscow, and Larin . . . Yes, yes—Larin. The fat, obnoxious, cruel Larin—nobody needs him. Little boy, what's wrong with you? You are crying? Don't cry. It won't hurt. Why— you're not here, you're far away, you're still playing in your quiet, sunny childhood. These loathsome thugs must be beaten, beaten, beaten. . . . Are there enough bullets? Five, six . . . Well, not for them all, but for the main ones! . . . So, look out, Veria! Look out, Larin! I'm going to shoot till the last cartridge, all of you dogs will get your own . . ."

Larin placed the revolver against his temple and pressed the trigger. Only one shot was heard.

CHAPTER 16

"RUDOY! So you managed to stay! That's wonderful!"

The open terrace was not lighted. Lida could barely see Rudoy in the darkness, standing behind a column. The night sparkled with stars, the Milky Way crossed the sky in an enormous white veil, shimmering as in the wind. On the large expanse of the terrace Lida saw only three young couples; snuggled close to one another, they stood by the railings in silence, yearning for love and the stars.

From the distant windows, above the whispering of the leaves, came the sounds of a tango.

"Quiet, Lida," Rudoy greeted her in a whisper. "I was able to stay. The lads are scattered over the city. They gave us leave until morning on account of the celebration."

Becoming used to the darkness, Lida was able to distinguish Rudoy's features.

"What a nice lad he is," she thought. "There's a frankness and directness about him, and he seems to be very honest. . . . Just like Andrei, only not educated, and rough." Breaking away from the tormenting thought of Andrei, Lida whispered excitedly: "Rudoy, have you heard the news—Larin shot himself."

Rudoy answered quietly: "They were talking about it here. Do you know why?"

"No, I don't know."

"Probably over a woman," Rudoy reasoned confidently.

"Why do you think that?" Lida was astonished.

"Quite obvious. Women are the most evil of all beings. . . . Half the deaths are over them. The devil himself doesn't understand them. They don't even understand themselves," replied Rudoy, thinking of Nina.

"Rudoy, how dare you talk like that! After all, now!—I'm a woman!"

"No, Lida, you're not a woman."

Lida flared up in the darkness. "And what am I then, according to you?"

"You're only a girl. No one will shoot himself over anyone like you," replied Rudoy quite seriously. "Men shoot themselves over women. Women—poison! Leeches! Who cling to the heart so tightly that you can't tear them away."

Lida laughed. "You're talking as tragically as if your heart was smothered in a dozen leeches right now."

"So what? It's quite possible——"

"Nonsense! Men gave up shooting themselves over women long ago. Ever since they thought up the Party line," said Lida sarcastically. "Now they shoot themselves over the line. Look over there! Sparks are flying out of the chimneys of the Party Committee. What do you think? Are they burning Larin's love letters?"

"Oh, sure! . . . Probably quite a commotion will begin now," said Rudoy with a sigh. "There'll be bloodshed."

"I'm afraid you're right," agreed Lida.

From the other corner of the terrace came seductive laughter. "What a lovely night," thought Lida listening to them. "How nice it is for all those lovers! How happy they are! But for me . . ." and pity for herself, pity for Andrei, filled her heart.

"Haven't you seen Nina yet?" she asked Rudoy.

"No."

"That's strange. I always thought you liked her."

Rudoy didn't reply. Hiding behind the column so that his face wouldn't be seen, he struck a match and lit a cigarette. For a minute his face was lit up. His dark eyes were alert, but his expression was sorrowful.

Lida was perplexed. "What's wrong with him today? He's not himself."

Drawing on his cigarette several times, Rudoy asked: "I thought you wanted to tell me something about your own troubles."

Lida didn't answer at once. Then she said quietly: "One of the students in my class was terribly beaten up. Absolutely for no reason.

And on top of everything, instead of sending him to the hospital, they threw him in jail."

Lida didn't want to mention Andrei's name. But from the way her voice shook, Rudoy felt at once that it wasn't simply "one of the students" but someone specially dear to her.

"Who the devil beat him up?" asked Rudoy with sincere sympathy.

"Remember that fellow who came up to me when I was talking to you in the chorus? Tall, red-headed, fresh? . . ."

"Oh! That one!" Rudoy exclaimed angrily. "He was the one who called us fools. I wanted to punch his face in for those words, but it wouldn't be proper in the ballroom."

"Rudoy!" whispered Lida with unexpected emotion. "Rudoy, could you avenge me on the scoundrel? Tell me, will you?" Lida caught Rudoy by the hand with a quick movement. Her fingers were shaking. Her eyes glowed in the darkness like two small coals.

"What's wrong with you, Lida? You're trembling."

"Rudoy, understand this; one can't remain calm when a wonderful person is perishing from inhuman sufferings in jail, while the scoundrel who isn't worthy to clean his boots, after committing a crime in front of everybody, runs around free. . . . That sort of brutality must not remain unavenged. It must not be!" Trembling from excitement, Lida pronounced her words with difficulty. "Rudoy, maybe my request seems strange to you, but if you don't punish the wretch, then I'll do it myself. . . . I'll think of some way." She spoke resolutely.

"There's nothing strange about your request," replied Rudoy grimly. "But it's not up to you to do it. You're a girl. That sort of thing needs skill and ability. You see this fist?" Rudoy brought his clenched hand up to Lida's eyes. In the darkness it looked very formidable. "I've put more than one jaw out of joint with it."

"So you'll do it?" asked Lida, her spine suddenly turning cold.

"Yes, I swear! I'll do it!" exclaimed Rudoy hotly.

And suddenly grasping Lida's thin little shoulders with his rough hands, he drew her to him, as if he wanted to examine her face better in the darkness. It held some secret, unknown to him.

"Listen, Lida, I see you *are* a poison girl," he said with surprise and unconcealed approval. "Apparently I was mistaken about you before."

Lida silently raised herself on tiptoe and lightly brushed his cheek with her lips. "That's for the student," she said softly, but grimly.

"All right, don't give the reward before time," replied Rudoy, a little confused, and added: "But why didn't the students beat him up?"

"The students!" exclaimed Lida with contempt. "The students are wet rags. You know what kind of people they are."

Lida felt that it was better not to explain the real reason for the students' cowardice. She could not be sure that Rudoy's courage would not crumble on hearing Durov's name. She merely warned him: "But please be very careful. Don't get into trouble yourself."

"Don't worry about that. We'll make a dark affair of it for him—cover him with a coat—and that's the end of it. It's very simple. We've got all night for it. Where is he now?"

"He's still dancing."

"Drunk?"

"Always drunk. But he can drink and stay on his feet."

"All right, Lida, I'll wait for him outside. Maybe I'll collect a couple of the boys, to make it merrier. They're probably loafing around somewhere not far away. Beating up city folks—that's real fun for a Cossack." Rudoy pressed Lida's arm. The whites of his eyes shone in the darkness. "Thanks for the job, Lida!" he said with unexpected gaiety. "Now, at least, I have an aim in life; before I was so fed up. I will justify your trust: We'll fix him so you won't recognize him."

"Be careful! Don't mention your name. He might remember it," Lida reminded him again.

"Don't worry! After we've finished with him, he'll forget his own name—let alone remember anyone else's. Well, so long. My! What a girl you are, Lida! What a time we'll have tonight!" And jumping over the terrace railing onto the iron platform of the fire escape, he flung at her—with respect:

"My girl, you *are* poison!"

CHAPTER 17

IT WAS EXACTLY a quarter past ten in the evening when Prokhor walked quickly across the ballroom to Veria, handed him an envelope, and reported: "Comrade Veria, this has just been received from the cipher branch. Very urgent."

"Now all telegrams will be urgent." Veria smiled crookedly and winked at Durov and Shcherbakov standing beside him. "Let's have it, let's have it! Let's see what's new. Who else is to be sent to heaven?"

The small face of the Second Secretary suddenly became serious, the drunken flush left his puffed cheeks. "Get my car out at once!" he ordered Prokhor. "I'm going immediately to the station. Comrade Durov, Comrade Shcherbakov, you will accompany me." And instead of explaining he handed Durov the telegram. The latter read: "Very secret. To Comrade Veria. En route to the Caucasus I will stop at 10:30 at Rostov Station. Must see you. Stalin."

The string of cars rushed through the dark streets of Rostov like a whirlwind. Veria sat in the first one, beside the chauffeur. Every now and then he glanced at his watch.

"I hope we're not late," he said, turning to young Shcherbakov, who was sitting in the back. Durov was traveling in the other car. "The reception committee isn't very big, but we had only ten minutes altogether—you can't do much."

"That's all right, it'll pass," the Moscow man calmed him. "The main thing is—shout 'Hurrah!' as loud as you can. He likes that."

They passed Engels Street, and with a scream of brakes drove around the station square, stopped at the side entrance. The whole station was already surrounded by NKVD troopers. Nobody was allowed either in or out. The commandant of the station, a fat Ukrainian with a worried face, met the delegation. He whispered softly, almost into Veria's ear: "The train will stop on track three. What do you want me to do?"

"Let's go to the track," answered Veria curtly.

The tracks also were jammed with troops. Lanterns were twinkling everywhere; thin bayonets flashed in their reddish light. The platforms were cleared of people. In the distance stood detained trains, with steam up and banked fires.

"How did you have time to send over so many guards?" asked Veria in astonishment of Durov, who was walking beside him.

"These aren't my boys. These are Moscow troops, from the Division of Special Assignments, Stalin's personal guard. One part of the Division usually travels ahead, takes necessary precautions. Local units are seldom warned."

Out of the darkness appeared a stocky, broad-shouldered military man in a long leather overcoat, girdled by a belt with a revolver. He had a lantern in his hand. Stepping over the rails, he came close to the group and without ceremony brought the lantern up to Veria's face. Without throwing the light on his own face, he asked curtly: "Are you Veria?"

"Yes. And who are you?" replied Veria angrily. He was not accustomed to such unceremonious treatment.

"I am the Chief of the Special Brigade, Shtokov," the latter replied and shone the light on his own face. It was a broad face, with prominent cheek bones, stern. "You'll be received in the car. Alone!"

He turned to the persons accompanying Veria, said tersely: "I suggest that the others leave the tracks. Wait, if you like, in the station."

"This is Comrade Durov, Chief of the Provincial NKVD, and this is Comrade Shcherbakov from Moscow . . ." Veria considered it necessary to warn Shtokov. But the latter didn't even blink an eyelid.

"The order was to clear outsiders from the tracks."

The "outsiders" Durov, Shcherbakov, Yudin, and a dozen others hastened back into the station. Veria and Shtokov remained alone.

Soon came the sound of an approaching train. Veria made an impatient movement, but Shtokov stopped him with his hand. "That's the first train. . . . Wait for the second one."

A train, blinding them for a few seconds with its powerful headlight, rushed past without stopping. In the doors and windows of the cars, flashing by with a rumble, Veria noticed many military men. It was the safety train. In case of damaged tracks or an explosion, it absorbed the crash.

The last car had barely passed when the light of the second train showed. But this train, approaching more slowly, soon came to a stop. The windows of all five cars were curtained. Immediately, shoulder to shoulder, the troops formed up smartly in their positions around the cars.

"Let's go, now," said Shtokov.

Beyond the line of the guard the commandant of the train met them. He saluted Shtokov: "In the third car, Comrade Major."

Shtokov and Veria went up the steps of the car, entered a brightly lit, small compartment—the antechamber, paneled in light oak. Everything glittered with varnish, nickel, burnished bronze. Underfoot a short runner led to a door covered with red leather crisscrossed with yellow cord. In front of this door, beside a little table, stood an elderly officer. He had a startlingly immobile face, almost wooden. At sight of Shtokov he drew himself up, saluted silently, and immediately disappeared behind the door.

Veria was going to follow him, but Shtokov stopped him with a sign. "Comrade Veria," he said crisply, "if you have a weapon I must ask you to hand it to me."

Veria hurriedly pulled a small Browning from his breeches pocket, gave it to Shtokov. He suddenly blushed. Only now he realized that all the time Shtokov had kept suspiciously close to him, stuck to him like a boy to a girl, going around from the right, then the left side. And on

212

the steps of the car he even encircled his waist respectfully—God forbid that he should stumble and break a heel. "They are well trained, the dogs!" thought Veria, with the respect of one expert for the neat work of another.

The officer reappeared from behind the door.

"Comrade Stalin asks you to come in," he said politely, and opened the door for Veria. While showing him in, he smiled. But the smile sat awkwardly on his frozen face.

CHAPTER 18

THE COMPARTMENT which Veria entered seemed dark after the brightly lit anteroom.

In the center of the room stood a long table of blond wood inlaid with mahogany along the edge. A lamp with a broad, dark blue shade hung low over the table. The light from the lamp fell only on the table, leaving the room in shadow.

From the manner in which the armchairs were placed around the table, the heavy curtains on the windows, the large writing set in the center of the table, made of some transparent Ural stone, and the well-sharpened pencils sticking fanwise out of a small vase, Veria realized that this was the conference car.

He did not notice Stalin at once. It was Voroshilov who first caught his eye—in green military uniform, sitting at the table in the full light of the lamp. His round face, with the sharply turned-up nose and short reddish mustache above a small mouth, was very red and noticeably bloated, as happens with people who drink a lot. He sat erect, keeping his left hand, in military style, on his thigh, as if it were resting on an unseen sword hilt, and looked with his slightly prominent brown eyes directly at the newcomer. This Commissar of War, Klementy Voroshilov, though not very brilliant, was savage and loyal as a dog to Stalin, and therefore he enjoyed his special trust.

There were rumors that Voroshilov was constantly quarreling with another member of the Politburo, also a favorite of Stalin's, Kalinin. They said that during one of these quarrels Voroshilov had chased Kalinin all over the Kremlin with a drawn revolver, frenziedly threatening to "smash the old goat's mug," and that Kalinin found safety under the table in Stalin's study.

This rumor, like many of the same kind, was impossible to confirm, but the picture of the furious Voroshilov, chasing his enemy with a gun, fitted in very well with the general appearance of the Commissar of War, whose whole face and figure suggested great energy which would need frequent outlets.

Stalin appeared from somewhere in the darkness rather unexpectedly. He came up to Veria, shook his hand. His hand was hot and dry. Stalin was short, but seemed taller than Veria. Apparently this pleased him. He slapped Veria condescendingly on the shoulder with his right hand, and did not hurry to invite him to sit down.

"I'm glad to see you, Lozo," he said, looking sharply into Veria's face, which seemed half-covered by his pince-nez. "It's over a year since we met. Your old boon companion, Klim," Stalin waved his hand towards Voroshilov, "can't forget the cherry brandy you served him in Gelendzhik. He thought that you had put dynamite in it."

Voroshilov opened his mouth and roared with barrel-like laughter. It seemed to Veria that he laughed louder and longer than Stalin's joke warranted.

Stalin, waiting until Veria had greeted Voroshilov, finally invited him to sit down, then seated himself beside him. His face, with the heavily wrinkled eyelids, seemed to smile, but Veria wasn't sure. All kinds of things could hide behind that large black mustache. However, Stalin's friendly reception calmed Veria. He waited anxiously for him to speak.

Stalin didn't hurry. He took his pipe from the table, filled it with tobacco, put it in the corner of his mouth. Voroshilov, well-trained, leaned across the table and obligingly handed him his lighter.

Stalin lit up. With a slow, searching look of his olive eyes he watched his two subordinates. He did not stand on ceremony. His intent look penetrated farther than they liked, as if it were plucking out the secrets of their hearts. Under this look Veria became ill at ease. He avoided it. But while doing so, he was able to study the face and figure of the dictator very carefully.

The oblique light made the traces of smallpox on Stalin's face particularly pronounced. The sharp shadows, the dark, uneven skin—as if it had been pitted by hail—made his face heavy and massive, like a sculpture of badly chiseled stone.

However, the black hair on his head, streaked with gray, the thick mustaches, and even the eyebrows were carefully combed and obviously oiled. Veria plainly smelled perfume. When Stalin lit his pipe this fragrance became mixed with the aroma of good tobacco.

Stalin was dressed for summer: a white military tunic, white trousers

214

tucked into black polished boots. The uniform was plain, but of the very best quality.

Veria noticed that the tunic sat very loosely on his short body. The material clung closely only to the little belly in front. On this animated hemisphere his left hand rested, almost motionless. It was the half-withered arm which saved Stalin from the trenches of the World War and perhaps from a German bullet.

The long sleeves of his tunic covered the small hands almost to the fingers. Veria had previously noticed this peculiarity in some of Stalin's other suits. He sensed in this strange whim of the dictator the desire to emphasize his aristocratic position: his hands were not for coarse work. It was unlikely that they lifted anything heavier than a pen.

Settling himself comfortably in the armchair, Stalin crossed one leg over the other. His right boot came under the light of the lamp. Veria was surprised at the unusually pointed toe and the thinness of the sole. "In boots like that it's possible to walk only on carpets and parquet floors," he thought.

Noting these details, Veria wondered how he might emulate the master. He knew that this must be done cautiously. Outright copying would be dangerous. Certain peculiarities of dress Stalin guarded as jealously as his own person.

"The telegram calling Larin to Moscow was sent, as you suggested. . . . Good," Stalin began unexpectedly, as if continuing a conversation started long ago. "And now it has been reported to us that Larin has killed himself. That, of course, is bad."

Stalin spoke quietly. Veria strained his ears to make out his words, although he sat close beside him. But Veria caught a barely noticeable shade of irritation in his voice. Although Veria, like Stalin, was a Georgian, the latter spoke to him in Russian out of respect for Voroshilov.

"Why didn't you watch Larin? Why did you allow him to shoot himself?" continued Stalin. "Larin was a very important link in the chain of treachery. Comrade Vishinsky reported to me just a week ago that it would be a good thing to have him in court as the representative of the Rostov center of the Trotzkyite conspiracy. . . . And now what? Will I have to send you instead of Larin to that Menshevik Vishinsky?" Stalin asked jokingly. Cold shivers ran up and down Veria's supple back. He froze in the armchair. With each word of the almighty sovereign, the blood drained from his face.

"How can he lie so calmly?" he thought, and was afraid of his own thoughts. "What the hell kind of a Rostov center, Rostov conspiracy?

215

And Larin—what kind of a conspirator was he? Why, he was your most faithful dog!"

Aloud, however, Veria hastened to say something different: "I very much regret what happened, Joseph Vissarionovich. I ask you to forgive me. I gave Comrade Durov precise instructions to watch Larin's every step. However, Larin managed to shake his shadow at the last moment . . ."

"He should have been disarmed, even locked up, if things had gone to that length," interjected Voroshilov, looking insolently at the little Veria. The Commissar of War was sober and therefore in a bad mood. He had been itching for some time to go to the dining car for a glass or two.

"Klim is right," Stalin approved. "Speaking frankly, I didn't expect such negligence from you, Lozo. I always considered you a clever devil. But now it turns out that a fool like Larin twisted you around his finger. Just like the fairy tale about the worker Balda." On Stalin's face appeared a strange smile. Voroshilov, with the alertness of a court jester, again roared his short, deafening laugh.

Veria, pale, got up. "Joseph Vissarionovich," he said in an excited voice, but full of determination. "That was my last mistake. Now no one will fool me!"

"No need to get excited, Lozo. Sit down!" Smiling, Stalin pushed him into an armchair. "I didn't call you to talk about Larin. I simply wanted to have a look at you, my friend. Never mind Larin! It's a pity, of course, that he was able to get away from us. Well, there'll be others. . . ." At Stalin's last words Voroshilov snorted like a horse at its oats.

Veria suddenly became frightened of these men—particularly of Stalin. "What contempt he has for people! How cheaply he rates them!" he thought.

In the meantime, Stalin, puffing away at his pipe, looked at Veria paternally.

"You know, of course, that Romain Rouen is coming to visit your city," he said after a brief silence. "I have had a chat with him already. An interesting personality. He says the object of his visit is to arrange an exchange of students with us. According to him, such an exchange will iron out immediately all the contradictions between our country and the capitalist west, like the wave of a magic wand. He's a crank. However, I agreed with him fully. I praised the idea, assured him that from our side there would be no obstacles, that we are always glad to learn from them and to teach them . . ."

"You said that to him? Why?" Voroshilov said, surprised. "Why, that's quite dangerous!"

Stalin's eyes screwed up in a sneer at such a naïve question.

"Promises, Klim," he said patiently, "are given according to motive, but are fulfilled according to circumstances." Then, turning to Veria, he continued: "Of course, Romain Rouen couldn't think of anything cleverer than an exchange of students. Like all westerners he's a rotten intellectual. He's worried in case we, God forbid, should forget the human being." Stalin took the pipe out of his mouth and mimicked the Frenchman: " 'Don't you think, Monsieur Stalin, that in the course of the great reforms which you are instituting so wonderfully in your country, you have forgotten the main thing—man, the individual personality?' I set his mind at rest as well as I could on that score and hastened to send him off to Gorin. Mikhail will put his soul at peace in no time. On the subject of the human personality Gorin is our greatest master." And noticing the scornful grimace on Voroshilov's face, Stalin added: "At least, up to now he has been."

Then he asked Veria: "I presume Romain Rouen will stay with Gorin?"

"No, he will live in a Government summer house."

"Why so?" Stalin asked.

"Some mix-up took place with Gorin's son," replied Veria. He considered it out of place and, in any case was afraid, to report the details of the scandal with Pavel. "Gorin is apparently embarrassed to show that crazy one to the foreigner."

Stalin raised his eyes and gave Veria a long, heavy look. "It's not his craziness that is dangerous, but his wit," he said thoughtfully.

Veria knew this habit of Stalin's—to interject short aphorisms into conversation with the air of deep thought, at times successfully, at others not. To play at being a philosopher, a thinker, was the dictator's favorite pastime.

"Excellent! Well put!" Veria hastened to praise and immediately showed keen delight on his monkeylike face.

Stalin sighed.

"I'm afraid that Pavel has a bad influence on his father," he said. His face suddenly became hard and unpleasant. In these words, pronounced as usual, dully and slurringly, Veria caught the hint which, apparently, Stalin was trying to give him.

Veria leaned his whole body forward and, catching Stalin's searching glance, hastened to show that he understood the hint. He even nodded his head so that Stalin would have no doubts. His tense pose, the drawn-out neck, the peering eyes, all seemed to say: "Here I am, dear master. I understand everything. Your loyal little devil will not make any more mistakes!"

Stalin made a wry face, puffed out a cloud of smoke, hid his eyes behind it. "Yes, many fathers are unlucky in their sons," he said in his usual tone. "The Durov brat, I hear, gives you a lot of trouble also." And he added with a sneer: "I myself have one such blockhead, Yasha. If only he would get married . . ."

"That's all right, he'll sow his wild oats and then settle down," Voroshilov assured him. "I always consider such lads better than the pampered ones. I can't stand a sissy."

"How naïve Gorin is," said Stalin after a slight pause, as if he were answering his own thoughts. "At such a serious moment he occupies himself with trifles, such as that woman . . ."

Veria glanced at him quickly with his small sharp eyes. "He already knows about that!" he thought in surprise. He was vexed that he had not told Stalin first.

"That incident can be considered closed, Joseph Vissarionovich," he said. "I have already reassured Gorin. I supposed that Gorin would have to be kept satisfied, in a good humor, particularly before the arrival of the Frenchman."

"You did right to reassure him," Stalin approved.

"But why stand on so much ceremony with him?" exclaimed Voroshilov, displeased. "He is, of course, a great writer, the stormy petrel of the revolution and so on, but there's a limit to everything. It seems to me that we exalt him too much. He'll be astride our necks soon."

Stalin shrugged his shoulders; in his stern eyes flashed a spark of contempt. "You don't understand a thing about it, Klim. To be rough-tongued is good only in battle. Here patience is needed."

"And how long must we wait?" asked Voroshilov, unappeased. His short nostrils dilated. "How long are we going to hang back?"

"Don't hurry events. . . . How long, you ask?" Suddenly taking a pencil from the little vase, Stalin began to bend it with his carefully tended fingers.

"What doesn't bend, breaks," he said. And, breaking the pencil, he threw the two pieces onto the table under Voroshilov's nose. "That's how it is in everything," he concluded significantly.

Veria and Voroshilov, as if at a command, straightened up in their armchairs, stared at Stalin, amazed, dumbfounded, full of silent admiration and the devil knows what else, as if Stalin had just made some extraordinary scientific discovery or performed a miracle.

"That's genius! That's genius!" These words were clearly on their faces.

Stalin accepted their slavish worship as his due. He would have been surprised if Veria and Voroshilov had reacted differently. In his gestures, in the cold expression of his eyes, in his reserved manner of speaking there was not a shadow of humor or irony. He spoke quite seriously. At that moment, more than at any other time during the entire conversation, his stubborn will and cruel character showed themselves.

"A striking lesson!" cried Veria at last. He was excited. "I'll remember this lesson for the rest of my life."

"You'll do well if you remember," Stalin remarked approvingly. "For many, life would be quiet, pleasant, and, above all, secure if they did not forget that truth. However, I do not think that it will be necessary to break Gorin. He has enough brains—to bend. . . . By the way, how is Professor Novikov getting along?" he asked Veria. "Novikov is good, not like the old intellectuals, all their idealistic bunk . . ." and Stalin cursed briefly, but strongly. Stalin's hatred of the old intellectuals was well known to Veria. He smiled approvingly.

"Oh, Novikov is prospering," he exclaimed. "We're going to make him Director of our University. He's a clever man, no doubt about that."

"It's not a matter of brains, but of convictions," Stalin corrected him. "With weak convictions the brain becomes a poor asset. That's why Novikov is good, because he has strong political vigor. I know that many historians disparage him among themselves, because he is breaking the faith in established truth. But that, I think, is tommyrot. Truth! Truth! What good is it to people who have convictions? From such people as Novikov all young specialists should take an example. . . . You, Lozo, give him plenty of help. In everything."

"Absolutely, Joseph Vissarionovich."

CHAPTER 19

DURING the entire conversation Veria had been waiting impatiently for Stalin to tell him what interested him more than anything else—his own future. But Stalin, it seemed intentionally, talked about everything else but that. After finishing with Novikov, he suddenly plunged into a discussion of the theatre, working in several witticisms. To the dictator's jokes Veria responded with laughter, as loud as Voroshilov's, although mice were scratching at his heart. He began to fear that Stalin, wishing to punish him for his negligence with Larin, had forgotten about his promotion.

Having finished with the theatre, Stalin switched to the ballet, jokingly reproaching Voroshilov for his interest in a beautiful ballet dancer. Stalin was evidently in a good mood and in no hurry.

At last Veria lost all hope. In anguish he watched the golden time passing, one minute after another, and still Stalin had not broached the subject. Veria felt a pounding of the heart and an impatient trembling in his legs. Such things seldom happened to him.

Possibly Stalin guessed at his agitation, but he gave no sign. Finally, in desperation, Veria decided to try to wring from the dictator the recognition so indispensable for him. He had not the nerve to ask him outright; so, in a very cajoling but subtly hinting voice, he said: "Joseph Vissarionovich, before I forget, have you any orders about a replacement for Larin?" This question Stalin was meant to understand thus: "Why don't you say anything about my transfer to Moscow, as you promised a year ago?"

Stalin understood exactly.

He smiled and said softly to Veria: "We are very satisfied with your speech today, Lozo. Very satisfied. The Politburo believes that the idea must be developed further. . . . What do you think? Could you write a book, taking your speech as the basis? Something like the history of the Party movement in the Caucasus?"

Veria, completely unprepared for such a turn of affairs, became confused. He felt deceived. He had not expected a delay. Apparently Stalin drove a hard bargain, he was not selling the promotion cheaply. He demanded new tests from him. Veria was ready to howl like a dog on a moonlight night. However, he mastered his confusion.

"I shall do everything in my power to fulfill your task," he replied firmly.

"Very good. As soon as you've finished—I think six months or a year will be enough for you—we'll call you to Moscow. It's important that the book should have its beginning here, in the local background, in the Caucasus."

"Thank you for your trust, Joseph Vissarionovich."

"Be careful that there are no more such mistakes as with Larin."

"There won't be, I can assure you, there won't be," Veria replied with some fervency.

Stalin rose. Voroshilov and Veria followed immediately.

220

"Well, good-bye, Lozo," Stalin extended his hand to Veria. "I wish you and your province success."

"Thank you, Joseph Vissarionovich. A pleasant journey to you. My meeting with you has been the best lesson of my life."

"Be a good pupil." Stalin slapped Veria on the shoulder and said, almost sentimentally: "Lozo, my friend, I am placing great hopes in you. . . . In the meantime you will take Larin's place. Young Shcherbakov will be your assistant."

Stalin slowly turned his head towards Voroshilov.

"What do you think, Klim, should I tell him our secret or not?" he asked the Commissar of War and winked.

Voroshilov shrugged his shoulders, began to laugh. "Why not? Tell him."

"Lozo," said Stalin solemnly, "the Politburo has decided to place your name on its preliminary list of candidates."

At these words of the dictator Veria's heart jumped joyfully. He drew up his small body like a tight cord, even clicked his heels in a military manner. He could say nothing from emotion. At last, at last, his dream was being realized. His crazy ambition was becoming reality.

The preliminary list of the Politburo, this most secret list, known only to Stalin and his closest assistants—was the first internal step to the Politburo. From this list were picked the candidates who, usually after two or three years, became full members.

"Satisfied?" asked Stalin, watching his agitation with pleasure.

Veria was silent, his cheeks flushed. Suddenly he bent and, raising the hem of Stalin's jacket, and unembarrassed by Voroshilov's presence, kissed the soft fabric, his little eyes dimmed by tears.

What was the use of words?

"I am your slave, wholly your slave until death," said his impetuous gesture. Stalin was not in the least surprised by such an unexpected display of gratitude. Throwing his arm around Veria's shoulder in a fatherly manner, he accompanied him to the door.

Voroshilov bade him farewell with unusual warmth, congratulated him loudly on his promotion. Of the previous dryness and arrogance, which had frightened and angered Veria at the beginning of the conversation, there was by now no trace.

When the happy Veria came out of the car Shtokov, with a smile that made him quite unrecognizable, returned his Browning to him.

Seating himself in the automobile, Veria heard Stalin's train pull out. Following the lights of the train with his eyes, he thought: "Yes, that was the best lesson for you, Veria! You thought you were smart, sly as the devil. But the real devil, there he goes. How he can lie, be the hypocrite, play with human weaknesses!" Veria frowned painfully, remembering his rabbitlike agitation under Stalin's icy glance.

"But, my God, what a brazen fellow Voroshilov is! Well, we'll see yet . . ."

"Where would you like to go, Comrade Veria?" asked the chauffeur. He had already repeated the question several times. But Veria, sunk deep in his own thoughts, hadn't heard him.

"Where? Home, home, of course . . ." replied Veria absent-mindedly. "No, wait!" he said suddenly. "Go along Sennaya Street. I'll tell you where to stop." Saying these words, he thought: "Such a night can't be passed so simply. . . . Impossible!"

"Sennaya it is!" replied the chauffeur, and smiled in the darkness.

Veria didn't notice the smile. He sighed, leaned back blissfully on the cushions of the seat, half-closed his eyes, so as to dream better.

"I am placing great hopes in you." . . . The words of Stalin repeated themselves in his head.

CHAPTER 20

WHEN VERIA LEFT the ballroom for his meeting with Stalin, he tried to do so unobserved, fearing that the dance might end. But the men, overheated by wine and the nearness of the women, stormed around and were enjoying themselves as before. Nobody was worrying about him.

Among the few who noticed Veria's departure was Oleg Durov. "Now we can raise hell," he thought, squirming with pleasure. "It was getting so dull, you might as well be dead." Larin's suicide didn't bother him at all. The whole province could shoot itself, as long as there was a full bottle of vodka.

He had drunk heavily. His face had become swollen in red blotches; under his eyes the bags puffed up. With a group of other spoiled brats of provincial bosses, he reeled from one end of the ballroom to the other. He pinched the young girls, pestered the women, made an uproar, egged people on.

"Hey, fellows! Did you see how Veria slipped away?" he said significantly to his friends.

They were crowded around an open window under the stairs leading to the balcony. They were smoking, refreshing themselves. From here the entire ballroom was visible as on the palm of one's hand. From the balcony the half-drunk musicians, cadets from the artillery school, played noisily the most decadent dances. Although it had just struck ten, this was already the second orchestra. The first one had been thrown out, too drunk to play.

Oleg was sitting on the window sill, moving his fingers in the pockets of his breeches. He was wearing the same shirt with the embroidered cockerels in which he had appeared a day ago at the University. But he had changed his Cossack trousers for cavalry breeches. He considered them better for dancing: their wide wings were smarter, more elegant. For full effect he had put spurs on his boots.

"You're right, Oleg. Veria has disappeared," remarked one of the lads lazily.

"Your father's not here either," another put in. "Nor the Moscow guests."

"Where could they have slipped away to?" asked a third.

"Probably to prepare Larin's burial," somebody suggested.

"Bury your grandmother!" Oleg interrupted. "It's none of our business anyway where they've slipped off to. The main thing is, they're not here. Now it's like having no supervisors. Do you get it?"

"Right. Right!" agreed the exulting lads.

"Hey, Khrenov!" Oleg suddenly shouted to a tall young fellow with a pale face. He was standing nearby with legs spread wide. "Don't keep your hands in your pockets in front of me."

"And where are you keeping yours?" the lad snapped back.

"I can, but you mustn't!"

"Fool!"

"What! What did you say?" Oleg jumped down off the window sill, stood in front of Khrenov and also spread his legs wide. "Do you want a slap?" he muttered through dribbly lips. They stood in front of each other, ruffled like a pair of cockerels.

"Cut it out! What are you scrapping for?" the others shouted at them. "Think up something more interesting."

Oleg, still looking wolfishly at Khrenov, went back to the window sill. Suddenly his face brightened. With a gesture he beckoned to his friends. "Come here. . . . I'll tell you something."

"Now what?"

"Listen, I'll do the talking." Oleg wagged his head excitedly. In the fresh air from the window the wine affected his brain more strongly. Sticking out his chest like a barrel, he asked: "Do you want to see a comrade shock worker in action?"

223

"How's that? What do you mean?"

"Very simple, my dull friends! . . . I'll show you how to break a wench. In one easy lesson."

"Oh! That's what you have in mind!" snickered one called Fat-Trust by his mates. He asked with keen curiosity: "Who?"

"Do you know Lidka?" asked Oleg.

"Sidorov?"

"Of course."

"A young girl!" The lanky Khrenov, son of the military commandant of the city, waved his hand fastidiously.

"Suppose she is young! That's what makes it interesting," Oleg answered coarsely and turned to the others: "Now listen. . . . I'll entice her into that room—the office of the physical-culture instructor. There are many floor mattresses there. You hide behind the desk. The exhibition begins soon. In full light."

"But won't Sidorov nail us?" asked one of them apprehensively.

"Sidorov is dreaming heavenly dreams. He's asleep in a plateful of gravy," Oleg reassured him with a sneer.

"All right, let's go."

"I won't go," said Khrenov suddenly.

"Why?" Oleg approached him menacingly. "Cold feet?"

"I'm not afraid, but I simply won't soil myself with young girls," Khrenov replied sullenly.

"You're a wet rag, you God damned sissy!" Oleg cursed him.

Khrenov's nostrils trembled. He came close to Oleg, seized him by the collar of his shirt, and hissed into his face: "And you can go—you know where." Then, shoving him roughly, he strode off into the ballroom, swaying a little.

"He's drunk, the fool! That's why he doesn't want to," said Oleg angrily. "Well, to hell with him! Are you going?"

"All right, we're going." The five, giggling foolishly and swearing at each other, went in a gang into the instructor's room, closed the door behind them.

Oleg remained alone, searching for Lida. She had just come into the ballroom. Standing only a minute and looking around as if she were seeking someone, she went toward the exit. Oleg hurried to her. Lida's face was sad and strangely unfamiliar.

"Are you lonely, Lida?" Oleg showed his yellow, tobacco-stained teeth.

"Leave me alone, Oleg. I don't want to speak to you."

"Lida, Lida," Oleg bowed before her, tottering a little, wheezing through his nose. "I know you're mad at me. So listen, I have decided to apologize to you. Forgive . . ." For full persuasion Oleg hung his head on his chest, looked guiltily at the floor.

But his appearance did not touch Lida. She left him.

"Lida, don't you believe me?" muttered Oleg, going after her. "Couldn't I make a mistake? In the heat of the moment anything may happen. You see, I was jealous of him . . ."

Lida stopped. She looked at him with almost physical loathing.

"You were jealous?" Lida laughed bitterly. "Why are you lying?"

"No, it's true. I love you, Lida."

These words sounded foolish and insolent, as one would expect from Oleg Durov. She wanted to strike him, so obnoxious was he to her. She turned away, her face contorted.

Feeling that his repentant words went badly with his drunken appearance, Oleg decided to act slyly. "Why, I've already helped Andrei," he said softly, playing the modest hero.

"How did you help?"

"I begged my father to transfer him to the hospital," lied Oleg. "Satisfied?"

Lida was silent for a moment, to quiet her joyful heart. "Surely that's not true?" she thought. And then she said, "It wasn't you who helped, but Gorin."

"Oh, yes, of course. A lot Gorin did! I'm telling you, I helped. . . . Why don't you believe me?"

"And in which hospital is he?" asked Lida quickly.

"That's a secret, but I know. . . . My God, what a noise they're making in here! Will you come into the instructor's room? It's quieter there, I'll tell you the whole thing."

"Are you sure you're not lying?"

"Honest Komsomol!" said Oleg solemnly. "I'll tell you how to get to him. Only—all this is a secret, nobody must hear. If they find out, they'll pull my head off."

Listening to his drunken talk, Lida hardly believed him. But so great was her desire to learn where Andrei was that she forced herself to believe. "He's drunk, and maybe he's telling the truth," she reasoned.

Thinking only of Andrei, she went with Oleg. She opened the door of the room, allowed him to pass. As he passed her he felt her small, firm breast with his hand, as though by accident.

The lights were on in the room. The exercise mats had been dragged in when the gymnasium was cleared for dancing; they lay around in heaps, hung over the table, were thrown on chairs.

225

Lida stopped at the door. "All right, tell me."

"Wait till I shut the door," said Oleg. "Now listen, your Andrei is in the military hospital. You know, that one at Nakhichevan."

"But will they let me in?"

"I'll arrange everything, don't worry."

"Well, if you're not lying, thank you." Lida took hold of the door knob. But Oleg caught her by the shoulders.

"Thanks? Is that the way to show gratitude?"

Puzzled, Lida looked at him. "But how?"

Oleg showed her with a gesture. "That's how."

Lida tore at the door. But Oleg stopped it with his foot. "Let go the door, Oleg!"

"Don't hurry, don't hurry, or you won't see Andrei . . ."

"Let go, I say!" screamed Lida.

"Don't be obstinate! What are you pretending for?" said Oleg through his teeth, pushing her away from the door.

"Let go! Oleg, I beg you to let me go!" She still tried to be calm, but two bright spots appeared on her face, which had turned pale.

"What are you playing at, being innocent or what? Didn't you fool around with Andrei?" He spoke in an excited voice. And suddenly snorting, he placed his hand on her breast.

Lida jumped away from him as if she had been stung. Her dress tore and through the tear the soft, rosy swell of her breast showed, scorching Oleg's eyes. Not taking his eyes off her, Oleg tried to push her towards a mattress. Her eyes wide with fright, she retreated from him.

"Why—all girls do this . . ." said Oleg in a strange, dull voice: "Look, here, . . . it's soft . . ." He pushed her roughly onto a mattress, throwing himself down after her.

In falling, Lida saw the lads hiding behind the desk. They looked at her with drunken, covetous eyes. She didn't understand at once. . . . But suddenly realizing, she screamed loudly and piercingly.

Oleg pressed her mouth shut, buried his lips in her neck below her ear. With his other hand he pulled up her skirt. In mad haste his fingers began to tear at her underwear. His yellow eyes became bloodshot.

Like a wild cat Lida, hissing with fury, twisted under his heavy body, scratched his flushed, distorted face, breaking her nails.

"Quit fooling! Quit fooling!" repeated Oleg, and trying to save his face from her nails, sunk his lips deeper into her neck. His breath came hotly. His spurs tore her stockings.

With all her might Lida fought against him. She was suffocating from the pressure of his sweaty hand. When, for an instant, she was able to tear it away from her mouth, she sank her teeth into his cheek so that it bled.

Oleg blew up.

"So, you'd bite!" he shouted, and struck her in the face with his fist. Blood began to flow from her nose. "Hey, fellows! What are you staring for? Help me!" croaked Oleg hoarsely.

The boys came from behind the desk one at a time, avoiding each other's eyes, caught hold of the half-naked Lida.

At that instant the door burst open with a crash. Into the room rushed Sidorov. Behind him in the doorway the face of Khrenov, twisted in a spiteful smile, appeared for an instant.

Sidorov was unsteady on his legs. But, on seeing his daughter under the pile of young fellows, he sobered at once. With a bound he threw himself at them, kicked Oleg with his heavy boot. The latter, howling, hopped out of the room practically on all fours. After him ran his friends.

Sidorov, no longer thinking of them, bent over the shuddering body of his daughter. His bronzed face was ash-like. He sat down beside her, to quiet her. Then he lifted her in his arms and, tottering, carried her from the room. From his expressionless eyes tears flowed, leaving white trails through the gravy stains.

Through the open door of the ballroom came mad music, the gay laughter of men, the shrill, drunken squeals of women.

CHAPTER 21

OLEG DUROV went outside, rumpled, his whole face covered with blood.

"I was kicked . . . Me, Oleg Durov, kicked with a boot! . . . All right, wait, you'll learn . . ." he mumbled excitedly. He wheezed, tottered, gazed around him. Right at the stairway he saw Sidorov's car. He approached, kicked it with his foot.

"Well! Scum!"

Picking up a lump of mud from the street, he painstakingly, sticking out the end of his tongue, drew on the shabby side of the old Benz, the words: "Before the revolution Director Sidorov sang in the church choir!" Then, after thinking a bit, he added: "What did we fight for, comrades?"

At once he felt better. And when he had smashed the front window with a brick, he calmed down completely. "He'll sober up in the draft, the swine!"

The boys approved of his work, and also revived.

"Where to now?" they asked Oleg.

"I don't know. Let's chase around town a bit. We'll think up something," replied Oleg and, spitting on his handkerchief, wiped the wound on his cheek with it.

They crossed the square in a crowd, went along Budenny Avenue. They laughed, shouted songs, threw stones at basement windows. Somewhere behind them another group of young fellows was walking —also probably recovering from a drunk.

On their way they went into a food store of the Party Committee. They were allowed in without question—friendship with Durov's son was cherished here. The fat storekeeper, who wouldn't have given a hungry Rostovian a crumb of bread, curried favor with Oleg. "Have you come for a hair of the dog? For a snack?"

"Wrap me up a lunch, a good one," Oleg ordered him.

His companions were surprised: "What do you want a lunch for?"

"I have an idea," Oleg replied curtly.

The storekeeper wrapped up some salt herring, sausage, cheese.

"Shall I add some sweets?" he asked, winking slyly.

"Yes."

"Very good." He put in a box of chocolates, and without being asked, added a bottle of port wine.

Outside, Oleg announced to his companions: "I'm going to Lily's."

"All right. We'll go along."

But when they stopped at the door of an old three-story house, Oleg brushed them off: "Well . . . See you tomorrow."

Treading heavily on the iron steps, Oleg came to the second-story landing. Without knocking, he opened the door. In a small room, filling it completely, stood a bed, a table with a mirror, a chair. On the bed was a great mound of pillows. On the chair alongside, in front of the mirror, sat a neat little blonde with full lips, plump hands, and the eyes of an innocent violet. On her knees lay an open book. On seeing Oleg she looked horrified.

"Oh, it's you, Marquis!"

"What do you mean—marquis?" asked Oleg. "Here, I brought a lunch. Do you want to gorge?"

Lily frowned. The coarse Oleg had smashed her dream world to smithereens. She was reading *The Three Musketeers*. Turning the pages impatiently, her face flushed with emotion, she had glanced into the mirror now and then. There, instead of the small room (six feet by ten), the luxurious drawing rooms of the Louvre Palace extended into the dim distance; from the window, instead of the smell of slops and the cursing of women, came the fragrance of flowers and the magic whisperings of a thousand fountains.

Lily had three lives. From nine in the morning to six in the evening she worked as a typist for the Party Committee. In the evening at home she entertained her bosses, exhausted by purges, by conferences, and by ill-tempered wives.

The third life, and the most important one, belonged to her exclusively. This was the world of books, always long, always romantic, always sentimental—a world of noble heroes and loving beauties. Among the heroes were the Frenchman d'Artagnan, the Spaniard Don Juan. The beauty was always she, Lily.

The big executives loved Lily tenderly. They loved her for her intriguing little skirt, which never quite covered her knees; for her pretty legs, light and obedient; for her small, full mouth and the merry dimples in her cheeks. But more than anything they loved her wide, dreamy eyes. These eyes belonged to the third world: unearthly, complaisant. After meetings, noisy to hoarseness, after dry figures and menacing editorials in *Pravda,* it was very pleasant to look into these innocent eyes. They brought back memories of childhood, a quiet pond with butterflies, a loving mama, a long forgotten tenderness . . .

For other men, who became so hard that even Lily's eyes called forth no special emotional disturbance, Lily meant merely full breasts and broad hips.

They loved Lily also for her adaptable character. In the morning—after an evening drinking party where any kind of prank was allowed, and where Lily herself never stood on ceremony—in the morning, everything was changed. Behind the small desk in the branch sat a neat young lady, tapping away on her typewriter, speaking respectfully to her superiors:

"Would you like three copies, Pyotr Petrovich?" . . . "It's ready for you now, Ivan Ivanovich." There were no familiarities. She was just a hardened shock worker, a modest toiler of the Five Year Plan.

To herself Lily called all men "tom-cats," "stallions," "counterfeits." The genuine ones were in the books. With them she carried on lofty conversations, in their strong embraces her heart stopped beating, over her they fought duels, while Lily from the Party Committee, pressing her hand to her heart, holding her breath, awaited the outcome. The hero, of course, was victorious. Lily rewarded him with a kiss and a

229

perfumed handkerchief. But could a clod-faced boy like Oleg understand this?

Lily sighed.

"Did you bring any candies?"

"There are candies. But you'll have time enough to stuff yourself,"
replied Oleg. "First, pour me some water."

Quite at home, he went over to the washbasin standing in the corner
by the door, above a pail. Lily got up lazily from her chair, went over,
dipped some cold water with a jug.

"Pour it over my head, Lilya—it burns."

"Who scratched you up like that?" asked Lily.

"Never mind! And tell me: are you expecting anybody tonight?" he
asked, splashing.

"No, no one. But who can tell about you tom-cats?"

"In that case, I'll spend the night with you."

"If you like," replied Lily, unconcerned.

She went over to the little table, opened the parcel with the lunch,
clapped her hands joyfully: "Little Bear Candies! I haven't had any
for a long time!" Biting a candy with her small teeth, she turned up her
eyes blissfully: "What delight! What do you think, did the marquises
eat 'Little Bears'?"

"I don't know, I wasn't acquainted with marquises."

"I've been reading about them. Oh! How wonderfully they lived!
And the men—certainly not like you, crawling onto the bed with your
boots on. You have no manners!"

"I'll take them off, don't worry," mumbled Oleg, stretching himself out on the bed. After all the commotion it was very pleasant to lie
on the soft mattress. "What are you reading?" he asked Lily, placing
his hand behind his head and looking at the ceiling.

"*The Three Musketeers.* It's thrilling. There are some pictures. Do
you want to look?"

"Here, let me see."

While Oleg was looking at the pictures Lily greedily ate the lunch he
had brought. The marquise was very hungry.

"Who mussed up the pictures like that?" exclaimed Oleg suddenly.

"With ink?" asked Lily. "Major Semyonov. He gave me the book."

"He sure made a job!" Oleg grinned. "What an artist!" On the en-
graved illustrations, full of gallant musketeers and elegant ladies, the
bold hand of Semyonov had inked in details that should have made the
paper itself blush.

Lily, munching sausage, explained: "Major Semyonov ordered me

230

to show him this book every time he comes to me. He says he needs it to excite him."

"Ha! I've never heard of such craziness. Why, he's not an old man!"

"I don't know," answered Lily calmly.

Oleg hurled the book away.

"Lily, stop eating. Surely you're not going to turn the whole night into a meal!"

Lily wiped her lips with a napkin. Unhurriedly she rose, sat down on the bed beside Oleg. Taking down a guitar from a nail, she began to pick at the strings. The small room filled with sobbing sounds. When Oleg grew tired of listening, he pinched Lily's rump competently. Convinced that everything was in its place, he grunted with satisfaction. Lily resentfully bit her full lips. "Don't pinch," she said, silencing the strings with her hand.

"Why are you so touchy?"

"For no reason. More important people than you don't pinch me."

Oleg laughed, drew her to him. Lily dropped the guitar on the floor.

"Don't be so rough! You'll tear my blouse!" she said, pushing away from Oleg.

A scuffle began. Oleg floundered about. Lily jerked with her bare legs.

Oleg shouted, flushed with pleasure.

Relaxed, he lay back on the pillow, spreading his arms wide. Lily leaned over him, gay, no longer hungry, with radiant dimples in her cheeks. Her blouse had slipped off her right shoulder. She pursed her full lips and kissed Oleg on the cheek, right where Lida had bitten him.

Oleg suddenly paled. With her ill-starred kiss Lily had reminded him with surprising sharpness of his recent humiliation. He pushed Lily away with fierce curses, as if Lida Sidorov were in front of him.

Lily was stupefied.

"Go to hell!" roared Oleg. "What are you looking at, you bitch?"

Crawling away from him on her knees along the bed, Lily kept her surprised eyes on his face, distorted with anger.

Oleg was choking with fury. "No," thought he. "I'll get even with Lidka, and her father! . . ." He got up from the bed, went to the door. Then, remembering, he turned back, took the lunch from the table—all that was left of it. Putting the still unopened bottle of port wine into the pocket of his breeches, he left the room, slamming the door loudly. He didn't even look at the terrified girl.

Lily sat motionless on a corner of the bed. When the door slammed behind Oleg she began to sob. She was sorry to lose the lunch, especially the Little Bears.

Oleg stood for a minute on the landing. When he began to go down he heard the sound of the outside door opening and somebody's hurried footsteps on the stairs. Oleg ran three steps up, hid behind a projection in the wall. From the shadows he looked down. It wasn't very light, but Oleg recognized the man coming up the stairs. It was Veria.

Obviously Veria did not suspect that he was not alone. The muscles of his face were relaxed. He was smiling. But his smile was strange, unpleasant. The thin lips of his large mouth were trembling sensually; in his eyes, under the pince-nez, a kind of restless, covetous fire burned. Several times he passed his small hand excitedly over his bald spot. A new, loathsome, almost indecent expression appeared on his face. Oleg became frightened. He had never seen Veria so hideous.

Waiting until Veria disappeared behind Lily's door, he went quietly down the stairs to the street.

"My God! What an ugly bastard!" he whispered, sighing with relief. "So, he also goes to her. . . ."

Oleg walked along the pavement slowly, trying to collect his thoughts.

Aimless in the empty street, he did not notice that some shadows behind him ran from one entrance to another. When he was about to turn off Sennaya Street into a lane, having decided to go home, somebody from behind threw a coat over him. At the same instant a strong hand struck him painfully on the head. He groaned and dropped to the pavement. Three prowlers threw themselves on him and began to beat him mercilessly. Oleg moaned.

They beat him silently and long. When Oleg stopped moaning and lay quite still, they picked up the coat and ran toward the Don.

BOOK II

PART FOUR

⎍⎍⎍⎍⎍⎍⎍⎍⎍⎍⎍⎍⎍⎍⎍⎍⎍⎍⎍⎍⎍⎍⎍⎍⎍⎍⎍⎍⎍⎍

CHAPTER 1

"WHILE DRIVING through the city I noticed a great number of queues. I was particularly struck by the queues in which everybody carried either bottles, tin cans, or jugs. What are these queues for?"

Romain Rouen smiled pleasantly. He was much afraid of embarrassing Gorin with this question. He was in a strange country, had been received very warmly, and like a well-bred guest, he didn't want to cause any unpleasantness. But curiosity consumed him.

"What you saw were queues for kerosene," replied Gorin.

Romain Rouen was surprised. "That means that a shortage of fuel is being felt?"

"Yes. Fuel is being used for tractors; that's why there isn't enough for the housewives' oil stoves. The fuel supply can't keep up with the mechanization of agriculture." Gorin explained word for word just as Veria had answered a similar question from him.

"Oh!" exclaimed the Frenchman, and raised his eyebrows understandingly. He was quite satisfied with Gorin's reply. In his imagination an absorbing picture arose: vast fields, on which thousands of tractors were moving, driven by cheerful lads and lasses. After this picture, the queues seemed as trifles to him. This was one of the difficulties of growth, excusable, inevitable! . . .

"How proud he must feel!" he thought of Gorin. "It has fallen to his lot to be an active partner in great transformations. An absorbing, a noble role! Yes, this is real life, heroic, never to be repeated, beyond the power of words, like Beethoven's Fifth Symphony. Ah! How I envy him!"

Romain Rouen, a great French writer and music critic of world renown, considered himself a broad-minded intellectual. He seldom agreed with generally accepted ideas. No matter how badly the majority of people might think about something, he was always ready to give it its due.

If, for instance, the majority of Frenchmen hated communists, calling them fanatics or agents of Moscow, he considered them as intellectuals championing their ideas, unjustly persecuted people, martyrs . . . If in his presence people began to talk about the inhumanity of the new laws in Russia, he frowned, brushed it off with a wave of his hands, said that one must understand the peculiar conditions in Russia and that these laws, if examined in their proper perspective, would not appear to be cruel at all but extremely humanitarian . . . If he was told that as the result of the collectivization in the Ukraine alone, six million people perished, he would exclaim: "Bah!" and not believe the speaker.

Rouen, without noticing it, had become infected with a disease very common among so-called broad-minded intellectuals—the disease of subconscious egoism. It expresses itself in a desire to stand apart from society, to contradict. As a rule it turns "broad-minded intellectuals" into narrow Philistines; into the exact opposite of what they imagine themselves to be.

Being a great writer, Romain Rouen possessed a strong, almost morbid sensitivity. He felt very keenly certain ugly aspects of French life. In his eyes these defects acquired exaggerated dimensions, casting a tremendous shadow on all that was good in his country, beclouding even what had made him a great writer. In all this Rouen was perfectly sincere. But his was the sincerity of a person with an ailing soul rather than of one with a sound objective mind. His indignation recalled the revolt of Mikhail Gorin against the Tsar's regime, years earlier, as a result of which he went to Italy. However, to be fair, Gorin had much more reason for his criticism.

Rouen viewed the revolution of 1917 and the events following it in Russa with unconcealed delight. He thought that in Russia lay the answer to his inner torments. He had written and spoken often on this subject. Soon he found himself surrounded by a chorus of enthusiasts, singing in tune with him, praising his "bold and progressive ideas." Very soon he became one of the pillars of the Council of Franco-Soviet Friendship. It never entered his head that he became at the same time

236

an obedient puppet in the skilled hands of the Moscow agents, who made use of his fame and reputation for their own ends. The "broadminded" Romain Rouen was too simple and naïve to understand that.

Thoughts of a trip to Russia often stirred Rouen's imagination. He had met Gorin in Italy. This self-taught man, who had risen from the lowest stratum of society to become one of the best modern writers, amazed and fascinated him. When Gorin, on returning to Russia, invited Rouen to visit him, he accepted immediately.

He had already been a week in Rostov. He was delighted and astounded with everything. He was pleasantly flattered by the luxury of the suburban villa in which he was housed. From the windows of the villa he admired the broad Don and the green steppe beyond the river, and sought musical comparisons for everything he saw and experienced each day. He had already been hunting and fishing. Most important, he had talked his head off with Gorin.

He had also been shown some of the sights of Rostov Province: the stud farm of pure-bred Don racehorses, and the Selmash Plant, where he examined completed seeders. Director Sidorov, however, had not shown him the main shops of the plant, where tanks were being produced.

Today was Rouen's last day in Russia. Tomorrow he was to fly to Paris. Someone proposed a visit to a school. Rouen consented eagerly.

The school was new, light, with large classrooms and a good gymnasium. The new schools were built larger than necessary so that they could be used as hospitals during a war. Of course, nobody said anything about this to Romain Rouen.

The woman interpreter who had accompanied the writer from Moscow, a very pretty young lady, drew his attention to the inscription over the entrance: Mikhail Gorin School. Rouen nodded. He had already seen Gorin's name on parks, steamers, kolkhozes, streets.

For the famous guests a pageant was being arranged at the school. Rouen sat beside Gorin among the children. Also in the hall were representatives of the Rostov Department of Education, Novikov and several other professors from the University, members of the Provincial Party Committee, and other important persons. Gorin's daughter Nina was helping the school organizers behind the scenes to prepare the show.

Childish hands had already tied the inevitable Pioneer ties around the necks of Gorin and Rouen. They were bright red. Both writers looked younger in them, gayer.

Rouen's large, long face, with its prominent eagle nose and his gray hair falling almost to his shoulders, gave him a noble appearance. With his thin fingers he stroked the bright head of the little girl leaning trustingly against him. She was looking up at his strange un-Russian face, her eyes filled with wonder. But not she alone—all the suddenly silent children gazed at them, fascinated. Mikhail Gorin particularly excited them.

His large portrait hung in the most prominent place in the hall. The children noticed the likeness. Every now and then they would point their fingers at the portrait and at Gorin, whisper to each other, laugh excitedly, then shyly hide behind each other when Gorin looked at them. A boy sitting beside Gorin continually felt the sleeve of his suit, the buttons; he even touched the gray mustache.

"They're real, they're real," Gorin reassured him, laughing.

The heads of the school were not less excited. The desire to please the guests, and fear of the local Party chieftains whom they had never before seen in such numbers, made them hustle about behind the scenes more than was necessary. The visitors had dropped in so unexpectedly that the teachers and the Pioneer leaders had had no time to prepare a special performance for them. It was decided to repeat pieces which had been played on the Mayday holiday, fortunately quite recent so that the children hadn't yet forgotten their poems, dances, and roles. The energetic organizers had managed, in some miraculous way, to prepare one new revue. But even with this they had a great deal of trouble; particularly in making costumes.

However, everything was ready now: the costumes adjusted, the roles memorized, the scenery in place.

CHAPTER 2

ONTO THE STAGE stepped the head Pioneer leader of the school—a sturdy girl in a white blouse, black skirt, and red tie, with a boy's haircut. In military style she drew herself up like a ramrod, made a solemn face and, raising her right hand, gave the Pioneer salute.

"Pioneers!" proclaimed the leader loudly. "For the cause of Lenin-Stalin—be ready!"

"Always ready!" a deafening chorus responded.

Romain Rouen looked around and smiled. "Wonderful, wonderful!"

When quiet was restored the leader announced: "Now the first Pioneer squad will present a play in one act, *The Court Opens.*"

The curtain parted. An expectant silence reigned in the hall.

In the center of the stage the audience saw a table covered with a red cloth. At the table, facing the hall, sat five judges. A real court, even in Moscow, would probably not have exuded such inhuman grimness as the deadly serious faces of these small guardians of justice.

The oldest, the president of the court, wasn't more than twelve. His rumpled hair and badly washed ink-stained fingers provoked a smile. But the face—the face was magnificent! Revolutionary vigilance, hatred of the class enemy, profound determination to carry out his proletarian duty were reflected in his unchildlike eyes. Even an adult would have felt uncomfortable under that look.

To the left of the table stood empty benches for the accused. What accused? For the enemies of the people? That remained a terrible mystery. But already the empty benches smelled of doom, of the death sentence.

Two baby sentries with large wooden rifles in their hands looked narrowly from under helmets pulled well over their eyes; only under extreme necessity did they wipe their noses with their hands. To one side, at a separate little table, sat the prosecutor, a small Vishinsky. He twisted his mouth into a sneer, wrinkled his brow wisely. The fate of the accused, whoever they might be, was already decided. Objections were irrelevant. There was no defense. If in the real trials in Moscow defense is play-acting, then in a play trial—what's the use? Here on the stage was the basic pattern, and the effect was real and convincing.

"The court is open!" announced the president of the court. "You have the floor, Comrade Prosecutor."

Little Vishinsky got up, poured water from a carafe into a glass, and began to drink. He drank slowly: so slowly that the real Vishinsky would in as much time have finished with a couple of enemies of the people.

"Comrade Pioneers!" began the prosecutor at last. "The Council has entrusted me with investigating and presenting before the Pioneer Court certain suspicious individuals who for many years, under all kinds of plausible and implausible pretexts, have tried to poison the consciousness of Soviet children. These individuals are the heroes of fairy tales. Some of them are Russian, some of them have been sent here by our enemies abroad."

The prosecutor spoke seriously, without a hint of irony. The wise-

239

acre from the Moscow Department of Education who had written his part probably considered Soviet children sufficiently experienced in life to understand thoroughly the significance of the charge.

And he was not mistaken. The audience understood every word of the prosecutor. A deathly silence reigned.

The president of the court called the accused.

Under a heavy guard the most unexpected and motley group of characters came onto the stage. Here came the Witch with her broom, the beautiful Cinderella dressed in a magnificent gown and with her slipper in her hand, a Princess in a golden robe, a Prince with a feather in his broad hat, Father Christmas, and Ivan the Fool.

The children, who had never in their lives seen any except ragged gray clothes, gasped at the sight of such bright creatures, and a great wave of irrepressible delight spread through the hall.

"Look, look! Father Christmas!" shouted one.

"But who is that in such a beautiful dress?" asked another.

"I don't know."

"Oh! How beautiful she is!"

An unhealthy mood had developed! The leader, who until now had been standing in the wings of the stage behind the curtain, came out to restore order. "Comrade Pioneers! Please observe silence! You should be ashamed of yourselves!"

Little by little the children quieted down, but their eyes shone with happiness as before; they looked with rapture at the heroes of the fairy tales, unable to tear their eyes away.

"Who are you?" the president of the court sternly asked the Princess in the golden robe. She stepped forward and suddenly stumbled. The Prince held her up.

"Oh! I stepped on something hard," she whined affectedly. "It must have been a straw."

The prosecutor explained to the judge: "This is the same Princess who felt a pea through twenty feather beds and twenty mattresses."

"Oh, dear! Oh, dear! I couldn't sleep that time; my side hurts even yet," the Princess whimpered again.

"If you are such a mollycoddle, how on earth do you manage to work?" one of the judges asked her.

"But I don't work."

"Who, then, prepares your dinner and clothes you?"

"Servants and maids."

"So, somebody works for you. That means that you are an exploiter!"

240

The judges whispered among themselves. The president raised his head.

"The next accused. Who are you?" he addressed Cinderella, who had stepped out to the front. She told her happily ending story.

"So . . . so . . ." drawled the president ironically. "That is how you betrayed the working class and became another exploiter like this Princess!"

Cinderella, covering her face with her hands in shame, sat down beside the golden Princess to await her fate.

Finishing quickly with the Witch, about whom the prosecutor merely explained, "She is a fable; there are no such beings," the court examined the case of Father Christmas.

"Name?"

"Father Christmas," answered the accused in a childish voice, adjusting the pillow under his red coat.

"Have you any other names or nicknames?" asked the president sternly.

"I have, I have," answered Father Christmas in a guilty voice. "I am called Santa Claus, Saint Nicholas . . ."

"A suspicious individual," remarked the president dryly. "What is your occupation?"

"On Christmas Eve I creep into houses through the chimneys to bring presents for the children."

"A likely story! We don't believe you. You creep into the houses to spy!" and the president thumped the desk threateningly with his little fist.

"Ay!" cried the unmasked Father Christmas in fright. He fell to his knees, begged forgiveness. But the merciless president waved his hand, the sentries caught him under the armpits, dragged him to the bench.

The last one was Ivan the Fool. He was dressed in rags, his face smeared with dirt.

"Your social status?" asked the judge.

"Peasant."

"Have you ever hired workers?"

"No. I have always been a worker myself."

"Have you any property?"

"No. I had one horse, but he was sway-backed."

The chief judge expanded in a satisfied smile. "Everything is clear. He is one of us. Free him."

Ivan the Fool, bestowing an idiotic smile on the judges, sat down beside the prosecutor.

241

The president of the court rose and, addressing the hall, announced loudly: "The Pioneer Court pronounces the following judgment: all these Princesses, Princes, Cinderellas, Witches, and Father Christmases are harmful elements. The stories about them are not for Soviet children. There should be no place for them in our books," and, clearing his throat, he added decisively: "They must be liquidated. Sentries, lead them away!"

The sentries began to drive the condemned ones from the stage with blows. They, in accordance with the script, defended themselves, wept, cried, smearing the make-up over their faces. Then as they went off stage, something incredible happened in the hall. The children, who had been sitting quietly, cried out desperately: "Don't! Don't!" "Leave them, they're good!" "Don't shoot them! Please, don't shoot them!"

An uproar followed. Many of the children cried, went into hysterics. The more courageous boys jumped from their places, ready to rush to the help of their loved ones. A girl sitting beside Romain Rouen begged him with tears in her eyes to save the unfortunates.

Rouen didn't understand her words, but sensed perfectly what she wanted, looked in confusion, now at her, now at Gorin. During the play Gorin, not knowing where to hide from shame, had been gloomily silent. "A silly play. And they put it on for a foreigner!"

Rouen had understood the meaning of the play even without translation. He felt embarrassed, as if someone had committed an indecent act in front of him. He was no longer able to smile even diplomatically.

The Pioneer leader in the meantime rushed about the stage like a frightened hen, cackling and fluttering. Her shouting could not be heard above the noise, but her distorted mouth and the swollen veins on her neck were visible. The situation threatened to become a scandal.

Novikov got up and hurried back stage. There he saw the completely flabbergasted and frightened teachers surrounded by the bellowing little artists. A young woman was calming Cinderella, who was crying from fright.

"The dressed-up children must be shown to the others at once!" exclaimed Novikov and pulled the girl's sleeve roughly to attract her attention.

The young woman turned around quickly. It was Nina Gorin. Novikov started and was at a loss at first what to say. Nina raised her eyes to him inquiringly. He saw that her eyes were gray, bottomless, and sad like a northern lake in autumn.

"I'm very sorry for treating you so roughly," he said, trying to cover

242

his embarrassment with a smile. "But it seems to me that we must show these Cinderellas and Princesses to the children as soon as possible. Otherwise they'll pull the hall apart."

"Yes, yes, please do something," said Nina, studying his face with interest. "Aren't you Professor Novikov?" she asked unexpectedly.

"Yes."

"Lida told me about you. And I recognized you from her description. . . . Oh! What a noise! I don't know who on earth suggested that play. If I had known what it was about I would have forbidden it."

"Yes, the play was quite out of place."

"Not out of place, just silly!" exclaimed Nina.

One of the women teachers rushed up, her face pale and tear-stained. Trembling with fear, she asked them to go out on the stage with the children. "I'm afraid to show myself! Oh! How terrible this is! How terrible! Whatever will they do with me now!"

Wasting no time on the teacher, Novikov asked Nina to take Cinderella by the hand, he himself took the Princess in the golden robe and, signaling to the others to follow them, they went out in front of the curtain.

"Here they are! Look, all alive and in good health!" he said loudly, raising the artists' hands.

A howl of delight rolled over the hall.

Novikov and Nina came down from the stage with the children. They made them sit around Gorin and Rouen. Gorin thanked Novikov with a glance. Nina sat down beside the professor, pressing a little blond boy to her side.

"Aunty, Aunty," the boy asked, "tell me: is there really a Father Christmas?"

"Why, of course there is such a kind old man," she replied. Suddenly the boy felt her tears on his fingers.

"Aunty, you're crying?"

"Am I? . . ."

The hall was quiet again. The program continued. The performance ended happily without any more incidents.

At the Paris airport a crowd of reporters met Romain Rouen. Among them the reporter of the communist paper *L'Humanité* stood out prominently.

"Do you consider your trip to Russia successful?"

"Oh, yes. A complete success."

243

"What do you think of Stalin?"

"All he wants is peace. He is all for peaceful collaboration among nations."

"How does the question of the exchange of students stand? Did he promise to help you?"

"Oh yes, oh yes! I am convinced that there will be no obstacles to this on his part."

Rouen answered questions in a confident tone, smiling broadly, joking with the reporters. But deep in his heart he was uneasy. The memory of the children's play in Rostov had not left him. The trial of the heroes of the fairy stories had touched his heart. Why? Perhaps because these heroes were bound up with his childhood? Or because the spontaneous reaction of the children in the hall awakened his conscience?

He always liked to talk with reporters, liked the attention of the press. Yet the happiness which he usually felt on such occasions was missing this time. Between his heart and his happiness were the grim unchildlike faces of the little judges, the weeping girl pressed to his breast and demanding justice of him. This seemingly insignificant episode had spoiled the whole trip for him. By all logic it was absurd. But feeling seldom gives way to logic. It depressed and irritated him.

He said nothing about this feeling or the Pioneers' trial to the reporters, or later even to his friends. But he remembered it all his life.

CHAPTER 3

MIKHAIL GORIN had one peculiarity not yet known to Novikov. Encouraged by his first successful talk with the writer during the chess game, Novikov considered the wheels well greased: that Gorin was simply bursting with impatience to begin work on the play, inspired by the idea which had been presented to him so subtly. (Novikov could not recall Glushak's role without a smile.)

One can well imagine how downcast the self-confident professor would have been if he had learned that the writer had completely forgotten his momentary enthusiasm, his conversation, even the professor himself.

But that was exactly what happened. Gorin seldom trusted sudden enthusiasms, having convinced himself by experience of their barrenness. He trusted only long-contemplated ideas, hard as rock. Only when he was convinced of their soundness did he seat himself at his writing desk.

Mikhail Gorin had forgotten about Novikov because the past week had been very full and muddled. Larin's suicide, the arrival of Romain Rouen, Pavel's illness, Nina's strange behavior. . . . Nina worried him particularly. During the past week she had not once been riding with the Cossacks and apparently was no longer interested in it.

"So the fresh air didn't help," Gorin mused, sighing. "Well, you can't go against nature. Sooner or later I'll have to part with her." In affairs of the heart, and especially of such delicate ones as those of his own daughter, Gorin felt himself so helpless that sighing was all he could do. "Maybe things will arrange themselves of their own accord," he thought. From all these anxieties Gorin was very tired and, more than anything else, he wanted tranquility and rest.

So when Feodor Novikov came to him, a week after the banquet, with a precisely prepared report expounding in detail his point of view on the epoch of Ivan the Terrible, Gorin did not at first understand what he was talking about.

Novikov had prudently taken Glushak with him. It seemed to him that his own appearance in Gorin's house would be more natural with the Academician along. Glushak was by now so afraid of Novikov that the young professor even found it necessary to comfort him, so that his behavior wouldn't arouse suspicion in Gorin's house.

"Why, this is a complete report!" Gorin exclaimed in surprise, turning over the pages of Novikov's work. "I never thought that you would take our discussion so much to heart. I must confess that I had completely forgotten about it. This week has been so terribly jumbled."

Novikov smiled understandingly. "I considered it my duty to set out on paper my thoughts about that epoch. As I promised you then, I intend to collect material for your play from the archives. These are merely my own views, but they may possibly be of some interest to you."

Gorin looked with embarrassment, now at Novikov, now at Glushak, not knowing what to say. "I suppose it's too late for me to retreat. If you have gone to so much trouble, I am obliged to read your report," he said, somewhat embarrassed. "Pyotr, just look what youth is like now! It's dangerous to talk with them: before you open your mouth you're already bound with obligations."

"In this case you must blame the Academician," Novikov hastened to interject with a smile, glancing at Glushak with the emphasized modesty of a young scholar before his elder. "It was Academician

Glushak who first gave you the idea of writing a historical play."

"Yes, yes, I remember," laughed Gorin, and shook a threatening finger at the Academician.

Glushak knew perfectly well that he was playing a fool's role: not wanting to do so, he was helping some secret scheme of Novikov's. The latter looked at him with kindness, even affection.

"Damn him! What an actor he is!" thought Glushak. "The devil himself is probably controlling his face." He recalled with a shudder the harsh tone in which this same Novikov spoke to him when they were alone.

Outside the door, a girl's voice was heard singing a gay Italian song and then Nina Gorin, in a blue dress, light and airy, came into the room. The song stopped abruptly. Nina looked at Novikov, a little embarrassed.

"How do you do, Uncle Pyotr?" she addressed Academician Glushak, evading Novikov's intent gaze. "Mama wants you to come see her; she's on the terrace. The aquarium there is out of order. Maybe you can help her fix it."

Glushak rose readily and, asking Gorin to excuse him, went out. Nina was going to follow him but Gorin stopped her. "Nina, meet Professor Novikov."

Nina approached Novikov, her silk dress rustling, and shook his hand firmly. "We are already acquainted, Papa," she said, and blushed slightly, recalling the scene at the school and the somewhat extraordinary circumstances of her meeting with the professor.

Gorin eyed Novikov and Nina up and down with half-closed eyes and suddenly laughed to himself. "What a fool I am!" he thought. "I seriously thought that this young professor prepared the report for me. It was merely a pretext for coming to the house to meet her."

Gorin, a moment ago annoyed by the unexpected appearance of Novikov, now rejoiced so much that, approaching the young couple, he put his arms around their shoulders in a fatherly manner. "While I'm reading your report, Professor, you'd better take a walk in the garden. Nina, show him our greenhouse and other interesting things. We have a beautiful garden, Professor."

Novikov looked at him in surprise, not understanding these sudden embraces. "Please, Comrade Gorin, if you do not agree with anything in my report, don't stand on ceremony: comment on it freely. I shall be grateful for it."

"Why such formality? Why do you call me Comrade Gorin? Just call me Mikhail. And about the report, don't worry, I'll read it criti-

246

cally," and Gorin, unable to restrain himself, winked at Novikov.

"Ah, youth, youth! What wiles they use!" Thinking thus and smiling beneath his mustache, Gorin propelled Novikov and Nina slowly toward the door. At the door he pressed them together, tweaked Novikov's ear painfully; and before the latter could figure out what it was all about, he found himself with Nina in the hall.

Alone in the room, Gorin laughed loudly and happily. Going to the desk he put a heavy paperweight on Novikov's report and winked again slyly. Then he lay down on the sofa, stretched out contentedly, and closed his eyes, smiling blissfully.

No matchmaker ever felt more satisfied and happy than Mikhail Gorin at that moment.

CHAPTER 4

HER FATHER'S sudden concern amused and irritated Nina. For devilment she decided to spoil his scheme. She led Novikov into the spacious greenhouse which adjoined the palace, and in a dry business-like tone, like a guide, began to acquaint him with its many-flowered aristocracy: "These are gardenias. They aren't very colorful, but have a lovely smell. Abroad, men often pin this flower to their lapels— doubtless to attract the attention of women." (Novikov didn't even twitch an eyebrow.) "And look there—the orchids. That is a woman's flower and the one I like best. Do you want to see them?"

"I do," answered Novikov absent-mindedly, wondering how Gorin was taking his report. Today's conversation and the conduct of the writer displeased him very much. He missed the former enthusiasm for his idea. Thinking about Gorin upset Novikov so much that he wasn't listening to Nina at all. Gorin would probably have lost some sleep from disappointment if he had known that the young professor was not thinking about his daughter at that moment, but about the foolish report, about Drozd, about his career.

"Why! you're not listening to me," said Nina, wrinkling her nose in surprise. She had a comic habit of wrinkling her nose when she didn't understand something. At the moment she didn't understand Novikov. Often she had spoken with men who were stunned by her beauty, looking as if they had lost their wits and hearing. But with this professor it was different. She saw that he was taking notice neither of her words, nor of herself! Of her, Nina Gorin!

"You were talking about the garden . . ." said Novikov uncertainly. They were walking out of the greenhouse into the garden.

"Of course not; I just asked you the second time if you like fishing," she exclaimed, and laughed. "Really! You're as absent-minded as a professor."

Novikov smiled guiltily. "How badly, how tactlessly this has turned out," he thought, vexed with himself. He decided to take himself in hand and for the time being to forget about Gorin.

He looked around at the park. What he saw stunned him, knocking out of his head everything except amazement.

"Is it possible! Is it possible that what I see actually exists?" he asked Nina, almost stuttering.

She laughed, unconcernedly tossing a light braid of her hair. "Everyone who sees this park for the first time can't believe his eyes. But I assure you, it really does exist."

The broad panorama spread out in front of Novikov was so fantastic in its splendor that his brain refused to accept it as of this earth, much less a production of human hands. Sweeping green terraces descended in broad steps toward the Don, their contours changing constantly, some curving smoothly, some zigzagging sharply, others falling straight. The mighty sweep of the huge masses of green was the motif of the park. Novikov had taken only a few steps when the landscape began to change, as if some magic had moved great masses of earth. If the terraces were the foundation of the landscape, the broad granite stairway, cutting deeply into them and descending to the Don itself, was the center of the composition. With its clear geometrical form the stairway held the park together.

Once satisfied with the soundness of the composition, the architect who planned this park perhaps a hundred years ago for the heirs of the Count Zubov had given free rein to his imagination. On the slopes of the terraces dark poplars, casting long shadows, rose toward the clouds; beside a pool green cataracts of willows tumbled; or mighty oaks, shutting off half the sky with their broad crests, shot upward in gigantic outbursts.

At the foot of these giants, graceful rows of trimmed bushes and small trees were arranged between broad carpets of flower beds, as varied in form and contour as in color. Circles, ovals, stars followed one another. Amid the foliage and flowers, graceful arbors in white marble, Greek statues of youths and maidens, enormous vases with flowers gleamed in the sun.

248

In the middle of the stairway, halfway down to the river, was the fountain—three bronze maidens strained in passionate transport toward the Don, bearing in their hands a great horn of plenty. Over the rim of the horn, water fell in a broad singing stream, turned to wine in the rays of the sun. Small winged cupids blew into long trumpets, surrounding the maidens in a merry ring. Thin streams of water came out of their trumpets, breaking into fine spray.

Novikov was convinced that the sun shone more brightly here, the foliage was more luxuriant, the shadows from the trees were deeper, the flowers bloomed more magnificently, as if nature herself had decided to help the talented artist. The broad Don, the steppe receding beyond it, served as a background for the park. A magic, fabulous picture.

Novikov, who rightly considered as the height of luxury his two rooms on Budenny Avenue with their view of the garbage heap, stood in a stupor.

"Surely it can't be that Mikhail Gorin, to whom this palace, this park, and a host of servants is given; who is surrounded with honor, fame, almost as great as the official glory of Stalin and certainly more sincere—surely after all this it can't be that Gorin is still discontented and even suspected by the Politburo of revolt? What more does he want?"

Novikov was a man of the Soviet regime. He knew well that most of the people dreamed of nothing more than a piece of bread, hot soup, and a pair of rubbers every three years. He prided himself that he had attained such social status that he could dream about the University Director's four-room apartment and even of such a priceless treasure as a pass to the special store. He realized the boldness of his dream and really had little faith in it, just as an ordinary mortal in Rostov might feel about his dream of getting a new pair of rubbers.

He would have to finish undermining the present Director, who was no fool and was holding hard to his job. And then, how many ambitious people beside Novikov were after the coveted job! A difficult struggle lay ahead. Novikov knew that for each piece of bread the Soviet man must strangle his fellow man, snatch it right out of his mouth. He knew also that for this piece of bread it was necessary to fight, not only figuratively but literally, with real blood flowing. How often had he seen terrible scenes in the queues where hungry people pushed each other around just to get a pound of barley or ten cubes of sugar! How often had he looked with fearful respect at the clerk, a guardian of untold treasure in the form of a sack of flour or a barrel of herrings, standing before the empty shelves and keeping order among hungry hands straining towards him. How often had he looked with envy at some lucky one who had been able, without losing his life, to get his ration. Novikov's own face had broken into a happy smile when he had worked his way out of a crush with an old herring in his hand, as if it were the largest pearl in the world, obtained at the risk of his life from the bottom of the sea. Peoples' tastes and desires had changed; they had learned to value dirt at its weight in gold.

That was why Novikov found absolutely absurd the idea that Mikhail Gorin who, before he was dead, was already living in paradise, could want still more from life. What could he want? Novikov was so used to thinking about human desire in petty, material terms that he was incapable of imagining a man who had everything material and still was unhappy. Moral values? Nonsense! One could write about them, read about them in the papers, argue for them before others at meetings, but surely no one in the whole of Russia believed in them seriously! Moral values disappeared long ago with the soul of the last priest, shot somewhere in a concentration camp on the Solovetski Islands.

Novikov began to doubt the deductions of Moscow about Gorin. So far he had noticed very little of what Drozd had spoken about so seriously, and about which he had warned him. What kind of indignation? What kind of revolt? The trivial remarks of a great man, used to expressing his thoughts aloud? Some discontent, a barely noticeable vexation which could be explained by age. It was more probably a feeling of dissatisfaction with himself, rather than with the regime or the policy of the Party.

The fact that Gorin had recently not written articles nor made speeches supporting Moscow's policy could be attributed simply to fatigue. Moscow could reprint his old articles, as had been done successfully. Then why the alarm? What was the need for Novikov's task?

As if searching for an answer to his thoughts, he looked closely at Nina. Now he noticed her beauty, but this did not surprise him. What else could one expect in this marvelous park, amid nature brought to perfection by the hand of an artist? Here her beauty appeared as natural as orchids in a greenhouse. The park and the palace were her world. But was she happy?

Novikov didn't notice that he had said the last words aloud. Nina raised her eyebrows, surprised to hear such a personal question from him. Then, thinking that he meant the park, she replied: "Oh, yes! I love this park. There are many mysterious corners in it with shaded

250

ponds where, as my father says, even when sober you can catch mermaids."

Novikov laughed. "Has he tried to catch them?"

"No, but there are a lot of carp here. Do you like fishing?"

"I was very fond of that sport in my boyhood."

"In that case I'll show you an excellent pool. It's not far—a real fisherman's paradise."

They turned toward the broad stairway. Nina moved lightly and gaily; now beside him, now attracted by some flower, she ran ahead, waited smiling.

"This main fountain which you see from here is called the Three Graces. It's very noisy, like a waterfall. When we get down to it we won't be able to talk."

"Wonderful, wonderful!" repeated Novikov. He noticed with satisfaction that not one of the bronze graces was lovelier than the lively Nina, also bronzed by the sun.

Looking at her, Feodor could not believe that the funny, uncouth, walrus-faced Mikhail Gorin was her father. He remembered now with a smile how he had pictured Gorin's daughter when Glushak mentioned her the first time. He had expected to meet some house plant, pale, drooping, boring. Instead, beside him was a completely unexpected being—merry, vital, blossoming in the full strength of youth. Nina's shining gray eyes sparkled with the joy of life; pleasure was reflected on her face in a smile, often changing into unexpected bursts of clear laughter. Her laughter was also special—melodious, infectious.

It seemed as though all the statues, flowers, and fountains had been assembled in the park to make her life comfortable and beautiful, and she took her pleasure among them joyfully. She was in her native element, like a swallow on the plains.

When she walked beside him Novikov noticed a faint fragrance of lavender coming from her and it seemed to him that this was not perfume, but she herself, her shoulders and arms enveloping him in an elusive cloud, tender, womanly and alluring. It disturbed his thoughts, and his heartbeat quickened.

"It is just the unexpectedness of it," he thought, vexed with himself for such weakness. "After all, one doesn't meet girls like her often; she is probably the only one in the whole country with such a favorable combination—foreign upbringing, elegant life, her father a celebrity, plus her natural beauty and character. Everything is explained very simply!"

Nina behaved naturally. She didn't talk the nonsense usual between

251

slightly acquainted people. Drawing her eyebrows together and driving a smile from her face, she questioned him about the University, about his work, told him about her own studies at the Conservatory. She treated him, not as a professor, but as an equal. Novikov, accustomed to seeing shy or flattering students around him, was struck by her free manner.

"Of course, they have all kinds of celebrities in their house. Why should she be shy with me?" he thought, and suddenly became jealous.

Nina had dropped the tone of a guide and talked now in a friendly way, although caution and mistrust still lingered in her large eyes. After they had passed the noisy fountain she stopped suddenly and looked searchingly at his broad face with its high forehead.

"Tell me, Feodor Pavlovich," she addressed him. "Isn't it true that Papa invited you to the house to introduce you to me?" She spoke seriously, but her eye was roguish.

"No, you're mistaken," replied Feodor, a little confused. "My visit was purely on business. I hadn't the slightest idea of seeing you."

"Give me your word of honor that it is so."

"Word of honor! . . . But why?"

"Oh, that's good! So you didn't come to woo me, as a suitor," she exclaimed and suddenly laughed. "And all the time I thought . . . In that case let's shake hands and be friends," and she added, in the tone of a conspirator: "I hate suitors."

Jokingly she shook his hand, her face beaming. Stupefied by such an approach, Feodor looked at her, smiled, felt a little foolish, a little embarrassed, but basically good. "Where have I seen such eyelashes?" he thought suddenly. "Like the wings of a night butterfly!" He wanted to say something nice to her, something in keeping with herself, and so he told her what he was thinking:

"You have lovely eyes, Nina."

Her eyebrows quivered; she freed her fingers from his broad hand, became serious, and said bluntly: "We'd better turn along this path. The pool is beside that grove."

Feodor gathered that he had committed a blunder.

In conversation with women Feodor almost instinctively adopted a half jocular, slightly teasing, slightly condescending tone. He found such a tone very convenient. It was easy to change from it to familiarity, a light flirtation, or an excuse for leaving a bore without offending her. But he discovered that his well-tried tone was completely out of place with Nina. More than that, she set the tone and he yielded to her with pleasure. This was the Novikov who, up to this time, had treated women with contempt. He suddenly discovered in himself a feeling of slavish rapture in her beauty, her voice, and even her mind. His brain protested helplessly while his whole being delighted in the contemplation of this surprising girl.

CHAPTER 5

WHEN THEY approached the grove Nina was again in a happy mood. It was not in her character to sulk for long. Among the slim birches the blue water of the pool glittered. The loud voices of men swearing and laughing could be heard coming from the grove.

"It's a little too noisy for paradise," Feodor remarked. "Fish don't like noise."

Nina smiled slyly. "I believe I know what's going on. It's Cheprok catching crabs again. We have an old man with us. A very amusing person."

They came out on the bank. Two lads and an old man with a red nose were fussing around in the water beside a large fallen tree. They were all shouting, but the shrill voice of the old man was heard above them all. He was cursing in an anatomical way—naming kidneys, spleen, heart . . .

On the bank, beside the scattered clothes, a stooped, thin man sat smoking a cigarette, watching the racket, obviously bored. On noticing Nina and Novikov he got up slowly and came to meet them.

"This is my brother Pavel," said Nina, introducing them. Shaking Pavel's weak hand, Feodor with difficulty restrained a grimace. He felt that in this park everything must be in harmony, like Nina. The lanky Pavel broke this illusion unpleasantly. Pavel's face recalled Mikhail Gorin, but in the bloated features the will and energy of his father were missing. In the sunshine his thin hair and sickly skin appeared particularly ugly. From his appearance Feodor guessed that he was a drunkard, although he was sober at the moment.

"Crabs again?" Nina asked him.

"Yes, but no luck. They've been fussing around for an hour without result," replied Pavel in a hoarse voice, looking at Novikov coldly.

The big-nosed old man—Feodor guessed at once that he was Cheprok—was shouting at the fat-faced lads:

"Hold him! Hold on! Don't be afraid! He won't bite off your finger! Hell! You've let him go again! . . . Here, move the tree over, I'll crawl under. Is that how you devils catch crabs!"

The devils sent him to hell, shook their fists at him.

Nina, seeing that Cheprok and the lads were so absorbed that they still did not notice her, and fearing that she might hear some incautious words from them, made her presence known: "Uncle Cheprok, have you caught anything?"

As soon as Cheprok heard her voice he ducked up to his neck in the water and shouted to Pavel: "Quick, give me my shirt! What the devil brought her here?"

Catching the shirt that was thrown to him, Cheprok put it on right there in the water. He buttoned it up carefully, as if he were going to a party, and again pushed his hand under the tree trunk to get the obstinate crab.

"You're being funny, you devil! None of your tricks—you won't get away! So! Pinch! Fine!" Cheprok flashed his eyes desperately, but now cursed in a low voice. Suddenly he jerked his elbows, wagged his head joyfully—he had caught the rascal. He threw the green monster onto the grass and then came out on the bank himself.

"Heigh-ho! I've tired myself out!" he puffed. "The youngsters are no good. They know how to eat them, but they're weak on the catching. . . . Come out of the water! What are you gaping at!"

Nina went behind a hillock so as not to embarrass the men. Cheprok, his wet shirt clinging to his body, began to pull his pants over his thin legs.

"Why did you put your shirt on?" Feodor asked with interest.

Cheprok frowned angrily, looked askance at Feodor from under his thick eyebrows and didn't reply. He turned to the boys: "Take the crab to the chef, and be quick about it. And don't fool around—the stable's got to be cleaned!"

Chuckling, the lads went slowly toward the palace.

"Why don't you answer about your shirt?" Pavel said to Cheprok.

"And to whom have I the honor of speaking?" asked Cheprok, and again looked suspiciously at Feodor. The latter introduced himself.

"So you're a professor? Well, well . . ." drawled Cheprok. "I knew a professor, only he was a specialist in breaking and theft—a housebreaker, that is. They called him professor because he wore glasses. I was in the same cell with him in Odessa. That was long ago—he's dead now, of course—God rest his soul."

254

Looking toward Nina, whose blue dress could be seen far away among the birches, Cheprok hurriedly pulled his shirt off his bent back and wrung it thoroughly. Now the puzzle was solved for Feodor. On the old man's chest a tattoo was pricked out in powder blue: a dogs' wedding—a picture not for tender girlish eyes.

Pavel explained: "That was a trick his friends played on him—in his younger days. He got terribly tight once, and while he was asleep they persuaded a specialist to decorate him, for a ruble. Now Cheprok has to deprive himself of showing his manly chest in ladies' company."

Cheprok took a pouch and clay pipe out of his pocket and leisurely began to light up.

"Yes," he confirmed, "I was quite a sinner in those days. I recovered and noticed nothing. Right after my drunk I went to a mixed steam bath—there were that kind at one time in Odessa—and the women nearly beat me to death with their tubs. I didn't understand at first what was wrong. But when I did, I felt like crying. You couldn't wash it off, nor rub it off. I wasn't going to pull off my skin, and so it remained."

"But you should have tattooed another one on top of it—it would have been a lot better," advised Feodor.

Cheprok scratched the back of his head in amazement. "Just think of that! How many years I've lived—and that idea never entered my head! . . . But it would be a pity: the man did his best, they paid him money. It would be too bad to spoil his work." Cheprok looked slyly at Feodor.

Feodor and Pavel laughed. "What a patron of art!"

Nina rejoined them, holding a bouquet of flowers in her hand.

"Have you finished with your secrets?" she asked Cheprok, looking at him with a mischievous, boyish smile. Cheprok merely scattered a thousand sparks from his pipe, surrounding himself in smoke.

Nina went over to the edge of the pool and lay down on the grass. Supporting her cheek in her hand, she gazed thoughtfully at the water.

"It's nice here, isn't it?" she said, and Novikov realized that she was putting the question to him. He nodded. He did not wish to voice his thoughts. Now that the lads had gone away it was quiet on the shady bank. Through half-closed lids Feodor saw how the reflection of the still water flitted over Nina's thoughtful face. From time to time she threw flowers into the water and watched the slow current in the pool bear them away.

"Feodor Pavlovich," she said. "Come here."

Not a professor, but an obedient boy came.

"Now, lie down. Here, beside me. Look at the water. What do you see?"

"Water," replied Feodor.

"No, no! . . . You see the sky. And when I throw in a flower, small waves come and among them appear strange visions. . . . Don't you see?"

"I see . . . your face," Feodor said softly.

Nina laughed.

Pavel suddenly got up.

"Let's go home, Cheprok," he said thickly and, touching the old man on the shoulder, walked slowly away from the pool. Cheprok jumped up and ambled after him.

"Uncle Cheprok!" Nina called, and got up.

Cheprok stopped, looking sly and a little guilty.

"Give this bouquet to Mama. Tell her I'm coming soon." She took a red flower and stuck it in a buttonhole of Cheprok's still-wet shirt. "This flower goes very well with your nose," she said smiling, and kissed the old man's cheek. On Cheprok's face a vast number of merry wrinkles appeared, and adoration shone from under his heavy eyebrows.

"Oh, Nina! Nina! You're an awful girl!" He shook his head and hobbled toward Pavel, who was waiting for him.

"Pavel's as jealous as Othello," she said. "He can't bear it when anyone is with me. Cheprok and I are his best friends. Pay no attention to his gloom; he's a very kind fellow and very unhappy."

"He drinks?"

"Yes. Because of a broken love affair. You see, he lived a long time in Paris. And there, the very air is somehow special, as if it had been created for romance. . . . Pavel fell in love with a woman. I've seen her. She was not beautiful—a pale face, with eyes large, black, and burning in a rather unnatural way. Perhaps she was ill. She used to laugh nervously, not sincerely . . . But he worshiped her, couldn't live without her. She was unfaithful and in the end left him. He began to drink then. When he left with Papa for Russia he thought he would forget, that it would pass. It was worse than ever."

Feodor listened to her attentively, with serious face and eyes screwed up in thought. Elusive images wandered through his mind, now arousing sadness, now perplexity. "What an unusual world Nina lives in!" he thought. "What good people they are here and how they love each other!"

Even the unhappy Pavel touched his imagination not by the tragedy

256

of his life, but by its strangeness. "Everything here is unlike everyday life. The Russian tragedy is coarse tragedy, simple and boring, like a toothache. Meager rations, death from starvation, political arrest, shooting, or suicide to avoid it—that is the everyday tragedy of the Russian people. But the tragedy of love! Where? In Paris!"

Novikov suddenly felt a yearning unusual for him. So unbelievably beautiful did this world appear to him that he already began to doubt its permanence. "Here people are kind and affectionate; there are warm feelings, precious traditions . . . This world reminds me in some way of my early childhood. But childhood passed long ago. I've already become used to the thought that it never existed, that it was simply a dream. Now this dream is living before my eyes. Is it possible that this fantastic island can remain unharmed for long, untouched by the raging ocean surrounding it?"

It hurt Novikov to think of its instability. It hurt him the more because somewhere deep inside him he felt that he had been sent here not to strengthen that world. There were no evident reasons for it, but Novikov knew that this was one of those feelings which he trusted more than the deductions of his mind. A foreboding shadow rose before his eyes, a menace of catastrophe. The treasures he had found, living but incredible as a miracle, threatened to vanish into an abyss . . .

"Why are you so silent?" Nina asked, looking anxiously at him.

"I'm thinking about your suitors. What are they like?" Feodor replied with a weak smile.

"Oh, it's not worth thinking about them!" exclaimed Nina. "They're all boring, all alike—they have no faces of their own."

"How is that?"

"Just so. They all say the same things. Their eyes have the same look. It's as if they were looking all the time into your class nature." Nina showed him what kind of look it was. She raised her eyebrows comically and peered gloweringly at him. "Before you know it, they find a dialectical error in you. And I know very well that such people can't see further than their own noses."

"And what kind of a look have I?" asked Feodor with interest.

Nina looked at him and, after a little hesitation said, blushing slightly: "You have a very strange penetrating look. It almost reaches the soul. I was afraid of you at first when you stared at me so angrily behind the stage at the school. And today in Papa's study, there seemed to be something strange in your look, almost frightening. . . . I don't know how to explain it in words."

257

"It just seemed so to you; there's nothing frightening about me," he hastened to say with a smile.

"Yes, now I see myself that it isn't so," she said, not noticing his agitation. "That came to me probably because, just recently, I was mistaken in a certain person. . . . Now I suspect all men."

In spite of the reassurance in Nina's words, Feodor was seriously alarmed. The thought came to him that it would be much more difficult to lie to her than to Mikhail Gorin. And because he would have to lie, to cheat, to wear a mask—he could not get along without doing so—he suddenly began to pity this girl, Cheprok, even Pavel, but more than anyone else he pitied himself. At that moment, as never before, he desired to be sincere, not to pretend—to be as she was. Something pure and fresh breathed from her, unlike anything he was used to among the people surrounding him, steeped in lies, intrigues, suspicions . . .

Feodor lay on his back and, half closing his eyes, looked at the sky. High above, through the sparse leaves of the birch, he saw a hawk. It was soaring, poised on widespread motionless wings.

"He has probably sought out his prey—he'll fling himself down in a moment," he thought. "There he goes!"

He sighed.

"What caused that?" asked Nina.

"Just . . ."

"There is something troubling you, isn't there? If there is, tell me—you'll feel easier."

Feodor raised himself on his elbow. "Can you cleanse the mind with words?" he asked.

"With words? Probably you can't," she said slowly. "But to keep your mind closed up is very bad."

"And is yours always open?"

"Always," she said, and gave him a direct and significant look.

"I envy you," Feodor wanted to say, but kept quiet. He rose. The talk had come to a danger line; it began to frighten him. "Maybe it's time we went back?" he said.

"Yes, I suppose it is time . . ." Nina also got up.

On the way they spoke little. When they had to cross a brook Nina asked his help with her eyes.

Feodor, happy as a boy at the chance of doing her a service, held out his hand, bracing himself as if to receive a weight. Nina leaned toward him, her elbow on his palm, and he nearly lifted her into the air.

258

But his hand was trembling.

She felt his agitation and knew it had some relation to their talk and to herself. She found nothing strange in the fact that such a chance acquaintance as Novikov, after talking with her for an hour or two, should be agitated and trembling.

But it did seem strange and not quite natural that at the same time his face was completely calm.

CHAPTER 6

LIKE ALL WOMEN, Gorin's wife Luba gave attentive heed to her feelings, especially when they were unpleasant and not clear. But unlike most women, who are capable only of analyzing them in the company of their friends, or tormenting themselves with them in private, but do nothing about them, Luba always tried to rid herself of unpleasant feelings as quickly as possible. To find their cause and eliminate it was her main anxiety.

For that reason she had called Glushak to her at the first pretext. An annoying uneasiness had taken hold of her from the moment that she first noticed the strange change in the Academician. Now, waiting for him on the terrace, she was glad that in a minute she would learn everything and be freed of the unpleasant feeling forever.

"What has happened to your aquarium, Luba?" Glushak came in, smiling respectfully and rubbing his hands. Everything about him breathed decency and propriety.

"The aquarium can wait, Pyotr. I want to speak with you alone."

"To talk? Very good. To gossip, and with such a pleasant companion as you—that is pure enjoyment." Glushak laughed, sweet as honey. His words, his honeyed laughter over something that wasn't funny, acted unpleasantly on Luba. Pointing him to an armchair opposite her, she began bluntly: "Pyotr, recently I have noticed a great change in you. Don't shake your head—I'm not mistaken. There's something disturbing you; you seem to be afraid of something. Maybe you have some personal trouble, in which case it isn't my business. But it seems to me that the change in you has some relation to Mikhail. As his wife, I want to know what is the matter. That's all. As you see, I'm speaking frankly; you are our old friend. I expect the same frankness from you."

After this disagreeable opening, Luba sighed with relief. "Now he'll answer me and everything will be clear," she thought with content and awaited his words with a smile.

But she was too late. Glushak, a week ago looking for an opportunity to warn Gorin about Novikov, now feared the slightest discussion as he feared fire. His previous intention now seemed crazy and he shuddered, imagining the results of such a revelation.

All he could do was lie.

But he was a poor actor, and his face was a bad mask. He blinked involuntarily as if from some inward pain, and began to speak hurriedly: "Forgive me, Luba, but I don't understand what change you are talking about. I haven't noticed anything in particular. . . . It's possible that the events of the past week have upset me: my report, Mirzoyan's departure from the Academy, and other things. . . . But all that has nothing to do with Mikhail."

Glushak stopped. Silently Luba looked at him, her face slowly flushing. She was ashamed for him. Her good friend was lying, and lying very clumsily. For the first time she noticed his small nose and his narrow eyes, evading her look. The pudgy fingers of his hands were trembling slightly. "How pitiful he is," thought Luba suddenly, and realized how right her vague feelings had been. Looking into the park, she asked softly: "Pyotr, how many years have you known Mikhail?"

Glushak felt the air with his fingers. "Thirty years or more, I can't remember now."

"Tell me, during all that time has Mikhail ever lied to you, even once?"

Glushak jumped up from his chair, on his face a look of injured innocence. His honor had been outraged. "Excuse me, Luba! Are you trying to say that . . . I——"

Luba turned to him abruptly. "Yes, that's exactly what I want to say. You're lying. You're lying unskillfully. I don't know why, but the worst of it is—this lie is torturing you more than anyone. So you're lying against your will!"

With her words it seemed that Luba had washed the mask from his face—it became again pitiful, dejected.

"Don't talk like that . . . don't," whispered Glushak. "Surely you know me! To tolerate such a thought . . ." Suddenly he covered his face with his hands, groaning.

Luba's heart winced. She went over to the Academician, removed his hands from his face. Glushak was crying. The tears were running down his puffy cheeks, along the sides of his little nose.

"Pyotr, Pyotr, don't torture yourself, tell me what's wrong!"

260

Glushak was silent. "If she asks me again—I won't be able to hold out," the thought flashed through his head, and his heart fell, his legs trembled. "So be it . . . I must warn them about Novikov, it will be better for me . . . Just his name, his name alone . . . Oh, my God! What am I to do?"

"Pyotr, speak!" Luba almost screamed.

Glushak was just going to whisper the dangerous word to her when a servant, a red-cheeked youth with a watering can in his hand, came onto the terrace.

"What do you want?" Luba asked, annoyed.

"I was going to water the flowers."

"How often have I told you not to enter a room without knocking! Go away!"

"Excuse me, I didn't know you were here . . ." The servant backed off the terrace, casting a quick glance at their agitated faces. "Excuse me!"

Luba looked at him with large cold eyes and shut the door behind him.

"Pyotr, speak," she said while still at the door, but there and then understood that her words were in vain. Glushak had come to his senses.

"If you don't mind, Luba, I'd better go . . . I'm exhausted, my nerves are all shot. I'm growing old. . . . And so, the tears . . ." Glushak spoke hurriedly, not looking at her. "You understand me . . ."

Luba nodded her head absent-mindedly. Yes, yes, of course, she understood a lot, even more than Glushak was going to tell her. Without bidding him farewell, she silently let him out the door, and herself went upstairs, in her heart a bitter, painful feeling.

Outside the door Glushak wiped away the sweat on his forehead; with a sigh of relief he whispered, almost surprised: "Why, I nearly ruined myself there." And imagining what would have happened to himself and his wife if he had spoken the fateful word, he groaned. "Never, not under any circumstances, will that happen again."

Then he was overpowered by the thought that from this moment a mystery would be hanging like a heavy cloud in Gorin's house, and that Luba and probably Gorin would see the key to the mystery in him. He realized that now everything would be different, that the tension would grow until it led to some kind of scandal or catastrophe. Now the loathsome vultures, which had released his heart for a while, seized it anew and still more violently with their sharp claws. Like a thief, glancing around, he slunk into Gorin's study.

"How on earth could I weaken so, give rein to my nerves? Oh, God! give me strength, don't ruin me . . ." he repeated to himself.

When Feodor and Nina returned, Mikhail Gorin, cheerful and gay, having slept his fill, asked them: "Did you have a good time?"

"Oh, yes," replied Nina. "I showed Feodor Pavlovich the pool, the one with the birches. Cheprok was catching crabs there."

"Excellent!" said Gorin and, noticing that Feodor was looking suspiciously at the report on which the paperweight still lay, he said, smiling: "I have read your report and I like it very much. But leave it with me, I want to look over parts of it more thoroughly. We can discuss it some time at our leisure. Drop in any time. Don't stand on ceremony."

Controlling his joy with difficulty, Novikov asked: "How do you like my idea about Ivan the Terrible's drive toward the open sea? That's something quite new."

"Oh, yes, of course. It is very interesting," replied Gorin, although he had no idea what the professor was talking about. So as not to smile too noticeably, he chewed the end of his mustache.

Novikov returned late to his apartment on Budenny Avenue, but was not the least bit tired. He was pleasantly disturbed by Nina, by Gorin's words, and by everything that he had seen.

When he was undressing before going to bed, he noticed a light hair on his sleeve. Smiling, he removed it carefully.

"How could it have got onto my shirt?" Feodor was surprised. "Ah, yes, when I was lying beside her at the pool. I lay beside her . . ." he repeated to himself. "Friend Feodor, you are getting too soft; in your work this cannot be tolerated. But then, why not?"

That night Feodor smoked for a long time, unable to fall asleep. But it was not of his career nor of his report that he was thinking. His open eyes saw a delicate profile, while in his hardened heart there appeared suspicious cracks. It yearned for a maiden's love, as the Don steppe in July yearns for a rain.

CHAPTER 7

IF ONE BELIEVED what *Pravda* wrote about the eye specialist Professor Filatov, one would think that this Odessian had never had a failure. According to *Pravda,* all his incredibly bold operations were crowned with restoration of sight to the blind.

262

Filatov was a good surgeon; but such a good one as *Pravda* described he had never been, and indeed, could not be. Like any successful doctor, he had his defeats and failures. One such failure was his operation on Andrei Demin.

But then, one didn't need to be a great specialist to be convinced, on the first examination, that the right eye of the unfortunate student was lost forever. The wound was too terrible, and worse, had been neglected. Filatov didn't ask under what circumstances Demin received the wound nor why medical precautions had not been taken at once. His ability to keep his mouth shut was valued in Moscow as much as his surgical skill. Filatov was able, however, to save the left eye, in which, almost from the moment of wounding, the sight had failed as the result of shock.

When Lida, accompanied by Nina, went to see Andrei in the hospital, the patient was lying with a huge bandage around his head, covering both eyes. Filatov had gone back to Odessa, leaving the patient in the care of a military doctor.

"Please, don't stay long," warned the nurse. "The patient needs quiet; it's bad for him to be excited."

"Now they're worrying," Lida thought, "but a week ago they threw him in jail, into a stinking cell."

Only in one thing could she find a slight trace of comfort: Oleg Durov had got his retribution. That plaguing boil had faded from the face of Rostov for a while. For a week now he had been lying in the hospital with a bashed-up face and broken ribs. No one in town knew who had beaten him up. The Rostov paper *Molot* inserted a note of sympathy for Papa Durov. "The despicable attempt of the enemies of the people," wrote the paper pompously, irrigating its pages with inky tears, "to frighten you with terror is doomed to failure. No matter how the class enemy rages, it cannot break your iron will. The toilers of the Rostov district sincerely wish a most speedy recovery to your son and the best of health to yourself, Comrade Durov, fearless fighter on the advance front of socialism!"

Among themselves, everybody whispered that the beating-up of Oleg had been done by Sidorov. Everybody knew the hot-tempered character of the Selmash director. Indeed, those who saw his face, when he carried Lida in his arms, had no doubt that he would personally punish the scoundrel without bothering to instigate anyone else to do it. Everybody was very pleased about this—everybody, not excepting the author of the published note of sympathy. Oleg had pestered Rostov to the limit.

Important persons who, like Sidorov, had daughters, were terribly shocked over Oleg's latest escapade. It was one thing when he roamed the workers' districts. But when he began on the directors' daughters! . . . The irate papas shook their heads in sorrow on receiving a negative reply to their hopeful question, "Isn't the son of a bitch killed?"

The inability of Durov to do anything to Sidorov, in spite of the general suspicions, was particularly piquant. It wasn't easy, even for Durov, to break the chief of the huge tank plant, who was directly responsible to the Politburo. The singular situation of the unpunished "punishment" intrigued the whole town.

Durov, in the meantime, gloomy as a devil, hardly left his son's bedside the first two days. Oleg had barely regained consciousness when Durov asked him eagerly: "Who, who beat you up? Oleg, sonny, answer me!"

In reply Oleg merely mumbled something incoherent or asked for water.

If Durov and Sidorov met unavoidably, the atmosphere surrounding them became charged. They didn't greet each other, and tried not to notice each other.

"There'll be trouble," the Party workers whispered among themselves. The situation became the more complicated as Veria— since Larin's death the all-powerful master of the Province—was equally friendly with Sidorov and Durov.

Durov knew perfectly well that suspicions alone were not enough. He carried out the most detailed investigation, personally directed the interrogations. Under torture, people incriminated themselves—and were shot for the sake of propriety—but Durov knew that this was not what he was after. He had not come across any actual leads. This maddened him and still further strengthened his belief in Sidorov's guilt. In his heart he swore to be revenged on him.

If Lida didn't know all this, she guessed it. Now the state of constant fear—for her father, for Andrei, for Rudoy, for herself—never left her. As often happens in such cases she sought the company of a good friend. Such a friend was, of course, Nina. They now met more often than usual.

264

CHAPTER 8

"ANDREI, it's Lida."

Andrei shuddered. The windows were hung with venetian blinds, the room was in semidarkness. Only a narrow band of light lit up the lower part of Andrei's face. What Lida feared most of all she noticed at once: this was another person. But it was not the bandage on his head that changed him. No, it was something else. At the kind, almost childlike mouth a wrinkle had appeared, one sorrowful little line. Lida's whole being shrank, she saw that this was the wake of horror, of pain and death. But then a violent joy filled her, which could be expressed only in the words: "He's alive!"

Lida came up to the bed, took his hand in hers, pressed it.

"Where's Mother?" asked Andrei hoarsely, breathing heavily.

"She's well, you'll see her soon."

"Why wouldn't they let her in here?" His voice shook painfully.

"Please don't be alarmed, Andrei. We were able to come to you with great difficulty. They're not allowing people to see you, so that you won't get excited."

"Poor Mother . . ." groaned Andrei. "Are you alone, Lida?"

"No, my friend Nina is with me. Gorin's daughter."

"Ah! I understand." The wrinkle at the edge of his mouth deepened. "She came out of curiosity, to hear words of gratitude from me. Well, give my best thanks to your father for saving me so generously," he said somewhat harshly and bitterly.

"Andrei!" exclaimed Lida reproachfully.

"Andrei what?" he said, not bothering to conceal his anger now. "There is a bandage over my eyes, but now I see hypocrisy better than before. In my cell were some men condemned to death. A few hours before being shot they looked after me like their own blood brother, eased my pain in every way they could. I value their care a thousand times more than the so-called charity of Gorin. You can tell that to your father!" Andrei turned his head toward Lida's voice, thinking that Nina was beside her. But she was standing at the other side of the bed.

"Andrei, calm yourself," whispered Lida. "You're having a hard time; we understand that very well. But you know yourself that Mikhail Gorin has done a great deal for you. Without him you would have died."

"I'll die anyway," said Andrei, so convincingly it seemed as though he was seeing into the future.

"Why are you talking like that?" protested Lida hotly. Her eyes became moist. "What kind of death are you talking about? When the doctors believe that soon you'll be quite well? The worst is over." Then, reflecting a little, she added: "And you've been avenged on Oleg. He was beaten up and is in this same hospital. It's not clear yet whether he'll get better. He certainly has something to worry about."

"I'm not thinking about him," said Andrei quietly. "Yes, I'm not thinking about him," he repeated—and suddenly, as if he were continuing his own thoughts, he asked: "I can't hear your friend. . . . Is she pretty?"

Lida was surprised by this question. "Yes, very."

"Prettier than you?"

"Much prettier. . . . But why, Andrei?"

"Ask her to come to me."

Lida looked at Nina in alarm. The latter came close to the bed quickly, cautiously touched his hand, which was lying outside the blanket, with hers. Her fingers were shaking.

"Bend down, please," Andrei asked her. "Like that." He began to pass his hand over her face. "Yes, yes . . . I see—your face is very delicate. But that other face was still prettier . . ."

"Andrei, which face? Who are you speaking about?" asked Lida, a little frightened.

Without answering her, Andrei lay back on the pillow.

"Say just one word to me, Nina," he asked.

"Calm yourself, you mustn't get excited," she said quietly, and suddenly turning away, went over to the window.

"Your voice is also good, clear. But her voice was still more clear, more musical," said Andrei thoughtfully.

"Lida, dear," exclaimed Nina by the window. With her fingers she touched her face, which had turned pale. "I think I understand. . . . Oh, this is awful, awful."

"What do you understand? What is awful?" Lida wrinkled her brow, trying to catch the meaning of what was taking place.

"I'll explain it to you myself," said Andrei. He began to speak hurriedly, excitedly. "This is very strange. I wouldn't have believed anything like it, if I hadn't seen it myself. She appeared in a dream. No, not even in a dream. You see, it's night for me all the time. She came to me three times and each time her coming filled my soul with a kind of extraordinary light, joyful feeling. I'll never forget that. This woman

266

—no, she was quite a young girl, probably not more than sixteen—
was so gentle, so clean, so beautiful . . . The first time she appeared
soon after I came to the cell. The prisoners explained to me that I had
been thrown into the death cell and that nobody goes out of there alive.
I gathered that my life was coming to an end and I was afraid. Very
much afraid. Unbearably, I wanted to live . . . And just at that terrible moment she appeared. I felt so good that the pain passed, and even
fear—yes, I was no longer afraid of death. And a strange thing, that
time she didn't say anything to me. Merely looked at me. But her look
was more understanding than any words. It spoke of love, yes, of
love . . . In the filthy, stinking cell love flamed like a bright sun and
conquered death." Andrei caught his breath.

"On her second coming she spoke: just a few words—I can't remember them. But I have remembered her voice: it sounded like the sweet-
est music. I think that she was calling me somewhere . . . There—
you see," Andrei finished with a sneer. "Would you have seriously
thought that Andrei Demin, who passed his examination in dialectical
materialism with honors, could meet a ghost?" Andrei laughed, but
his laughter was bitter. He turned toward the window, as if he could see
the light.

"The third time, what did she say to you?" Nina asked him.

"What? You . . . you believe me?" shouted Andrei and laughed
loudly. "That's something I never expected . . . I really never expected that. Do you actually think that I keep company with a ghost?
Why, that was merely a mental phenomenon, a manifestation quite explainable. In moments of danger or shock the brain can create much
greater marvels! And you ask so seriously! Really, that's very amusing."
Andrei choked with laughter. "However, if you are so impatient to
know what happened the third time, I'll tell you. Only, don't think that
this has any importance. It's simply fantasy, delirium . . . All right.
The third time she opened my eyes, metaphorically speaking, of course.
She explained everything to me, absolutely everything. Life became
understandable and clear. I saw the real truth, as this girl was the embodiment of it. So, at least, I gathered. This time I remembered everything she said, everything to the last word. Only I can't tell you her
words. I gave her my promise . . ."

"You gave your promise to the convolutions of your brain?" asked
Lida with a smile.

Andrei laughed. "You caught me . . . But let's leave that. Tell me,
Lida, can you get me out of here?" Andrei pronounced the last words
very grimly.

267

"Why?" Lida was surprised. "It's clean here, and nice; good doctors are looking after you. You're really in the best hospital in Rostov."

"That's not the point," insisted Andrei stubbornly. "It's like a prison here. I can't even see my own mother."

"I'm afraid, Andrei, it won't be possible to do that. No one would listen about your transfer to another place."

"But try it."

"And here's another thing: where would we transfer you? To your mother? To that damp and dirty basement? You mustn't think of it. Of course, I would gladly have you with us at the summer house, but my father—he'd go out of his mind. No, it wouldn't be possible at our place either."

"And what if we transfer Andrei to our house?" asked Nina unexpectedly. "There are plenty of people to look after him there. Besides we have a house doctor. Andrei won't feel any worse there than here. No, as a matter of fact, that's a good idea; I'll persuade my father, without fail."

"Thank you," responded Andrei. "If you do that, I'll probably break my promise and tell you more about the third visit of the beautiful ghost."

Nina laughed. "Now that will be interesting."

The nurse looked in at the door. "It's time to end the visit, girls. The patient needs rest."

"Good-bye, Andrei! Get better quickly!" Lida squeezed his hand and went toward the door.

"Tell my mother that everything is well with me; tell her not to worry."

"I'll certainly tell her."

"Good-bye, Andrei," said Nina softly, also squeezing his hand. "I hope to see you soon at our house."

Nina left the room. But Lida—Andrei felt this—remained. The sly one, she came up to his bed quietly, bent over him. But her perfume—lilac, probably—gave her away. Without seeing her he imagined her face clearly, dear, beloved, never to be forgotten.

"Lida, darling . . ."

"What, Andrei?"

"Just . . ."

Andrei raised himself slightly on his elbows. Sharp pity pierced Lida's heart. Loving and suffering with every smallest particle of her being, with every thought, she whispered: "Andrei, I love you very, very much . . ."

268

Andrei was silent, smiling gratefully in his darkness. Then he dropped his head back onto the pillow and said in a weakened voice: "I'm a little tired . . . Wait, don't go! Kiss me, Lidochka. You know, we've never kissed each other properly . . . You don't mind?"

Lida threw her arms around his neck and kissed his hot lips hard, hard.

"My darling . . ."

"Beloved . . ."

Words were whispered from mouth to mouth, from heart to heart, setting afire the bright flame of love and passion, making them one and binding them. It was suddenly light in the room. The sun came from behind the clouds, the bars of sunlight from the venetian blinds lay clearly over Andrei's bed.

A week later Andrei was transferred to the Gorins'. Wishing to please his daughter, Mikhail Gorin arranged everything without much trouble.

CHAPTER 9

"PLAY US something lively," Sidorov asked Nikolai, who was picking at the strings, tuning up his mandolin.

"A Ukrainian hopak?"

"Let's have a hopak."

The Novikov brothers were visiting the plant director. In the first week of July, while resting after the feverish examination days at the University, Professor Novikov remembered his invitation. Taking his brother with him, Feodor appeared at the now familiar summer house. Sidorov received him cordially. After a full dinner on the open veranda, he led them proudly to his yacht. This was an old but very graceful small vessel, with sails and an auxiliary engine. With an expansive gesture the director invited them on deck. The sails were raised, the yacht heeled a little, sailing lightly in the wind toward the Azov—the wonderful banks of the Don began to pass slowly by.

However, they could not admire the view very long. Before the sun set, an unexpected shower drove them into the cabin. Only the chauffeur, Ivan, who composed the entire crew of the yacht, remained on deck.

Sidorov's wife and daughter were in the cabin with the men. Lida was in a happy mood. She had visited the Gorins that morning and had seen Andrei. The latter joked, laughed, felt incomparably better than in the hospital, and this gladdened her greatly. Besides, a great worry had fallen from her shoulders: last week she had passed her exams successfully in the Faculty of History and now two summer months awaited her with their freedom and recreation.

"You can really play!" Sidorov praised Nikolai, and added down-right affectionately: "You rascal!"

The director, fierce and distant in his own plant, was relaxed and kind in the cabin. He smacked his lips contentedly, his hands were beating time, flapping like two heavy shovels. His face was slightly Mongolian, browned from the sun, and his stony cheek bones stood out like knobs. His eyes were bright when he was drunk, but when he was sober they looked stubbornly with a gloomy sternness from beneath his black eyebrows.

A varicolored skull cap, sewn from a priest's confiscated vestment, stuck tightly to the director's shaven head. Such skull caps were fashionable at the time; great heaps of them were sold in the stores in Rostov. Usually Sidorov wore the Party shirt with the inseparable Order of Lenin on his chest. But now, on a free day, he had on a Ukrainian shirt, embroidered with bright designs.

Sidorov was distinguished by the rough directness of his character, but did not lack craftiness. They said about him at the plant that, when necessary, he could appeal to a man as "my dear fellow" and at the same time throw him into the devil's teeth.

The director was sincerely glad of the visit of the Novikovs. During the past week the officious faces of his subordinates had annoyed him beyond endurance. With these brothers, on the other hand, he was in no way bound; better company was not to be found.

When Nikolai finished playing, his host poured him a glass of cherry brandy: "Just what a young man needs—a cup of vodka with a kiss as a snack."

Nikolai emptied the glass at one gulp and suddenly began to argue fiercely with the director about the shortcomings of a tank which he had seen only in the blurred pictures of the papers.

It was gay and noisy in the cabin. The whole company sat close together around a little round table covered with a tablecloth, their faces lit by the hanging lantern. Wine, fruit, and *hors d'oeuvres* were piled high on the table. Along the walls of the cabin, paneled in red wood, the Sidorov trophies were displayed: bottles and flasks of all kinds and sizes. A warm wind, bringing with it the smell of the rain and the aro-

270

matic freshness of the meadows along the river bank, blew in through the two open portholes and mixed with the tobacco smoke of the men and the perfume of the women.

Rolling slightly, the yacht sailed like a toy boat on wavelets. The lantern swung with the motion and a great number of moths and beetles, saving themselves from the rain, circled around the light and fell onto the white tablecloth. The talk, mixed with laughter and jokes, jumped from one subject to another.

"And now, Professor, are we going to get a party from you soon?" asked Sidorov, taking a breath as if after heavy work. He had just succeeded in proving to the obstinate Nikolai that it was not worth while throwing the tanks out as scrap—they might still be useful in a future war.

"What do you mean by that—a party?" smiled Feodor.

"You know yourself quite well what I mean." Sidorov screwed up his eyes slyly. "You'll be the Director of the University soon. All Rostov is talking about it. Such an event must be celebrated."

"Oh! So that's what you mean! Well, that's just a rumor. Don't believe it. I can't understand myself where people got such an idea."

"There's no smoke without fire. I heard it from very good sources. You can expect the appointment any day now. And I tell you—it's a very wise decision. In the first place, you're a Rostovian. In the second, the present Director, Belosiorov, is no damn good as an organizer——"

"And in the third place, he's a very nasty person!" exclaimed Lida hotly. "Isn't that true?" She turned to Nikolai, who was sitting beside her. "Nikolai! You're not listening to me."

Nikolai, whose gaze was wandering somewhere on the ceiling of the cabin, started at her words and, opening his mouth, looked at Lida.

"What are you dreaming about?" laughed Lida. "You looked very foolish."

"He's in love, you can see that at once," said Sidorov.

"Nikolai in love? Nonsense!" exclaimed Feodor. "He doesn't even know what that word means."

Nikolai smiled and silently listened to their jokes. Indelible good nature shone in his eyes. The fact was that he had made an important discovery. Lida, on whom he had looked at first with such contempt, caught his imagination. "Ah, Feodor, Feodor!" Nikolai exclaimed to himself. "Now I understand why you tied yourself up to this girl. . . . Well, one can only envy you: her dad's important, they have a summer

271

house and yacht, and Lida herself is so simple, without any airs. She's not conceited." Nikolai valued the last trait especially. "But why has she all of a sudden become so pretty?" he wondered to himself.

It was easily explained—Lida was in love. Andrei had upset her quiet inner life. It was after her visit in the hospital that Lida changed, although she had grown thinner and there were shadows under her eyes. But her eyes shone with an inextinguishable light. It was these brown eyes, radiant with an inner joy, that made her so unrecognizable, so attractive.

Nikolai was never able to treat the near presence of a pretty girl with indifference. "If Lida didn't belong to Feodor, I would have made a try for her long ago," he thought. Even so, Nikolai could not refrain from a mild flirtation. Now and then he gallantly poured her some wine—Lida didn't drink cherry brandy, it was too strong—or he showed her clever tricks with his handkerchief; or he read her palm roguishly.

Apart from his pretty neighbor, Nikolai could not look calmly at such an abundance of food on the table. But, being a man of the world who knew how to conduct himself in company, he behaved as if he had passed all his life on yachts, drinking expensive wines and eating fruit, although it was hard for him to keep from shouting with pleasure. Nikolai was used to brushing the crumbs into a small heap and bringing them carefully to his mouth. But here! Bread—that treasure—nobody even noticed it. From bread, Nikolai's thoughts were led to the University dining hall, from the dining hall to the tray of the waitress Nadya, which she carried so well, from the tray to her rounded arms with which she embraced him so warmly in the evenings. From these sweet memories Nikolai's mouth dried up; he looked warily at Lida, in case she was reading his thoughts.

Sidorov merely laughed, looking out of the corner of his eye at Nikolai. "Nikolai, would you like to smoke a foreign cigarette?" He handed him his open cigarette case. "The writer Romain Rouen gave them to me when he was at my plant."

Nikolai lit his cigarette, passing the smoke through his nose contentedly. *"Merci beaucoup . . ."* and, immediately forgetting the Director, moved so close to Lida that his shoulder touched hers.

Poor fellow, his innocent game didn't fit into the plans of Lida's mother, Natalia, at all. For some time she berated herself for not having the sense at the very start to seat Lida beside Feodor. Wondering how to correct this mistake, she at last decided: "I'll make them change seats!"

272

"Leonid, go outside and see if the rain's stopped," Natalia asked her husband.

Sidorov went out obediently and returned in a minute. "It's still raining, but lightly. It'll probably stop soon." His wife was sitting in his chair and looking at him with innocent eyes. "How about a game of cards?" he was going to propose, and hesitated. At a loss, he shrugged his shoulders and sat down in her place. Now Natalia was beside Lida.

"Lida, go and find out from Ivan if we have gone far from the town?" she asked her daughter.

"Why?"

"Don't be lazy! Go and find out."

Lida, raising the pretty line of her eyebrows slightly, left the cabin. As quick as a quail her mother jumped over into her place, beside Nikolai.

"Now, young man, tell my fortune." She extended her pudgy hand to Nikolai. "Let's see what is in store for me." Nikolai merely blinked his eyes over such a sudden change in the scenery.

When Lida returned and reported that they had just sailed past the village of Vishnevsky, she had to sit between her father and mother. To her horror, Natalia realized that her operation was far from finished. She was about to take new steps, but Sidorov, who had caught on to his wife's stratagem, forestalled her.

"Professor, let's change places," he asked Feodor, "otherwise Natalia will send me out in the rain again."

Feodor smiled understandingly and sat down beside Lida. Her cheeks flushed slightly. Natalia sighed with relief and snatched her hand away from Nikolai. "You're a bad gypsy."

Her full red lips smiled affectionately, her face seemed unworried. But her mind was in a haze. Lida had scared her badly. "Is that how to charm a suitor!" thought Natalia, trying with her look to raise her daughter's modestly lowered eyelids. "Doesn't even look at him! No play or coquetting. I certainly never expected such ignorance from my own daughter."

When Natalia first learned about Andrei, she attached no importance to him. "Lida has tied herself to him out of pity. That will pass. She's surely not so stupid as to think seriously about some jailbird . . ." However, just in case, her parents scolded their daughter thoroughly for her foolishness, while Papa Sidorov passed the strap lightly over her tender spot.

And now, instead of sidling up like a sly vixen to Feodor, Lida either sat like a log, or suddenly started up some fun with that empty vessel

Nikolai. "Oh, dear, as long as she doesn't get lost among the three of them. That's what it means to be still young, without experience."

Natalia had cause to worry.

Feodor had captivated her completely. "He's well built and broad-shouldered, clever and a good talker, and his face doesn't spoil him: straight dark brows, light hair, it's obvious at once he's got breeding. And his eyes! Lively and sharp. Who better could one wish for Lida? And they say he'll be the Director soon—and him so young!"

"Where do you intend to spend the summer, Professor?" Natalia turned to him with an amiable smile.

"Most probably in Rostov. Some urgent matters have piled up. I wanted to spend a month in the Crimea, but as you know, man proposes—God disposes."

"In that case come and visit us as often as you can. We'll be only too glad to have you. This summer we're going to remain here. Usually Lida spends her vacation with me at Sochi, but this year she wants to stay at home for some reason. And I don't want to go away alone. You see, these are Lida's last few years with me, then she'll fly away like a bird from her nest . . ." Natalia spoke in a tearful voice, even brought her handkerchief to her eyes for full effect.

Feodor understood her game perfectly. Her Cossack attack on a suitor merely evoked a smile from him. He was good-natured, in an excellent mood, felt free as never before. Particularly with Lida. She sat beside him, her hands folded in her lap.

"What a difference there is between her and Nina," he thought, looking from the side at Lida's animated, almost childlike face, her innocently sloped shoulders and the two unspoiled hillocks of her breasts, shyly bulging out the rose material of her blouse. "Nina is superb, unrestrainedly coquettish, arch, almost womanly; but her beauty is dangerous, it takes hold like a fever. Even yet I feel a shiver after meeting her . . . Lida is simple and clear as a spring day; there's nothing to fear from her. She's affectionate, trusting—not like Nina, with whom one has to be on the watch all the time. At the Gorins', everything is complicated; there I have to lie and pretend. Here I don't need to act, here I'm simply a professor of the University and that's all. My twin—the agent of the Politburo—has remained outside the threshold of the Sidorov summer house. That's wonderful! Isn't it a pleasure, God damn it, to relax properly in this noisy company, so simple and at ease!"

Lida barely touched her wine. She watched the two brothers closely, not hiding her smiles and curiosity. Nikolai seemed to her at times funny, at times nice, while she was just a bit afraid of Feodor. Her fear was not of him as a professor, stern and exacting at examination time; this fear was of something new, unknown. Lida didn't understand him. He seemed too strange to her, too unusual, not at all like other people—frightened rabbits or soulless automatons. She could never forget how Feodor had brought her the pass, how friendly he had been, how kindly he had reassured her. "What could be the reason for his unusual behavior," she thought, "if it weren't his brave and kind heart!"

Since then Lida, without noticing it, had been watching Feodor more closely, and the more she watched, the more surprised she was. How clearly she remembered a conversation with him at the University. It was during the examinations. They were alone in the room. Lida had taken her card and begun to answer excitedly. Her subject had been Peter the First's war with the Swedish King Charles, and the significance of the battle of Poltava. The professor listened to her attentively; and suddenly, when she stopped to catch her breath, he asked her quietly: "Tell me, Lida, why do you love Andrei so much?" Strange to say, his question did not surprise her. As if she had been expecting it, Lida began to talk about Andrei, all the time looking trustingly into the professor's eyes.

"He's kind, honest . . ." repeated Novikov after her, and suddenly asked: "But you've said nothing about what he looks like or his position . . . Do you mean, that's not important?"

"No, it's not important!" Lida replied firmly.

Novikov looked closely into her eyes and said, smiling: "You're lucky, Lida, you love with a real love." He was smiling, but his smile didn't hide the pain in his voice.

Surprised, Lida thought: "But can't you have real love?" and immediately the professor became dear to her, almost her kin, although he remained even more mysterious.

In a childlike way Lida was glad of her acquaintance with Novikov. After all that had happened to Andrei, to herself, she had stopped believing in people. Now this tall, energetic man with the straight and honest look of his clever eyes had returned her lost faith to her. There are still honest people in the world! There are still people with lively human feelings and kind hearts, so there is still hope. And Lida, burning with her first maiden love for Andrei, could not live without hope.

Poor girl! Trustingly and with gladness she saw in Feodor Novikov qualities that were not in him and could not be. What would Feodor himself have thought if he had been able to read her thoughts? He would probably have smiled with pity. Whom would he have pitied?

275

Her? Himself? Or perhaps he would have looked in the mirror with pride, surprised how well his face could hide the awful emptiness of his heart, while his actions, thought out with cold calculation, could call forth dreams of the unattainable in the mind of an innocent girl. . . .

CHAPTER 10

"HOW DID YOU LIKE that Frenchman?" Sidorov asked Feodor.

"Romain Rouen? I just saw him briefly, when he was in the school. I didn't get a chance to talk to him."

"He's a queer one," said Sidorov confidently. "He even thought the new prison being built was a hospital. 'What a beautiful building is going up there!' he exclaimed to the interpreter. 'That's the best architectural structure I've seen yet in your town. What is it?' The interpreter up and told him: 'That's a hospital, M'sieu Rouen.' And he merely smiled approvingly. Of course, not all foreigners are such simpletons as that writer. You begin to show them the agricultural-machinery shop, and all the time they're darting their eyes around and ask what's being produced in the other shops. Romain accepted everything as the genuine article."

"Leonid knows foreigners well," explained Natalia. "He lived a whole year in America."

"You don't say!" Feodor was surprised. "That must have been very interesting."

"Yes, very interesting," drawled Sidorov, for some reason with a sigh. "I was sent there, as a good Bolshevik, to learn the technical end. Well, you can't deny it, they know the technique, the devils. . . . But what really surprised us was their attitude toward us. We went around freely whenever we wanted. They showed us everything! There were no secrets."

Feodor shook his head incredulously. "They probably deceived you in the same way that you deceived the Frenchman at your plant. They simply showed you what they considered safe to show."

"No, no; just imagine! They didn't deceive us. At first we didn't trust our eyes. We were looking for a trap all the time. Everything seemed so unbelievable. But after we had looked around a bit, we saw that it was all above board. Then we were really surprised!"

"Did you learn English?"

276

"No. There wasn't time. And then, I had a rotten teacher. We'd begin our lesson in English, but finish up in Russian, under the table—dead drunk. And, strange to say, the drunker we were the better we understood each other."

"Papa, tell them how you wanted to teach the American workers proletarian solidarity," Lida asked him, with a smile.

"Yes, that was a real comedy," laughed Sidorov. "We, of course, arrived there as though in an enemy camp. Every passer-by seemed to be a capitalist. Naturally we kept ourselves on the alert. Our attitude toward life was strict. At the least sign we were ready to man the ideological barricades.

"Well, they taught us technique, these solid craftsmen. They did everything without red tape, but without hurrying like crazy cats—and everything ran smoothly, as it never runs here with all our meetings and slogans. That threw us into a cold sweat. How is it that there the workers are working for the capitalists better than our workers for their own State? All right. We decided to enlighten the workers. That is, by way of barter: you teach us American technique and we'll teach you our Russian revolutionary spirit. We began to explain the revolution and the class nature on our fingers, somehow. The others smiled, listened. They even nodded their heads very sympathetically: 'Good, good.' So, we thought, everything's going well—the heads of the capitalist slaves are being enlightened. We were just going to tighten up the talks, when one of the workers took his pipe out of his mouth and asked: 'Mister Sidorov, and how about strikes with you in Russia?' We, of course, explained to him according to the book: 'We don't need to strike because the workers work for themselves.'

" 'Well, if strikes aren't needed, we don't need the Soviets,' said the worker, stuck his pipe in his mouth and went off to his lathe as if nothing had happened. Our political talk ended."

Everybody laughed, but Nikolai shook his head sadly: "You can see at once they're pretty ignorant people."

The director looked at him strangely, either with contempt or with pity and, reaching across the table, tapped his forehead with a finger: "Kolya, it's your head that's ignorant. Better have a drink," and he added hopelessly: "Tank engineer——"

"How did you pick up the American technique?" asked Feodor with interest.

"Couldn't be easier," Sidorov replied. "But everyone in his own way. One of our comrades, of all that he saw in America, for some reason only noticed a little dog in a wheel at a Chicago circus, which caught his fancy. On his arrival in Russia, while his memory was still fresh, he erected a water pump on his own plant: a huge wheel, into which he put a horned bull to turn the wheel the way the dog did. But the bull, of course, is an ignorant animal—doesn't understand American technique, would rather ride cows than wheels—he smashed one of his horns in the first hour and at the same time the whole construction."

They all laughed. The story teller himself laughed more than anyone.

"Of course, not everybody understood American technique like that ill-starred engineer," said Sidorov, smiling. "There were some lads with heads among us. The year in America wasn't wasted for that kind. Only, not all of them were able to use what they had learned," he added, but without a smile.

"What do you mean by that?" asked Feodor.

"This: of the five of us who went to America, only two are working now at their specialty; the others were sent to hell and gone. They returned from America as good technicians, but bad Bolsheviks. You know yourself where that kind goes." A note of pride sounded in the director's voice. Yes, he wasn't one of those; America didn't spoil him; he was and remained a staunch Bolshevik.

"Is that true?" thought Feodor, and answered himself: "Probably it is; he's of the thick-skinned breed, not quickly perishable goods."

As if he wanted to dispel the last doubts of his guest, Sidorov reclined self-contentedly in his chair and said cheerfully: "Yes, damn it, I live well! I'm satisfied with everything, I enjoy life. I'm happy myself and my family is happy!" and turning to Lida, he asked her: "Isn't that so, little daughter?"

Lida didn't answer her father. She frowned, bending over her glass.

"Well, why are you silent? . . . Surely you're not badly off? Is it really so hard for you to thank your father for everything he has done for you? Such a happy life didn't fall into your lap from heaven, you know!" Annoyance sounded in Sidorov's voice.

Without taking her eyes off the glass, Lida said softly: "Papa, how can you talk like that. Aren't you ashamed of yourself?"

Sidorov was dumbfounded.

"What do you mean, ashamed? Why should I be ashamed?" He cast a puzzled glance at the others: "That's a nice state of affairs! And isn't it yourself who is ashamed of me, my little daughter? If so, then why? Have I killed anybody or did I steal all this stuff, the summer house, the yacht, your education at the University? Why, of course not!"

"An honest person cannot be happy when the whole country is suf-

278

fering," said Lida, still as softly, but her words fell like a heavy stone in the quiet of the cabin.

For a whole minute her father couldn't say a word.

At last Sidorov spoke, but somewhat hoarsely, with difficulty: "So, according to you I have no right to be happy! Oh, no, little daughter! You're mistaken, greatly mistaken! I have earned my happiness honestly, with my own hands, with my own blood . . . Yes, with blood!"

Sidorov jumped up suddenly and began to unbutton his shirt. But his thick fingers wouldn't obey him, they were shaking from excitement. He pulled the shirt so that the buttons flew, and ripped it off.

"There you are! Look at that!" shouted Sidorov, showing them all his broad, hairy chest. On the left side, a little above the heart, he indicated a small white scar, obviously from a bullet. "And here's another!" Sidorov's face became pale, but his eyes burned with a mad fire. "And another! No, Lida, don't turn away—look!" Sidorov turned his back toward her. Right across the director's broad back, like a furrow in a field, ran an ugly scar. "That's from a Cossack saber! That's how I got my happiness! If the bullet had been two finger-breadths lower, or the saber blow stronger, neither I nor you would be here now. And you . . ." Sidorov didn't finish, he bent over the table and poured a glass of cherry brandy. His hand shook; in the deathly silence that had set in, the bottle tinkled wickedly against the tumbler. After pouring it out, he drank it at a gulp, and dropped heavily into his chair.

Natalia rose abruptly from the table, nodded severely to her daughter: "Come on deck, Lida. I think the rain has stopped." Lida hurried after her mother. Sidorov didn't even look at her.

For a long time he sat motionless, staring heavily at one point. When he had calmed down a bit, he poured Feodor and Nikolai a glass each.

"You see, Feodor, we're all from one nest, but the fledgling, it seems, is of quite a different breed," he said with bitterness.

Nikolai again took up the mandolin and began softly to pick at the strings. The whisper of the wind in the portholes now sank, now grew stronger, like the sleepy breathing of the river. Under the melancholy motif of the mandolin and the casual creaking of old wood, Sidorov began to talk, at first slowly, with difficulty, then more hotly and bitterly.

Feodor gathered that the director had to get something off his chest. He didn't interrupt him, listened in silence. But to Sidorov it didn't matter whether anybody was listening to him or not . . .

His own daughter had stung his very heart, his very soul. He had

279

heard, he had heard this reproach about happiness before. But the poisonous words passed by his ears, didn't bother him. He thought, people are just jealous and so they invent all kinds of rubbish, imagine a shadow on a clear day . . . But here his own child had pricked him with the old reproaches.

"I had a friend; his name was Vaska," said Sidorov between gulps of vodka. "I loved him like my own brother. I couldn't help loving him. With him I had gone through all the fronts in the Civil War, we went side by side into the attack, we drank the same sorrow and the same joy . . . We both had a close friend—Death. And she played with us! Like a hot-blooded girl with a simpleton, this way and that. At times she would twist so hard that you'd ask her yourself, with anguish—take me, along with my life. No, she didn't take us; she spared us all the time. It turned out worst for Vaska. A White-Guard bullet knocked his eye out—but he lived.

"And then the Civil War ended; peacetime life began. We opened our arms wide, you understand, to accept that happiness for which we had fought. And here the real test began. What remained behind us began to look like a merry game. There our bodies were tortured; the soul was hard as steel. 'What are you shedding your blood for, Comrades?' the Commissar of the regiment used to ask us on formation. And without hesitation we would answer: 'For the Soviets, for the happiness of all the toilers in the world!' With such firm faith death wasn't frightening. And then suddenly, right under this same steadfast soul they placed dynamite and cracks appeared in all directions. Vaska and I returned to our own plant, began to work at the same lathes we had worked on before the war. But around us was ruin, hunger, the darkest hell . . . Everybody was barefoot, naked. There were no clothes; we went around in sacks—you made three holes, pushed your head and arms through, and there you were.

"But that was still understandable—the effects of the war. Something else was not understandable. We looked around and saw that the workers' happiness had turned wrong side up. While we were fighting, others had fixed themselves up with soft jobs. They were sitting pretty; you couldn't knock them off. One was the Commissar of Food, another the director of the plant, still another the Chief of the Cheka. . . . There was hunger around, but for them—not even a puff of wind. They were carousing. You'd walk down the street from work, barely dragging your feet, and one of these fat mugs would drive past you with a black racer in the shafts—like a blue streak. He'd have a cigarette in his mouth, a Mauser on his knees, a couple of whores grinning—heading out of

town, for a sail on the Don, for a big spree. Then the cracks began . . .
At that time Vaska spent nearly all his spare time at my house. He sat
behind a tumbler of vodka, his one eye glittering while it grinned, as it
were—and never said a word. I didn't like this one-eyed grin of his.

" 'What,' I would ask, 'are you grinning about?' And he up and
answers me once: 'They fooled us, Leonid Stepanovich; they fooled us
so good that it's funny.' 'Wait now, how is it that they fooled us?' I ask
him. 'What do you mean by that, you one-eyed devil?' 'Just so,' he says:
'You and I were fighting for the happiness of the toilers. I lost an eye;
they scratched you up a little bit too. But happiness—well, we haven't
seen it . . . The years are passing, but for us workers it's getting
worse and worse.' Ah! How his words aroused my anger! 'You drooling
idiot!' I tell him. 'What the hell kind of Bolshevik are you? You're
afraid of hardships, you can't see the bright future beyond temporary
failure.' 'No,' says Vaska, 'I can't see it. I see the peeling walls, I see
the filthy rags, but of brightness I see nothing.'

"At that time I lived in a damp basement, in one room with my wife
and Lida—she was a baby; she cried. It stank, it was stuffy. But I was
obstinate, I couldn't believe that Vaska was right. I went over to Lidka,
picked her up. I could hold all there was of her on the palm of my
hand. I brought her up to Vaska's eye. 'Look,' I ask him. 'What do you
see?' 'Well,' he replied. 'I see your daughter. She's crying—obviously
she wants to be fed. And you have nothing to give her. And that's all.
I see nothing else.' 'Look into her eyes,' I say. 'See how clear, how
bright they are. And with these eyes she will see the happy future.' "

Sidorov got up, went to the porthole and inhaled the river air. Feodor
and Nikolai looked at him silently. Nikolai muted the strings with his
hand. . . . Still looking through the porthole, Sidorov said: "And
now this same Lida doesn't consider my happiness honest. Why?"

Sidorov suddenly turned to Nikolai: "What were you playing just
now?"

"Love Letters."

"It's a very nice tune, sad but nice. Go on, go on, only not loud."

"And what happened to your friend Vaska? Did you convince him?"
Feodor asked.

"No, I didn't. He ended up badly, very badly. These vodka debates
began to repeat themselves, every free day. And always hotter, and
more spiteful. Sometimes we swore at each other, at others we would
be kissing each other, or suddenly we'd strike up a song, like *Love
Letters*. We would sit, our arms around each other, and howl like a
couple of dogs at the moon. That's how depressed our souls were. And

we disclosed things to each other that up till then we had kept cautiously to ourselves, locked up. And we didn't notice how we were drifting away from each other, always further and further.

"And then, once, it burst.

"We had been drinking heavily that night. My wife had gone with Lidka to her relatives. We were left alone in the room, and so we let ourselves go. I called Vaska a traitor, he called me a fool and a flunky. . . . We were both cold mad—ready to go at each other with our fists. Vaska got up and shouted at me: 'You're no longer my friend!' 'And you're not my friend, and I'm damn sorry that bullet only knocked your eye out. You should have been killed altogether, because you're a class enemy!' 'Ah! So that's how you think of me!' Vaska shouted. 'If you're such a staunch Bolshevik, run and tell them what I've said to you—you know a real Bolshevik should do that. And if you can't, then you're just the same kind of an enemy as I am.' As soon as he said these words to me, something tore loose inside me. I don't know what happened to me. I stood in front of him; he even stepped back. 'What's the matter with you, Leonid?' I must have looked terrible to him. And I hissed right into his face: 'All right, snake, look out . . .' I put on my cap and ran out. I went staggering along, not even knowing rightly where I was going, but I came to the Cheka and blurted out everything. 'Only,' I said, 'don't do him any harm, just give him a good lesson.' They grinned, smiled, promised anything. From that time I never heard of him again. I got into an awful state. I wanted to do away with myself. And just at that moment, the Secretary of the Party Committee of our plant sent for me. 'Comrade Sidorov,' he said, 'we have decided to send you to study engineering. We need such loyal Party people as you!'

"I was standing in front of him, trembling with joy. 'Now,' I thought, 'good luck has come at last. Ah! What a pity that Vaska isn't here now. How happy he would have been!' "

Sidorov stopped in sorrowful remembrance.

Feodor was shocked. He could not understand whether Sidorov was talking seriously or making fun of him. Nikolai also opened his mouth in amazement.

"Doesn't he realize that they sent him to the Institute because he turned his buddy in and showed his loyalty to the Party? Of course he knows, even though he's drunk and pretending to be a fool."

The door of the cabin opened. Natalia shouted: "The rain's stopped. Come up on deck, it's such a fresh night up here!"

282

CHAPTER 11

IT WAS AS IF there had never been any rain. The sky was clear, starry. Only at the very edge of the broad river a few belated clouds played tag with the gypsy moon. The light breeze around the mast stirred the little pennant lazily, dried up the last of the rain drops.

The transparent July night hung over the Don. The Milky Way bespattered the floating yacht with stars, dreams wandered over the sleeping river, there was the monotonous chirping of crickets, the rustle of birds in bushes along the bank, and the echoes of a dog's bark in some distant village. The yacht sailed quietly in the middle of the river. To the left, vanishing in the moonlit swell, ran hazy meadows; to the right, in the deep silence, rose the white silhouettes of the chalk cliffs.

Lida stood at the helm beside Ivan, silently listening to the light breathing of the boundless, ancient river. The warm breeze blew on her, bringing with it the fancies of daydreams.

"Maybe we should stop?" asked Ivan.

"What for?"

"Aren't you going to swim? After the rain the water's always warm as new milk."

"If you like. Ask Mama."

Ivan's idea pleased Natalia. "Let them swim under the night sky," she thought. "They'll come closer together, as if they were under one blanket."

The yacht stopped, the anchor was dropped. Lida and her mother went to the cabin to change. The men remained on deck.

"Some night!" sighed Sidorov, looking at the sky. "On a night like this you regret that you're not about twenty years younger. I used to paw the earth with my hoofs like you do, Nikolai—I lived not without sin. We used to finish our work at the plant and go straight to a dance or on a spree. And was I lucky with the girls! They clung to me like fish to live bait. And of them all, there's one I'll never forget; that was before Natalia. What a hot one she was! On a night like this, and with a moon, we'd get in a rowboat, tie it up to a quiet bank, and play from sunset to sunrise. And in the morning, as if nothing had happened, off to work. Our young people can't do that nowadays; their muscles are too weak."

"Why, of course, with the food you get now you can't play much," Nikolai agreed.

"How far are we from Rostov?" asked Feodor.

"About twenty miles. All around here are government summer houses. Those lights there, behind us—that's the Gorin palace."

At the director's words Feodor remembered Nina. "What's she doing now? Maybe she's admiring the night and the gypsy moon."

"He's a funny fellow, Gorin," continued Sidorov. "I just can't understand him: he must be blind or pretending to be. He delivers a sermon in *Pravda* as if he took us for a bunch of fools. But no matter how much you shout 'candy,' it doesn't make it any sweeter in your mouth."

Feodor was surprised at this appraisal of Gorin. "The Party, however, values him greatly. In the ideological struggle his voice is very influential," he remarked.

"Maybe it was, but not now. Ideological sugar has almost gone out of use. They don't persuade the stubborn now; they shoot them."

"He's right," thought Feodor, and said: "You're wrong. I can't agree with you. Gorin's influence now is just as important and significant as it has been all along. Take, for instance, abroad. There, his voice is listened to."

"But only abroad. Literary men and other intellectuals like Rouen come to Gorin from the ends of the earth and argue with him enthusiastically about such lofty things as individuality and art in socialism, while sadist Durov is reflecting how he can devise some better torture to appease his flesh. These are two different worlds, and Gorin is just as far from reality as the sky is from the earth." Sidorov didn't speak loudly, but his voice was saturated with hatred and sarcasm.

"Good Lord! How fiercely he hates Durov!" thought Feodor. On the other hand, Nikolai 's eyes lit up at the plant director's words.

"Comrade Sidorov, is it true what they're saying, that Durov is getting ready to gobble you up?" he asked gaily.

Sidorov frowned: his cheek bones quivered grimly. "That's all right. He won't gobble me up! He'll choke; I'm bony. And anyway, my young friend, it's none of your business."

Natalia came out of the cabin, and after her, as if she were hiding behind her mother's broad figure, came Lida—both in bathing suits.

Feodor's eyes ran over the girl's whole figure. She had on a short white suit. In her very modesty there was the yielding simplicity of a girl of seventeen. Feodor suddenly felt a longing, a strange melancholy. His sadness was for the lost innocence of his childhood.

284

"Lida, is that really you?" exclaimed Nikolai, dumbfounded. His eyes popped in amazement.

Sidorov smirked, while he seemed to be stroking his daughter with his look.

Lida ran to the side of the yacht, but hesitated before jumping into the black water, sparkling with stars. Then she bent and, with a squeal, dived.

"Ah!" exclaimed Nikolai and strained his whole body after her.

"Here—hey! Where are you going?" Sidorov stopped him and, taking Nikolai by the elbow, led him gently into the cabin, like a delicate piece of china. "Change your clothes, you silly ass, then dive."

When the men came out of the cabin in bathing trunks, it was Natalia's turn to appraise the bodily prowess of the guests, especially Feodor's. She looked him over without ceremony, critically, without missing one detail, in a businesslike way; she was preoccupied with her daughter's future happiness. But everything was in its proper place and harmoniously formed. Feodor wasn't a Hercules, nor was he puny either—just rightly muscular, a man in the prime of life.

"Be careful! Don't swim far from the yacht—a *som* fish may catch your leg. There are a lot of them at night. If you keep together they won't come near; they're afraid of noise." Ivan warned them and jumped into the water with such a splash that he probably deafened all the *soms* within a mile.

A moment later the entire population of the yacht was in the water.

"Professor Novikov, Nikolai, where are you?" cried Lida from the darkness. The brothers swam toward her voice. "Don't you think it's easier to swim at night? As if the water held you up, almost like the sea," she said when they came near her.

Feodor laughed, not knowing why. Lida swam toward the shore with surprising speed, easily, throwing her thin arms out like a man. On the background of the dark water, in the large drops sparkling like rubies, she looked like a large golden fish, fabulous, unreal—as if it were a deceptive play of the moonlight. Feodor and Nikolai hurried after her. Feodor felt boyishly happy, though a bit foolish. "I'm like a schoolboy chasing a girl. What for?" flashed through his head. "However, I'll think at home—now I must catch up with her and that's all."

He came up with Lida, caught her cold fingers with his hand, laughed gaily.

"You're the first one who has caught me," said Lida and freed herself from his hand.

285

At the shore, laughing and puffing, they threw themselves down in the dark shallow water and lay still from exhaustion. The quiet water washed the sand lazily and tiny fish darted in all directions. Lida raised her dark eyes and, supporting her chin in her hand, looked at the low-lying moon, her face delicate and fine. Deeply moved, Nikolai didn't take his eyes off her.

"When I look at the stars it takes my breath away," he said to Lida.

"Look at me then."

"You stop my heart beating completely," whispered Nikolai in her ear.

"Poor boy. It's positively dangerous for you to look at God's world," laughed Lida. "In that case, you'd better shut your eyes."

"And your mouth too," added Feodor, without looking at his brother.

From the yacht came Natalia's voice: "Nikolai! Nikolai! Swim here, I need you."

Annoyed, Lida shrugged her shoulders: "Don't go, Nikolai . . ."

"No, you'd better go when they're calling you," said Feodor, his teeth flashing in a smile. "Maybe she's drowning."

"Who—Mama? She swims like a fish!" exclaimed Lida.

Nikolai winked and swam off to the yacht. "It's quite clear," he shouted over his shoulder. "Two's company—three's a crowd."

Nikolai's joke left Feodor alone with the girl in an awkward silence. Lida hastened to break it.

"How did you like the Gorins' park?" she asked. "Nina told me you had been at their house."

"The park is magnificent. I was quite astounded."

"And you surprised Nina. She never imagined you like that. According to her a professor must positively wear glasses and have a beard."

Feodor laughed. "What else did she say about me?" he asked with interest, and was disappointed to hear:

"That's all. Tell me, don't you think that she's a very interesting girl?" remarked Lida and, to his surprise, Feodor noticed a little note of pride in her voice.

"Yes, she's a very beautiful girl."

"She gets that from her mother. Luba has kept her youth very well. She's as graceful and lively as a young girl. You know, of course, that she's a countess?"

"How's that? What countess?" Feodor was astonished.

286

"Gorin met her in Italy. She went there just before the revolution. When the storm broke in Russia she remained there—practically a pauper."

"What an interesting fate!" exclaimed Feodor. "She had been a countess, the revolution ruined her, but on marrying the 'stormy petrel of the revolution' she again became a person of quality and rich, more so than before."

"But I think that didn't make her happy," Lida remarked.

"Why?"

"I don't know. Sometimes it seems to me because of her feeling of insecurity in the future. You see, she's from an entirely different world. That strikes you as soon as you see her."

"What exactly?"

"Well, everything. In any simple conversation. It's very difficult for her among us. The kind of people around—coarse, hard, as if they had grown an iron casing. And all their talk is about evil, hatred, enemies." As usual, Lida expressed herself brusquely and definitely.

"Not all people are like that," Feodor remarked.

"Nearly all. . . . Now you, for instance, are sensitive, but you're an exception. If everybody were like you, how nice it would be to live!" said Lida warmly, and looked into his eyes with innocent trust.

He found it hard to bear her glance. More from this childlike innocent glance than her words, something irremovable and heavy dropped in Feodor's chest. He felt suddenly that he feared Lida's trust and loyalty in the same way as Nina's archness and shrewdness.

"Tell me, Lida, how is Andrei coming along?" he asked, knowing that this would change the conversation.

"Andrei's improving; he feels much better now, especially since he moved to the Gorins'."

"To the Gorins'!" Feodor exclaimed in surprise. "Why to the Gorins'?"

Lida was a little astonished at his agitation, but she explained everything. Dimly realizing the reason for it, Feodor felt that Andrei's presence in Gorin's house would somehow hamper the fulfillment of his task. "Yes, of course," he thought with annoyance, "this Andrei will be an eyesore to Gorin, will act as a bad reminder for him. Ah! How badly that has turned out. Very untimely."

"Who arranged that?"

"Nina."

"But why didn't you put him up in your house? It would have been much handier for you."

"Of course. But my father wouldn't have allowed that on any account. Surely you can see what kind of man he is."

"If you like, I'll talk to him," Feodor suggested with some heat. "I'm sure I could persuade him."

Lida raised her eyebrows naïvely, like a little girl. "What a considerate, wonderful man he is," she thought to herself. "How ready he is to help his neighbor in any misfortune!" And without taking her eyes off him, she said: "Try if you like. Only I'm convinced that you can't do anything with my father. You don't know him yet; he's very obstinate."

"Well, one way or another, I'll talk to him."

"And then, there's my mother," Lida added with sudden embarrassment. "Surely you see that she looks on you as my suitor. . . . I don't know where she got the idea. I can imagine her face when you begin to talk to her about Andrei. You'll kill her."

"I—a suitor?" repeated Feodor.

"Why, of course! Isn't that funny? You—my sweetheart!" and Lida laughed gaily.

Her laughter offended Feodor. "What's so funny about that?" he thought with sudden annoyance. "Why the devil couldn't I be her sweetheart?" Aloud he hastened to agree with her: "Yes, of course, that's very amusing."

"But Mama'll get over that," Lida assured him. "Her mind was temporarily disturbed."

"I doubt it," thought Feodor to himself, remembering Natalia's maneuvering in the cabin.

When Feodor and Lida swam back near the yacht, her mother looked closely at them, as if she were trying to guess from their appearance what had happened between them, and apparently she wasn't pleased.

"Well! Is that the way to play?" she thought. "Keeping herself about half a mile away from him. . . . Is that the way I used to swim in my young days with all my suitors? Not a spot on my body was left whole, they pinched and pawed me so. While that fool swims like an iceberg!" To herself Natalia talked vividly and strongly.

"Well, if she's a fool and doesn't know what to do, I'll help her," she decided and waited for a suitable moment. When, of all the bathers, only Lida and Feodor remained in the water, while her husband, with Nikolai and Ivan, went to the cabin to change, Natalia, trying not to make any noise, slipped over the other side of the yacht to the water

288

and suddenly, with the agility of a dolphin, dived. Swimming unnoticed under the water toward her daughter, she pinched her leg very hard and pulled her under with all her might.

"Oh!" Lida screamed in a piercing voice. "A *som!*"

At this scream Feodor's heart jumped suddenly, painfully, as if it had been torn loose. (Later he recalled this with astonishment.) He was already climbing onto the deck but, when he heard the scream, he threw himself into the water. In three or four strokes he was beside the girl. Her face was scared and she was already swallowing water.

With his left hand Feodor held her so that her head was above water and swam to the yacht. Feodor's heart beat from blissful dismay; he barely understood what had happened. As he swam, fairy tales appeared to him, white swans flew before his eyes. He realized that such miracles happen once in a lifetime, and that he would never forget that moment.

"Lida, you haven't choked?" he asked in alarm.

"N—no, just a little," she replied, her whole body still trembling, and she clasped his strong neck more firmly with her hands.

Greatly excited, Feodor helped her to crawl onto the deck. Her figure was clearly outlined for an instant against the background of the huge red moon. Panting, she placed a hand on her small breast. "Oh-h-h! How scared I was!" Then she turned to him and exclaimed: "What's wrong with you, Professor? You're so pale!" And suddenly she laughed; her teeth flashed and her eyebrows rose. "What an adventure!"

Sidorov ran up from the cabin. "What happened?" he asked, alarmed.

"Something pulled me under the water," Lida answered.

"Not a *som,* surely?"

A lantern was brought; there were no traces on Lida's leg.

"What the hell!" said Sidorov. "Are you sure something snatched at you?"

"Why should she lie?" Natalia asked her husband sternly. She had just appeared from somewhere beyond the cabin, but water was dripping from her as from a drowned person.

Everything became clear. Feodor understood perfectly, and thought with annoyance: "No, better not say a word to her about Andrei."

Sidorov merely spat overboard fiercely.

"Ivan, weigh anchor. It's time to go home."

CHAPTER 12

BUT THEY DIDN'T return home at once. From somewhere on the river the distant, faint, barely audible sound of a steamer's paddles was borne to them.

"I know who that is. That's my workers coming," shouted Sidorov, pleased.

Natalia waved her hands hopelessly. "Lida, let's go to the cabin and sleep—now we won't be going home till morning."

Soon the silhouette of a small steamer could be distinguished. It was moving slowly, laboring.

"Ahoy!" shouted Sidorov, cupping his hands to his mouth like a trumpet. "Sereda, is that you?"

"Oho—o—o!" someone responded. "How are you, Leonid Stepanovich?"

Presently the steamer came up to them, its lights reflected in the water. Now Feodor saw that the little tug was pulling a large barge behind it. He shuddered. There, behind barbed wire stretched along the sides of the barge, could be seen the motionless figures of people, silent, slouched, closely crowded together.

"Where are they from?" he asked Ivan, who was standing beside him, fear in his voice.

"They're coming back from Comrade Sidorov's plant after work. About ten miles from here there's a large concentration camp."

Feodor didn't say another word. He noticed how Nikolai's face, usually carefree, suddenly became serious and paled in the darkness.

"What do you say, Sereda, shall we sing?" cried Sidorov merrily, taking absolutely no notice of the barge.

The man he was addressing came to the side of the tug and was clearly visible in the light of the lantern. "Probably the chief of the guard," thought Feodor. Sereda was held together with belts; from his side, dragging the deck, dangled a curved Caucasian sword. Spurs flashed on his wornout boots.

"Impossible, Leonid Stepanovich," he replied in a singsong Ukrainian voice. "It's against the rules to——"

"To hell with rules. No one will know, unless you tell them yourself. As for me, you surely know—like the grave."

"Impossible."

290

"There you go harping! 'Impossible!' 'Impossible!' Just one song!" insisted Sidorov. From his voice it was obvious that he was sure of success. Apparently this bargaining had taken place many times before. "I'll give you some brandy," the director promised in a soft voice. "Ivan, run and bring a bottle." Sidorov wasn't miserly. He was passionately fond of choral singing, and in his youth had sung in the church choir.

When Ivan appeared with the brandy, Sereda shouted to someone in a stern voice: "Stop the tug, we'll take a breather!"

From what kind of work Sereda wanted to rest wasn't clear, but the steamer stopped and the barge was quite near the yacht.

The director flung the bottle to the officer and the latter caught it with a practiced gesture. "Thank you, Leonid Stepanovich."

Sereda drank from the neck of the bottle, then gave it to his assistant. The bottle passed around and eventually it was handed over to the barge where three sentries, with rifles, finished it.

"Now, let's sing," said Sidorov.

"What'll it be?"

"What about *Oh, my Don, my peaceful Don?*"

"Right."

Sereda struck up first in a thin, clear voice. The director and the sentries caught it up.

After the first couplet Sidorov stopped and said to Sereda: "Not bad, but rather watery. Get the whole barge to sing."

"I can't, Leonid Stepanovich, the enemies of the people are forbidden to sing."

"And who'll know?"

"Well, in any case."

"Come on, come on!"

"All right, just one song . . ."

The sentries on the barge, who obviously knew to a nicety the diplomatic talks between the two chiefs, raised the butts on the prisoners. "Sing, you rabble! But in harmony!"

The dark figures of the prisoners stirred. Some of them got up, supporting themselves on each other. One old man with a white beard, like the martyrs painted on ikons, caught Feodor's eyes. With one hand, misshapen like a twisted root, he leaned on a stick: The other was bandaged crudely—probably it had been damaged at the heavy work. He was standing tall, thin, grim. The wind ruffled his gray hairs.

The chief of the guard struck up the second couplet. The prisoners caught up the tune, at first shakily, not all at once, but after a moment the whole barge was singing. By their willingness to sing, in spite of their tiredness, by their brightened faces, a moment ago looking almost dead, it was apparent what joy the singing gave them. Their director's whim opened, if only for a brief moment, the coffin lid of silence.

Frightening it was to hear from them the words of the song:

> Oh, free-flowing Don, accept the salute
> Of your loyal Cossack . . .

Feodor saw how the tears flowed from the old man's eyes, dropped onto his white beard. What was he crying about? About his ruined life? About relatives, sons, about himself? Or about the Don which was no longer free?

One powerful voice in this awful choir filled the darkness, hovered over the water, and must have been heard far beyond the distant bend of the river. Feodor looked towards Gorin's house, wondering if Gorin heard this singing and what feelings it aroused in him. In the singing, boundless as the Don itself, there sounded yearning, tenderness, and anger. . . . Yes, anger. At that moment, not so much in words as in the passion of their voices, the prisoners were able to express what had been forbidden them under pain of death to say. They sang as if they were speaking aloud their secret thoughts.

The stars moved slowly across the sky. The singing at times sank low, at others, like a terrific whirlwind, it rose to the very stars. Sidorov stopped singing, listened to the choir, half-closing his eyes, apparently sobered.

Feodor was seized by a chill every time the prisoners responded to the couplet with a single cry, like the wind in a dark forest. But more than anything, the look of the people themselves, with their staring eyes and wide-open mouths, frightened him—they looked like dark apparitions appearing here in the middle of the night to remind Feodor of the other great world, where millions of people were rotting alive and where Feodor himself might perish.

Nor was he alone in being shocked. If he had looked closely in that moment at Nikolai, he would have noticed the expression of suffering on his face, which suddenly became tense, almost petrified. Nikolai's fists were corded with swollen veins. He could no longer look at the wretches. Their singing became torture for him. He turned away and went to the other side of the deck, afraid lest the sea of his fierce anger, which filled him to the limit, would splash over. If Sereda or Sidorov had been in his path just then, he would certainly have killed him.

292

But now the singing was stilled; and in an instant it was as if everything had become still. The prisoners stood, holding their breath. The song had twisted their hearts, as fire twists birch bark. It again became bitter and dark inside them, probably worse than before.

"Gr—ea—at!" said Sidorov slowly and very thoughtfully.

Suddenly Feodor noticed the old man on the barge stagger and begin to wave his arms weakly and nervously, as if he were drowning.

"Oh, brothers, I can't go on!" he moaned quietly and dropped slowly to the deck. Then he stuck his face into the barbed wire and was still. "He's sung himself out," said one of the sentries. The prisoners around crossed themselves devoutly. One could hear the murmur of prayers, a hoarse cough, mixed with sobs.

"Comrade Chief!" shouted a sentry to Sereda. "Looks like an old man here has died. What are your orders?"

"Died?" asked Sereda, annoyed. "Take him to the stern; we'll straighten things out at the camp," and turning to the engine room, the chief of the guard ordered: "Get her going! It's time to move!"

"Well, so long, Leonid Stepanovich," he said to Sidorov a little apologetically. "I'll see you at the plant tomorrow."

The wheels churned and the tug began to pull the barge behind it. The long, black mass passed the yacht slowly. Feodor saw two prisoners lift and carry the old man to the stern.

The barge passed on. The sentry at the stern waved his hand to Sidorov, smiling. The latter did not respond; he stood looking gloomily into the darkness.

The water eddied astern of the barge, the reddish gleam of the gypsy moon slid over the waves. It seemed to Feodor that it was not a barge, but some huge wounded animal that was crawling away with difficulty to its lair, leaving a bloody trail behind.

CHAPTER 13

MIKHAIL AWOKE early with the sunrise. During these morning hours an extraordinary stillness hung over everything, as if all living things were hushed in the expectation of very important events. But Gorin knew that nature was mistaken. It would be just another day, the same as the one before, like a link in a chain.

He dropped his long sinewy legs onto the carpet, but did not get up, just remained sitting on the bed, thoughtful, his head sunk on his chest—a large, awkward figure, with his bony shoulder blades sticking out sharply under the white cloth of his nightshirt.

In an old, wonderful time, waking full of joyful energy, he used to go impatiently to his study where, at the open windows, his manuscripts, damp from the morning dew, awaited him. In those days, intoxicated by spiritual uplift, full of impatient thoughts, he would take up his work immediately. That time had passed. Where was the creative impulse, the sense of unlimited strength and confidence in himself? Where?

That was when he wrote his poem about a lonely hero who tore his heart out of his breast and with it lit the way for people who had lost themselves in their own lies and greed. At that time he had thought that he was writing of himself—so great was his desire to do something big, unforgettable, to help people to find the truth of life, to accustom their eyes to the bright sun of justice. His heart had been lit by the flame of love for the people, and he thought that flame would never die. Surely that wasn't a delusion? Could it be that his heart was being covered with ashes and was incapable of lighting up even his own soul? No, that couldn't be! What he was going through now was merely a temporary weakness . . . It would pass, as a cold passes.

Gorin sighed loudly and, raising his head, looked out of the window. A breeze moved the blind slightly, bringing with it the refreshing smell of the garden. But the breeze did not blow away the shroud of yearning from his soul, did not dispel his heavy thoughts . . .

Every morning was for Gorin the beginning of a trial, and most frightful of all, he was not sure he would emerge victorious. He was preparing himself for the new day as a soldier prepares for battle, checking his arms, putting on his armor. At that early hour, when Gorin was alone with himself, he recalled the past day, judged himself. He was not yet wearing his armor, but his shoulders felt its weight—this need to hide his thoughts and doubts in front of people. Gorin frowned, recalling the details of his talk with his wife about Glushak, and Pavel's recent outburst. His son was an old wound; its pain was familiar and by now he was accustomed to it. But Luba's strange, not quite understandable words about Glushak brought a new pain to his heart. Glushak's collapse, it seemed—and Mikhail Gorin considered that his friend had simply become old and tired—had brought new doubts of his own strength.

"No, no, never!" said Mikhail aloud and got up, rang the bell.

294

Cheprok, who had been waiting on the other side of the door for his signal, came in.

"Well, Cheprok, is everything all right?"

"Everything, thank God," answered the old man. "Only Vanka, the warehouse man, was caught stealing yesterday and they're throwing him off the estate this morning." And Cheprok, helping him to dress, began to gossip at length and in detail about Vanka's villainy. Apparently Mikhail was listening to him attentively. But it wasn't Cheprok he was hearing, it was the sound of passing time, the voices of acquaintances which resounded in his head.

Then he recalled a recent incident that took place in the forest when he was hunting boar with Romain Rouen. That was a tense moment. Ahead of them in the dense forest they heard the noise of the beaters; at any moment the excited animal, dangerous in his fury, might appear. A light rain had just fallen; it was hot in the forest; steam was rising from the glade where they stood. Above their heads flew birds frightened by the beaters. Gorin stood beside an oak stump out of which sprouts shot up on all sides, not taking his eyes off an opening between two wild gooseberry bushes. He figured the boar would come from there. Several paces from him Romain Rouen was frozen in a tense pose beside a birch tree, holding his rifle ready, consumed with hunting ardor. Suddenly, at the most dangerous moment, when the snapping of branches could be heard ever closer, he lowered his rifle and, turning to Mikhail, said: "This is how, with beaters and noise, they hunt the independent intellectuals in the West. Amid the howl of the reactionary papers, amid the hisses of scoundrels. . . . You're lucky! Here they only hunt animals."

Mikhail's face twitched painfully. Not because the untimeliness of the conversation irritated him, but because the Frenchman's words, spoken, of course, to flatter him, grated on his taut nerves. To his own surprise he replied, without taking his eyes off the gooseberry bushes:

"If they don't hunt them here, it's simply because there's no longer anything to hunt. All the independent boars have been killed off long ago. I alone remain, and even at that it looks as if I have become tame . . ." The end of the phrase was drowned by a shot. Gorin felled the squat, panic-stricken animal with his first shot—he was bearing down straight on Rouen. The boar fell two paces from him.

"You have saved me from the tusks of that monster," said Rouen with a smile on his pale lips.

"That's a good lesson for us," replied Mikhail, going over to the blood-spattered boar. The bullet had entered his heart. "You can't mix politics and hunting." Gorin was speaking in his poor French; from excitement it was worse than usual.

People rushed up, noisily began to congratulate Mikhail on his successful shot; the conversation with the Frenchman could not be continued. Gorin was glad of that. He himself was afraid at his unexpected outburst because, in his excitement, he had expressed his inner condition with extraordinary clarity. On the journey back from the hunt he intercepted Rouen's searching look.

Gorin, thinking about Rouen, recalled his own youth. In the same harsh and merciless way he had judged the society of that time—in the same way he had thought freedom and justice were hemmed in, while their defenders, the advanced intellectuals, were persecuted by the Tsarist regime. He had been just as sure of his own rightness and as childishly naïve as this gray-haired Frenchman.

What an irony of fate! Rouen had come to him like a pilgrim to the promised land—to glimpse in the sunset of his life the marvelous incarnation of his dreams—and Gorin could give him only doubts and bitterness. Somewhere a fatal mistake had been made; somewhere a monstrous lie was hidden. He strove to find it—but now even the hope of solving this devilish problem frightened him.

"So what's the matter, Gorin? Have you already lost courage, or are you ashamed of your own belated repentance?"

"I won't, I don't want to believe in my mistake! It is not I, but the people surrounding me who are mistaken, while I am simply blinded temporarily and do not see the real life; it is passing me by. All these people close to me—Pavel, Glushak—they don't belong to the present world. They are weak shadows from an old smoky candle. It is they who are confusing my mind, in them lies the evil, not in me . . . I am among people, but I am alone."

Gorin began to walk about the room in long strides, the crease of suffering between his eyebrows growing deeper. Cheprok, making the bed, glanced at him distressfully.

"Why this piling up of torments? . . . Look at Shchusev: he isn't afraid of a lie. He bathes in it as if it were his native element and laughs at it. Yes, it's easy for him; he keeps his feelings under a good lock."

Mikhail recalled Shchusev's face, his eyes, sparkling all the time with lazy humor. From Rostov he went to Tiflis, to fulfill some routine government job. Then to Gori, in Georgia—Stalin had ordered the small house where he was born to be enclosed in crystal and marble, to make this house a second Athos, a place of pilgrimage for believing communists of the whole world.

"I'm going off to build a glass case," said Shchusev before his departure. "Stalin doesn't trust to the grateful memory of his heirs and, without waiting for them, is building monuments and museums for himself."

"Shchusev, of course, will build a magnificent case and will get his routine Order of Lenin," thought Gorin. "He's a sly cynical careerist." But Mikhail could not help but appreciate the bold outspokenness of the architect.

Nevertheless, when Shchusev left he had sighed with relief. That man, whose screwed-up eyes prevented one from peering into him, could see everything that was going on in Gorin's mind. He had annoyed and confused Mikhail. It was as if the architect's whole demeanor said to him: "Why torture yourself? Why get excited? Be like me, Mikhail, and everything will be all right." He had tempted him with peace of mind, but the price of such peace frightened Gorin.

Never before had Mikhail experienced such depression. There had been one awful period in his life—after the death of his first wife. But that was a personal tragedy. It was not doubt that slowly tore his soul to pieces, throbbing like the agony of a toothache, but the sudden sharp sorrow that came on in a moment—then, the life of a friend whom he loved more than himself, more than his work, had been cut short—then, love was broken.

The history of that love was strange and significant. He—a vagabond, a tramp, wandering along the shores of the Black Sea in the company of Cheprok and others like him—had stopped once at the port of Odessa. His soul he had long ago besmirched in vice which vodka alone could wipe out, and vodka he zealously used. But if his soul craved vodka, his stomach demanded food and lots of it, for he was a big healthy young man. In the company which he kept, work was regarded as a degrading occupation, while theft was honorable. Enthusiasm for this profession brought him in contact with a circle of smugglers. There in Odessa, in one of the dens of thieves, he met a wonderful girl, daughter of a smuggler, a bright, wild being, a real child of the sea and like the sea unpredictable—at times quiet and affectionate, at others stormy and passionate. The meeting took place one morning following a drunken party, in a tumbledown hut, in which the noise of the waves resounded as in a seashell. This noise woke him and when he opened his eyes he met the glance of a young girl—curious and wonderfully tender. A golden radiance poured out of her dark eyes and, charmed by this radiance, he blissfully lowered his eyelids. He thought that he had died and that God, forgiving his drunkard's soul, had sent him to heaven and that an angel was before him—so beautiful were her eyes and hair in the silvery dust from the light of the window, and so great was the contrast between what he had seen the previous night—Cheprok's ugly nose and a pair of protruding drunken eyes.

It would be hard to say what attracted the young girl to Mikhail, but in the evening of the same day they were sitting with their arms around each other on the high shore above the sea, And in the morning, when the first rays of the sun, not yet above the water, lit the emerald mass of the sea as if from within, she was already his wife.

It was a sudden and bright love. Mikhail remembered clearly how time stood still, how the noise of the waves disappeared and their hearts stopped beating each time their lips met. He would never forget her first cry of pain, shame, and happiness—when he, proud in his strength, stood before her naked, and the sun rising over the sea shone on these two people drunk with love, and with its scarlet rays hid the flush of shame on her face and the blue shadows of love around her enraptured eyes.

In a voice full of tenderness he had asked her, then: "You're not sorry, Mira?"

And she, all atremble from desire, drew him to her breast and whispered in his ear: "I'm sorry only for every second that I haven't been in your arms; hold me closer, my darling . . ."

Thus did a tender and passionate love come to Mikhail. He had known many women before Mira. How did this one differ from the others? This girl with the childlike pure heart not only gave him the gift of love about which other men could only dream, but she also changed him completely; she enriched his soul with an unknown happiness, awakened in him the desire to leave an imprint on this frightful and wonderful life—the desire to write. He was never sure where love ended and creative work began. It was then that he wrote his first works, those short stories in which earthy realism was strangely interwoven with romanticism. It was as if Mira, who until the end of her life was more lover to him than wife, had opened his eyes. In apparently simple and coarse people he learned to see beautiful human qualities. In repulsive tramps, from whom people usually turn away with horror, he found high and noble feelings, at times roughly expressed, but always sincere. Such was the style of his stories—rugged, often naïve, but always truthful and sincere, like the word of a child.

Gorin sent the first collection of his stories to a journal published in Rostov, never dreaming that they would make him famous overnight. The stories were reprinted in a St. Petersburg journal and published as a book. People began to pronounce Gorin's name with the same delight as Chekhov's and predicted the fame of Tolstoy for him. From the very beginning he became a semilegendary figure around which were built a variety of facts and fancies. Much of this was brought about by the unusual subjects of his stories. He described his friend Cheprok, his smuggling acquaintances, thieves, tramps, prostitutes, and wanderers like himself with restless souls, always looking for new impressions, and also like himself, hungry with love for mankind. He also described Mira, told people what rich feelings were hidden in the simple, uneducated girl, born in a miserable cabin on the seashore; described how passion and spiritual beauty created in her a wonderful harmony of soul and body—unheard of by city people with their weak chicken bodies and satiated desires. He belabored these people, and strangely, they who hated the bitter truth like ill-tasting medicine took his blows with gratitude, with the religious exaltation of repentant sinners. They extolled him as a new prophet who had seen with his young eyes all the sweetness and all the bitterness of life, had drained this cup to the dregs. His stories breathed of the salt wind of the sea, threatening to blow to pieces the frozen charm of old Russia. They uncovered new breathtaking horizons; their realism elevated the soul. As an artist, Mikhail Gorin not only worshipped the beauty, strength and goodness inherent in man—he was also a rebel. With all the might of his young soul he hated the Tsarist regime which, it seemed to him, hindered the development of the best qualities of man, destroyed him, cast him backwards into the obscurity of a thousand years, into the beastly reign of slavery.

His *Ode to the Stormy Petrel* glorified the approaching revolution and became a symbol of the times. Students, teachers, engineers, all the intellectuals, considering themselves the bearers of the idea of the revolution, declaimed this ode to each other with faces pale and eyes sparkling from excitement. In it sounded the triumphant thunder of coming events, and its rhythm reminded one of the music of Beethoven. Wealthy lawyers, raking in thousand-ruble fees while defending some pimp who had robbed an old woman, thought it good taste to wind up their speeches with Gorin's *Ode* and invariably called forth tears from the accused—this "victim of environment"—applause from the men, and swooning sighs from the smartly dressed ladies in the court.

If the historians set themselves the task of picking out the one man who had done most to make the revolution of 1917 possible they would have to decide on Mikhail Gorin. For men like Lenin merely reaped the harvest which this naïve giant with the power of a genius and the heart of a child had sown. The fact that after the overthrow of Tsarism Lenin took these same intellectuals, these amateurs of pretty declamations who had welcomed the revolution with the rapture of inexperienced calves, into an iron grip; and the fact that Stalin later let them rot in concentration camps or simply shot them—these facts are history. The history passed Gorin by and only in the later years of his life did it touch him painfully. In those days, indeed, no one could have foreseen the evil joke of fate—no one, least of all Gorin himself.

Encouraged by his first success, he devoted all his time to literary work. Mira, on the other hand, having become a woman, a wife, was even more beautiful, as if it were the first time she had felt the inner coursing of her hot blood. Unthinking, unreasoning, with the unrestrained force of her awakened womanhood, she gave her whole being to her love of Mikhail. Like the deep ocean, her passion almost drowned him in its waves. Mikhail, strong and life-loving, at times was almost overpowered by her love and was glad when she quieted down. At such times she used to sit on his knees, pressing her head to his broad chest, singing songs softly and tenderly, like the lapping of waves in clear weather.

She bore him a son. It seemed as if there were no end to happiness. But the end came suddenly and harshly; she died of tuberculosis. That thirst for life, that hot passion which had shocked Mikhail, these were hidden symptoms of her disease. It was evening when she passed away; her face seemed illuminated in the darkness and she had never looked more beautiful.

Then the light dimmed for Mikhail. He felt that he would never again be able to work—life was empty and meaningless. But the writer in him could be stopped only by death. He had not died nor surrendered. The journey to Italy, the sharp change, helped to heal his wound. When he met Luba, some years later in Florence, this clever, gentle, and calm woman seemed to give him what he sought more than anything else—a quiet haven. But he found that the shadow of Mira had not forsaken him. Feeling the burden of his memories, Mikhail was particularly attentive, affectionate, especially ardent in his love for his wife, as if he

300

were convincing himself that the past was forgotten, crossed out forever . . .

And then Nina was born. Perhaps Mikhail had suffered too much; perhaps it was not a woman's, but some other's, caresses that his tired heart needed. So when Nina appeared in the world, greeted with the salty winds of Capri, her first cry smothered Gorin's endearing words to his wife. Nina became a new sun for him, driving away forever the shades of the past. In her beautiful eyes hope was reflected; not pain, but a quiet joy grew in Mikhail's heart.

With Nina's birth began the most fruitful period of his creative work. He worked evenly and calmly, without looking backward into the past, without fear for himself.

Thus the troubled period of his life ended. He was convinced that never, never again would doubts assail him, never again would he experience that terrible feeling of loneliness. The future appeared to him cloudless and bright, like an autumn day in Naples. And now? . . .

Gorin drew aside the light curtain with his hand, looked out of the window and suddenly felt his heart flutter, as if it were laughing. Nina was walking along a path in the park. She was in shorts, with a towel over her bare shoulders—returning from her morning swim in the river.

"How beautiful she is!" he thought, admiring her. "How light and smooth are her movements!"

Slowly he dropped the curtain, turned to Cheprok, and putting his arm around his stooped back, went out of the room with him. His steps were even and firm. His face was calm; on his breast, which a moment ago had been full of doubts, he wore an unseen but strong armor. Mikhail Gorin was ready to meet the new day.

CHAPTER 14

"HERE'S A TRUE story: once at a lecture I began to explain Pavlov's theory on reflexes to my students—I noticed that they weren't understanding. I explained again and again without result. I went on explaining, explaining—until at last I myself understood, but they still did not. Ha-ha-ha! . . . Here's Mikhail Alexeyevich. Having your morning swim? Have you heard the new story, or shall I repeat it?" asked the doctor.

"I heard, I heard . . . no need to repeat it. Only you can explain what you yourself don't understand," replied Mikhail with a smile.

"Good morning, Doctor. Good morning, Luba, Nina." And after kissing his daughter's still damp hair, Mikhail sat down at the table.

They were having breakfast on the terrace at a round table, covered with a white tablecloth, in Russian style, with a samovar and turnovers. Luba, shivering from the morning coolness with a lace shawl around her shoulders, poured the fragrant tea. Spots of sunshine, reflected by the mirrorlike silver samovar, the silver spoons and the fine cut glass, played on her smiling face.

It was a pleasure to look at Luba: she was growing stout, but still had a pliable waist, back and shoulders of rare grace, and fine and delicate features. Beside her daughter she looked like a copy executed in quite different tones—dark and deep.

Between the widely spaced white Doric columns of the terrace the park could be seen, still wrapped in a blue morning haze. The pigeons were cooing, strutting importantly on the paths and leaving a clear imprint of their feet in the sand, damp from the dew. The splashing of the half-closed fountains could be heard—their silhouettes stood out ghostly, framed in the sunlit jets of water. The air was filled with the wonderful fragrance, evoking grateful smiles in the people.

"Mikhail, you look wonderful," Luba remarked, handing him a glass of tea. "How is the water? Cold?"

"Yes, it's cold. Not so much on the surface, but underneath—like ice. Brr! I saw Nina when she was coming back from bathing and I was quite envious," explained Mikhail and, glancing at the vacant chair, asked: "Why on earth hasn't Pavel come for breakfast?"

"He asked to have it served in bed."

"What's wrong with him?" Mikhail turned to the doctor in alarm.

"Nothing serious," the latter replied. "He's just in the dumps. He should swim more, as now, early in the morning, and he would be healthy and fresh as a dandelion, exactly like you." And, biting a biscuit with his large teeth, he said, working his eyebrows: *"Sehr gut,* as little Fritz said when he drank a barrel of beer."

The doctor and his jokes were an inevitable part of every breakfast in Gorin's house. A very active, lean man of about forty, with red hair neatly brushed back of his ears, and a surprisingly white, feminine skin which would not tan, he filled the fresh air of the terrace with his quick speech and not always fresh stories. When he laughed, throwing back his head and opening his mouth, full of gold teeth, he looked like a neighing horse. His name was Tsibik, but everyone called him simply the doctor.

He appeared in Gorin's house during their first days in Rostov—the

302

ailing Pavel needed a doctor's care—and he remained to live with them, becoming something in the nature of a house doctor. Tsibik worked in the main Rostov hospital, was regarded as a fairly good pathologist, sometimes gave lectures at the Faculty of Medicine. Every morning after breakfast he went to the city, where he had dinner in the service dining room and returned home in the evening. He was the only member of the household allowed to sit at the Gorin table. This came about almost unnoticed, thanks probably to a certain brazenness of the doctor. In the end Mikhail became accustomed to his presence and even found it convenient: at table the doctor reported to him on the health of his family, of the members of the household, and of the racehorses, of which Mikhail had a full stable.

Justly mistrusting the quality of the city dinners, the doctor always ate a hearty breakfast—the abundance of the Gorin menu was not regulated by any ration cards. Luba, knowing his appetite, purposely ordered the table to be set in country style, turnovers with many different fillings, pancakes, and fritters.

The doctor never got used to the new life—all this food, fountains, unheard-of luxury, such fantastic luck to fall so unexpectedly on his red head! The state of blissful dizziness never left him for a minute. It seemed to him all the time that fate—that unpredictable fairy—was light-heartedly playing with her delicate fingers in his fiery mane and, apparently, would never tire of doing so. How precious, for example, had been the kiss it bestowed on him at the very beginning of his new career! When Pavel became bored last year and decided to refresh himself abroad, in France (this was arranged for him without any difficulty), it happened quite naturally that the doctor accompanied him. Then Tsibik definitely believed in his lucky star.

They stayed in France for two months, mainly in Paris. Paris, the city of light! Within its walls, ancient as history itself, young life beat always. Something mysterious and attractive about it makes people, young and old, forgetting their duty, their family, and even themselves, reach out toward its magic lights. Even those arriving for the first time throw themselves at Paris as at a lover after a long parting: some, in mad passion, burn up their lives, deafened by the music, drunk from the wine, charmed by the beautiful women; others, in quiet joy, caress with their eyes the palaces, the boulevards, the paintings of the Louvre, and the wonderful sunsets of Montmartre. But no matter what their temperament, people in Paris do not live—they love.

Doctor Tsibik alone suffered there. He spent all his time in Paris in a dentist's chair, contorted by torture. But however great the pain, his soul exulted, for he was getting himself gold teeth! Not one, not two, but both rows; he changed them all, bad ones and good. The pain vanished altogether when he imagined with what respect and envy they would look at his golden maw in Rostov.

At first he thought to realize the unattainable dream of every Soviet person—to buy himself a gold watch—but changed his mind. He distrusted the border guards too much. "In two winks they'd take it away." There remained the second dream—gold teeth. "They'll hardly take them out at the border; too much trouble." With the rest of his money the doctor bought himself a cigarette holder, studs, and tie pin made of transparent rose amber. The amber cigarette holder, amber studs, red mustache, red slicked-down hair, the two rows of gold teeth—all made him bright red and transparent from head to foot.

But the outward change in him paled in comparison to the inner change. The foreign air really went to his head; he suddenly imagined himself a European, a proud representative of a great civilization, enriched by an advanced culture and amber studs. Now he looked down on his own countrymen, and in his heart he considered even Gorin beneath him. Though Gorin had spent half his life abroad, Tsibik saw that the writer remained an incurable Russian.

Tsibik had always distinguished himself by a special neatness. (When he went to bed, the doctor folded his pants, bachelor fashion, under the mattress, and put them on with pride in the morning—razor-edged, as if straight from the press.) But now he became scrupulously neat, almost sickeningly courteous, and haughty to the point of the ridiculous. He even grew long fingernails and carried a nail file with him; when not engaged in telling stories, he filed them importantly, sticking out his little finger coquettishly.

However, the "foreigner" Tsibik kept to the well-known Russian rule at table: reach for what you want! At first he was shy; but later, seeing that nobody rapped his greedy knuckles, he began without ceremony to rake in everything his eyes saw. Before taking a piece, he aimed at it with his eyes and, smacking his lips, stretched out his long hand, plentifully overgrown with red hair. But in spite of his wolfish appetite he remained gaunt as Pharaoh's cow.

Everything about the doctor was mixed up half and half—sincerity and falsehood, simple-mindedness and affected haughtiness—but his main characteristic was flippancy. When he took off his white smock he also shed the dignity so necessary to him in the hospital.

Pavel liked him because he didn't insist particularly on medicines, didn't bore him with a diet—simply left him to himself. Mikhail got used to him, Luba tolerated him and tried not to notice his shortcomings. But Nina simply couldn't stand him. At first she had liked him; he amazed her with his extraordinary neatness, his courteous manners and lively speech. But after a while she saw through him. On one occasion she complained to the doctor of a headache. He immediately asked her to undress, so that he could examine her. She was beginning to unbutton her blouse when she suddenly noticed how convulsively his huge Adam's apple jumped. Nina blushed deeply; she didn't undress and from that time avoided the doctor, hating him with her whole heart.

Tsibik, to hide his embarrassment, always spoke with her in a half-joking tone. But only Cheprok really scared him. A kind of weakness seized him when the old man fixed his eyes on him. Cheprok used to say that "for the doctor the whole world is covered by a woman's skirt."

But the weaker sex was not the doctor's main passion. He had four most precious, most secret desires: to become director of the hospital, to own a gold watch, to learn the fox trot, and to make another visit to Paris. The first three were possible, although difficult, and depended on himself; the last desire depended on Gorin, and Tsibik had little faith in its realization. However, just in case, he curried favor with Gorin, tried to charm him, and considered it his duty to entertain him at breakfast, sometimes with jokes, at others with stories, or simply by making him laugh a little. Like all palaces, Gorin's palace could not do without its jester.

"Well, Doctor," said Mikhail with a smile, "soon you won't need to go to the city—we have our own hospital now—patients galore: Pavel, Andrei . . . It only remains for me to catch a cold in midsummer and take to bed."

"It will be an excellent hospital," responded the doctor. "For a nurse I'll take Nina, as long as she doesn't become interested in the young patients," and with a playful ripple of laughter the doctor looked at Nina but, seeing the almost angry look in her eyes, he turned quickly to Mikhail. "H—m—m. . . . Oh, yes . . . As for a cold, I have a deadly prescription: vodka, black currant liqueur. An old forester taught me how to make it. First the berries are infused in spirit, and then it's diluted with water. For you, of course, I won't dilute it. . . . Heh—heh—heh!"

"Fool!" said Nina suddenly.

"What?" The doctor looked at her, offended. With her eyes she indicated a small butterfly that had flown into a bowl of honey. It was stuck and unable to get out.

The doctor broke into a smile.

"What is sweet is dangerous—isn't that so, Nina?"

Mikhail, inhaling deeply of the fragrant air, said: "Last night I heard somebody's excellent male choir singing on the Don. However, I was just going to sleep; possibly I dreamed it."

"No, I heard it also . . ." Luba remarked, and her voice suddenly broke. "You know, when you're falling asleep, at that wavering moment between sleep and wakefulness, all singing seems to be heavenly, especially if it comes from a distance. I always liked listening to the night singing of the fishermen on Capri. Night softens even a coarse song, it imparts a kind of mystery to it; everything worldly vanishes, only the song and the stars remain. . . ."

"How remarkably you express yourself!" murmured the doctor, and even clicked his heels under the table from emotion.

"I haven't heard anything like that for a long time," Mikhail resumed. "Who could it be? Whoever it was singing, it's a good sign— people sing like that only when they are happy."

"Most probably it was Cossacks from the village," Luba remarked, and for some reason looked searchingly at her husband.

Mikhail noticed her glance. "They're all expecting something from me," he thought with annoyance, and changed the conversation. He turned to the doctor. "Tell me, how is Andrei feeling?"

"Excellent! Andrei's grit amazes me. He jokes, makes wise cracks, behaving as if he hadn't lost an eye, but was at a resort."

"Please look after him as well as you can," said Mikhail. "And don't hurry his convalescence—let him lie in bed as long as possible."

"Nina's looking after him," replied the doctor. "She reads books to him, as a real Sister of Mercy should."

"That's excellent."

"Poor boy," said Luba softly, sighing. "I'll never forget the moment when the doctor took the bandages off his eyes. Imagine, Mikhail, the doctor did it on purpose when it was already getting dark, but it was still quite easy to distinguish the park. You should have seen the expression on Andrei's face! He grew numb for an instant, then suddenly broke out into such loud, happy laughter—"

"Laughter?" interjected Mikhail. "Why should he laugh?"

"I don't know. Probably, simply the joyful feeling of the light, the knowledge that he could see."

306

"That was his reflexes," announced the doctor with a thoughtful air, at the same time catching sight of his reflection in the silver samovar. "Irritation from light, acting on the nerves, is at times able to evoke involuntary laughter."

Nina bit her full lips, looked at the doctor disdainfully.

"He's silly," she thought. "It's your own laughter that comes from your involuntary reflexes to lickspittle. It wasn't reflexes, and not the park, but Lida that Andrei saw, and he laughed from sheer joy."

She remembered that moment well. Lida was standing beside the window, half turned toward Andrei. Nina was convinced that he saw nothing but her. At that moment she envied her friend terribly: "That is real love!"

Nina was in a state of confusion. Rudoy was a thing of the past, and she didn't want to remember him. Ahead of her rose unexpectedly the tall figure of Feodor Novikov. The meeting and talk with Feodor had roused her deeply and joyfully. He was quite unlike the men she had met before. He was clever, bright in conversation, completely fearless in his thoughts. She had noticed his agitation in the park and the knowledge that she was the cause of it filled her with a vague alarm and pride.

At first she treated the young professor like a pleasant discovery and as such she intended to store the meeting with him in her mind, among other pleasant thoughts and pictures. But once when her father mentioned Novikov's name by chance she felt with astonishment how her heart began to beat quickly. Unexpectedly, she discovered that she was awaiting his coming with impatience. But the days passed, and he did not appear.

"What am I getting worked up about?" she thought with annoyance. "That meeting was casual and without significance."

However, she could not reconcile herself to the thought that it was to remain the first and last, merely teasing her with a hazy promise of happiness. Her nights seemed to become transparent, the border where wakefulness ended and sleep began merged, while before her closed eyes rose the scene of their meeting, in her ears sounded their voices, her own gay with laughter, his restrained but full of inner excitement; in her imagination beautiful visions scurried in a sweet whirlwind, catching her up in one absorbing feeling—love.

Nina was in love. But so sudden and unexplainable did this new feeling seem to her that she had little faith in it.

A gay little bird flew onto the terrace, dropped to the railing and began to hop along it, looking alertly at the people.

"If she hops to the fourth pillar, Novikov will come today," Nina

307

guessed. The little bird took wing before reaching it, and hid behind the lilac bushes. "So, he won't come. What a pity."

Mikhail also followed the little bird with his eyes.

"Yes, Doctor, moral life has its limits, but only daily experience teaches us to fumble for them," he said thoughtfully. "To step beyond these limits, without leaving a trace, is impossible—it's not like a bird flying from bush to bush . . ."

Nina gathered that she had missed the beginning of the conversation and was sorry. She liked to listen to her father. He spoke in a special way, not with words but in pictures, and to listen to him was as interesting as witnessing live scenes. But at the moment it irritated her that her father was talking, not with her, nor with her mother, but with this insignificant doctor. "He's throwing pearls before swine," she thought bitterly, unable to imagine that the doctor, whose main interest seemed to consist in gorging himself, could understand her father's words.

The doctor, glancing around the table with his honeyed eyes, replied to Mikhail with a joke: "In my childhood my father taught me to feel out the moral limits. When I began to get interested in our chambermaid, he lambasted me with a strap."

Mikhail laughed. "The lessons of life are at times more harsh and painful than the most merciless lambasting."

Mikhail spoke in a cheerful voice, joked, laughed more than usual, but stubbornly avoided Luba's glances and talked almost all the time to the doctor. It seemed as if he wanted to show his wife that her talk about Glushak yesterday had not bothered him at all. But it was difficult to deceive Luba. His vivacious speech merely reminded her more sharply of his mental suffering, his torturing loneliness and sleepless nights. However, she showed no sign either—she concentrated on watching Nina. Recently the latter had astonished her.

Nina was drinking tea, dreamily eating turnovers, and looking at her mother affectionately with shaded eyes; but she answered her absent-mindedly. Luba decided that Nina was in love.

As always, the doctor said aloud what the others were thinking: "I notice that Nina has changed noticeably: she has become silent, thoughtful, absent-minded. . . . As a doctor I can diagnose her illness from these symptoms—she is in love. But to identify the lucky one, science is helpless."

Nina's gray eyes opened in surprise; her cheeks flushed deep red under her tan.

"You don't know how to read symptoms, Doctor. I'm not in love,

308

but simply disgusted," she said, looking with hatred at the doctor's Adam's apple.

"Who, then, is so loathsome to you?"

"You are."

Luba tinkled softly with her teaspoon, calling Nina to her senses. But the doctor laughed loudly, flapping his arms like wings.

"That is still another sign!" he exclaimed. "To a girl in love, all men except one are loathsome."

Nina got up from the table. Without looking at the doctor, she said to her mother in passing: "I will be practicing in the sitting room. If you like, come and we'll play a four-handed piece."

Mikhail, smiling with his eyes, asked his wife: "What's the matter with her today?"

"I don't know." Luba shrugged her shoulders.

The doctor made a wry face. "The usual girlish emotion—a storm in a teacup. Nina, as always, is much too passionate."

"By the way, Mikhail," Luba said, rising from the table. "Pavel wanted to speak to you about something."

Mikhail looked at her questioningly and, it seemed, with annoyance. "The ordeals are beginning," passed through his mind. His whole being was straining to avoid them. But Luba insisted: "You'd better go and find out what it's about."

Mikhail rose, and then immediately turned to the doctor: "Let's go together. It may possibly concern you . . ."

He didn't want to go alone. He was afraid of conversations with Pavel, afraid and not sure of himself.

CHAPTER 15

PAVEL WAS PACING from corner to corner of the bedroom, a dressing gown thrown over his shoulders, smoking a cigarette nervously and following the design on the carpet with lowered eyes. The outline of his long profile was dark and harsh, with his scanty hair, his flabby lower lip. He had asked for breakfast in bed to avoid appearing at the table on the terrace—he knew that he was repugnant to everybody.

"So what? I don't need you either," he repeated to himself irascibly but, remembering Nina, he realized that he was not quite right and made a mental reservation: "Well, if not repugnant, at least pitiful, and I hate your pity still more."

Pavel hadn't slept; he had smoked and thought a great deal. There was a bitter taste in his mouth. A headache racked him and made it hard for him to think. And his thoughts were very important and precious.

. . . How was it now? It was spring, a windy, rainy day, and he was driving with her in a taxi from St. Denis, a suburb of Paris. The seats of the taxi were upholstered in worn green plush and were warm and comfortable, like a mother's knees. The rain was falling in such a fine drizzle that only a moist wind blew on his face through the open window. The houses, the trees, the passers-by, hurrying with their many-colored umbrellas which now and then tore out of their hands, were reflected by the wet sidewalks in a bluish sheen. Everything appeared to Pavel unusually gay, familiar, and dear. Even the humid air gladdened him, reminding him of something in the past. But more precious than anything was the woman sitting beside him in a dark blue cloak, a small hat whose veil half covered the tenderly sorrowful yet happy face. He looked and could not see enough of the dear features, familiar to the point of heartache.

She had not been surprised by his unexpected appearance in Paris. She didn't even ask him how he was able to come from Russia specially to see her, as if that were as simple as arriving in the train from Lyon. Nor did he ask her how she was living, with whom, whether she had thought of him—he wanted everything to be as before their parting. He wanted to live again the precious moments of the past.

When he had kissed her cold lips she smiled trustingly and whispered, a little sorrowfully: "Darling, you are exhausted, I can see that." But she did not pity him and on that account was specially dear to him. Once she had asked him: "Why should you go back to Russia, if it's terrible there?" And he had answered her solemnly: "I am going away to think about you."

Oh! How foolish he had been, how naïve!

Pavel closed his eyes and with sharp clarity imagined the whole scene —the blue curtain of rain, the noise of wheels on the brick pavement, the expressive face of the taxi driver. This chauffeur, like all chauffeurs in Paris, considered himself the skillful director of the act being played in the back seat of his little theatre. Now and then he turned his dark face around to them, smiling slyly, clicking his tongue, and with his free hand making signs—obviously encouraging them. It didn't please him that they were sitting quietly, merely looking at each other—he wanted action. When he caught their rare kisses in his mirror, he slowed down, he knew that lovers are never in a hurry.

310

He was a funny, amusing chauffeur. How funny he seemed to Pavel then, and how dear he was to him now.

Pavel still remembered the springy smell of the fields, sharp and sweet, which they both suddenly caught in the very heart of the city when they were lunching in the open garden of the little restaurant Lucas on the Place de la Madeleine. It seemed to Pavel that even now that arousing smell blew in through the open window of the bedroom, so fresh was his memory.

Yes, memory often plays tricks with people; like opium, it poisons the imagination of the unfortunate and even paints the mud of the past in rainbow colors, while the merciless blows dealt out by life are transformed into brotherly kisses. With Pavel it was even worse. He possessed a special sensitivity, he could see much and seal it up. But all this weighed on his soul like a precious burden, without any hope of finding expression. His memory unconsciously stored up all the pigments, all the colors that his eyes encountered—the roofs of Paris were his palette, the flowers of the rhododendrons on the Champs Elysées were stowed away in his brain in bright strokes—priceless and full of a special disturbing meaning, but for him alone. He had no close friend with whom he could share his memories. That was why he bore the parting with the one whom he loved, and who remained in Paris, so poignantly, like his own death. Here in Rostov, he was pining from yearning, grief, and solitude.

At times the most dangerous thing happened. Numbness seized him, a desire to dissolve, to leave this earth without trace. But to get away from himself was as difficult as forgetting all that was dear and important to his heart. He had to drink, and drink hard, to forget himself even a little, forget that he was sick, repugnant, and of no use to anyone. . . .

Pavel didn't notice when his father and the doctor entered the room.

"Did you call me?" asked Mikhail, looking with anxiety at the thoughtful face of his son.

Pavel shuddered and raised his eyes. When he saw the doctor he frowned and asked irritably, with twitching lips: "What's he doing here? I asked for you, alone."

"I thought . . . maybe it was something that concerned the doctor."

"Are you afraid to talk to me as man to man? Am I so repugnant to you?"

"Pavel!"

"Yes, yes! . . . Don't think that I don't notice that you avoid me like a leper. For weeks at a time you don't come near me."

Mikhail turned red. His son spoke the truth. He felt a sharp pity

311

for the young man. "How is he to blame?" passed through his head.

"Forgive me, Pavel." Mikhail whispered softly and took his son's hand. It was hot and covered with sweat. "You need the doctor, though."

The eyes in Pavel's yellow face flashed. "The body can be cured, but who will cure the soul? Yes, it's too late now. Perhaps one must be born again to learn to live in present-day Russia. For what we have— tastes, feelings, and moral ideas—all must be buried . . . forever . . . without trace . . . And one must bring out the animal in one, the primitive instincts—without any sentimentality. Otherwise you're an enemy . . . an enemy of the people!"

"Excuse me, Pavel, but you're talking nonsense," said Mikhail sternly. Against his will a sense of irritation with his son rose in him. "That's not true."

Pavel moved closer to his father and, drawing his breath in quickly, whispered: "No, I'm speaking the truth and you know it. Only you fear the truth worse than death . . . But I'm not afraid, it only hurts me, as if the lie of life is corroding everything inside me, like rust. . . . I can't stand hypocrisy! Everybody is pretending, shouting about virtue, while they kill people by the thousands openly. . . . Thousands, did I say? No, millions! Maybe others can look on calmly, but I can't. I feel that I should do something, but what? I don't know. . . ."

"You need a woman," said the doctor, and winked at Mikhail. He tried to look as if Pavel hadn't uttered these dangerous words. "If you like, I'll get you one. I have pretty little nurses in the hospital—they'll treat your mental wound in a trice, like a prescription. . . . Have you had a woman recently?"

Without replying, Pavel went to the window. Looking into the park, he said curtly: "Father, I want to go abroad."

Mikhail sighed, it seemed, with relief. He was expecting something different. In a confident voice he began to dissuade his son. "Pavel, you were abroad last year. Did that help you? No! And it won't help you this time. . . . That's all imagination. In what way is it bad for you here?"

Pavel bared his yellow teeth nervously.

"Bad?" he exclaimed. "I tell you, it's not bad—it's like the grave here!"

"Don't get excited, Pavel. Ask the doctor's advice whether you need to be abroad or not. Tell me, Doctor, would it do any good?"

Although Pavel's sudden whim made the doctor's heart leap with

312

joyful hope, he managed to shrug his shoulders indifferently. "There's no special need for it. However, a complete change of surroundings is always desirable. Do you intend to go to Paris again?" he asked Pavel. The doctor pronounced the word Paris with an anxious heart; it held his unattainable dream.

"Yes, to Paris."

"Oh!"

"What do you mean—'Oh!' "

"Paris, a torch city! Women, belles, charm!" twittered the doctor, no longer able to restrain himself. At the thought of Paris he went to pieces completely—began to rub his hands excitedly, smacked his lips as if he were sucking candy.

Mikhail waved his arm hopelessly. "After all, Pavel, you're a grown man and not a child. You can decide for yourself. If you want to go— then go. When do you want to go?"

"The sooner the better."

Suddenly the doctor ran to Pavel and began to shake his hands, looking into his eyes beseechingly, like a dog. "I congratulate you! I congratulate you!" He was, of course, congratulating himself in anticipation, and not Pavel.

"I'll take you with me," said Pavel, understanding the doctor, but disliking his exuberance. "Father, please arrange a visa for the doctor also."

"Thank you, Pavel!" beamed the doctor. "You're a good friend. You know, I can guess whom you want to see in Paris," he added in the tone of an intimate friend. "I'll bet it's that little, dark . . . I know, I know, I saw her . . . Ah! You playboy! She's all right, but a bit on the small side. You have an original taste, Pavel. That's like the story, you know, about the bear and the honey bee! . . . Ha—ha—ha!" And the doctor threw back his long bony head, choking with laughter.

Pavel turned purple.

"If you don't get out I won't answer for myself!" he said between his teeth, taking a bottle from the table and raising it threateningly at the doctor. The latter, looking fearfully at the disheveled Pavel, backed towards the door. He was going to stop there.

"Out!" roared Pavel.

The doctor slammed the door just in time. The bottle smashed against it with a crash.

Behind the door the doctor wiped his forehead with a handkerchief, took a deep breath.

313

"What a disorganized being that Pavel is!" he said to himself. "But Paris!"

When they were alone Mikhail said to his son sternly: "You've lost control of yourself. What is it that's destroying your life?"

"Anguish, Father . . . terrible, draining anguish. Especially at night, when I can't sleep, and lie alone with my thoughts. . . . But what about you? I have eyes, you know; I see everything."

"What do you see?" asked Mikhail, barely holding his irritation in check.

"Admit it, Father, that you counted on something different when you returned to Russia two years ago."

Mikhail flew into a rage. His dislike for his son, which had been growing against his will, of which he was ashamed and which he was powerless to overcome, suddenly poured forth. Choosing his words poorly, he shouted at Pavel: "That's a lie! An idle fancy! I don't need to admit anything. You are merely blaming me for your own weaknesses—you are sick, and you think that everybody around you is sick. . . . But you are mistaken. I am well! Yes! Yes! Healthy in mind and body! Don't cast me in the role of Hamlet! I have no doubts, I firmly believe in the rightness of my life. I certainly never counted on finding heavenly manna here when I left Italy. Many people are grumbling about the difficulties—just such weaklings as you. I, on the other hand, welcome them, for beyond the difficulties of the present I see the greatness of the future."

Pavel looked closely and sadly at his father's large face, distorted in anger.

"You know that's not what I'm talking about," he said quietly. "The trouble isn't in difficulties. I'm speaking about corruption . . . about the fact that there's no room now for an honest man in Russia. When a man's conscience is eroded by red-hot iron, no reform can justify that."

"It's not true that there's no room for an honest man in Russia. Take me, for instance: I occupy a very prominent place. According to you— I am not honest?"

"The Politburo has tolerated you so far, but their path and yours are different. You feel that yourself."

"My path is with the Russian people, Pavel. The Politburo has nothing to do with it."

"And who knows where the path of the people is? The people don't choose their own path—they go where they are pushed, with a bayonet

314

in their backs. . . ." Many hard thoughts had accumulated in Pavel's mind. But he was speaking with difficulty. He did not feel at all well, his fingers shook, on his cheeks a feverish flush appeared, and the perspiration had come out on his brow in large beads. Through his parched lips, twitching spitefully, he spoke dangerous words.

Mikhail listened to him distractedly, looked at his convulsively quivering face, at the damp wisp of sparse hair sticking to his pale forehead, and thought: "I should have left with the doctor."

The words that Pavel was saying, and which came to him with obvious effort, evoked only irritation in Mikhail—he had no need of them.

Pavel apparently felt this. He stopped talking, went over to a small table, poked a cigarette into a seashell—a present from his father—watched how the ash softly dwindled in its mother-of-pearl convolutions. And like the ash in the seashell, his sallow face wrinkled and darkened.

"Father . . ." he said at last dully, as if he were reluctantly bringing out of the depths of his being some weighty thought.

"What, Pavel?"

"Let's all go abroad . . ."

"What do you mean—all?"

"You, Luba, Nina, and I. The whole family . . ."

Mikhail became cautious. "Why?"

"We'll see when we get there. . . . What's the use of guessing now."

"Speak more plainly, Son."

"Is it necessary? Recently you have resented plain speaking."

Mikhail shook his head.

"No, Son, the Don doesn't flow backwards. And don't forget, we're both Russians. Even though I have spent a great part of my life abroad, I have remained a Russian. You're the same. We're thick-skinned Scythians, Son . . ."

"That's it, that's it, Scythians!" Pavel caught him up bitterly, taking long strides back and forth. "In my childhood I read in the history book that when the Scythians saw an enemy stronger than themselves, they hid in the river under the water and breathed through reeds. It's like that now! all Russians have been given the right only to breathe, and that through a reed; to sit motionless and tremble each succeeding minute."

Pavel suddenly stopped in front of his father, spread his long legs. Straining his voice, injured through coughing, he said, with unconcealed hatred: "No! I want to breathe with my full chest, and not through a

315

reed. I am weak, but I'm not a coward. . . . I can't understand why you want to be a slave, even a very valuable one."

Mikhail shrank under the blows of his son's merciless words. He could not contradict him; his resistance was weakening; the ground was slipping under his feet. What he had feared more than anything else when he went to Pavel had happened . . .

"I want my eternal rest to be in my native land," he said quietly, as if he were apologizing to his son. And now indeed, begging for mercy, he approached Pavel and took him by the elbow.

"You're partly right. I've lost courage, my friend," he murmured, trembling and infecting Pavel with his shiver. "I've lost courage. But there's no need to beat me down completely. I'm grieved enough already . . ." and sitting down heavily on the bed, he added in a barely audible whisper: "I've already entered the autumn of my days. I am old. My breast is too weak to bare it to the hatred of those in power."

His father's last words pricked Pavel painfully. As never before, he felt that his father was the only human being dear to him. With desperate compassion, as if he were doing it for the first time, he looked at Mikhail's bent gray head, at the broad shoulder blades, sticking out like those of an old man under the light cotton shirt, and at the strongly molded hands, clenched hard into fists—his father was clearly holding himself in.

"Forgive me . . ." said Pavel, and faltered. Something gurgled in his throat. He coughed, a dull bark. "Forgive me . . . I wasn't fair to you."

There was a moment of silence, broken only by Pavel's coughing. Each was afraid to speak first. Then, as if overcoming something inside him, Mikhail got up slowly:

"I'll go now."

Pavel didn't reply. He looked down at his feet and saw nothing. Tears filled his eyes. When the door closed softly behind his father, the sharp thought stung him with the old familiar pain: "Now I'll have to get drunk, terribly drunk—otherwise I'll go mad."

CHAPTER 16

MIKHAIL GORIN went to his study to fulfill a necessary but boring duty—to receive the visitors who came every day with presents and with requests, or merely out of unconcealed curiosity.

316

His secretary showed him the list of visitors. There were the writer Vladimir Bedov; a group of young correspondents from the paper *The Kharkov Bolshevik;* a delegation of frontier guards who wanted to present Gorin with a rifle, famous because, as they announced proudly in their letter, exactly one hundred enemies of the people had been killed by it while trying to cross the State boundary.

Hearing this, Gorin thought of Pavel: "Just so, I suppose they killed people like him . . . But he will get his visa. What nonsense!" And he asked his secretary: "Are they serious?"

The secretary, probably thinking that Gorin doubted the number of enemies killed, hastened to assure him: "The certificate of the commander of the frontier district is attached to the rifle."

A reciter of folklore was also mentioned in the list. Gorin ordered her to be received after the writer Bedov.

The more Gorin thought about Pavel's words, the more he was convinced that he intended to remain abroad for good.

"I must refuse him," Mikhail decided, imagining what a scandal such a step by his son would arouse.

But then he remembered his own shameful weakness, displayed so unexpectedly in his talk with Pavel. Now he blamed him for everything, even his own weakness. Every minute his irritation against his son was growing stronger.

By the time the secretary finished with the list and asked him if he had any orders, Mikhail felt that he must be rid of Pavel. He gave the secretary instructions to arrange a visa for Pavel and the doctor:

"For France. The object of the journey—for medical treatment." And suddenly he sighed with relief, as if he had thrown a heavy load off his shoulders.

While he was talking with the writer Bedov, Gorin kept wondering into which category to put him. He had evolved three categories of writers: the first—careerists; they tried to obtain letters of recommendation from him to open a way to success. The second—frightened souls; they came running to him with a cry for help, begging him to drive off the pack of "critics"—armed not with pens, but with rifles and orders for their arrest. It had fallen to Mikhail's lot to save many such unfortunate fellows from jail. This was the most disturbing category. To the third belonged the beginners. They had published very little, had not yet gone through the grim school of censorship and therefore were,

317

as a rule, childishly naïve, full of great plans and therefore interesting.

Bedov didn't fit into any of these categories. He did not ask for a recommendation, nor did he beg him for protection and it was clear that he was not a beginner. Bedov simply came to exchange ideas with him about his new book. That was all.

He enlightened him on the subject of his work, called *On the Happy Path*. The book was about kolkhoz life. A mean kulak, consumed with fury against the Soviet regime, tried to burn down the kolkhoz granary. But his son caught him at the scene of the crime, and making a speech full of noble anger, gave his father up to the authorities. To everybody's joy, the father was shot.

Now, as a writer, Bedov was faced with a delicate problem: Should he make the son of the kulak a hero and award him a medal? Or, because of his family tie with an enemy of the people, should he send him for a short term to a labor camp, where he could be helped to get rid of the last traces of his hostile origin?

With such a delicate problem the writer Bedov had come to the great Gorin. Maybe the latter would be kind enough to give him his advice.

Mikhail looked at Bedov with amazement, hardly believing his own ears. But on being convinced that the man was deadly serious, Mikhail, assuming as thoughtful an expression as possible, said to him: "Why shouldn't you—just before the end of your novel—let the reader into a little secret? Let us say, for instance, that the kulak was not really the hero's father at all; the chairman of the kolkhoz was his father, but only the chairman and hero's mother knew this, and she modestly kept quiet. In that case there would be no need to send the young man to the concentration camp—he could be awarded a medal and even taken into the house of his real father, the chairman, who might marry him to his pretty secretary."

When he finished, Mikhail expected a burst of laughter. But it didn't follow. Bedov's face showed the highest degree of surprise; he had even paled from excitement.

"That is genius, genius!" he whispered. "Why didn't I think of that before? Thank you, Mikhail Alexeyevich! A thousand thanks!" And the writer groaned with rapture. He hastened to retire, holding his head in a stiff position, as if he were afraid of losing the precious thought just received.

Escorting him to the door, Mikhail thought distressfully: "I'd better make a fourth category: the writer-optimist."

318

The author was replaced by the reciter, a large elderly woman in a speckled kerchief, with a broad-nosed face in fine wrinkles and with quick, crafty eyes.

After a warm greeting, Mikhail asked her to recite some folk tale that she herself liked best. He leaned back in his chair and closed his eyes blissfully, completely abandoned to listening. He loved the creative power of the people, finding in it often surprising gems of humor, subtlety, and directness. But in the next minute Mikhail nearly jumped out of his chair, so unexpected was the bass voice of the woman. Looking fixedly at the corner of the room, she announced: "The tale of the Eagle-Lenin and his friend the Falcon-Stalin," and, without stopping, droned monotonously: "And when the Eagle-Lenin was dying he called to himself the Falcon-Stalin, and bequeathed to the Falcon . . ."

Gorin frowned in agony. The crafty old woman was simply narrating the official history of the Party, adding wherever she could to the name of Stalin such words as "falcon," "sun," "light." It was clear that this "folklore" had its origin somewhere in Moscow in the department of propaganda. Without allowing her to finish the routine struggle of the Falcon-Stalin with the Snake-Trotzky, Gorin escorted her to the door.

Irritated, disillusioned, and aware that he was already tired, Mikhail instructed the secretary to stop the reception until the next day.

CHAPTER 17

NINA HAD GONE to Andrei Demin's room to continue the reading of Tolstoy's *War and Peace*. The room looked onto the park. Instead of the huge bandage he had worn in the hospital, Andrei now had a neater one, covering only one eye. He was sitting in an armchair opposite Nina and listening to her attentively. But the ideas of the book, spoken aloud in Nina's melodious voice, interwove themselves with his own thoughts. While he was listening to the story of Natasha Rostov he thought about Lida and his love for her. Imagining what Lida would have done in Natasha's place, he was sure that she would have conducted herself much better than Tolstoy's favorite . . .

For Nina, looking after Andrei, reading to him, was a peculiar expression of her love for Feodor. She grieved for Andrei's sufferings sorely, but at the same time felt within herself an abundance of kindness, tenderness, and love. "How kind and good I am! What happiness to live on earth and bring happiness to others!" she thought and, as "others," she had Feodor alone in mind.

Mikhail Gorin dropped in to see Andrei just when Nina had finished reading and was getting ready to leave. "Surely this isn't her new infatuation?" thought Mikhail, following her with a surprised glance.

When he was alone with Andrei, the conversation switched imperceptibly from Tolstoy's book to humanism. Andrei, carried away, began to talk excitedly. He took a book from the little table—Dzerzhinsky's *Letters*.

"Take an admiring look at Felix Dzerzhinsky's ideas, that celebrated chief of the Cheka. You extolled him in one of your articles. Here are his words; I remember you quoted them once. Here they are from beginning to end. 'One must have the inner consciousness of the necessity to meet death for the sake of life, to go into slavery for the sake of freedom, and have the strength to survive the whole hell of life with open eyes, feeling in your heart the great, sublime hymn of beauty, truth, and happiness wrung from life.' "

"What are you trying to prove with that quotation?" asked Gorin. He noticed that Andrei read this part of the book with a quaver in his voice.

"I want to put one question to you. You quoted this part two or three years ago in Italy, when you were far away from Russia. Apparently you liked it. Tell me, do you like these words of Dzerzhinsky now?"

Gorin was silent. His glance, clouded by inner pain, avoided Andrei.

"You don't answer."

"No. Now why . . ." replied Mikhail at last. "The phrase is as good to my ears as before . . . and logical. One must look at things objectively."

"All right. Let's translate this phrase from poetical language. To me, in this phrase the whole horror of our regime is apparent. That is the program. That is the program for Dzerzhinsky himself, for the members of the Politburo, but more than anything it is intended for those who execute their will, for such henchmen as Durov. It's as if the program said to them: 'You must be firm and convinced in the rightness of your terrible work. It must be clear to you that your crimes are necessary. Destroy thousands; put them to death without hesitation; it is necessary for "life." Drive other millions of people into slavery; it is necessary for "freedom"!' When Durov and other scoundrels like him break the bones of their victims in the dark cells, up to their elbows in

320

blood, cripple innocent people, hear their animal howls, they must—to express oneself in the words of Dzerzhinsky—'have the strength to survive the whole hell of life with open eyes, feeling in your heart the great, sublime hymn of beauty, truth, and happiness wrung from life.' There you are, Mikhail Gorin—the real face of Soviet humanism!"

Gorin paled. "Silence! Silence! Don't say any more! You've been sent by the devil himself to torment my soul."

"Ah! You don't like it!" shouted Andrei. "But I have been there. I have the right to speak. My father perished there. And it's possible that he, when he was screaming with pain, remembered the article you wrote in sunny Italy. . . . The blood of others, Gorin, is cheap!"

Mikhail recalled how he had yielded to weakness in his conversation with his son, now he wanted above all that this should not be repeated. "What is it they want from me? Of what are they all accusing me?" A wild obstinacy seized him. He lost control of himself and began to shout at Andrei: "I don't want to see you any more! I don't want to, do you hear!"

"Don't worry, Gorin, I won't burden you long with my presence."

"That's it, that's it . . ."

Mikhail left the room, slamming the door with a bang. The conversation with Andrei was the last drop in his overflowing cup. All the stored-up irritation, vexation, anger poured out. Shchusev, Glushak, Luba, Pavel, that insignificant writer Bedov, and the crafty fake reciter . . . It seemed to him that each of them had added a drop of poison to his soul—it was an ordeal that he was no longer able to bear. All his wrath turned against Andrei.

"He shouldn't be in my house, he shouldn't . . ." he repeated to himself. At that moment his angry outburst didn't appear to him heartless or unjust. He felt hatred growing and boiling inside him. "Vulgar, good-for-nothing people surrounding me! This has got to be stopped! And Demin, he must be the first to leave my house!"

But however convinced Gorin was of his own rightness, somewhere deep inside he dimly felt that with his shouting, his angry outburst, he had proved nothing to anyone and never would. He knew that he lacked a sound argument, solid ground. And the more helpless he felt the more furious and unreasonable was his anger.

At midday Lida brought Andrei's mother to him. The visit was quiet and joyful. Rough and harsh as Andrei had been with Mikhail Gorin, he was just as tender and affectionate with his mother. Lida noticed

321

that Andrei was upset. When he told them that he was going to leave Gorin's house, they were surprised.

"Of course, I would like very much to have you with me," his mother said to him. "But it's so much better for you here; a clean room, nourishing food . . . I advise you, my son, to remain here a little longer."

"No, Mama, I can't. One shouldn't bother people, no matter how kind they are. No matter how kind they are," he repeated slowly.

Andrei embraced his mother with particular, impetuous tenderness. The latter broke down, cried: "Your father . . . he is dead, you know, Andrusha."

"Don't cry, Mama, don't!"

When they parted, Andrei kissed her, looked long into her eyes. When she was on the way home, Andrei's mother recalled that look and suddenly something pricked her heart. She stopped on the sidewalk and groaned, catching at her heart with her hand: "Oh, Andrei, my little son . . ."

She didn't know what was upsetting her so much, but she felt that there had been something strange and wonderfully sad in her son's look. She raised her eyes to heaven and, looking at a large white cloud, motionless at that height, she crossed herself:

"Lord! preserve my son . . ."

On the second Sunday in July Mikhail Gorin, uneasy about what seemed to him Nina's new infatuation and because it might become an obstacle to Andrei's departure, invited Professor Novikov to visit him.

He had a talk with his wife before Novikov arrived. Luba approved of Pavel's proposed visit to Paris. She herself had noticed that Pavel's presence irritated Mikhail. About his suspicion that Pavel might not return to Russia, Mikhail said nothing.

When the talk turned to Nina, Luba smilingly expressed her surmise that their daughter was in love. Mikhail told her that he had already discovered that secret. In humorous words he described the professor's ruse with the report—which the latter had written, as Gorin believed, only as a pretext to see Nina. Mikhail told how he had had to lie when the professor asked him about the contents of the report, about which he had not the slightest idea.

After calling Novikov, Mikhail again remembered the report. It was still lying untouched in the library. Believing that it was impossible to deceive the professor any longer, he decided to look over Novikov's work. After dinner he shut himself in the library, gave orders that he was not to be disturbed, and began to read, yawning in anticipation: "Just what can a man in love think up?"

He read through the first page without particular interest; on the second page he exclaimed "Ah!" several times; and, beginning the third, he became completely absorbed.

The report produced an unexpected impression on him. In it he found what he had been dimly seeking. Before him lay the answer to his doubts—he felt that at once. Novikov had presented the period of Ivan the Terrible with such new and unexpected force that Gorin was dumbfounded. He got up from his chair and walked up and down the library in excitement.

"Yes, yes, certainly that period resembled the present. Certainly blood was spilled then, even if innocent . . . How often have I myself shuddered at thought of Ivan, whom I imagined as a monster! And now this young professor presents Ivan and his epoch in an entirely new light."

Mikhail recalled the poisonous words of Andrei, remembered Pavel's sorrowful reproach, and thought, almost with malice: "All right, I'll answer you. I'll reply to your every word, every reproach, every look. I'll prove that you are blind, seeing no further than your noses."

He sighed with relief. "Enough of despondency! It's time to end doubts. I was right; I was surrounded not by the people I need. I don't need Glushak, Pavel, Andrei, or Shchusev. I need more people like this young professor . . . And as for the play, it will be my test."

After marking the more interesting places in the report Gorin went out into the park to refresh himself before Novikov's arrival.

"Ah, my lovesick professor," thought he, smiling, "when you wrote your treatise you never thought what a valuable service you were rendering me. No wonder they say love is blind!"

CHAPTER 18

FEODOR NOVIKOV was expecting a call from Gorin. He awaited it with excitement and prepared himself for the occasion carefully. First of all he decided to buy a new suit. To appear in his shabby jacket amid palatial luxury seemed to him out of place. Besides, Nina . . .

Advised by Nikolai, who knew more about these things, Feodor

323

went to the only place where it was possible to buy a suit—the black market. Knowing approximately the market price, Novikov took all his savings—about four thousand rubles.

The market was near a cathedral which had been closed for several years. The crowd, the dust, the hard-faced militiamen with their revolvers, at first frightened him. He began to push around among the people who, constantly feeling the near presence of the militia, walked with the appearance of having come into the oppressive air and dust for an outing: they all wore indifferent looks, directed to the side, or above. But, passing one another, they whispered: "A pair of boots for two pounds of flour" or "A gold brooch for a loaf of sugar." To Feodor's vexation nobody asked for money. When the militia noticed a suspicious group of people, they approached quickly with a shout: "Hey! You! What are you peddling there?" The people would show their empty hands. Nobody brought anything to the market; the goods were hidden elsewhere.

Novikov walked around, listened, looking for the right moment. At last he found it where he least expected it. A little old woman in a ragged shawl whispered to him, barely audible: "A good suit for two sacks of flour." Novikov had no flour, nevertheless, like her, looking up at the sky, he asked in a whisper: "Will you sell it for two thousand?"

"I don't take money; flour or sugar."

At that moment Novikov was sorry that he had no friend in a food store. However, he didn't retreat from the old woman: "All right, I'll find the flour, but first I'll have to see the suit."

The old woman looked at him suspiciously. "You're not a stool pigeon?" she asked him, and added: "But you're too clean-looking for a stool. An engineer or something?"

"Yes, an engineer. I'm getting married, Mother. I need a suit."

The old woman relented and, looking around, said quickly: "Well, all right! Follow me, only keep at a distance." And she shuffled through the crowd. Novikov, trying not to lose sight of her black shawl, followed her. The old woman walked ahead without turning around. Obviously she knew the ropes.

She led him to a vacant lot where some old logs were lying among a bunch of tall nettles. Two people were sitting on the logs. When they came up to the logs he almost stopped from surprise. One of the young men was Oleg Durov. His arm was still bandaged; a fresh scar on his cheek looked raw.

"Ah! Professor!" Oleg greeted him gaily, apparently not in the least

324

surprised at his appearance, but even glad of it: "Going in for speculation?"

Novikov came to himself quickly and asked dryly: "Now, where's the suit?"

"The suit'll be here right away. . . . Vanka!" Oleg turned to his companion. "Get the portmanteau."

At his words the little old woman began to look uneasily around: "I'd better depart from evil . . ."

"Go on, go on. I'll pay you afterwards," Oleg advised her.

"Only, don't forget—two pounds of flour."

"I know, I know! Beat it."

When the old woman hurried away, Vanka took a good leather portmanteau from under the logs and opened it in front of Novikov. In the portmanteau lay a neatly folded suit, absolutely new, light gray with a blue pin stripe. There was no doubt the material was from abroad. Novikov's eyes lit up. "If only it's not too small," he thought hopefully.

"Can I try it on here?" he asked Oleg.

"Go ahead. There's nobody around," the other said off-handedly and spat out his cigarette. Novikov noticed that one front tooth was missing. "My God, somebody beat him up well. Whoever it was did a good job," he thought. Feodor excitedly put on the jacket. The sleeves were a little long, but otherwise it fitted him like a glove. The trousers he merely placed against his legs to see that they were long enough.

"I'll take it!"

"My! But you're quick!" replied Oleg roughly. He was being rough with Novikov on purpose. The meeting with the professor under these "intimate" circumstances put them on the same level, even gave Oleg the advantage. "The suit is being sold for two—no, three sacks of flour," he snapped.

"Unfortunately, I have no flour," said Feodor. "I can give you two thousand cash."

Oleg actually jumped with surprise. "No flour? Then what the hell did you come here for, wasting time, trying to pull our legs? What the devil do I need your money for? It's lousy even for toilet paper!"

"And what the devil do you want flour for?" Feodor asked him as roughly. "Doesn't your father feed you enough?"

"That's our business. But if you're really interested, Professor, I'll tell you: any girl will lay for a sack of flour—the best there are, even an actress!"

Oleg's friend laughed. "She'll lay and she'll thank you!"

325

"I have no flour, boys. I can add another five hundred rubles. That's all," said Feodor.

"No, that's no good!" Oleg shook his head but did not, however, close the portmanteau.

"Three thousand! I have no more money. Search me if you like!"

Vanka nudged Oleg with his elbow: "Why drag it out? Let it go! It's a good price."

"Four thousand!" insisted Oleg, and stared expectantly at the professor's mouth.

"What carrion!" thought Feodor, and again looked into the portmanteau. There, under a newspaper, lay something. Feodor raised the newspaper and saw a pair of new shoes.

"Give me the shoes and throw the portmanteau into the bargain for four."

Oleg reluctantly agreed. "All right, take them. I don't want to lug that grip around. Otherwise I'd never have given them to you."

Although Feodor knew that he had paid little in comparison with the usual prices on the black market, nevertheless he counted out the money to Oleg almost with tears—the entire four thousand. Putting the suit into the portmanteau, he noticed the trade-mark under the collar. "English?" he asked Oleg, indicating the trade-mark with his eyes.

"No, American. It's never been worn," replied Oleg and added, so that the professor would have no doubts on that score: "An engineer returned from America. They caught him before he had time to put on the new suit. Now he's got a different worry—it's not the suit, but his own hide he's got to save. Ha—ha—ha!"

Feodor carried away the portmanteau, happy; to the fate of its former owner he gave no thought. Now he could go to Gorin well dressed. Imagining what an impression his suit would make on Nina, he began to whistle a lively tune.

A few days later a tailor turned up the sleeves and shortened the trousers. The suit, as well as Feodor, was ready for the important event.

CHAPTER 19

WHEN NOVIKOV entered the Gorins' estate a noisy scene was going on: Cheprok was driving out two servants who had been caught stealing.

"They'll shake the fat off you in the army!" he shouted spitefully,

326

helping the guard to load their trunks into the britchka. The fat-faced lads snarled and told him to go to hell, but looked gloomy—apparently they believed the old man.

Mikhail Gorin was looking out of the window, chuckling, well satisfied with the bellicose appearance of his friend.

Nina, told by her father about Novikov's visit, ran out to meet him, beaming happily. She didn't notice his new suit at all. All that she saw was Feodor's face—in the first moments uneasy, agitated, and then heartened by her warm welcome.

Gorin, shaking Novikov's hand firmly, invited him into his library. But first he said jokingly to his daughter: "Don't get excited, Nina, I won't keep him long—I'll return him to you. Look how your eyes have lit up!"

Nina, who was standing beside her father, kissed his cheek in amused silence, at the same time looking at Feodor.

"Didn't you make a mistake in identity there?" her father whispered into her ear. She blushed deeply and ran upstairs to her room.

With great satisfaction Novikov heard from Gorin that the latter liked his report very much. More than that, it appeared, justifying Feodor's best hopes, the treatise had inspired Gorin to an important undertaking.

"Yes, yes, I'm going to write a play, *Ivan the Terrible,* and I tell you frankly—without your report I would never have had the courage to do this."

Novikov beamed, silently bowed his head.

"You surprised me," continued Gorin with frank amazement, examining Novikov's broad-shouldered figure. "I always figured that scholars expounded their ideas in dry, boring language, useful only for stimulating the after-dinner snooze. You write as if you were declaring your love—with heat, with passion."

"This is my favorite subject, Mikhail Alexeyevich," replied Feodor with a smile. "Perhaps on that account I overdid it a little."

"No, no, you didn't overdo anything. It is all very good," Gorin hurriedly interrupted him. "I'm afraid, you know, that I've slackened up this last while. I've become disagreeable to myself. That's why I've felt myself drawn to you, especially after this treatise."

"One of these days the material selected by my friend in Moscow will be here from the archives," said Feodor, noting Gorin's excitement with surprise. That the "friend" was Drozd Novikov did not mention.

"I see that you have anticipated everything. You really want me to write this play, don't you?" said Gorin banteringly.

"Yes, I want it very much," replied Feodor firmly. "I am convinced that it will be the best thing that you have ever written."

"Well, hardly the best. To better what was written in one's youth is a tough job in the sunset of life."

"It is impossible to compare what was written long ago with what will be written at present. The times are too different," said Feodor.

"You're right. I have become quite different myself, quite different . . ."

Novikov had his own special game which he played simply to satisfy his own curiosity. He wanted very much to know why Gorin had become as he was now. So far he had not found the answer. As during their first meeting, when he played chess with Gorin, the writer appealed to his imagination—his outward appearance, his extraordinary energy and vitality—although often Novikov caught an inner sadness in his eyes.

His first meeting with Luba took place in the same library. Mikhail called her to introduce the young professor to her. Feodor saw at once that Luba was a woman of strong character, with whom he must always be on the alert. "From her I may expect more unpleasant surprises than from Gorin," he thought.

Luba liked Feodor but she felt dimly something strange in his behavior, particularly when she listened to his conversation with Mikhail. She asked herself: "Who interests this professor more—my husband or my daughter?" But when Nina entered and Luba noticed her eyes, radiant with joy, and at the same time caught a similar look in Feodor, full of rapture and adoration directed at Nina, she answered herself: "My daughter."

Feodor and Nina went for a walk in the country. On the way they met Pavel and the doctor, who were returning from fishing, both very contented—in the doctor's pail were coiled several large fish.

Pavel was not surprised when he saw Nina with Feodor. The doctor, on the other hand, looked at this person, unknown to him, with unconcealed curiosity. However, noticing Feodor's cold manner, he did not blurt out his usual jokes.

During their conversation Nina mentioned that Pavel was getting ready to go abroad and that the doctor was going with him. "What luck that kind have!" thought Feodor enviously, at the same time looking with surprise at the thin figure of the red-haired doctor.

After talking a little with Pavel and the doctor Nina and Feodor went toward the woods, which showed on the horizon as a blue band.

On the edge of the woods they sat down on the grass. However insignificant the words they were exchanging may have appeared, for them they were full of interest and special meaning. Together they were happy. To both it was clear that they loved each other, but a frank declaration had not yet taken place.

Suddenly Nina's eyes froze, fixed above Feodor's head. The latter, wondering, was going to turn around to see what had attracted her attention. But in the instant she screamed, and something hit Feodor on the head. He fell to the grass and lost consciousness for several minutes. When he came to and raised his head, he saw a thin, dirty man in ragged clothes, sitting on his chest and holding a club threateningly.

"Get up and take your clothes off!" the man ordered. His eyes were dilated, staring, almost crazy. Feodor realized that the man in front of him was a convict.

The convict held Feodor by the arm as he sat up and looked around, rubbing the injured place on his head. Another one, even more frightening—his mouth was torn—held Nina by the arm.

"Don't make a noise!" hissed the torn lips in a hoarse voice. "You, girl, don't get panicky—we only need clothes. These are no good—they'd catch us right away," and he pointed to his own rags.

With one hand his companion began to take off Feodor's suit, holding the club ready in the other one. "Take it easy, or I'll give it to you again," he said harshly. He was nervous, hurried, jerked at the suit, pulling off buttons. After taking Feodor's trousers off and leaving him in his shorts, he began with the shoes, and then, as if remembering, he ordered: "Take your shoes off yourself!"

While the convict was undressing him, Feodor considered whether it was worth while putting up a fight. He could not reconcile himself to the idea that his new suit should be lost so easily. His head was buzzing; he dared not touch the large bump that was swelling there. The convicts, although they looked starved and weak, were armed with knotty clubs and in a fight they would kill without a thought. Nor would they likely spare Nina. Feodor decided to sit quietly, hoping that something would happen and his suit would be returned to him. The convicts were obviously in a hurry.

"The clothes are too clean, too noticeable," one of them said critically, unceremoniously tying Feodor's neatly pressed suit into a bundle.

"That's all right! We'll roll them around—they'll pass," the other one reassured him. "Anyway, they're better than ours."

In the meantime Nina had relaxed. Convinced that her life was in no danger, she began to wait patiently for the convicts to go away, and even to look waggishly at the discouraged Feodor.

"Have you anything to eat?" asked the man with the torn mouth, who still held her by the arm.

"No, nothing. We were only going for a walk and didn't bring anything with us," she replied almost with regret.

"Let's go! Let's go!" the other convict urged his companion. He had already finished with Feodor and gripped the tightly rolled bundle in his hand.

"Wait!" the man with the torn mouth replied, and suddenly ordered Nina: "Take off your clothes!"

"Why?" His companion was surprised. He was very nervous, afraid of delay, kept listening for sounds in the woods.

"We can exchange her finery for bread . . . Come on! Come on! Don't keep us!" And the torn-mouth convict shook his club threateningly at her.

She took off her blouse, seemed to hesitate an instant, and then, determinedly—to get rid of them quicker—took off her skirt and handed it to him. Without waiting for their orders she took off her shoes, very expensive ones, saying in an almost apologetic voice: "That's all."

"Thank you! . . . Forgive us!" And the fugitives vanished into the woods.

When the crackling of branches ceased behind them, Nina, remembering, hid behind a bush. She had only her panties and brassiere—of all too transparent material. But peering from behind the bush she laughed at Feodor.

"And now, how will we get home?"

"It'll soon be dark; then we'll go," Feodor replied almost roughly. The whole incident had upset him greatly. To lose his brand-new foreign suit, for which he had paid out all his savings—and on the first day at that!—was too much even for his strong nerves.

"What an adventure!" Nina exclaimed gaily. The whole incident now seemed to her very interesting, if not amusing. She regarded the loss of her clothes as the funniest happening in her life, and had no idea how precious the suit was to Feodor.

"I'm not going to sit here all day," she said at last, resolutely. "You go ahead, and I'll come behind you. But don't look back."

"All right."

They went into the open. It was still light, although the sun was already hidden behind clouds on the horizon.

330

Suddenly a playful mood seized Nina; every now and then she laughed, recalling details of the attack in purposely exaggerated and humorous words, teasing Feodor unmercifully, calling him the "Knight of the Mournful Mien."

"How is it you were unable to save your lady from such unheard-of humiliation—from losing her clothes?"

Feodor at first was silent, sulked. Then her happy mood infected him. Suddenly he felt that the adventure had brought them closer together in a way that dozens of evenings and conversations could not do.

Only his striped shorts embarrassed him. It seemed to him that Nina never took her eyes off them and probably was laughing at his absurd appearance.

Suddenly she exclaimed: "Ouch! Feodor!"

He turned around. Nina was jumping on one foot, holding the other one in her hand: "I stubbed my toe on a stone!"

Feodor ran up to her. "Where, Nina?"

"Right here."

But Feodor looked into her eyes. They were opened wide, gazing steadily at him. Feodor took her by the shoulders and drew her to him. He kissed her on the lips. Her eyes looked at him as before, neither afraid nor surprised. Then they closed.

"How grand everything is . . . everything, everything," she said at last. "What wonderful, kind people they were. Isn't that true, Fedya?"

"What people?" asked Feodor, wondering, kissing her eyes.

"In the woods, the convicts . . . Kiss me here, Fedya."

"Oh, yes, very good people and kind . . . And here?"

"Fedya, why am I so happy? And I'm not at all frightened. It is as if I had known you all my life!"

"My dear . . ."

"We'll always be happy, won't we, Fedya?"

"Always."

From the road came the sound of horses trotting. A minute later a Cossack squad of ten riders appeared around the bend, raising the dust, golden in the rays of the setting sun. The Cossacks increased their pace and came to a halt in front of Nina and Feodor, smirking at catching them in their underwear. The Cossacks' eyes burned with the peculiar light of hunters in a chase. Among the riders Nina saw Rudoy. He didn't take his sullen eyes off Feodor. However, he kept silent.

"Did you happen to see any fugitives—a pair of convicts?" asked the first rider, apparently the leader.

Feodor, overjoyed at the opportunity of recovering his suit, was going to direct them to the woods, but Nina anticipated him: "No, we haven't seen them. Nobody passed us."

She was trying to hide behind Feodor's broad back, noticing the more than curious looks of the Cossacks. She prodded Feodor to make him keep quiet.

"All right, boys! Let's go to the Don. Maybe they're hiding in boats," said the leader, and the squad wheeled from the road toward the river.

When the Cossacks had ridden off several paces, Feodor heard one of them say spitefully, and loudly on purpose: "I guess we interrupted them, boys. Did you see how he'd already dropped his pants?" The squad responded with a ready laugh.

Feodor, realizing that Nina had heard every word, was afraid to look at her. Nina not only heard; she recognized the voice of Rudoy. But Rudoy's words caused her no embarrassment, nor anger. She was happy, and nothing could mar her happiness. Even if they had begun to throw dirt at her or swear in the lowest language, she would still have remained happy. She only thought about Rudoy wonderingly: "How on earth could I have loved a man like that?" Now her past intimacy with him seemed absolutely incomprehensible.

The sun was hidden completely below the horizon. Strange shadows ran over the steppe—the first presage of night. Nina walked beside Feodor. Both were silent. Then she took his hand. A little later, still silent, they turned off the road near a large wild cherry bush, where two little birds were fussing and twittering. . . .

PART FIVE

⊔⊓⊔⊔

CHAPTER 1

AT THE END of July Feodor finally received the material on Ivan the Terrible from the Moscow archives. He looked over the old, yellowed sheets with excitement, carefully checking them as a warrior checks his weapons before a battle. Everything was in order.

He sent them to Gorin, first compiling a commentary on each one. A few days later he received a letter from Gorin, thanking him for the documents in the warmest terms, but half jokingly remarking that the material had been selected with somewhat of a bias. Reading these lines, Novikov became alert, but Gorin went on to say that probably it was just what he wanted.

Novikov smiled. He felt at ease. Even before the receipt of the material he had learned from Nina—they met often now—that Mikhail had already begun work on the play, putting down his ideas, selecting material in the library, thinking a lot.

"You wouldn't know Papa now. He's full of inspiration. Thoughtful and gay, as we haven't seen him for a long time," she said once to Feodor. "What have you done to him?"

"I?" Feodor was surprised.

His surprise was genuine. He himself didn't understand why his luck was so good, why Gorin had taken so quickly to another's idea, why his treatise had such a strong effect on the writer. Feodor had expected difficulties, but everything had happened quite simply. At first this simplicity frightened him. He was afraid that Gorin's first impulse would pass before he had written the play, that he would cool off.

Novikov did not know that Gorin had been on the verge of collapse and that his treatise proved to be the life-belt thrown at the very last moment, when Gorin was nearly drowned in the sea of doubt. And Feodor, of course, did not know that half of his work had been done for him by Pavel and Andrei who, without intending to do so, had pushed Gorin into his embrace.

In the same letter Gorin invited the professor to visit him more often, ". . . not to see an old grumbler like me, of course." Mikhail apparently didn't know that Feodor and Nina had met several times in the city and that they tried to spend every spare moment together. At the Conservatory the yearly examinations were being held and she had been preparing for them diligently. Feodor was also fairly well occupied, although the work at the University was finished; on the order of the Party Provincial Committee he was giving lectures on Russian history almost every week. The Party was definitely not going to forget the question of the Slavs. Once, Nina went to one of these lectures, because she wanted so much to hear Feodor speak. When he asked her after the lecture if she liked it, she did not reply right away. Feodor saw at once that she looked anxious.

"This may seem strange to you, Fedya, but I was frightened at the lecture." She tried to choose her words as carefully as possible, fearing that Feodor wouldn't understand her. She herself didn't understand her bewildered feeling. "I didn't recognize you, there on the rostrum; you seemed such a stranger that I was frightened. You seemed to be fighting with someone, beating him mercilessly."

"Nonsense," said Feodor, smiling and kissing her forehead. "I advise you not to go to any more of my lectures—they are, in any case, not for your musical ears."

"Well it seemed like that to me," she said, responding to him with her warm smile. "You're very kind, Fedya. I know that well."

"I have an idea," Feodor suddenly cheered up. "To make us even, I'll go with you to the Conservatory and see you take your examination. That will be on Thursday, won't it?"

"You know?" Nina was surprised, and then her face clouded. "Maybe it would be better if you didn't go, Fedya. I'll feel your presence and perhaps lose my head."

"Most certainly I'll come," insisted Feodor. "And why should I distract you?" He knew that she would have to play the piano in the main auditorium before hundreds of students, parents, and prominent musicians of the land.

334

That evening in the Conservatory was one of the happiest for Feodor. The music she played (it seemed to him that she played superbly) for the first time revealed to him her inner world, and explained much that he had not suspected. Although the music had been written a hundred years before, it sounded to him like the latest revelation of life.

Nina told him afterwards that she had played for him alone, forgetting completely the hundreds of people in the audience.

Cheprok tightened the saddle, then turning aside, said gloomily: "Ready, Nina."

"What's wrong with you?" Nina asked. "Why have you been frowning at me recently?"

Feodor, already mounted, was waiting for Nina with reins loose, at the gate of the estate. They were going into the country for a ride. It was not the first time.

Cheprok, still looking aside, replied—to her surprise with a catch in his voice: "I wish you happiness, Nina . . . I see how you like to be with this man. But listen to an old man: don't hurry. Examine Feodor well, study him, then decide. You mustn't jump into a pool without knowing what's on the bottom."

"Ah! So that's what it's all about," exclaimed Nina. "You may as well know that I'm not jumping into a murky pool but into the clearest water! And I can see each grain of sand on the bottom of it." Then, after kissing the old man's wrinkled cheek, she added reproachfully: "I'm already grown up, but you still think of me as I was on Capri."

"Now, now . . . That's the whole trouble: we're not on Capri, but here. Here people are different, Nina."

But she was no longer listening to him. Vaulting into the saddle, she rode up to Feodor.

"Was he picking on me again?" Feodor asked. He felt Cheprok's unfriendliness and tried to treat it with the tolerance of the young for the peculiarities of old age.

"Cheprok wasn't picking on you, but he still regards me as a child," replied Nina absent-mindedly. Then, as if she had remembered something, she began to laugh. "Fedya, let's go to the woods! Remember? Where we lost our clothes."

"All right," Feodor replied and they rode out of the yard. Nina waved her hand gaily to the guard.

Cheprok stood, squinting his old eyes against the sun, looking after them. He was thinking of those far-off days when he used to carry

Nina in his arms, bathe her in the sea; when he used to dream about living to see her happiness, her first child. . . . It looked as if that time was approaching, but it seemed to him that this cold man with the terribly piercing eyes (why didn't Nina see that?) would never bring happiness to his favorite.

Feodor was happy and proud in his love for Nina. He was happy because, with her, he began to be himself, the man he always secretly wanted to be: the man with a kind heart, harboring evil toward no man. He was proud, as any man may be proud with whom a very beautiful and clever girl is in love.

Feodor could not withstand the temptation of showing Nina to his brother, imagining beforehand his surprise. Although Feodor treated his brother scornfully as an irresponsible, as a man unable to hide his feelings and keep his mouth shut, in this situation he was drawn to Nikolai more than to anyone else, because he knew how frankly and with what noisy delight Nikolai would express his admiration.

And Nikolai justified his expectations fully. The three of them went to swim in the Don, having arranged a picnic. Nikolai, not in the least backward with Nina, loudly admired her. Feodor, very pleased, never tired of listening to his brother, whose outspoken words were the most beautiful music to him.

Although Nikolai behaved toward Nina with frank student boisterousness, he felt that she belonged to another world, completely unknown to him. And because such a girl could love Feodor, he became filled with still greater respect for his brother.

Thus Feodor's masculine vanity was fully satisfied and he bade Nikolai farewell that day more warmly than usual. Nikolai returned from the picnic very excited. It was only when he was on his way to the communal boarding house that he suddenly thought: "And what about Lida? How does she fit into this picture?"

He was so surprised by his unexpected question that he waggled his head. Up to now he had been convinced that Feodor had designs on the plant director's daughter, although he didn't understand his strange coolness toward her. He could only ascribe it to his brother's temperament. But now he was not sure. Without realizing it, he was pleased. He didn't know why, but he wanted to see Lida free, not bound to anyone.

Nikolai entered his room in the boarding house in the happiest mood, undressed quickly, lay down on the bed and soon fell asleep, although his two room mates went on playing cards for a long time, talking noisily to each other.

CHAPTER 2

EVERY TIME Feodor stepped over Gorin's threshold he regretted his suit, so ingloriously lost. By good fortune the weather remained sunny and he could go about in summer clothes.

Sometimes he met Glushak at the Gorins'. The Academician seemed fairly calm, but sat mostly with Luba, talking quietly about the weather. Novikov noticed that Gorin avoided Glushak, although Mikhail met few people these days: he was working hard in his library.

Glushak saw that Gorin was charmed by the professor. He could not understand Novikov's power. Once the thought entered his head that he might be a hypnotist; Glushak had heard of such. From all these thoughts his head ached—and his fear of Novikov became so great that even at the mere mention of the professor's name his heart contracted painfully.

Feodor dined at the Gorins' several times. Mikhail no longer hid his thoughts about marriage. Winking at Feodor, he spoke to Nina about grandchildren; Nina blushed and lowered her eyes. Luba, seeing her happy look, was as glad for her daughter as was Mikhail. Only Feodor seemed to her to be either secretive or too reserved. But she could not help notice and appreciate his politeness and courtesy.

Every time he was in the Gorins' house Feodor listened to everything around him, as if by the sounds he could determine whether everything was in order. Quietness pleased him. That meant that Gorin was working.

Only once, at dinner, Mikhail frightened him a little. "I will have to talk with you," the writer said. "But it's early yet—perhaps in a week."

But a week later he still said it was too early. Apparently, whatever it was hadn't matured yet.

One incident nearly wrecked this favorable course of events. Glushak, who was still trying to figure out Novikov's purpose, forgot himself again. No one was bothering him, but . . .

Feodor was sitting in an arbor in the Gorins' park, waiting for Nina, who was with Andrei in another part of the park and did not yet know of his arrival. Not wishing to interrupt them, Feodor was waiting patiently for her to come.

With eyes half-closed he was watching a pair of butterflies frolicking above a lilac bush. Suddenly he heard talking not far away. It was Luba and Glushak walking along a path. Feodor stood behind the lilac bush and they didn't see him. Soon he could distinguish their words.

"What do you think of the young professor?" Luba asked Glushak.

Glushak was silent, apparently embarrassed by her question. At last he replied, but only with a question: "What do you mean by that?"

"Nothing particular. I see Nina's love for him, but sometimes I think that Mikhail interests him more than Nina."

Glushak turned around several times, as if he were afraid that he might be overheard, then said quickly: "I know nothing about the professor, Luba, but to me he seems a strange person. I advise you to be more careful of him . . . I repeat—I know nothing definite, but I have heard evil rumors about him."

"What kind of rumors?" asked Luba quickly, looking sidewise at the Academician's face.

Glushak became confused. "Well, now, how shall I tell you? . . . He attained his professorship in an unclean way . . . Above all, Mikhail should be cautious of him."

Luba, disappointed, shrugged her shoulders. She gave the Academician's words no importance. "He is jealous of Mikhail," she thought.

Novikov smiled in his concealment. The coward Glushak was trying to play safe. "Look what he thought up—evil rumors!"

About fifteen minutes later Feodor saw Glushak shuffling hurriedly along the path. He had left Luba with Nina and Andrei.

When Glushak walked past the arbor, Feodor took two leaps down the steps and, seizing Glushak by the arm, dragged him behind the bush. "I heard everything!" he said threateningly between his teeth. And suddenly, with all his might, he slapped Glushak across the cheek with his hand.

From the unexpectedness of the attack Glushak collapsed like an empty sack. But Feodor yanked him to a level with his own face and snarled, "Are you asking for death?" Then he threw the Academician, half dead from fright, onto the grass.

Novikov purposely feigned anger. He knew that the Academician was no longer able to harm him. Even if Glushak had broken faith and told everything, hardly anybody would have believed him—and least of all Gorin. However, even harmless scandal was undesirable and it was best to avert it.

Glushak was so frightened by the incident that he took his vacation a week ahead of time and went away to the Crimea for a cure. A nervous twitching appeared in his face.

CHAPTER 3

THE CONVERSATION about which Gorin had warned Novikov finally took place. In the middle of August, Novikov found Gorin in a state of high excitement. Mikhail invited him to go for a walk in the park. Feodor waited with impatience for what Gorin was going to say.

"I've come to a place where it is necessary to solve an old controversy—power and coercion," said Mikhail. "In your treatise there is the thought that the reign of Ivan for the first time solved the problem of authority in Russia. But can one accept coercion as the solution of that question?"

Novikov nodded his head understandingly. "The first doubts are beginning," he thought excitedly. "And along with them, my real work."

Speaking as calmly as possible, he said: "The problem of authority has for a long time engaged the minds of the greatest dramatic writers. However, they approached this problem from the wrong side. They considered coercion the curse of authority, like the mark of Cain, to obliterate which they thought was their first duty. But that was more the approach of cheap moralists than of objective thinkers. . . ."

Feodor spoke in the tone of one whose thoughts were not in opposition to Gorin's, but on the contrary, fully coincided with them. His whole bearing said, as it were, "We understand each other, you and I are not cheap moralists."

". . . Submitting to historical necessity, Ivan executed by the hundreds the boyars who were against him. But, even when resorting to coercion, Ivan remained a human being of great spiritual purity and mental nobility." At the last words Novikov could not restrain himself and looked searchingly at Gorin, afraid that he might overdo it and excite his ridicule. But the writer was listening to him attentively, looking down at his feet. Even if he was smiling, his smile was hidden deeply under his mustache.

"In that aspect," concluded Novikov, "coercion is not the curse of authority, but the inescapable duty of the progressive statesman, particularly at a critical period for his nation. It clears life of its dead layers and paves the way for the new."

"And the human being? . . ." asked Gorin with some doubt in his voice. "I have in mind the sufferings of individuals—if you tear them out of the heartless historical design and examine each one separately as a being of flesh and nerves—how do you justify coercion in relation to them? How can you forget their sufferings?"

"Each man is mortal; the people are immortal. Ivan was probably the first Russian Tsar to sense the immortality of the people and mentally merge himself with their fate," replied Novikov. "Ivan saw, of course, the sufferings of individuals and there were times when some men, even under torture, hurled words of wrath and curses into his face. But there is where Ivan's strength lay: that he understood the significance of his historic role better than any of his contemporaries. His iron will, however merciless it may have appeared in relation to individuals, was in essence the incarnation of the will of the people. He felt this. He also saw how often his own role was thankless. This embittered him, but he never repudiated one of his actions. He was immeasurably greater than those who, barely glancing into the eyes of history, trembled at what they saw."

Gorin became more cheerful. Obviously Novikov's words pleased him.

"Tell me, do you think that Ivan suffered at the sight of the cruelties committed on his orders, no matter how just they may have appeared to him?" Then he explained: "I must portray his inner feelings in my play."

"Unfortunately Ivan was only human . . . He felt it very keenly and it caused him the greatest suffering. His idea, hard as rock, was imprisoned in a human envelope which, alas, nature created weak and short-lived. He regretted that he was merely a human being. At the end of his life Ivan attained fully the unity of the spirit with the flesh, or rather, almost completely dissolved his carnal entity. You noticed, I hope, that chronicle which I sent to you among the other documents, in which the monk Tikhon describes Tsar Ivan the Terrible during the last period of his life. This spirituality of the ascetic, the almost unearthly appearance of the Tsar, struck him at once. He wrote that 'Ivan the Terrible had the eyes of a seraph.' Ivan rises before us as a man living an exceptionally high, tense spiritual life, so universal that it——"

"But the poets extolled Nero as a demigod—for money," Gorin interrupted skeptically.

"That's true," replied Novikov, smiling. "But the chronicler Tikhon was not, in the first place, a poet; and in the second, he wrote for such as you and me and not for the eyes of Ivan the Terrible. For this he had very good reasons because, as is well known, Ivan did not like flatterers and executed them as mercilessly as he did cowards. As for Nero, you can't compare him with Ivan the Terrible. Nero's insane orgies, with their unsurpassed cruelties and voluptuousness, were an expression of a distorted understanding of the enjoyment of life, established even before Nero, and a subconscious expression of the doom of his world. Actually, Nero's reign proved to be merely another step on the path of the final downfall of Rome. Ivan, on the other hand, laid the foundation of Russia by uniting a large number of small principalities into one mighty empire. This in itself, without the services of flattering poets, proves Ivan's greatness."

Mikhail could not but appreciate Novikov's skill in argument, in lucidly proving his points, and the clarity of his expression. "A clever lad," he thought to himself.

He was quite satisfied with the conversation, although he felt rather tired. Without realizing it, he was for the first time feeling the impact of Novikov, physically rather than mentally. He noticed his aggressive manner in speaking, but ascribed this to the fervor of youth, or perhaps to his desire to prove himself.

Later, the conversation turned to Andrei Demin. To his surprise Novikov learned that Gorin didn't like Andrei. On learning the cause of the dislike, he understood fully what had puzzled him before—Gorin's inner condition and why he had taken to Novikov's idea so readily. For the first time Feodor noticed a surprising trait of Gorin—his almost unexplainable naïveté. It amazed him.

"How can an almost childlike naïveté be combined with the realism of an experienced writer in such a talented and great man?" he asked himself. This discovery astounded and gladdened him because it lightened his task immeasurably.

CHAPTER 4

DOCTOR TSIBIK had been sitting for an hour in the reception room of the First Party Secretary of Rostov Province, Veria.

He could not figure out why he had been summoned. Smoking a cigarette nervously, the doctor tried not to notice the narrowed and seemingly mocking eyes of Veria's bald adjutant.

Veria made him wait a long time, but received him kindly, courteously inviting him to sit down in an armchair opposite him. Leaning back in his chair unconcernedly, Veria began to question him about the hospital.

The doctor's habitual self-assurance returned; hope flared up in him, causing a pleasant tremor in his heart: "Surely not a promotion? . . . It may be they are going to appoint me chief of the hospital."

The doctor began to talk with self-confidence, floridly, sprinkling his speech with medical terms, as if to say, "You'd better realize who you're talking to."

Suddenly Veria interrupted him: "I hear that you are preparing to go abroad?"

"Necessity, Comrade Veria," replied the doctor, modestly lowering his eyes, but blushing deeply. "Pavel—Gorin's son—needs medical observation."

"You're lying," said Veria softly, looking straight into the doctor's face. Something broke inside the doctor. His heart fell.

"Excuse me, Comrade Veria, I probably didn't hear you right . . ." The doctor tried to assume the perplexed air of an intellectual not accustomed to rough treatment.

"You're lying, I say," Veria repeated. "And very clumsily. You're altogether too anxious to go abroad. Why? Do you want to see Paris again?"

The doctor was silent.

"Tell me about Paris. It will be interesting."

"But there's nothing to tell . . . It's a boring city."

"Don't be bashful. Tell me: what do you expect to see there that we haven't got?"

The doctor said nothing. His fingers shook. Veria sighed distressfully: "I'm sorry for you, Doctor. You're a Soviet man, but you've lost the look . . . Surely it's clear that your outrageous desire to go abroad places you on a level with the renegades, with those whom they catch on the border and shoot within twenty-four hours."

The doctor, white as a sheet, looked blankly into Veria's small face and moved his lips soundlessly. Veria pulled a paper out of his desk drawer. It was Gorin's request for a visa.

"The Government refuses to grant Pavel a visa," said Veria and, sneering crookedly, added: "There's no sense in sending you alone to Paris. Is there?"

Receiving no answer, Veria said dryly, flourishing his pince-nez: "You are threatened with serious consequences."

342

The doctor began to slide slowly from the chair. He saw and heard Veria hazily. Veria said suddenly in a loud voice: "Doctor Tsibik, you will save yourself if you kill that scoundrel Pavel."

Veria pronounced the word "kill" firmly and precisely. He was neither hinting nor standing on ceremony. He knew that shocking directness would affect the doctor now more than anything else. He saw his helplessness and enjoyed it.

Unable to restrain himself any longer, Veria jumped up from his chair, ran around the doctor, rubbing his small hands; and, his eyes glittering strangely, he said quickly: "Killing is too good for him, the damned wretch! He's an enemy, the worst enemy of the people, the kind they grind into powder! . . . That his father is Mikhail Gorin doesn't mean a thing. He's a very dangerous person—he might even kill Gorin! But we'll get him first. Hee-hee-hee! . . . You, Doctor, know how to do that. Don't hurry—think everything over, so that there'll be no suspicion. But in a year, not later, there must be no Pavel. . . . You hear? There must not be."

Veria lost control of himself completely. His face became excited, blotched with red spots, his movements jerky and nervous. He came up close to the doctor, took his face in his hands, and said—smiling convulsively and twisting his large mouth: "Dare to sin, and you'll enjoy the sweetness of repentance." He repeated this phrase several times. In it there was, apparently, a meaning known only to himself.

It seemed to the doctor that he was having a terrible dream. He didn't remember how he found himself on the street. Whether he said anything to Veria or not, he didn't know.

Pavel's words, "That's all right, Doctor, your turn will come," said to him not long ago, suddenly sounded with piercing clarity in his head. He cried, walking along the street to the hospital, unable to keep back the tears, but he wasn't thinking about Pavel. He was feeling sorry, miserably, for himself.

That same day Veria received Feodor Novikov. Veria had calmed down after the scene with the doctor, although his eyes were still darting about, like two little mice. Veria announced to Novikov that he had been appointed Director of Rostov University and congratulated him on his promotion.

While talking about Gorin and his new play *Ivan the Terrible,* Veria said: "You know, I'm also writing a book, the history of the Party movement in the Caucasus." And grinning, he added, "So there's something in the nature of a secret competition between us. I'm writing in full consciousness; he's writing in complete delusion. Let's see whose work will be the better. But I consider my work more honest."

From these words Feodor realized that Veria knew about his task— and perhaps on that account wanted to emphasize the contrast between himself and Gorin. He hoped that Veria would not expound about his work, considering the matter too secret and too unpleasant. But Veria not only talked with him as he had with the doctor, directly and openly, but even raised a subject about which Novikov had no suspicion.

Suddenly he spoke about Nina. "I hear that you have fallen for the girl, as the saying is, up to the ears. Considering her natural qualities —that's understandable. What is not understandable is your short-sightedness."

"What do you mean?" asked Novikov, at once on the alert.

"Your position. . . . You want to combine business with pleasure!" said Veria, looking sharply into the professor's face. "That is not the path of a real Bolshevik."

"But allow me . . ." Novikov tried to object, realizing what Veria was hinting at. But Veria didn't let him.

". . . And then, you can see for yourself, if your work is unsuccessful your connection with Gorin's daughter will place you in a very awkward position. Very awkward," repeated Veria, turning a pencil in front of his eyes. "I'm afraid, Professor, that you didn't think about that. To some extent that's understandable, as Nina could turn anybody's head. However, it's never too late to come to one's senses and I advise you to do that as quickly as possible. Cool off, Comrade Director."

Noticing the confusion on Feodor's face, Veria got up from the desk—he didn't gain in height thereby—and in a friendly tone said: "Don't be offended at me for mixing in your private affairs. But a Bolshevik has no private affairs—there is only duty, responsibility to the Party. Your position is more serious and . . . more delicate, than an ordinary case. If you had not been bound by your special work, I would have congratulated you on your happy choice. But you are not free—and you must find the strength to crush your feelings for the sake of duty."

"I understand perfectly, Comrade Veria. That was a mistake."

Veria now spoke more freely: "Of course Nina is a fresh flower and tempting, and to play around a bit with one like her isn't a sin. But playing and serious feeling are two different things."

After the conversation with Veria, Feodor felt both soiled and frightened. He was used to taking orders. But that concerned his work. Now, for the first time, the unceremonious hand of authority had crept into his personal life and this hand seemed to him dirty, slippery, and frightfully repugnant.

CHAPTER 5

DOCTOR TSIBIK became unrecognizable. He was thoughtful, surprisingly untalkative, forgot his stories, seldom even pressed his pants. At the same time he began to pay unusual attention to Pavel, every now and then asking him how he felt. Gorin had not yet received a reply to his request from the Government, but no one in his house doubted that Pavel would in a short time get his visa. The doctor, of course, said nothing.

He was very anxious that Pavel should follow a definite regimen, and once even gave him a medical examination. Pavel was surprised at this unexpected activity.

"What's happened to you, Doctor? Are you well yourself?"

"I have to take you abroad strong. God forbid that you should break down on the journey!" the doctor answered, with a strained laugh. To himself he thought that Pavel was probably right—he really felt sickly. Even the excellence of the Gorin breakfasts no longer cheered him.

Forbidden fruit is always sweet. Feodor felt, after his talk with Veria, that his love for Nina was growing stronger. This frightened him and, recalling Veria's words, he tried to crush his love, as if it were a shameful feeling.

This turned out very awkwardly. Nina was perplexed: alone with her Feodor was particularly affectionate and tender, yet with other people present she did not recognize him. He was noticeably cool, tried to keep as far away from her as possible, even avoided her glances. For the first time she experienced the inexplicable but terrible pain of jealousy. Though realizing the senselessness of it, she was jealous of Lida.

Once Nina, Feodor, and Lida gathered around the piano in the Gorin drawing room. Nina was going to tell Lida about Nikolai's latest escapades, but suddenly stopped, began instead to pick idly at the keys—a melancholy motif floated in the air. Such moodiness attacked her often now. Lida, on the other hand, was particularly happy and carefree these days. Nina knew that she was happy because of Andrei and that Feodor had nothing to do with it, but every time Lida smiled at him, Nina felt her heart contract painfully. She lowered her eyes to the keyboard and was afraid to raise them.

Lida saw her friend's emotion and guessed its cause. But she was quite unable to understand how Nina could be jealous of her. It was so strange and unworthy of Nina. She went over to her and put her arm around her shoulders.

"What, Lida?"

"Oh—nothing," said Lida softly. "I'm happy. If only it would be always like this, with all of us together . . ."

Nina nodded her head in silence. Feodor enjoyed watching both girls.

"Nina, play us something a little livelier," he asked her.

"I'm not in a mood for a lively tune," she replied in an unexpectedly irritated voice.

"Then let Lida play to us," said Feodor and laid his hand on Lida's shoulder.

Nina suddenly got up from her chair and, without saying a word, went out of the room almost at a run. Feodor and Lida exchanged glances. Lida's face turned red, deeper and deeper each second.

An uncomfortable silence set in. They were glad when Mikhail came into the room with Luba, both looking very perplexed and excited.

"Andrei has disappeared," said Mikhail, in an almost frightened voice.

Lida paled. "What do you mean, disappeared? What do you mean?"

"He went away and left this note," said Luba. "It's for you. See what he says." She handed the note to Lida.

Lida, bewildered, began to read:

"Dear Lida: I'm going away for good, because I don't want to upset your life and that of others. You mustn't bind your fate to mine. The son of an enemy of the people has a very insecure and dangerous fate. Forgive me, but in time you will understand that I am right.— ANDREI."

Lida was at a complete loss. "What foolishness! . . . How could he write such a thing?" she said. "No, he's probably joking. But if he's serious, he'll come to himself; he'll come back soon."

"I think so too," said Mikhail. He spoke sincerely. If Andrei had appeared then in the doorway Mikhail, probably more than anyone else, would have been glad.

346

He had been wishing all along that Andrei would leave his house. Now it had happened. But it had not happened at all in the way he had wished.

CHAPTER 6

IT WAS AUGUST, dry and windy. Two people were making their way through a deep ravine overgrown with nut trees and birches. They were walking in silence, carefully, trying to make as little noise as possible, avoiding dry branches, stopping often to listen. When the water of the Don appeared blue through the foliage of the trees—the ravine was near the bank of the river—the elder, gray, with his left eye bandaged, said quietly: "Now we'll have to wait for darkness, it's dangerous to go farther; they'd spot us."

"I'm pretty hungry to wait so long," his companion sighed, but sat down on the grass beside him. "If only we had a piece of bread and some salt . . ."

A week had passed since Andrei Demin had hid himself in the woods, where he had suffered from hunger and exposure. But he did not regret the step he had taken. More than ever before he was convinced that he had to go—not only leave Gorin's house but go away altogether, from all his friends, from his whole former life. This may have looked like impulse, but he had sound reasons. He knew that he was an unwanted guest at the Gorins'. But with Lida also he had to make the break. He knew that his rescue from Durov's hands by Gorin was only temporary. The son of an enemy of the people has a short life. To bind Lida to his own uncertain fate he considered dishonest, egotistical, even criminal.

When he left the Gorins' he had no definite plans. But a sort of plan formed itself: it was necessary to hide from the authorities because he had no documents, and to search for food so as not to die from hunger. Then in the woods Andrei ran into a young lad, still a boy, not more than sixteen. His name was Volodya. In tears Volodya told him how, a month previously, more than a hundred families had been arrested in their village, loaded onto trucks, and sent away under guard to the railway station to be transported in freight cars to the north. On the way to the station Volodya tore himself free from the hands of one of the guards and ran into the woods. They fired at him.

"But I got away," said Volodya, smearing the tears on his face with a dirty hand. "My father ordered me. He whispered: 'Break for it, son! With us you'd die anyway.' "

So Andrei and Volodya became partners in their new life. It was far easier for them together. Each keeping watch for the other in turn, they were able to sleep more peacefully, and it was easier to get food.

When dusk came, Andrei and Volodya went out onto the river bank. They planned to make their way unobserved to one of the food barges and stock up—with luck, for a couple of days. Such an undertaking was very risky; the sentries shot without warning. But hunger isn't a godmother, and they were used to risks—this wasn't their first. Placing a bag on the ground, Andrei took out an auger. In the darkness they found a boat, got into it, and quietly floated toward the grain elevator towering dimly upward. Soon they could distinguish the dim lights on the barges and the tinkling of bells. Before reaching the first barge, they stopped at the bank. Volodya got out of the boat and went toward the barges. His job was to divert the attention of the sentries. Andrei then rowed away again, listening in the darkness.

Soon he heard Volodya, whimpering and sniffling, shout from the river bank in a terribly pitiful voice: "Uncle, give me some grub . . . a chunk of bread!"

Steps sounded on the barge; someone in heavy boots was going to the right-hand side, next to the bank, with a lantern in his hand. "Who's there?"

"Uncle, a little bread . . . For three days I haven't eaten."

"Get to hell out of here!" shouted the voice from the barge. "There's too many of you loafing around. Don't you know it's forbidden to come near the barges? We have orders to shoot!"

"I want to eat! . . . Uncle dear, give me a little piece."

The man on the barge cursed. "Hey! Vanka!" he called. "Go ashore and catch that son of a snake—we'll show him bread!"

"Oh, to hell with him!" someone responded lazily from the bow, and Andrei, to his surprise, heard a female voice saying sleepily: "You hear so many of them now . . ."

"A little bread, Aunty, a little bread!" shouted Volodya, still more loudly, encouraged by a note of sympathy in her voice.

The sentry apparently lost patience. He swore long and foully. "For God's sake, I tell you, go away or I'll shoot!"

Andrei decided it was time: Volodya had drawn the sentry into a loud wrangle by now. He rowed quietly up to the barge and hurriedly began to bore a hole in its tarred side. Judging by the depth of the barge in the water, it was probably filled with grain, awaiting its turn

348

for unloading into the elevator. The work went on slowly, Andrei stopped often, listening to the voices on the barge.

Volodya was now shouting loudly: "I hope you croak, you bastards! You misers! I hope you choke on your own bread!"

Andrei at last bored through the side, took out the auger and felt a warm stream of grain flow into his hand, falling onto the bottom of the boat with a steady rustling sound. He froze: cold sweat came out on his forehead in beads. It seemed to him that the grain was falling with the thunder of a waterfall—and for miles around everybody would hear it. Volodya, in the meantime, now screamed, now swore, now teased—somebody was already chasing him along the bank of the river. On the barge the sentry was still threatening to shoot.

The boat filled up quickly with the grain, sinking ever lower in the water. Andrei had barely time to level it off. When the water had almost reached the gunwale, he stuffed up the hole in the barge with a rag and pushed off quietly. The boat went quickly with the current. At a safe distance, Andrei shouted as loudly as he could: "Ferry! Bring the ferry!" That was the signal agreed on, and on hearing it Volodya was to run from the barge—his job was finished. But from the direction of the barge shots sounded, two in succession. Andrei, uneasy over his friend, tied the boat to the bank and ran towards the barge, but soon almost collided with Volodya—running headlong, smashing into bushes, tripping over roots, and whimpering mournfully like a puppy.

"Volodya! What's wrong with you?"

"The blackguards! They did fire! Got me in the arm . . . It's bleeding." There was no pursuit. Having driven the bothersome youngster off, the barge people quieted down. Andrei bandaged Volodya's arm. The wound was not dangerous, a mere skin crease. Volodya, tired, lay on the grass.

"Well, Andrei, did you get anything?"

"Yes, some grain."

"Good, we'll trade it in for groceries."

After resting a little, they hid the boat well, covering it with branches and grass.

"I hope it doesn't rain . . ."

After this night operation the two friends revived. Not only had they stocked up with food for themselves; they were also able to help others. They met a group of fugitives like themselves in the woods. Among them was an old man, with a young daughter of Volodya's age. The unexpected help saved them from almost certain death—the old man was already barely able to move. The affairs of the group were in a bad way. Three of the men, on whom the fate of the entire group depended, were weak and dull-witted people who could do nothing better than beg in the villages. It was dangerous and mostly useless; there was starvation in the villages no less than in the woods. One of the men had a revolver, and the old man a Berdan rifle, but they were afraid to use these arms.

Volodya became attached to the girl and helped her in every way he could, often denying himself his piece of bread. Andrei somehow became the leader of the group. He took on this unexpected responsibility with full consciousness of his duty.

The fugitives lived in the thickest part of the woods, taking turns keeping watch. They cooked only during the day, lit no fires at night, slept in a dugout to warm each other with their bodies. They talked little, thought much. And their thoughts were all about winter. Winter, like a terrifying specter, loomed before them; they all knew what frost would bring.

But misfortune came sooner than winter. Through stupidity two of the men were followed when returning from a sally. When they were all eating thin gruel from one pot in silence, shots suddenly sounded on every side. "Surrender! Or we'll kill you!" sounded voices.

The fugitives were silent. The old man snatched the revolver from Andrei who, as leader, now carried it. "Lead them away! Maybe I can hold the cops off for a while."

"I'll stay," whispered Andrei sternly. But the old man knit his brows: "Do what I say. It's easier to die than to lead them out. I'm going to die soon anyway."

"Follow me," Andrei ordered, more with his eyes than in his whisper, and dived into the bush.

Just then a military man in a blue cap showed himself. The old man calmly fired, almost point blank. Without a sound the military man fell. The old man crawled towards a tree, crossed himself, and awaited the attack. He did not reply to the shots; he fired only at a certainty.

In the meantime Andrei was leading his group out of the encirclement, sometimes crawling, sometimes lying flat. Then in a glade, where the trees were rather sparse, a bullet suddenly dropped the girl. Volodya, forgetting himself, dashed to her, but on the way fell, cut down by another bullet and dying within a pace of her.

Andrei gestured the remaining three men to hide themselves and not move. But they couldn't hold out. When they stood up, raising their arms for mercy, three shots in succession mowed them down. Andrei remained alone. Cursing the three fools under his breath, he quietly crawled into the bush, straight toward the rifle that was sounding out death. Instinctively he felt that this would be the best thing to do.

"I must see him, I must see him," the burning thought repeated itself in his brain.

In a few minutes he saw him: a red-haired youth with a good-natured, almost humorous face, lying behind two birches. The blue cap was pushed back onto his neck. The birches were growing like a crotch, from one root. The rifle lay between the two trunks. The soldier was looking tensely into the glade. Each mound and shrub was visible to him. Andrei could see him lick his dry lips. Noiselessly Andrei crept toward him from one side, then fell on his back with the whole weight of his body. The soldier tried to turn his rifle on him, but it caught in the crotch. Encircling his neck from behind with his arm, Andrei squeezed with all his might. The soldier began to choke. Andrei gradually drew his head back until he heard his spine crack—the soldier shuddered and slumped to the ground. From his bluish mouth the tongue hung out, but Andrei still squeezed and squeezed his throat. Then he let go and ran—erect, without bending, for a long time, until he dropped from exhaustion on the rotted leaves. Seeing a hole in the ground, he crawled into it and began painstakingly to cover himself with branches. Then he froze motionless, crouching. In the distance was the dull sound of continued shooting. Sharply and loudly, Andrei heard his heart beating. Then the shooting stopped. That meant the end of the old man.

"They've killed him, or he's killed himself," thought Andrei. "No, they probably killed him. He wouldn't spend a bullet on himself."

Andrei thought about the struggle going on in his country: just so must the Russian people die—with guns in their hands, like this old man, in battle, giving his life dearly; not like his own father—in the cells, helpless, under the exulting laughter of his torturers. Then he remembered Volodya and the young girl and a terrible pity seized his heart.

When darkness fell he crawled out of the hole and worked his way out of the woods into the open, into the city. He was alone and knew what difficulties lay ahead of him.

A week later he ran into a patrol. He was unable to escape and was arrested. When interrogated he called himself by another name and refused to tell where he came from. The questioning officer hit him on the head with the butt of his revolver and Andrei lost consciousness. He came to in a concentration camp.

CHAPTER 7

SIDOROV had difficulty persuading Feodor Novikov to celebrate his promotion at the family's summer house. Feodor stubbornly refused, knowing why the plant director wanted to arrange this celebration and imagining how badly it would affect Lida's low spirits. But Sidorov persisted. He already regarded Feodor as his son-in-law. Now, indeed, inexpressibly pleased over Novikov's appointment as Director of Rostov University, he wanted to conclude the whole affair with the wedding as quickly as possible. He was imbued with an extraordinary respect for the young professor. As for his daughter, her wishes were of secondary importance.

Before this, Sidorov had a stormy scene with Lida. She didn't even want to think about marriage. "I love Andrei and I will be faithful to him!"

"Show me your Andrei! Where is he?" thundered Sidorov.

When Feodor came to the summer house with his brother, Lida looked at him coldly. After her father's words, their former simple relations seemed to her impossible. She blamed Feodor as well as her parents, and to spite them she talked to Nikolai. Feodor understood her condition perfectly, and tried to leave her in peace.

Nikolai remained as before, good-natured, unconcerned. Natalia treated him with bantering indifference: she saw that he was in love with Lida, but considered him no longer a danger to her ideal, Feodor.

Surrounded by all these submerged currents and intrigues, fine and coarse, crafty and naïve, the object of them sat sorrowful and aloof—thinking of Andrei and his unknown fate.

Natalia was uneasy over Feodor's cool manner. Although she blamed her daughter for her inability to "inflame the young professor," the professor himself seemed not to be the passionate type. "It's time the fools were getting together," she thought.

Secretly she had managed to have a talk with a fortune teller—an old woman who lived on the edge of the city. The old woman was very much afraid of the authorities (for telling fortunes, her property could be confiscated and she could be sent to the north), but Natalia

Sidorov was an old client and she talked with her for a long time beside the samovar, drinking one cup of tea after another. To loosen her tongue, Natalia had brought with her a pound of sugar and a bottle of vodka. The old woman hid the sugar away carefully, but the vodka they drank. Natalia explained her problem. The fortune teller nodded her head sympathetically.

"You can hardly kindle the passions of the young ones with sooth-saying nowadays," she said thoughtfully. "There's no better method than the Spanish fly."

"What kind of fly is that?" Natalia became interested. "Must it bite them, or something?"

"No. You put it in the food," explained the old woman.

"For whom?"

"Better the man. . . . If you excite the man he'll climb the wall and no matter how much your daughter tries she won't have a chance to hold out against him."

Natalia was overjoyed. Then she asked anxiously, "Where could I get such a fly? I've never seen one."

"I have a dried one," said the fortune teller. "Only that will cost you another bottle of vodka."

Natalia promised the bottle and, on getting the fly, looked at it with respect. The fly, as a fly, was not particularly distinguished, except that it was green. Natalia thought that she had seen its like on a manure pile.

On parting, the old woman gave her some advice: "The best way is to put the fly in a turnover. And make him eat it on an empty stomach, just after he has eased himself. That's the best time."

Everything was carefully prepared. The turnovers were on the plate in the center of the table, right opposite Feodor. She had marked the turnover containing the fly with a little cross and watched it jealously, not taking her eyes off it.

"Try the turnover," Natalia invited Feodor affectionately. "Lida baked it. Decide for yourself whether she's a good cook."

Feodor thanked her and took a turnover—but not the one with the little cross! Sidorov also wanted to try his daughter's handiwork; reaching out to the plate, he looked over the turnovers to see which one would be best—and took the marked one! Natalia almost screamed. Forgetting herself, she smacked her husband's hand, like a misbehaving schoolboy's. "What are you doing, you old devil? You don't need that yet!" she said, and added in an apologetic voice: "Leave those for the guests."

Sidorov, thinking that he had broken some fine rule of etiquette unknown to him, obediently dropped his spoil. After thus saving the unlucky turnover, Natalia put it in a saucer and placed it in front of Feodor. "Try another one."

Feodor, thanking her, took a bite of it, smiled, and said it tasted very good. Then he ate it all.

Impatiently Natalia awaited the results.

As on the first visit, Sidorov took his guests for a cruise in the yacht. And, as before, they met a barge carrying prisoners. But on this occasion an unlooked-for incident took place. Lida suddenly recognized Andrei among the prisoners.

"Andrei! Andrei!" she shouted, beside herself.

He was sitting close to the barbed-wire fencing the edge of the barge, bent over—dirty, wasted, like an old man. At Lida's shout he raised his head. Then, as if some unknown force were drawing him to Lida, he sprang up; and before the guard could catch him, he jumped over the barbed wire into the water. He swam towards the yacht, his solitary eye fixed on Lida. Convulsively seizing the rail, Lida leaned her whole body toward him.

"Andrei, my darling . . . faster, swim faster," she whispered, never taking her eyes off him, as if her very watching could save him. Suddenly there was a shot, then another—two spouts of water spurted up beside Andrei's head.

"Don't shoot! Don't dare to shoot!" shrieked Lida piercingly.

Nikolai suddenly dived into the water, as he was, in his clothes, and with quick strokes swam toward Andrei.

"Where are you going?" shouted the frightened Feodor. "They'll kill you!"

One more shot sounded. The water behind Andrei turned red and he sank, but came up, still trying to swim. Nikolai caught him under the armpits, dragged him to the yacht. They lifted him onto the deck.

"Andrei, darling!" Lida threw herself on him.

Andrei looked into her eyes, smiled weakly.

"I didn't leave you after all, Lida . . ." he said softly, and died.

354

CHAPTER 8

LIDA was confined to bed for a whole week. She became thin and taciturn.

The Sidorovs had already moved from their summer house to the city apartment. A hush reigned there. It rained nearly every day, bringing to mind the approaching fall. Natalia wandered about noiselessly from one room to another, aimlessly changed knickknacks from place to place—a box, a plaster of Paris dog with an ear hanging down —while she listened for sounds from Lida's room. But there all was quiet.

Every evening Lida's father went in to see her. He sat heavily on the bed—the springs squeaked woefully—and, passing his heavy hand over his daughter's soft hair, said in a confused way: "Now then . . . now then . . ." He was afraid to reason with her. Once he tried to tease her to make her laugh, as he had often done when she was a little girl and naughty. With his horny finger he tickled her behind the ear, blew into her eyes. But Lida merely turned her head to the wall, pressed her lips tight to keep from crying.

"Well, I'll be damned!" thought Sidorov, shaking his head. "She was really in love with that convict."

Once Nikolai came to visit Lida, but they wouldn't let him in to see her. "The doctor said not to disturb Lida," said Natalia, looking away.

Nikolai wandered about outside, squinted up at the closed window of Lida's room, and went back to his communal boarding house, kicking at small stones.

Nina brought a noisy liveliness, and Natalia welcomed her every visit. Nina, better than anyone else, was able to drive away, as she said, "Lida's autumn melancholy." She purposely burst into her friend's bedroom without ceremony, opened the window, and paying no attention to her spiritless, almost stark appearance, chattered loudly, persistently asked her about trifles and, without waiting for an answer, told her whatever came into her head, as if nothing had happened.

On the Monday of the following week Nina arrived greatly excited. She found Lida in the kitchen helping her mother to unpack the things they had brought from the summer house.

"Thank God Lida is better," she thought with joy, but gave no sign that she had noticed the change.

"Lida, get dressed at once: we're going to the theatre! I've brought you a ticket!" she cried from the door. "Stop fussing. Fedya bought three tickets and has arranged everything for your sake. He said he wouldn't go unless you do."

Lida drew her eyebrows together painfully: "Why does he want me to go?"

"Ask him yourself. But you simply must come with us. I don't want to sit alone on three empty seats."

Lida shook her head stubbornly, but Natalia took Nina's side: "What's the sense of pining at home? It will brighten you up a bit."

There was only an hour before the performance. Natalia and Nina quickly dressed Lida, who submitted indifferently like a doll. "It's useless, all this . . . it's no good . . . ," she repeated in a weak voice, but they dressed her and literally led her out by the hand.

"Understand, silly, this is an event: the first presentation of *Anna Karenina* in Rostov," said Nina, pulling her along. Lida merely responded to her friend's delight with a weak smile. She walked beside her mechanically. Wherever Nina might have led her she would have followed just as submissively.

Feodor met them at the entrance to the theatre. He looked at Lida with curiosity, didn't ask any questions, but seemed glad she had come.

It turned out that Feodor had bought tickets for the most expensive boxes. When they entered, Mirzoyan and two other prominent Party officials were already sitting there with their wives. The men recognized Feodor and bade him a good evening, while the women looked Nina up and down intently and coldly, either envying or disapproving her foreign dress and unfamiliar hair-do. Mirzoyan could not restrain himself and, unobserved, winked at Feodor as much as to say, "You're aiming high, brother."

The curtain parted and silence fell in the theatre. Nina sat in the front row of the box between Feodor and Lida, leaning her graceful arms on the red plush of the balustrade. She looked stealthily at Lida, then stroked her hand. "Don't worry, Lida, everything will be all right," she whispered. "The main thing is, you and I have remained friends . . ."

Lida looked attentively at the stage but one persistent thought consumed her—Andrei. How could anything remain the same when he was dead? What is that woman on the stage talking about—doesn't

356

she know that death has passed over Rostov? She's laughing! . . .
How dare she laugh?

"The scenery is beautiful, isn't it, Lida?"

"Beautiful?"

"Don't you like it?"

Nina was in an excellent mood. What she was seeing on the stage
and what was happening around her merged for her into one happy
and exciting feeling, in which the main thing was the nearness of
Feodor. In the semidarkness she caught his tender and loving glance.
She blushed, and smiled in response. She noticed that many of the
men in the pit were looking up at her.

"I am looking my best," she thought. "And Feodor sees their
glances. Let him. That's good. Of course, he's very proud of me. . . .
And how unfortunate Anna Karenina was, married to a man she did
not love . . . No, my husband will be Fedya, whom I love, a most
remarkable man. Only, why is he so shy today? He has moved away,
as if he were afraid to touch me. . . . And Lida—how sorry I am
for her . . . But who is that looking so intently through his opera
glasses from the Government box? I believe it's Shcherbakov. He's a
queer fellow. All right, whoever it is, I'll smile to him . . . I'm so
very happy. Dear Feodor, dear Anna Karenina and everything around
me . . ." Nina was as if intoxicated; only the presence of the sorrowful Lida restrained her.

During the intermission a student acquaintance of Lida's, son of
the chief prosecutor of the Province, came to them in the box. A
thin and lanky lad, with slicked-down hair, he was under the influence of the play and imagined himself to be Count Vronsky. He
came in on parade, as if it were not a suit he was wearing but a uniform
with epaulets. Clicking imaginary spurs and casting a glance full of
respect in Nina's direction, he sat down beside Lida and froze into
a refined pose. Had it not been for the presence of the others he
would have kissed Lida's hand, exactly as on the stage.

"Tarasova! What charm! How finely she interprets Anna's feelings.
And Khrulev, there is acting! Did you notice how he cracked his fingers
when he was nervous, or how he smoothed down his hair—words
were unnecessary to show that this was Karenin . . ." The student
was talking loudly so that everyone in the box would hear him. "By
the way, Lida, have you heard the story about a pupil at a Rostov
school? In his class composition he wrote this: 'Vronsky gathered all
his feelings into one point and directed them at Anna.' "

Nina laughed, not because the student had said something funny,

357

but because she was feeling happy. Mirzoyan broke into the conversation: "That's all rot—feelings, experiences, and other soulful mush," he said pointedly. "The trouble is that Anna hadn't any discipline. If the secretary of the Party Committee had summoned her, bawled her out thoroughly, and loaded her down with social work, she would have forgotten Vronsky quickly. And, believe me, she would have been happy."

"Yes, I wouldn't mind talking to her alone," interjected one of the Party officials amid general laughter.

Lida was nervous. She was disgusted with the student. His eyes, honeyed and greasy, were particularly unpleasant. The fat Mirzoyan was fatter and more stupid than ever. She didn't even recognize Nina.

"How can this be? Andrei is dead . . . and still they can joke and laugh as if nothing had happened . . ."

Suddenly all the men in the box rose and drew themselves up respectfully. In the doorway appeared Shcherbakov. He was wearing, as usual, a well-pressed semimilitary suit of gray material, but his haughty, cold face showed excitement.

"He's probably had a few drinks," thought Feodor, at the same time bowing to the young but influential visitor.

"I saw you in the box," Shcherbakov told Mirzoyan, without responding to the greetings of the other men, "and remembered that your report is scheduled for tomorrow."

"Very good, Comrade Shcherbakov. Everything is prepared," replied Mirzoyan with a servile smile on his round face.

Shcherbakov murmured something in reply and, as if noticing Nina for the first time, smiled to her: "Ah, Comrade Gorin, how do you do? How is Mikhail Alexeyevich?" Inviting the men with a gesture of the hand to be seated, he said to Nina in a pointedly official tone: "I hear that you passed your examination at the Conservatory successfully. It wouldn't hurt you to take on some social work now—for instance you might organize a concert for the military garrison. But we'll talk about that again. In the meantime, remember me warmly to your father," and, smiling once more, he left.

The men were silent, but each looked perplexed, while the women buzzed like a wasp's nest. It seemed strange to everyone that instead of summoning Mirzoyan to his box, the Second Secretary had come to him. Mirzoyan was more surprised than anyone, as Shcherbakov had already spoken to him about his report by telephone that morning. Nina blushed. She was certain that Shcherbakov had come to the box because of her; and in spite of the official manner in which he had spoken to her she, like any woman, felt that his dry tone was merely a screen behind which he was unskillfully hiding his confusion. She felt that Feodor also noticed this.

"Let him . . . it will serve Fedya as punishment for his recent fickleness," she thought.

When the second act began Lida decided to take herself in hand and follow the performance more attentively. But every word spoken on the stage beat painfully on her strained nerves. The words of the actors, now shrill, now dull, resounded in her ears in a strange, distorted manner. As if the stage had begun to rock, the audience, the actors, all merged into one whirlwind and Lida suddenly saw the Don shining in the sunlight. Andrei was swimming toward her, gazing at her with his single eye; and his lips moved.

"Andrei!" screamed Lida. In the silence of the theatre her scream sounded unexpectedly loud and sharp, like a shot. Everybody, audience and actors, turned in her direction. But Lida saw nobody; she was looking straight in front of her with wide-open staring eyes. She did not remember Nina and Feodor leading her into the corridor, or how Feodor calmed the people who came out, assuring them that he could manage, or Nina bringing her a glass of water. When she opened her eyes, Nina asked her excitedly: "What's the matter, dear?"

"Nina, everything is over for me," she said in a resigned voice.

"What foolishness!" exclaimed Nina hotly. "I understand your grief. . . . But you're still young! Your whole life is ahead of you!"

Feodor stood beside them, nervously biting his lips. "I'd better take you home," he said to Lida. "You, Nina, stay and see the play through."

Nina raised her eyes to him. He was surprised to see that they were shining with happiness.

"Fedya," said Nina, placing her hand on his shoulder. "Fedya, kiss me . . . at once!"

Startled, Feodor looked around. There was no one in the corridor. Without embracing her, he kissed her impulsively, afraid to look at Lida, who was sitting on a sofa with bowed head. Nina, radiant, responded. Even the presence of Lida and her sorrow didn't interfere with her happiness but rather excited her to enjoy it.

CHAPTER 9

NINA'S BIRTHDAY was at the beginning of September and Mikhail decided to celebrate it with an excursion into the woods. He arranged a picnic with snipe shooting. "The fall is the best time in the woods," he said. "Nature then wears her brightest clothes."

Nina was joyful, yet uneasy. For some reason she thought that Feodor might propose at the hunt.

Mikhail noticed her agitation and asked his wife about it. Luba told him that Feodor's strange behavior during recent days ("Something is preventing him from being himself with Nina") was the cause of their daughter's anxiety. "That's all nonsense," Mikhail assured her. "Young people are always doing that sort of thing."

At the hunt Mikhail was very friendly with Feodor, clearly accepting him as a future member of his family. Only Cheprok looked at Novikov with open suspicion and once even spoke to Mikhail about it. But the writer was deaf to his grumbling.

The party met a young peasant couple; they lived with the forester, father of the young man. This family was an odd remnant of the past, a surviving island in an ocean of misfortune. Through a lucky set of circumstances—the forester arranged hunts for such important men as Veria and Gorin—collectivization had not touched them. And so they remained in the forest, in their own cabin, far from the village life so full of sorrow and confusion.

Nina saw how the peasant and his young wife exchanged loving glances, not abashed by the presence of the guests. They lived in their own world. "It seems that such love is not for me," she thought bitterly.

The day passed and Nina had not yet received the expected proposal from Feodor. Feodor appeared gloomy, uncommunicative, avoided her noticeably. Before night the women busied themselves preparing the beds in the forester's house, while the men gathered in the old bath house which stood on the bank of a deep stream. They drank, recalled former hunts, discussed life. The forester poured vodka and more vodka. Their gray heads together, the old friends struck up a song, so old that Feodor had never heard it.

In the small bath house there was a smell of mint and steamed

360

birch leaves. The logs, old and blackened, had absorbed this smell over the years.

It was getting dark.

Feodor was talking to the forester's son at the other end of the long table apart from the older people. He asked him at length about his wife, how they got married, where he met her, how they were living now. The young man told him in detail and with pleasure. Every time he mentioned his wife a broad smile appeared on his good-natured face, and his eyes, even though drunken, shone with happiness.

"You, Feodor, aren't you marrying his daughter?" he asked, nodding his head toward Mikhail.

"Sh—sh! Not so loud!" said Feodor, a look of fright in his eyes. "I love her, but I can't get married."

"How's that?"

"Don't ask!" Feodor poured him a glass. "Drink!"

The lad shook his head sympathetically. "She's a lovely girl. I'm sorry you can't marry her. Perhaps some of the higher-ups are courting her?"

"No!" whispered Feodor. "I simply don't want to—or no, not that . . . But, as I told you, I'd rather you didn't ask."

Gorin and the forester got up from the bench and went to the door, their arms around each other. Mikhail, looking particularly tall in the low cabin, stooped to keep from bumping his head against the ceiling. Passing Feodor he slapped his shoulder: "Let's go to bed, Fedya . . . my son . . ."

Feodor didn't reply.

When they had gone Feodor talked for a long time with the young man. Then the lad went onto the porch for fresh air, and slumped there on the threshold—dead drunk. Feodor finished the bottle alone, looking dully at the window, where in the dark glass his ruffled head was reflected.

Nina, in the meantime, unable to sleep, tossed about on the bed.

Feodor had not proposed to her. He had even avoided her. She felt the crimson flush of shame cover her cheeks. Jumping up, she lit the lamp, took off her nightdress and went over to the mirror. In wonder, as if for the first time, she looked at herself.

"How beautiful I am! Beautiful!"

Throwing on her coat over her naked body, she left the cabin. It was very dark; the forest soughed uneasily: in the distance sheet lightning flashed. Running along the path, overgrown with fragrant grass, Nina went toward the river where a single little window shone in the bath house.

"Fedya, you don't know me yet! You don't know me!" she repeated over and over again as if in a fever.

She went onto the porch. The door was open and the feeble light from an oil lamp showed the forester's son sleeping on the threshold. Nina stepped over him and went inside, closing the door behind her and shaking the coat off her onto the floor.

"Fedya, I've come to you," she said softly but firmly.

Feodor raised his eyes, without surprise, as if he had been expecting her. He looked long and silently at her, then rose, tottering. Nina saw at once that he was very drunk.

"A gift from the empress," said Feodor bitterly. "Let me have a good look at you." He raised the lamp above his head to throw more light on her. She stood motionless, naked, beautiful.

"A gift from the empress," Feodor repeated. The lamp wavered in his hand. The shadows, like the fingers of a lover, nervous and hurried, glided over her young body.

"Stand like that . . . don't move!" exclaimed Feodor, as if he had sobered up for a moment. "What a pity I'm drunk! When I'm sober I'll think this was a dream."

"This isn't a dream, Fedya. I'm here with you."

"Your eyes, your breasts, your . . . legs . . . You remember Solomon's Song of Songs: '. . . thy belly is like an heap of wheat set about with lilies. Thy two breasts are like two young roes that are twins.' But Solomon hadn't seen you! And I, unfortunately, am not Solomon and cannot speak in verse. But you are beautiful, Nina!"

The blush of joyful shame covered Nina's face, her eyes were radiant. "Speak, speak, Fedya," she said softly, and took a step toward him. But Feodor stopped her with a movement of his hand.

"You are beautiful, but you are not for me . . . unfortunately. Let us regard this as a dream." He dropped onto a bench, placed the lamp on the table, and bowed his head.

Nina ran to him and, pressing his head to her breast, whispered passionately: "Fedya, darling, this is all yours, to the last particle, to the last drop of blood. All, all, is yours . . ." She spoke hurriedly, covered him with kisses, ever pressing her quivering body closer to his. But Feodor got up and pushed her aside with an irresolute hand.

"No, Nina, I can't accept your gift. I love you! You know that! . . . But I have run onto submerged rocks . . . yes, submerged rocks."

362

And suddenly he struck the table with his fist in a terrible rage. The lamp jumped and nearly went out.

"Nina, you're living in another world!" he shouted. "Come to your senses! Open your eyes!" And then, mocking himself, he said: "Perhaps we could arrange a wedding in a church? In the big cathedral on the square in Rostov, where the black market is? They would open the cathedral for us and clean it. And the wedding dress? We'll make it from a good poster about a Soviet family! And instead of a priest, my best friend Veria will marry us better than any. 'My children!' he will say: 'Unite your flesh and your spirit in happy wedlock and bear fruit and multiply like rabbits.' And instead of an ikon he will make us kiss the mustached portrait of the master. And such a merry peal of bells will sound all over Rostov that the devil himself in hell will turn green from envy. Veria, my kind friend, will read us a sermon. Not once have you, Nina, talked with him as you should have. And that's bad: you've missed a great deal. He knows many secrets of life. For he is, of course, its stage manager. Ha—ha—ha!"

Numb with horror, Nina looked at his distorted face. But Feodor laughed drunkenly.

"There's only one thing this Veria—this evil dwarf—doesn't know: what love is."

He embraced her head, drew her to him. "Do you remember, Nina, that day on the steppe?"

"I remember, I remember, dear . . . You said that we would always be happy."

"And I didn't lie to you, Nina. . . . Remember that!"

"I believe you."

Lightning flashed and thunder pealed suddenly with terrific force. The lamp seemed to fade and the naked Nina became, for an instant, like marble.

"Nina, go away, go away! . . . I can't be your husband."

"Why? Is there someone else? Lida?"

"No, no one. And not Lida! You know that yourself."

"Then what's the matter?"

"Go away, Nina, and forget everything," he shouted. "Go away, I tell you!"

Involuntarily she backed away from him. Feodor swayed—and suddenly, as if he had been mown down, fell to the floor. Nina bent over him—he was already in a drunken stupor. She placed his head on her knees, stroked his hair.

"You will be mine, Fedya," she said. "You're drunk now, but you will be mine."

But however persistently she repeated the words, she felt in her heart that something more serious than his sudden drunkenness had arisen between them. She put a pillow under his head and kissed his forehead. Then she went out.

The storm was raging and there was a downpour of rain. But Nina didn't hurry. Back in the cabin she lay down on the bed and cried, covering her mouth with a pillow.

To convince Veria completely that there was nothing serious between himself and Nina, Feodor Novikov openly courted Lida. But Lida was still under the impact of Andrei's death. Feodor's attention seemed to her strange and cruel. With tears in her eyes she asked him to leave her in peace.

Feodor's sudden attention to his daughter cheered Sidorov. Following the rule of "Strike while the iron's hot," he cornered the University Director and spoke to him "man to man." Novikov gave him his word that he would marry Lida.

"The ice has moved," Sidorov told his wife after this talk. Natalia smiled. She was certain that the success of the affair had been clinched long ago by the turnover with the Spanish fly.

CHAPTER 10

FEODOR, waiting until the door closed behind his visitor, turned to Nikolai with a laugh: "Did you see how he bowed? . . . Well, how do you like the set-up?" Feodor reclined in the armchair with exaggerated importance, glanced around the large office with a satisfied look. "You see this carpet—from wall to wall? It cost three thousand rubles at Government prices—that's no joke. And the desk? Just look at the work. The fortress of a bureaucrat, a Gibraltar, not a desk. Ha—ha—ha! Have a cigarette; they're from Moscow."

Feodor beamed. This was the first time Nikolai had come to his office and he wanted to show himself in all his glory. He had even received the visitor on purpose while Nikolai was there, so that his brother could see what respect and fear he caused among his subordinates.

Now, spreading himself with a satisfied smile, Feodor expected to hear noisy exclamations of delight and envy from his brother. But for some reason Nikolai sat scowling.

Feodor was surprised. "Are you sure you're well, Nikolai?"

"I want to talk to you about a serious matter," said Nikolai.

"You must be sick," laughed Feodor. "Nikolai—with serious business . . . That's good! Cut it out, dear brother; seriousness doesn't go with your face. That's why you're such a good sort; one can relax with you. Otherwise: you saw that visitor." Feodor waved his hand towards the door. "Bores you to death."

Involuntarily Nikolai smiled at his brother's words. Nevertheless, he said stubbornly: "Feodor, I want to ask you about Lida."

"About Lida?" Feodor was surprised and his face became serious. "What—has anything happened?"

For a moment Nikolai was silent. Obviously it wasn't easy for him to express his thought.

"I don't understand your intentions toward her," he began at last. "I know, of course, that you love Nina Gorin. Yet you've become so . . . so attentive to Lida. Haven't you noticed that Sidorov and his wife look on you almost as a son-in-law?" Nikolai sighed deeply. He felt suddenly that his words didn't fit the circumstances in which he found himself—this official office, the portrait of Stalin on the wall, the bust of Lenin in the corner. And Feodor himself seemed such a stranger and so distant that he became embarrassed. "I shouldn't have spoken, I shouldn't . . . it's useless," he thought with regret and vexation at himself.

If Feodor had asked him to leave the office, he would have left without a word. But Feodor made a mistake. Apparently his brother's face looked very comical at that moment—he merely asked sarcastically: "How does this concern you?"

Nikolai flared up: "I am your brother——"

"And therefore I must give you an account of everything I do?"

Nikolai suddenly got up and walked to the front of the desk. His first feeling of awkwardness had passed.

"How can you talk like that?" he exclaimed with heat. "Nobody's asking you for an account. I know you look on me as a windbag. But it so happens that your empty-headed brother has noticed that the serious-minded and thoughtful Feodor is carrying on a very mixed and two-faced game. You love Nina and are going to marry her, and at the same time you find it possible to turn Lida's head—although you have no feeling for her. In any other circumstances I wouldn't have taken any notice. It's your business. But here . . . You know yourself how much Lida has suffered recently, how deeply she felt Andrei's loss, and you saw how intensely she can love . . . What do you want—to deliver her another blow and beat her down completely? Suppose she becomes attached to you? How will you break the news of your marriage to Nina? For you, this may be an amusing game; for Lida it may be the fatal blow . . . As her friend I ask you—leave her in peace."

Feodor was stunned. He could barely control his rage. How dare this boy, this feather-brain, lecture him on ethics and morals? Feodor was the more furious because he knew that Nikolai was right.

"You've mixed everything up," he said at last, almost maliciously. "Your outburst of noble wrath is altogether out of place. I intend to marry Lida and if you must know, I have given my word to her father. Now everything is up to her. . . . What more is needed? Mama and Papa are informed, the honor of their daughter is already safeguarded."

If a bomb had burst in the room, Nikolai would have been less surprised. Seeing his amazement, Feodor exulted. But Nikolai rallied quickly, and sighed ironically: "Do you think I believe your fairy tales?"

"Fairy tales? It's the absolute truth."

"Listen, Feodor, I know you too well to believe that you would trade gold for silver. To give up Nina, Gorin's daughter, who lives on the fat of the land, in palaces and in luxury, without any fear of her soul; Nina, who is up to her ears in love with you—for Sidorov's daughter? . . . That isn't like you."

Feodor flew into a rage.

"I see you have a very bad opinion of me," he said, then regaining control of himself, added dryly: "In any case, you will soon be convinced . . . but to quiet your mind I can assure you—I love Lida."

"And Nina?"

"What about Nina? Everything is over with her. Our personalities were not in harmony, as they say in novels. There are no bridles for feelings." Feodor was almost stuttering over these last words.

Nikolai looked closely into his brother's eyes. Feodor became uncomfortable. He hid his confusion behind a contemptuous laugh: "Listen, Nikolai, aren't you in love with Lida yourself?"

Nikolai blushed. Feodor had said aloud what he had not admitted to himself, let alone to others. But Feodor was still laughing, leaning back in his chair—his laughter was artificial, unpleasant. "You should have said so in the beginning, you fool, instead of adopting such a moral tone."

366

"There's no need for you to laugh," said Nikolai. "As her friend, I wish only happiness for Lida. It seems that I was pleasantly mistaken in you, Feodor. Forgive my foolishness."

"That's all right, we all make mistakes."

The brothers parted, after shaking hands. However friendly their handshake may have appeared, both felt depressed. Nikolai found it hard to believe his brother, doubted his sincerity. His laughter seemed especially strange and unpleasant.

Feodor was furious. His brother had touched him on his sorest spot. He had reproached him for something over which he had no power, for Feodor was no longer the master even of his own feelings. Without knowing it, Nikolai had reminded the important and influential Director Novikov how weak and helpless he really was.

CHAPTER 11

WHAT FEODOR strove for, happened: his relationship with Lida Sidorov became the talk of the University, if not of the whole town. It was something to talk about—the young Director was courting, apparently very seriously, a student of his own University, the daughter of an important plant director. Feodor was pleased: that meant that Veria would hear about it.

But Feodor did not suspect that he had, at the same time, made a dangerous enemy for himself in the person of Oleg Durov. Oleg could not forgive Lida for her obstinacy. On leaving the hospital he swore to avenge himself on her. As soon as he learned that the new Director was courting her, following the well-known rule of the dog in the manger—"if not for me, not for others"—he decided to frighten Novikov. Remembering the previous Director, a timid and servile being, Oleg didn't doubt that Novikov would be the same if pressure were put on him properly. And he thought it would be a good thing to clip the comb of the too arrogant new Director.

Two men detached themselves from a tree and began slowly to approach Novikov. Feodor became alert. On the vacant lot across which he was returning from the Don not another soul was to be seen. The tall yellow grass was dry and dead. A cold wind was blowing. One of the approaching men was wearing a yellow leather jacket on which the rays of the setting sun shone weakly. Under the jacket a shirt with open collar showed. Tall and thin, he reminded Feodor of someone. The other, stocky, kept a little distance to the rear, his hands in the pockets of his military trousers. Feodor noticed their sullen, threatening manner. As they approached, Feodor recognized Oleg Durov and his bodyguard Ivan—the same one who had been with Oleg when he had sold him the suit the previous summer.

Oleg stopped in front of Feodor, spread his legs, spitting the cigarette from his moist lips. His face was insolent, with protruding eyes.

"Let's talk straight, Director!" said Oleg harshly, with sneering emphasis on the title. "Stop running after Lida! She's not for you!"

"Go and sleep it off; you're drunk," Feodor said, as calmly as possible, although his whole body was trembling.

"Who's drunk? Me?"

"Don't get excited, Durov. Go on your way."

"Threatening, eh?" Durov's bodyguard moved closer.

Wondering how he could get rid of them with the least fuss, Novikov said: "Keep away. Nobody's touching you, and don't you touch anybody."

"How about Lida?" asked Oleg, and a stream of the most shameless cursing lashed Feodor's face.

Novikov now watched their every move. The stocky Ivan, who kept his hands in his pockets, worried him more than anything else. Oleg appeared to be drunker, and therefore less dangerous.

Novikov was trying to gain time, hoping that somebody would appear. But no one came. Oleg in the meantime was already pushing close to Feodor and waving a dirty fist under his nose: "If you touch Lida— I'll kill you. That's easy for me!"

"What the hell are you talking for?" interjected his friend. "Sock him! That'll teach him not to run after somebody else's girl."

Novikov now realized that he could not get rid of them by persuasion—that only inflamed them. When Oleg touched his face with his fist, which smelled of filth, a desperate rage seized him.

"You whelp!" Feodor cursed, and to his own surprise shoved Oleg with all his might. Oleg's lanky body fell against his stocky friend, throwing him off his feet. But before they both toppled, a shot rang out and Feodor felt a sharp pain in his left shoulder. Ivan had fired without taking the revolver from his pocket. Feodor fell on top of them, caught the hoodlum's arm, and twisted it above the wrist till it cracked.

"Ay—ay—ay! You bastard!" wailed Ivan, and dropped the revolver from his useless hand.

368

Feodor picked it up and before they could recover he hit Ivan on the head with the butt. Blood spurted; Ivan groaned and slumped like a sack onto the grass.

Oleg in the meantime had got up, snarling. "Now you've asked for it!" His right hand was reaching into his pocket when Feodor hit him over the ear with the revolver butt. Oleg staggered and bellowed with pain, baring his yellow teeth. A second blow, harder than the first, toppled him to the ground. "I'll kill you!" he howled, spitting blood. "I'll find you even if I'm dead and buried, and I'll kill you!" Helpless rage choked him.

Feodor was now in a savage fury; victory and rage blinded him. He went up to Oleg, who was on his hands and knees trying to get up, and with his heavy boot kicked him in the crotch from behind. Oleg screamed and fell in a heap to the ground, twitching his legs and clawing the ground with his hands.

Shaking, Feodor rolled him over and looked in his blanched and howling face. "That's all right, you'll get over it," he said.

Putting the revolver in his pocket, Feodor went quickly to the Don, feeling the pain in his shoulder more and more. "I'll have to wash up. I'm in a hell of a mess!" he thought. "My God! The dogs! They nearly killed me . . ."

Suddenly Feodor stopped, as if he had been stunned. His face turned pale: sweat came out on his forehead in large beads. "What am I doing? What am I doing?" he repeated aloud. "I must have gone crazy! . . . Why, Oleg and his father can be the death of me!"

He returned to the groaning lads, and taking out the revolver, shot first Oleg and then his bodyguard. Oleg's eyes were closed, but the other lad saw everything. He looked with horror at Novikov and his lips moved, begging him not to shoot. But two shots rang out. Novikov was surprised how calm he was at that moment. He wiped the butt of the revolver with his handkerchief and threw it into the long grass. Then, trying to keep to the bushes, he went quickly to the city, holding his blood-soaked shoulder with his right hand.

CHAPTER 12

TRYING TO KEEP out of sight in the darkness, Feodor went to the students' communal boarding house where his brother Nikolai lived. He knew that alone he could do nothing with the wound. The bullet had to be extracted at once and the wound cleansed. "Surely they've taught him something at his medical faculty," he thought.

Nikolai's room was on the ground floor and Feodor saw through the window that his brother was lying on the bed reading a book. He was alone. Feodor tapped on the pane. Nikolai jumped up from the bed and, opening the window, looked into the darkness.

Feodor said softly, "I must see you alone."

"What's wrong, Feodor? Why are you here?"

"You'll find out at once. Help me in. . . . Will your room mates be coming soon?" With Nikolai's help, Feodor climbed into the room through the window.

"They went into town . . . Blood!" exclaimed Nikolai in a fright, noticing Feodor's bloody arm for the first time.

"What did you expect—ink?" retorted Feodor, and added: "We've got to get the bullet out and bandage it, and quickly!"

"B—bandage?" Nikolai questioned, stammering and looking dully at his brother. "B—bullet?"

"Move! Don't stand around! And cover that window! . . . Quick! And not a word to anybody."

"Right away, right away . . ." Nikolai hustled around the room, not knowing where to begin.

Feodor sat down on a stool. Nikolai covered the window with a blanket and, teeth chattering, ran into the corridor. "You sit there. I'll run for a basin of boiling water," he whispered.

In a few minutes he returned with a basin under his arm and a kettle in his hand. "I told them in the kitchen that I was going to wash my head," he explained to Feodor.

Pulling out the drawer of the night table, Nikolai began to search hurriedly among all kinds of odds and ends—forks, spoons, rags for cleaning shoes, combs, spools of thread, and other bachelor rubbish—for the instrument he needed most now. But all he found was a pair of tweezers. Nikolai rushed over to a neighboring table; there he was lucky, he pulled out a lancet.

"I quite forgot that I gave it to Petka a week ago," he explained to Feodor in an apologetic voice, showing him the lancet. "He needed it to sharpen his pencil."

Throwing the instrument into the boiling water, Nikolai began carefully to take off Feodor's jacket. Then he ripped up the sleeve. "Turn away now, and if it hurts, bellow . . ."

While Nikolai was making incisions around the wound Feodor could still bear it, but when he began to take out the bullet he groaned.

370

After extracting the bullet Nikolai was going to throw it into the basin, but Feodor took it out of his hand and put it into one of his trouser pockets. "Have you gone crazy?" he hissed. "Now hurry up and bandage it, or somebody will come."

Nikolai made the bandage from Feodor's shirt.

"Lie down, now; rest. I'll clean up."

"All right, but hurry! I must get away from here as soon as possible. You'll have to take me over to my apartment."

When everything was cleaned up and the blood stains washed away, Feodor climbed out the window. To go by way of the corridor was dangerous; some of the students were sure to meet him.

Feodor was completely white and shook as if he had a fever. He swayed as he walked and Nikolai supported him. Trying to keep to the dark streets, he took his brother to his apartment on Budenny Avenue. Feodor had not yet moved into the Director's apartment at the University. The family of the former Director was still living there.

After laying Feodor on the bed, Nikolai started for the door.

"Where are you going?" his brother asked.

Nikolai was a little confused. "I thought of calling Lida . . ."

"No-no, there's n-no n-need! Not under any circumstances!" shouted Feodor, and even tried to raise himself on his elbow. "Nobody must know about this! . . . You understand, nobody!" His head fell back on the pillow. Fever set in.

Nikolai reflected, shook his head, and cautiously left the room: "No, I'll still call her," he decided. He trusted Lida completely.

Going to the nearest phone, Nikolai called Lida. She came in half an hour, very much alarmed. "What's wrong with him?"

Nikolai told her all he knew.

Suddenly a voice on a radio nearby announced: "Oleg Durov, son of the Chief of the NKVD of Rostov Province, has just been brutally murdered by vile enemies of the people. An investigation is being conducted. Several suspicious persons have been arrested already . . ."

Turning pale, Lida looked with horror at Nikolai. Slowly and silently Nikolai sank into a chair.

CHAPTER 13

FEODOR became delirious. In his raving he repeated the names of Nina, Gorin, and Drozd. Lida, listening to his rambling talk, tried to catch the thread of his chaotic visions. In these wanderings, Gorin ap-

371

peared at times as some kind of hazy but definite obstacle which he was continually trying to overcome, at others as the convict who had attacked him and Nina in the woods. He was sitting on his chest, waving a club threateningly over him. Feodor tossed about on his bed.

Lida could not help but pity him. And from pity to love, everybody knows, is but a step . . .

Nikolai and Lida knew that leave from work for any sick person is legal only when it is supported by a certificate signed by a doctor especially empowered by the authorities.

"But how will we get the certificate?" Lida wrung her hands, pacing up and down the room. "A doctor won't give one without first examining Feodor, and that is absolutely unthinkable!"

Suddenly Nikolai struck his forehead: "I have the solution! I'll pretend to be the sick Feodor!" he exclaimed. "I'll lie here in this first room. It's not likely the doctor will know Feodor by sight and everything will go off without a hitch."

"And if he knows him?" Lida was afraid.

"We'll call an old one, who's working in some small hospital and has no connection with the University. The probability that he might know Feodor is very small. In any case, we've got to risk it; otherwise we won't be able to manage."

"Yes, I guess you're right. Only, you're not sick, you haven't got a temperature."

"That's a detail. We can grease his palm—he'll write out the certificate," Nikolai reassured her. "For the doctor it's important to see the sick person, and not his temperature."

So it was decided. They blocked the door of the room where Feodor was lying by putting the bookcase against it, so that it would look as if it were not used.

Two hours later Lida returned with a very old and angry-looking doctor. When they were still at the door, she slipped a fifty-ruble bill into his hand. Without looking at it the doctor shoved it in his pocket and went into the "patient." With a habitual gesture he put a thermometer into his mouth, began to fill in the certificate. Lida gave him the necessary information. When she answered the question about place of work: "Director, Rostov University," the doctor raised his eyebrows and looked closely over his glasses at Nikolai's face.

"You look very young for your years," he said to him.

"Yes, Fedya is probably the youngest University Director in the country," Lida interjected smiling, with a definite tone of pride.

372

The doctor asked nothing more. Taking the thermometer, he said calmly that the temperature was high and wrote the corresponding figure in the certificate. Lida beamed. "What a nice old man," she thought.

"The Comrade Director may stay in bed for a day or two," said the doctor in the tone of a judge, and was going to write this sentence into the certificate.

"Two days!" cried Lida, horrified. "He will have to stay in bed for a week at least. Please, Doctor, give him a week."

"You're joking," said the doctor, looking ironically at her from under his brows. "They don't allow a week even to the dying. Don't forget that I'm putting my signature on the certificate and I'm responsible with my head."

"Well, give him at least another two days," pleaded Lida and slipped another fifty-ruble note into the doctor's hand.

"All right," he consented unwillingly. "I'll put down five days. Only he must remain in bed. Otherwise, you know . . ." The doctor signed the certificate and was just going to leave when from the next room came the sound of Feodor groaning.

"Who's there?" asked the doctor, surprised.

"That's a neighbor. He's an awful drunkard," Lida explained, her whole body trembling.

The doctor hurriedly took his leave. Lida accompanied him to the stairway. "See that he stays in bed," the doctor reminded Lida again. "Sometimes they catch that kind of sick person at the market, and then off come our heads."

"Don't worry, Doctor. Thank you very much," said Lida, and added in a confidential whisper: "We're going to be married . . ."

The doctor smiled for the first time. "Well, in that case, of course, there's nothing to worry about: he won't want to get out of bed," and the doctor winked at Lida.

Returning to the room, Lida exclaimed joyfully: "We've got our certificate!"

On the other side of the wall Feodor again groaned deeply. Nikolai, throwing off the blanket, jumped up from the sofa and helped Lida to move the bookcase. They were just on the point of opening the door, when the doctor came back into the room. Seeing Nikolai up out of the bed, he showed no surprise. Trying not to look at him, he explained dryly: "I forgot my gloves."

"Oh, here they are." Lida hastily handed him the gloves that were lying on the table.

The doctor left.

"Did he notice that the bookcase had been moved?" Lida asked Nikolai excitedly.

"I don't think so."

"I hope not . . ." said Lida, locking the outside door.

CHAPTER 14

WHEN FEODOR was better and able to go to work, he decided to visit Gorin, to see how things were with him. They had not met for nearly a month.

He noticed many changes. The first thing that caught his eye was the depressed mood of the whole family. They had learned of the refusal of the visa for Pavel. The Government had replied to Gorin that in view of the complicated international situation it was forced, to its regret, to stop the issue of foreign passports to all without exception who wished to go abroad for medical treatment. The letter was written in a very mild form and Mikhail pretended that he was satisfied with the explanation. He tried to raise Pavel's spirits, advising him to take himself in hand, to busy himself with some useful occupation. Pavel stung Mikhail by saying bitterly that the refusal of the Government was equivalent to a straight insult to himself. Mikhail felt, inwardly, that this was true.

"He's always right!" thought Mikhail.

To his astonishment Feodor saw a new face at the Gorins'—young Shcherbakov, Second Party Secretary of the Province, after Veria the most influential person in Rostov.

"Does he visit you often?" Feodor asked Nina with an unexpected touch of jealousy in his voice.

"Yes, often . . . But does that matter to you?" she replied, and looked at him almost challengingly.

"You've changed——"

"And haven't you?"

During his illness, Feodor had thought that he had overcome his love for Nina. But now, when he saw another man beside her, jealousy burst upon him with unexpected force.

Feodor decided that Shcherbakov's presence was the work of Nina's mother, who apparently had great plans on that score. Feodor noticed

374

that Luba had become cooler with him, although she seemed at the same time twice as respectful.

He noticed with satisfaction that Mikhail didn't like Shcherbakov and that Nina apparently merely suffered his presence. He saw none of that happy radiance that had shown in her eyes when she used to meet him.

Only one thing at the Gorins' gladdened Feodor: Mikhail was working with great enthusiasm on his play. The work was progressing quickly and Gorin had already passed the halfway mark. Mikhail was experiencing that joyful satisfaction a man feels when he overcomes difficulties. They fascinated him. Even the new form—the historical play, which he had never written before and which he had previously disliked—had opened up much that was interesting and new.

The tasks he had set himself were to present the figure of Ivan the Terrible objectively and make him a flesh-and-blood character through the words and action of the play. He did not say to himself: "I must whitewash Ivan the Terrible, because that is what Stalin wants." If such a thought had occurred to him for an instant, he would have abandoned the work. Although this was precisely what Novikov required from the writer, he had conveyed this idea to him in an entirely different light. "It is not necessary to whitewash Ivan the Terrible, but to reinstate him in his true significance, to make him as he really was. For this, one thing is necessary—to clear away the dirt with which the slandering historians have bespattered him." And Novikov skillfully supported his position with carefully selected documents from the archives.

Gorin at once noticed this new and audacious approach, noticed and valued it. If it hadn't been for Novikov's treatise Mikhail Gorin would have taken quite a different attitude toward the play and, if someone else had begun to write it, he would have suspected the writer of a slavish attempt to please the contemporary ruler.

But his task seemed to Gorin bold and noble. It inspired him. He sincerely believed that with his play he would solve the problem of an objective description of historical events and in their light help such blind men as Pavel to understand contemporary Russia.

But the deeper he went into his work, the more often he stumbled onto difficulties. The first difficulty was the problem of authority and coercion. The result was his talk with Novikov. It couldn't be said that Feodor had convinced him and overcome his perplexities, as

375

with the wave of a wand. It was simply that some remarks of Novikov were fixed in Gorin's memory: for instance, his words about the chronicler Tikhon struck his imagination more than anything else, and at one time he even wanted to include him in the play.

Gorin did not intend to deny Ivan's cruelty. But he was soon convinced that such an approach would be very difficult to combine with his main object—to picture Ivan as the Tsar-Reformer, the far-sighted statesman. Every time he tried to introduce a cruel episode he became convinced that the whole structure of the play collapsed. Acts of cruelty impress themselves on an audience with particular force. Sensing this, Mikhail threw them out of the play and in that way, against his wish, whitewashed Ivan the Terrible.

Only when he had passed the halfway mark in his work did he feel an uneasiness, a heaviness in his hand when he portrayed Ivan the Terrible, as though he were writing about an enemy.

At such times he particularly wanted to see Novikov, sensing him to be a support. But he had heard that Novikov was sick. When Feodor arrived he was delighted, even though he knew about his falling out with Nina. He wanted to talk to Feodor about that too.

Mikhail noticed Feodor's paleness, his unusually serious, even tense appearance. They were sitting in the library. Serving tea, Mikhail recounted his difficulties with the brutal episodes and explained why he was compelled to throw them out.

"I have struck out that scene of the execution of the boyars at the Kremlin," he said. "Only a mention is made of it in the play."

To his surprise Novikov exclaimed, almost in fright: "Why are you doing that? Ivan's cruelty must be emphasized, not kept in the background. And having been emphasized, it must be justified. Otherwise the whole idea of the play will be lost." Feodor stammered a little and hastened to add: "At least, that's what I think."

But Mikhail noticed his confusion, and for the first time a nasty taste remained with him from Novikov's words. Because of the strange heat with which Novikov responded to his words; the emotion, almost fright, with which he pronounced the words "the whole idea of the play will be lost," Mikhail could not help noticing that the Director had a more than academic interest in the play—and this seemed wrong, although he didn't know why he felt it was. It was a passing feeling—and the thought that perhaps Novikov had not yet quite recovered from his illness, and was therefore excited, reassured Gorin and made him able to continue the conversation. He tried to explain to Feodor why it was difficult to combine Ivan's cruelty and his virtues

376

in the play. "It's very awkward after the scene with the execution, where Ivan looks like a madman, to change to his monologue about the unity of the State and other words of wisdom."

Feodor, having regained his self-possession, said calmly: "I'm not a dramatist, but it seems to me that to justify Ivan's cruelties in the eyes of the audience, the negative qualities of his victims must be shown in a particularly striking manner; in the present case, the boyars—their reactionary ideas, their rift within themselves, their love of power, and their greed. Once these qualities have been sufficiently clearly shown, the audience will forgive Ivan his cruelty against them."

Mikhail saw that this was probably the only way out of the situation, but at the same he noticed with irritation Novikov's efforts to influence and press him. He hurried to change the subject:

"Feodor Pavlovich, I would like to talk to you about Nina. As I understand it, some quarrel has taken place between you. Perhaps it's not my business, but I'd like to know the cause, as I may be able to help. It seems so strange, so sudden."

"I am sorry about it," replied Feodor. "As you know, in such cases it's very hard to find an explanation. The simplest explanation, although a hackneyed one, is that our temperaments are different."

"Nonsense!" exclaimed Mikhail. "Visit us just the same: perhaps you'll make it up. And you'd better look out—you've got a rival." Mikhail winked significantly. "To tell you the truth, I don't like him a bit."

Mikhail parted with Feodor that day in the most friendly manner. But when Cheprok later spoke about the Director in his usual bitter way, Mikhail suddenly felt pleased with him and approved his words.

When Luba asked Doctor Tsibik how the refusal of the visa was affecting Pavel, the doctor shook his head: "I'm very worried about him."

Pavel's condition really had become worse recently. When the doctor suggested a course of treatment to him, he refused, but later agreed to go with him to the Crimea.

Cheprok insisted stubbornly on being allowed to accompany Pavel. It was only with difficulty that Pavel persuaded him to remain with his father.

377

CHAPTER 15

THE MYSTERIOUS wounding of Feodor, his ravings, his temporary helplessness, requiring care and kindness, opened Lida's closed heart. She fell in love with Feodor. And Feodor, seeing such a change in her, humbly accepted it as inevitable. In his heart, apart from a warm, friendly feeling for her, there was nothing. But he saw that the course he had been forced to take must be followed to the end.

In the meantime, Sidorov became furious at Novikov for delaying the marriage. He little realized that his nervousness was a reflection of troubles at his work. The powerful hand of Durov was already making itself felt. Unpleasant rumors began to spread around his plant. Feeling for the first time the insecurity of his own position, Sidorov tried to assure the future of his daughter as soon as possible. At last, to Sidorov's joy, the first open declaration took place between Feodor and Lida. The wedding was set for the end of October.

Before the wedding, amid the general fuss and preparation, Natalia gave her daughter some advice and nearly frightened her into a faint with her frankness. Sidorov wandered about the house, getting into people's way, but was in an excellent humor. He took a long time making up a list of guests and invited nearly half the town, the very cream of the authorities—Veria, Shcherbakov, Mirzoyan, but not Durov. To Lida's deep regret Nina was unable to come—she had gone with her father to Moscow.

Feodor felt his first yearning for Lida, who had grown much prettier recently. One day when she tried to explain to him that her love for him was, as it were, a continuation of her broken love for Andrei, Feodor comforted her. "Our love will be happy." Lida pressed herself to him trustfully.

The wedding was in full swing. Nikolai, quite drunk, wished Lida happiness: "Feodor is a good man! I'm the only one that can't get along with him," he told her. Lida's mother laughingly persuaded Nikolai not to grieve, while Sidorov generously poured him more wine. Now that Nikolai was no longer dangerous, he felt kindly toward him. Probably drunker than anyone else, Sidorov talked too much, spoke about Durov with hatred. Some of the guests began to exchange significant looks. His father-in-law irritated Feodor. For the first time he had misgivings about the stability of the plant director's position and was rather scared by it. But it was too late now. Lida's mother cried a little, as mothers do at weddings, but her tears were, of course, the tears of happiness: Feodor was her ideal.

On the first night, when Feodor and Lida went to their room, Natalia crossed herself affectionately. Sidorov, dead drunk, slept.

Feodor's eyes suddenly reminded Lida of the frightful eyes of Oleg Durov, when he tried to rape her at the banquet. "Men are all alike," passed through her head. But immediately she thought: "No, my husband, my Fedya, is different. He is the best man in the whole world."

CHAPTER 16

TIME PASSED, leaving deep traces behind. The purge which everybody had expected after Veria's speech at the opening of the Marx-Engels Institute in Rostov took place and embraced the whole country. Rostov alone was spared, to the general surprise and joy of its inhabitants. A dozen or more second-grade leaders from among those close to Larin were arrested, and that was all. It wasn't worth while talking about such trifles, much less comparing them with what happened in other towns and districts of the country where no one had any assurance of his fate. A judge who drove the condemned to their death today, himself took the last steps of his life on the morrow.

The idyllic quiet of Rostov seemed strange and unexplainable. Only those close to the top authority knew the real reason: Veria and his staff were so busy with work on the new political book that they were physically unable to devote any time to the purge. Moscow, waiting impatiently for the appearance of this important book, demanded nothing more from Veria. So, at a time when the whole country was enduring one wave of terror after another, in Rostov justification for the atrocities committed was being carefully sought and formulated.

But even in this unnatural calm, somber events were brewing. Durov, after the murder of his son, was in a rage and fury. He no longer looked like a human being. Desperately he sought the murderer and swore that he would leave no stone unturned in Rostov until he found him. Frightful rumors went around the town about tortures of people suspected by him. They said that he had choked more than one victim with his own hands, strong as a gorilla's.

Feodor lived well. He was not sorry that he had married Lida. She was deeply in love and there seemed no end to her happiness. They were living in Novikov's new apartment at the University.

He visited the Gorins often, not as a suitor now but as an old friend. There he spent nearly all his time with Mikhail, discussing the play. It was nearly finished. Once Mikhail read it to him. Novikov saw with joy that the result exceeded his best hopes. He imagined the sensation this play would create.

"Ivan the Terrible is your greatest work!" Novikov exclaimed, and noticed with surprise that the writer remained sad.

"If you only knew what labor it has cost me," replied Mikhail, and Novikov understood what he had in mind.

It was then that Nina's first suspicions were aroused.

Once she asked her father: "What does Feodor Novikov mean to you?"

Mikhail replied that he was a clever man, very useful to him as a walking historical reference. "But he is more than a reference. Not only has he a wonderful memory, but an almost artistic imagination. I have never before met anyone who could talk so vividly about historical facts."

When he was alone, however, Mikhail became thoughtful over his daughter's question.

Pavel and the doctor returned from the Crimea. There had been an accident. Pavel nearly drowned when he fell out of a boat far from shore. Fortunately some fishermen rescued him. But on the whole, the trip raised his spirits. The doctor, on the other hand, looked rather confused. On his arrival from the Crimea he was summoned by Veria who, in spite of being so busy, found time to bawl him out properly. With the malice of a snake Veria first expressed delight at his sunburned appearance, and then, as on the former occasion, fell on him with the foulest curses.

"You're a jackass and not a doctor. I entrusted an important matter to you, and what have you made of it? A circus number with the sudden appearance of a drowned man in the second act. . . . I thought you would carry out the operation with finesse, without traces. If you don't understand what is required of you, I'll explain in simple language: that's why you're a doctor—to know how to doctor him to death. You understand, to doctor him to death?" and throwing an annihilating look at Tsibik, Veria added dryly: "You haven't much time

380

left, Doctor. Figure it out. We still remember about your trip to Paris . . . we still remember."

When Tsibik took his shaking body out of his office, Veria mumbled "Jackass!" and rang up Durov.

During the first month after the incident with Oleg, Feodor was greatly alarmed. Every minute he expected arrest and the terrifying meeting with Durov. At times it seemed to him that he felt his long arms on him. But time passed, Durov continued to rush about after false leads and Feodor gradually calmed down, although he remained careful. This had become a habit. He never undressed in the presence of acquaintances anywhere, on the beach or in a bath house, so that no one would notice his wound and ask too many questions.

In the course of that year Mikhail Gorin finished his play and in November it appeared in print. It was received with the greatest acclaim. Moscow surpassed herself in the matter of propaganda. The play was shown in all the theatres in the country at the same time. It was broadcast on the radio. Millions of copies were published in a cheap edition. Steps were being taken to produce a film *Ivan the Terrible,* with the scenario based on Gorin's play.

Gorin himself looked tired. He was not satisfied with his work. It was not at all what he had intended. He had wanted to justify Ivan and he *had* justified him in his play, but in his heart Ivan had become repulsive to him. To Novikov this was now a matter of indifference. He had done his job. Gorin could not help noticing a strange expression on his face, as if Novikov and not himself were resting after hard work.

CHAPTER 17

SO MONTHS passed, and Durov still did not know who had killed his son. The best investigators spent many weeks trying to solve this problem, but all in vain. When Durov himself had begun to lose hope, chance put him on the right trail and he found the murderer. At the time Feodor Novikov was working quietly in his study at the University and did not suspect the deadly danger threatening him.

There were many reasons why Durov, for a whole year, had rushed around unsuccessfully on false leads. A group of the very best investigators whom he had detailed to work exclusively on this problem became victims of their own training. Beginning the investigation, as usual, by photographing the bodies, taking prints, analyzing the blood, and carrying out a medical investigation and autopsy of the bodies, as well as other things necessary in such cases, they compiled a report on the basis of the data obtained, then quietly filed it and gave full rein to their imagination, arriving a hundred miles from the true picture.

First they laid down a firm Marxian foundation: Oleg was killed by an enemy of the people. There were at least two murderers (who would have gone alone against the armed Oleg and his bodyguard?).

This was supported by one circumstance. There were many footprints at the scene of the murder. The bodies were found by some children, the children called some adults and, before the police arrived, a hundred pairs of feet had trampled all over the place. The investigators concluded that the murderers were most probably the same criminals who had beaten up Oleg in June. In this way they were faced with a conspiracy. The investigators introduced this imaginary conspiracy very handily into the framework of the class struggle in the country in general, and as a result of the Larin regime in Rostov in particular.

Guided by such a profound thesis, the investigators set about their basic task: to find the criminals, or rather, the conspirators. The motive of the murder was, of course, obvious: revenge on Durov himself. Here at once the widest field of action opened up before the investigators: Durov had more enemies than a sultan has wives. However, the investigators were not scared by this and began making arrests, soon after which a rich flood of confessions started to come in.

If this had not concerned Durov personally he would have been very satisfied. After getting the confessions he would have issued orders to shoot the criminals, closed the file, and hidden it along with others, first sending a copy to Moscow. But now Durov needed real truth and not State truth.

Not trusting the investigators, he himself questioned the "criminals" and was convinced at once that they had simply slandered themselves under torture. Not one of them could give an accurate description of the scene of the murder, or the appearance of Oleg and his bodyguard. Like automatons they repeated over and over again something about instructions from the "center," about secret meetings where they planned their murder, and other tommyrot suggested to them by the investigators.

Durov was furious. The man whom he suspected more than anyone else, Sidorov, was out of his reach. He was unable, to his regret, to arrest and torture him like the others. However, Durov conducted the

382

investigation personally, guided by the idea that Sidorov, in avenging his daughter, had killed his son. And that of course was far from the truth and brought him nowhere except that it served to spread unpleasant rumors about Sidorov around the town.

Then, after losing faith in his investigators, admitting his own helplessness, Durov decided to summon to his aid a man whom he would usually not have trusted with the simplest affair. This was the famous Rostov investigator Protopopov, who had earned his fame in uncovering the most complicated crimes before the revolution. Now he was living in jail, arrested almost fifteen years previously for belonging to some liberal or radical party.

Protopopov was brought to Durov. His appearance disillusioned the grim chief. Before him stood a bent little old man with a dirty bald head, weak eyes that were unaccustomed to the light, a thin gray face, and hands twisted by rheumatism. He was shaking like a poplar leaf—obviously very frightened by this unexpected call. Durov sent away the two ugly-faced escorts and explained to Protopopov what he wanted. In conclusion he said significantly: "Find the murderer—and you'll get your freedom. But I remind you once more, the whole investigation must be conducted secretly and you will report to me personally. You will be given all the help you need."

The little man was terribly pleased. He seemed excited not so much by the prospect of freedom as by the opportunity of again working at his favorite job.

Protopopov was bathed, shaved, given clothes; two majors were appointed his assistants; then he got down to work. First he took out of the safe the file which Durov's investigators had prepared. After studying all the data with almost jealous attention to detail, and approving their accurate work (he was greatly surprised by it), Protopopov went to the scene of the crime. He spent a long time taking measurements, walked back and forth along the road across the vacant lot, bent down, made intriguing little jumps, then made the two assistants lie on the ground exactly in the positions of the bodies when found. He compared them with the photographs, made them get up and, going up to them, looked at them for a long time, thinking deeply. Then he drew the first one, who represented Oleg, close to him and suddenly shoved him with all his might. From the unexpectedness of this the latter stepped back and knocked his colleague to the ground.

"The shot!" cried the little old man, beaming.

The officers exchanged looks of wonder. But the little man ran

383

straight to town, dragging his suite along with him. "It's all clear! It's all clear!" he mumbled to himself under his breath.

He examined carefully the bodyguard's suit, Oleg's leather jacket, and then laughed with joy—he had found what he was looking for. The bullet hole in the pocket of the bodyguard's trousers was already described in the report and the shell, ejected from the revolver, had also been found in the pocket. But the investigators had not noticed, or had attached no importance to, a scratch on Oleg's jacket. But this scratch helped Protopopov to rebuild the whole picture.

An hour later he was reporting to Durov: "There was no conspiracy to kill your son. On the contrary, it was probably your son and his bodyguard who attacked one man—yes, just one man!—and he, in self-defense, killed them."

"You're joking," said Durov sternly, his heavy jowls quivering.

"That's the truth. The first shot was fired by the bodyguard from his pocket. Before this there was probably a fight, the unknown man shoved Oleg, Oleg fell onto his bodyguard, and at that instant the latter fired at the unknown, but the bullet grazed Oleg's jacket. Judging by this scratch the bullet must have entered the upper part of the unknown's body. In spite of his wound this man threw himself on the bodyguard with a single aim—to take away the revolver, which he did, having first dislocated the guard's right arm as the medical evidence showed. This must have been a powerful man; a weak man could not possibly have done such damage. Then the unknown hit the bodyguard on the head with the butt of the revolver—hit him very hard—the skull cracked."

"Sidorov!" thought Durov, and very nearly plunged out of his office to throw himself on his enemy.

Protopopov continued: "The action following this was a short fight with Oleg; he hadn't time to pull out his revolver. The unknown gave him two blows in the face with the same revolver and then, when Oleg fell, kicked him in the crotch. The kick was terrific—Oleg lost consciousness."

"Then?"

"Then the unknown decided to kill them. He was probably afraid that they would revive and turn him in. He shot them in the head in succession, close up—the wounds are powder burned. This alone shows that the two fatal shots were fired after the fight—as an afterthought."

However unpleasant it was for Durov to hear the words of the old investigator, he realized that he was right. Knowing his son's character, Durov could easily imagine that he had started the fight.

"And who is the murderer?" asked Durov.

Protopopov shrugged his shoulders. "For the time being that is not known. We must now look for the cause of the fight and the person with whom Oleg could have quarreled so seriously. . . . But all this can be found out in time. The man must be tall, strong, with big hands —and, of course, with a wound in the upper part of his body."

"But why tall?" Durov questioned. He kept trying to fit Sidorov to the description given by the investigator. But Sidorov was not tall— on the contrary, he was stocky. "Maybe you're mistaken?"

"Hardly. The blow on Oleg's face is evidence. Only a tall man, approximately the same height as Oleg, could have done that."

"And how are you going to go about finding the criminal?" asked Durov.

"We'll have to look into Oleg's personal life," said the little old man, sternly.

Durov frowned, but replied: "All right. Do whatever you want— but without any noise."

When Protopopov took up the second and most important part of his investigation, as an experienced investigator he first looked for the woman in the case. But here he ran into difficulties, as great as those that had led the Durov investigators off the track. Oleg had as many "women" as his father had enemies, and nearly all of his "romances" had within them the seeds of hate and revenge. The only exception, probably, was Lily—for whom he would hardly have avenged himself on anyone. She was recognized as common property. In passing, Protopopov found that she served the entire upper Party group, headed by Veria.

During the week that the murder took place, Oleg had had a scandalous affair with one of the actresses of the Rostov Theatre, and the circumstances were very suspicious. Protopopov spent a whole month on this affair and, of course, got nowhere. Now he saw the real difficulties of his work: Oleg was mixed up in scandals, fights, rape, nearly every week; and to make head or tail of this mess would be quite a problem.

However, he scrupulously analyzed each separate case. In time he came to the affair with Lida. But it was no different from the others. Besides, Andrei—obviously Oleg's enemy in this case—had died; Oleg, clearly, had obtained satisfaction and the matter appeared to be

385

closed. On learning that Lida had married the Director of the University, Protopopov was completely reassured. He imagined the Director as an intellectual in glasses, harmless as a fly—such were the University directors of his time, meek occupants of office armchairs. Here Protopopov made his first mistake and, as with Durov's other investigators, it was the result of his upbringing. Fifteen years of isolation in jail had made him a Rip van Winkle of the Soviet regime.

Another six months passed and Protopopov was still examining Oleg's past and saw no end to it. He reported his difficulties to Durov and was already preparing to go back to jail, when unexpected circumstances solved everything.

CHAPTER 18

THIS MUST BE credited as a merit of the Soviet regime: its police character has been brought to a height of perfection. If the executives of this system are perhaps weak, unimaginative, and blinded by their own propaganda, the system itself is built without a flaw: the most commonplace act of a man cannot but leave a trace. The Soviet man cannot receive bread without having a bread card with three stamps on it—from his place of work, from his house administration, and from his co-operative store; he cannot leave town without obtaining the permission of his boss, witnessed by the militia; he cannot be sick without obtaining the official medical certificate. Like a fly in a gigantic spider's web—no matter how carefully it jerks its legs, its movements are transmitted along a hundred threads to the spider and he at once fixes his greedy eyes on it—so the Soviet man, a pitiful fly in the intricate web of the State, cannot make one movement without its being recorded somewhere on paper.

In this case, no matter how cautious Feodor was, how thoroughly he knew all the dangers, and how carefully he tried to avoid them, he eventually became a victim of this soulless, methodical, and brutal system, from which there is no escape. Slowly but surely the fatal ring narrowed around him.

Two circumstances caught the eye of the chief of the Special Branch (NKVD) of the University. The first was a secret report from the waitress in the University mess, Nadya. In appearance a harmless creature with whom Nikolai was friendly and whose expansive backside he liked to pinch, Nadya was in the service of the Special Branch. Every day she handed in a short report, illiterately written. Her task included watching the behavior of the lecturers and students in the mess, taking note of such things as nervousness, loss of appetite, and so on. The day following the murder of Oleg she wrote of individual remarks overheard at the mess—in the main people complained about the poor food. Then she noted that Professor Ploshkin had no appetite—he didn't eat all his portion and left half a meat ball on the plate. And the student Nikolai Novikov also didn't eat his meat ball, which was indeed an unheard-of event.

"It seemed to me very strange, for the first time Nikolai didn't clean his plate and ask for more," wrote Nikolai's loving friend.

The chief of the Special Branch read this report along with many others received from agents—students, lecturers, janitors, and others —and filed it away. He paid no particular attention to Nadya's words. The reason for Professor Ploshkin's loss of appetite was no secret to him. Ploshkin's wife's brother had just been arrested and now Ploshkin was worried. Nadya's words about Nikolai Novikov he simply underlined with a red pencil—which meant that this needed some explanation. But he knew Nikolai well and did not expect anything dangerous from him. "More than likely he's got a belly ache," he thought. Thus this report remained lying without attracting its recipient's attention in any special way.

About a year later a strange circumstance made the chief recall Nadya's information.

The manager of the administrative branch of the University, on going over the medical certificates that had collected during the year before sending them to the Department of Higher Education, recalled one of his blunders. On Director Novikov's certificate, giving him the right to five days' rest, the doctor had forgotten to place his rubber stamp. Without the stamp the certificate was invalid. In such cases, the manager usually returned the certificate, but inasmuch as the affair involved the Director, he accepted the certificate, intending to send it off to the doctor one day for him to correct his mistake. And then he had forgotten all about it. Now the manager recalled his blunder and, not wanting to show it to others, decided to go to the doctor himself.

The doctor received him at the hospital. At first he was frightened, but on learning what it was about, he readily stamped the document. Then he turned to the manager: "I would like to ask you one thing. You see, I have a niece. She is taking the first year at the Medical

387

Institute in Kharkov. But recently her mother—her sole parent—died, and she is alone. If she were living in Rostov, my wife would look after her. But that would be possible only if she could be transferred to the Medical Faculty at Rostov University."

"You'll have to ask the Director about that," replied the manager. "Only he can arrange such a transfer."

"And why shouldn't I?" thought the doctor. "I did him a favor with the certificate—let him now place my niece."

Soon the doctor appeared at the University. The manager took him to Novikov's office and was greatly surprised when the doctor and the Director apparently didn't recognize each other. Novikov was first to realize what was up and hastened to invite the doctor to sit down. The manager left the office thoughtful. Ten minutes later, the doctor came out of the office, looking perplexed. When the manager asked him if the Director had agreed to place his niece, he forced himself to smile and said that he had agreed. The manager thought for a long time about this strange episode and eventually decided to tell the chief of the Special Branch about it.

"Bring me the certificate," said the chief shortly. "And be careful that everything is done quietly. Don't make a fuss. It's quite possible that they simply didn't recognize each other. That happens . . ."

When the certificate was brought to him he read it carefully, but found nothing suspicious. Only the date of the certificate seemed familiar.

"It's possible that the doctor made out the certificate for Novikov without seeing him," decided the chief. "It won't do any harm to send a report to the Special Branch of the hospital; let them watch the doctor there," and he wrote a letter: ". . . there's a suspicion that Doctor —— is engaged in illegal dealings, issuing certificates for bribes."

It never occurred to the chief of the Special Branch to connect the certificate with the murder of Oleg. The incident with Oleg had happened almost a year before and apparently was closed. He had heard that there had been arrests in connection with the murder, and shootings—that is, the incident had ended normally. Nobody had told him about the new version of the murder developed by Proto-popov.

In due course his letter put in motion a secret mechanism in the hospital. The Special Branch began to watch the doctor; finally, laying a trap for him, they caught him in the act of taking bribes. The doctor was stunned. He admitted everything. Regarding the

388

affair with the Director, he told all he knew about it. He described in detail the man who was lying in the bed and who, he discovered later, was not the Director. The obliging Special Branch at the hospital in turn sent this new data to its colleagues at the University: "It's up to you to deal with your Director. Our work is finished."

Now the chief of the Special Branch had a new problem—to find out who had impersonated whom, and why? He called the doctor. The latter was already convicted and awaiting his sentence. The completely distraught doctor gave him all the necessary evidence. The chief guessed that the impersonator was Nikolai, and the girl Lida Sidorov. When he showed him their photographs, the doctor recognized them at once.

All was clear, except one thing—why had all this been arranged? Why did the Director need a certificate if he wasn't sick? And if he was sick, why didn't he ask the doctor for one instead of arranging a masquerade with Nikolai? However, he decided that Novikov probably needed to go somewhere on personal business, and to arrange leave for himself, had asked Nikolai to fix everything up. But here one circumstance caught the chief's attention. The doctor spoke always about one room, whereas it was of record that Novikov had two rooms. He cross-questioned the doctor thoroughly about this.

"In the other room, the girl told me, some drunkard was living. I heard groans there, as if the man was mumbling, as in a delirium or drunken stupor . . ."

"What the hell?" thought the chief, and hurriedly opened two files on Feodor and Nikolai Novikov. On Feodor's file there was nothing except that he had been sick. On Nikolai's, on the other hand, he noticed Nadya's report and that put him on the alert. The affair smelled of something serious.

Knowing Feodor's reputation and the confidence the authorities had in him, and being afraid of putting himself in an awkward position, the chief of the Special Branch, without questioning anybody or alarming anyone, compiled a detailed account of what had happened and sent it to Durov, asking his superior for instructions on what to do next: to carry out an investigation or to leave things as they were.

A day or two later Durov suddenly summoned him. An elderly man, unknown to the chief of the Special Branch, was sitting in his office. This was Protopopov.

"Tell us everything in order," said Durov, and by the impatient light burning in his eyes the chief of the Special Branch gathered that his report had proved important.

389

He told everything he knew and was about to express his own surmises, but Protopopov couldn't restrain himself and asked him: "Tell me, have you ever seen the Director undressed? Did you notice any signs of bullet wounds on his body?"

"No, I never had an opportunity," replied the chief, and suddenly realized why the date of the Director's illness had seemed familiar. It was the day of Oleg's murder! How could he have forgotten that? That day he had made several arrests among the students in connection with the murder, and it remained imprinted on his memory. He also understood why Durov had called him so quickly and why he listened to his every word so attentively.

When Durov and Protopopov were alone, the latter said: "We must see if Feodor Novikov has traces of a wound. That will be sure proof. If you will allow me, I'll investigate him myself."

In the meantime Feodor, at first badly frightened by his meeting with the doctor, gradually composed himself. He considered the matter settled.

A month passed and everything was as before. Nobody bothered him. Once Feodor went to the steam baths. He purposely chose a bath house at the other end of the city, so that he wouldn't meet an acquaintance there. At the baths a feeble little old man sat beside him on the bench and beat himself vigorously with a birch whisk. Several times Feodor noticed that the old fellow seemed, as it were, to probe his body with his eyes. Feodor didn't like his looks at all. He hastened to leave the bath house. The old fellow remained seated. It was Protopopov. He didn't need to investigate Feodor any more. He had noticed the wound on his shoulder, pinkish from the hot water, the obvious trace of a bullet. He gloated—the crime was solved.

That same day Nikolai was arrested. Durov realized that Director Novikov, a professor well known throughout the country, was not an easy prey. With empty hands, without solid proof, he couldn't be taken. But after Nikolai's confession, and he didn't doubt that he would get that right away, Durov intended to arrest Feodor.

Durov personally questioned Nikolai. To all his threats Nikolai stubbornly repeated that the doctor had been mistaken, that he had seen not Nikolai, but Feodor, that Feodor had been really ill and that he and Lida had nursed him. He accused the doctor of shameless lying.

"Don't lie or it will be worse for you," Durov threatened Nikolai. "You don't know our methods—people talk with us."

390

Strangely enough, Nikolai was not afraid of him. Only hate, mixed with a wanton, almost gay eagerness, grew in him. As if he had longed for the opportunity of making a fool of this Rostov scarecrow, he continued to stick to his story: Yes, the doctor examined Feodor thoroughly, found that he was sick, and made out a certificate for him. About some "drunk" behind the door in Feodor's apartment or about his wound, he knew nothing—that was all nonsense.

"All right," said Durov ominously. "I'll give you a day to think it over. Better confess right now. Tomorrow will be too late—tomorrow we'll talk to you in another way."

That same day Durov told Veria that he had at last found Oleg's murderer. He gloated.

"Yes, I've found the criminal!" he shouted. "And just imagine, it's none other than our famous Director Novikov!"

"What?" Veria nearly jumped out of his chair. "What did you say?"

"Director Novikov," Durov repeated triumphantly. "There's no doubt whatever. Here, I have written an order for his arrest."

"Wait! Wait! Give me more details," said Veria, still hardly able to believe his ears. "How on earth did this happen?"

Durov told him. He described all the proof, the doctor's evidence, and the wound on Novikov's shoulder. Veria listened attentively and suddenly laughed aloud. He squirmed in his chair, held his belly; the tears streamed from under his pince-nez.

"No, no, it can't be . . . The Director, unarmed, drove off two armed men! That's something! That's really a professor!"

Durov looked at him gloomily, not understanding what Veria found funny in this affair. Suddenly Veria said: "You can forget about the arrest."

"What do you mean—forget?" shouted Durov and drew himself up. "Why, I'll throw him in jail right away, the son of a bitch!"

Veria got up, and in the tone of an order, said: "You won't arrest him. Do you understand? You won't arrest him. And further, I'm ordering you to forget this affair. The enemies of the people killed your son. And what kind of an enemy is Novikov? And as for all your careful detective work, it's not worth a blown egg. If it's necessary for the Party, we can always prove that you're Napoleon. You would be the first to offer your hand to be cut off, to prove this."

Durov stood in front of Veria, pale, his jowls working ominously, his hands clenched into fists.

"But he killed my son!" he shouted, beside himself.

Veria shrugged his shoulders, took off his pince-nez, and began to clean them with his handkerchief.

"It's strange how you, a Bolshevik, can put your personal affairs on such a high level," he said suddenly. "In fact, I was about to tell you that you spend too much time on this detective business that has nothing to do with your duty. You're diverting officers needlessly, creating unnecessary panic, alarming people (Veria was thinking about Lily), and generally occupying yourself with something that is unnecessary. Your task is to detect enemies of the people—never forget that. I don't want to hear about this nonsense again. Not a word. And further, you will answer to me personally for the safety of Novikov. You can go."

Durov turned on his heel and left the office, but couldn't control himself and in his fury slammed the door.

As soon as Feodor learned of the arrest of Nikolai he thought that his end had come. He didn't doubt that Nikolai would betray him. He knew the methods used by such people as Durov too well to hope that his brother would be able to hold out against them. And then suddenly, the evening of the same day, Nikolai came to his apartment. There was a bruise under his right eye, one tooth was knocked out, his shirt collar was torn. He had been thoroughly beaten up, but he was alive and free. He told Feodor everything that had happened to him, what kind of questions they had asked and how he had answered.

"Surely they didn't believe you?" asked Feodor, not knowing which surprised him most—Nikolai's shrewdness or his bravery.

"Probably. Otherwise why did they let me go? Although to tell you the truth, I didn't expect it. Durov was quite convinced that I was lying, and he appeared to know everything."

Feodor didn't know how to interpret Durov's strange behavior. Probably Durov was preparing some clever trap for him, leaving him free until a chosen moment.

During that frightfully tense time, when every knock at the door caused a cold shiver all over his body—Feodor was called to Moscow to a conference of historians. Fear has large eyes. Feodor saw treachery in this, considered it the work of Durov, felt that he was being enticed to Moscow like a mouse into a trap. But he learned from the papers that the conference was really projected and that he was mentioned as one of the prominent scholars. He was encouraged by this. How-

392

ever, just before his departure he asked Nikolai to help Lida if anything happened.

On the train he was nearly killed. At night, when he was crossing the platform from one car to another, a hoodlum tried to knock him under the wheels. Feodor was able to beat him off. Suspecting that this was Durov's work, he became very cautious.

CHAPTER 19

FEODOR ARRIVED in Moscow at 10 o'clock in the morning. He hired a sleigh and gave the driver the address of the Hotel Metropol, indicated on the invitation.

They drove slowly. The driver and his horse, both old like memories of childhood, stopped every now and then to let a street car pass, with black clusters of people hanging on, or a company of soldiers marching to the steam baths with bundles of clean underwear under their arms, or simply to argue with garrulous pedestrians.

Feodor, pale, with a slight fever as if from a chill, looked gloomily at the town. "I wonder what it has prepared for me?"

Around the street-car stops the public loomed thickly, surging in an assault on each car. The street car moved on, listing to one side from the weight of the people clinging to it, springs down, the bumper rattling on the paving. People ran after it, losing their hats, dropping behind, wandering meekly back, again joining the crowd waiting for the next car and another skirmish.

Endless crowds of people moved along the sidewalks on the dirty snow, in black or gray jackets and huge felt boots; in kerchiefs, in caps with ear flaps under which the face was almost hidden. The wind drove into their backs, pushed them into drifts piled along the edge of the sidewalk. Nobody noticed anyone else. All hurried silently, alone; seldom were two people seen in conversation. Each was shut up within himself, bore his fate alone over the snow and the cold, as on the desolate steppe.

Feodor looked at the passers-by, at the uneven line of houses, pressed closely against each other as if against the frost, and the whole town appeared to him like the people—gloomy, sullen, soulless. "I might perish, disappear for nothing and not even a dog would care," he thought, shuddering.

393

On Theatre Square, around the House of the Trade Unions, horse guards stood right on the sidewalk, with rifles and sabers. From the papers Feodor knew that a trial of the long-forgotten Opposition was going on. There the accused told in detail how they had prepared to overthrow the Soviet power, repented, begged for mercy, and received the death sentence. Feodor turned his eyes away from the unpleasant building.

"Overthrow the Government! Who will believe such nonsense?" he thought bitterly. "Just try to overthrow these patrols, grown stiff from the frost! Try to make a conspiracy with any of these passers-by, silent, frightened, and faceless . . ."

At the hotel a shining automobile overtook them, long, black, such as Feodor had never seen before—it flew toward the Kremlin, throwing up snow, without any roar from the motor, no stream of smoke behind, like a chariot in a fairy tale. At the front fluttered a flag, possibly American. A face appeared at the window for an instant, young, well-groomed, happy. The passenger looked with interest at Feodor sitting in the sleigh: he was probably surprised at his high caracul hat. Feodor followed the automobile with envious eyes. That is life! Such a diplomat would serve his time in Moscow and return to America to eat oranges—what did he care? No axe hanging over him! With what pleasure would Feodor have sat in his place in the automobile, under the armor of diplomatic immunity.

From his room Feodor immediately went to the Academy of Sciences. There an official, receiving the delegates in turn, gave to each a package of necessary documents—passes, bread and food cards, books, and buttons. Hearing Novikov's name he looked at him with unconcealed curiosity. Feodor's heart trembled.

"There are instructions for you, Professor Novikov," he said, taking a paper out of the desk. "You are called to the Kremlin, to see Comrade Malenkov. You will get your pass at this place: the address is shown here." And the official, holding out a paper to him, added, smiling: "You're a lucky man, Comrade Novikov."

"Why?"

"Why! Man, you're going to the Kremlin! That's a great honor! Tell me, perhaps it's Stalin who is calling you?"

Feodor left without answering. He didn't know what to think. The official's tone wasn't ironical, but the address where he was to get the pass to the Kremlin seemed to him very ominous. It was the NKVD.

"A trap? The cat's play before the death blow?" Benumbed by horror, he arrived at the NKVD building half dead, but there they gave him the pass, explained in detail through which gate he must go, at what hour, and warned him particularly not to have any weapon with him.

On the street again, Novikov relaxed. But he could not understand why he was called to the Kremlin, nor who Malenkov was. He had never heard of him.

The reception was set for 12 o'clock midnight. Feodor was not surprised at the late hour; he had already heard of this Kremlin whim.

Half an hour before midnight Novikov was on Red Square. It looked deserted, like an abandoned field. A few pedestrians, alone and silent, crossed it hurriedly, like black birds, so small did they look on the wide square. The cupolas of the Cathedral of Vassily the Blessed stood out in silhouette. The severe and squat marble mausoleum gleamed dully; two sentries stood in frozen stiffness at the entrance, their thin bayonets burnished to a blue light. Fir trees, trimmed with snow, stood like other enormous sentries along the battlements of the Kremlin.

The dark sky hung low over the square, whose limits receded into the frosty haze. But above, on the tall pointed spires, red stars burned brightly. The silence was oppressive. Suddenly the quarter hour struck in the Spassk tower and at once, with an angry cry, the old crows rose from it. The same that picked out the eyes of the musketeers whom Peter the First had hung on the Kremlin battlements, they flew up and settled again. The loud, heavy toll of the bell pierced the haze, hung suspended over the square, frozen in a thousand-year torpor.

Shrinking from the cold, Feodor went to the gate of the Spassk tower. Sentries in gray caps and warm greatcoats checked his pass carefully, looked over the documents, compared him with the photograph on the passport and, after showing him where to go, released him. Their faces were businesslike, stern, unsmiling. Feodor passed on a few paces and was again stopped by a sentry, just as stern and imperturbable, who also checked all his papers although he must have seen that Feodor had already gone through the procedure. Soon he was convinced that this was a system. The sentries stood in sight of each other and each one checked Feodor's documents with fresh caution, as if the latter had dropped before him from the sky. It was like this right to the door of Malenkov's office.

Feodor didn't have to wait. He was conducted at once to Malenkov. Behind the desk he saw a full-cheeked young man with dark hair, a small strand of which fell over his forehead. He had a small, almost turned-up nose and small, slightly piggish eyes. He got up and shook hands with Novikov.

"Sit down, Professor," he said. "I am Georgi Malenkov, Comrade Stalin's personal secretary." Malenkov's hand was plump and soft. "Have a pleasant journey?"

Feodor became alert. Was this possibly a hint about the night incident on the train? But Malenkov appeared to be sincere; his tone was friendly. Feodor sat down and, after saying that he had had a pleasant trip, waited for what Malenkov had to say.

Studying his face, he felt at once that he would never forget it. Malenkov was very young, apparently younger than himself. He was thirty, no more. But his appearance, his whole expression, was that of an old, experienced bureaucrat. Malenkov's stout body was dressed in a loose Party shirt.

"How did he, so young, become Stalin's trusted man?" thought Feodor to himself with the curiosity of one careerist seeing another, more successful one. "He is younger than I, but has reached such a high position. What has he got that I haven't?" Feodor asked himself, looking at the round, plump, even slightly swollen face of Malenkov. So far he was struck with the heaviness and peculiar gloom, which even his smile did not iron out. But that was still not an answer to his question.

In the meantime Malenkov was also studying Feodor's face with his small eyes and, apparently, was satisfied with it.

"I called you on the instructions of Comrade Stalin," began Malenkov. "Comrade Stalin would like to talk with you personally, but he is very busy and instructed me to tell you the following: First of all, he is very satisfied with your achievement in the field of Russian history, rates your bold innovation highly, and considers that your effort is worthy of being copied. On behalf of Comrade Stalin personally, I thank you, Professor Novikov."

Feodor rose at these words and drew himself up in military style. "Thank you for your confidence," he said with emotion. He was exultant. So his fears had been groundless. It was not to execute but to praise him that they had called him to Moscow. Novikov's joy was written on his face, and Malenkov smiled understandingly.

"Tomorrow at your conference you will yourself be convinced how highly Comrade Stalin thinks of you. He intends to point you out as an example for the other historians."

Then Malenkov asked him to sit down and in a more everyday tone began to question him about his work at the University. He mentioned Gorin's play. "The Government very much appreciates your work in this field also," he said.

Feodor replied merely with a nod of his head. Malenkov evidently approved of his reluctance to say much on this subject. He rose and held out his hand.

"That's all, Comrade Novikov. But, just a minute! It's good to support words with deeds," he said smiling, and handed him a packet. "Here is the Government's award to you. Don't tell anybody about it, but spend it to your heart's content. Have a good time in Moscow. You have earned it."

On the way to the hotel Feodor could hardly restrain a shout of happiness. He guessed that there was money in the packet. But it wasn't the reward that gladdened him, it was the feeling of release from fear, from that wearying burden. He was free. He had nothing to be afraid of. Now he looked at Moscow with quite different eyes. There was the gloomy Lubyanka prison—no one had pushed him into its deep cell. There was the tall NKVD building—he had no need to jump out of its window to save himself from torture. There was the frozen Moscow river—no one had thrown his cold corpse under its ice.

In his room he opened the packet and whistled with surprise. There were twenty thousand rubles in beautiful, iridescent hundred-ruble bills. Beaming, he gazed at them and suddenly, for no apparent reason, said aloud:

"But his eyes were evil."

Then he realized why Malenkov surprised him. His eyes were small and merciless, exactly like those of an infuriated boar, ready to devour even its own offspring. Novikov understood now what Malenkov had that he lacked: ruthlessness, complete, absolute, unthinking ruthlessness.

"Yes, his eyes are strange, not normal," he thought. "And how could it be otherwise—a man accustomed from youth to hold the lives of people in his hands cannot remain normal."

And Novikov thought further that it was a good thing that he had been summoned to Malenkov, not for torture, but to receive a reward.

CHAPTER 20

IN THE MORNING of the following day the first session of the conference of historians was opened, and in the evening the Government gave a great dinner in their honor in the Andreyev Hall in the Kremlin. Stalin and most of the Politburo were present.

At the dinner Novikov sat next to Yudin, the same famous Moscow propagandist whom he had seen at the opening of the political Institute in Rostov. Feodor was satisfied; he was sitting beside a man whom he had recently envied. Yudin, apparently, could not remain silent for a minute. He jabbered without end and Feodor had to look at his thick lips and large popping-out tongue. But Feodor was in an uplifted mood and did not even notice his neighbor's ugliness. Like all those present, his eyes were trained on Stalin. The latter was sitting at the center of the main table. On his left hand was Voroshilov, his first favorite at that time, while on his right sat the president of the Academy of Science, Komarov. Beside Komarov sat Molotov, and then other members of the Politburo, intermingled with prominent Academicians.

Stalin talked mostly with Komarov and was obviously in a good mood. He frequently raised his glass of red wine, but Feodor noticed that he took small sips.

Then Stalin rose and everybody became silent. Stalin cast his eyes over the hall—deliberately, seeming to stop on every face.

"Comrades," he said, not loudly, but everybody heard him. "Scientists-historians! You have gathered in Moscow to sum up the total of your work and lay out paths for further development of historical science. I will not say exactly what these paths should be and how your science must develop, I will not take the bread out of your mouths." (A servile little laugh passed through the Hall.) "I will merely say that without the correct understanding of events of the past we Bolsheviks would not be able to orient ourselves in current politics and, even more important, know how to meet the threatening storms of life without panic. However, not all of us know yet how to interpret correctly historical events; many still cling to the heritage left by bourgeois scholarship, are unable to live through a day without repeating some old, outlived formula, which we need about as much as last year's snow." (More laughter.) "And as a rule it is such people that panic

398

first. Somewhere a cockroach rustles and they immediately shout about the downfall of Soviet power; somewhere a masked enemy whines pitifully and they immediately fall into hysterics and shed their tears in rivers, mourning over the victims of the policy of the Party. It's a pity, indeed, to waste words on such woebegone historians. Just now I want to talk about a different kind of historian, about scientist-innovators, scientist-historians who are able to strike fearlessly along new paths, who are leaders in their own field . . ."

Novikov, listening attentively to Stalin's speech, thought involuntarily: "Surely that's not about me?" He looked around at his neighbors; they were all listening, necks craned, a fawning expression frozen on all their faces. Probably in many heads the same ambitious thought flashed.

". . . We Bolsheviks are often accused of putting special eye-glasses on truth," Stalin continued. "But the glasses have nothing to do with it; the fact is that we have our own truth. Our enemies in the West do not understand this. But it is not for them that our truth is written. It was created by people, the like of whom they do not know and never will. Our truth was nursed by people of a special, rare breed—Soviet man. As an example of such a man, a historian-scientist, a Bolshevik, I wish to name a Rostov professor, Feodor Pavlovich Novikov. This young scholar was not afraid of our truth, he boldly smashed old traditions, ancient grandfathers' legacies. I raise my glass to Feodor Novikov and scientist-innovators like him."

Stalin emptied his glass and the entire hall rose and drank with him. Feodor noticed many people looking around, searching for him in the hall. Stalin nodded at one of the waiters and whispered to him. The latter came up to Novikov.

"Comrade Stalin invites you to sit beside him," he said, smiling respectfully.

Novikov rose, and accompanied by the envious looks of his colleagues, followed him.

"Sit down, Professor Novikov," Stalin said, taking him by the sleeve and seating him on a chair, placed there by the foresighted waiter. Academician Komarov made room for him. "Sit here, so that everyone can see you." He squeezed Novikov's arm. The hall responded with loud applause. Molotov extended his hand and greeted him also. Voroshilov did the same, saying gaily: "You and I are Rostovians, fellow townsmen."

The dinner continued. One after another the toasts were drunk. Stalin himself poured some wine for Novikov, questioned him about

399

his work. "If you need anything, don't hesitate to ask us; we will help you," he said.

And although Feodor was in an uplifted state, he nevertheless watched everything that was going on. Every detail imprinted itself clearly on his brain. And he noticed that throughout the whole conversation Stalin never mentioned Gorin's name.

CHAPTER 21

FROM SHEER JOY Feodor rushed all over Moscow, looking up old acquaintances. He began with his sister, Olga. She was living in a small room on the Vozdvizhenka with her girl friend—a small, likable brunette. Their room was one of many that had been made as the result of repeated division of a large drawing room by partitions of thin plywood. At one time it had been part of a large private residence. On the ceiling there remained traces of its former luxury: a sentimental painting of a nymph soaring on clouds and roses. As their share, the women had the legs and plump buttocks of the nymph; the other half disappeared intriguingly behind the plywood partition, where an accountant of the Commissariat of Non-Ferrous Metals lived noisily with his numerous family.

Although Feodor's room at the hotel was luxury compared to their cramped apartment, their place became for him, nevertheless, a little bit of home in noisy Moscow. The two girls took him under their wing and conducted him like a rustic provincial to the theatres, museums, the picture galleries, although Feodor had seen much of this before when he was studying at Moscow University. He, of course, paid for all three. He was staying in Moscow for only two weeks, up to the New Year, and he hurried to see everything.

He spent the days in various sessions, sometimes at the Academy of Sciences, at others at the Marx-Engels University, and sometimes in historical museums. In the evenings he was free. Whatever had been said at the sessions, in which he himself took an active part, flew out of his head completely at exactly six o'clock. In contrast, the least word spoken by his sister or her friend or by some chance-met acquaintance he remembered and often repeated to himself.

He was very much surprised at his sister. He had not seen her for nearly three years and she seemed to him to have changed greatly. The main thing he noticed was that she had many of his own traits

400

and, strangely, this was unpleasant to Feodor. What he considered virtues in himself—coldness, calculation, ambition—all these were present in Olga, but in her they were a travesty. Perhaps because she was a woman? In any case, after each meeting and conversation with her a faintly unpleasant taste remained with him, as if he had just looked into an ugly mirror in which his likeness had appeared but with his traits exaggerated to the point of caricature.

Feodor decided that such traits, unpleasant in a woman, were the reason why Olga had not married. Olga, however, explained it to him otherwise. Indicating with her eyes the partition, behind which there was pure hell—weeping, screams of children, cries of the accountant's wife, the hissing of the primus stove—Olga said, compressing her lips fastidiously:

"Get married, and live like that accountant? Breed, fight in the kitchen with the neighbors over some kettle, comfort my husband when he has been frightened to death by his boss—you should hear what they say at night when they are engaged in the propagation of children. No, I'd rather stay single!"

"But not everybody lives like your neighbor. Surely you could find a husband with a better position, with a more decent apartment?" Feodor asked seriously. "You're a pretty woman and clever. That uncommon combination should provide opportunities for your personal happiness."

Olga flared up and looked at him almost with dislike in her lovely but cold eyes. "You've never been a girl and you wouldn't understand what that means. A man can always make a more or less decent life for himself—like you, for example. But for a woman . . . Today you think you are married to a good successful man; tomorrow he'll throw you over, and leave you with a bunch of kids. I myself have seen many such instances among my friends. No, Fedya, married life carries a lot of evil in it."

Feodor, who was under the influence of his unexpected happiness with Lida, could not agree with his sister. However, he nodded his head in understanding. "Yes, it is very important to find a man you can trust," he said, sighing.

Olga smiled at him ironically. "The trouble is, a lot depends not on the man. Often a good man has to behave like a swine. You can't foresee everything . . ." and, noticing a watchful expression on his face, Olga asked quickly: "Tell me about yourself, about your wife. What's she like? How did you meet her? And how do you live yourself?"

"I'm very happy with Lida," replied Feodor. "I couldn't wish for anything more."

"If you only knew how I envy you! Why on earth wasn't I born a man? We are living in a man's world."

However much Feodor sympathized with his sister, he couldn't help noticing how his antagonism towards her grew. But on the whole Feodor felt rested; he even, for a time, forgot Gorin, his relations with Nina, and the whole tense Rostov atmosphere.

Only once was he reminded of it. The three of them went together to Gorin's play, *Ivan the Terrible*. Coming out of the theatre when the play was over, Feodor overheard someone in the crowd saying: "Well, Gorin turned out to be an easy nut to crack."

So somebody, knowing nothing about Novikov and his task, understood the meaning of the appearance of Gorin's play.

At the end of the second week of his stay in Moscow, on the very eve of the New Year, Feodor met Drozd. When the latter learned that Feodor had spent his time in visiting theatres, museums, and such institutions, he burst out laughing.

"Is that the way you have a good time?" he exclaimed with sincere astonishment.

"How else?"

"I'll show you. It's a pity you've so little time left, but never mind. Better late than never."

He took him to his own apartment—it turned out to be really luxurious by Moscow standards—called a number, and soon two young ladies appeared. One of them was brown-haired with a surprisingly beautiful profile. A bright comb was stuck in her modishly dressed hair. Both were dressed decently, even fashionably. One was wearing a nicely tailored coat, trimmed with gray caracul; the other a seal-skin coat.

"Meet Tania and Valerie, members of the corps de ballet of the Bolshoi Theatre. This is my friend Feodor. Be kind and gracious to him," Drozd introduced them.

Feodor hardly recognized his boss. It seemed to him that the latter was currying favor with him. The girls sat down on the divan, quite at home. Valerie, the owner of the beautiful profile, never took her caressing eyes off Feodor.

Drozd, seizing an opportunity, whispered to him: "Devote yourself to Valerie. Take note of her figure, her legs! Magnificent!"

"Where are they from?"

"They've both just finished the school of ballet. Not Ulanovas, of

402

course, but we're not going to dance with them on the stage," and Drozd winked, making a quite understandable gesture.

"But surely you know that I'm married," Feodor considered it necessary to warn him. He was still shy with his chief. But the latter laughed.

"Married! Ha! Why, so am I."

"But where's your wife?" Feodor was surprised.

"Oh, that's a long story," Drozd frowned. "Briefly, she doesn't live with me any more . . . All right, let's go to the girls," and, taking a bottle from the cupboard, Drozd went into the next room. "Let's down one before supper."

Following Drozd, Feodor recalled his sister's words.

They all went together to a restaurant for supper. When the mirror-doors of the restaurant, sparkling with temptation, opened, Feodor was deafened by the noise of the orchestra and blinded by the brilliance of the dancing couples. He understood what Drozd meant by "a good time."

They sat down at a table. Drozd beckoned to a waiter, whispered something to him. The latter quickly brought some vodka. Feodor drank his and looked around.

"Foreigners?" he asked Drozd guardedly, indicating with his eyes the well-dressed dancing couples.

"Some are foreigners. But there are a lot of ours among them. They're burning up life: some from joy, like you, and some from sorrow, like that one there," and Drozd nodded towards an elderly man with gray hair and a gray beard, sitting a couple of tables from them. He drank hurriedly, as if he were stabbing himself with the glass.

Leaning over to Feodor, Drozd explained: "He's a chief engineer of an automobile plant. He was abroad—he'll be shot, of course, although it's a pity—he's a clever man. And the other one, who's writing something—he won't be shot, but he should be."

"Who's he?" asked Feodor, looking at a small individual bent over a sheet of paper. Without taking his eyes off the paper, the latter from time to time reached with his left hand for his wine glass and raised it to his lips. The noise of the orchestra apparently didn't bother him.

To his surprise, Drozd named the famous Moscow journalist, Burgov. "You see he's scribbling, writing some correspondence from a kolkhoz. Tomorrow the article will be in *Pravda*. You know the kind . . ."

Yes, Feodor knew. He had read Burgov more than once, knew his style: ". . . right now a column of tractors is passing by me. On the first one is the shock worker Ivan Vedro, a red-cheeked lad; he's shouting something to me, waving his hand gaily. Beside him is his young sweetheart, a shy smile on her healthy face. They have just finished plowing their hundredth hectare, have fulfilled the plan 112 per cent, and are now returning to the kolkhoz, singing. To your success, shock worker Vedro! The whole country is proud of you! . . ." and so on in the same vein for four columns. All the journalists of *Pravda* wrote like that, only Burgov was the best at lying about the high percentages and the shy smiles.

"And to think that he was at one time a Menshevik!" said Drozd. "But his tongue is well hung; that alone saves him."

As if he felt that someone was talking about him, Burgov raised his dreamy eyes, overcast with a drunken haze, emptied his glass, and then went on with his work.

"Have you forgotten about us?" Valerie asked Feodor coquettishly.

They ordered a sumptuous supper—over a hundred rubles for each. With the generosity of a wealthy provincial Feodor paid for all. When Valerie saw his fat billfold, her eyes became very endearing. Drozd caught Novikov's inflamed look. Again he leaned over to his ear: "It's all right. If you want to sleep with her, you can. But it'll cost you money."

Feodor was going to answer, but at that moment a strange hush fell on the hall. Everybody looked toward the door. In the entrance appeared a medium-sized young man with red hair and large, somewhat melancholy eyes. He was well dressed; a diamond flashed on his tie. A pretty girl was with him, taller than he, while behind him and a little apart were two well-built men. The young man looked over the assembly with a mocking glance, whispered something to the girl, who wrinkled her brow coquettishly. The whole company passed into an inner room. The hall buzzed like a wasp's nest.

"Who is that?" Feodor asked Drozd.

"Yasha—Stalin's son," replied Drozd. "He is a frequent guest here."

"And the girl with him is Nadya Vlasova," said Valerie, and envy sounded clearly in her voice. "I know her well. She's nothing special . . ."

"There's competition everywhere," laughed Feodor to himself.

"Well, let's drink to your success!" said Drozd a moment later. "The second and last phase is now ahead of you."

Feodor clinked glasses with him, but inside he wondered: "What kind of last phase? What's he hinting at?"

404

But Drozd said scornfully: "Don't pop your eyes. You know your-self what it's about."

His words were drowned in a hubbub. "New Year! New Year!" they were shouting all around. All in the room rose and raised their glasses.

Feodor's face, pale from vodka, showed his emotion. He was just going to extend his glass to Drozd, but changed his mind and turned to Valerie.

"Well, Valya, here's to the New Year! Obviously fate has bound me to him."

"To whom?" asked Valerie, trying to make herself heard above the noise.

"Forget it. . . . It doesn't matter," and leaning over the table, Feodor kissed her full red lips. Valerie laughed; in her eyes greedy little lights flashed, catlike.

The night was quiet and solemn. High up in the sky shone the moon, circled by a frosty halo. The snow creaked under foot. Feodor, taking Valerie's arm, went to his room in the hotel. They parted from Drozd and Tania at the restaurant.

There was nobody on the stairs. Valerie laughed, showing an even row of teeth, fell drunkenly on his arm. "Oh! Hold me up!" Feodor caught her, kissed the warm hair on her neck. He felt as if he were in a pleasant dream, floating on air. Supporting Valerie with one hand, he opened the door of his room with the other and switched on the light. At once he noticed a letter on the floor; apparently it had been pushed under the door. The address was in Lida's handwriting. This reminded Feodor at once of Rostov, of a different, sober life. He frowned. "I'll read it later," he thought. But he had already lost his gay mood.

Valerie noticed the change in him. She sat close to him on the divan, raised her leg higher than was needful, and bared her knees. "How do you like it: with the light on or not? . . ."

In the morning Feodor woke up first. Valerie was lying with her broad back toward him, her nose stuck into the pillow. "How much should I pay her?" thought Feodor and regretted that he had not found out from Drozd.

Then he remembered Lida's letter. Lying in bed, he read it: "Dear Fedya, I'm very sad, terribly lonely without you. You haven't written to me, why? . . ." Between the lines Feodor imagined Lida's face, trust-ing . . . his own, his dear, loving wife. Feodor unconsciously moved away from Valerie's hot side, as from something dirty. Pity pierced his heart. He was drawn to Lida. Lida wrote about life at the University, what was going on there without him, what the reaction was there to Stalin's words about him. She was obviously very proud of him. Then, at the very end of the letter she wrote: "Come home as soon as possible. I have great news for you. I'll tell you when you come. A thousand kisses, I love you, your LIDA."

"News? Good?" asked Feodor aloud. "Really? Really?" he smiled. "Of course, it will be a son, my son." And strangely, he imagined his son suddenly as a tall, well-built young man.

He jumped up from the bed. Valerie, curled up in a ball, was licking her bright lips in her sleep. Feodor looked at her in astonishment. Valerie appeared to him very disgusting with her rapacious cat look, her agile, experienced hands, her vulgar tricks, this whole whirlpool of mercenary caresses out of which he had just emerged with a buzzing head and guilty conscience.

"Of course, I love only Lida, with my whole heart."

He dressed, touched Valerie's shoulder. "Get up. I've got to go." He woke her roughly. She sat up in bed without covering her legs, stretched lazily.

"It's early yet," she said, yawning.

"How much do you want?" asked Feodor with aversion.

"Of what?" Valerie drawled, surprised.

"How much money must I pay you?" repeated Feodor.

"My God, you are asking . . ." Valerie was offended. Then apparently she remembered the fat billfold and said snappishly: "A thousand!" And afraid of her own words, she stared at him with her made-up eyes.

"All right," Feodor took several hundred-ruble bills out of his billfold and without counting them, threw them onto her knees. "There's more than a thousand there. . . . I'm going out for breakfast; get out before I return to the room!"

Not listening to him, Valerie looked unbelieving at the money. She thought he had gone out of his mind.

But Feodor, going down the stairs, sighed freely. No matter what she had asked, he would have given it to her—so anxious was he to get rid of her as quickly as possible.

He was glad: "Soon I'll see Lida!" Now, as never before, Lida seemed to him the dearest, most precious thing in the world.

PART SIX

CHAPTER 1

TO FEODOR'S surprise a large delegation met him at Rostov station—representatives from the University and the Department of Higher Education and several Party functionaries. When he stepped onto the platform the band struck up, and Lida threw herself on his neck. But she was pushed aside and the Secretary of the Party Committee of the University shook his hand: "Congratulations, Comrade Director, on your happy arrival!"

Following him, several hands were stretched out to him.

"Congratulations! Congratulations!"

The passengers traveling with Feodor, not knowing what it was all about, asked in surprise: "Why the celebration?"

"That's our Rostovian, Director Novikov, about whom Stalin spoke," they were told.

It was evening before Feodor was left alone with Lida. He was carried off to a dinner, speeches, replying to speeches. His hand ached from handshaking. But as soon as they were alone everything was forgotten.

Lida asked: "Did you get my letter?"

"Yes, I did, and I think I can guess what it's about." And, unable to restrain himself, Feodor drew his wife to him, kissed her warmly on the lips. "I was lonely without you, Lida . . ."

Lida looked up at him: "What have you guessed?"

"You're expecting a baby?"

She blushed. "Yes, we're going to have a baby."

407

"What do you think—will it be a boy?" asked Feodor seriously.

Lida laughed in spite of herself. "How should I know? But does it matter?"

"I would like to have a son . . ." replied Feodor anxiously, but caught himself quickly: "But it doesn't really matter. The main thing is, now we'll have a family. You know, Lida, when I was in Moscow alone, and especially when I received your letter, I felt most sharply how lost I was without you. How truly they say that absence makes the heart grow fonder!"

Happy tears appeared in Lida's eyes. Blinking her wet eyelashes and pressing herself still closer to him she said: "Darling Fedya! And I . . . I couldn't live without you."

From that moment Feodor was in a strange state. The smile almost never left his face; he was indulgent with his subordinates, almost affectionate. He was greatly excited about Lida and didn't know what to do for her that he had not already done. He tried to persuade her not to attend lectures, to rest, but Lida merely laughed at his extraordinary concern. "Women in the plants work up to six months, and nothing happens. Studying is easy in comparison."

They were both very happy. Looking at them people envied them, but it was impossible to watch them without smiling.

Then suddenly disaster struck. It came with a monstrous crash, with inhuman cruelty and pain.

One evening Feodor was sitting alone in his apartment reading a magazine. Lida had gone with her girl friend from a lecture to the city library to get some books she needed. Suddenly the door opened and Natalia rushed into the room. She was almost unrecognizable. Her usually self-satisfied and calm face was white as snow, her eyes dilated, staring. For a minute she was unable to speak.

"What's the matter? What's wrong with you?" Feodor asked her in alarm, getting up to meet her, the magazine in his hand.

"Leonid has been arrested!" she exclaimed at last, and dropped sobbing into a chair.

Feodor paled. His arms became heavy. The magazine fell to the floor with a thud.

"W—what for?" he could barely utter.

"I don't know!" Natalia raised her tear-stained face, terribly ugly at this moment, and spoke through her sobs. "Four of them came just now and took him away. They wouldn't let him take anything—one even struck him when he wanted to say good-bye to me . . . You can find out what's wrong and save him. You have connections, you're a well-known man, Stalin knows you . . . But please hurry, or it will be too late!"

"Save?" asked Feodor, as in a dream. "You think that I can save him?" And then, as if he had still not caught the full significance of her words, he added, at a loss: "But they'll probably release him in any case. Probably there's been some misunderstanding . . ."

Gradually he pulled himself together. Natalia noticed this and was frightened by his appearance. He stood in front of her, unnaturally tense, his face pale and expressionless.

"All right, Natalia, I'll try to do something. . . . You go home and calm down. . . ." He spoke with difficulty, but his voice was cold and unfriendly.

Natalia got up slowly, went towards the door, stooping, as if she were carrying an unseen but terribly heavy burden. At the door she stopped and, avoiding his eyes, her own dulled by tears, said pleadingly: "For Lida's sake, save him."

"Yes, yes, of course . . . I'll do what I can." Feodor hurried her out.

Natalia understood. She looked searchingly at him and said, quite sharply, in her usual tone: "Watch out, Feodor. Don't pull a double cross," and went out.

Feodor locked the door and began rushing up and down the room. "What should I do? What should I do now?" he mumbled aloud.

He suspected that Sidorov's arrest had a direct connection with his encounter with Oleg Durov. Now he was married to the daughter of an enemy of the people. What could be worse or more dangerous than this? He imagined the glances of the people, his acquaintances, colleagues. Their guarded manners, frightened movements on meeting him: ready to run, to shy to one side, as from the plague.

"What should I do? Go at once to Veria and frankly ask his advice?" But Feodor knew how he would reply. He would say—you yourself should know what Bolsheviks do in such cases.

"So—a divorce."

At the mere thought of this Feodor shuddered. "Break up my family, destroy my happiness . . . Yes, but an end has come to happiness in any case . . ."

Feodor looked at the clock. Lida should be coming soon.

"How can I tell her about this misfortune? And most important, what shall I do about it? Ask her to leave me of her own free will? But would she understand?" and Feodor, imagining Lida's face, trusting, childishly open and innocent, knew well that she would not understand. "But it is the only solution," he thought, feverishly. "To wait until others force me to do it, until they call me to the Party committee for a 'heart to heart' talk, until I have to make a speech at a Party meeting, thump my chest and publicly wash my hands of Lida, listen to the vicious hints of my enemies—no, that would be disastrous. Better to make the break at once, before it's too late."

By the time Lida arrived, Feodor had definitely decided what to do. Lida at once noticed his strange appearance.

"What's wrong with you, Fedya?" she asked, putting her books on a table.

Feodor went up to her and, embracing her from behind, said to her as calmly as he could: "Lida, don't get upset, but your father has been arrested. Natalia was just here and said——"

Lida instantly turned her face, rosy from the frost, to him. "Impossible! Fedya . . . What for?" she exclaimed, and the color left her face.

"I don't know, but it is so."

"Where's Mama?"

"She went home."

"Home?" Lida was surprised and suddenly began to hurry into her fur coat. "Fedya, let's go to her at once! We'll find out what's the matter. We'll have to go to the Provincial Committee of the Party, to Veria, to Shcherbakov. We must do something as soon as possible . . . Get dressed and let's go."

Feodor stopped in front of her.

"Lida, we'll have to separate," he said gently but firmly and, seeing her perplexed look and interpreting it in his own way, he hastened to add: "Temporarily, of course . . . you understand, until things quiet down . . . And afterwards . . ."

Lida looked at him as before, surprised. She was trying to grasp his meaning. "What are you talking about?" she asked at last. Feodor saw that she was completely at a loss.

He sighed painfully.

"Why can't you understand such a simple thing! We must separate! . . . By good luck we haven't registered yet, so we won't even need to get a divorce. You simply return to your mother, and that's all . . . it's very simple . . ." Feodor spoke with difficulty and with every word was convinced that it was far from simple.

Lida listened to him attentively, looking with astonishment into his restless eyes—his eyes seemed particularly strange—and at last she understood.

410

"You're throwing me out?"

"No, not at all . . . Understand, Lida. You are now the daughter of an enemy of the people——"

"Surely you don't believe that my father is an enemy?"

Feodor threw up his hands hopelessly. "Can't you understand? It doesn't matter what you or I think—the important thing is what others think. Your father is an enemy of the people—to go on living together now would be dangerous for us, for my job and, in the end, for you."

"You don't love me, Fedya?" Lida suddenly asked, and to his astonishment Feodor saw that this was the only thing she was concerned about.

"Of course, I love you! But for us—if you like, for our love—for the sake of our happiness, we must part, and the sooner the better."

Lida suddenly went into the bedroom. Feodor, not understanding what she was going to do, followed her.

"All right, Fedya, I'll go . . . I'll go, I'll just take my things and go . . ." she repeated hurriedly. Her lips were trembling like a child's. "Right away . . ."

Feodor felt terribly sorry for her. If she had thrown herself at him with shouts, had made a scene, smashed dishes—he could have controlled himself. But her helpless appearance, her small figure and the guilty look on her face—they worked on his nerves. He ran to her, dropped beside her on his knees, took her little hands in his and kissed her fingers. "Believe me, Lida, this is necessary . . . It is hurting me terribly! You don't know how it hurts me, but there's no other way."

"Yes, I understand . . ." Lida freed her hands and hurriedly began again to pack her clothes in a suitcase.

"Lida, I'll see you, nobody will know about it."

Lida looked at him, her eyes dark and swollen by tears. She smiled pitifully: "Thank you, Fedya . . ."

Feodor rose. "I'll get a cab. I'll send your other things to you tomorrow."

He put on his coat, took her suitcase and went out. Lida walked resignedly behind him. She was in a strange, numb condition.

There was a cab almost at the gate of the University.

"I'd better see her home." Feodor was going to sit down beside her; but, remembering Natalia, he changed his mind. He gave the address and money to the driver. Then he kissed Lida on her stone-cold lips.

"Don't worry, Lida . . . Everything will be all right."

Lida was silent, looking straight ahead of her. She noticed neither his kiss nor his words.

411

CHAPTER 2

THE FOLLOWING day Feodor found out what had happened to Sidorov. Although not a word was printed in the paper about his arrest, rumors were all over the town. The charge was very fear-inspiring—sabotage. Naïve people said that he had been an agent of some western power almost from the time he wore diapers, while those who knew the real reason were silent. Feodor had an opportunity of talking with the chief engineer of the plant, whom he knew well. The latter, looking over his shoulder, whispered: "Sidorov is as much a saboteur as I am a Spanish king. For two months now the plant has not fulfilled the plan because of poor supply of materials. There are, of course, other technical causes, but that's the main one. They could arrest me as well as Sidorov for that. It's simply that someone wanted to get rid of him and took advantage of the lag in production at the plant."

Feodor knew who that was. Durov, evidently, had been waiting impatiently for this opportunity and had framed the hated Sidorov. Moscow wouldn't want to intercede on behalf of the director of the lagging plant.

That same day the Secretary of the Party Committee of the University came to Feodor's study.

"I have a matter to discuss with you," he said. "We have received news that your wife's father has been arrested as an enemy of the people. The point is that she is a student and a Komsomol. You understand that in such cases the children of enemies of the people are expelled from the Komsomol at a students' meeting. It may be, however, that the Provincial Committee will make an exception in this case and decide to leave this matter to us. But you'll have to get busy yourself . . ."

Feodor became watchful. "Durov's trap," he thought and said as dryly as possible: "You are mistaken, Comrade Ilyenko. The student Sidorov is not my wife and never was. I don't intend to plead for her before anybody and I do not consider that this matter concerns me at all."

At first the secretary was surprised, but then nodded his head understandingly. "But you haven't an official divorce yet, Comrade Director,"

412

he said in an admonishing tone. "She is still Lida Novikov, not Sidorov."

"Again, I say, you're mistaken," said Feodor, almost gloating. "We never registered. And as far as the wedding is concerned, to which, as I recall, you were invited—that is not an official act. Right?"

The secretary screwed up his eyes slyly. "Guess that's right . . . But you see, they will expel her from the Komsomol and the University. You know the secret order from the Central Committee about student-children of enemies of the people."

"Of course I know. Precisely on that account I insist that everything should follow a normal course, without any leniency and exceptions to the rule."

The secretary looked in perplexity at the Director's dry, official face, and said with compassion: "It's too bad. She'll be lost in the twinkling of an eye. I'll tell you, as a friend: I believe that everything can be arranged quietly; nobody need know anything. She can remain a student and she won't even be expelled from the Komsomol. If you like, I myself will speak to the Provincial Committee. Your name is very highly thought of there and they will arrange everything for you."

"No, thank you."

Ilyenko got up. "Well, just as you like. It's your business."

"No, now it's your business and not mine."

When the secretary was at the door Feodor stopped him: "Comrade Ilyenko, when will the meeting be?"

"Tomorrow, after studies. I'll have to prepare the resolutions and the speeches of the students."

"A general faculty meeting, or simply of her courses?"

"The courses will be enough for this affair."

"So I won't need to attend," said Feodor. "That's good. And by the way, remind those concerned that the student's name is Lydia Sidorov. You understand, Sidorov."

The secretary looked once more into the cold, impenetrable eyes of the Director, then went out.

Lida was expelled from the Komsomol. The meeting was oppressive, silent. The secretary of the Party Committee had to speak several times to spur the discussions. But the formal procedure was preserved faultlessly: there were the usual speeches by the activists, prepared previously by the secretary. They called for "merciless measures against the student Sidorov, bound by family ties to an enemy of the people"; a resolution was read, demanding in the name of the meeting her expulsion from the Komsomol, and hands were raised in unanimity. Lida, as stunned and unresponsive as when she left Feodor, handed back her membership card and left the classroom. But however mechanically the students conducted themselves, the news that the Director's wife had been expelled from the Komsomol and, of course, would now be expelled from the University, shocked them all.

At the meeting Novikov's name was not mentioned once, an omission which was accepted by everybody as a sign that her connection with him had been officially recognized as not existing. Still more important, Director Novikov remained in office. And more than that— he had passed the test: he had conducted himself like a true Bolshevik.

A week later Lida was expelled from the University. When the manager of the administrative branch brought Novikov the order for her expulsion he looked searchingly at him. But the Director's face was composed. He signed the order and, raising his eyes, looked straight into his subordinate's face, as if he were challenging him. The latter left hurriedly, very much embarrassed.

Two weeks later, Lida was mobilized to a chemical plant as a worker, and Lida and her mother moved to a workers' barracks at the plant. The luxurious home in which they had lived previously with her father was confiscated, with all their property.

CHAPTER 3

WHEN FEODOR saw Nina's face he realized at once that she knew everything. The meeting took place on the military rifle range. It was Sunday, and the senior classes at Rostov University had come out to ski and to practice shooting. The students from the Conservatory were also there. Novikov looked for Nina, feeling that he must see her. He found her at the third station, near a shed where the skis were kept. Nina, in a dark blue ski suit, red cap, and red mittens, was putting on her skis. The students were crowded around, talking noisily with each other and laughing. Some were waxing their skis, others were raising the right ski high, then the left, practicing turns.

Again, as when he last saw her, the sight of Nina caused him pain, a withering anguish. Nina was fastening her ski harness and didn't notice his approach. He spoke to her. Nina raised her face, and the smile that had been on her lips vanished. It was then Feodor realized that she knew everything.

414

"How do you do, Nina? I haven't seen you for a long time."

"How do you do?" she said coolly; and then, as if considering something, added: "Feodor."

"You have the same program as we: an excursion and target shooting?"

"Yes. But, of course, I'll fall behind: I'm very poor on skis."

"That's fine," said Feodor, trying to speak cheerfully, pretending that he didn't notice her cool manner. "In that case I'll also fall behind —and have a talk with you. You've no objection?"

Nina shrugged her shoulders.

"Well, I'll have to go to my crowd; I must be present at the start of the excursion," said Feodor. "I'll find you later."

Nina did not reply, but looked closely at him. Feodor knew what she was looking for. "Of course, she considers me a beast now, inhuman," he thought. "As if she could understand."

Feodor, as Director of the University, not only attended the start of the ski run, but took part in it himself. The students formed into a column, over a thousand of them, men and women. On the shoulders of each one hung a soldier's complete equipment—rifle, pack, spade, mess gear, and a rolled greatcoat. This equipment was loaned by the military garrison. The task was to ski ten miles over rough country. At the end of the run, target practice on another rifle range awaited them, along with the judges—officers of the Rostov garrison. Each one, on arriving at the rifle range, had to lie down at a line, get ten rounds of ammunition from the officer on duty, and shoot at the target with his own rifle. Whoever arrived first at the rifle range and had the best shooting score received the most points. The competition was hard, and not only students took part in it but also the professors and the entire service staff.

At exactly ten o'clock in the morning an officer of the military garrison gave the signal by firing a shot from his revolver. The whole tremendous mass, their skis squeaking on the dry snow, moved forward.

At the start the entire throng of skiers seemed to be monolithic and moved slowly, unevenly, with frequent stops. Then, one after another, individual skiers began to break out of this huge mass and forge ahead, trying to outstrip each other. The trail led down a gentle slope to the river and Feodor, who was the very last on the hill and was waiting his turn to move, could see the whole column. The sun was shining brightly and the many bluish trails left by the skiers looked from there to be straight, as if they had been drawn with a pencil and a ruler.

Feodor had remained last on purpose, so as to swing at a suitable

415

moment into the path of the third section, Nina's column, which almost paralleled his. He was listening, expecting to hear the shot signaling the start of the excursion. But there had been no shot as yet.

One after another, the skiers passed him, and their quick movements and excited faces fascinated Feodor. He couldn't hold himself back and began to drop down the incline. The slow movement of the main column irked him. Like many impatient ones he turned out to the side and began to outrun the column.

"That's all right, I'll meet Nina at the crossroads," he thought, having in mind a place about five miles distant, where the third section's trail joined theirs.

Soon he had outstripped the column and saw in front of him only about a hundred students, who were advancing in a fairly scattered chain. Right ahead of him was a stocky student, a good skier. He took long, strong strides, what is known as the Finnish stride. From the side it looked as if he were waddling from right to left. He had on a gray shirt and ordinary gray pants tucked into black ski boots. Everything else—the rifle, rolled greatcoat and so on, was the same as the rest. For some reason the longer Feodor looked at him the stronger became his desire to see the face of this good skier. At last he overtook him, glancing at his face in passing. He had high cheek-bones, a short, slightly turned-up nose which gave him a comical appearance, and surprisingly deep blue eyes.

"Like a girl's," thought Feodor, and ran ahead.

But in a hundred strides the lad had overtaken him. Now—Feodor felt this at once—a tacit competition began between them. They were approaching the river, and here it was necessary to make two or three jumps; the lad made them awkwardly, was delayed, and fell behind Feodor. Feodor, feeling with pleasure the desire to win this competition, went with long strides, overtaking one after another of the skiers. Someone shouted to him: "Where are you hurrying, Comrade Director? You'll be played out before time!"

Feodor didn't look back, but he was sure that the stocky student was running right behind him. Feodor didn't feel any tiredness yet, though already the perspiration was coming out on his back under the equipment; but so far that was rather pleasant, a warm feeling.

Feodor ran another full mile in this way, the stocky student behind him all the time; he could hear his breathing clearly. Then the student overtook him and began to draw farther and farther ahead of him. Feodor increased his pace, but another skier came between them and, for the first time, Feodor was surprised to find that he felt tired. Soon he almost ceased to feel his body, moving his legs mechanically, pushing with the poles.

At the outset he had been thinking. Or rather, separate and disconnected thoughts were running through his mind, scraps of thought, and—as was usually the case recently—they were sad, unpleasant, depressing. He thought of Lida, of his pity for her, of his rage—against whom he was uncertain; then he recalled, or rather relived, his fear when he first learned about her father's arrest; then again, the whole scene of Lida's departure from the apartment, her pathetic, resigned figure, her mouth, twisted, childlike. Driving away these thoughts, he recalled his talk with Nina and her coldness, her silent accusation of cruelty; in his mind he explained his position to her, justified himself to her—although he felt that neither she nor he himself believed his explanations. Every time he caught himself at these thoughts, Feodor noticed that he had fallen behind. Then he would increase his pace and try not to think about anything.

To his surprise he saw the stocky student again. Evidently he had slowed down a bit, for Feodor would not admit that he himself had been going faster. At sight of the student, Feodor increased his stride and overtook him, deciding not to give in any more. He was so fascinated with this race that he didn't notice when he passed the crossroads where he was going to wait for Nina.

Now he was going freely and evenly. Strangely, he felt no fatigue whatever, and this feeling of special lightness, even though the equipment had not been lessened, astounded him. Sweat was pouring down his face and ran into his eyes, his body was steaming. It was cold—he could tell by the peculiar color of the snow, by the sound of the skis, and by other signs—but he did not feel the cold at all. He raced, and was afraid only that the stocky student would overtake him.

On the sixth and seventh miles he had a particularly joyful feeling of lightness and a strange inner emptiness, wonderfully pleasant. He didn't try to explain this phenomenon or find reasons for it—he was not thinking of anything, though he knew instinctively that something extraordinarily good had taken possession of him, some long-forgotten spiritual exaltation. The fact that he felt no fatigue, was so surprisingly at peace and joyfully uplifted, together with that astonishing inner lightness—all this was a sensation of his fast-beating heart and tense muscles, rather than his brain. If someone had asked him later the meaning of this overwhelming feeling, he would hardly have been able to explain. Perhaps it could be expressed best by saying that he had, as it were, been born again, that he had become, for a time, a part of nature, part of the silent forest he was passing, one of the trees standing here eternally. His movements also seemed to him as everlasting as the road. And even the stocky student seemed the same; Feodor was sure that he also was experiencing the same joyful feeling.

In such an uplifted mood Feodor came to the gates of the rifle range and remembered Nina. At once he felt the weight of the load on his back and his free, happy feeling vanished. He stopped at the gate and suddenly realized that he was dead tired. The stocky student ran past him and looked at him in astonishment, unable to understand why he had suddenly stopped at the very finishing line and given up the first place to him.

But Feodor had lost all interest in the contest. His whole body ached terribly, but his heart more than anything else. Anguish and emptiness were there. Breathing heavily, he removed his rifle and all his equipment, unrolled his greatcoat and, throwing it over his shoulders so as not to catch cold, he sat down. He scooped up a handful of snow and ate it, feeling how it melted in his dried-out mouth. Along with the snow, his recent joyful feeling seemed to melt away and was replaced by a heavy, pressing sensation, like a weight on his shoulders. Not knowing why, perhaps because he was now tired, Feodor found that he was crying.

He was crying over his dream, his fate, and the feeling of joy and freedom which had just mocked him so and which he knew he had lost, never to regain. The tears trickled slowly, the frost caught them and stung his eyes. Feodor took another handful of snow and rubbed his face so that people wouldn't see his tears and guess his weakness. Then he took out a cigarette, lit a match with difficulty, his fingers trembling from the recent tension, and, smoking, waited for Nina.

CHAPTER 4

THE MEETING with Feodor had upset Nina greatly. What she had been thinking privately now flared up with new strength. She knew that he and Lida had parted, but she didn't realize the reason at once, although she heard about Sidorov's arrest. It didn't occur to her to connect this arrest with their separation. She had tried to find Lida, but it was as if the latter had dropped into the earth.

It was during her search that Nina found out from the students the real reason. She was stunned. No matter how suspicious she had been of Feodor recently, she could not believe that he would descend to such meanness. When he stood before her, the man of whom she had been thinking as a monster, he astonished her with his confused, even pitiable appearance.

She tried to find in his face traces of the evil of which she had been thinking and which, she knew, must exist in him, and could find none. His face was as usual, but his eyes were less calm. They seemed to evade her glance.

Full of this unsettling emotion, Nina followed the other students on her skis. She carried only a rifle on her shoulder, having left the rest of the equipment at the base. Her whole being protested against anyone making her into a pack mule. Nina was regarded in the Conservatory as an exception from all rules and was allowed to do many things for which another student would have been expelled. She was treated like a strange curiosity, was even called a "foreigner." She missed meetings, took no part in social work—all these things that were obligatory for every Soviet student she regarded as absurd.

Nina was skiing now, not because she had been ordered to, not for any official reason—to prepare the students for a future war—but simply for the pleasure of being in the fresh air.

It was a beautiful winter morning. The river, along which they presently traveled, was covered with snow, and the bushes on its banks formed fantastic grottos, hillocks, silhouettes of strange beasts—complete sculptural groups—all motionless and silent as in a dream.

When the trail went through the forest the scene became even more majestic. That strange peace which envelops one on a clear winter morning overwhelmed Nina. She had not been brought up religiously; Mikhail Gorin was an atheist and wanted to bring her up as one. But when Nina was quite small Luba took her several times to the cathedral in Rome. Now, looking at the silent fir trees surrounding her in their trimming of snow, Nina recalled the tremendous, solemn cathedral. And the feeling of peace reminded her of the long-forgotten words of a sermon.

"Yes, I must forgive, forgive and understand . . ." she thought, looking with a grateful smile at the silent forest, at the tops of the trees sparkling in the sun under the bright blue sky. Whom to forgive, whom to understand, she didn't quite know. But she felt an all-pervading, noble feeling of grace filling her whole being.

When she caught sight of Feodor sitting under the greatcoat, she

419

wanted to be gentle with him, to try to understand him. "Maybe I was wrong. There are probably more reasonable explanations for his strange step," she thought, approaching him.

They walked together to the rifle range and, selecting a place opposite two targets, lay down. An officer gave them shells. "Take aim before you fire. Don't hurry," he told them.

They lay silent, getting into a comfortable position.

"What did you want to talk about?" Nina asked, looking at him sidewise.

"Oh, just . . . You know, of course, that Lida and I have parted."

"Yes, I heard about it . . ." Nina was not looking closely at the target.

"You blame me, of course?" said Feodor.

"Blame you? I don't really know yet what the trouble was . . . Maybe submerged rocks again?" Suddenly her voice shook. She fired, probably to hide her agitation, and slammed the bolt roughly.

"No, it wasn't submerged rocks," said Feodor. "You see, Sidorov was arrested."

Nina laid down her rifle in amazement. "So?"

"One must live, you know, Nina . . ."

Nina lowered her eyes and thought, holding her breath: "Let him, let him talk. Let him unburden himself to the end." But already she was trembling inside.

Feodor, however, was very anxious that she should understand: "Lida didn't understand; she was resentful. But you were always reasonable, you would have understood. There are things in this world stronger than us, and to bash your head against a wall is foolish . . ." Feodor placed his hand on hers. "This morning, back there, I realized how I long for you, Nina. If you had come to me, we could have talked as we used to . . . What's to hinder us now from restoring our former relations?"

Nina rose and looked him up and down: "One victim is too few for you?"

An officer came up to her and asked her why she hadn't used all her shells. Placing the shells in his glove, she said bitingly as she moved away: "It's a pity to waste them . . . on that target."

The officer shrugged his shoulders, not understanding her.

Returning to the base, Nina no longer noticed nature's magnificence and experienced no feeling except one of disgust, as if she had come in contact with something foul and slimy. Remembering her recent feel-

420

ings of grace and good will, she set her lips, thinking bitterly: "That's a good lesson for you, Nina—a very good lesson."

CHAPTER 5

TWO WEEKS had passed since Lida and her mother began working in the chemical plant. The plant was beyond the city limits and produced explosives. They lived over two miles from the plant, in barracks. By now Lida had become used to it, but at first she had been afraid to step over the threshold.

Accompanied by a petty clerk, a skinny man with greasy eyes who bore the grand title of Superintendent of the Branch of Communal Apartments, they had arrived at the barracks, slipping in the darkness on the garbage-strewn yard. In Lida's hand was one suitcase, all that they had been allowed to take from their former home. When the door opened, Lida involuntarily stepped back. A fusty, sharply sour, almost suffocating odor hit her. By the light of bare electric bulbs, fly-specked since summer, Lida saw a long corridor with dirty, peeling walls and a series of doors on each side, knocked together from rough, unpainted boards. Every now and then the doors opened and men, women, and children ran into the corridor, hurrying toward the far end. At the very threshold a boy—without pants and with a large, bulging stomach and thin little legs—was sitting on the warped floor which was covered with inches of dirt. He was pulling the tail of a silent, pitiful-looking cat, obviously used to torture. Other little children like him, and some older ones, were scattered along the corridor, crowded in groups near the stoves, crawling along the floor, crying.

The superintendent noticed Lida's panicky movement and couldn't restrain himself; he said spitefully: "This, of course, is not a director's villa; but one can live." He knew by their papers who they were, and their first fright gave him genuine satisfaction. Not without pride, as if he were showing the barracks to prominent visitors—but with the sole difference that now he wished to draw their attention to everything that was most unpleasant, ugly, and dirty—he conducted them to a room at the far left, in the women's half of the barracks. Without knocking he opened the door and, leering into Lida's face, gestured her to go in first. Several pairs of frightened eyes fixed themselves on the intruders. Lida was by now so stupefied by the terrific poverty, dirt, and

421

noise, that she did not at once make out the faces—she merely noticed that there were many of them.

The superintendent announced loudly: "New tenants for you—be kind and gracious to them! You, Musya," as he turned to a girl who had come out to meet them. "Give them two cots."

In reply a dissatisfied muttering sounded in the room; someone shouted from a corner: "As it is we're living like herring in a barrel! Where are you going to fit more in!"

"That's all right! Crowding won't spoil the harmony," the superintendent quieted them cheerfully.

When he went away Lida expected fearfully that reproaches would be heaped on them: angry words, even curses. But to her amazement the muttering stopped, the women crowded around them and began to ask questions without ceasing—where they came from, their names, where they had worked before; they spoke about themselves and gave them advice on how to live. Musya—a big girl with straw-colored hair, who turned out to be the senior in the room—was barely able to lead them away to their cots.

"You be careful with that super, he's woman crazy," she advised Lida. "Did you see how he looked you over? He won't leave our room —hangs around the girls."

Lida, listening to her words, noticed three men in the room. Musya caught her suspicious glance. "They're all right; they're family men. They live on the other side of the partition."

Four cots in various parts of the room were partitioned off with ragged blankets hung on strings.

Little by little Lida began to distinguish the faces. Mostly they were young, snub-nosed, with prominent cheek bones—clearly belonging to peasant girls. But on all, the traces of the heavy plant work were already apparent: they were pale, tired, their eyes lackluster. Lida noticed red blotches on their hands and faces, as if from a scald. She asked Musya what they were.

"That's from the acid—you'll find out yourself tomorrow."

Musya also took her and Natalia to the communal kitchen at the end of the corridor, where she explained in a businesslike way in what order they should use the oil stove, how much water they were allowed to take in the morning, what pots they could use, and for how many weeks a piece of soap should last—in fact, she initiated them into all the secrets. When there was nothing left to explain, Musya asked Lida: "Now, tell me frankly, who are you? I can see that you're not a worker."

422

Unwillingly Lida told her. She was afraid that they would be hostile toward the daughter of a director, even a past one.

But Musya was not even surprised. "That's all right. Don't worry. We have the daughter of an Academician. How she cried the first days—it was awful! And she was awkward, too. She accidentally burned her face with acid. Luckily she wasn't blinded."

Musya, with a nod of her head, indicated a girl sitting two cots over from them. The whole right side of her face was drawn together by an ugly red scar. Perhaps on that account the left side of her face appeared to Lida particularly beautiful. The girl raised her eyes and smiled at Lida.

Lida noticed that the cot next to hers was still empty. When they were all in bed and had put out the light Lida saw somebody come and undress quietly. By the light of the moon, and already half asleep, Lida saw the profile of the girl and it seemed surprisingly familiar to her. With this last impression she fell asleep.

Early in the morning someone wakened Lida. She opened her eyes and saw before her a young girl, thin as a rake, and not more than fourteen years old. She guessed at once that this was her neighbor. And she realized why her profile had seemed familiar—the girl looked like her. There was unchildlike fatigue on her face, dark rings under her eyes undispersed by sleep. Her eyelashes were long and thick, but her eyes weren't dark like Lida's—they were blue, and so sad and depressed that Lida's heart contracted. "Like a quiet little sister," she thought.

"Get up, get up, or you'll be late for work! You mustn't be late," the girl said, bending over her. "You arrived yesterday, but I came in late and missed you. My name is Tonya."

Lida got up and looked closely at her new acquaintance, and felt sure that they would become friends. Tonya was dressed very poorly. She wore an ugly dress, long ago cast off by someone, light summer shoes too big for her, tied with string to keep them on her feet, and on her head she wore an old woman's kerchief, the whole turning her into a pitiful scarecrow; but her face remained delicate and attractive.

They ate breakfast in the bedroom at a long table—rusks, and tea with saccharin; and they talked—hurrying to say as much as possible before the whistle blew. Lida and Natalia, as newcomers, were silent, listening.

"Yesterday the brigade foreman told me that he had received five clothing coupons. They should be distributed today," said Musya, sipping her tea. "I'd like to get a skirt—this one is as full of holes as a

423

sieve. But then there was a breakdown in my unit yesterday—now he won't give me a coupon."

"He'll distribute them all right! We know how," a girl called Lena put in with anger. "He'll give Pashka the best again—either a skirt length or a shawl."

"But Pashka's a shock worker," said Musya reasonably.

"We know what kind of a shock worker—flirts with the foreman, then he fulfills her plan for her on paper and doesn't list the breakdowns. She's the first shock worker—from the bottom!"

"Now you're just lying, Lena!" shouted another girl, and from her incensed face Lida guessed that this was Pashka herself. "I didn't work, eh? And who remained after work three weeks in succession? I! Who took Olga's place when she was sick? I! And nobody overlooks my breakdowns—the brigade foreman nags me more than anyone else."

A hubbub arose; they all made a din at once, the tea tumblers jarred angrily. Lida looked at Tonya. She was sitting on her cot, with her tumbler, unnoticed, silent. When she had finished her tea she came to the table on tip toe, poured some tea quietly and, again on tip toe, went to her own place. "Why is she so frightened?" thought Lida with a sudden pang.

"No, I must say that Pashka works well," said Musya in the meantime. Her words evidently had weight. "Why, last quarter she received felt boots as a premium . . ."

"Through pull," Lena interrupted. "It wasn't for nothing that she slept with the Party organizer."

Pashka, upsetting her tea, reached out to pull Lena's hair, but at that moment the whistle sounded. They all jumped up from their places and ran outside. Lida walked with Tonya. The latter ran along in the snow, shivering and hopping. She had only her thin shoes on her feet, without galoshes.

"Why don't they give you felt boots?" asked Lida.

"That's all right, they'll give me some," replied Tonya, her whole body shaking. "Today they're going to distribute coupons and I heard that there are some boots, so they'll give me a pair. I made out an application away back in the fall. The brigade foreman promised me then . . ."

At the plant Lida was really frightened. They made out her pass, handed her a suit of overalls, already burned in a dozen places, put a paper helmet on her head to keep her hair in, and rubber boots on her feet. Then she went out into the shop and for the first few minutes she nearly fainted. The acid vapor hung in a pungent haze throughout the

424

shop—people ten paces away were barely visible. The acid, it seemed, was everywhere: it squished under foot, where it was sprinkled with lime for neutralization; it dripped from weird towers, pipes, valves, and almost from the walls. The compressors with their tremendous fly-wheels, the towers, and the overhanging bridge—all were lost in the poisonous haze.

The brigade foreman came to Lida at once—a stocky man of about forty with a pale, bloated face, splashed with lime. He saw Lida sway and put her hand to her forehead, then sit down on a barrel.

"It's all right. You'll get used to it," he encouraged her. "It's not so bad here—in the fifth shop it's worse. . . . I was told that you are Sidorov's daughter; is that true?"

"Yes."

"I knew him . . . Well, I'll give you lighter work at first to get you used to it. Stand over there and watch this pressure gauge: see that the needle doesn't go up to 30. If it does, just open this valve. That's all. I'll tell you later what it's all about. In the meantime understand this: If you slip up, there'll be an accident, and here punishment for accidents is very severe—you'll make the acquaintance of the prosecutor. . . . I used to know your father," he repeated for some reason and, patting her shoulder, he went over to Natalia, who was waiting for him, her face pale and frightened. Her imposing carriage and pompousness had left her long ago.

The time until lunch seemed to Lida everlasting; and the work, which she at first thought was very easy, became more and more of a trial with each succeeding hour. Her head ached; her whole body was sore. The brigade foreman came to her several times, encouraged her, and even brought her a sort of wooden shield and placed it at her feet.

"Stand on this—the acid here is strong; it even eats through rubber overshoes, against all rules," he said. "If you feel like fainting, try to fall on the shield, or the acid will spoil your face. It has happened to one already."

Lida thanked the brigade foreman and noted that at least he was well disposed towards her, possibly from respect for her father.

CHAPTER 6

SO BEGAN a new life for Lida. During the first day her thoughts about her own fate, about Feodor and her father, were heavy but disconnected. When she felt like crying she looked at the other people around her, with their own sorrows and cares, and restrained herself.

She and her mother came home tired that day, ahead of all the others, who remained for the distribution of the clothing coupons. Soon they began to come—most of them wearing a dissatisfied look. Then a noise was heard in the corridor and a group of women workers came into the room with Musya at their head—they were practically carrying Tonya. She was crying, covered her face with her hands. In the room she fell on the bed, sobbing, her small shoulders shuddering.

Alarmed, Lida asked what was the matter.

"The brigade foreman didn't give Tonya boots, and she needs them more than anyone." Musya handed Lida a paper. "This is Tonya's coupon! Just look!"

On the paper, with three signatures and a large seal, was written: "Child's kerchief—one."

Lida couldn't understand what all this meant. The brigade foreman seemed to her to be reasonable; how could he permit such foolishness, smacking of insult? She decided to talk to him the following day.

But the next day he surprised her still more. He listened to her unwillingly, embarrassed, then said: "Tonya Polenov has too many accidents. We have shock workers for whom there aren't enough coupons."

"But she may catch cold, even die!"

The brigade foreman waved his hand fretfully. "That's not your business. Don't butt in with your advice. You'd better get to work," and, muttering something under his breath, he went away.

Lida was stunned. From yesterday's talk among the girls she gathered that Tonya was one of the best workers, very accurate, never late for work; even in the fiercest cold she arrived in her light shoes on time. The main thing was that she had no accidents; they said so yesterday. What was the matter then?

After the first week Lida was able to size up her surroundings better. She saw what held this seemingly unbearable works together, what forces moved the people. They had many bosses in the shop—the chief engineer, three shift bosses, the Party shop organizer, the youth organizer—but the immediate boss was the brigade foreman, and a lot depended on him. Although he remained kind to Lida, she did not trust him for she saw how often the girls cried at night because of his unreasonable demands and his nagging—he knew how to punish them quietly but painfully.

426

It seemed to Lida that the plant was in a continual fever, in a perpetual state of emergency, like an assault in war. From the people, as well as from the machines, the impossible was demanded. Nearly every day, during the lunch hour or after work, meetings were held; the Party organizers spoke, the engineers spoke, and one word was repeated more than any other—"accidents." Every day big and small accidents broke down the plan, threw back the fulfillment of the norm, and drove the managers almost to a state of frenzy.

The plant was apparently in a special category with the leadership of the Provincial Party—important officials came often, while in the administration building a state prosecutor was always present, with the widest powers, including the sentencing of people to the firing squad.

Actually, only one thing was needed: capital repairs. All the machinery and equipment was terribly worn, not so much from age as from overloading. While sick and dead people were replaced with fresh ones, the machines remained the same. It would be necessary to stop the whole assemblage for capital repairs. This would put off temporarily the fulfillment of the plan, and the Government authorities didn't want to agree to it. Instead they made the workers work under unbearable conditions, driving them with threats, with Party speeches, with impossible norms and laughable "bonuses." Repairs were done on the run. Every day something was feverishly soldered, welded, patched in Lida's shop. They even decided to carry out capital repairs without interrupting production—the work of the systems being repaired was added to that of the others so that the general output of the shop would not be lowered. Then the shop became a hell: freed hot acid threw itself at the workers with revengeful fury, caught their breath, bit their eyes, burnt their fingers as if tearing the flesh off their bones. Their clothing and hair smoked.

The fifth shop, the so-called nitrogen shop about which the brigade foreman had told her, became famous as a graveyard. People tried to avoid going near it—a cloud of acrid smoke hung like a curse over this wing, and people came out of there, if they were not carried out, looking like corpses. The prosecutor was afraid to go into that shop, even for a minute, to conduct his investigations—and that was probably the only advantage it had over the others.

Even so the people working in this cursed place were called lazy, shirkers, and saboteurs at meetings. The Secretary of the Party Committee—a great lover of fresh air—used to shout at the meetings: "Labor discipline is dropping impermissibly! There is one accident after another! In Petrov's air compressor the pressure dropped to the danger point. Setting of the critical mixture took place. But that wasn't enough: after criminal neglect he uncharged the cold mixture, thereby stopping his aggregate for a whole hour. For that kind of trick, Comrade Petrov, the prosecutor won't pat your head." Petrov turned as pale as a sheet. "Crane operator Vanin fell asleep at her crane." Lida and all those present knew that Vanin had fainted—it was particularly stifling where she worked. "Tool operator Musya Lobov burned out a bearing and she put a compressor out of action."

That was how they blamed the workers, as if they were the criminals, not those who drove them. Lida felt this unceasing, stubborn pressure on her the whole time, every minute.

"Yes, our bosses never overlook anything. They know how to get their own out of a person, without discount," Musya said to her once bitterly.

Lida was still quite unable to stand the barracks although, to her surprise, Natalia became acclimatized to the conditions. She was already arguing in the kitchen over pots and oil stoves like the other women, and her voice was beginning to be more and more influential there.

Lida became very friendly with Tonya. Although the girl was not talkative, Lida learned that she was an orphan, that her parents had died of starvation in the Ukraine. She landed in Rostov by traveling illegally, under the seat of a railroad car. But she was caught at the station and, as she had no documents, she was mobilized for work in this terrible plant.

After the incident with the coupon, Tonya became more silent and often cried at night. Hearing her sobs, Lida was unable to control herself and also cried quietly—life seemed to have come to an end. Nevertheless, she forced herself to believe that all this was temporary, that Feodor would take her from here and they would again live together as before. Indeed, he had promised her this.

Natalia, on the other hand, couldn't speak of Feodor without hatred. What angered her was not that he had left her daughter—that, actually, she could understand. It was the crude way in which he did it, without any apparent emotion. Worse, he was making no attempt to see Lida secretly and help her; this was plain treachery. If Feodor had previously been her ideal, he had now become her worst enemy and all the curses she could think of she heaped on his head. Thus the days passed—in hard work, in fear for oneself, in feverish thoughts about one's future.

The brigade foreman was always polite to Lida in spite of her talk about Tonya. But once . . .

Once Lida was working on the night shift. Passing by the tool room, she heard a strange smothered cry, as if someone were sobbing. Lida opened the door and to her surprise saw Tonya sitting on the foreman's knee. He was covering her mouth with his hand and only her distended eyes, filled with tears and fright, were visible on her face. Tonya's skirt was pulled up and her white, quite undeveloped legs were pitifully pressed together.

The brigade foreman, flushed, with excited eyes, stared at Lida. Something strange happened to her. Without thinking, she ran up and silently slapped him in the face with all her strength. Tonya slipped to the floor and, covering her face with her hands, sobbed.

The foreman didn't run away. Only, while adjusting his clothes, he said to Lida in a dull voice: "If you say anything, you'll be sorry," and added, as he was going out: "There is little faith in the daughter of an enemy of the people. Remember that."

CHAPTER 7

THE FOREMAN'S words, uttered with biting contempt, reminded Lida with sudden acuteness of her real position. Yes, she had become an outlaw. She was unable to defend even herself, let alone someone else. She did not tell the authorities what had happened. Everybody in the barracks advised her not to.

"Nothing will happen to him in any case. You'll only ruin yourself," Musya told her.

The foreman changed at once. He became furtively hostile, nagging. Lida was afraid that he would frame up an opportunity for revenge, but so far nothing had happened.

Tonya now behaved very strangely. Sometimes, for no reason at all, she suddenly started to laugh weirdly, then as suddenly became silent.

On nearly every free day at the plant extra work, so-called "volunteer effort," was organized. On one of these days, when Lida returned from the plant to the barracks, she heard a familiar voice calling her. Lida turned around and her heart jumped: Nikolai was running toward her. Shrinking, Lida hurried her pace. But Nikolai caught up with her.

"What's the matter with you, Lida? Why are you hiding? Why didn't you leave an address?"

Lida was silent, hanging her head.

"I've been looking all over the place for you. Only found you by chance. Where are you going now?" he asked, looking her over steadily.

"Where else—but home . . ."

Nikolai kicked a chunk of snow with his foot. "Lida, believe me, I sympathize with you, very much . . . But this hiding from your friends the way you're doing—that's not nice."

Lida looked at him, was going to say something, but kept silent. Nikolai saw tears in her eyes. Her face looked to him terribly tired and pale. "It's hard on her," he thought with bitterness.

Lida, holding her breath, waited for him to say something about Feodor. Perhaps his brother had sent him specially. But Nikolai was silent. At the barracks Lida stopped hesitantly.

"Nikolai, you'd better not go in. They'll see you—it's dangerous to be with me. I'm like a contaminated person."

Nikolai looked at her reproachfully and, without saying a word, took her arm and went to the barracks door with her.

It was as if Lida was seeing the barrack room for the first time—never had it looked to her so squalid and loathsome. On the wooden table, leaning crookedly, the unwashed dishes lay scattered; at the very edge of the table a bowl yawned, overturned on its side, its maw showing some liquid inside, perhaps jelly or just slops. The beds were made of three boards, with their patched blankets and greasy pillow cases gray, almost black. Trunks, baskets, and bundles of clothes stuck out from under the beds. On a string in the middle of the room, almost above the table, somebody's ragged underpants were spread out shamelessly.

Natalia was very surprised to see Nikolai. Also on guard at first, she asked in an unfriendly voice: "Now, I expect you'll forget the way to us?"

"No, Mother, I won't forget."

Natalia shook her head. "You and Feodor are brothers, but different . . . I don't understand it."

That was the first time Feodor's name had been mentioned. Lida looked at Nikolai inquiringly, almost fearfully.

"You mean that Feodor hasn't come to see you?"

Lida barely whispered: "No. But he promised to come . . . He'll come."

Nikolai was silent. He had seen his brother and he hadn't seemed to be getting ready to do anything.

430

Excusing themselves, Natalia and Lida left the room. Nikolai realized that they wanted to prepare a lunch. He did not stop them, knowing that they wouldn't listen in any case. He sat down, crossed his legs, smoked, and looked intently through the dusty window, behind which a bare tree was swaying. All around was squalor, poverty, and fearfulness. Nikolai had not been in the plant, but he felt that it must be still worse there.

"Oh, Feodor! Feodor! What have you done?" he repeated to himself, and anger against his brother rose in him with new force.

Lida returned, bringing with her a bottle of vodka she had dug up somewhere.

"There was no need for that," he reproached her. "It costs money . . ."

From the kitchen Natalia brought a black frying pan with fried potatoes and dried fish, and the tea pot. "It's not sumptuous, but it's the best we have," she said and, wiping a corner of the table, laid out the food. Then she poured Nikolai and herself a glass of vodka.

"Pour Lida some too," said Nikolai. "This is a holiday."

But Lida took away the tumbler.

"I . . . you see . . . I have . . ." She was confused, but her embarrassed appearance and sudden blush explained everything more clearly than any words.

Nikolai drank his glass with emotion, his face gloomy. "Soon?"

"Not yet—about six months."

Nikolai jumped up, clenched his fist, and beat it into his left palm. "We've got to get you out of here at any cost," he said through his teeth, and beat his palm again, as if he were crushing something.

"It's no use talking about that," Lida objected sadly. "How on earth can you help? . . . Impossible!" But she could not look at Nikolai's face without a tremor. It was very dear to her now, almost like her own kin. And his excitement scorched her like heat. Here was a friend who thought of her, worried about her. So she was not completely alone!

Nikolai placed his broad hand over Lida's. "Lida, don't worry—all this will pass . . ."

Then she leaned towards him, as to a protector. "Nikolai, I'll tell you about Feodor. You ought to know."

When she had finished, her head was bowed and she was nearly crying, biting her lips. Nikolai was silent. Then, very seriously he said: "I'll have a talk with Feodor. Yes!"

431

The talk took place the following day.

"I was at Lida's yesterday."

Feodor raised his right eyebrow, looked at Nikolai expectantly, even threateningly. "So . . ."

"The rest is up to you."

Feodor was silent for a minute, then asked: "Where is she?"

"At the chemical plant." And noticing the sudden tremor on his brother's face, Nikolai added: "There, as you know, a year or at most two is all they can live." Saying these words, he tried to fix Feodor's eyes with his own, but couldn't. "Since when have his eyes become so shifty?" he thought.

"What do you want me to do?" asked Feodor, having taken hold of himself and made his voice purposely harsh. "As you know, we have separated."

"I'm going to save her from certain death, while you, it seems, want to kill her."

Feodor knit his brows. "Why such terrifying words? Nobody wants to kill anyone. She is living her own life, and I mine. We don't interfere with each other."

"Yes, everything is lovely!" Nikolai remarked sarcastically. "Only, your eyes are shifty for some reason or other." Nikolai kept his temper with difficulty. Feeling aversion for his brother, indignant at his heartlessness, and unable to pierce his case-hardened armor, he rose to leave. "But you promised to help her. Surely you can keep your word!"

"I promised? I promised nothing!" said Feodor, pretending surprise. Then he added: "Look, Nikolai, before it's too late, listen to my advice—don't visit Lida."

"Keep your advice to yourself! I don't need it."

"Independent, eh?" Feodor jeered. "So you've become brave? You've forgotten your pleasant visit to Durov?"

"I was there. But you weren't, and you're afraid . . ."

"Don't deceive yourself. You were lucky once—you won't be a second time."

"You're afraid that I'll compromise you?" asked Nikolai. "Maybe I should announce that you're not my brother. Would you like that?"

Feodor compressed his lips. "Get out of here!" he said ominously.

"Have you sealed your conscience, eh?"

"Out!"

Nikolai stopped at the door and said evenly: "I'm afraid we'll have to meet again some time on a narrow path, Feodor . . . dear brother!" and he slammed the door violently.

432

CHAPTER 8

DOCTOR TSIBIK'S face showed despair and disappointment. Yes, his work was thankless, his efforts not appreciated, his advice not listened to.

"Understand, Mikhail Alexeyevich, an impossible situation has arisen. Pavel absolutely refuses to obey me, he won't take medicine, he won't follow a regimen. In fact—he does everything opposite to what I tell him. It can't go on like that. I would have given up long ago and left only, you understand, I'm sorry for him. Why! He'll kill himself!"

Mikhail shook his head sorrowfully and looked at Nina almost with entreaty. She was sitting at the piano fingering the keys softly, apparently not listening to what the doctor was saying.

"Nina, maybe you would talk to Pavel," Mikhail said to her. "You're probably the only person Pavel listens to."

Continuing to pick at the keys, and without raising her eyes, Nina said: "Papa, if you want to know my opinion, it's better to leave Pavel in peace. Since he returned from the Crimea he has changed for the better. The Crimea had a definite improving effect on him—excepting, of course, that he nearly drowned there," and Nina shot an annihilating glance at the doctor.

"Of course Nina believes I tried to drown Pavel," scoffed the doctor nervously.

"Stop! Please stop quarreling!" said Mikhail angrily. "Nina, don't talk foolishness. No, this continual state of sickness must be ended. After all, we must cure him with our combined efforts. And here he is—talk of angels and they flap their wings."

Pavel came into the sitting room. He was wearing high felt boots, half covered in snow, a blue windbreaker, and a squirrel cap with ear flaps. His longish face, reddened from the frost, was smiling.

"I was helping the lads to clear the snow from the road—what a pleasure! That beats all your medicines, Doctor," said Pavel; and, placing his mittens on the radiator, he asked Nina: "Will there be a ski run today or not?"

"Of course there will," she responded eagerly, and, unable to restrain herself, she looked triumphantly at her father: "You see, I told you so."

433

"It looks as if she is right," Mikhail thought. "Better leave him in peace. Although the doctor probably knows best."

The doctor turned to the window and pressed his lips together in resentment. His whole appearance said, as it were: "All right, rejoice. You'll see for yourselves soon."

Pavel took off his windbreaker and cap, threw them on the parquet floor, and sank with a loud sigh into an armchair.

"How tired I am, though. Not used to it, probably."

He looked around the room with cheerful eyes, but noticing the inquiring looks, frowned. "Well, why are you so quiet? . . . What do you think, Father, shouldn't we have a drink before the ski run?" and he winked at him.

Mikhail couldn't help smiling—his son's appearance pleased him. But the doctor, turning quickly from the window, said spitefully: "That's it, that's it—drink! You know nothing else. You'll kill yourself, Pavel."

"Ah! Quit grumbling!" Pavel waved him aside. "You'll die sooner than I. Bring out the bottle, I say. And Nina will have a drink with us. Won't you, Nina? A little won't do any harm."

Mikhail knit his brows. "I wanted to talk to you about that, Pavel. You've got to stop it."

"To stop what?"

"Oh, you understand me perfectly. You've got to stop drinking."

Pavel shrugged his shoulders. "What harm is there in drinking a glass before going to ski? And further, I don't like guardianship."

"Don't get angry. We're talking sense to you. You may be all right now, but if you slip . . ."

"When I slip it'll be time enough to get excited."

"It may be too late then," the doctor remarked gloomily.

"You're lying, Doctor. I'm not sick. I was sick, yes, but not from vodka, you know why yourself. But now, everything has passed. I have decided to strike out the past. Yes, it has passed!" said Pavel, noticing the doubting look of his father. "I'm going to work, as a translator or something, and forget everything completely."

"It's high time!" exclaimed Mikhail. "I thought myself of offering you some work—you know two languages perfectly. You could do literary translation very well."

"Right, right! . . . And as for you, Doctor, don't come near me when there's no need. If I get sick, then you can cure me. But just for spite, I'm not going to get sick," he scoffed.

"I will only be happy over that," remarked the doctor, but his whole

434

appearance showed clearly that he didn't believe one word of Pavel's.

Mikhail looked doubtfully first at Pavel, then at the doctor—and didn't know whose side to take. Pavel seemed to be right—but the doctor appeared to be really worried.

"All right, we'll wait and see. Indeed, maybe it's not worth worrying about," he thought.

Pavel rose in the meantime, and going up to the doctor, slapped his shoulder: "If you pester me once more with medicine—I'll throw you into the snow. So help me God, I will!" and he added, with a laugh: "All right, let's have a drink, Doctor Killjoy!"

CHAPTER 9

THAT WINTER was dry, and the snow unusually deep, something rare in Rostov. Mikhail, as if he were afraid of being alone, surrounded himself with company, the noisier the better. The Gorin house was always full of people. Lights shone in its large windows until late at night. If any famous artist was passing through Rostov, Mikhail at once invited him to visit and would hold a dinner in his honor. Of the local people, besides the old acquaintances like Glushak, one of the new and frequent guests was Shcherbakov. Talk about his interest in Nina was quite open now. The servants in the Gorin house, accustomed to decorous, almost monastic quietness, were tremendously pleased with the change. The holiday bustle, the possibility of drinking with impunity, of gossiping, and particularly of stealing food—all these raised their spirits and filled them with unusual forethought and attention. Holding up their heads like high-spirited colts, they rushed about the house. The local authorities also found Gorin's open house handy. When they were unable to think up some way of spending government money on a banquet, they simply went to see Gorin—his food and wine left nothing to be desired. Besides, one could often see famous persons from Moscow at the Gorins' table, and arrange one's career along with the drinks.

The fine winter favored the people. All kinds of entertainments were arranged; sleigh rides on the river—purposely in Russian style, with troika and bells, as well as rabbit shooting, fox hunting, ski excursions.

Enjoying it himself, and trying to stifle an unpleasant feeling which had sprung up in him since the appearance of the play, Mikhail found pleasure in entertaining. Besides that, he noticed with satisfaction

435

that Pavel was drawn into this holiday boisterousness and was less thoughtful. Mikhail was afraid only that the drinking, unavoidable in that manner of life, might awaken in Pavel the slumbering devil.

Mikhail noticed, of course, that Feodor Novikov did not visit him. However, he was rather glad of this. Feodor reminded him of his sore spot—his play—and at present this was an unpleasant thought.

For Doctor Tsibik this unexpected liveliness was torture: in the gay, often drunken, company he had to play the part of a fool, to laugh, to make jokes, while inside he was trembling with fear and terrifying forebodings. He himself saw quite well that Pavel was getting better and that his sickness—whatever it was—had apparently vanished. Two or three times Veria had come to dinner at Gorin's. Once, during a noisy dance, he cornered the doctor unobserved. Smiling brightly— from the side it looked as if they were merely exchanging empty phrases—he said between his teeth: "I see your patient has improved. . . . I congratulate you!" The doctor was going to answer, to explain, to justify himself, but Veria had already gone to another guest, wearing a gay smile. Only behind the pince-nez the doctor caught a terrible glint. There was no mercy there.

That evening the doctor spent a couple of hours in the lavatory— he sat there, his teeth rattling as with a fever, afraid to appear in the drawing room. He realized that he was on the brink of destruction and to save himself he must at all costs kill Pavel. Like a story-book murderer he began to watch for an opportunity, and was naïvely surprised by the ways he was able to hide his tense condition, and by what terrible and ruthless thoughts came into his head. He was surprised, but he was also afraid for himself. This fear came to him at night—it seemed to him that then he lost the feeling of reality, that he was falling gradually into a world created by himself, where oft-recurring thoughts of abnormal deeds—killing, poisoning, doctoring to death—were becoming too common and habitual. At one time the doctor had dabbled in psychopathology and he knew the danger of such an abnormal mental condition.

During the day another thing frightened him—the impossibility of fulfilling his terrible role. In the first place Cheprok was in his way. He literally walked on the heels of the doctor, not hiding his suspicion, intercepting his glances, trying not to leave Pavel alone under any circumstances.

Nina was also suspicious of the doctor, although her suspicion was not dangerous—she merely didn't believe in his medical efficiency. As for Pavel, the doctor felt that he had become cool toward him, and less frank than formerly. He explained this change by the fact that Pavel was drinking less. But there was also the possibility that after the incident with the boat in the Crimea, he instinctively shunned him. Everything put together could at any moment result in Mikhail Gorin—wishing to avoid unpleasantness—asking him politely to leave his house. For the doctor this would mean falling into the fearsome embraces of Veria. He understood clearly that there was little time left and every minute threatened him with disaster.

The opportunity for which he had been waiting impatiently occurred at the beginning of February. One day a noisy company, including Shcherbakov, went on a rabbit hunt. In the evening, after a successful hunt, they stopped for the night with the chairman of a sovkhoz. The chairman had roused the entire sovkhoz and arranged a real celebration. The guests had brought their own liquor. To decline refreshment was impossible, and nobody thought of refusing.

A noisy dinner dragged on late into the night. The doctor watched Pavel. Neither Cheprok nor Nina was with them. The entire company was composed of men. Pavel was happily drunk, talked a great deal with Shcherbakov.

When they went to bed Pavel was placed in the same room with the doctor. With foresight the doctor had whispered to the chairman of the sovkhoz that it was his duty to be with Pavel.

Pavel fell asleep at once. It was a frosty night and the moon was shining brightly—the doctor could see Pavel's face clearly. He was lying on his back, his arms thrown wide. Convinced that Pavel was sound asleep, he went over to the window and cautiously opened it. Then he pulled the blanket off Pavel. When Pavel began to turn in his sleep and shiver, he closed the window and covered him with the blanket, then Pavel quieted down. The doctor repeated this three or four times during the night. In the morning Pavel was unable to get out of bed—he was shivering as from ague. Sick as he was, he was taken home to the estate. Mikhail didn't attach any special importance to it. Like everyone else, he thought that Pavel had caught cold at the hunt. He remembered that he had been lightly clad.

But the doctor was exultant. Now Pavel needed his care—now his life was, indeed, in his hands.

But a difficulty arose at once. Cheprok began to sit beside the sick Pavel, leaving the room only when Nina or Mikhail relieved him. He asked Mikhail insistently to call another doctor, but the latter refused. "This is a simple cold—it will pass. Doctor Tsibik isn't any worse than others."

Cheprok remained on duty at night. The first night the doctor waited for Cheprok to become exhausted and fall asleep. At last the moment came. He walked on tiptoe to Pavel's room, in pajamas and bare feet. This also was part of his plan. The doctor, opening the door, looked in—Cheprok was asleep, had dropped his head on his chest. Pavel tossed on the bed, only half conscious. The doctor went up to him quietly and took hold of his hand. It was perspiring. The customary treatment flashed through the doctor's mind. He sneered at this professional atavism. "Now you are not a doctor, but a murderer." With a quick movement he stuck a hypodermic needle into Pavel's arm and pressed it, then withdrew it. Now he had to get out of the room as quickly as possible. But some force or other made him stop at the door and wait. He had to wait less than a minute. The doctor knew what should happen, but what actually happened was worse than all his conjectures. Pavel raised himself on the bed as if some burst spring had stuck him in the back, and sat like that for a second looking straight ahead. His eyes were wide open and staring at the doctor, but he could tell that Pavel saw nothing—it was as if he were looking into himself. Suddenly a terrible animal howl sounded in the room, filling it completely, and like a wave, overwhelmed the house.

Pavel's mouth twisted, he fell on the pillow, beat his head on it and howled—this howl did not stop for a second, but seemed to get louder and more horrible. Pavel's eyes were rolled back, showing the whites, and froth issued from his twisted, howling mouth. Cheprok jumped up, threw himself at Pavel, not noticing the doctor. Doors banged, people were running to them. The doctor, biting his fingers, wanted to scream, to run away, to cover his head, but stood stunned, trembling—only at the last moment had he sense enough to hide the needle in the sleeve of his jacket.

The first to arrive was Mikhail.

"What—what's the matter?" he asked, and his frightened face showed his extreme excitement.

"I don't know yet," answered the doctor. "I've only just run up."

He went to Pavel and touched him cautiously. "Most likely it's delirium—nervous upset . . ." he said something else, apparently in Latin, he didn't quite remember.

From that moment the doctor again became a doctor. He did everything he could to ease Pavel's pain. Toward morning Pavel calmed down. He lay in a coma until midday—then he came to himself. He remembered nothing that had happened to him, only complained of a dull pain in his head.

438

Thus began a double life for the doctor, and torture for Pavel. The doctor treated and watched over Pavel in order to inject the painful drug into him at every opportunity. Each new seizure was more terrible and more prolonged. Between them Pavel improved, even got up from his bed, walked—but the doctor now knew that his days were numbered. It only remained to deliver the final blow.

CHAPTER 10

A STRANGE feeling took hold of the doctor and kept him from inflicting his final blow. He suddenly felt drawn to Pavel and that Pavel was necessary to him *alive*. This was not from twinges of his conscience—no, the doctor knew that with his whole being. It wasn't even compassion—he watched the disintegration of Pavel's body with indifference. It was something else. This drunkard, this live corpse, suddenly became infinitely dear to his heart. It seemed to him that he had entered into a secret alliance with him, and this bond with him gave him an astounding power. But mainly, he felt he could learn something from Pavel, something very important, that was hidden from him. The doctor felt this attraction most keenly after the second injection. That time he tried to bring Pavel back to consciousness with special zeal, feeling sure that Pavel would disclose his secret to him. The second day after the seizure their first conversation took place, the beginning of a whole series of talks. The three of them—Pavel, Cheprok and the doctor—were sitting together, drinking.

Pavel was still weak. On seeing the doctor he tried to get up, but fell. He vomited. The doctor cleaned up after him diligently, put him to bed again, wiped his face.

"What is hurting you, Pavel?" he asked him with emotion. Cheprok, helping the doctor, recognized genuine pain in his voice, was unable at that moment not to trust him.

When everything was cleaned up and Pavel himself, pushing aside the doctor's help, lit a cigarette, the doctor and Cheprok sat down and took a good look at the patient. Lying on his back, with one hand behind his head, Pavel was looking at the ceiling through whiffs of smoke. From somewhere or other a bottle appeared in the doctor's hands. Hesitantly, almost guiltily, he looked at Cheprok and opened it. The doctor was now practically unrecognizable: there was absolutely no insolence in him, nor the former jauntiness; even the gold teeth in

439

his mouth seemed to have dulled. Very quietly, he poured a glass for Cheprok first, then for himself. Without taking his eyes from the ceiling, Pavel asked for a glass. The doctor fidgeted:

"You can't have one—you're still quite sick."

"Pour one out, I tell you," ordered Pavel curtly.

The doctor looked questioningly at Cheprok, the latter shook his head negatively. But the doctor wanted very much to hear Pavel talk, and nothing would loosen his tongue better than vodka. He poured him a glass.

Pavel was the first to begin to talk; he spoke to Cheprok. The doctor understood this, they had a common past.

"Do you remember, Cheprok, that fisherman on Capri? I forget his name. He used to dance so well?"

"Gigotto?"

"Yes, I think that's the one. What do you think, is he alive now?"

"I don't think so. He liked to fight with a knife; people with a passion for that don't live long."

"It's a pity," said Pavel. Every now and then, wiping his face with his hand as if he were pulling off a cobweb, he drank with short gulps, two, three, drowning his sorrow. The glass in his shaking hands rattled softly against his teeth. "I had a dream, I remembered how a little girl drowned in the sea. Do you remember that?"

Cheprok shook his head. "You have no children of your own, so you pity other people's," he said wistfully.

"No, it's not that. Such happenings usually remain in my mind sharply. Another's sorrow affects me more strongly than my own. I shut my eyes and it seems to me that I hear human wails—millions of people crying, damning the moment of their conception. I'm ashamed for the human being: he has been living a long time, but he hasn't learned how to live. One man mastered the great art of making fire, to warm himself, to cook his food, to light his way; another roasted the soles of his feet with that fire. Since then it hasn't ceased to smell of singed human flesh. One man thought up an axe, so that he could cut down trees and build himself a house or a boat—another, with a triumphant snarl, split his head open with that axe. And that's how it goes. Why is it that from the very beginning people follow the path of violence and evil, and not the path of brotherly love?"

Cheprok, not used to abstract talk, merely snorted. But the doctor, anticipating an objection, said roughly: "The struggle for existence, that's why!"

"No, you can't explain it by that alone. The animals have that, but they are without reason. Man, on the other hand, after attaining the sunny heights, should be able, it seems, to contemplate the truth—that it is better to live in friendship." Pavel was silent for a minute, wrinkled his forehead, fearing that his skull would not stand the bursting pain.

"I'm especially sorry for children. Why should they suffer? For instance, one man thought up collectivization. In the name of some theory, which has not yet been proved, millions of bushels of grain are sold abroad to pay for a dam. Starving's a terrible sight—but the most terrible of all is to see it in the children! Each one of these Russian children is imprinted on my brain to the least detail; dead of hunger, each one of these little corpses, paving the way for the diabolical idea of collectivization. They haunt me night and day. When my father and I were passing through Kharkov, a boy of about seven ran up to the window of our car—the authorities apparently were not too efficient there, and he had slipped through the guard. He stretched out his hands, thin as reeds, and asked for bread. My father turned from the window and began to talk about the Dnieper Hydroelectric Station. I, on the other hand, could think of nothing but this child who was old enough to ask us: 'Why am I suffering?' Not with thousands of Dnieper Dams can the icy horror in his eyes be justified."

"You're a sponge," said Cheprok. "You soak up all the national grief like a sponge, and you're as helpless as a sponge. Squeeze you and only tears come out. . . . That's bad."

"I can't do otherwise."

"Andrei Demin was different," said Cheprok, and suddenly exclaimed, "Too bad! If only we had more like him!"

Pavel's face lit up. "I understand what you mean. Now I understand —yes. But when he was in our house, he seemed to me like a simpleton."

"That kind are always simple," replied Cheprok grimly.

The doctor couldn't restrain himself and objected: "Your Andrei was just foolish. Without any reason he went away from a house where he was warm, well fed, and secure. He left and perished— and that's all. What is there so special about that?" The doctor was extra fidgety. Cheprok asked him, surprised: "Why are you so fretful— as if you needed to go to the toilet? Or else your corn hurts?"

Pavel, however, twisting his lips in contempt, replied to the doctor: "Yes, at first sight it looks as if he had been foolish—he went away from a warm place, he even left his mother, broke her heart . . ."

"And how he loved her!" Cheprok interrupted. "I saw it."

"But when you think it over well, you'll see that without just such foolish deeds there is no way out for Russia—a blind alley," Pavel continued. At that moment he was very sorry that he had not had a proper talk with Andrei. "Yes, I remember, there were no tears in his eyes, as in mine. His look was dry, burning; great rage had accumulated in him. He said little, but when the time came he did what every Russian should do. Multiply his action a million times and there would be a free Russia. That is who Russia is waiting for: men like Andrei must be born among us, with dry eyes, but full of an avenging will!"

Pavel's words became more furious with each swallow of the spirits. His lips, cracked from the fever, formed the words painfully.

Cheprok, with sudden emotion, placed his hand on the young man's shoulder: "Pavel, my friend, at such moments you are more dear to me than anything else on earth," he said with heat. "Only believe such people will yet be born—you'll see."

"You and I, however, won't see it," said Pavel sadly, and added: "Recalling Andrei makes me particularly ashamed of myself, of my helplessness. I suffer from inaction. Andrei seemed inconspicuous, but now I see the clarity of his soul and look, directed toward the future . . . He was an eagle. As for us, we sit and wait for help from other nations. But Andrei didn't wait; he himself began . . ."

Although the doctor feared such conversations, he had become used to them. It was something else that was bothering him now. He was waiting for Pavel to talk about that most important thing, for the sake of which he had so far preserved his life. For some unknown reason he was sure that sooner or later Pavel would approach the heart of the matter.

". . . for us, a lying caress is warmer than the truth," said Pavel. "We are the slaves of our bodies and the people in power take advantage of that."

To this, Cheprok answered: "I used to know a book-learned man. He was in jail with me in Odessa, for theft. He told me something about that—the flesh and the spirit, that is—and explained it very interestingly."

"A book-learned man! In jail for theft!" sneered the doctor. He was angry because Cheprok was dragging out his conversation. But Pavel asked Cheprok with interest: "What did that book-learned man say to you?"

"It was a story he told me, something like a fairy tale. I didn't understand it all; but that learned man really expressed himself cleverly. I'll tell it as well as I can."

442

CHAPTER 11

"ONCE UPON A TIME there lived a great, great scientist, and he wanted to learn the meaning of life. He read many books, but didn't find the answer. He learned everything, even such secrets which, without knowing the first, you can't learn the second, and that a woman can be hotter than a burning log in a stove . . ."

"What a scientist!" exclaimed Pavel gaily. "All right, go on!"

"And so, after this the scientist decided, in spite of all his degrees, to ask the common people how he could learn the meaning of life. And of course he was put on the right path at once. The people told him that in a certain forest there lived a little old man who knew *everything*. Fine! The scientist found the little old man in a glade flooded in sunshine, adorned with flowers; all manner of blessings abounded. The little old man was thin, with a white beard to his navel, sitting and smiling, his little hands folded on his belly. He seemed simple, one of those who idle away the time bothering no one, twisting twigs and sniffing the woodland scents. But the scientist had a sharp eye; he realized that the little oldster was simple only in appearance. His eyes were wise and not clouded with the mould of books.

"Well, the scientist greeted the oldster respectfully and explained his trouble to him. The oldster fired a question at him at once: 'Why do you want to know?' As much as to say: 'If it's for fun or out of curiosity, you won't get an answer—just sniff the flowers and go back to where you came from. But if it's for a good purpose, that's a different story.'

"The scientist explained that he wanted to learn the meaning of life in order to free people from all their troubles—they tear around, you know, in the cities, like blind mice and do themselves much harm. If one were to teach them the meaning of life, then they would live peacefully, and instead of climbing all over their neighbors, they would find an easier way to happiness.

"The scientist's reply pleased the oldster. 'Truly,' he said, 'they live restlessly in the cities. The last time I was there, I went as a boy with my father to sell some cabbages, and they nearly tore his beard off. Right in the middle of the city a little pig was lying in a puddle and was too lazy to get up, so our wagon ran over him. But, it turned out,

443

the pig belonged to the mayor, so my father got hell for that; we left the city barely alive . . .'

" 'You've been sitting here a long time,' thought the scientist and was filled with still greater respect for him. Aloud he said: 'Pigs don't lie in puddles in the cities now, but the confusion is much worse and they can tear off your beard just the same.'

" 'I quite believe that,' agreed the little oldster, and at once unfolded the heart of the matter: 'In human life everything is set in motion by one thing: the struggle between the spirit and the flesh. The spirit wants to break out of the body and be free, but the flesh prevents this, holds the spirit in bondage, as in an iron cage . . . If the spirit is at peace—everything will be at peace.'

" 'But how to pacify it?' asked the scientist. 'You can't pacify it,' replied the little oldster, 'until it is freed.' 'But that's impossible!' exclaimed the scientist. The little oldster screwed up his eyes craftily and replied simply: 'Possible or not, that's the way everything goes.' The scientist was quite astonished and looked at the oldster mistrustfully: 'He's been drinking home-brew, the old grouch.' But the other led him to a shady nook where a birch and an oak were entwined: there, at the roots lay a stone, transparent, like marble, in the shape of a small cup, and in this little cup there was water from the last rain, as clear as a baby's tears. 'Look!' said the little oldster. 'In this water you will see many things.' The scientist looked, and as he looked it was no longer a little cup before his eyes, but a whole sea, and in another moment he saw life itself."

Cheprok stopped to take a sip from his glass. By now his story had begun to interest the doctor.

"He saw life, but how he saw it!" continued Cheprok. "As if he had suddenly become possessed of a million eyes: all life, to the smallest grain of sand, passed before him, as with a drowning man in his last moments. Only this wasn't his life alone, but the life of the whole world from the very beginning. And it not only passed, but with understanding, as if someone's voice were explaining it to him. Much that the scientist had previously read in books he understood now quite differently. He learned that his wife had been unfaithful to him with a neighboring professor whom, in his presence, she had always called 'that bald devil.' But now the scientist had other things to think about—events of such magnitude passed before him that the evildoer, the professor, was consumed in them like a mosquito in a bonfire.

444

"Then suddenly there came unfamiliar things and people in strange clothes.

" 'What's that?' the scientist asked the little oldster. 'That,' he explained, 'is the future. Look, look—look sharp! . . .' and the scientist saw that the farther it went on the more strikingly did the appearance of the earth change; fantastic buildings, gigantic canals appeared, and all this the scientist understood very well, as in a dream, where everything is clear to the last detail, but in the morning it's impossible to remember. The scientist saw how terrible catastrophes took place, how mountains of corpses and the smoke from a conflagration stretched along the horizon, and then again new buildings arose and canals, much better than the others and more beautiful, only to be turned again into ruins . . . And it went on like that for a long time. People began to look not like people, they became transparent and could fly like birds, only without wings. And suddenly—many years had passed—suddenly everything vanished. There were no buildings, no people; only the earth remained, the trees, the grass, and the flowers. The scientist was about to ask the little oldster what the trouble was, when he himself understood. Something like music sounded in his ears, and not in his ears really, but in his soul: so tender, so tranquil, so surprisingly clear that he did not know whether to laugh or to cry . . . Although the scientist didn't see anything, he realized clearly that the human spirit was flying in front of him.

"Then the little oldster explained: 'Yes, that's the spirit, free from flesh, triumphing . . . You see, the soul flies during sleep and here at last it has begun to fly in reality, but that won't happen soon.'

"The scientist looked closely and saw that the place over which the spirit was flying was very like the little glade where he was standing with the little oldster. The trees were almost the same, the sun was playing and the breeze was swaying the grass, only there was nobody around, and an unusual peace and contentment reigned in the air. And the scientist felt suddenly as if something inside him had been disturbed and wanted to break out. That, of course, was his soul, it had become envious and wanted to run away and join the choral dance. . . . The scientist couldn't hold out, he said: 'Ah! how beautiful! If only I could live there! . . . No worries, no sorrow . . .'

" 'Many years, millions,' said the little old man, 'many millions separate us from that.' 'But can't we cut into them?' asked the scientist. The oldster was silent for a while, then he said curtly: 'We can.' 'Then why haven't you done so, if it's possible?' The scientist was surprised.

445

The little oldster was somewhat embarrassed; his child-like little cheeks flushed, but he explained as well as he could: 'Well, you see, I'm used to my sinful body. I love it—healthy or ailing—and I like my vodka.' The scientist thought and thought and then he agreed with the little oldster. He thanked him for the lesson and returned to his home in the city without telling anybody that he had learned the meaning of life, so as not to embitter the people for nothing. Let them go on drinking their vodka . . ."

Pavel laughed: "So the flesh is still stronger than the spirit, is that it?" and added with a touch of bitterness: "Tyrants take advantage of this. We tremble for our bodies. The fear of pain governs us. Therein lies our weakness."

"But how can we cut across this frontier of millions of years?" the doctor asked Cheprok. "The little oldster didn't tell the scientist?"

Cheprok answered roughly: "He didn't have to tell him, the scientist understood. Get wise to yourself and you'll understand too."

"It's clear enough from the story," said Pavel.

The doctor got quite excited. "Ah, he's sly, the drunkard, but he has brains."

But Pavel, suddenly turning a twisted face to Cheprok, said bitterly: "I don't know about others, but my weakness is explainable . . . at least to me. I live as if I were at the foot of a mountain, always in the shadows. Oh, if you only knew what a misfortune it is to have a celebrity for a father! You can't preserve yourself, your individuality. No matter what you do, it's useless, you merge with the shadow and become a blank. In the years when a man wants to create, to do something, even evil, he is capable of nothing—he has been born like a mouldy growth in a cellar. This curse hangs over him all the time and he can't save himself from it."

The doctor noticed the feverish light in Pavel's eyes. On his cheeks appeared the earthy shadow of exhaustion. The doctor realized that he must hurry. And Pavel, as if he were replying to the doctor's thoughts, finished: "I have grown weak, and the weakened ones, like the laggards in the death march, are killed these days."

The doctor shuddered. His Adam's apple, big and pointed as if a large nut had stuck in his throat, jumped convulsively. Suddenly he asked Pavel:

"And what is death?"

The doctor was scared that he had given himself away with his question, but his curiosity, brought to white heat by horror, was stronger than he. Pavel, watching the doctor's mental convulsions with

446

interest, replied with a question: "Is life dear to you, Doctor?"

"The fear of death makes it precious and sweet."

Pavel sneered: "But still more sweet to watch the death agony of another? Yes?"

A silence set in, more terrible than a scream. The doctor felt as though he were hovering over a bottomless pit, exactly as in childish dreams. "Surely he doesn't know everything?" he asked himself in cold horror. Suddenly he murmured incoherently: "Yes, yes, how can one, while loving a man dearly, at the same time desire his ever-lasting torment? Where is the borderline between the joy of living and the agony of death? Where is the solution of the devilish riddle? Can it be there is no way out?"

Cheprok noticed the doctor's terrible agitation, and couldn't understand what caused it. Pavel suddenly laughed. "Where, Doctor, did you acquire this mental spinelessness?" And he added seriously: "There's something strange about you. You're fidgety."

"You're dodging, you're dodging," said the doctor, and winked understandingly at Pavel.

Pavel and Cheprok looked at each other. "What's eating the man?" Pavel asked. "Is he losing his mind?" Cheprok shrugged his shoulders.

On the next and following days the doctor caught himself thinking only about Pavel. And every day, impatiently waiting for evening, he hurried home to continue the conversations.

If the doctor had previously put on the face of a jester to hide his awful emptiness, there was no need for this now; he was ready to burst from an excess of his own importance. Joyfully he watched his self-confidence growing. How clear and free from fear his life had become! The change was obvious. While shaving in the morning the doctor drew his hand away from his face: so painfully new was his skin. He was exultant, but said not a word to anyone about his amazing transformation; but in front of the mirror, smirking furtively, he winked to himself with a crafty eye. Thinking of himself as a calculating miser who had received a legacy, he kept his secret to himself. In this way February and March passed.

CHAPTER 12

SPRING WAS early that year and, as always on the Don, it came suddenly. At the end of March the Don seemed still to be full of its winter somnolence, although at night people heard the quiet rustling and cracking of the ice on the river, and distinguished in the dim gleam of the moon the water forced through tortuous cracks, dark as oil. Then, on one of the first April days the ice moved with a loud crashing and the liberated river overflowed the left bank, pouring over the steppe, farther and farther. For many miles, as far as the eye could see, stretched watery space. The current dragged into the open water tremendous trees with the earth washed from their roots, lumber, barrels that had come from God knows where, boats, old chairs, and whole roofs, as if the river had undertaken to clean the steppe of all kinds of rubbish.

No sooner had the ice passed, than the spring days began to run, one after another, in a merry dance. The sun, light red, sank so low that it nearly touched the roofs; from the sun-bathed cornices loud drops began to fall quicker and quicker. Babbling brooks boiled over the earth, the first grass appeared, young and translucent —its delicate texture blooming with dewdrops. Flocks of sparrows flew excitedly from one tree to another, chirping deafeningly, while in the great oaks the rooks went about building their frugal homes. On the pulsating, vibrating air the scent of the birch buds and lindens was wafted, while in the clear blue sky white clouds, like lambs in a field, gamboled over each other in disorder, and the spring birds frolicked and bathed, filling the surrounding air with their passionate cries. All things took on a lightness and transparency, their shadows became bluish, everything was full of a special spring animation, everywhere was an overflow of radiating gladness, and in each cry and rustle the passionate urge of life was heralded.

During these days Pavel made Cheprok open his window and he lay with his face toward it, his head propped high on a pillow. His eyes no longer saw clearly: beyond the curtain, stirring in the fresh breeze, he distinguished only the chestnut tree which stood nearer than the others. But he felt the caress of the spring air on his face and hands; it induced a strange calm which deadened the pain for a time: it blew softly with the breath of eternal life, but even in the joyousness of the spring he felt a delicate sorrow of atonement and parting. Pavel knew that he would die soon, that the inevitable could happen at any moment, and this feeling of the nearness of death sharpened his thoughts to crystal clarity. But strangely enough, instead of thinking of death, he stubbornly recalled the distant past, the long-forgotten precious trivialities and quiet joys of his childhood.

He slept a great deal now. His dreams were varied—during the day they were peaceful and reflective, the continuation of his thoughts. At night, when his fever rose, there was delirium. After one such night, while he was still sleeping, Mikhail came quietly into his room. He approached the bed and, without taking his sorrowful eyes off the patient, asked Cheprok, who was sitting in his usual place in the corner beside the window: "Well, how is it? Is he better?"

Cheprok shook his head. "Pavel was delirious all night," he replied softly. "He was remembering some girl, some Jeanette. They were gathering flowers together, but the flowers were strange—glass or something. He was urging her to be careful, not to break them and not to cut her fingers. He tossed about, excited, repeating the same thing all the time. Then he lost her, called and called for her; then, toward morning, he quieted down, became calm, probably found her . . ."

Hollow-cheeked and awkward, his face twitching, Mikhail said hoarsely: "I'll come when he awakens."

Jumping up from his chair, Cheprok sidled up to him quickly and silently touched his elbow.

"What is it, Cheprok?"

The old man's eyes, red from a sleepless night, puckered pityingly. He could not restrain himself, leaned his old head against Mikhail: "I'm sorry for him, Misha . . . His heart is so gentle: if a little fluff touches it, it leaves a scar, and what goes on here . . ."

Mikhail hurriedly patted the old man's stooped shoulders and went out without speaking.

When he awoke, Pavel listened to the sounds. In the park there was the usual bird festival—he smiled. It was quiet in the house—only once in a while from the far wing came the sound of a piano; it would be Luba or Nina playing. Luba played, defiantly, loudly, as if she were intentionally stifling unpleasant thoughts; Nina played sadly and softly. When Nina played, Pavel closed his eyes. Fear and excitement melted away and a calm, quiet sadness filled his whole being. Each time it seemed that he had heard that music in some childhood dream that had faded from his memory. He tried not to move, for fear the movement of his body would break the heavenly charm of the sounds and the transparent chain of memories and quickening scents, fluttering and fragile, like dried flowers in an album.

In the evening the sun sank into the flooding Don, tinting the water purple. Such moments were the most difficult for Pavel. He knew that soon the pain would come, terrible, draining, dark. He hurried to think, wanting to remember all the precious happenings before the dreaded end, and was never able to. The pain always came first. The air became thick, as if it were filled with mercury, and began to ring in his brain. The ringing changed to a crash, filled the room, and, breaking down the walls, burst out. Things split into pieces, the pieces dissolved into ugly forms, everything visible vanished.

Then the pain passed; rather, he dissolved into it. In his tortured body rose an unsteady feeling of devastation and keen sorrow. He lay with open eyes, watched how the red flames of the sunset glowed. It seemed to him that in its red flames eternity was reflected. The sunset and the clouds filled his whole being: his empty body was able to house the entire world, to the last atom. He was calm—as the universe, for which human life is an insignificant moment, is calm. But whence the sadness? Why was it not enough to merge with the world? What could be more important? Still not knowing the answer, Pavel felt that the answer must be astonishingly simple and bright, like a hope realized. And it must also be supremely human and therefore immeasurably greater than the universe and more majestic than eternity.

CHAPTER 13

WHEN NINA came in to take Cheprok's place Pavel suddenly asked her: "Help me to write a letter. You can write French, can't you?"

"I can, from dictation, but there'll be mistakes."

"That's fine. Get some paper, please, the better kind."

When Nina had everything ready, Pavel leaned back on the pillow and, half-closing his eyes, began to talk. Nina started at his first word —not because he was speaking in French, unfamiliar to her ear, but because Pavel's voice was strangely far away, as if he had conquered boundless space.

"Dear, unforgettable Jeanette, now I am beginning to understand how profoundly right you were and how wrong and terribly unjust I was. The circle is closed, and I am returning to the inevitable dust. But the lesson has not been in vain. On parting from you I thought with naïve pride that I was going away to find myself. I wanted to test happiness—if it came, I would have enough courage to live it through to the end. But it didn't come. Not happiness, but the fatal potion of loneliness did I drink. It is terrible and cold, like the icy silence of the universe. 'We mustn't part, we can't try the patience of fate thrice,' you told me then. I didn't understand your words. I was too blind and self-confident to understand the great truth: the wisdom

450

of life is born in the heart of woman. It was a painful lesson. It has cost me my life. But I was lucky: at the last minute, in my last despair a new star shone for me. How brightly and cheerfully it glistens. I am entering the twilight but it seems to me that I am only beginning to live.

"Darling, unattainable friend, now I know what your eyes were saying, your jet black hair, your cloak, fragrant with the spring rain and that wild flower which you plucked with me at St. Denis. They spoke of what is most important in life—the living joy of love."

Pavel stopped. "That's all," he said after a minute.

"Where shall I send this letter, to what address?" asked Nina. Her voice was shaking and she spoke with difficulty.

"Address?" asked Pavel. His thoughts were far away. "I'll tell you afterwards, for I must first correct your mistakes," he smiled weakly. "Now, go away, I want to sleep, I'm very tired . . . No. Go and call everybody: Father, Luba, Cheprok."

When Nina had brought all those he had asked for, Pavel said: "I want you to forgive me. I know you are angry with me."

"We? Angry!" they exclaimed almost in chorus.

Pavel tried to raise himself, but only groaned. Mikhail helped him, supporting his shoulders. At last he said:

"Father . . . I have a request. I will die soon . . ."

"What nonsense! You'll get better," said Mikhail, while Cheprok interjected hurriedly: "We'll marry you off yet. We'll choose such a beauty for you that one look from her and all your sickness will vanish like magic. I'll dance at your wedding yet."

"No, I'm dying," said Pavel calmly. "And I want a funeral service in a church. There must be a church open somewhere."

Mikhail was not surprised. "There's no sense in talking about death, Pavel. But I promise to fulfill your request." The last words Mikhail pronounced firmly, as if he were opposing someone beforehand. Then he took Pavel's hand in his. He felt no animosity now, only pity. "Pavel, it's not for us to forgive you, we should ask your forgiveness. Forgive me, I have been inattentive to you and unjust. It's a late repentance, but . . ." Mikhail was unable to finish. Suddenly Pavel's face lit up: "Don't, Father. Everything's fine. Where's Luba?"

"I'm here, Pavel." Luba came up and kissed his forehead. "Forgive me, Pavel."

"Now, now, what foolishness . . . Give me your hands, all together, all together . . . like that."

They were standing around him, silent: Mikhail with trembling chin, Luba distressed and sad, Nina with an almost rapturous face; and

Cheprok, pathetic, even comical, his broad nose particularly red and ugly.

Pavel pressed their hands to his heart. "We mustn't part, we mustn't forget each other," he said softly, gazing out of the window. "What is that light? . . . Ah, that's my star. How nice, no remembrances, no sadness . . ." Pavel fell into slumber. A little later, as if from a great distance, he heard Nina's tender, beautiful voice: "He's falling asleep, we'd better go."

Pavel had a dream: his father was standing on the high shore of the sea, young, well built, as he had seen him in the portrait by Repin. He was dressed in top boots and a blue shirt, worn outside his trousers, and gathered with a narrow belt. His light, flaxen hair stirred in the wind. He was standing half turned to Pavel but his face wasn't visible. He was talking quietly with a slim girl whom he was embracing, his broad hand pressing her tightly to him. Pavel realized that the slim girl was his mother. He couldn't remember her, but now, for some reason, he was sure that it was she. Like his father's, her head was uncovered; her chestnut hair was laced with sunlight and her long dress touched the rocks of the shore. Suddenly the girl turned around and looked fixedly into his face with her large dark eyes. She was not surprised, just smiled broadly and sympathetically and beckoned with her hand, as if she were inviting him to join them. Pavel, overjoyed, wanted to run to his parents, but stopped. "Papa, are you crying?" he asked reproachfully. He didn't see his father's face, but he knew that he stood with his back to him to hide his tears. With a kind of second sight Pavel saw how the large drops rolled slowly down the cheeks of the young face. "Don't, Father, I'm feeling so well . . ."

At that moment the girl turned away and talked with Mikhail again calmly, pressing her head to his shoulder affectionately, as if Pavel weren't near him. Pavel wanted to rush up and pull them apart roughly, to talk with them about something cheery and noisy; but he groaned, waking up.

Cheprok was sitting on a chair beside the window, snoozing. Beyond the window the sunset was blazing—that meant the pain would come soon . . .

He lay thus all through the night and the following day. Only late in the evening did Pavel open his eyes. On seeing Nina he asked uneasily: "Where's the letter?"

"Here," she answered quickly. "Do you feel easier?"

"Nina," Pavel said, moving his lips with difficulty and feeling that little time remained. "Send the letter to . . . to . . ."

452

Nina put her ear to his very lips to catch the address, but Pavel was already silent. To his wide-open eyes appeared an astonishing vision: a sunny glade, dotted with wild flowers, spread out at his feet. A warm breeze swayed the tall grass like waves. And it seemed that a melody was borne on the breeze, tender and strangely familiar. Then, with gladness he saw that the melody had a face and figure. Jeanette! She was smiling, and she was standing in the glade, at the other side of the young birch and the young oak, entwined like a pair of lovers, but the tresses of her hair, stirring in the breeze, brushed his face. They were soft as light. Only they were dark.

"Come to me!" Jeanette urged, making an impatient gesture with her hand. "Oh! How clumsy you are!"

"So, you're here already?" asked Pavel, and his heart fluttered joyfully.

"Of course; didn't you know? Hurry, I'm impatient to embrace you."

"At once, at once," replied Pavel apologetically. "I was delayed by the letter: I wrote to you about my star. But now the letter won't be needed, I'll tell you myself, everything, everything . . ."

Jeanette was already embracing him.

"Jeanette!" exclaimed Pavel, feeling a growing rapture. "Jeanette, I am here, forever!"

CHAPTER 14

MIKHAIL GORIN fulfilled his promise. A funeral service was held for Pavel in a small church on the outskirts of the city, after which he was buried with full Christian rites in a cemetery. No matter how Veria tried to persuade Gorin not to do this, the writer insisted on having his own way. Pavel's wishes were sacred to him now. When Veria saw that he could not overcome the Gorin obstinacy, and that he could not avoid a church service, he decided to take the affair into his own hands, at least partly. The road to the church was cleared of traffic and lined with soldiers. Somewhere they found a priest, who turned out to be the former Bishop of Rostov and had, God knows by what magic, brought his mortal body through the purges, firing squads, and exile. To avoid unforeseen incidents, Veria ordered a dozen responsible Party men to escort the coffin to the church and even to attend the service. They were to act as representatives of sympathizing organizations.

453

The townspeople who were able to see the funeral procession from their windows, or from the roofs of houses, were particularly touched by the tall figure of the writer walking, with head bent low, behind the coffin. He seemed to hear and see nothing that was going on around him. On his left hand walked Luba, strikingly beautiful and austere in her mourning dress, and Nina with tear-stained face. The townspeople decided that she was Pavel's wife. On Gorin's right hand walked Academician Glushak with his wife. He had intended to walk in the middle of the procession, so as not to intrude himself on Gorin's eyes, thinking that the unfriendliness of the writer would be particularly apparent now. But Mikhail noticed him and with sudden impetuosity and determination, as if he were rectifying an unforgivable mistake, took him by the arm and asked him to walk beside him. Glushak, surprised by such long-forgotten attention, was moved. His eyes were moist. Behind them shuffled Cheprok with Doctor Tsibik, and farther back walked the household and close friends of the writer, many of whom had managed to come from other towns. A little apart from this group were the "representatives," all stolid, dressed on the same pattern, and looking somewhat embarrassed by their role.

The church service was solemn and decorous. The Bishop, with his thin ascetic face, black beard, and astoundingly clear blue eyes, was in good form; he read the prayer reverently and with feeling. Even the "representatives," attending on Veria's orders, who in the first moments in church had felt some awkwardness and even bashfulness from the unfamiliar church atmosphere, felt the importance and solemnity of the moment. So much were they carried away by the service that when the Bishop, as if he were addressing the deceased Pavel, exclaimed passionately: "Tell us what you see there? Will our sorrow be eased soon?" they didn't notice the significance with which the Bishop, taking courage from the circumstances and his own eloquence, tried to endow these words. However, some of those in the church understood his meaning and later there was much talk in the city about the Bishop's courage and his prayer.

Doctor Tsibik, who up to then had been standing motionless, suddenly paled at these words of the Bishop and seemed to reach out toward him. After the words: "May his soul rejoice, oh Lord! Array him in the vestment of salvation and in the raiment of gladness clothe him," when everybody in turn began to approach the coffin to take leave of the deceased, the doctor couldn't stand it any longer. He dropped slowly to his knees in front of the coffin, his face drained of blood, and whispered regretfully: "Thank you for everything, Pavel.

454

Only why did you take your secret with you, without telling me the most important thing?" Then the doctor rose and, stepping evenly in his private world, went slowly to the exit, not noticing the surprised glances that followed him.

About all this, even the church service itself, there was not a word in the papers. But a notice of condolence signed by Stalin and the other members of the Politburo was printed on the front pages. When later that day Gorin saw the paper on his table, he thought with a pang, "It would be better if they hadn't written anything!"

Doctor Tsibik entered Veria's reception room as if it were his own, familiar from long usage. What a difference from his first visit! Not a shadow of fear nor the slightest nervousness. With a calm, almost imperious voice he asked the adjutant to inform Veria of his arrival and sat down in an armchair, crossing one leg over the other. Prokhor, the bald-headed adjutant whom the doctor already knew, asked respectfully if he would not like a cup of cocòa while he waited.

"No, thank you," replied the doctor and smiled, showing his gold teeth.

The doctor hadn't long to wait. A moment later Veria was seating him in an armchair, offering him a Kazbek cigarette, excusing himself for being unable to call him in sooner. The radiance of his smile vied with the doctor's teeth.

"It's a great pleasure to see you, Doctor," he said, looking affectionately at the doctor's spare figure in the immaculate blue suit. A ray of sunlight played on the red crown of the doctor's pate. "It's so seldom I have the chance to talk with an educated man."

The doctor accepted the compliment with dignity. "Aha! It works!" he smirked to himself, content. "What a pity I didn't meet Pavel earlier and wangle that priceless wealth from him. It's much more peaceful and profitable to live like this." He even looked with concealed compassion at Veria. "Poor fellow, he doesn't know the secret. Most likely he shakes like a lamb's tail in front of his superiors in Moscow or pretends to be a fool, the way I used to." The consciousness of his own personal excellence made the doctor a splendid conversationalist. His talk was bold and refined, his movements confident and calm. He enjoyed his new role and intentionally set himself more and more difficult tests, awaiting the results with a feeling of acute curiosity. His new character withstood all the tests, emerged with flying colors—the doctor knew now that he was capable of anything!

As if confirming his conclusion, Veria told him: "Doctor Tsibik, I

455

called you to tell you the glad news personally and to congratulate you on your promotion. The Government has decided to appoint you Director of the main Rostov hospital." ("The Government!" exclaimed the doctor to himself.) "You fully deserve this responsible position. Your education, your excellent organizational abilities, your knowledge of the most up-to-date methods of treatment, your prestige among the medical profession, and finally, your surprising character and firmness, make you the obvious choice. I sincerely congratulate you, Doctor Tsibik!"

Veria got up and, going around the desk, extended his hand to the doctor. The doctor gloated. So, at last his dream had come true! So, at last he had become the Director of the hospital. As for the gold watch and the fox trot, these could be acquired later. But even his boundless inner triumph did not shake the doctor's balance. He parted from Veria as one equal from another. Accompanying him to the door, Veria slapped him on the back and whispered, winking slyly: "As for the other thing, you did a great job! A great job!"

The doctor smiled modestly: "It was, indeed, a pleasure," he said, and again pitied Veria to himself: "Poor fellow, he doesn't know a thing . . ."

Veria obligingly opened the door for him. With head held high the doctor went into the reception room, smiled condescendingly to Prokhor. Two serious-looking men with bristling mustaches, wearing white smocks, rose to meet him and, taking him by the arms, led him into the corridor, raising him gently off the floor.

From behind came Prokhor's barking laugh and the shrill, gulping chuckle of Veria . . .

CHAPTER 15

THE CONNECTION between Pavel's death and Doctor Tsibik's madness was too obvious. Luba became panicky; she felt as if a heavy shroud of darkness had been dropped over her.

"Why did Misha come back to Russia? We'd be living abroad, not so luxuriously, not so noisily nor with so much honor, but without fear. If we had tired of Capri, we could have gone to America. But here . . ." Luba sighed loudly. "How will all this end?"

However, she kept a grip on herself and didn't voice her thoughts to Mikhail; he had recently become dark as a cloud. Gloomily, and without ceasing, Mikhail thought about Pavel. The circumstances of his son's death seemed to him suspicious. At night, lying beside her husband, Luba heard how he often groaned in his sleep. During the day Mikhail wandered about the rooms, slowly dragging his slippers on the floor, unable to find a place to rest. He acquired a new, unpleasant habit: screwing up his eyes as if he were afraid of the bright light or as if he kept remembering something shameful and blameworthy.

Luba, however, decided definitely to speak to her daughter. She was more afraid for her now than anything else. One morning when Nina came into her room as usual, Luba said quietly: "Shut the door. I want to talk to you."

"What is it, Mama?"

Luba, already dressed and with her hair up, rose to meet her, her black dress rustling—she was still wearing mourning. She looked closely, almost sternly at her daughter.

"Nina, you are grown up and, I hope, will understand me. I want to say that it's dangerous for you to stay any longer under this roof. There are too many mysteries in this house."

Nina was not surprised: "I understand, Mama. . . . Will he understand?"

"I'll talk to Mikhail. He'll understand. For he, as well as I, wants your welfare." Luba came close to her daughter and asked softly: "How is your affair with Vassily?" That was young Shcherbakov's name.

"You mean you want to know whether I love him or not?" asked Nina, almost angrily. "Of course not!"

"I see, I see . . ." said Luba sadly and twisted her fingers in despair. Dark spots appeared on her olive cheeks. Placing a hand on Nina's shoulders, she said hurriedly, and somewhat perplexed: "But understand, my friend, in this case that may be not at all important. . . . It sometimes happens that love for the husband comes with habit."

Nina removed her mother's hand. "Don't, Mama. I've already made my decision."

"You have?" Luba was surprised, as if her daughter had increased twofold in stature before her eyes.

But Nina, turning very pale, said bitterly: "Yes, I have decided. You know how sometimes you can feel so much in one second, when everything becomes clear all at once, as if a bandage had been torn off your eyes. That's what happened to me when I saw Novikov the last time. Oh, Mama, if you only knew what a scoundrel he is, how

457

cleverly he conceals his beastly face beneath the mask of culture and breeding. My conversation with him was a good lesson to me. I used to believe in everything that was noble and honest. But now I know the other as well: how easily an honest and good person can be trampled in the dirt in this country, how terrible is the revenge of scoundrels." Nina drew herself up suddenly, as if she were throwing a challenge: "No, I will not allow myself to be crushed, as Lida was crushed. There is no other recourse in this world but to become merciless and heartless, and above all, one must be heartless toward oneself, to everything dear that blossoms in the soul, killing everything that remains of the former days. If one can't get out of the country, one must change oneself. In Rome do as the Romans do!"

Luba moved away from her daughter in fright. Nina's face was suffused in a raging fire, distorted, her large eyes dry and hard.

"Stop, stop, Nina! What are you saying?" she said in a low voice. Her hands were shaking so much that she intertwined her fingers and squeezed them. "Quiet! For God's sake! The walls may have ears." The usually calm and confident Luba looked pitiful. It was several minutes before Luba was able to ask Nina: "Are you sure of Vassily?"

Nina scoffed: "One word from me and he will jump into the river."

Then Luba embraced her and kissed her with a long kiss on the cheek. "Nina, do you remember how nice it was on Capri?"

"Don't, Mama! You can't return to that—better forget it."

"Of course. But oh, how heavy it is here!" Luba pointed to her heart. "Heavy and fearful." Then, as if recalling something, she asked her daughter: "And so you have come to an understanding with Vassily? When do you intend to get married? You see, everything must be done properly, and you haven't told me a thing yet."

"There's nothing to be told. I'm going to him myself . . . tomorrow."

Luba recoiled in astonishment. "Yourself? Tomorrow?" she repeated as if stunned.

But Nina was already going out of the room and only when she reached the door, she replied quietly: "I know what I'm doing. You had better go and warn Papa." And she left, holding her head high and compressing her lips.

CHAPTER 16

YES, NINA KNEW what she was doing. Next morning when Luba caught her in her room ready to leave, she cried out in surprise. Never had she seen her daughter look so lovely. She was dressed in a cream traveling suit, simple but elegant. From under the white collar of her blouse, two short wine-colored ribbons showed. A small hat, also cream and also trimmed in the wine color, was tilted to one side, setting off her hair, arranged high in the new style. The little hat and the coiffure suited her well. Her small hands were encased in gloves.

Nina seemed to Luba to have grown suddenly taller, more slender, and somehow mysterious: there was a new dignity, a new beauty, simple yet impressive, even severe, not only in her suit, in her coiffure, in her figure, but also in her face—tender and thoughtful with darkened gray eyes—as if she had just had an icy shower. If it had not been for the familiar shadow from the eyelashes on her cheeks, and the starry spark in the depths of her eyes, it would have been impossible to recognize her.

"A woman, a real woman!" exclaimed Luba, at once defining in one word the new quality in Nina. Looking at these clear, family features Luba recognized herself, recalled her own youth. She herself had dressed with emotion just like this at the crucial moment—preparing to step into the dizzy unknown which lures and frightens every girl, like the first kiss. But where did Nina get this severity? This determined, almost haughty smile?

While the servants were carrying down the suitcases, Nina went to say good-bye to her father. But he was already standing at the door, nodding to her, smiling benignly, somehow cumbersome, a little comical, abandoned, alone. Nina suddenly felt so sorry for him that she ran to him, threw her arms around him, pressed herself to his breast.

"Papa dear, forgive me for leaving. But I will be seeing you every day. I promise . . ."

Mikhail stroked her fair head and bending, kissed her half-open, cool lips. "So you're going away from me," he said in a sinking voice. "You're going away, and you'll forget us. Isn't that so?"

Squeezing her eyes tight, Nina shook her head.

"Now, now, I was only joking," said Mikhail, seeing her damp eyelashes. "Let me see how you look." Taking her hands in his own large ones, he pushed her away so as to look her over better, even inclined his head to one side. "What a beauty!" he exclaimed in wonder. "Wait a minute . . . Luba! Why! She's cast in your mold—you remember, when I saw you the first time in Florence. Ah!" he sighed with longing. "Ah, those were the days!"

Luba, badly upset, tried to smile. "I was also thinking about that . . ." she said and cut herself short, took a handkerchief out of her cuff.

"Well, enough of this sniveling." Mikhail pulled himself together and added a little gruffly: "I suppose it's better this way. Actually, why should Nina live with us old grumblers? Cheprok!" he called loudly. "Bring us a glass each! Let's have a drink before parting."

When Cheprok brought the wine and each had a glass, Mikhail, still standing, said: "So you and Luba had decided on Shcherbakov. Well . . . I don't know modern young people. Of course, I'm not a girl, so there's nothing for me to know."

Nina, afraid of what she read in her father's eyes, said hurriedly: "Vassily is neither better nor worse than the others." Her lips were trembling. "Yes, Papa, a year ago I thought that I loved the best man in the world. I felt an abundance of tenderness, I was preparing to plunge head first into happiness . . . Everything turned out in vain. It's hard for me. It hurts: you see that yourself, Papa. But don't think that I'm weak. I have simply decided to live without illusions."

Mikhail wiped his forehead. "Yes, I have no objection. Only, it's all so sudden. When on earth did you have time to come to an understanding with him? Is he coming for you?"

"No, I haven't even rung him up."

"Good gracious!" Mikhail was astonished. "You're certainly sure of yourself. . . . Look out! To be spurned is the most terrible injury for a woman."

Nina's hand, holding the wine glass, shook.

"I've gone through that once already," she said quietly, and taking a small sip, placed the glass on the table with a quick movement, as if she were putting a period to something. "Well, I must catch him before he goes to work."

Nina kissed her father again, then Cheprok. "Mind you look after Papa for me, Grampa," she said to him.

Apparently sensing a reproach in her words, Cheprok said heatedly: "You may kill me. I'm to blame. I failed with Pavel."

"What kind of nonsense is that?" said Mikhail. "Nobody's blaming you."

460

"Nobody will ever deceive me now. Only over my dead body," said Cheprok with trembling lips.

An open car, a high-powered Italian one, was waiting in front of the steps, a present from her father. It was light blue, gleaming, like a holiday. A chauffeur respectfully held the door open. Nina stopped a moment beside a column, leaned her temple against it. Luba was standing beside her. "Mama," Nina said softly, "someday I'll take my revenge for Pavel on the right person . . ."

Luba, turning pale, whispered: "For goodness' sake, Nina, don't think about things like that," and, apparently full of a new fear for her daughter, added: "Maybe it would be better for me to go with you?"

"You don't need to," replied Nina, and went down the steps.

When the car was out of sight beyond the ornamental gates, Mikhail, putting his arm around his wife's waist, drew her to him. "Well, and so we are alone, Luba."

"Are you sorry?"

"Of course. But if you think about it, Nina is right. Only . . . only, will her heart hold out?"

CHAPTER 17

GOVERNMENT VILLA No. 6, in which Shcherbakov lived, was already familiar to Nina. It was the same villa in which the French writer, Romain Rouen, had stayed when he came to visit Gorin. Nina had visited him several times with her father. But then the guards had been concealed along the road in the bushes; now they were in the open. Soldiers with rifles and fixed bayonets and officers with revolvers, all in blue caps, stood singly and in groups within sight of each other. This was a closed road. In addition to the Shcherbakov villa it led to the residences of Veria, Durov, Kashirin, and several other leaders of the Province. The soldiers and officers watched the racing automobile with an attentive glance, but did not stop it. The Gorin car had a government license plate.

"Out of one prison into another," thought Nina, and a momentary feeling of fear oppressed her heart. So as not to see the soldiers, she leaned back in the seat. Gay white clouds floated in the blue sky. How she envied them! Now her past seemed beautiful and distant, like them. Life then had seemed light, happy and untried. Nina thought about her brief love for Feodor, who appeared to her now not as one person,

461

but two. The one who had loved her and whom she had loved was not at all like the other—vile and despicable. Her brain refused to merge them into one person, so contradictory were they. All right, then! she was not successful in love, so she didn't need love. Enough of wandering in a syrupy fog, enchanted and happy.

But somewhere in the depths of her a thin voice asked, as if it were mocking: "But don't you want to be in love again? Don't you want to recapture that former lightness, the sparkle of the eyes, to hear again your own gay, pealing laughter? With what else can you replace them?"

No, carefree life and happiness had gone forever. She was already convinced of the vulgarity of life and the impossibility of happiness. And it was not happiness that she was seeking now! One simply had to live. With a bitter sneer she remembered that these were Feodor's words. "One must live somehow," he had said then.

"But he is a man, and the world belongs to them. You're a woman. Are you able to stand that test?" the restless little voice asked.

It seemed to Nina that already her strength had failed her. A ticklish shiver of fear penetrated her soul. "Perhaps I should go back before it's too late, perhaps I am really taking too much on myself?" she thought, but then told herself: "No, I must be firm, I must be firm." Her hatred, her whole proud will rose.

Before her eyes appeared her father's stooped back, his embarrassed smile. "Oh, how I pity him . . ."

Her mother, unrecognizable, with frightened eyes: "I'd give anything if only that look of fear wasn't in her eyes."

The face of her dying brother Pavel distorted by pain: "They wouldn't let him go abroad, they finished him off here!"

And Lida, her dear friend Lida, whose heart of gold they threw into the gutter and trampled: "Where is she now? Is she alive? . . ."

"Oh, no, I will not submit!" She squeezed her hands so tightly that her gloves stretched, ready to burst. "I won't submit! I may even be able to avenge them some time!" Her heart shrank into a heavy, icy ball. "From now on—not a drop of feeling, I shall be cold and calculating, like a soulless, avenging machine."

"The Veria summer house," said the chauffeur at this moment, pointing a hand at the open gates beside which was a particularly large number of soldiers. "The next one is the Shcherbakovs'."

A large gray building in modern style showed beyond the thin woods, with large windows and a flat roof, and beyond it the Don,

462

shimmering in the sun like the scales of fish. A moment later they were driving into the garden.

Shcherbakov, pale, his face creased from lack of sleep—there had been a party the night before and they had caroused until early morning—rushed out in his unbuttoned jacket when he was told of her arrival. When he saw Nina he stopped, didn't believe his eyes, became more pale; his mouth hung open. Then, coming to himself, he leaped down the steps, pushed the chauffeur aside, and opened the door of the car himself.

"Nina! You came of yourself?" he repeated, almost stuttering. His narrow face, with its slightly protruding lower lip, was excited, almost silly looking. He began suddenly to button his jacket.

"Excuse my appearance . . ." He left the buttons, threw himself at the suitcases; then, embarrassed by his own haste, stopped and smiled confusedly; his pale mouth slipped to the side.

"Vassily," said Nina firmly, looking at him sharply. "I have come to live with you."

"Thank you, Nina, thank you . . ." replied Shcherbakov like a boy. He was going to kiss her but apparently something in her glance frightened him. He ran into the house, throwing over his shoulder: "I'll be right back! Just one minute . . ."

In the hall he rushed up to his major-domo, hissing: "Vanka, kick the girls to hell out of here! Through the back door! And be quick! There mustn't be hide or hair of them around!"

"What's wrong? Has your father come from Moscow, or something?" Vanka was surprised.

"No, my wife . . . I'm getting married!" Shcherbakov mumbled as if in a faint. "Get busy, you devil, she's already here." He rushed back to Nina, who was coming in the door. "This way, Nina. Sit down for a minute, while they're making your room ready," he said, leading her by the arm to his study.

While this was going on, three girls—just as they were, sleepy, in their underclothes, heads tousled—were rushed into a truck. With his own hands Vanka helped Lily, from the Party Committee; he pushed her up by her broad backside and slapped her in fun. "There's a smooth heifer!"

The half-dressed, confused girls, not understanding the reason for the hurry, were furious and chattered angrily; Lily began to whimper. As the truck was moving away, Vanka threw their clothes, slippers, and stockings, rumpled into a bundle, onto the girls' knees—everything he had time to collect. "Go, like hell!" he ordered the driver. "Throw them out somewhere along the road. And don't stay long! Come back as quick as you can!" The driver grinned, raced his motor.

Tidying himself up, the major-domo went to show Nina to her room. Shcherbakov had already disappeared somewhere in the depths of the house; his cracked voice could be heard giving orders.

CHAPTER 18

THE FLUNKY Vanka, sharp-nosed, pock-marked, and brazen, was Shcherbakov's favorite—he knew how to please him better than anyone else. He walked ahead of Nina with the suitcases, opening doors deftly with his foot. Once in a while he turned around, baring his yellow teeth in a smile, his red face showing a desperate anxiety to please.

"I'll bet he's a thief," thought Nina, having learned at home to analyze the characters of the servants.

At last they came to a large room with a carpet on the floor, and with a bed and a dresser in Karelian birch.

"I hope the accommodation will please you," said Vanka in a honeyed voice. "Vassily Alexandrovich prepared this room for you a long time ago. 'Vanka,' he said, 'when I get married, I'll put my wife in here!' The best room in the house, I can assure you."

The major-domo spoke with feeling, but his self-satisfied smirking face hid a certain nastiness. With a swinging step he approached the bed; he pressed the mattress with his hand to show that it was soft, and giggled. Nina stood motionless in the center of the room waiting for him to go. Looking around, she saw a bundle on the carpet. Vanka intercepted her glance, threw up his arms:

"Oh, the devils! They didn't tidy up! . . . I'll show them!"

Twisting his body he bent down and picked up the bundle, but dropped it, spilling the contents. Nina saw high-heeled slippers, a woman's blouse, panties, a bra . . . Vanka, knitting his narrow brows and not taking his eyes off Nina's face, began to stuff the clothes into the bundle, but again, as if accidentally, dropped it. Then with affected zeal he began to clown on all fours on the floor.

The blood of fury rushed to Nina's face.

"Get out!" she said quietly through her teeth, but so ominously that the flunky hurried to back out the door with his bundle.

464

Nina dropped into a chair in front of the dresser and unhurriedly began to take off her gloves, not moving her eyes from her reflection. Looking at her was a stern, beautiful girl with flaming cheeks and frowning brows. The line of her shoulders and proud head was like that of a conqueror. Her inner little voice was whispering encouragingly: "Now, keep your head, Nina—what just happened was only the beginning." "I'm ready," she replied mentally, and relaxed her eyebrows. The angry flush receded from her face. But in the depths of her heart the still uncooled lava boiled.

A cautious knock at the door, and Shcherbakov entered. He was as if on parade: straight and tall, with buttoned-up jacket, military breeches whose wings hung loosely in the new style, low to the very tops of his brightly polished boots. But his eyes looked at Nina rabbit-like, confused and tender.

"Nina, the whole house is at your disposal. I have given the necessary orders." He became silent, blinking his eyes, wondering what to say next to break the foolish awkwardness, but could think of nothing, only wiped his flabby nose and shifted from one foot to the other, like a goose. Then taking out his cigarette case and asking her permission, he began to smoke, inhaling deeply.

"I'm afraid I've kept you. You have to go to your work?" asked Nina, noticing his car through the window.

"Not at all—they can wait." Shcherbakov flipped his unfinished cigarette through the window and said almost dramatically: "Nina, for a long time I have dreamed of this moment and, truth to tell, had little hope . . . It always seemed that you didn't love me." The last words sounded quite gloomy. To her own surprise, Nina suddenly smiled broadly.

"The workings of a woman's heart are as unpredictable as the flight of a bat," she said, and turned her face to him. Sparks of mirth were all over it. He took an impulsive step toward her, his dejected eyes rounded. Nina looked into them and suddenly blushed: "Vassily," she said cautiously, "we'll live apart until we register and celebrate the wedding."

"Let's register tomorrow then!" exclaimed Shcherbakov hotly. "And the wedding will be tomorrow also! . . . But no—next week. I want to tell my father, so he can come from Moscow."

"Why! He respects his parents!" thought Nina, and became quite gay. Several times she had seen how subordinates twice his age paled and trembled at his angry words. Yet this haughty, cold man had melted before her, like a wax candle from heat. Half jokingly she said:

465

"I'll try to fall in love with you. In the end that will be better for us, won't it?"

Shcherbakov drew himself up and said solemnly: "I'll try to be worthy of your love."

From a person like that one could mold anything, it seemed. "Maybe I'll be able to influence him, make him more human?" But at once Nina drove the thought away: "Don't be a fool. You've been burned twice; that's enough." She merely said, with a sigh: "No, why should you? Be as you are, I don't demand much. . . . But, I don't want to see any more of your major-domo, whatever his name is."

Shcherbakov drew himself up. "Has he done anything wrong?"

"He's a boor," she answered simply.

Without asking anything more, Shcherbakov opened the door and yelled: "Hey! Vanka!"

Vanka appeared at once, as if from out of the earth; obviously he had been standing nearby. His sly face was spread in a smile, his eyes were eager. Spoiled by his nearness to authority, he believed in his own power and indispensability, had no idea that something more powerful than he had come into the Shcherbakov house.

In a hoarse bass, Shcherbakov asked him, "Don't you know yet how to behave? You wretch!" and suddenly hit him in the teeth with his fist. It was so unexpected Nina jumped from her chair. But Shcherbakov, infuriated, shouted: "Go at once to the personnel branch and report that you're fired."

Vanka turned white as a sheet. Nina was alarmed, especially when he fell to his knees and, as if threatened with the death sentence, begged for mercy: "Vassily Alexandrovich, forgive me! I made a mistake! I won't do it again! Don't fire me! I'll serve you like a slave."

"Get out!" roared Shcherbakov, and kicked him into the corridor.

Nina expected that Shcherbakov would be upset or ashamed of showing his temper. But, turning a broadly smiling face to her, and very satisfied with himself, he came toward her jauntily and on the spur of the moment put his arms around her shoulders.

"Ah! Nina, we'll get along together, you and I!"

He felt easy now. The former awkwardness had disappeared. Stooping slightly, he kissed her for the first time. His moist lips touched hers. With difficulty she hid her repugnance. She freed herself from him gently and shook her head.

"I'm afraid I've detained you from important government work. You'd better go. Come, I'll see you off." And she went ahead, stepping lightly, erect and calm.

466

BOOK III

PART SEVEN

LⅡⅡⅡⅡⅡⅡⅡⅡⅡⅡⅡⅡⅡⅡⅡⅡⅡⅡⅡⅡⅡ

CHAPTER 1

NIKOLAI met Lida at the door of the barracks. She was just going for a walk with Tonya. It was Sunday, a fresh April day. The spring wind drove the frayed clouds, which vanished before the eyes under the rays of the sun. Both girls were dressed lightly and in holiday attire. Nikolai was sure that he had seen the light dress with the lilac flower on Lida previously at the summer house. But she was not wearing the belt now because of her already prominent stomach.

"We do not work today, so we decided to get a breath of fresh air," said Lida, smiling. As always, she was very glad to see Nikolai. Here he was again; he had not forgotten her. He was growing thinner, worried, but he was still the same light-haired and blue-eyed boy.

Nikolai approved: "That's an excellent idea and today is just the day for a walk. If you don't mind, I'll go with you. But first, let's go back to the barracks. I've brought a treat with me—we'll have some tea. Natalia is at home, of course?"

Nikolai spoke in a cheerful tone, but Lida noticed that he was gloomier than usual. That meant there had still been no results. Poor fellow, this treat of his was simply to soften the bitterness of failure. For more than three months now Nikolai had been trying to get Lida out of the cursed plant, had descended to all kinds of guile—and he was shrewd and sly as a harmless snake—but everything seemed to be in vain. Lida was not allowed to quit the plant. Nikolai began to feel as if everybody was conspiring against him. Lida herself guessed what was wrong—Durov. He had laid his heavy hand on her fate, and of

469

course, no such poor student as Nikolai could snatch her from under his paw.

Realizing the foolishness of his efforts, Lida was all the more filled with gratitude and compassion for Nikolai. Several times a week he came to see them, was exceptionally anxious and attentive, and each time his arrival was like a holiday to Lida. Often she thought that if it were not for dear, kind Nikolai she would not be able to bear her terrible ordeal.

It was particularly noisy and smoky in the barracks that day. Everyone was dressed up, and the girls, besides washing the spots of lime from their faces, had rouged their cheeks with beets and tinted their eyebrows with charcoal into fantastic curves. Lida's room was chockfull of people. From early morning the young men, who had managed to have a few drinks, had been sitting on the beds with their girls. Here and there careless words were heard, the affected squeals of the girls, and the stallion-like nickerings of the young fellows. Somewhere in a corner an accordion wheezed out a tune. On one of the beds a girl, forgotten by everybody, tossed about in a high fever. Her damp hair was sticking to her burning forehead, her head was thrown back, her lips moved soundlessly in delirium. At a long table the more sedate older people were drinking tea, gossiping, while those who had already had their tea stretched themselves out on the cots, belly up, blissfully happy. The supervisor circulated through the room, squeezed himself as close as he could to the girls, while they chased him away with curses. In a word, everything was as it should be.

Nikolai immediately ran to the kitchen to make tea. He was by now at home in the barracks. They all knew and liked him, and he also liked them. Everybody approved of his care for Lida, followed his efforts to get her out of their rotten barracks with interest and sympathy, but had little confidence in his success.

In the kitchen, Lida's mother Natalia was washing clothes in a small wooden tub. At sight of Nikolai she beamed—he was very dear to her, like her own son. Wiping her sweaty face with her hand and grumbling, "Tea! Tea! All they know is to slop tea," she split a match in two—economy—then lit the primus stove. While she was heating the water, Nikolai, trying to make himself heard above the hissing of the battery of primuses, prattled away with Natalia to his heart's content.

"Be a bit more careful with Tonya," she said significantly. "Don't say anything to hurt her by mistake. And don't joke—she doesn't like jokes. There's something wrong happening to her. We're all afraid for her."

470

They drank tea all together, inviting Tonya. Another permanent member of the tea parties, Musya, the senior in the room, went for a doctor to get a certificate for the sick girl: she would not, of course, be able to go to work next day.

Natalia drank her tea gravely, staidly, sipping it from her saucer. Between sips she leisurely reported the news to Nikolai: who had died, who had got married, who tried to commit suicide, who had disappeared without a trace, and who was caught and handed over to the prosecutor. Then she changed to small talk: "Yesterday the director of the plant ordered the supervisor to exterminate all the bugs in the barracks. You see, the doctors have found out that the people are becoming weakened from loss of blood during sleep and that this lowers productivity. The bugs are threatening to disrupt the plan. The supervisor stubbornly resisted and tried to convince him that a campaign against bugs was destined to failure. 'The bug,' says he, 'is Russian and therefore it is impossible to exterminate him. He is crafty and sneezes at all the subtleties of science.' And now the chief of the chemical laboratories himself has been ordered to prepare a sure remedy against the insects . . ."

Nikolai wasn't listening to Natalia. He sat opposite Lida and looked on happily while she ate the cakes. These cakes were his treat. By what miracle he was able to get them, nobody knew. He himself kept quiet about that.

"Very, very tasty!" repeated Lida delightedly, to give him pleasure. "Have some yourself." Indeed, she liked the cakes very much; but now, for some reason, she craved something salty more than anything else—dill pickles or mushrooms. But how could Nikolai be expected to think of that? And she hesitated to ask him.

Nikolai, on the other hand, looking at Lida, was thinking: "What are a few cakes? I'd give everything I have, if only you were happy and content. Darling Lida, inexperienced, timid, beaten down by sorrow! Such as she can only submit humbly to fate, resignedly, and quietly fade away . . ." With sharp horror Nikolai remembered that the workers were fed only once a day in the plant mess hall.

Every effort cost Lida a great deal. Once, when she was hanging out clothes in the yard, everything turned dark before her eyes and her legs gave way. The barrack children looked surprised when, for no apparent reason, she dropped to the ground and sat there for a few minutes unable to move. Her thinness made her look like a little girl. On the other hand, her eyes had doubled in size and her whole appearance had become grave and serene.

471

This gravity frightened Nikolai. With aching pity he recalled how in his presence Lida modestly concealed her stomach in the folds of her dress, and again he was ready to shout a protest with all his might: No! It was impossible to allow her to remain here one single day more! At all costs, she must be snatched out of here! But how?

CHAPTER 2

THE SUPERVISOR, seeing the cakes from the far end of the room, approached and hovered in their neighborhood, clearly trying to thrust himself on their company. But nobody invited him. Then his small faded eyes, separated by a long nose, blinked aggrievedly while his mouth twisted pathetically. He was wearing a bright red shirt and white pants which had slipped down over his gaunt belly; Nikolai, looking at them, was somewhat afraid that they would fall right down and expose his dirty underpants. Finally, without invitation, the supervisor sat down on the bench.

"Well, Nikolai, how's the world using you? Still tearing around without success?" he said, smiling mockingly and fingering a pimple on his neck. "You're trying in vain, old boy—just wasting your time. We won't give you Lida. She's one of the shock workers—the best Stakhanovka."

Nikolai was going to answer him roughly, but at that moment a woman's piercing scream rang out and silence fell at once. Even the accordion choked itself in the middle of a scale. The only thing heard was the rattle of the teapot in Tonya's hand. From behind a curtain, beyond which some family was living, a saucepan flew out like a rocket and landed with a bang on the table in front of the supervisor's nose.

"Damn it! The Orlovs are fighting again," observed the supervisor, and settled himself more comfortably, so as to observe further developments better.

Obviously the Orlovs were crowded: the curtain—a bright colored blanket—tossed about turbulently, ready at any instant to tear itself free of the nails in the ceiling; and in fact it did tear itself loose presently. Orlov was beating his wife on her emaciated bare back with one hand, while with the other he gripped her by the hair and shook her head from side to side. Three children, scrambling onto the red

472

pillows, were howling bloody murder all together, as if at a command, their large mouths open wide.

"Hit me! Hit me!" screamed the woman heartrendingly. And suddenly breaking free from him, but not running away, she thrust her ugly distorted face at him and screamed, full of consuming hate: "Now hit me! Here, you forgot to hit me here yet!"

"Aha! I forgot, eh? All right, here you are—take that!"

Blood flowed from her nose, but she continued to scream: "Hit me, hit me again! Why have you stopped? Are you tired?"

When the man, in a complete frenzy, eyes blazing wildly, reached for a bottle to finish her once and for all, Nikolai and two others pulled him away. The suffering woman was given some tea to drink. The man wheezed and wheezed and began to hang up the fallen blanket.

"Alas! The human race doesn't know how to live," sighed the supervisor, disappointed that everything had ended so quickly. He was already munching the cakes—he had snatched some during the uproar. "D'you know, Nikolai, you should stay and live with us. We'll set a splendid apartment aside for you, there in the corner, and when you get married we'll curtain you off with a blanket. You can knock off kids for yourself in complete privacy. It'll be really nice! And it's cheery here: every day a show; they can't live without a bully. Barbarians, in short."

Suddenly Tonya burst out laughing. She laughed long, hysterical, unchildlike, womanish laughter, and shouted: "He's right! It's merry here. See that one, lying there!" Tonya pointed at the sick girl. "It's funny for her! She'll die of laughter yet!"

Just as suddenly, she cut off her laughter. A sharp spasm passed over her face. She got up abruptly from the table, accidentally upsetting a glass of water with her elbow over the white trousers of the supervisor. The supervisor hissed fiercely, but she didn't even look at him as she left the room. Wiping up the water, the supervisor scowled in contempt: "A spoiled girl. She won't end well, believe me."

Nikolai got up. "Lida, let's go out," he said dully.

Outside they overtook Tonya. She was leaning against the board fence and looking straight ahead with a fixed stare, like a blind person.

Beside her on the fence was a tremendous poster—a young man and a girl, red cheeked, laughing, holding hands, were walking into the happy future; pictured on the horizon was a town made of crystal. At the top of the poster was a bright slogan: "Hail! to Soviet youth!" Across this sparkling vision of happiness someone had already managed to scribble an obscene word with charcoal.

473

Without saying anything, Lida took Tonya by the hand, walked with her ahead of Nikolai. The short-lived southern snow had disappeared long ago. It was wet Rostov April weather. A strong wind blew, swayed the girls—they were so light and weak. Tonya's face looked out pitifully from her ragged kerchief. As always, she looked like a garden scarecrow, although her clothes were clean. The old-womanish dark dress, too large for her, was drawn in by Lida's belt. At the back, the hem of her skirt hung almost to her heels, while in front it climbed upward. And where the former owner's obviously buxom breast had been, the dress hung now in pathetic folds. To crown it all, on her feet and over her girlish socks, Tonya wore men's boots of monstrous size—they had issued them to her at last. But at what a price! Nikolai, to whom Tonya's story had been told, knew. As if in a delirium, she had told the girls in the barracks how the foreman raped her: she had begged him, cried, had kissed his boots, but no—he had raped her.

Nikolai squeezed in between the girls, took their arms: "Let me lead you, or before you know it the wind will blow you away."

Lida smiled warmly at him, but Tonya shrank away—she wasn't used to friendly touches. They walked by squalid houses, passed the same kind of barracks they had just come out of. It was crowded; the workers with their families poured into the street to warm up under the spring sun, to breathe the fresh air. Sparkling puddles were ruffled by the wind. With quick hands the girls caught at their skirts, blown up balloonlike. The heedless sparrows flew up right under their feet.

With head high, Nikolai, smiling, led the girls in the very center of the sidewalk. They attracted attention, especially Tonya. But from these glances she cowered still more.

Nikolai wanted very much to drive away the hurt look from Tonya's face. He began purposely to talk all kinds of nonsense, and more foolish things happened to him in a week than to another in the course of a whole life. Tonya, walking uncertainly as if she were tripping over invisible stones, smiled. But when Nikolai wasn't looking at her the smile left her face, as if she smiled only for others but for herself there was no laughter. Then, suddenly, she said: "Let's turn into the park, it's very noisy here."

Nikolai understood—it was hard for her in front of people.

CHAPTER 3

THEY WENT into the vacant lot which for some reason was called a park—perhaps because a dozen trees grew there. Crossing the park, they stopped beside a broken-down shed. From its open door came the smell of rotting sawdust. From here a street car could be seen, at the other side of the park, turning at the loop—it was the end of the line. People were strolling about, but here, beside the shed, the park was deserted.

"I'm tired," said Lida, and sat down on some boards piled into a heap. "I'd like to sit like this all day, in the sun. It's wonderful."

Nikolai sat down beside her. About ten paces in front of them was a gully, overgrown with wild, bushy weeds. Tonya went near the edge and looked down.

"Look out! Don't fall! You'll hurt yourself," said Nikolai.

"It's all right; it's sloping."

None of them wanted to talk. Each was thinking of the other. From time to time Lida looked with surprise at Nikolai. "What a dear friend he is! Why does he still come to us? Why doesn't he give us up as hopeless?" she asked herself. Lida knew very well that this kind-hearted man, who had shown the world his courage, was the only person who was interested in their existence. And she thought: "There is nothing more precious than a good friend. Everything can be borne, even the unbearable, if one friend stands by you. One tender look, one kind smile—and faith in yourself, in your own strength, begins to grow, to broaden." Lida loved Nikolai now in a sisterly way and was grateful for his patient anxiety.

Nikolai was drawing lines on the ground with his shoe, subconsciously expressing thereby the gravity of his thoughts. In despair over his fruitless efforts, he felt all the more sharply the suffering of his beloved Lida. With her resigned eyes, and her soul like a child's—affectionate, impetuous . . . would it take long to crush such a one?

From the moment when Nikolai found Lida at the plant and began to visit her, he had noticed many changes in himself. He had stopped going out with his girl friend at the University. It had happened quite naturally. He had become friendly with her after Feodor's marriage, when he decided to forget about Lida and his dream. The girl turned out to be simple and amorous, and allowed him to do whatever he liked with her. Now, somehow, he never thought of her. Actually, he felt that it was out of place, shameful to snatch a little happiness for himself when such things were going on in the world. In his helplessness Nikolai slashed the air with his fist.

"What is it, Nikolai?"

"The same old thing . . . I hate them, I hate those ugly punks!" he exclaimed with fury. "Well-fed, inhuman as stone—you can't break them. Just yesterday I went to see one such bureaucrat. I know him very well. I told him about you, that you were a capable girl, perhaps he could place you somewhere with him. At first he smiled, was glad to promise everything; but when it came to *this*—period! At once, before my eyes, he froze, became as cold as stone. 'I can't, I can't do anything, there are no jobs available,' he repeated in a wooden voice. Well, all right, the time will come when they'll thaw out. . . . They'll recognize us yet, the scoundrels! I'll get revenge! I'll show them!"

He spoke so fiercely that Lida shrank back, frightened. She knew that he was discouraged and hurt because of his vain efforts to help her. But was he, Nikolai, capable of avenging anyone at all?

Quieting him, Lida pressed his hand. "Don't get excited, Nikolai. It really makes me ashamed when I think that you are suffering so much on my account. Now tell me about your studies. You know, I often think of the University."

They sat thus, warming themselves in the sun, until midday. Nikolai, carried away, began in a lively way to tell all the news which he thought would interest Lida. Purposely he did not mention his brother.

During all this time Tonya said not a word. The more enthusiastic Nikolai became, the more aloof she seemed to be. Lida glanced at her often; Tonya frightened her.

At midday Nikolai had to hurry to the students' mess for his dinner; he had to go all the way across the city on the street car. He got up: "Well, it's time I was going. Meantime, until the next free day, if not before. So long, Tonya, be a good girl and don't be downhearted. Honestly, sometimes I look at you and you seem like sisters."

Both girls also rose.

"I'll go along with you a little way, Nikolai," said Lida, and turned to Tonya: "You sit here, dear, I'll be back soon."

Silently the girl nodded her head.

As Nikolai walked away with Lida the last thing that struck him was Tonya's figure—such a child, small, reserved, deserted. She was standing beside the door of the shed, as if she had forgotten them, looking

476

at the flying clouds almost greedily. A strange, stabbing foreboding of trouble oppressed Nikolai's heart. But he tried to shake it off.

"Lida, I think you should take Tonya to the doctor," he said when they had gone some distance. "She's too quiet . . ."

"Yes, you're probably right," agreed Lida.

A little later Nikolai said dully: "Forgive me, Lida, for having accomplished nothing. I'm ashamed to remember how I shouted: 'I'll do everything, I'll pull you out of this cursed place!' As you see, nothing has come of it. Forgive me."

Tears started in Lida's eyes. "Dear Nikolai, I don't need anything. Honestly, I don't. Everything will turn out all right, somehow." She took his arm. Nikolai looked at her sidewise. Lida walked lightly, inhaling the fresh air deeply and apparently with pleasure. Her sweet face, usually tired and sad, now was rosy and animated. The corners of her lips were almost smiling. "What's wrong with her? She doesn't understand the whole horror. How can she be so forgiving?"

But Lida was thinking about her child. She felt its movement and suddenly imagined "him" as a boy—light-haired, merry, looking, of course, like Feodor. She caught herself at this thought, so unexpected, alarming, as if the spring wind had scattered the clouds of despair and opened before her a radiant vista, very like the one which she had seen in the Crimea. Her thoughts went stubbornly to that unforgettable moment when she and Feodor had been happy together. There, on the shore of the Black Sea, he had embraced her and it seemed to Lida that over the sea, into which the tremendous globe of the sun was dropping, golden threads were drawn from their hearts and reached to the very sun. Lida knew happiness then. Neither what happened later, nor the black torture of the present, could obliterate from her memory that magic vision.

"Lida," asked Nikolai, looking into her dreaming eyes, "Lida, why are you smiling?"

Lida shook her head in embarrassment. "Oh, I just thought of something . . . Tell me, have you seen Feodor?"

"You still think about him?" Nikolai asked in surprise.

"Why, of course. You see, Feodor hasn't seen *him* yet . . ."

Nikolai didn't reply. Thoughtfully he looked at her hair. "It is more delicate than fine smoke," he thought.

Lida smiled: "You probably think that I'm crazy?"

"I'm crazy too," replied Nikolai. "I also want to be happy."

A street car came along, clanking and rocking from side to side.

Nikolai shook Lida's hand hard, then jumped onto the platform. From there he waved, shouted: "Lida, keep up your courage; I haven't lost hope yet!" The street car moved off.

Lida went back to Tonya, smiling to herself on the way: "What a surprising person Nikolai is. At first I thought he was quite different . . ."

Tonya wasn't beside the shed. Sudden alarm seized Lida. She ran to the gully, but stopped half way, sighed with relief: "Why, of course! Why didn't I think of that before—she was exhausted, poor thing, by the fresh air and now she's sleeping in the shed, on the sawdust."

At the door of the dark shed Lida called: "Tonya! Tonyusha! Where are you?"

Then she took a step inside and suddenly cried out wildly: there, from the narrow belt strung over a rafter, hung Tonya.

CHAPTER 4

FROM THAT moment Lida's panic began. Tonya's childlike head, tilted over helplessly toward her left breast, was imprinted on her brain as if with a white-hot iron. This terrible picture broke the thin ice of her hopes; fear—monstrous, primitive—gushed to the surface. Lida started to rush to the street-car stop; she wanted to overtake Nikolai, to get him to help her, and for company, so that she wouldn't be alone. But she didn't reach it; she slipped helplessly to the ground beside a thin woman with a face full of suffering, who was sitting cross-legged, darning a stocking. Near her on the ground a bloated child with crooked legs was crawling around.

"Has something happened?" the woman asked quietly.

"Yes, Tonya has hanged herself," Lida replied dazedly, not taking her eyes off the child. He crawled to her awkwardly, put out his hand, smiled an old, wise smile.

"What do you want?" asked Lida, and suddenly realized what it was she feared so terribly and unconsciously. It was not fear for herself, but for her child. What awaited him? He would be so small and helpless. They would crush him with a heavy boot. How could she protect, save him?

People started running toward the shed. It seemed to Lida that the whole scene—the running people, the clouds above, the bare trees and the dark shed by the gully—all this was taking place far, far away and

478

had absolutely nothing to do with her. She didn't even hear the shouts of the people. The woman rose, picked up her child, and said in the same quiet voice: "Let's go."

"But I don't want to, I'm afraid," replied Lida fearfully.

"No, no, not there. Come with me; you must rest, calm down."

Lida went with her submissively. The woman walked without haste. She led her to a little log house, where her room was. It was poorly furnished, but clean, lighted by a single small window.

"Here—lie down here." The woman pointed to a narrow bed. "I'll get something to eat," and she began to tinker with the primus stove.

Lida lay on her back and closed her eyes. It was unbelievable that Tonya, alive a few minutes ago, whom she had loved like her own sister, was being taken down now from the noose, dead. So there was no room for illusion. Tonya had realized this before Lida had. She had counted the cost and decided that there was no other way out. Lida didn't notice when she began to talk aloud. Probably it was her unconscious desire for contact with a living being. The woman didn't interrupt her, didn't ask questions. She poured some kvass into a bowl, crumbled black bread and onion into it. When the potatoes in the pot were ready, she called her: "Let's eat. Please sit down. It's not much of a meal, of course, but . . ."

While they were eating the woman told Lida her name: Elizaveta Rubakin, a school teacher. She told about herself in sparing but accurate phrases. "My husband died last year. I live alone."

She placed the child on her knee, began to feed him some potatoes. He ate greedily. Suddenly the woman sighed deeply: "I pity the child. He has rickets; he should be fed and fed—but with what? There's barely enough food to sustain the spark of life."

She asked Lida, while they were drinking tea: "If I'm not mistaken, your friend's name was Tonya?"

"Yes."

"I'll pray for her."

"Surely you're not a believer?"

The woman nodded her head. "Are you surprised that I'm a teacher and a believer? They don't know about it at school. But I trust you, of course."

"Why?"

"Why not? Sorrow and despair are imprinted on your face. People with such faces don't inform . . . Tell me, are you expecting your first child?"

"Yes."

479

"I had three, but two died of starvation."

Lida shuddered. The woman pronounced these words in such a frightfully resigned voice that Lida shrank back in her chair. "That's terrible . . ." she whispered.

"Yes, it's awful. They died almost at the same time, lying so small, like two curled-up yellow leaves. We buried them side by side. And afterwards, when I was sweeping up the room, I found a small bootie—such a little one, so pitiful; and at once the child, as if alive, rose before my eyes. And I fell on the floor, drowned in tears. . . . Volodya—my husband—couldn't stand it when the second child died. He killed himself. He wanted to kill me first, and this one, but I begged him not to. It's not right, to take your own life. It's wrong and sinful."

She became silent; then she asked Lida: "You said you had parted from your husband. Why?"

"He left me," replied Lida and her lips trembled. It was the first time she had pronounced the word "left" aloud. It was impossible to lie to this woman.

"Did he love you?"

"Yes, he loved me," replied Lida with heat.

"Then he'll return. Love is stronger than anything, believe me."

Elizaveta got up from the table and opened a small cupboard in the corner; inside was an ikon. She dropped to her knees and softly began to say the words of a prayer. It was quiet in the room, water was dripping somewhere from a basin. Lida set her lips, to keep from moaning. She closed her eyes. The consuming anguish of her own desolation was bursting her breast.

The woman rose from her knees and, going to the window, looked through it. Her whole figure expressed the deepest, most concentrated sorrow.

"Well, I'll be going," said Lida hesitantly. The woman didn't reply, didn't even move. Obviously she was far away. With a desperately beating heart Lida left, closing the door carefully. The little boy tried to catch hold of her skirt but fell on the floor with his weak little body, and cried. Lida bore that cry away in her like a stone.

The barracks were scarcely different from usual. The people were just the same, sitting around, gathered in groups, lying on the beds. But less laughter and shouting was heard among the young people. Many were thoughtful, moody.

On seeing her daughter, Natalia threw herself at her: "Where did

480

you disappear to? I looked all over the place for you. . . . Don't you know that Tonya has hanged herself?"

"Yes, I know," answered Lida in such a dull voice that her mother looked at her in alarm.

The rest of the day and most of the night Lida thought and thought. There was so much she couldn't understand. Tonya had killed herself, while that woman whose husband committed suicide had much greater sorrow—her husband and two children dead and probably the third would die soon, which meant that she had no future. And yet she preferred to live! What on earth supports her? What gives her strength? Religion?

Lida rubbed her temples where her blood was coursing feverishly, thumping dully in her ears. Life was so terrible. It was as if she were living not with humans but with wild animals who were devouring each other. Why is there no room in the world for good, honest, innocent people? Like Andrei and Tonya? Why must they perish, become victims of human cruelty? Cruelty is terrible in animals, but unbearable in humans.

Human fury was raging around Lida like a hungry pack of dogs. Flashing their eyes, showing their teeth, the dogs were approaching nearer and nearer for the final leap, after which there is a short scream and death. With what effort she had tried to bring herself, her independence and pride, through this monstrous life! But she had found only bitter despair for her youth, her outraged dream. What more could be done? One thing was obvious: it was impossible, unthinkable to leave everything as it was before. Toward morning Lida decided she must go to Feodor. She was sure that if she explained to him the whole horror of her position, he would understand. Wasn't it his child that was threatened? Wouldn't he feel this? Of course he would feel it— surely he was not a beast! Lida fell asleep toward morning. She didn't hear Natalia come to her and look long, with wistful, motherly eyes at her thin little face, lit dimly by the dawn.

In the morning Lida didn't go to work. That was a crime, she knew. But in this there was a measure of desperation: either Feodor would understand and their life together would be resumed, or—then there was only one end, and she wouldn't need to worry about being absent.

Lida dressed in the woodshed which was in the barrack yard. She had not yet become used to dressing in the barrack room where at any time a family man might come out from behind a curtain, or the syrupy-faced supervisor might open the door without knocking. It was crowded

481

in the shed where, in addition to the wood, there was all kinds of trash. Lida was going to put on the dress with the lilac flowers which she had worn the previous day, then suddenly remembered that it was with the belt to that dress that Tonya had hanged herself. All atremble, Lida tore the dress off and, throwing on her coat, ran into the dormitory. There, in her suitcase, among blouses, skirts, precious photographs of friends, she selected the very best that she had—a blue dress. This dress was specially dear to her; she had worn it when Feodor kissed her the first time. When the police ordered her and her mother out of their house with only one suitcase of clothes, she had snatched this dress first.

Lida returned to the woodshed and put on the blue dress. Then, in front of a sliver of mirror, she touched up her eyelids slightly with a blue eyebrow pencil. After hesitating a little, she put on some turquoise beads. Stealthily, like a thief, she went out of the shed. It was still early. The sun, cold and wrapped in morning mist, was barely rising above the roof of the barracks. Lida, shuddering in her bare shoulders as from a chill, ran to the gate. At this moment, Natalia, who had been looking for her to go to work, saw her. She cried out in fright: "Lida, where are you going?"

Lida stopped, but immediately thought: "Oh, it doesn't matter!" and waving her hand to her mother, she ran to the street car.

CHAPTER 5

THREE MEN were waiting in the Director's reception room, a professor and two students. They looked at Lida in astonishment; probably her appearance was strange. She wanted to go straight into Feodor's office, but at that moment the manager of studies came out. He didn't recognize her at once, but when he did, he was embarrassed —he couldn't think what to say to her, how to treat her. He decided to be neutral, not boorish—just fairly respectful, his own particular brand of treacherous respect.

"What can I do for you?" he asked, feeling that something extraordinary was about to happen. Lida's face, drawn from despair, her cold, clasped fingers, spoke most eloquently of this.

"I've come to see the Director," said Lida.

"But he's engaged. Allow me to tell him," and the manager disappeared into the office, not closing the door behind him. Lida heard

Feodor's voice and her heart contracted, his low voice resounding in every fiber of her body. Involuntarily she took a step forward. The familiar voice, like a stone falling into a pond, aroused waves of unforgettable feelings in her. How joyfully her eyelids flew open, with what childlike trust her eyes brightened, how pathetically her lips smiled!

The manager came out quickly, and completely changed. In a very dry and official tone he said: "The Comrade Director cannot see you."

Lida stood abashed, not understanding. As if in her sleep, she repeated: "He cannot receive me? But I must see him! Do you understand? I must!" Then, as if coming to herself she threw herself at the door, but the manager blocked her way.

"You mustn't, Citizeness Sidorov," he said with great emphasis. There was an ugly inference in the "Sidorov." The manager enjoyed being a cad, and knew how to be one.

Lida fluttered about the reception room like a wounded bird. Suddenly she stopped: "All right. Then I'll write him a note."

The manager shook his head in dissent, but then said, shrugging his shoulders: "Write one if you like. It's all the same to me."

But it wasn't all the same to him. He looked forward with delight to the impression his report would make on the chief of the Special Branch, how the darling Director's former wife, with a big belly—obviously near her time—visited him right in the University, how he did not receive her and how she wrote him a note. Scandal! Scandal! The manager was afraid of and did not like the too cold and haughty Director (hard-as-stone Bolshevik! That's what he thinks!) and considered it a pleasure to drag him into a scandal.

Lida took a pencil and pad from the desk. Her thoughts tumbled over each other in her agitation. One thing was certain: she must write only what was most important, and briefly; her life would depend on that. The pad shook in her thin little hand.

"Dear Fedya," ("Yes, that's true—he's dear, even now," thought Lida)—"I do not ask your love, but pity the child . . ." The pencil broke. What a nuisance. She must write quicker, quicker. Lida ran from one student to another, asking for a pencil.

"Yes, yes, I must say the important thing," thought Lida again and wrote: "Yesterday Tonya perished. I will be next if you don't save me and our child. You mustn't be a murderer—you must not. LIDA."

She tore off the page; a tear fell on it.

"There." She handed the note to the manager. "Give it to Feodor." The manager took the note, brazenly read it and, raising his eyebrows in amazement, vanished into the office. She heard him turn the key in the lock from the inside.

Lida sat down. Her heart was beating as if she were awaiting a sentence. The students and the professor looked at her with fear and curiosity. The professor turned to her: "Tell me, aren't you Lydia Novikov, the Director's wife?" Lida didn't hear him.

The manager came out. His lips were twisted. Silently he handed the note to Lida, looking with interest at her face. His interest changed to fright—Lida's face turned pale as the paper. He knew what was wrong: across Lida's note Feodor had written: "Leave me in peace. F. NOVIKOV."

Clutching her heart, Lida stood for several moments; then, holding onto the wall, she went into the corridor. She was shaking all over; the floor had dropped from under her feet.

The rumor about Lida's visit had preceded her. The curious poured into the corridor. But no one approached her, no one supported her as she walked down the steps, almost fainting. Lida herself noticed no one. Her face was transparently white, with deep blue circles under her eyes.

She found herself on a street car. A young man, with a flush of excitement on his cheeks, had squeezed himself close to her in the crowd. Lida paid attention to him only when his fumbling fingers began cautiously to lift the hem of her skirt. She turned to him and said, in a faraway voice: "Leave me in peace."

As she pronounced these words, her face twisted in a spasm of pain, such pain that the young lad forgot even to be embarrassed.

There was nobody in the barracks except children and old people. Lida went into the dormitory and threw herself on the bed. She was trembling like an aspen leaf. She still squeezed the note in her hand, then dropped it on the bed.

"Leave me in peace, leave me in peace . . ." These words, cold and monotonous like the fall of rain drops, repeated themselves in her head.

CHAPTER 6

AT SEVEN o'clock that same Monday evening Nikolai, passing the Rostov Theatre in the street car, saw Nina Gorin from the window. She was just driving up to the theatre entrance in an open automobile. Beside her sat a man whose face was familiar to Nikolai. A joyful feeling came over Nikolai—at last the long-expected luck had come. Of course,

Nina would help Lida. Nikolai jumped off the street car while it was still going and ran toward Nina's car. She was already getting out. The man —Nikolai remembered now that it was Shcherbakov, Second Party Secretary—held her arm. Running toward them, Nikolai cried:

"Nina, Nina! Wait!"

Nina turned at his shout, but then frowned and walked on. Nikolai, in despair, quickened his step but was unable to catch up to her— somebody's strong hands caught him by the wrists: "Where d'you think you're going?"

"Hey! What's wrong?" Nikolai protested; but looking at the two men holding him, he realized that they were NKVD in plain clothes. However, Nikolai had time to shout to Nina: "Please listen to me! I've come from Lida!"

Nina stopped at once. "Let him go, I know him. . . . Do you know where Lida is?" she asked Nikolai quickly when he came up to her.

"Yes, I saw her only yesterday . . ."

"Why on earth hasn't she called me?" Nina asked, surprised.

"It's a long story. I'll tell you later."

"In that case I want to see her at once. Vassily," she turned to Shcherbakov, "I won't go to the concert. You stay, but I must go to my friend. It's very important."

Shcherbakov, frowning angrily, asked Nikolai: "Where does this Lida live?"

"At the Obukhov barracks."

"In the barracks?" exclaimed Shcherbakov. "Nina, do you realize where you are going?"

"Yes," replied Nina. "And you are going with us. Yes! Yes! Right away!"

Nikolai rode in an automobile for the first time in his life. Under different circumstances he would have enjoyed the luxury, but now he had no time for that. He hurried to tell Nina about Lida.

"I'm afraid for her. That plant will break a strong man, to say nothing of her, and she with child."

Nina listened to him and a sob rose in her throat.

At the barracks the people poured out to see the glittering automobile. The frightened supervisor appeared and decided that some important inspection had arrived, stood drawn up importantly, saluting with his right hand while holding up his drooping pants with his left.

Nikolai led Nina straight to Lida's room. Nina looked around her in horror. The dirty floor, the old walls saturated with the smell of sweat and bedbugs, the multitude of haggard people, silently making

485

way before them, shocked her. This was the first time since her arrival in Russia that she had been in a workers' barrack. Shcherbakov walked behind, his fleshy nose sniffing fastidiously.

In the room, at sight of Natalia, Nikolai felt at once the hot breath of trouble, although he knew nothing yet. He asked where Lida was.

"She left the room a few minutes ago. I myself have just come back from work," replied Natalia in a tired voice. "She's probably sitting somewhere alone. Being so terribly upset over Tonya, she didn't even go to work. I'm afraid they'll punish her for staying away . . ."

"But what happened to Tonya?"

"Don't you know? Why, she hanged herself."

"Hanged herself!" exclaimed Nikolai.

Nikolai noticed a crumpled piece of paper on Lida's bed. He took it, read it through, sensed everything, and suddenly shouted: "Where is Lida, for heaven's sake!" He caught Natalia by the arm and by the force of this impulse she felt the full measure of his love for her daughter.

Natalia became alarmed: "Has something happened? Lida didn't tell me anything! She just kissed me suddenly and went out."

Forgetting himself, Nikolai ran out into the yard, feverishly asked the first boy he saw: "Have you seen Lida Sidorov?"

"I saw her," replied the boy. "She went to the shed to change her clothes. She always changes there."

Nikolai rushed to the woodshed. The door was locked on the inside. He pressed his ear against the door.

"Lida, are you there?" Nikolai called. There was no answer.

Nikolai knocked, but, seeing an axe stuck into a chunk of wood, he snatched it up and began to break down the door.

"Hey! Easy there!" shouted the supervisor angrily. "That's government property! You'll have to answer for it."

In his rage Nikolai roared at the supervisor, knocked him aside roughly and broke into the shed. On the earth floor, face down, lay Lida, her left arm twisted under her.

Nikolai dropped to his knees beside Lida and turned her toward him. A deathly pallor covered her beloved face; her eyes were shut tight, as if she were ashamed for the people standing around her. There was blood on her left arm. Nikolai only then noticed the bloodstained knife lying beside her.

"She's cut a vein," he said in horror.

Tearing open the collar of her dress, Nikolai placed his ear to her

486

small, firm breast—her heart was beating weakly. "She's alive!" he shouted joyfully, and began to bandage her wrist swiftly.

Nina, pale, stood leaning against the wall, not taking her eyes off Lida. "Why? Why?" she repeated, and spasms of despair tightened her throat.

Lida groaned.

"We must get her to the hospital at once," said Nikolai. Nina came to herself. She turned abruptly to Shcherbakov, who just stood, staring, confused.

"Vassily," she said in a shaking voice, "I don't know how you're going to do this, but Lida must live." Then she turned to Natalia: "Get all your things together, you'll go with us. You won't come back here any more."

The supervisor, who had been hanging around, couldn't restrain himself and broke in: "If I may make so bold as to inform you, Comrade—I don't know your name—just in case you may not know it: Natalia Sidorov's husband is an enemy of the people, and today Lida, her daughter, was absent from work without permission, for which she is liable to punishment in accordance with all the severity of the labor code. That she tried to evade punishment by committing suicide doesn't mean a thing . . ."

Nikolai turned to the supervisor, and baring his teeth, hit him on the ear. "That's for the enemy," he said, and hit him again: "And that's for being absent. I've wanted to do that for a long time."

The supervisor rushed to the lanky Shcherbakov for protection, but the latter kicked him.

They placed Lida, still unconscious, in the automobile. A minute later Natalia got in with her suitcase on her knees; the crowded automobile, splashing garbage around, flew out of the filthy yard.

At the hospital they had to wait a long time. Nina sat on a divan, tense, ready to get up at first sight of the doctor, while Nikolai sat on a chair beside a small table, smoking nervously. They were silent. Each thought his own thoughts. Shcherbakov paced with long strides up and down the reception room, cast reproachful looks at Nina, still puzzled: Why, instead of being at the concert, had he found himself in the hospital among these unknown crazy people? From one corner of the divan Natalia vacantly followed his boots, glittering in front of her eyes.

When at last the door opened and the doctor appeared, they all looked at him with dread: the doctor's face was worried, tired. Turning to Shcherbakov, he said sullenly: "She will live."

487

Nikolai inhaled deeply, dropped his head onto the table, sobbed and laughed.

CHAPTER 7

FEODOR NOVIKOV, returning late in the evening from a Party conference, opened the door of his apartment, switched on the light and almost shouted with surprise: in the armchair directly facing the door sat Nikolai, looking at him with eyes of hate.

Feodor took a step forward. "What are you doing here?"

"I've come to square accounts with you, Feodor," replied Nikolai, without getting up. "Do you remember, I said that we would meet again on a narrow path? And so we meet. But now we won't part."

Feodor's steel eyes measured Nikolai contemptuously and coldly. "You know I don't like jokes, Nikolai. I'm tired, I want to go to bed. Get out!"

"Not before we square accounts. Shut the door!"

Not moving, Feodor looked at his brother. Nikolai's face astonished him—grim, frozen in rage. It seemed unbelievable that not so long ago this same Nikolai was eating the leavings from his plate in the University mess, chattering about girls, was proud, jealous, and respectful of him, while Feodor considered Nikolai a light-minded boy and empty vessel. At that time he had been afraid of him, afraid that Nikolai would somehow spoil his career with his frivolity. Now he was also afraid, but of something quite different. Nikolai—tired, thin, with two slowly stirring muscles in his cheeks—was fearsome with an inner righteousness. In his eyes Feodor read unconcealed contempt for himself.

Feodor shut the door.

"And how do you intend to square accounts? I'm trembling with curiosity." Feodor sneered, still with an air of superiority. It was difficult for him to keep up this pretense.

Nikolai got up and, from a distance, showed him Lida's note. "I read your resolution," he said hoarsely. "And you are to be congratulated! You have become a real hard-as-stone Bolshevik and learned how to carry out death sentences."

Feodor's jaw muscles swelled wickedly. "Easy, easy," he threatened: "It doesn't count with me that you're my brother."

Nikolai paled in anger, came up close to Feodor, not taking his angry eyes off him. "You scoundrel!" he said. "Why are you posing? You haven't been my brother for a long time."

Feodor took a step forward. "Nikolai, cool down," he said in a conciliatory way. "Let's come to an understanding. We aren't boys— there's no need for us to get into a fight." Feodor was smiling ingratiatingly now. Nikolai, his whole body leaning forward as if he didn't believe his eyes, looked into the smiling face of his brother. Then he caught his brother by the arm and gripped it painfully.

"Let's be calm. . . . Let go of my arm, Nikolai," said Feodor. "Why should we quarrel? There's nothing on earth that can't be settled peacefully. Lay out your thoughts and I'll lay mine out. We'll reach a solution."

"I'm afraid, Feodor, that we won't understand each other."

"We'll understand; we'll understand."

Avoiding Nikolai's persistent stare, Feodor went into the kitchen and returned with a bottle and two glasses, taking a fleeting look at his brother in passing. Nikolai was sitting in an armchair, his head bowed. Feodor stopped in front of him, clinked his glass.

"Would you like some vodka?"

Nikolai took the glass, his teeth rattling against the edge, and drank it. His thoughts were as concentrated as the detonator in an explosive. "Feodor, do you know that she tried to kill herself and the child? That's where you have driven her."

Feodor's sunken gray eyes looked at Nikolai heavily, without blinking. "There you are: you're always in a hurry with conclusions," he said coldly. "I have nothing to do with that."

"Ah . . . so you have nothing to do with it?" Nikolai opened his eyes wide and asked, holding his breath: "And who's to blame?"

"What do you mean—who? That's life."

"I see, I see."

"Mind you, I sincerely pity Lida."

"Ah! You pity her."

Nikolai looked at the hateful face of his brother and thought with a pang: "I should have hit him at once, in passion. . . . Now he'll talk my head off—he's an expert." Placing the tumbler on the floor he rose, went to the door and turned the key, then swung around toward Feodor who was standing beside an armchair. Nikolai's eyes were bright and wicked. Feodor at once drew himself up, paled.

Nikolai went at him silently, breathing hard. He didn't know what his own face was like at that moment, but Feodor's face expressed

489

horror. All that had accumulated in Nikolai for the past few months burst out in mad fury. He could no longer hold in check the feeling of hate and revenge. His face knotted, his clenched teeth grinned, he even hissed. Feodor retreated before this terrible vision of hatred, snatched at his revolver. At that moment Nikolai rushed at him and caught his arm, preventing him from raising it.

"Throw it away!" he cried out, not recognizing his own voice, it was so high-pitched and strained. "Drop it, you bastard!"

The revolver thudded to the carpet. With a roar the brothers grappled, like a couple of mad dogs. They drove their fists at each other. They fell, got up, fell down again. Nikolai's muscles strained and an old, forgotten, vulgar, primitive joy of physical strength overwhelmed his consciousness. His muscles, swollen from anger, were ready to burst.

"Ha! You swine! This isn't making a fool of the helpless Lida!"

Feodor replied with a curse, tore himself free for an instant, snatched up a chair and threw it at his brother. But Nikolai dodged; the chair missed him and crashed into the door, flying into splinters. With a leap Nikolai reached Feodor and hit him in the teeth. On the Director's lip a scarlet stream appeared. Evading the second blow, Feodor again seized Nikolai in his arms—they clutched at throats, tore at flesh, rolled and kicked on the floor. But they were of even strength. At last they reached that point of mutual exhaustion when a puff would have tumbled the enemy, but neither had enough strength even for that. They lay on the floor locked in a close grip, motionless—just breathing heavily. Nikolai recovered first. With his last strength he rose over his brother and hit him hard on the temple; Feodor grunted hoarsely and rolled over.

Nikolai got up with difficulty, swaying as if he were drunk, covered with blood, and went into the kitchen. He washed up somehow. When he returned to the room Feodor was sitting on the floor shaking his head. Both his eyes were swollen and his shirt was ripped. Nikolai saw his bloody lips part with difficulty, baring his teeth in a spasm.

"Nikolai," Feodor said huskily, and stopped, slowly licking his lips. "I'll tell no one about this fight, and you keep your mouth shut."

"All right," replied Nikolai. Feodor looked pitiful, but there was no pity for him in Nikolai's heart. He took the bottle, filled a glass, was going to drink it; but he changed his mind and brought it, spilling in his shaking hand, to his brother's lips.

"Here, drink."

490

"Thanks. . . . It's funny, Nikolai, we're brothers, but we fight like two dogs, like enemies."

"We are enemies."

"Like that?"

"Yes."

A minute or so later Feodor asked: "How's Lida?"

"She's all right now. She's in a hospital."

"Tell me, do you love her very much?"

Nikolai started, frowning, but replied: "It's impossible not to love Lida. You don't know her—nor is it likely that you ever will."

"Yes, when you think of it, you're right. Apparently, I'm not fated to have a family. I've burned my fingers twice. The first time with Nina . . . I am unlucky . . . I'm unlucky, Nikolai," he repeated dejectedly. "Oh! If somebody would only point out to me the man who made my life like this, I would choke him with these hands . . ."

Nikolai went to the door. He was still quite hot after the fight. His eyes shone; his teeth flashed. The whining of his brother didn't move him. He knew that Feodor was weakened, so he was whimpering like a beaten dog. Tomorrow he would pull himself up, become hardened again—Nikolai no longer deceived himself.

"I'm going," he said. At the door he stopped: "Now, I suppose you'll kick me out of the University?"

"Why? Are you afraid?"

"No—just curious."

"No, I won't kick you out. Only, only . . ." he waved his hand weakly. "Don't think badly of me."

Nikolai left. It was light outside, every now and then the moon peeped from behind the swiftly flying clouds, and each time it seemed younger and brighter. Nikolai's steps sounded hollowly on the deserted street. Suddenly the wind brought the damp smell of the river. Nikolai inhaled it with pleasure and smiled. Why was he so happy? Because Feodor acknowledged his superiority? Because he had chosen the right way in this difficult life? Because he had always realized that he had a heart? Yes, there was all that. But the main thing was that Lida was alive. His own, dear Lida. Tomorrow he would see her again, she would look at him—and in her eyes, as always, an amazing world would be revealed, clean, sunny, human, a world toward which his soul was striving so stubbornly and joyfully.

THE WEDDING, to Vassily Shcherbakov's great disappointment, had to be postponed for two whole months. His father, Member of the Politburo Alexander Shcherbakov, was busy with some particularly important affairs in Moscow and couldn't come before that. In a letter to his son he warned him that on no account was he to celebrate the wedding without him. And here he added that he was bringing him some good news, a present from the "boss" to the newlyweds. His father spoke warmly about the bride, writing that he had met her two or three times in Moscow when she was visiting there with Mikhail Gorin. "Nina is a beautiful girl and evidently clever. I approve of your choice. The boss is of the same opinion. As to the wedding—we'll put on such a feast in Rostov that all the devils in the world will be green with envy."

Vassily read, and bit his lip in chagrin. The cursed delay! Apparently nobody cared a hoot about how he felt. Urged on by passion, Vassily had promptly registered with Nina in the registry office the day after her unexpected arrival. His friends had congratulated him, winked significantly; one or two had knocked off a joke suitable to the occasion—but they, arriving home, lived like two strangers in a hotel: Nina did not allow him in her room. She suddenly turned to stone. "I'll be your wife after the wedding," she repeated, as if splashing ice water on his impassioned heart. Vassily was ready to yowl like a stray cat. He began to smoke a lot; when he met Nina he would start and swallow saliva, even get headaches. "This is like a monastery," he thought angrily. "It's all right for her, the virgin, to control herself— she doesn't know what she's missing."

The very first week his patience broke. He began to watch Nina like a peeping Tom. He got a key to her bedroom and when she wasn't there, went in stealthily, with trembling fingers pawed her dresses, lingerie, ashamed of himself, kissed the silk cloth. Once, in secret, Vassily climbed up an oak tree that grew opposite Nina's window, sat there one whole evening. What he saw through the window he alone knew—he, and a crow roosting on a branch right over his head. Vassily would not have come down from the tree so quickly had not the cursed bird begun to caw loudly—apparently she was tired of his uninvited presence. Swearing like the devil, Vassily climbed down the tree hurriedly, tore his pants, scratched his cheek, and clambered through the bushes in the darkness, drunk with aroused passion. He only had to shut his eyes and before him appeared Nina, naked. Her gleaming body lit up the whole world. To drive away the delightful vision, Vassily got terribly drunk that night. He drank until morning in his study. Toward dawn he saw a little devil—a little green female devil sitting on the leader's portrait, like a crow on a branch. Teasing him, the devil showed him her green tongue. Vassily threw a bottle at her, but missed her—shreds of paper remained of the leader, while the devil sat as before on the frame and made altogether indecent gestures. Only on the third day did Vassily calm down. In the end, quite upset, he was sorry that he had fired the major-domo Vanka— the latter would without doubt have arranged something with the girls.

Only the promise of pleasant news eased his inhuman sufferings. He guessed what his father was hinting at. And even before the arrival of Alexander Shcherbakov the Provincial Committee of the Party received official notification from the Central Committee: Veria was elected a candidate-member of the Politburo and must soon leave for Moscow to take up his new duties. In his place, as First Secretary of the Northern Caucasus Committee of the Party, Vassily Shcherbakov was appointed.

On the day he received the news Vassily, barely taking time to accept the congratulations of his subordinates, arrived home in a triumphant mood and hurried to tell Nina the good news. So he hadn't suffered in vain: It was going to be a double celebration—there was great revelry ahead, friendly meetings with honored guests, the pinnacle of his young but rich fame. Knowing how his father liked to carouse, Vassily anticipated the pleasures of the celebration: "There'll be a feast, by God, big as a mountain! We'll fill the Don with wine!"

To his surprise Nina showed no joy whatever.

"You told me long ago that you would get Veria's place," she remarked in an indifferent tone.

She was sitting on a divan in the parlor, a number of letters on the small table in front of her and on her knees. She was wearing a plain white dress; her arms, bronze from sunburn, bare to the shoulders; on her breast a round, silver medallion. As always, Vassily was astounded by her beauty and stood in front of her for a minute or two in silence, powerless to tear himself away from her large eyes. Then, remembering, he exhaled loudly through his nostrils.

"Yes, but that was just talk, while this is the actual fact!" he exclaimed. "Here's the telegram from Moscow. Read it. Tomorrow the

493

announcement will be printed in *Molot,* and maybe *Pravda* will squeeze in a line or two. Ah! Nina, don't you see what this means? Now I'm boss of the whole province, absolute boss!" Vassily began to walk quickly up and down the parlor, in joyful excitement waving his arms, rumpling his hair. "Is the door closed? Good. So, Vanka Popov will be the first one I'll get rid of. Let him go to the devil! He congratulated me today more warmly than anyone else—'the cat knows whose meat she ate.' In general, this little nest will have to be cleaned up! I'll bring all the tainted ones to account. If I ever seize someone by the scruff of the neck, he'll never get away from me—neither cross nor pestle will help him. And with Semyonov—he's one of these smart alecks in the Special Branch—I'll talk turkey seriously. I'll put the question point blank, broadly and on principle, so that he'll feel who the boss is now. And if he resists, well—I've got some interesting evidence on him too. Don't worry. I'll clean up the apparatus—it'll work like a clock. They'll know me yet, the devils. They'll run around like squirrels!"

Vassily was carried away, his eyes sparkled, he choked over his words. Nina wasn't listening to him. Vassily looked askance at her. "She doesn't understand her own good luck, the queer little thing," he thought, smiling to himself. "Well, that's all right, she'll find out soon . . ."

Happy, he sat down beside her, put his arms around her. His eyes dimmed with tenderness. "Nina, my dear little friend, why are you so gloomy today?"

"Why is it, with us Russians, that when someone is thoughtful we consider that he is gloomy?" asked Nina.

Vassily leaned close to her, fawningly impatient, looked into her eyes. "You mustn't be pensive, darling . . ." he murmured and suddenly was unable to restrain himself. Pushing aside the silver medallion with his soft lips, he kissed her breast at the oval cut of her dress. His groveling kiss evoked an unpleasant chill in Nina. "He's alien, quite alien to me," she thought in fear, glancing into his face, familiar to the smallest feature. "And soon he'll be my husband and I must yield to his desires."

Pushing Vassily gently aside, Nina lifted a letter from her knee. "Look, I received a reply from Lida. She writes that she and Nikolai can't come to the wedding, but I know—they don't want to."

Vassily rolled his eyes in astonishment.

"That's why you're sad!" he exclaimed. "So what if they don't want to come? No great loss! As a matter of fact, it's very good that they

494

won't be at the wedding; they would be out of place. And Nina, for some time I've wanted to tell you——"

Nina, flaring up, interrupted him: "Don't dare talk like that about my friends!"

Vassily had no desire to argue. "All right, all right, don't get excited, I was joking. But the fact that she isn't coming is quite understandable: she is pregnant. She'd be embarrassed, of course. Now you see, everything is explained simply."

Vassily got up, lit a cigarette, again paced up and down the room. He couldn't sit still. Stamping time as he walked, he sang merrily: "Oh, Marie! Oh, Marie! . . ."

Nina frowned. Vassily had no ear for music. "A bear must have stepped on his ear," she thought.

"Tell me, who else is invited?" asked Vassily, breaking off his song.

"Only three girl friends from the Conservatory."

"Why so few?" he was surprised. "Invite more, before it's too late. It'll be merrier."

"Do you mean it?" asked Nina, with doubt in her voice.

"Of course. Your friends are my friends," answered Vassily and, making a sweeping gesture with his arm, left the room.

Alone, Nina felt how flushed her face was. With shame she recalled her words: "Don't dare talk like that about my friends." They were false, contemptible words; the fact was that she had lied. When she received Lida's letter declining politely, instead of the expected disappointment, suddenly, to her own horror, she had been pleased. She was glad that her best friends, Lida and Nikolai, weren't coming! It was difficult for her to admit this herself, but that's how it was. From the time when she had been an involuntary witness of Lida's attempted suicide, when with her own eyes she had seen her condition, when with unexpected envy she had noticed Nikolai's love for Lida, a love whose existence she had herself considered impossible, she had been restless and unhappy.

Lida suddenly became a living reproach to Nina. Her feeling of righteousness, which she had felt with such pride, had dimmed. Her soul had become cold and misty. A belated remorse for her mistake seized Nina—a fervent warning voice was telling her that she had stepped onto a crooked, lying road. Lida's moral superiority became too evident. Against it Nina felt herself to be a nonentity, and involuntarily she became in her thoughts more and more irreparably and irrevocably separated from her friend, who perhaps already hated

495

her. "Why, of course, you made a mistake, my dear," she heard the punishing inner voice. "You intended to save your body at the price of your soul. But look at Lida: through terrible trials, much more difficult than yours, she has brought her heart clean, unspoiled. You, Nina, are bankrupt."

She drove these thoughts away, struggled desperately with them, crushed them as insects are crushed, but all the time they crawled and crawled and there was no place to hide from them. They found her even in sleep. Recently she had had an awful dream: She herself, Lida, Feodor—they were all naked. Around was radiant nature, the woods, the fields, bathed in sunshine. Feodor was holding Lida by the hand and smiling at her. But on seeing Nina he snatched away his hand and reached out to Nina. Lida started to cry. Then Feodor and Nina together began to drive her away, shouted at her, threw stones at her, while Nina (afterwards she recalled this with horror) even snarled spitefully, she hated Lida so much. They drove Lida away—she stopped at a distance from them, her whole body shuddering from bitter sobs. But Feodor and Nina, completely happy, sat down on the grass, looked tenderly into each other's eyes, kissed, caressed each other, and surrendered to love.

Even when she awoke, the bright, proud feeling which the dream gave her did not leave her at once. But following this she shuddered with horror and repugnance. What a lying dream! Didn't she know what kind of man Feodor was, what baseness he was capable of? Why wasn't there even a shadow or a hint of this in the dream? Why was she completely, supremely happy in his arms? And then, whence came this awful, beastly hatred of Lida? Why! She hadn't a more sincere and better friend! Perhaps Feodor also had dreams like that? Then was it possible that her hatred of him was born not of her heart, but from dirty, envious life? Or perhaps it was her conscience, with sharp memories of her former love for Feodor, trying to emphasize the emptiness of her present relations with Vassily. Did she not feel her whole being protesting, not wanting to yield itself to the mercy of this moist-lipped bureaucrat? Maybe for that reason she had never dreamed of Vassily, as if he did not exist. Yes, yes, it must be so: her conscience told her so. Conscience? Who invented it? Was it born in the timid thoughts of humans or truly created by Providence to stand up before the affairs of man, like a judge at a trial?

Thus was Nina tortured, and the approaching wedding began to grow in her imagination into a menacing specter.

496

CHAPTER 9

WHEN Alexander Shcherbakov arrived on Saturday, without warning, Mikhail Gorin and Vassily were in the kitchen selecting the wines. Cheprok was helping them. Luba had shut herself up with Nina and the dressmaker in the bedroom, making the final preparations. The wedding was to take place the following day.

Shcherbakov, a huge old man with a strong neck and sloping shoulders, horn-rimmed glasses gracing the turned-up nose on his fat face, immediately filled the spacious rooms with his deep bass and the stamp of his elephantine boots.

"Ah! Mikhail Alexeyevich!" He extended his hand to the writer cordially, without taking the white cap off his large-boned head. "I never thought that you would become a relative of mine. Where's the bride?"

"She's locked herself with her mother upstairs. They're contriving something there," said Mikhail, smiling. Shcherbakov's stout figure breathed of exceptional energy. "He can give his son a hundred points any day," thought Mikhail, comparing the energetic old man with the flabby Vassily.

Vassily, suddenly excited, ran around his father aimlessly.

"Alexander Pavlovich, maybe you'd like a drink after your journey?" he asked subserviently. Vassily addressed his father by his name and patronymic, as his chief. He was going to get some expensive cognac from a cupboard, but his father stopped him.

"Wait a minute. I brought some Moscow stuff with me."

The sturdy, brisk Shcherbakov himself ran for the bottle. He returned beaming, shaking a sparkling bottle temptingly. "You haven't got anything like this here. It's fresh." The spirit was clear, like the first spring rain. Even through the cork its exciting bouquet could be sensed. Vassily's eyes sparkled. Cheprok cackled. With the palm of his hand against the bottom Shcherbakov expertly knocked out the cork. The vodka poured merrily into the glasses. Mikhail noticed that his manicured fingers were short, but quick and knavish. Shcherbakov raised his glass.

"Let's drink to the friendship of our families."

At the table he was gay, joked, looked keenly at Nina, who was sitting next to him, loudly praised Vassily for his choice. At the end he kissed Nina on the cheek and ordered Vassily to kiss her too. "Ah! Youth, golden time! I'll tell you a secret ahead of time: You will spend your honeymoon at Sochi, at the sanatorium of the Central Committee of the Party. I have already arranged everything."

After dinner, when Vassily wanted to slip away unobserved from the parlor to his own room upstairs for a nap, his father stopped him. "Where are you going? Better stay with us. Show me the list of invitations."

He sat awkwardly, like a haycock, in a luxurious armchair. At his feet lay a German shepherd dog, Vassily's favorite. When the list was brought Shcherbakov took it in his thick fingers, twitched his nostrils upward and began to read aloud: "Veria, Durov, Kashirin . . . Well, well . . . Mirzoyan—how is he, the old dog, still growing fatter? . . . Nadezhda Alexandrov . . . Who's she?"

"People's artist; surely you know her?" Vassily was surprised. As usual he was walking back and forth in the room, tall, drawn out, looking spiteful or perhaps upset. "She's passing through from Moscow," he explained.

"Oh, that one! . . . Khrenov . . . Glushak . . . Novikov——"

"Feodor Novikov?" exclaimed Nina. "You invited him?" She turned to Vassily in surprise.

From under his glasses the elder Shcherbakov raised his eyes to her questioningly. He regarded Nina's meddling as clearly out of place. Greatly embarrassed, Vassily stopped in front of her: "Yes, I invited Director Novikov. You see I consider——"

"And you did right to invite him," his father interrupted him. "Surely you have no objection?" He turned to Nina and it seemed to her that for an instant a savage glitter appeared in his eyes. Luba, afraid for her daughter, looked at her warningly.

Nina shrugged her shoulders: "It's all the same to me."

However, the thought flashed through her: "Surely Novikov hasn't become such an important personage that even Vassily found it necessary to invite him?" She knew of Vassily's dislike for Novikov, whom he could not forgive for his previous relations with her. Therefore, it wasn't personal reasons that guided him. Nina began to realize that the wedding had a political character. The elder Shcherbakov confirmed her guess.

"We hold Feodor Novikov in great esteem. Comrade Stalin prizes him highly," he stressed with his voice, turning his broad face toward Nina. "Vassily was quite right in inviting him."

Then, as if he had forgotten about Nina, he addressed Mikhail:

"Now we must arrange the order of the wedding. Soviet etiquette hasn't been established yet, so we'll have to create it ourselves."

"That's fine," said Mikhail. "Personally, I haven't anything against the old etiquette."

Shcherbakov understandingly nodded his head, even rolled his eyes dreamily. "My God, how many weddings have I seen! We used to celebrate for weeks on end, and then we could barely revive the guests by dousing them with cold water. Mikhail Alexeyevich, you should tell the young folks about the old-time weddings."

"Yes, Papa! Tell us, please," begged Nina. She wanted to cheer her father up. Recently she had noticed in his eyes, in his movements and actions, a kind of inner struggle. Even his speech was strange, full of unspoken thoughts.

"In the olden times they arranged things this way," began Mikhail, and gay wrinkles furrowed his gloomy face. "The matchmakers would go to the bride's house and arrange the dowry. The bridegroom would be with them, but he looked at the bride merely in passing—no kissing, nothing. All in all, up to the wedding itself, the bride and bridegroom were like saints——"

"I'm afraid in this case we're late," Shcherbakov interrupted him, winking merrily to Vassily. "We should have warned them earlier. Am I right, sinner?"

In response Vassily laughed woodenly and to avoid looking at Nina began to play with the dog, tickling it behind the ears.

"Go on, go on, Mikhail," said Luba hastily.

"All right. Before the wedding, the bride's women relatives sew her linen, while the bride herself embroiders a pretty tobacco pouch or knits a pair of woolen mittens for the bridegroom; in short, she shows her talents. Then, a week before the wedding, the young man visits the bride, but not alone—in the presence of her girl friends. He hardly talks to the bride, more with her girl friends, and only just as he leaves she gives him her handiwork. At last comes the wedding day, and the bridegroom goes for the bride. Several carriages are fixed up—some people have tambourines, accordions; in the manes of the horses—ribbons; on the shaft-bows—little bells; and everybody, of course, is drunk . . ."

"Oh! What a time!" Shcherbakov clicked his tongue.

"Yes, everyone is drunk as a lord. Only the bridegroom is sober. In a merry mob they arrive at the bride's house, but they are not allowed in. The bride's friends cry out that they must pay the ransom. Well, the young man's side ransoms the bride with silver coins or nuts. The girls sing songs, something like this one." Here Mikhail suddenly bawled in womanish falsetto:

> "Matchmakers generous,
> You are rich,
> Broad are your beards,
> Your pockets are deep.
> Accept these nuts,
> Love the young son-in-law."

Everybody laughed, while Shcherbakov exclaimed in surprise: "How can you remember these songs?"

Mikhail smiled: "I'll sooner forget my daughter's name. . . . And so, let's go on: Well, they give presents to the matchmakers and then open the door to the bridegroom and his friends. They gather up the bride with all her dowry and drive to the bridegroom's house. There the parents bless them, and incidentally, the bride's father beats her with a whip, then hands the whip to the bridegroom. That signifies the authority of the husband over the wife."

Displeased, Luba remarked: "It seems to me that you've taken very old examples, right out of Demostroy. In my time there was nothing of the sort. So we'll have to throw the whip out."

"If it's got to be thrown out, throw it out—that's your affair," said Mikhail. "After the blessing the bridegroom and the bride drive to the church——"

"Stop!" interrupted Shcherbakov. "We'll have to by-pass the church somehow."

"Of course. But formerly a wedding without the church was invalid. . . . And so, from the church—back to the house and there a regular feast is already in progress. The guests make the young couple kiss each other, they shout 'bitter' until they're hoarse. And every time they shout 'bitter' the bridegroom and the bride must kiss each other, otherwise they will offend the guests. After the kissing, the main gaiety begins. In the evening the young couple go into the bedroom and the guests break the dishes, bowls—that's for good luck. Then they go on celebrating until morning. Of course, it doesn't go off without fooling around. It's a tempting time. Each one is thinking what the young couple are doing. In the morning the matchmakers show the guests the sheets of the newlyweds, so that everybody can see with their own eyes that the bride had watched herself and was a virgin . . ."

Mikhail suddenly stammered, realizing that he had said too much. Vassily jumped away from the dog's snarl; he had stepped on its paw.

500

Shcherbakov coughed and began to fidget in his chair. The color rushed thickly into Nina's face. She didn't understand her father. She was ashamed and afraid for him. Of course, he was talking so recklessly on purpose. Apparently he wanted to try her. "But why? Surely he's not angry with me?"

Then Vassily stood up determinedly in front of his father. "I suggest that we conduct the wedding in a cultured manner, without the beating of pots and other nonsense," he said hoarsely and looked stealthily at Nina. "Otherwise, if you give our people their heads they'll kick up such a crazy racket that we'll all be ashamed later."

Alexander Shcherbakov shook his head in doubt.

"You could hardly hold them back. As the saying goes—it isn't good that's good, but what people like. However, how do you propose to celebrate?" he asked with interest.

"Well, the way they do in Europe. Decorously, with dignity. The guests arrive and offer their congratulations. Then they go into the drawing room. Some dance. Some go to the buffet for refreshments and drinks. They drink moderately, of course, not to excess." Here Vassily became a little embarrassed, remembering the recent visit of his green friend.

Alexander Shcherbakov frowned: "Where did you see that?"

"Well, I read it or saw it in the movies, I can't remember exactly. That's how it is, isn't it?" he turned to Mikhail as to an expert.

"Sure, sure. . . . But Alexander Pavlovich is right—our boys wouldn't stand for it."

Vassily scowled.

"That's all right. We'll make them. They'll behave themselves like honorable young ladies," he said heatedly. "When all's said and done, they must remember where they are. And whoever doesn't understand I'll throw him out!"

"All right, all right, don't boil over," Shcherbakov reassured him, understanding at last why his son was stressing this point. "We'll have it your way! We'll give you the European wedding."

At last they agreed that Luba would remain to complete the final preparations, while Nina would go away with Mikhail. Tomorrow at two o'clock her father would bring her back, along with Academician Glushak, when the guests would already be gathered. Mikhail himself suggested this arrangement. Several times he looked sidewise at his daughter and her look was like that of a bird in a cage. He suddenly felt unbearably sorry for her—he wanted to be with his daughter as he used to be, and as they probably would not be able to be any more.

501

Nina agreed willingly. She was also drawn to her father. She remembered with pain her mother's words about him in private: "Mikhail is silent all the time; he's growing thin. His eyes have sunk in. At times he scares me."

Yes, since Pavel's death her father had changed a great deal. Nina felt that he needed her and that maybe on that account, instead of saying things straight out, he was capricious and stung her with words.

Shcherbakov also looked at Mikhail as if he were expecting something unusual and dangerous from the writer. He was particularly courteous and respectful to him. During the conversation he gave him Stalin's greetings, repeated word for word the remarks of the dictator about his play: "Gorin's *Ivan the Terrible* is worth hundreds of thousands of agitators. It's a brilliant play."

Mikhail replied to Shcherbakov absent-mindedly. He was thinking his own thoughts. The latter noticed this and when he was accompanying him to the door, he said cheerily: "Well, Mikhail Alexeyevich, tomorrow we'll have a good time at the wedding. Now I must have a little chat with Vassily. I'll teach him a little common sense while we're both still sober. Tomorrow it'll be too late."

When Nina went away with her father, Vassily looked after her affectionately and uneasily. She turned around and their glances met. Vassily's face was agitated, his eyes wide. He inclined his head to one side and quickly, like a dog, licked his lips. Nina became frightened; she turned away and hurried to her father.

After their departure Shcherbakov shut himself in the study with his son and kept him there for three whole hours. Through the closed doors only a dull "boom—boom—boom" came to Luba. That was the elder Shcherbakov's resonant bass. Nobody knew what advice he was giving the new boss of the province; but Vassily himself wasn't heard.

Then the door of the study opened and, behind curling clouds of smoke, Shcherbakov came out, stern, his face red, Vassily following him with a nervously twitching lower lip.

CHAPTER 10

AND SO they decided to celebrate the wedding in the European way, with dignity, not following the Russian custom. But as Vassily had only a hazy idea of a western wedding, the result was a jumble. Shcherbakov,

Vassily, and Luba received the guests. The elder Shcherbakov was tense and wore an officially stern expression. Nor did Vassily breathe warmth: he looked keenly, almost hostilely at the guests, expecting beforehand all kinds of coarseness from them. The guests were shy. Only the hospitable smile of Luba softened the impression. All the same the guests, after shaking hands with the hosts and murmuring congratulations, hurried off with vast relief to the drawing room. There a second blow awaited them. There were no wedding tables. Mirzoyan, arriving at the same time as Feodor Novikov, whispered to him in perplexity: "What the hell's this? Where are the tables? By God, the Shcherbakovs have gone crazy!"

Instead of tables, there was a buffet. The guests crowded around the bar; in the right hand of each was a glass; the left clutched *hors d'oeuvres*. Not being used to this, the guests dropped sandwiches on the floor, tried to push them unobserved under the furniture with their feet, blew the dust off them, swore. Vassily, who was tired of standing around in the reception room, began to wander among the guests, admonishing them: "Everything must be done in a cultured way, without piggishness." The guests choked on their sandwiches, goggled their eyes at the young boss.

One of the last to appear was little Veria with his wife on his arm, a large and fierce-looking woman. Behind Veria came Drozd, in the uniform of the NKVD, with the sign of the sword on the sleeve. His eyes were smiling mysteriously. Feodor, standing beside Mirzoyan, started involuntarily. In his heart a heavy foreboding stirred: Drozd had not appeared for nothing.

Mirzoyan noticed his agitation, asked with eager curiosity: "Who's that?"

"I don't know. This is the first time I've seen him," answered Feodor evasively. He went to a far corner of the drawing room to be out of Veria's view.

At last the bride arrived. There was a rumble of excitement in the drawing room. The guests poured out into the reception room. Vassily, forgetting himself, looked over their heads at his future wife, stretching his neck like a goose and gaping. On Nina's right walked Mikhail Gorin; on her left was Olga, Glushak's wife, with laughing eyes, her turned-up nose comic. Glushak himself came behind with a huge bouquet of roses.

The elder Shcherbakov began to look for his son uneasily. Catching sight of him in the crowd, he boomed in his bass: "Hey! Vassily, what are you doing there? Quick, come here and receive the bride."

Someone in the crowd laughed. Shcherbakov took his son by the elbow, reproachfully glared at him from under his glasses, and at once smiled broadly at the approaching bride. The guests, many of whom had already had time to get tolerably drunk, looked, goggling their eyes at this unfamiliar ceremony. When Nina stepped onto the carpet runner the music burst out.

Feodor, squeezed on all sides by the hot, crowding people, could not tear his eyes from Nina. Dressed in a white satin wedding gown, she seemed light and transparent, like cold air. But Feodor noticed that her eyes were swollen; on her fine brow there were signs of suffering; in her face grief was written. As Feodor looked into that painfully familiar face his heart stopped. Across the carpet walked the girl whom he loved and who loved him. How close she was to him! Could he ever forget the first time he kissed her, while she responded with a look of confusion and tenderness? Live, throbbing memories—enough to make you shiver! How recent all that was! And couldn't he himself have been the bridegroom now? Unconsciously Feodor moved his gaze to Vassily Shcherbakov. Vassily was standing tense as a string, his eyes wide, looking at Nina.

"I wonder, has he had her yet or not?" thought Feodor suddenly, and a sharp feeling of jealousy pricked him. "Probably not—otherwise he would not be looking at her so greedily."

Nina was led to the bridegroom. Veria was the first to shout: "Bitter!"

"Bitter!" howled the guests, finding at last something familiar in this shout. The pompousness of the ceremony depressed them.

"Nina, kiss the bridegroom," said Mikhail softly. Tears glistened in Luba's eyes. Vassily embraced Nina awkwardly, kissed her cold lips. The kiss was brief. They stood opposite each other, embarrassed, not knowing what to do next. First to recover was the elder Shcherbakov.

"Bravo!" he shouted. "Hurrah!"

His shout was drowned in the storm of enthusiastic roars. The drawing room shook from the joyful rumble. Feodor's glass fell to the floor and shattered. He didn't notice it. Old Shcherbakov raised his hand and asked for silence.

"Dear Comrades!" he began. "We Bolsheviks have little opportunity to think about our personal lives. We have given all our time, all our energy, and often our lives to the affairs of the Party. That is quite understandable: the difficult times, the struggle with the class enemy, leave no room for a personal life. But to conclude from this that we Bolsheviks object to a personal life is a great mistake. When there is an opportunity we think about our happiness. And so I came here

504

yesterday from Moscow for two days—affairs won't permit me to stay longer—to be with my son, like any other father. Today is really a double holiday for me. In the first place, my son Vassily, invested with the trust of the Party and the people, has been elected First Secretary of the Province of Northern Caucasus."

"Hurrah!" sounded a lone drunken voice.

Shcherbakov drew his eyebrows together and continued: ". . . In the second place, today he is marrying Nina Mikhailovna Gorin. It is hard for me, an old man, to look at the young folks without emotion. In our time, under the cursed Tsar, was it possible for young people even to dream of being as happy as this—in love? And that my son would be marrying—whom? The daughter of Russia's foremost author, a world celebrity! Who was I? A hired hand. And so, of course, my son would have had a hired hand's life . . ."

Mirzoyan leaned over to Feodor and whispered waggishly: "The old man's lying like hell. He was never a hired hand, but a priest's son. That's a fact; trusted people told me."

". . . But now, under Soviet power, my son, having every opportunity, and thanks to his organizational talent and persistent work, has attained a high post and has won for his heart the beautiful Nina. Joseph Vissarionovich Stalin said to me when I left: 'You must celebrate such an event handsomely. Bolsheviks aren't monks. Don't cramp your style.' These are proper words!"

Shcherbakov turned heavily on his heels, embraced Nina and Vassily. "I wish you both a happy life! I give you my paternal blessing! Beget and multiply to your hearts' content! Hurrah!"

"Hurrah!" the ballroom shouted with two hundred throats. The orchestra began to play. The elder Shcherbakov, trying to outshout the uproar, yelled gaily to Mikhail Gorin: "It's your turn to speak, brother!"

Mikhail looked over the guests slowly. A sea of beasts stormed around him: bearish faces, foxy snouts, wolfish eyes—they growled, they hooted. Mikhail pulled his mustaches, smiled. When the noise quieted a little, he said in a gruff voice: "I am giving my daughter in marriage, but I feel here," Mikhail placed his hand over his heart, ". . . here, the same as when my son Pavel died. Why?"

At once everyone was silent. These unexpected words put the ballroom on the alert. Luba, suddenly turning pale, reached out to her husband, took him by the sleeve, but he pushed her aside.

"Since I lost my son, I can find no peace for myself. All the time I feel that I am to blame for his death. I am convinced that the older generation suffers from this feeling of guilt for the fate of the younger——"

"Maybe you killed Pavel?" Veria's laughing voice resounded. "Repent, Mikhail Alexeyevich! We'll drown all our sins in wine."

The ballroom laughed, the elder Shcherbakov louder than anyone, glad of the chance to turn the awkwardness into a joke. "Finish, Mikhail Alexeyevich," he whispered to the writer. "It's time to begin the celebration."

Mikhail, not listening to him, turned on Veria's lying voice: "Yes, I am to blame for his death. I am a criminal, but my crime cannot be drowned in wine, nor tearful repentance, and therefore, I am probably the criminal of criminals. My words are the frank confession of an old man, friendly advice, which may even serve as a warning to the younger generation. There was a time—many of those present here were not born then, and of course neither the bridegroom Vassily nor the bride Nina—we were young then, strong, full of inexhaustible energy, we thought of the future, looked ahead and pictured to ourselves this time, when our children would be grown and the masters of life. We walked in the season of our ecstasy; sensing keenly our historic destiny. We walked, barely touching the earth! Everything seemed possible! Passionately, almost with anguish, we dreamed of making our lives useful, enlightened, necessary. We dreamed of miraculously winging all Russian souls, of raising them on high, from evil to goodness. It seemed that the breath of decay could never touch our sacred ideas. I myself wanted to live until their fruition, aging neither in memory nor in heart. And everybody around me awaited patiently the blessed time, and died hoping for it.

"Our hopes deceived us. Life played a cruel joke, gave birth to a strange, unforeseen generation. Our dreams and our hopes receded together with the revolutionary songs about stormy petrels, the slogans which were like songs, and the heroes whose fame was louder than the slogans. And so we old men who in our time put into the bosoms of youth our sacred ideas of justice, our noble thoughts about humanism, our faith in the future, like a loaf of bread for a long journey, like a second heart—now we look with distrust on the men of the new generation and ask them: 'Have you carried the loaf to the end? Show us what is in your bosoms. Are you not keeping the stone of hatred there, instead of a burning heart?'

"But the new generation is strangely secretive. Instead of an answer they give us a skeptical sneer. They obviously do not believe in our alarm. They don't speak about their cynicism, but it is clear without

506

words. To live among this strange, cold generation makes one feel crowded and fearful. The whole country is squeezed in the vise of hate —life has become the shadow of death; human blood, shed by savage hands, has lost all value. People suffer, people perish. But they are not satisfied with that. They require that under each roof, in every family, someone should be killed. And killing, they name us as their teachers. Stubbornly they repeat our words. And therein lies the irony of fate— for yes, we spoke these words. But I swear to you they had a different meaning, a different spirit. Yet we spoke them—so the blame lies on us too.

"That is why I said that I was to blame for my son Pavel's death, why I am to blame for my daughter Nina's sorrow. Do you think I don't see how she is suffering? She wants happiness. Yes, why deny the natural instinct within us, the longing for happiness? Nina wants happiness in spite of everything and, in her own way, she is right. Can she, a young girl, calm the raging ocean of hate around her, destroy injustice, save the doomed? Of course not. But if she can't, must she, therefore, choke and drown in this terrible ocean, forget about happiness? Again, no. She is right, but she is unhappy. And she isn't alone . . ."

Red spots slowly covered Nina's face. Her eyes darkened. With a brusque movement she went to her father and said clearly: "Papa, please, talk about something else."

"He's drunk," sounded a voice.

Mikhail shuddered, shook his head. But he continued: "Yes, we old men thought a great deal about the future of the new generation, but we overlooked something. So, where lies our fault?" he asked, raising his voice. The ballroom waited in fright. Mikhail slowly looked around at the frozen faces and smiled. "Please don't be afraid." (But everyone became even more frightened.) "Our first offense was that we broke contact with the new generation. Cut off from us, how could youth feel the passion and spirit of our ideas? Our second offense was that we did not hand over to youth the stern school of comradeship through which we ourselves had passed. How can youth know about loyalty, about the great principle of mutual respect and trust, without which it is impossible to live on this earth? Living too softly—at times with everything given them—they closed their hearts and hardened them to the needs of their brothers. So now, belatedly, I say to the young people: Vassily and Nina, remember my words and carry them through your lives like your second heart, like a cherished loaf of bread. Do not lose it. And now, will you allow me, the criminal of criminals, to kiss you both and sincerely wish you happiness."

Everybody sighed with relief. Luba smiled. Mirzoyan again whispered to Feodor: "He turned that neatly, the devil."

CHAPTER 11

THE FRIGHT passed. Old Shcherbakov shouted his "Hurrah!" The orchestra played as before. The guests rushed to congratulate the newlyweds. Feodor was going to join the others, but was afraid. "Later, when the chance comes," he thought. He went to the buffet. Quite close to him in the crowd he saw Durov, and his whole body shuddered inside, as if at sight of the execution block. Durov was very glum, thoughtful—dark clouds passed over his coarse face. By chance he turned toward Feodor; he wiped his face as if with a wet rag—his look was vague, unrecognizing. Feodor looked for Veria, instinctively feeling him a protector. Veria's eyes were sharp, as if he were clairvoyant: even though he was standing with Drozd in the other corner of the room, he noticed Feodor at once and with a nod called him over.

"Are you envious?" he asked, laughing, when Feodor came up to them.

"Envious? Of what?" Feodor was surprised, pulled himself together, afraid of stepping into an invisible trap. Veria was always surrounded by them.

"Don't pretend," said Veria. "I was watching you from the beginning of the wedding; you're walking around as if you were drenched in water." He giggled, his small eyes full of slyness, and turned to Drozd: "The Comrade Director was head over ears in love with Nina."

"Oh, I see!" remarked Drozd. He was noticeably drunk, nodded to Feodor as to an old acquaintance, unrestrained by Veria's presence. The military uniform which Drozd found it convenient to wear also spoke openly of some sharp change, still unknown to Feodor. Besides that, there was his mysterious smile . . .

"Of course, Nina is very beautiful, as nobody can deny," continued Veria. "It's hard enough for a woman to resist her physical charms, let alone a man. She's a rare specimen. Novikov here was in love with her and she had lost her heart to him completely. Nothing could have been better; all that remained was the wedding. In short, faithfulness till the grave, the most passionate love. Yet I froze their love." Veria smirked contentedly, drank a mouthful of wine, openly probed his

508

favorite with his eyes. "I can just imagine how the Comrade Director cursed me!"

Feodor frowned. "I realized my mistake," he said sharply. "I cursed no one, except myself."

Veria smiled still more broadly and shook his round head, like a musician catching a false note. "Don't lie. You realized nothing then and cursed me roundly. 'Veria is a son of a bitch, won't mind his own business.' Right?"

Feodor was silent, considering it better to pretend not to have heard the question.

"And you're cursing me right now," Veria went on. "You're asking: 'Why, indeed, can Vassily Shcherbakov marry Nina without anybody bothering him? But immediately I flirted with her a bit, Veria started climbing up the wall.' You're offended, yes?"

"My feeling for Nina cooled long ago," said Feodor stubbornly, trying to appear calm. But Veria's words stung him painfully. "What does he want from me?" Feodor wondered. He looked at Veria's small face with its frozen smile, at his wide toad's mouth, into his yellow eyes, glittering under his pince-nez, and he became uneasy. Veria patted his shoulder affectionately and in his own deceitful way, winked at him.

"If you like, I'll explain to you why Vassily can and you can't!" he said suddenly.

Feodor put himself on guard; the glass in his hand shook. "How he looks!" he thought, watching Veria and not recognizing him.

Yes, Veria was in form today. His book, *The History of the Party Movement in the Caucasus,* had come out a week before with a bang. The ideas he had proclaimed a year ago at the opening of the political institute in Rostov were developed boldly and sharpened. In Veria's clever hands history was like an obedient girl, like Lily of the Party Committee. The monstrous lie breathed of primitive virginity. The task Stalin gave him had been brilliantly fulfilled and Veria's book was already spoken of as the reference book of the Bolsheviks. Besides that, Pavel Gorin had been killed—that was also to his credit. Veria was not going to Moscow with empty hands. He was standing on the threshold of his new life—no! not standing, but rolling along in a troika at a gallop. Wonderful, breath-taking visions flashed in front of him, making him drunk with more than wine.

Veria suddenly brought his glass up to Feodor's eyes.

"Look at the light. You see, the wine is clear as a tear. However, here, at the bottom there are dregs, barely noticeable, but they're there.

So, what is on top? Vassily Shcherbakov and others like him—the new generation, the favorites of fortune. Mikhail Gorin was just speaking about them, although he meant to say something different, to frighten us a little. Hee—hee—hee . . ." Veria seemed to become drunker with every word.

"But we'll talk about that later. Men like Vassily Shcherbakov have not reached their exalted position through talent and persistent work, as old man Shcherbakov would like us to believe. We all know that. But that isn't the point. The point is that Vassily is enjoying life while men like you and me do the dirty work. We are the dregs, we know the undercurrents of life, but we must not talk about them. To enjoy life so, just skimming the cream of it, one must be born the son of Shcherbakov—or better still, the son of Stalin. The chances for that are very rare.

"Vassily is marrying Nina Gorin today. What is she to him? A beautiful flower, the daughter of a world celebrity with whom even the Party must reckon. That is all that Vassily needs to know. For him life always wears a smile. He doesn't suspect its other side; he has nothing to do with it. A happy fate, isn't it? When Gorin dies they'll bury him like a Tsar, and they'll sing songs about him, and Vassily will be proud of his wife, the daughter of the great Gorin. We, on the other hand, although we know differently, must remain silent so as not to cast a shadow on Vassily's mood. Naturally one envies him!"

Veria flourished his pince-nez. In his little eyes cunning lay concealed. Feodor, standing in front of him, was completely dismayed by his frankness. What was this? Envy? Hidden enmity toward the Shcherbakovs? Or simply a game played on his nerves, an attempt to test him? Veria, in the meantime, changed his expression: his eyes smiled contemptuously as before, but his mouth was stern and serious.

"But don't worry, Comrade Director, we also have our advantages. During heavy storms, such light ballast as Vassily goes overboard." Veria jerked his glass slightly and a few drops fell onto the carpet. "Just like this . . . They need us at such times. It is good to feel you are needed. Isn't it?"

"Remarkably well put, Lozo Pavlovich," laughed Drozd approvingly.

Veria, on the contrary, became quite serious: "Comrade Director, come to me on Tuesday. We'll have a little talk. Drozd will tell you some interesting things also. Meanwhile, have a good time. Don't worry about anything."

Immediately Feodor's and Drozd's glances met, but Veria intercepted them quickly: "Didn't I tell you not to worry about anything? . . . But here comes Glushak. Comrade Glushak, come here a minute," Veria called.

CHAPTER 12

GLUSHAK started at the call, minced toward them. Feodor had never seen such a gait in a man, drunk or sober. Veria's glance seemed to shrivel Glushak.

"For some reason Mikhail Gorin has become very friendly with him recently," said Veria softly. "We'll have to shake this bag of filth well."

Glushak came up to them, rubbing his pudgy hands.

"Comrade Veria, I believe I have to congratulate you—you are running away from us, as it were, into a higher sphere, almost unearthly. Hee—hee—hee!"

"I'm running away, I'm running away, Comrade Academician. But it's dangerous to leave you alone—you'll be lost without me."

Glushak smiled, inclining his gray head respectfully. His blue, watery little eyes looked at Drozd hesitantly several times. "I don't think I know you . . ." he said, turning to the NKVD man, although he recognized him perfectly. He was exhibiting caution in front of Veria.

"You need not become acquainted," said Veria roughly, but his face feigned kindliness as before.

Glushak was embarrassed. A pathetic smile trembled on his puffy face; he hurriedly dropped his right hand, which he had extended to Drozd. Veria sneered.

"However, there's no harm done. Who knows, perhaps tomorrow Drozd will come to arrest you? Then you can become acquainted. Drozd is a very pleasant conversationalist. Of course he isn't an Academician, but he is rich in experience. He has passed more than one life through his hands into kingdom come." Veria spoke sweetly, almost endearingly, but Glushak became frightened by his words. A sickening shiver shook his corpulent body. With tremendous effort he forced out a hollow laugh: "You're a very merry fellow, Comrade Veria."

"But you've nothing to be afraid of. You're not guilty of any sins," continued Veria. "Though one can't depend on you intellectuals; at the least trifle you go into hysterics, or a temper. Who knows, maybe you feel like a secret criminal too, having killed your son or daughter, for example?"

511

Veria's hint was obvious. Glushak, however, preferred not to understand him. "What an idea, Comrade Veria! I wouldn't raise my hand against a fly, let alone a human being." He laughed again, but only with his mouth; his eyes were dead.

Feodor felt disgusted. He turned away from Glushak and was about to speak to Drozd. But Veria's next words forced him to be on the alert.

"The Comrade Director has just complained to me about you; he says you babble far too much. I consider it necessary to remind you, Comrade Academician, that in your position this is a most dangerous weakness."

The dismayed Feodor was going to interrupt, but Veria stopped him with a sign. Glushak became very pale.

"I don't know . . . don't know what the Director had in mind . . . I definitely do not feel that I am in any way guilty," he whispered in a woolly voice. His heart was beating madly, and his whole body seemed to be crawling, tortured by a sickening shiver. At that moment he hated his sweating body, his wheedling voice. He cast a helpless glance across the hall toward his wife—Olga was talking animatedly to Luba. Passionately Glushak wanted to go home at once, to lie on the sofa, to calm himself, to snuggle up to his wife. He hunched his shoulders as if from the cold, began to button his jacket but stopped at once, nodding his head, then took a deep breath and snapped his fingers. Veria pretended that he didn't notice his condition and continued to talk. On his little face, touchingly affectionate and threatening glances alternated quickly.

"I can't understand these intellectuals. They appear to be well educated, cultured people, brains without end, but they blabber like old women on the market. Silence is great wisdom—one must learn to be silent. And what is simpler? Bite your tongue and shut up; nobody forces anyone to blabber. But no, they can't restrain themselves. It is as if they suffered from verbal diarrhoea. Even Mikhail Gorin, a man of wide experience, couldn't hold himself in check, but burst forth, ridding himself of useless thoughts. . . . Tell me, did you know about his speech beforehand?"

"No, of course——"

"That's not good enough. It's your duty to know and to warn." Veria's voice was jagged, threatening. Feodor froze. In Veria's words there might be a hint for him also.

"Is it true that at present you are living with the Gorins?" Veria suddenly asked Glushak.

"Yes, Mikhail Alexeyevich asked me to move in with him."

512

"Why didn't you report that to us, and get our permission?" asked Veria severely and roughly. At this sharp thrust Glushak cringed. Fascinated, he stared into Veria's eyes.

"Excuse me, but Mikhail Alexeyevich and I are old friends and I considered I had the right——"

"Nobody gave you any rights," Veria cut him short. "All the same, tell me, have you noticed anything strange, anything particular in the writer's conduct?"

"No . . . unless you count the fact that he has become gloomy and thoughtful since his son's death."

"Unless you count!" Veria mimicked him. "You're a blunderhead, Comrade Academician, that's what you are!"

Glushak shuddered and looked very strangely at Veria. "Excuse me, what are you saying, Comrade Veria?"

"I'm saying what I think necessary."

Feodor watched Glushak with alarm. He recalled how he himself had been rude to the Academician. At that time he believed he had the right to say what he liked to him. But now, looking on from the side, he was painfully ashamed. "Veria is too rough with him. He has gone beyond all the bounds of decency," he thought, annoyed. A feeling akin to pity arose in him. Involuntarily he put himself in the Academician's place. After all, there was nothing to hinder Veria from jeering at Novikov in the same way, from being rude to him in front of everybody. Apparently Drozd felt the same. He stopped grinning and stood, shrinking into himself, as if from a chill.

Feodor saw Glushak's wife Olga look uneasily across the hall at her husband, realizing that something was wrong. Veria emptied his glass in one gulp, looked the Academician over with his little narrowed eyes.

"In short, Comrade Academician, your ears should be pulled, notwithstanding your age, so that you'll be smarter in the future," he said with downright provocation, even extending his hand towards the Academician's left ear.

Glushak turned pale and stepped back. Suddenly he became unrecognizable. Some inner cord had snapped. He drew himself up and, fixing his glance on Veria's face, he said with an old man's tremble in his voice: "It pleases you to make fun of me, Comrade Veria, but I'm too old for such jokes. Find yourself somebody younger."

Veria's face reddened. His eyes became round and colorless like a fish's.

"Shut up!" he barked.

513

But Glushak's whole being breathed desperate resolve. It seemed to Feodor that a joyous convulsion flitted over his face; it became triumphantly calm, as if Glushak had suddenly freed himself of something terrible that had been oppressing him.

"Excuse me. You're drunk, Comrade Veria. I'd better be going," he said quietly but firmly.

"All right, go. I think your wife is calling you," said Veria abruptly, but without anger. Not raising his eyes, Glushak left. Veria followed him with a contemptuous glance.

"Watch and suspect," he said to Feodor and Drozd, nodding in Glushak's direction. "A question mark is the favorite sign of the Bolsheviks."

The repulsive scene had caused Feodor to lose his balance. He couldn't overcome a feeling of disgust at Veria mingled with fear of him. It was obvious that Veria had stirred up the quarrel with the Academician on purpose. When his coarse taunts and open derision had roused Glushak to revolt, Veria was pleased, as if that was exactly what he wanted. What kind of cruel game was this?

Veria, in the meantime, satisfied with himself, licked his lips like a gourmand after a tasty dish, and said affectionately: "I thought he was going to fight. When you make an intellectual white-hot he always fights."

At that moment Nina passed them, walking slowly.

"Look, the bride isn't very near the bridegroom," said Veria, indicating with his eyes the solitary figure of Nina. Not noticing them, she went out onto the veranda. Veria winked at Feodor. "Go on and talk to her. It's not nice to forget one's friends."

Feodor shook his head. "I doubt if we could make conversation . . ."

"Go and try. You've nothing to be afraid of now."

"Well, with your permission." Feodor smiled crookedly: he had been seeking an opportunity to get away from Veria for a long time.

When he left, Veria said thoughtfully to Drozd: "That lad's made of flint, but there are soft veins in him."

Drozd grunted understandingly.

CHAPTER 13

NINA was standing by the balustrade, facing the garden. The sun was hidden behind clouds; there were no shadows, the turquoise twilight seemed to sprinkle the trees, the river, and the fields with ash. Nina's white figure dissolved in the strange light, outlined against the background of the distant band of the river. Feodor stopped three paces from her. She didn't notice him.

"I am helpless, helpless," said Nina softly all at once, leaning back from the balustrade as if she were pushing herself away from someone with her hands.

"What's wrong with her?" thought Feodor quickly, and called: "Nina!"

She started violently, turned, and on seeing Feodor backed away. The slope of her shoulders and the swell of her breasts, outlined by the low cut of her dress, were white, while her cheeks were aflame.

"What do you want?" she asked with a tremor in her voice.

"I wanted to thank you for your invitation. I admit that I didn't expect——"

"It wasn't I who invited you, but Vassily," she interrupted curtly. Her beautiful eyes were unrecognizable—the color of cold steel—no fire, no joy.

"Then I was gladdened by the vain hope . . . that nothing had changed."

Nina turned away. Her left shoulder gleamed softly as she moved. Feodor was drawn to press his cheek against this shoulder. He felt sure that she would not have repulsed him. But he froze in his place, powerless to take a step.

"Nina, I came to the wedding with a profound feeling," said Feodor hoarsely, forcing the words from the depths of his heart with an effort, "that I simply must talk to you about something very important. From the time we parted at the rifle range, one thought has never left me: no, you did not understand me then, you condemned me too hastily."

Without turning Nina said: "Words, words. Apparently you have forgotten that you have a wife—and I have a husband."

"I remember that, but I also remember that we should have belonged to each other."

Nina turned abruptly. Her gray eyes looked at him from under her lashes with cold hatred.

"Feodor, go away . . . What you are saying is not important."

"Forgive me, Nina."

She stepped back to the balustrade. "Why do you need my forgiveness? Why, as a matter of fact, this talk at all?"

"Then, why did we love each other?" asked Feodor. "Remember how clearly and joyfully your eyes sparkled—they don't sparkle like that now. Why? Because everything that has happened since has been diabolic, needless, stifling delirium . . ."

Pale, agitated, she stood in front of him. As if recovering herself, she passed her hand over her eyes and he saw then that tears were pouring down her face.

"Nina, you are suffering . . ."

But Nina pressed herself still harder against the balustrade, her breast tightening the silk of her dress. Feodor's throat became dry. Yes, of course, that was a familiar feeling: as if the tight silk had molded the former Nina—his lover—in front of his eyes. He swallowed and took a step forward.

"Nina, forgive me," he repeated again.

Nina looked at the broad figure of the Director and everything about him seemed hateful—his dry face, his imploring, tender eyes, his timid smile, his needless words. She was afraid of everything connected with him now. But suddenly a thought caught sharply at her heart: "And what about the dream? In the dream you were happy with him . . ." And instead of the angry and cutting words which she had prepared for him, she said softly: "Feodor, perhaps we are all to blame in our lives. I forgive you, but . . . but go away, please."

CHAPTER 14

ALL AFLAME, Nina passed Feodor, who stood with humbly bent head. At the doors of the hall she stopped, frightened. A regular riot was taking place. Mirzoyan, the collar of his shirt open, was standing on a wide window sill with a bottle raised in his hand, shouting as loud as he could:

"To hell with dignity! To hell with western fashions!"

Around him crowded men as drunk as himself.

"Where's Vassily? Bring on the tables, our legs are failing!"

"If we're to celebrate, let's celebrate!"

"Bring on Vassily!"

Catching sight of Nina, they rushed toward her in a drunken wave. Mirzoyan jumped heavily from the window sill and, his bald head and varnished boots glistening, ran up, butting her with his belly and breathing vodka in her face.

"Nina Mikhailovna, be so kind as to order the food! It's time to start the dinner. But first of all—more drink!" His eyes were oily, like an overfed boar's, his thick lips drooled. Nina, numb with disgust, pushed him aside with her hand. At that moment Vassily pressed close to her, shoving his dear guests aside with his elbows and knees. "What's the matter? Why all the noise?"

Mirzoyan's eyes flickered and he began to back away from him, but the drunken men shouted with renewed force:

"Is that the way to celebrate! Where's the vodka?"

"Why have you arranged such black boredom!"

"You're not drinking yourself, saving your strength for the night, but why should we?"

Vassily turned purple.

"You, Vlasov, simmer down! Don't make a damned swine of yourself!" he shouted at the noisiest one.

"Who are swine?" the men advanced on him, swaggering, bold beyond reason because of the vodka.

Vassily was confused, scared, but his father rescued him. Alexander Shcherbakov appeared unexpectedly—huge, hot as a steam boiler. He grasped his son's shoulder with his pudgy, hairy hand, and bent him abruptly to him.

"The guests are right. No need to play the fool, to pretend to be aristocrats!" he barked hoarsely. "All right, boys! Set the tables. Bring out the plates!"

The guests roared in approval. The servants began to bring the tables, the men drunkenly trying to help but merely hampering them. At last five tables were set in a row and covered with tablecloths. Chairs were brought up and they sat down, making a racket from sheer happiness. "Aha! Damn it! We won!"

The gloomy Vassily stood at a distance, afraid to look at Nina. The guests, in the meantime, were shouting: "Bring the young couple to the table!"

"Let's drink up!"

"Where are the singers?"

"Where are the dancers?"

"I'll dance!" Mikhail Gorin's voice suddenly sounded. Everybody looked around. Pushing the crowd aside Mikhail led the actress Alexandrov, a buxom, mature woman, to the center of the floor. Her face was flushed; she looked merrily and indulgently at the writer. Mikhail was quite drunk.

"Our boys couldn't stand it! I told you so," he laughed. "And now, make a circle. I'm going to dance! At my daughter's wedding I can do anything!"

Nina wanted to go to her father, but the crowd pushed her to one side. Those sitting at the tables jumped up—they were impatient to see the rare sight. An accordion player appeared from nowhere. Mirzoyan walked around the circle and sticking out his backside, began to make drunken steps. Mikhail pushed him away roughly.

"Step out, Nadezhda," he called to the actress. "You go first, I'll follow you!"

She tied a kerchief on her head like a peasant woman, made a sad face, sighed and, suddenly putting forward the toe of her slipper, cried:

> "I'm not so pretty,
> And I'm poorly dressed,
> No one wants to take me
> To his manly breast!
> Yee—ee—hee!"

She whirled madly—left hand at her side, right hand waving above her head, heels beating a tattoo. The musician, gladdened by the familiar tune, grinned from ear to ear, drew out his accordion still further and caught up with the dancer.

"Quicker! Quicker!" shouted Mikhail. Gay, looking younger, bending his right knee, he clapped his big hands deafeningly almost at the floor, stamping his foot in time, looking fervently from under his gray eyebrows at the whirling woman. Nadezhda floated over to him, billowing out her dress like a bell. Luring him with an eyebrow, she stepped back, stopped at the other side of the circle to catch her breath. Taking a small handkerchief out of her ample bosom, she wiped her face daintily.

"Your turn, Misha."

"All right, hold it!"

To feel freer, Mikhail ripped off his necktie with violent delight—the diamond stud sparkled on the floor. He flew out himself, rat-a-tatting on the parquet, shaking the floor and the walls.

"Go on! Go on!" the guests encouraged him.

Mikhail's feet flashed with surprising speed.

> "Go on hut, go on stove—
> The master wants to rove!"

Putting two fingers in his mouth, he whistled like a vagabond, as he used to in his youth.

"Wow!" responded the astonished crowd.

Above the noise Nina heard someone behind her say: "Mikhail's

518

not the same, though." She turned around quickly and saw Veria. Meeting her alarmed glance, he hastened to smile, but in his eyes she caught spiteful exultation. She herself felt that her father's noisy dance was probably his last outburst. With affected gaiety he seemed to be smothering some oppressive feeling. Suddenly Nina felt very sorry for her father, as she never had before.

But the crowd yelled: "Dig up the floor!"

"Weak! Weak!"

Mikhail dashed about harder, but tripped and nearly fell.

"The stormy petrel's drunk!" one husky voice shouted scandalously. Somebody else jerked the skirt of the writer's jacket.

"Look how he plunges!"

Veria, small, excited, impudent as a flea, jumped into the circle. Unceremoniously he jerked Kashirin's sword out of its gilt scabbard. Kashirin, commandant of the military district, was standing in the front row of the spectators.

"Make room there! I'll show you a real Cossack dance!"

Swaggering, Veria brandished the sword, too large for him, in the air. "Careful! Stormy petrel! I might clip your wings!"

"Ha—ha—ha!" Servile throats cackled with laughter.

Nina's lips trembled. Holding back her tears, she ran out of the hall. Nobody noticed her leaving. In the reception room she stopped in front of a large mirror. A girl, her eyes red from weeping, looked out at her.

"Tell me, what are you going to do now?" she asked furiously. "Who will you run to, who will understand your troubles?"

Instead of an answer, the girl in the mirror repeated her hateful grimace. Nina went outside. From the open windows floated snatches of the revelry—whistling, singing, hooting. She trembled from head to foot: her father, the wedding, melted away in her inflamed consciousness, and before her wide eyes rose the silent figure of Lida. She looked at her reproachfully and tenderly. Nina groaned with self-pity and ran to the garage.

The garage was crowded with chauffeurs. While their masters were carousing in the house, they had arranged their own celebration here: they were sitting cross-legged on the floor, passing a bottle of vodka from hand to hand, drinking straight from the neck, embracing each other and bawling songs. They were all husky young fellows of military age, many of them in uniform—leather coats and revolvers. From somewhere they had dug up girls, though just a few. They gave the girls drinks, and after the drinks pawed them. The girls, as they should, squealed affectedly, beat off the naughty hands. Right at the very door Nina saw her own chauffeur. He and another were sitting with a plump girl, pawing her from both sides. The girl was singing a ribald song:

> "The doctor asks: 'What ails you, then?'
> I alone love seven men."

Such words made the chauffeurs press closer to her, and add a little heat themselves:

> "A pitch-dark night and a snow-white breast—
> Till the very dawn they give no rest."

Beside them an elderly woman, the gardener's wife, with her cheek in her hand, dragged out an old, plaintive tune:

> "Tell me, then, my darling bride,
> Is it good among strangers to abide?"

They noticed Nina, became silent, stared at her in drunken surprise. Her chauffeur jumped to his feet, drew himself up startled in front of her, sticking out his chest. The girl also got up lazily, setting her skirts to rights. She looked challengingly, almost spitefully, at Nina.

"Nina Mikhailovna," mumbled the chauffeur, "please don't be angry. We're making merry with permission. We're celebrating . . . the happy event . . . Allow me to kiss your cheek heartily," and he extended his wet lips towards her. But his friend drew him back by the tail of his coat: "Have you gone off your head?"

"Forgive me for disturbing you," said Nina. "But I need the key to my car."

The chauffeur, rummaging in his pocket with unsteady hand, finally found the key. "If you like, I'll drive you. Don't think I'm drunk."

"No, I prefer to drive myself," said Nina with a smile. Noticing the girl's strange look, she addressed her softly: "Tell me, what is your name?"

"Nadya. Why?" replied the girl guardedly.

"Just so . . . I haven't seen you before."

"She's from the University mess room, a waitress," someone explained.

"How pretty you are!" Nina said with great sincerity. Lonely herself, she felt an unexplainable tenderness for her, for all these people. Suddenly, on impulse, she kissed the girl's cheek. The girl was embarrassed, blushed. Nina turned to the gardener's wife: "You sang very nicely. How does it go? 'Tell me, then, my darling bride . . .' I never heard that song before."

"It's an old one, a wedding song."

"That's very, very good . . . Well, I'll go. Please have a good time; don't restrain yourselves," and smiling gently at them all, she went out of the garage, followed by wondering glances. Just outside the door, she heard Nadya say something in a low voice, and everybody laugh loudly.

"That was probably something bad," she thought dejectedly. "Why? What have I done to them?"

Still trembling from excitement, she drove her car out of the yard onto the road, stepped on the gas, gathering speed—50, 60, 70 . . . The guard on the road looked around in wonder at the madly racing car. The speedometer nervously warned her of the limit. She saw the road only hazily. She raced aimlessly, in a kind of stupor. It seemed that the speed and the oncoming wind bore away her body and soul, and that it was no longer she who sat in the automobile, but some other girl, strange and incomprehensible. Nina felt neither fear nor surprise, only an aching pity for this girl . . . And besides, she wished with all her heart that the road would never, never end as now she was running away from herself.

CHAPTER 15

THEY REMEMBERED Nina only when the guests again sat down and were preparing to shout "Bitter!"

"Where's the bride?" Veria was first to ask. And, drunk as he was, his eyes were sharp.

"Scandal! Scandal!" clamored the guests.

The elder Shcherbakov tried to turn it into a joke: "She got scared and ran away. Just as before a bayonet charge."

"Ha—ha! A bayonet charge!"

"She's probably hiding in the bushes."

The guests poured out into the garden.

"Whoever finds her first—she'll be his," laughed Veria.

At the door Shcherbakov caught his son by the arm and, barely concealing his anger, whispered to him: "You, Vaska, entertain the guests while I go and look for her . . . She's not in the garden," and squeezing his elbow until it hurt, he added viciously: "My God, couldn't you look after her, you crow!"

"How am I to blame that she went away?" asked Vassily, embarrassed.

"Sure—the gobbler is to blame," hissed Shcherbakov, and his scathing glance drove Vassily out.

In the fresh air the guests became quite drunk. They forgot about the bride. In the twilight they began to romp, to wrestle, to catch each other. The Secretary of the Taganrog City Committee climbed up a tree and cawed like a crow on a branch. With his empty scabbard Kashirin tried to knock him off his perch. The director of the Selmash Plant, the one who had replaced Sidorov, skipped in the light of a window, his boots glistening, and tried to jump over his own shadow. But he was too short, and his shadow too long. Annoyed, the director fell on the grass, twitching his arms and legs. At once about ten men piled onto him with a shout—"Pig pile!" Three solid old boys, drunk to stupefaction, their arms about each other, went into the garden, right across the paths, over flower beds, trampling down the tender plants. They bawled a marching song, they fell, got up again, went on, tripping and grunting. The uproarious trio, at times twirling around on one spot, at others flying headlong as if the earth had slipped from under their feet, fell into a shallow basin; the goldfish flew onto the grass with the splashes of water. The chauffeurs, themselves drunk, began to pull their wet chiefs out. The fat Mirzoyan, watching them, wanted to get into the basin too, but his wife kept him back.

"Let go!" howled Mirzoyan. "I want to swim!"

"Oh, what a pity Sidorov isn't here! He would have raised all kinds of hell!"

"Now he's raising hell in the other world."

In half an hour the garden was unrecognizable, as if a tornado had swept over it: everything was mutilated, strewn with wreckage, broken glass, and muck. It was empty. The drunken cyclone had passed on to the river. In the end the furious Vassily himself led the guests there. "I'll drown them all, the bastards!" he thought, raging.

Feodor went down to the river by the bushes, still hoping to find Nina. In the bushes he unexpectedly collided with Durov. It was as if the police chief had been waiting for him there. No one was around. The guests were raising a racket at the river, bonfires were lit—the sparks rose in sheaves to the dark sky. Feodor froze. In the darkness their faces paled uncertainly, their eyes weren't visible. Durov's right hand was hidden in his pocket.

"Now it comes," thought Feodor, but his resistance to death seemed to have disappeared. His will, caught unaware, dissolved and flowed from his heart.

"Comrade Novikov," said Durov hoarsely, "why is Drozd here?"

Feodor was not so much surprised at the question as at the perplexity he noticed in Durov's voice. Perplexity and Durov—they somehow did not mix. Feodor would have been still more surprised if it had been light: he would have detected the shadows of fear in Durov's sunken eyes.

"I don't know why Drozd came to Rostov," he answered, still watching Durov's right hand. "I thought you knew."

Durov smiled grimly. He looked as if he might bare his teeth at any moment. . . . Feodor began to feel odd.

"You're lying!" said Durov roughly. "You know Drozd well, you saw him in Moscow and you were talking with him just a moment ago. You know everything."

"Is this an interrogation?"

In the darkness Feodor didn't see, but felt, Durov's fierce glare. Durov, however, remained silent. They stood thus for a moment, motionless. Feodor was the first to move.

"Excuse me, I'm going."

He passed Durov, expecting a shot in the back. But the shot didn't follow. After taking four paces he looked around—Durov wasn't there.

"What kept him from killing me?" Feodor wondered. "Whatever it was, Durov is definitely not himself."

Feodor didn't know that Veria had given Durov a clear hint recently: that he should sit quietly on his high and dry place if he didn't want to lie in a low and damp one. The unexpected appearance of Drozd, whose rank was equal to Durov's, made this hint a direct threat.

CHAPTER 16

LUBA ASKED Cheprok to take Mikhail into the study, while she went with old Shcherbakov to look for Nina. Mikhail and Cheprok, arms around each other's waists, made their way from the hall to Vassily's study. Mikhail's shoulders were still twitching from the excitement.

Cheprok lit the fire, while Mikhail sat at the desk and smoked.

"And so I danced at my daughter's wedding. From her birth I have dreamed of this. Yes, dreams, dreams, where are your sweetness? . . . Bring me some brandy, I'm chilled to the marrow," said Mikhail. He inhaled his cigarette several times, then crushed it nervously in the ash tray.

"Maybe you'll go to sleep?" asked Cheprok.

"Do what I tell you," Mikhail replied roughly.

Left alone, he sighed, then smiled. His glance moved over the walls on which the light from the fireplace gleamed, and suddenly he shuddered: "Pavel, my boy!" He dropped his face onto the table and cried out piteously and horribly in a thin, ear-splitting wail. Cheprok came with a snack and some wine and Mikhail raised his head, looked at his friend closely, noticing for the first time the deep wrinkles of old age around his mouth.

"Tell me, Cheprok, how long is it since we came from Capri? Two, three years?"

"Surely you haven't forgotten! In September it will be three years."

Mikhail sighed, mixed some vodka with the cognac in the tumbler. He started when the transparent liquid gurgled in the glass, gulped it down, and covered his mustache with his hand. He broke off a small piece of bread and flipped it into his mouth. The room smelled strongly of liquor.

"So we've been three years in Russia," he said thoughtfully. "Have I aged a lot?"

"We're all growing old," replied Cheprok evasively.

"No, I mean mentally. Physically, of course, we have to grow older, but mentally—mentally you can remain young till the grave. I feel very melancholy, Cheprok. My heart is empty, like a nest deserted by a bird."

"And the bird, of course, is Nina. Who else?" said Cheprok.

"Do you remember, old friend, how you and I used to follow the Don, barefoot, hungry, but happy as the birds of the air? I wasn't a writer then, nobody knew me. And, by God, when you think of it— that was a wonderful time! Just like a dream. A very nice dream. But for some time past my personal life has become like a heavy, endless dream. I try to break it off; with impatience I say: 'In a minute I'll wake up, in a minute I'll wake up.' But I can't wake . . . Sing something old—you used to sing not too badly."

"I've sung my song," said Cheprok. But he sang—softly, only a little hoarse.

524

"Aha! 'The Twelve Robbers.' That's a good one." Mikhail listened, his gray head lowered. ". . . But what's the reason for my uneasiness?" he thought. "Surely not Pavel? No. Nina? No, it's not that. Then where is the crack which is causing my inner world to crumble—the world whose strength I never doubted?"

Mikhail clenched his jaws, his whole body shuddered. The pain was desperate; it was tangible and sharp, like the sudden prick of a needle. To Mikhail it seemed as if someone were actually pricking him from inside, piercing the tissues of his body, his heart, and his brain, all at once with a thousand needles.

Cheprok sang on, sitting on a chair and leaning his head against the marble fireplace. "This is a good place," he said, taking a breath. "Listen, listen:

"The tempest rose—my ill fame!
This storm will crush me—this shame!"

Mikhail pricked up his ears. "Aha, I understand! The words are good because they touch me right in the heart," he said, obviously hurt, and in annoyance pushed away his plate. The plate rolled along the floor.

"Fool! A slobbering weakling! A ram led astray! An eagle plucked by jackdaws!" Mikhail got up ponderously, upsetting the chair. The mirror in the door drew his attention. With an unsure gait he approached it. He studied, without recognizing it, his own face: it reflected the complete dismay of his soul. Mikhail drank another glassful. The floor rose slowly and receded as slowly.

"Open the window, Cheprok! It's stuffy."

Cheprok opened the window and then hobbled into a corner of the room and was lost in the shadows. At once, out of the wall crawled a red-haired stranger, red-haired and clothed in red: a red cloak, red boots. Mikhail, swaying, stared with dull eyes at the uninvited guest. The latter also began to sway, mimicking him impudently.

"Who are you?" asked Mikhail. His curiosity was pricked to the point of horror.

"Don't you recognize me?" He heard Cheprok's voice. And, in fact, Cheprok came out of the shadows—the stranger disappeared. Where he had been standing, the reflection of the flames from the fireplace played.

"Aha, I understand," smirked Mikhail. "Hallucinations, an optical illusion. I've drunk too much. . . . Cheprok, go and call Nina. . . . No, don't bother her, she has no time for me now. But who has time for me? No one. Soon I'll be left alone with the red-haired specter. Ha—ha! I don't need him, I don't believe in ghosts!" Mikhail poured out still another glass, drank it, stared dully at the floor.

"Wake up! Wake up! Why sleep?" hissed the flame. "I was just getting set for a talk with you."

Mikhail started, raised his head. Close beside him stood the red-haired stranger.

"Been here long?" asked Mikhail in a wheedling voice.

"I always come after the tenth glass," replied the stranger simply.

"But I haven't drunk more than five," objected Mikhail.

"Your glasses are large," explained the red one. He sat down easily on the edge of the table, crossed his legs, looked at Mikhail sharply: Mikhail became frightened. He turned away—Cheprok was sitting beside the fireplace, looking into the fire, soundlessly moving his lips. Mikhail calmed down.

"I'm not afraid of you," he said.

"Why be afraid of me? You should be afraid of people," replied the stranger and winked his red eye.

"Yes, you're probably right. I'm a little disturbed on that count myself." Mikhail began to speak, lowering his voice mysteriously. "It seems to me, sometimes, that something is going on around me. All these people . . . while I see them and talk with them, I can't believe that they could deceive me. But when I'm alone———"

"But still more, you should be afraid of yourself," the guest interrupted him.

"What do you mean?" Mikhail asked, surprised.

"Don't you ever feel evil within you?" asked the stranger sternly.

"No . . . but, yes—partly. . . . By nature evil is a stranger to me. But if life arranges itself so that evil is everywhere, so that it surrounds me closely and I can't take a step without encountering it, as one can't walk dry in the rain, and so that I feel completely drenched in evil—then I am not sure that I myself am not evil."

"That is no justification. Man must know how to conquer himself. You know that very well, Mikhail."

"There's no support; that's the whole trouble." Mikhail shook his head sadly. "And without support man, even were he an Archimedes, is powerless. But believe me, I know that I myself am above all to blame for my weakness."

"Good! Good! Your conscience is awakening." The guest brightened up. "When you're sober it sleeps soundly. That's why drunkards are nearer to the truth than a thousand sober prophets. Now say: 'Let the

526

past disappear! I have changed!' Choose for yourself a new, shining path. And with a light heart, like the pilgrim, go along it joyfully."

"Yes, yes, like a pilgrim with a little pack on his back," Mikhail repeated after him dreamily. Then suddenly he became uneasy. "But wait! What kind of road? How can I find it?"

"They're in your heart, millions of roads. Choose the most open one."

Mikhail shook his gray head in doubt. "I'm afraid it's late for me to make a choice."

"There is no late nor early in the universe; the universe is eternal."

"I don't believe that!" Mikhail cried out. "There is a beginning to everything! There is a beginning even to baseness! Let us arm ourselves with patience and start looking for the beginning of all beginnings. Let us rise from beneath the clouds of abstraction! We shall see more clearly from there." Mikhail flopped on his backside onto the floor. The stranger laughed; laughed, and jumped into the fireplace. Mikhail beat his forehead, looked around. Empty—he was alone, on the floor. From somewhere far away, penetrating the walls and his consciousness, came the laughter of a drunken piano, and the shriek of the actress Alexandrov.

Mikhail got up with difficulty and stumbled over to the door in which, as he remembered, there should be a built-in mirror. Rumpling his hair with his fingers, he began to look into it. And suddenly his eyes rounded wildly: his face was not in the mirror. Nor was his hair, nor his lips—nothing! The room was reflected, the table was visible, the window, the bookcase—but himself he could not see. At once he felt a chill under his skin. Breathing rapidly, he began to feel the mirror with a trembling hand. His fingers slipped over the smooth surface; but, as if the mirror were mocking him, it did not reflect his hand. The mirror ignored him. Mikhail snorted, stepped back, and suddenly shouted furiously at the top of his voice: "Where am I? Why am I absent? You lie! I'm alive! I'm alive!"

"You lie! You lie!" the echo responded inside his skull.

Mikhail shook his head violently. The echo faded away. Mikhail winced and groaned deeply, in despair: "Nina, cruel Nina, why did you leave your father?"

CHAPTER 17

RUNNING, stumbling, Mikhail went to the window, looked into the garden and suddenly shouted with joy: "Feodor! Feodor Novikov!"

"If only he would come! If only he would come!" thought Mikhail feverishly. "Even he is better than that red-haired companion."

Feodor started, turned at the shout. In the light of the window his face was somber.

"What do you want? Oh, it's you, Mikhail Alexeyevich?"

"Yes, it's me. Come here. I'm alone and I'm frightened."

"Where are you?"

"In Vassily's study."

Mikhail sat down at the desk and smiled. He raised his eyes—in front of him stood Feodor, but a red Feodor.

"You're mighty quick. Did you climb in there?" he asked, nodding his head toward the window.

"That's not your business!" replied the red Feodor harshly. "Where's Nina? Where are you hiding her?" He thumped the desk with his fist.

"I—hide?" Mikhail was surprised. "What would I want her for?"

The red Feodor, his face distorted, reached for his throat, but at that moment the door of the study opened and Glushak entered. The red Feodor hid in the shadows.

"Pyotr!" exclaimed the relieved Mikhail. "The Director is going for me with his fists, asking where Nina is. How should I know?"

"Director?" Glushak started. "There's no Director here."

"There he is, hiding in the shadows."

Glushak looked in the corner. "There's no one here but you and me, and Cheprok there by the fireside."

"You're sure?"

"Of course."

"Then that's a joke of the red-haired fellow," Mikhail laughed. "But I'm not afraid of his jokes. They are not at all frightening. What is frightening is that I have mad dogs inside me. They gnaw my guts, tear my soul into pieces. I hear their snarling, I see the terrifying baring of their teeth, I know—only the last breath of my life can satisfy them. I'm ruined, I've lost everything! . . ."

Mikhail went over to Glushak and whispered hotly in his face: "Listen, Pyotr: tonight I'm going to run away. Would you like to go along with me? Of course, it's dangerous: they shoot on the border. But in any case, freedom is worth the risk."

"Mikhail! Sit down! You're not well."

Mikhail again saw Feodor Novikov. This time he entered by the door and was of normal color. "Well, well . . . he's being sly," thought Mikhail wickedly. In mad fury he jumped up, waved a bottle at the Director.

528

"What's the matter?" asked Feodor, frightened.

"Mikhail's a little drunk," explained Glushak.

"Aha! Feodor Novikov was here!" cried Mikhail triumphantly. Glushak began to explain something to him, but in vain: his words flew over Mikhail without touching his consciousness. He looked guardedly at Feodor. The latter, in a black suit, well built and tall, watched keenly from under his lowered eyebrows.

"Pyotr, aren't you afraid of him?" asked Mikhail.

"I'm afraid of nothing," replied Glushak confidently. He spoke the truth. The constant evil companion of his life—fear—was no longer with him. But Mikhail didn't know that. With his sliding gait Glushak slipped up to the desk, drank a glass of vodka.

"Mikhail Alexeyevich, Misha, listen to me," said Glushak, a change coming over his face suddenly. "I am not afraid of anybody. For instance, the Director is standing here, hears everything, and I want to make an important confession in his presence. I have betrayed you, Misha. You have considered me your friend, but I have betrayed you —wrote dirty reports against you. Forgive me, Misha!" Glushak dropped to his knees in front of Mikhail. "I am hateful to myself, but am I to blame? Is a man to blame who was not born brave? My brother Vladimir—you must remember him—the Chekists tortured him in the next cell. He howled so horribly that I lost heart. I don't know—perhaps someone else could have stood it, but I couldn't. The Cheka made me its servant—if they'd sent me to clean out the toilets I would have gone. But they did far worse than that—they made me betray my friends, and this I did, betrayed . . ."

Glushak's confession took Feodor unprepared. For several seconds he stood with open mouth, afraid to take a breath.

"Yes, I betrayed you too in my fear, in inhuman fear. I repent. It's late, but I repent, Misha!" exclaimed Glushak, and a hot exultant joy burned his heart. His whole being beamed from his smile, from the secret revealed at last.

Mikhail looked down at him, seemed to listen closely, screwed up his eyes, tried to open his mind to the excited words of this man, bruised by fate. "What's wrong with you, Pyotr? Why are you talking so jubilantly? And your eyes look so strange . . ." Mikhail raised his clouded, faraway glance to Feodor. "What's he talking about?" he asked, bewildered.

Immediately Glushak and Feodor spoke at the same time: Glushak joyfully, almost exultingly; Feodor, harshly and confused.

"I repent, Misha, forgive . . ."

529

"He's lying! Don't believe him! He's drunk."

"I betrayed you, Misha—I know, everyone's against you: the Director, Veria, and Drozd, all are your enemies."

"He's lying! Lying! Lying!"

Their voices rose and, suddenly drowned by the terrific cursing of Cheprok, became silent. The old man stood between them, tousled, prickly. "You've made your racket, you bastards! Don't you see that Mikhail Alexeyevich isn't himself?" All three stared at Mikhail. He went slowly toward a window, looked at the sky. Yes, at last he understood what Glushak had been talking about so excitedly. He sneered, twisting his lips just as if he were sober. But the look he directed at the sky was strange, resigned. "A soul without wings. A soul without wings," he said softly. Mikhail was dreaming of wings now. They would have borne him on high into the starry distance, away from these people, from the Director, from Pyotr, from this life, bitter as wormwood. Only in the recesses of the sky could he find purity, joy, and everlasting peace. Holding his breath, he watched the dreamy play of the stars. Each one of them was beautiful, each one lured him with its starry eyes, each one promised the fascinated Mikhail its love and heavenly bliss. Only to join them! Only to abandon this dreary world forever! For all eternity!

But fatigue overcame him, plunging him into deep sleep. Mikhail dropped his head onto his chest and slipped heavily to the floor.

"Lift him up carefully. Carry him to the divan," ordered Cheprok, closing the window.

Feodor and Glushak, without looking at each other, lifted the evenly breathing Mikhail.

CHAPTER 18

FEODOR returned to the ballroom. There the guests were crowding in small groups, whispering to each other. All you could hear was: "What a disgrace! What a disgrace! Shame!"

Suddenly the door opened and into the ballroom stumbled the elder Shcherbakov; he was leading Nina by the arm.

"I found her!" he shouted joyfully. "The girl simply decided to get some fresh air! And you people raised a panic!"

Feodor glanced at Nina. She was unrecognizable. All color had left her face; her large, frightened eyes burned feverishly.

Someone shouted: "It's time for the young couple to go to the bed-room!"

"We want to escort them!"

"Beat the pots!"

Somebody caught up an expensive vase and crashed it to the floor. Vassily, the muscles of his face working nervously, went upstairs first, stopped at the landing and looked down at the guests, who were staring at him with their drunken goggle eyes, then jerked his head angrily and went through the door. Nina followed him. The elder Shcherbakov, with Luba, escorted her to the stairs and stopped there. Nina began to go up alone, looking down at her feet as if she were counting the steps. It was quiet in the ballroom. Luba brought her handkerchief to her eyes.

While she was shutting the door Nina heard somebody downstairs whistle shrilly and Mirzoyan's voice bawl: "Bring on the girls!"

Loud laughter drowned his voice.

CHAPTER 19

ONCE THE YOUNG couple were in the bedroom the party began to break up. But Mirzoyan's drunken shout did not remain without notice. On the veranda a group of revelers gathered—Mirzoyan himself, tight as a drum; Veria, merrily excited; the gloomy Durov, and several other men. Here also was Drozd, who had kept apart in the meantime. They had sent their wives home long ago.

"Where's Shcherbakov?" repeated Mirzoyan. "Let him get us some girls. If we're celebrating, let's celebrate!"

Shcherbakov entered, swaying and wiping his hands. "I've locked them in the bedroom—she won't run away now."

Mirzoyan scurried over to him, putting his arm around his waist. "Look, Alexander Pavlovich—how about . . . you know what," and he made a quite obvious gesture with his hand.

"But where will I get them? You're the hosts here, while Vassily is busy."

At that moment Feodor glanced in at the door of the veranda. His face was agitated.

"Hey, Director! Come in!" shouted Veria.

Feodor approached and whispered to him: "I want to speak to you about a serious matter. Glushak has disclosed everything. There's only one hope: Gorin was drunk and may forget."

531

Veria's eyes lit up.

"I knew that would happen!" he exclaimed merrily. "One can read these intellectuals like an open book. But don't be afraid—it's not important now."

Winking to the perplexed Feodor, Veria led him up to the men. "The boys here are interested in girls—have you got a practical suggestion, Director?"

Feodor became confused. "Maybe there are some in the neighboring Cossack village?"

"The village girls are too dirty! Who wants them?"

Veria suddenly slapped his thighs: "I have an idea! Let's make a raid on the boarding house of the ballet school!"

For a second everybody was silent, then they chattered delightedly: "Why didn't we think of that before?" . . . "What a man, Veria! Everybody to the cars!"

They got into two open cars, loaded them with wine and refreshments. The chauffeurs, also rather drunk, fussed around more than all the others. The girls' boarding house of the Rostov School of Ballet, a two-storied building, was situated on the outskirts of the town. They drove up with great noise and honking. Veria waved his cap in the air, gave orders as if he were on the field of battle.

"Surround the house! . . . Hey, Vanka!" he shouted to his chauffeur. "Stand at the door, don't allow anyone in, or out. Pull out your revolver, and stay on duty till morning."

In the entrance hall, into which the frightened girls had poured, Veria kicked over a chair, roared, waving his Browning around: "Stand where you are! Whoever moves'll get a bullet in her forehead. All girls are confiscated until morning!"

The elder Shcherbakov buzzed behind him: "Easy, Lozo! You'll frighten them—they may die. What good's a dead one?"

From a bedroom issued a sleepy old woman. "What's happened! Why are you making such a noise?" she asked sternly. On seeing the drunken men she threatened them with a skinny finger: "Get out of the boarding house at once, or I'll call the militia!"

Veria scowled at her. "Where did you come from? Durov!" he yelled. "Tie up the old hag! Lock her up in the store room!"

They bound the panic-stricken old woman, gagged her with a rag, and dragged her to the store room. The frightened young ballerinas threw themselves at the doors, but the chauffeurs chased them away from there. Veria really let himself go. He shouted, waving his arm as if in attack: "Forward! Follow me! To the rooms!" and he ran up-

532

stairs. Mirzoyan, grunting like a pig, rushed into the first room—at once two young voices screamed. "Bring the wine! Bring on the bacchanalia!" shouted Veria from upstairs.

Feodor, no less excited than the others, entered a room with Drozd. He took bottles and a parcel of refreshments with him. They switched on the light. Two girls, still quite young, were trembling under the sheets—only their eyes, blinking with fear, were visible.

"Come now, girls, get out of your beds. We're going to put on a party," Drozd addressed them gaily.

Feodor approached the one whose eyes seemed to be larger and pulled off the sheet. The girl sighed, pressed her arms to her satiny belly, as if he were bearing down on her with a knife. Throwing back her head, she looked pleadingly at him, powerless to say a word. With the sheet in his hand, Feodor froze for an instant, astounded—the girl was very beautiful and somehow reminded him of Nina.

"So much the better," he thought spitefully, and laughed. The girl trembled still more from his laughter.

"Veria was right," said Drozd meanwhile, spreading out the refreshments on a small table. "No mistake here! All the girls are as if selected. Well now, Black-Brows! Enough of blinking your eyes—sit down here on my knee. And don't be afraid. We're just like a couple of tax collectors. The Government keeps you, pays you, looks after you without end. Now you're going to pay some of it back. Come on! Let's see what you have to offer . . ."

CHAPTER 20

VASSILY WAS waiting for Nina, standing with closed eyes beside a dresser. On hearing the creak of the door he opened his eyes, fixed, terrible; and suddenly, snorting wildly, he rushed at Nina. All atremble, he caught her shoulders with his moist hands and threw her down on the bed.

Nina was too frightened to resist. He seemed to be going to tear her to pieces—he ripped her dress, burrowed his face in the lace, cursed senselessly and filthily. Nina closed her eyes in shame, cried out loudly.

Sated, Vassily rolled to one side and snored. Nina, her legs trembling, got up, took off the torn, rumpled dress, and cautiously lay down on the edge of the bed. When Vassily put his leg over her in his sleep, Nina didn't move away. The limit had been reached.

PART EIGHT

⌐⌐⌐⌐⌐⌐⌐⌐⌐⌐⌐⌐⌐⌐⌐⌐⌐⌐⌐⌐⌐⌐⌐⌐⌐⌐⌐⌐

CHAPTER 1

"The password?"

"Bolt."

The sentry opened the ornamental gates. Drozd and Novikov, in the cab of a truck, a squad of soldiers with rifles in the body, drove into the estate.

It was Wednesday, the third day after the noisy wedding. What they were about to do was the result of a secret conference with Veria. Yesterday, after the conference, Veria had left for Moscow. Drozd—in military uniform, straight as a new pin, the collar of the tunic cutting deep into his fat neck, his thin lips firmly pressed together, his eyes insolent—was outwardly calm. Feodor looked glum. After the talk with Veria (a long conversation behind closed doors) he hadn't slept all night. His face was gray, tired, but inside he was alert, like a cocked gun.

The truck stopped at the main portal. Drozd nudged Feodor with his elbow: "They live well, the devils!" He was seeing Gorin's estate for the first time. Feodor looked at his watch: it was nine o'clock in the morning. He knew that Mikhail Gorin was still sick in bed after his spree. Alarmed, Luba came out to meet them. On seeing Feodor Novikov she frowned, while the sight of the heavily armed soldiers frightened her.

Drozd introduced himself gallantly.

"My name is Drozd, Commissar of State Security, First Rank. These soldiers are the new guard. We are increasing the guard as the result

534

of evidence of the preparation of an attempt on your husband's life by enemies of the people. But please don't worry. Everything is under control. If you have no objections, I'll explain the details inside. Can we see Comrade Gorin?"

"Mikhail's in bed. He's sick," replied Luba, reluctantly and coldly. It was obvious that she did not believe Drozd.

"It will take only a minute," Drozd again brought his hand to his cap, his face spreading into a smile, like butter in a hot pan.

Cheprok was on duty at the door of Gorin's bedroom. When he saw Feodor Novikov and the unknown man, he rose threateningly to meet them. In his hands, red as the claws of a boiled lobster, he held a big hunting gun. The old man's bushy eyebrows twitched grimly; his piercing eyes bored into the uninvited guests.

"Cheprok, these people are here on business about the guard. Let them in," said Luba.

"What guard?" snapped Cheprok, and blocked the doorway. The barrel of his gun was stuck into Drozd's stomach. The latter quickly brushed the gun aside and poked the old man in the shoulder.

"What kind of a circus is this? Where did this scarecrow come from?" he asked, devouring the old man with his narrowed eyes.

Feodor explained: "This is Mikhail Gorin's old friend. The old man's a bit odd, but harmless."

Cheprok was not appeased. He spoke heatedly to Luba, emphasizing each word with a fierce, sidewise look toward Feodor Novikov: "You shouldn't allow all kinds of people in, Lubov Dmitrievna. That's how we trusted the doctor, and then he up and killed Pavel——"

"Be quiet, Cheprok," Luba interrupted him, and knocked on the door.

Inside, Drozd repeated to Mikhail everything he had said to Luba, and added that it was desirable that Mikhail not leave the estate for a while. Mikhail, with half closed eyes, as if he were sleepy, waved his hand weakly: "It's all the same to me: I'll probably stay in bed for a whole week." His fingers were shaking and from his face it was evident that he had a bad headache.

"That's excellent," purred Drozd smoothly. "It's an ill wind that blows nobody good. In a week everything will be settled—your health as well as our worries." Drozd's eyes were caressing, but in their green depths there was something evil and merciless. Luba noticed this concealed play, and the constricting foreboding which had enveloped her from the first moment of the appearance of Drozd and Novikov remained. Frowning, she stood beside the bed looking at her husband.

535

Her face was like stone, but at the corners of her lips two little lines formed and in them was everything: great tenderness and great alarm. The sickness had sunk Mikhail's eyes deep into their sockets, his large mustaches seemed especially enormous, and his prominent cheek bones were still more sharply pronounced on his wasted face; above his right eyebrow beside the gray temple his pulse beat noticeably. The warm air barely stirred the curtains; the clouds, light as smoke, floated slowly by. Mikhail followed them with a far-away look.

The change in the writer shocked Feodor, but now it was all the same to him that Mikhail was so pale, that he had such a pathetic, wasted neck. More than that, in fact: instead of pity, he looked at him with an unaccountable dislike.

"Luba, where is Pyotr?" Mikhail asked about Glushak. "I haven't seen him since the wedding."

"They didn't come back here. I called them yesterday at their apartment but nobody answered," replied Luba with alarm in her voice, and she looked questioningly at Feodor. "You haven't seen Academician Glushak, have you?"

Feodor shook his head. He had indeed not seen Glushak, but he knew what had happened to him. On Monday Glushak, with his wife, had been arrested on Veria's orders and the very same day had been sent off to jail in Moscow. At the same time Alexei Dorogov, Olga's brother, had been arrested. Veria himself had told Feodor about it.

After a short conversation with the writer, Drozd personally detailed the guard. "Nobody is to be allowed to leave the estate," he instructed them. The guard was placed, not only along the fence, but at the outside doors of the house. To the chief of the guard, a young sergeant, decked out in belts (cartridge belt, revolver belt, belt for map case, belt for whistle) and spurs for the total corruption of the girls, Drozd explained that Luba could drive out as usual. "But aside from her—no one. And keep a sharp eye on that old grumbler Cheprok," added Drozd. "You can expect anything from him. He's too smart for his years."

CHAPTER 2

THEN DROZD ordered all the household to line up: the servants, the gardener, the chef, and the other cooks. They all gathered in the yard, puzzled, upset, looked timidly at the menacing uniform of Drozd, at the sergeant's belts. But more than anything the familiar but grimly mysterious face of Novikov frightened them.

"Where's Gorin's secretary?" asked Drozd. The secretary was called and Drozd ordered him to stand in line with the others.

Drozd walked up and down the uneven line, looked sternly into their faces, as if he were taking aim at each one, smirked at something two or three times and at last said loudly, so that everybody started:

"Attention, Citizens! From this moment none of you will be allowed to leave the confines of the estate. Anyone who dares to go even one step outside the fence will be shot. So my advice is: Better sit quietly; don't make a row. And there's no reason why you should: the groceries and all other necessities will be delivered here by the guard. Whoever has a sweetheart in town, put off your meeting for the time being. Nothing is going to happen to you. Nobody ever died from abstention." At these words of Drozd's the sergeant grinned broadly. "You must send no letters, nor make any telephone calls." Drozd turned to the sergeant: "Comrade Polikarpov, bring the telephone from the entrance hall into Comrade Novikov's room. Disconnect the others. Do that at once."

"Right away!" The sergeant, his belts squeaking, went off.

Drozd again addressed the line-up: "Comrade Novikov is in charge. If you need anything, ask him or the sergeant. You must not talk with the guard. Remember that! Now, are there any questions?"

"But what's happened?" . . . . "Why such strictness?" . . . "What about relatives—can we see them?" . . . "D'you mean we can't go into town for a couple of hours?"

Drozd made a wry face. "And don't argue. These are temporary measures. In a week or two, everything will be as it was before. The measures taken are for your own security."

The household was somewhat reassured—or rather, forced itself to feel reassured, stifling a sharp foreboding of trouble. The gardener, noticeably pale, said to his wife in a whisper: "Mother dear, it looks as if we're in for it."

When the line-up was dismissed, Drozd called the secretary: "Let's go and have a talk. Where's your office?"

The secretary, biting his trembling lips, conducted Drozd and Novikov into Mikhail's study. "Sit down, please." With a shaking hand he pushed armchairs toward them. He remained standing himself, tried to smile pleasantly, but his wide eyes filled with the turbidity of fear.

537

"Do many people write to Gorin?" Drozd asked him, without inviting him to sit down.

"A great many. Particularly since the appearance of his play *Ivan the Terrible*. But the number of unfriendly, anonymous letters has also increased. Usually I don't show them to Mikhail Alexeyevich; I consider it needless to disturb him . . ."

"And do visitors come often?"

"Often and many. During week-days about ten to fifteen people; on Sundays sometimes up to a hundred come—whole delegations. Of course, Mikhail Alexeyevich is unable to receive them all. Two or three a day; the rest he leaves to me. I pass the time with them somehow, so that they won't be offended."

"Well then, from today on there will be no receptions," said Drozd brusquely. "You will explain to visitors that Mikhail Gorin is sick and can't see anyone."

"But what will I do if Mikhail Alexeyevich himself wants to see the people?"

"In that case consult with Comrade Novikov. He will take the necessary steps and speak to Gorin. And as to correspondence, you will answer it as usual—but everything, incoming and outgoing, you will give to Comrade Novikov for checking."

"I understand. But how about the foreigners?"

"What foreigners?"

"Well, all kinds. Correspondents, for instance. They come to us nearly every week to inquire about Mikhail Alexeyevich. If I tell them that he's sick and can't receive them, they will at once print in their papers that the Bolsheviks are keeping Gorin a prisoner. That's easy for them."

Drozd looked closely into the secretary's eyes: "Maybe you yourself think that Gorin is a prisoner?"

The secretary was confused. "No—of course not! But the foreigners, they like sensationalism."

"All right, I'll think over this question," said Drozd. "Comrade Novikov will give you the necessary instructions on that score. The main thing at the moment is that everything should go on normally, as usual—but no receptions."

"I understand," replied the secretary and, in a humble voice asked: "May I ask a question?"

"Go ahead."

"I have a sweetheart in Rostov and I would like to visit her once a week, otherwise she'll be worried . . ."

538

Drozd's look became cold and foggy. In a gruff voice he said: "You heard what was said in the yard? Well, that was an order, and we aren't going to change it specially for you." And suddenly, his face changing, Drozd bellowed: "Why the hell are you shaking like a lamb's tail! Nobody's killing you!"

The secretary shrank into himself, caught hold of the back of a chair—his legs were failing him. "Pardon me . . . I just asked . . ." he mumbled.

Drozd and Novikov left the study.

"And now, Comrade Director, let's find nice quarters for you. I'm afraid that you'll have to spend more than one night under this roof."

They selected a room next to Mikhail Gorin's bedroom for Novikov, explaining to Luba that this was a precautionary measure. "Perhaps the Comrade Director will find it necessary to spend the night under Mikhail's bed," Luba said sarcastically.

Shrugging his shoulders, and with a look of injured innocence, Drozd replied: "We're worrying on your account, you know."

In the room, Drozd shook Feodor's hand in farewell, and looked searchingly into his eyes: "Well, Comrade Director, I guess this is the beginning."

"Yes, this is the beginning," Feodor responded gloomily.

Without answering, Drozd left. In a few minutes the hum of the truck taking him to town was heard.

CHAPTER 3

THE VERY FIRST night Cheprok managed to steal out of the estate. Pretending to be sick, he lay in bed all day, but with the approach of darkness, he climbed out of his window into the park. He crawled for a long way on his belly, stopping to listen often. At last he reached the bath house on the river and, when the moon went behind the clouds, he got into a boat and noiselessly crossed. It took him three hours to walk to town. In the first mail box he dropped a letter to Nina, written in his shaky hand: ". . . Come as quick as you can, Mikhail is in danger." He described in detail how she should get in touch with him so that he could take her unobserved into the estate. "The house is surrounded. They won't let anybody in, but I'll get you through."

After mailing the letter, Cheprok returned home. Climbing barefoot up the brick projections of the wall to his own window, and happy

539

that he had deceived the guard so cleverly, Cheprok was quite bewildered on seeing Luba in his room waiting for him. However, he collected his wits quickly. Knowing that Luba didn't want to write to Nina so as not to alarm her, Cheprok explained that he had run into town on his own business. "I hid my bits of savings. It's dangerous to keep them here now."

"Watch out, Cheprok, if you warned Nina. There's no sense in doing it. Our life must no longer concern her. It's better that way."

Luba embraced the old man impulsively. "He risked his life," she though with gratitude. Only now did Luba feel how isolated they were, that she and Mikhail had no friends on whom they could depend. For the three years of their stay in Russia, a circle of official adoration, which she always knew could turn into enmity in an instant, had surrounded their family tightly.

It was as if a corpse had been carried into Gorin's magnificent house. The corpse was fear. It spread quickly. Its poisonous vapor stole into every corner, caught the breath of the people. Fear penetrated into the soul of everyone; no one escaped it. A general numbness set in. With sinking hearts they all expected some tragedy. Actually the curtain to the tragedy had already opened. The people in the house now felt the betrayal by the Government. Mikhail alone suspected nothing. Fearing for his health, Luba did not mention her own forebodings.

Most of the time Feodor Novikov was engaged in checking the correspondence, settling questions about visitors. He handed over the matter of the guard completely to the dashing sergeant. Everybody in the house treated the Director as an uninvited but dangerous guest. Luba seldom met him, and when she did she said practically nothing. Feodor also behaved with emphasized coolness. Mikhail was still in bed, but was improving noticeably. Feodor knew that as soon as Mikhail got up his real worries would begin.

A week later, when Feodor was looking through letters in the study as usual, the door opened. Feodor raised his head and jumped up, astounded. In front of him stood Nina. In her right hand was a revolver, which she held aimed straight at his chest. The barrel was trembling, and Nina's pale face was trembling, her eyes narrowed with hate.

"Nina! It's you? Nina?" he breathed, and stepped backward. "How . . . how did you get here?"

"I want to ask you, myself: How did you get here?" said Nina. "What are you doing in my father's house?"

Not he, but someone else, with Feodor's face, with Feodor's voice,

540

said evenly: "Nina, drop that revolver, it's not a toy. And there's nothing to be excited about. I've been entrusted with the protection of Mikhail Alexeyevich."

Nina's lips twisted in complete aversion. "That's a lie!" she said. "You came here to kill my father. But I won't let you. Once we trusted people and lost Pavel. But now we're wiser, Comrade Director. I have sized you up very well and I've decided to kill you. Don't move!" she added in a strangely calm, and therefore dangerous, voice. "It will be interesting to see how they will explain your death. They won't say, of course, that the wife of the Secretary of the Province killed the Director. Of course not! They may put it down to chronic drunkenness, as they explained Pavel's death."

While Nina was talking, Feodor watched her revolver. "She pulls the trigger and that's the end," he thought feverishly, fearing through some careless word or movement to break the thin thread on which his life hung. "And she's right, there's no danger for her. Hell! What a crazy situation!" His cold hands were bathed in sticky sweat. Listening to the mad thumping of his heart, he awaited his chance.

"Nina, don't be naïve," Feodor said softly, so that his voice wouldn't shake from agitation. "If somebody really wants to kill Mikhail Alexeyevich, you surely don't think that they would give me the job? Surely there are plenty of cutthroats, people with the hands of murderers? And my hands, are they that kind?" As if with an involuntary gesture Feodor extended his hand to her.

"Don't move, Feodor!" she warned him. "And keep quiet!"

Feodor drew back his hand. Nina at once turned into steel. Her teeth were clenched, the revolver was firmly gripped in her hand, her steady stare fixed on Feodor's eyes. Feodor froze. The very life in him wanted to cry out in a last despair: "Have mercy!" but he could only tremble faintly. His fingers caught convulsively at the desk. He had almost stopped breathing. Thus they faced each other in a kind of fantasmal, dreamlike silence. In Feodor's consciousness the thought suddenly flashed: "If only she'd shoot quick! Why this torture?"

Somewhere beyond the door, in the depths of the corridor, Mikhail's voice sounded: "This is monstrous! Has everybody gone crazy? Where's that idiot Novikov?" The voice was coming nearer. Nina trembled, listened, and at that very moment fired. Feodor, taking advantage of her momentary confusion, grabbed at her revolver. The bullet flew past, and the revolver was in his hand. With a dull groan Nina fell onto the corner of the divan. Like a drowning man emerging from a

541

whirlpool, Feodor took a deep breath, then sank into an armchair. The door opened and Mikhail entered. He was in such a rage that he didn't even see his daughter.

"What does all this mean, Comrade Director!" he launched out at Feodor. "Why are you in my house, and where have all these soldiers come from?" Mikhail's white face was terrible: his gray eyes flashed fire, his hoary tousled eyebrows bristled, his voice lashed and was hoarse. He had a gnarled stick in his hand and threatened Feodor with it savagely, prancing over him like an angry bear. Feodor shrank into the armchair.

"But we explained to you, Mikhail Alexeyevich," he said disconcertedly. "The guard was increased as a precautionary measure, for your own safety."

"But why is some sergeant giving orders in my house as in a barracks?"

"Again, I say, we explained all that to you in detail, Mikhail Alexeyevich, and you agreed. Surely you remember?"

"Yes, but I never suspected that your measures would go to such idiotic extremes." Mikhail suddenly fixed his eyes with particular intensity on Feodor's face, as if he had suddenly remembered the most important thing: "And why did they entrust you with all this foolishness, Director?"

Without answering his question, Feodor said hurriedly: "I can assure you, Mikhail Alexeyevich, these measures are temporary. Another week and everything will return to normal."

"Don't believe him, Papa," Nina said, getting up from the divan. Mikhail turned to her quickly, recoiling with surprise. "Nina! How did you happen here?"

"Don't believe him, Papa," she repeated, tears ringing in her voice. "Surely you can see that you're imprisoned. Oh, Papa!" With a dull sob his daughter threw herself on his breast.

"Is that true?" Mikhail's voice was grim, with an unfamiliar quaver.

"Of course not!" exclaimed Feodor heatedly. "What nonsense! Nina's nerves are simply wound up. She's imagining all kinds of——"

"All right. That's easy to prove. I'll go out of the grounds right now and we'll see if anybody stops me. I'm not afraid of bullets! Let them kill Mikhail Gorin!"

Feodor turned pale. "I wouldn't advise you to do that, Mikhail Alexeyevich! Why make a scene? Surely you can wait another week——"

542

Mikhail turned sharply toward the door. "Let's go, Nina."

When the door slammed behind them, Feodor rushed to the telephone in his own room and called Drozd.

CHAPTER 4

"HALT! Where are you going?" The sentry raised his rifle. Without answering, Mikhail Gorin continued to go down the steps. The soldier —a Tartar, small, with prominent cheek bones, bristled like a lynx, snapped the lock: "Halt, I say! Or I'll shoot!"

Mikhail continued walking calmly but, when he came up to the soldier, he stopped. "What's your name?" he asked the Tartar suddenly.

"Yusupov," replied the soldier, not expecting the question.

"And my name is Mikhail Gorin. Did you ever hear it?"

"Hey! Your head talk foolish! Mine not listen!" shouted the soldier; and remembering himself, he jumped away a pace and brought the bayonet up to Mikhail's chest. His short legs tensed, his squinty eyes blinked, surprised and frightened at the tall man. "No people leave house. I shoot!"

"So you don't know me," said Mikhail. "Or perhaps you do, but it's all the same to you: once you've been told to shoot, I suppose you'll shoot." Mikhail waved his hand, turned his back on the soldier and went toward the gates.

"Halt!" For the third time, and very piercingly, the Tartar shouted. He raised his rifle and fired into the air. Mikhail shuddered, stumbled, but continued to walk on. He even raised his head higher. At that moment Nina appeared on the steps with her mother.

"Mikhail! Misha! Stop! They'll kill you!" cried Luba, terrified, and tried to throw herself forward to protect her husband, but a heavy numbness struck her. Nina, in a blind rage, jumped at the soldier and before he had time to defend himself, tore the rifle out of his hands. With a blow from the butt she beat him to the ground. In a fit of anger and desperation, she continued to beat him as he lay.

"How dare you shoot at my father!" she cried in a breaking voice, wide-eyed with horror.

Feodor Novikov ran out of the house with the sergeant. The sergeant waved his hand to the soldiers: "Seize him!"

Three soldiers detached themselves from the gate and ran up to

543

Gorin. One of them recognized him. "That's Gorin! Mikhail Gorin," he shouted, stunned. The soldiers stopped in confusion.

"Well, why have you stopped?" cried Mikhail loudly. "Take me, bind me! Clip the wings of the stormy petrel!" Beside himself, Mikhail laughed into the alien, unfriendly faces, into the abyss of his fate unfolding before him.

Then the sergeant, twisting his mouth, came up to Gorin. Hitting him a stunning slap in the face which rocked the air and jarred Mikhail's very soul, he shouted: "That'll teach you!"

Mikhail threw himself at the sergeant, but the soldiers, emboldened by their chief's example, seized him from behind. Outraged, driven to frenzy, Mikhail scattered the soldiers hanging onto him except one fellow, stalwart like himself, who held him, twisting his left arm painfully behind his back. Mikhail struggled in the iron hold, unable to believe that he was caught. He strove to free himself from the gripping hands, silently and frenziedly; he ground his teeth, not wanting to waste breath on useless shouting; but all his great body cried out, howled for freedom, tried to tear itself out of captivity. And only when they brought a rope and bound him did Mikhail slump to the ground. From his split lips and nose blood flowed freely over his mustaches. Breathing heavily, his eyes roaming wildly, Mikhail sought Nina. Her arms held by the Tartar soldier, Nina met his glance with a horrified stare.

Someone lifted Luba, who had fallen in a faint, and led her into the house. Then Nina, whom the soldier had reluctantly released on the orders of the sergeant, came up to her mother and took her by the arm. Her hair disordered, her eyes flashing, Nina whimpered, raged incoherently, swore hoarsely.

Stunned by the whole scene, Feodor did not at once come to himself. Only on the repeated question of the sergeant did he order Mikhail Gorin to be shut up in his bedroom. Luba and Nina were not to be allowed to leave the house until the arrival of Drozd. "And keep them as far away as possible from Mikhail."

CHAPTER 5

CHEPROK also was refused admission to the writer, but he broke a way through for himself by sheer will. In a mad rage he went after the

Director with his fists. "All my life Mikhail and I have been together and if you have even a scrap of conscience left you'll allow me to look after him now." Cheprok's voice was nervous, shaky, broke into a high, piercing falsetto.

"All right, all right! . . . Go to him! But don't make a noise," replied Feodor with emotion, stepping back from the advancing old man, so terrible and so pathetic.

Just in case, Feodor ordered the sergeant to search the old man and to take away anything that might serve as a weapon. While they were searching Cheprok he never took his sharp eyes off the Director. Feodor frowned and threatened him with a glance. Cheprok stubbornly continued to look straight into his eyes. They stood thus, glaring at each other, like a tamer and a beast. Feodor gave in first and turned away.

Mikhail was sitting on the floor, already freed of his bonds, but completely exhausted, crushed, staring straight ahead of him with a look of dull stupefaction. Cheprok rushed to him, put his arms around him, and shaking like a leaf in the wind, looked into his eyes. Mikhail was silent. It was hard to recognize him. Usually majestic and vigorous, he was bowed, his hands trembled, his tortured eyes were half closed. Cheprok put Mikhail to bed, wiped the blood from his face and hands, rubbed his chest, his temples with eau de Cologne, put a few drops of spirits of ammonia in a glass of water. "Drink this—you'll feel better."

Mikhail drank with labored, noisy gulps while Cheprok supported the bottom of the glass with his fingers. Mikhail turned his eyes toward the little table. Cheprok, guessing, got him a cigarette. Greedily Mikhail brought it to his mouth. His whole body was shaking and he was unable to light the cigarette even from the lighter which Cheprok offered him. Cheprok lit the cigarette and placed it between Mikhail's parched lips. After three drags, Mikhail asked: "Where are Luba and Nina?"

"Here in the house. They're all right——"

Mikhail groaned.

"They haven't been touched. Don't get downhearted, Misha." Cheprok wiped the beads of sweat from Mikhail's face and eyebrows, with an impetuous tenderness stroked his hair with his rough hand.

"What do you think, Cheprok dear? Things are pretty bad?"

"It's all right——"

"They're bad?"

"It's all right, it's all right, it's all right." Cheprok threw his arm around Mikhail's shoulders. "Misha, my friend, my everlasting friend

545

. . ." His voice trembled pathetically; he pressed himself closer to Mikhail, as if he were afraid to lose him.

Mikhail became still. He looked sidewise at the thin, tired face of the old man, and only then felt how everything in himself had been shattered and smashed. His head buzzed from a blow on the back of the neck. In his confused consciousness disordered thoughts and figures crowded. "Tell me, Cheprok, right away, between us here—is this reality or a nightmare? I've lost the thread . . ." Mikhail closed his deadened eyes; his voice was far away, barely audible.

Cheprok didn't answer.

Mikhail lay without moving, waiting. Only when he felt something hot on his hand did he slowly raise his eyelids. The bowed head of his old friend Cheprok was shaking silently, his hot tears falling on Mikhail's hand.

"We've lived too long, old friend," murmured Mikhail. "Oh, how right Pavel was! . . . And now you alone are left to me——"

"I'll never leave you. I'll die with you," said Cheprok in a gurgling whisper, and his face suddenly lit up. Mikhail took the twisted, red hand of his friend and with silent gratitude pressed it to his lips.

CHAPTER 6

AFTER GIVING final orders to the sergeant, Feodor remained alone in the study. For ten minutes he sat in petrified immobility. The events had stupefied him. His stunned mind jumped back to a scene in Veria's office. Drozd was with them. Veria's new orders had already been discussed. It was Veria who had discussed; Drozd and Novikov merely listened.

"The time for negotiations and psychic manipulations has ended," said Veria, pacing up and down the office. "Now we need action. I have the permission of the Government to use force if necessary. But we Bolsheviks aren't barbarians; we do not want to harm anyone. What is suggested is a simple restriction of Mikhail Gorin's movements, and that's all. Something in the nature of a straitjacket, which we will be putting on his body rather than on his spirit. I sincerely hope that during this period of trial Mikhail Gorin will revise his hasty and disastrous opinions and will return to the former peaceful fold, as our repentant brother, frequently erring, but dear to our heart." At the last words Veria even folded his hands reverently on his little belly.

Even then Feodor had considered the order to restrict Gorin's freedom, not allowing him to leave home, as open provocation, like Veria's evil game with Glushak at the wedding. He did not doubt that this idea was Veria's. One could feel the similarity of the pattern and the hand of the expert. He also clearly foresaw where this measure would lead. But why Veria entrusted him to carry out this betrayal—that Feodor did not understand, as yet.

Dismissing Drozd, Veria kept Feodor alone with him. He took a green file out of the safe. Smiling playfully with his eyes, Veria extended it to Feodor. This turned out to be the record of Oleg Durov's murder. Here were the report of the state investigators, the report of the old sleuth Protopopov, the information of the chief of the Special Branch of the University, the confession of the old doctor who took bribes, the information of the waitress Nadya, and, finally, the report of Durov senior himself.

Feodor did not at first understand why Veria was opening all these secrets to him. He began to read the papers as he would a novel, with heroes imagined by a talented author. But soon he saw that the principal hero and murderer was himself, Feodor Novikov. His fingers stuck to the paper. The report of the investigator Protopopov was particularly strong and deadly. Reading it over, stumbling over each word, Feodor went cold; an animal fear squeezed his heart. Unable to read more, he raised his eyes to Veria.

"You . . . you knew all the time?" he exclaimed. Feodor understood that to deny, to disavow would be useless.

"Yes, I knew," Veria smiled. He took the file and suddenly, without saying a word, he began to tear it up, page after page, throwing the scraps into the fireplace. "Give me a match, please," he said, when not a single page was left in his hands. Feodor, still not understanding, like an automaton handed him a box of matches. Veria set fire to the heap of papers.

"You see, I am destroying the traces of your stormy past. We shall consider that as a mistake of youth and, as they say, 'Who brings up bygones loses his eye.' Now, Comrade Director, I hope you are convinced that I trust you to the limit. Do not betray my trust," and with an impulsive gesture, full of theatrical grace, he extended his hand. True to form, he then outlined his thoughts picturesquely and in the grand manner.

In this way Veria conducted Feodor to a new door in his fate, merely opening it a little. With the confidence of a teacher in his best pupil he left it to Feodor to open the door fully and enter. There was no doubt that Veria looked on Novikov as a specialist on Gorin. But now this specialist was transformed from a clever mental surgeon into a jailer, and Gorin from an interesting patient into a tortured prisoner. This thought stunned Feodor. With all its obviousness it just would not fit into his head. Since Feodor's childhood, at school, all his life, Mikhail Gorin had been to him, as to all the young generation, the symbol of the new epoch, a rebellious soul, breaking through to freedom.

And now? Now Feodor wasn't sure that the evil that had brought him to this absurd situation was not hidden all the time in Gorin himself. But one way or another the new situation demanded from him guile, caution, vigilance, and above all, boldness. Feodor even repeated to himself several times: "May my will turn into steel, and my heart into flint."

CHAPTER 7

THE ARRIVAL of Drozd interrupted his thoughts. Not more than an hour had passed since he had called him, but to Feodor it seemed like an eternity, so many stupefying events had taken place during that short time.

Drozd appeared cheerful, confident, and in his own way even inspired. Obviously he felt in his element. On learning that Mikhail Gorin was shut up in his own bedroom and that Luba and Nina were not allowed to go to him, Drozd approved.

"For Nina I have a pleasant surprise," he said. "Just look out of the window." The perplexed Feodor went to the window and saw a convertible car in the yard; in it was Vassily Shcherbakov. He sat beside the chauffeur, looking expectantly at the windows of the palace.

"Why doesn't he come inside?" Feodor was surprised.

"I told him to wait in the car," said Drozd, self-satisfied. "Although he's the First Secretary of the Province, in the present case we're more important than he is. Our task is of State, even world dimensions. You remember what Veria said about the critical time? Such a time has come to us———"

"But how did you locate Shcherbakov?" Feodor interrupted his rhetoric.

"We met on the road here. He raced up from the Crimea after Nina. Guessing rightly that she might make things awkward for him, although he didn't know what had made her break away so unexpectedly from

548

his embraces, Shcherbakov hurried to gather her up before she had done any damage. Of course he knew nothing about Gorin, but I explained a few facts of life to him—or rather, I advised him to keep as far away as possible from Gorin's house. Now he's sitting meekly."

Unhurriedly Drozd lit a cigarette. "How is Luba Dmitrievna?"

"Poorly," replied Feodor.

"I'm depending on her common sense," said Drozd thoughtfully. "I believe she'll understand that for her, and in the end for Nina, it will be better if they both leave here quietly. We'll have to try to persuade them to go away with Comrade Shcherbakov. Their further presence in this house is entirely superfluous."

"I'm afraid it won't go over very well," Feodor doubted.

Drozd narrowed his eyes on a stream of smoke. "You'll be surprised how simple everything can be. Human nature is a complicated and mysterious mechanism, but there's always a combination that fits. The whole trick lies in finding the right combination," said Drozd with great significance—and there was no doubt that he believed he knew the secret.

"As to Nina, that's Shcherbakov's responsibility. If he can't control the girl, what the hell kind of a leader of the Province is he?" exclaimed Drozd.

"I'm pretty sure that she'll follow her mother," said Feodor. "It's very unfortunate, though, that she came at such an awkward time and raised all this rumpus. Luba Dmitrievna must have warned her?"

"I doubt it. That's not like her. I'll bet it was that old grouch Cheprok," said Drozd. "Incidentally, where is he?"

"With Mikhail Gorin," replied Feodor.

"What!" Drozd jumped up. His green eyes looked at Feodor with an outraged glint. "How did you allow that?"

Feodor was embarrassed. "He's harmless—I searched him. All he had was a pipe, some tobacco, and the key to his room."

"That's not the point! . . . Let's go in right away and throw the dirty bastard out!"

"And what about Shcherbakov?"

"He'll wait."

A sentry stood at the door of Gorin's bedroom. "What's new?" Drozd asked him.

"Everything's quiet so far, Comrade Commissar of the First Rank. The old man put the patient to bed," replied the soldier, drawing himself up taut in front of his superior. "The patient"—that's how they were ordered to refer to Mikhail Gorin.

549

Drozd's eyes hardened vindictively. He pulled his revolver out of the holster. "I'll scare Cheprok a little. This'll be more frightening than his elephant gun." Before Feodor could say a word, Drozd opened the door roughly and stood inside the room in a silent, threatening pose, his legs spread wide.

Over his shoulder Feodor saw how Cheprok started, how he jumped up from the chair, and how his face changed. Feodor almost read his thought, it was so clear: Cheprok was convinced that they had come to kill Mikhail Gorin. Cheprok retreated, shielding Mikhail, who had raised himself on his elbows. The old man's black eyebrows were frowning, his eyes, red from lack of sleep, looked into Drozd's face boldly and with hate. Suddenly he jumped on Drozd.

Not expecting the attack, Drozd stepped back, tripped, and fell. Cheprok seized him by the throat with both hands and began to choke him. Drozd floundered desperately, wheezed. With difficulty Feodor pulled off the crazed Cheprok. His old body was dried out and light, but his clawlike hands did not readily release Drozd's throat.

Frightened badly, Drozd got up, swaying. From rage his eyes had become round as a falcon's and dully evil. He picked up the dropped revolver and at once smashed the butt in Cheprok's face with such force that it opened the cheek to the bone. Blood spurted. Cheprok broke out of Feodor's hands, but Drozd hit him again and Cheprok fell. In a voice hoarse from pain, he shouted: "God curse you, hangmen!" The soldiers seized him roughly and started to drag him out of the room. "Misha, my friend! Farewell!" Smothered cries slipped out of his clamped mouth.

Mikhail leaped from the bed, but Feodor held him. Shaking, Mikhail looked with horror at his friend.

"Halt!" Drozd ordered the soldiers. "Lay him on the floor."

The soldiers threw Cheprok onto the floor by the door. Drozd went up to him and, without taking aim, fired twice—in the chest and head. The shots echoed in the corridor and before they had stilled, Luba's far-away cry was heard. Then everything was still. Mikhail, like a lifeless sack, as if the bullets had gone into his body, hung limply in Feodor's arms. He whispered with white lips: "You're a murderer, Director! May you be damned."

550

CHAPTER 8

IT WAS AS IF the murder of Cheprok had loosed the dark forces in Drozd: his movements became violent and nervous, like a drunkard's; his face was agitated and repulsive; his eyes became glassy; he looked through people. When the sergeant ran up on hearing the shooting (he had been with Luba and Nina, trying to charm them with ill-timed gallantry), Drozd ordered him in a gruff voice to bury Cheprok in the park. "Lock up the whole household, including the secretary, in the basement."

"What will we do with them?" asked the sergeant.

Drozd looked at him strangely: "Isn't it clear?" he asked, nodding his head toward Cheprok. The sergeant turned quite pale, drew himself up, and, louder than was necessary, said: "Exactly!"

Drozd reinforced the guard at the door of Gorin's bedroom, and also ordered a guard outside the windows. "And listen, no talking with the crazy one." So, from a "patient" Mikhail Gorin became "the crazy one."

"Now let's go to the women," said Drozd.

On the way to Luba's room Feodor couldn't restrain himself and cautiously warned him: "Comrade Drozd, aren't you taking too much on yourself in arresting all the household indiscriminately? You might get it in the back of the neck for that."

"Arrest—nonsense! I have full authority to adopt the most harsh measures. This is a State affair—witnesses aren't needed!" growled Drozd resentfully. "In any case, they're all spoiled by luxury and are no good by Soviet standards. No need to pity them. If we don't shoot them, then others will."

In the meantime, stunned by the catastrophe, the harassed Luba was lying on the sofa. A wet towel was wound around her head. There was a smell of vinegar in the room. Everything that had happened, in spite of its manifestness, remained to her incredible, unnatural, wild, inhuman. Her wan face was drawn by the degrading grimace of fear. Deathly tiredness and fear, deep, chronic, ingrained.

Nina walked nervously about the room. She took six steps forward, stopped, jerked her left shoulder, then six steps back. Not raising her eyes from the floor, she frowned, as if she were striving to concentrate. There was by now no hate in her eyes, only perplexity and confusion.

551

Both women were silent. Both thought the same thing: "What about Mikhail? What can we do? What will happen next?"

During the past two hours so many hopes had been shattered that the entire future receded. There was no place where help could be expected. There was no one to trust, nothing to depend on. One thing alone was clear: they were both helpless.

Then Nina's resentment on account of her father, her mother, her outraged family blood, became stronger. Her whole being strove to rush somewhere, to do something, to undertake anything, only not to sit here between four walls, only to fill somehow this wilderness of horror. But nothing could be done.

And Luba had two wounds in her heart: husband and daughter. Both wounds were bleeding and hurt unbearably. She no longer doubted the possibility of a violent death for her husband. "Poor, poor, Mikhail . . ." whispered Luba, turning icy cold from the mere thought of what awaited him. She was ready to fall on her knees and ask—beg!—for mercy. But before whom? Before this smirking sergeant, who was sitting impudently with them in the room here? Before Director Novikov, that gloomy demon of their home?

Suddenly Luba slipped from the sofa to her knees on the floor.

"Lord, King of Heaven!" she whispered passionately, blessing herself with the sign of the cross. "Protect Mikhail! Save him from death!"

Something broke loose in Nina. She rushed to her mother, caught her, hugged her, laid her face on her breast and sobbed. Luba's very heart split. "My poor little girl! I won't let anyone take you!" she crooned, the tears of despair pouring down her cheeks. At that moment the two shots sounded. Luba screamed in a shrill wail that rent Nina's whole being. Her body trembled; she pressed herself to her daughter as if she were protecting her from danger. Now fear for her daughter drowned out all other feeling. The sergeant jumped up from his chair and ran out of the room, leaving only a soldier on duty.

"This is the end," said Luba a minute later. She sank down on the sofa, sliding her fingers over its smooth material. "Nina darling, forget everything! Just save yourself! That is the most important thing—for my sake do that! Be careful, don't argue . . . You can't argue with them——"

Not listening to her, Nina whispered: "Save Papa, O Lord! . . . and Cheprok also! . . ."

Drozd and Novikov entered the room.

Luba moved forward with her whole body and froze in a new expectancy of horror. She already had the look of a widow.

552

Drozd sat down insolently and lit a cigarette. Novikov remained standing. "Sit down, Feodor Pavlovich," said Drozd, pushing a chair over to him.

"We've come to you on business," Drozd addressed Luba. "Our conversation with you will be short and possibly not quite pleasant."

Luba turned pale and exchanged looks with her daughter.

"What have you done with my father?" asked Nina sharply.

Drozd didn't even look at her. "So, Luba Dmitrievna," he continued, "as you have been convinced yourself today, your husband is sick with a very serious nervous disorder. He must have treatment, and the Government, rightly fearing for his health, has ordered him to be provided with the most expert medical care. Right now Mikhail Alexeyevich is under observation by two Rostov doctors. Besides that, a famous psychiatrist is leaving Moscow. But all this, of course, is between ourselves; no one must know of Mikhail Alexeyevich's sickness. However, I ask you, Lubov Dmitrievna, not to be afraid. The doctors consider his condition quite curable. But they insist that you leave the house. Yes, they are convinced that for you to see Mikhail Alexeyevich might have a disastrous influence on him. Therefore, they have entrusted me with persuading you to leave this house temporarily. I repeat, temporarily. Actually, the doctors give assurance that in a week his mental balance will be completely restored and you can see him again. No longer than that. You won't even need to take any clothes with you. Fortunately Comrade Shcherbakov has just arrived for Nina Mikhailovna, so that you can go away together. You can stay at the Shcherbakovs' or, if you like, we'll reserve the best room in the Rostov Hotel for you. You'll live there for a week comfortably." Drozd pronounced each word clearly, leisurely, watching the reaction on the women with sadistic pleasure. After finishing his speech, he bared his yellow teeth in a syrupy smile.

"Tell me, what was that shot I just heard? What were they shooting at?" asked Luba in a resigned voice. It seemed that she hadn't been listening to Drozd at all.

"Shooting?" repeated Drozd and, pretending surprise, he asked Novikov: "Did you hear any shots?" Then suddenly he remembered: "Oh, yes, of course . . . That was one of the guards who took a notion to shoot at the crows. I can assure you that he will be reprimanded, so that he won't make needless noise and frighten people . . ."

Luba and Nina watched this masquerade in dumb horror. Finally Luba got up from the sofa. "I want to see my husband," she said with a nervous quaver in her voice. "By what right do you not allow me and my daughter to see him? You say that he is nervously upset. That's a lie! This morning he was quite well, but on the other hand I saw with my own eyes how your blackguards beat him. And now, after your words, I'm convinced that you have killed him. Yes, yes, killed him! And if you haven't killed him, then show him to me. Show me Mikhail!" screamed Luba in desperation, and the tears poured out of her eyes.

Drozd frowned sorrowfully, shook his head with mock regret. "Calm yourself, Luba Dmitrievna. I deeply sympathize with you. I understand your condition, and only on that account I forgive your none the less insulting remarks. I kill Mikhail Alexeyevich? Why! If you want to know, he is very dear to me—like my own father!"

Luba hurriedly waved her hand at him. "Stop! Stop! Don't talk like that!" She didn't know with what gesture or with what words she could stop this nightmare. Everything was too unnatural and absurd. Only by getting out of this sticky slime of absurdity would it be possible to carry on a normal conversation in which logic had at least some meaning.

"Well, all right," said Luba. "Let's say that he is actually ill. Who ever heard of a wife not being allowed to see her sick husband? Why, that's sheer mockery! It's inhuman! Comrade Director," Luba turned to Novikov. "It's not of your own will that you are permitting such monstrous injustice. Tell me, who ordered you to arrest my husband and us? I must know . . ." She spoke rapidly, her voice breaking, a feverish glitter in her eyes, a harsh expression in her wasted face.

"Nobody is arrested," Drozd hurried to reply for Novikov. "Mikhail Alexeyevich is ill, while you are free to leave the house. Really, consider the situation. It seems that you alone want to kill Mikhail Alexeyevich. . . . I respect you greatly but, dear Luba Dmitrievna, I find you incomprehensible. I understand Nina Mikhailovna's unforgivable foolishness because of her inexperience—but you? You aren't a girl."

Luba looked at him with the eyes of a suffering animal, as if begging him to end this torment. "At least, may we exchange notes with Mikhail?" she asked.

Drozd suddenly leaped up and with a vicious kick knocked his chair over. "You don't understand me!" he shouted. "We didn't come to you for diplomatic negotiations. We brought you our conditions—very liberal conditions! It remains for you to accept them or . . . or——"

"Or I'll report you!" Luba interrupted him. "I'll institute proceedings against you! I'll go to court!"

"Court? I am the court!" snapped Drozd.

554

Squat and bull necked, he looked into Luba's face. And Luba understood that from his hard, animal force she would be unable to defend herself, either with persuasion or with prayers. She was cowed; her whole being shrank into a ball.

"Nina, let us go. You can't argue with these people . . ." she said in a weak voice and went to the door.

"I won't go!" said Nina firmly. "I won't go anywhere until I find out what has happened to Papa and Cheprok."

Drozd looked at her with contempt. "Nina Mikhailovna, make no mistake," he said threateningly. "Don't think that you are a very important person. This is not abroad—here values are different. I advise you to go with your mother. I'll open the door," Drozd actually went to the door and opened it. "Either you'll make use of it, or . . . you'll find that it's stronger than steel and even your husband, Shcherbakov, would smash his head against it!"

"Nina, come!" cried Luba, scared. Her face was deathly pale. "For my sake, come!"

Nina shuddered, looked searchingly at her mother, at the furious Drozd and the frowning Novikov, and slowly went towards her mother. "Mama, only for your sake . . ." she said softly and went out of the room with her.

"Escort them to the car," Drozd ordered the soldier on duty at the door. Going into the corridor, he looked after the two women again, to make sure. Luba and Nina walked thoughtfully and heavily, their heads bowed. Yes, they were dutifully bearing the invisible burden on their shoulders.

CHAPTER 9

SO MIKHAIL GORIN was under arrest. His meals were served in the bedroom; he even had to relieve himself there. A pail stood stinking in one corner—the lazy sentry would not empty it. At the door, the guard had been strengthened. In the corridor the passing steps of other sentries were heard. All the servants had disappeared; there were only military men in the house now, aside from Director Novikov. The whole palace was surrounded by soldiers. Mikhail already knew they had been told that he was a lunatic. He didn't even try to refute that: what they thought was of no importance.

There is a form of torture in which a man is thrown from hot water into icy cold. That is what had happened to Mikhail: from fame to arrest, from honor to disgrace. This sharp change blinded his soul. He said not a word for a whole day. With lackluster eyes beneath the knitted gray brows he watched the entering sentries. He plowed the floor with his steps, smoked one cigarette after another. Tiring of walking, he sat down at a table, supporting his chin heavily in his hand and gazing fixedly ahead. How slowly the time passed! It seemed to Mikhail that each second was separated from the next by an endless emptiness. In this void Cheprok's last cry rang: "Misha, farewell!" Mikhail's face twisted painfully, his lips trembled. His leaden head craved rest. He opened the window carefully and sat on a chair beside it. Outside was the flowering park and the Don. The Don was like a broad blue road in the night, amid fragrant grass and trees, under the warm July sky, thickly sewn with stars. Mikhail breathed deeply of the soft air. Along with the fragrance there burst into the room a motley flow of sounds. From every corner of the park the jealous trilling of nightingales could be heard; down by the river a lonely snipe twittered, from the grass and flowers rose the mysterious music of crickets, by the pond many thousands of frogs burst into an overflow of love. All things lived free and without restraint, proclaiming loudly, for all to hear, their lawfulness and right.

"Get away from the window!" the sentry on the terrace shouted suddenly.

"Shut the window!" the sentry in the corridor echoed and, running into the room, pointed his bayonet at Mikhail's stomach. Mikhail left the window without closing it. The sentry himself slammed the casement and pulled down the blind. "Cut that out, you old devil!" he threatened, "or you'll get steel instead of supper!"

The slightest wish of Russia's favorite was thwarted by the bayonet of a soldier.

Mikhail undressed. When he lay down and stretched out on the bed he had to wipe the perspiration from his brow several times. After the fresh air the suffocating stink seemed even stronger. In his drowsiness it seemed to Mikhail that somebody heavy, sticky, leaned on him and pressed his chest, breathing the reeking odor into his mouth.

Sergeant Polikarpov was the first to come to Mikhail in the morning. He cleaned his boots there in the room with gloomy energy, the smell of the boot polish drowning for the time being the other stench. Outside, along with the sun, the clean, fragrant morning awoke; from the river a blue haze rose. But in the bedroom there was the fustiness and darkness of an abandoned well. Mikhail, waking with a headache, asked permission to go out, but the sergeant merely snorted: "What next?" About ten o'clock Drozd came. Apparently he had just had breakfast. He was gay and self-satisfied and slapped Mikhail in a friendly way on the shoulder.

"Aye, aye! You had quite a game yesterday, Mikhail Alexeyevich. Well, enough of that! God will forgive you. How do you feel?"

Without answering, Mikhail turned away from him.

"You're sore because I shot your friend Cheprok yesterday. But the law isn't written for fools. In my place, would you have waited until he choked you? Of course not . . . I know it would have pleased you better to see me dead, but that's a question of self-defense. Yes, the great principle of self-preservation——"

"What do you want from me?" Mikhail asked in a hoarse voice, without turning.

"Oh, how rude you are! I bring you greetings from your wife and daughter, while you——"

"Where are they?" asked Mikhail quickly, turning his face toward him.

"With Shcherbakov. They're awaiting your recovery with impatience. Honest to God, you don't need to worry about them."

"Listen, whatever your name is——"

"My name is Drozd."

"Listen, Drozd. You can do whatever you like with me. Your sergeant can keep me in this stinking room, refuse to let me go outside; he can be rough; he can even kill me. But just leave my wife and daughter in peace."

"But nobody's bothering them," said Drozd. "Nor does anybody intend to kill you. There is no need to get excited. And as for the sergeant, he shouldn't be rude. If he is, we'll fix that quickly." He called Sergeant Polikarpov over and when the latter stood in front of him at attention, Drozd slapped his face smartly. "You see, our friend is complaining about you," he explained to him.

Rubbing his cheek, the sergeant glared at Mikhail.

Drozd laughed. "Any more complaints, Mikhail Alexeyevich?"

Mikhail merely waved his hand. "No, it's better without complaints."

"Well, just as you like. As for fresh air, there shouldn't be any difficulty. Get dressed, Mikhail Alexeyevich, and let's go. I'll even have a swim with you in the river."

When Mikhail was dressed Drozd himself opened the door onto the terrace, with a generous gesture invited Mikhail to go out first. But,

557

in allowing him to pass, he waved a hand behind his back to two soldiers. They quickly crossed their rifles: "Halt! Where are you going?"

"Oh, hell! That means we can't," Drozd regretted. "It's a pity. Well, maybe some other time. In the meantime, let's avoid trouble and return to the room. They might beat us up—they're a tough bunch. No doubt it's Feodor Novikov who ordered such severity."

"Novikov?" sneered Mikhail bitterly. "No, not Novikov, but Stalin himself."

"Oh, no, you're wrong there," replied Drozd. "You should just see how they're writing about you." He took two papers out of his pocket, *Pravda* and *Izvestia,* handed them to Gorin.

In a prominent place in both papers there were printed congratulations from the Government to Mikhail Gorin on the occasion of the award of the Order of Lenin to him. There were also laudatory reviews of his old books from before the revolution and of his new play *Ivan the Terrible,* which they called his best work. On the front page of *Pravda* the well-known photograph appeared; the smiling Stalin with the trustful-looking Gorin. This photo was taken at the Kremlin in the first days after Gorin's return to Russia.

"Well, you can read, while I go and check up to see how well they're guarding you."

Drozd found Novikov a bit worried. "There are fresh troubles," said the Director. "The foreign correspondents have presented their respects."

The usually impassive Drozd was perturbed. "Surely the devils haven't sniffed something?"

Two men were standing at the gate of the estate. The sentries would not let them in.

"You, Novikov, go to them alone. It would be awkward for me; I'm in uniform," said Drozd. "Hell, we've slipped up there! We should have taken care of them before, at least hidden the sentries in the bushes. Tell them that Gorin has gone for treatment to the Crimea. Tell them anything. Get rid of them somehow."

When Novikov reached the gate he saw at once that there was only one correspondent; the other man was obviously a native, detailed to him as a chauffeur.

"What can I do for you?" Feodor addressed him. "I am Gorin's secretary."

The foreigner replied himself. He spoke a little Russian. He gave his name, which Feodor at once forgot—it was so unfamiliar to his

558

ear. Then the correspondent explained whom he represented, naming a famous British press agency of which Feodor had heard and read in the papers often. He was a tall, serious man in glasses, with a somewhat absent-minded look.

"May I have an interview with Mikhail Gorin?" he asked, looking over Feodor's head at the palace.

Feodor explained to him as well as he could that Gorin had gone to the Crimea. With his first words the correspondent began to write something in his notebook.

"Tell me, where is Mister Volkov, Gorin's former secretary?" he asked. "I knew him well and, incidentally, he usually received me in the house and not at the gate."

"Volkov went with Gorin to the Crimea. I am in the meantime performing his duties," replied Novikov curtly.

The correspondent smiled, wrote something in his notebook, looked at the sentry at the gate, noted other military men in the yard, and smiled again. "Nevertheless, where is Gorin?" he asked with the same respectful smile.

Feodor raised a surprised eyebrow. "Why, I told you that he is in the Crimea. Now, if you will excuse me, I won't keep you any longer. Come in about a month; Mikhail Gorin will be back by that time. I'm sure he'll receive you and you will meet your friend Volkov." Feodor bowed to the correspondent and, unobserved, made an impatient gesture to the chauffeur, as much as to say, "Get to hell out of here as quick as you can." The chauffeur hurried over to the car.

But the correspondent didn't follow him at once. With a slow movement he put his notebook away in an inner pocket of his jacket, looked over the windows of the palace, one after another. Suddenly taking off his hat, he stood for a moment motionless, with bowed head—exactly as people do at an open grave.

CHAPTER 10

NOVIKOV and Drozd dined together in the Gorin dining room. Sergeant Polikarpov, currying favor with his superiors, served them himself. Drozd was talkative and unnaturally gay. He ordered the best wines brought from Gorin's cellar and, like a host, treated Novikov. "Drink, Feodor Pavlovich! Enough of sulking!"

"I'm not sulking, I'm thinking," objected Feodor. His voice sounded harsh and without feeling. Feodor had aged greatly during these last days. The wrinkles had furrowed deeper into his brow, his cheek bones were more sharply outlined, his eyes had sunk under his eyebrows. But he was calm and firm.

"I wonder if we did right with Gorin. Haven't we made a mistake?" he asked dryly.

"So, you haven't learned anything from life yet?" replied Drozd.

"On the contrary, I learned long ago——"

"Maybe you regret Nina?" and Drozd, still smiling scornfully, looked straight into the Director's eyes.

Feodor bit his lip. In spite of himself, at Drozd's words, he was seized by tormenting shame and regret. He saw his reflection in the large mirror that hung on the wall opposite. He was ashamed before Drozd and annoyed that he had seen him in that condition.

"I regret no one," he said stubbornly, but his voice unconsciously sounded as if he were justifying himself. "I regret nothing, except business. I simply doubt that with such methods good results can be obtained. I believe more in the strength of the will and the power of thought than in naked force."

Drozd drained his glass at one gulp, and jumping up from the chair, sat down beside Feodor and whispered hotly in his ear: "Cut it out, Feodor! Don't fool yourself! You damn well know how all this will end." Throwing his arm about his shoulder Drozd felt Feodor shudder at his words. "Personally, I also consider force superfluous, but that is how Veria ordered it. He knows best."

The fork in Feodor's hand shook and clattered against the plate. An unpleasant thought about the provocator flashed through his mind. "I am not at all disputing Comrade Veria's decision. But he said nothing about force," insisted Feodor with cold emphasis.

"All right, all right," Drozd reassured him. "Here—read this telegram. I just received it this morning." Drozd handed him a paper. Then he got up and walked about the room, stopped in front of the window, rocking on his heels. Feodor knit his brow while reading Veria's telegram: "I approve measures taken. However, further action entrusted entirely to Novikov under his personal responsibility."

"As you see, from this day on, Gorin is completely yours," said Drozd, and to his surprise Feodor heard resentment and spite in his voice, as if this callous beast had been infuriated by the thought that a rich spoil had fallen to another's lot. "Now you can carry out your theories to your heart's content."

"These theories smell of a corpse," replied Feodor darkly.

Drozd laughed. "What? Turning yellow, you great soul-shatterer? Not sure of your own strength? Look out, Director! They'll flip you in the head."

"I didn't grow my head for flipping," said Feodor roughly.

"For what, then? For a bullet, I suppose?" asked Drozd.

Feodor saw quite clearly that Veria's order had hit his chief hard. Drozd was offended that Veria didn't trust his skill to break Gorin and, in fact, had pulled him off the job. But Feodor didn't interpret the order in that way at all. To him it seemed this was a new trick of Veria's —it wasn't so much that he mistrusted Drozd as that he wanted to test Novikov. He was leaving him alone to cope with his task.

CHAPTER 11

IMMEDIATELY after dinner Feodor went to Mikhail Gorin and spent the rest of the day in his room.

Drozd, very drunk, went into town that first day to be out of Feodor's way. But before he drove off in the magnificent Gorin car, he couldn't resist saying to Feodor, with a sneer on his face: "If you need me, don't hesitate—give me a call. We're not proud, you know—always ready to help." Then he poked the chauffeur in the back: "Get a move on! Don't fall asleep!"

After his departure Feodor was complete master of the situation— nobody could interfere with him now. Well . . . almost complete master. He could not escape the unseen glance of Veria, close and searching. Besides, he was convinced that secretly Drozd hoped he would fail. Nothing would please Drozd more than to fly back in response to the Director's call for help. All of which Feodor found disheartening. Although he remained undisputed master in the house, the presence of a large number of armed soldiers with wooden and impenetrable faces, coarse manners and sinister uniforms (why the blue of the NKVD caps should seem sinister was not clear to Feodor) —all had a very depressing effect on him. At times it seemed to him that he had become as much a prisoner as Mikhail Gorin.

More to destroy this unpleasant likeness to a prison than to ease Mikhail Gorin's situation, Feodor ordered the slop pail taken out into the corridor and the room aired and cleaned. But when Mikhail asked him to leave the blind up on the window opposite his bed, so that he could see his beloved Don, Feodor refused. He refused roughly, as to an enemy, and was surprised at his own roughness. But this window blind was the first line drawn in his new relationship with Gorin.

Feodor knew that Gorin's dependence on him, which should have eased his task, was actually a handicap. The human mind, particularly such a highly developed and proud one as Gorin's, when it is driven into a corner, is capable of unexpected and desperate outbursts. Feodor would have preferred to deal with a free mind, a mind unfettered, in the open where it would have the chance (even if it was only an illusion) of resisting, retreating, and maneuvering. It is easier to lead such a mind into a mental labyrinth. But the mistake (and what else could it be!) had been made, and Feodor had to deal with an accomplished fact: Gorin was a prisoner and his mind was now the mind of a captive in a cage. Only one approach remained: the direct one, the shock treatment.

"Let us be frank, Mikhail Alexeyevich," said Feodor. "There must be trust between us. This is no time for misunderstandings. Isn't that so?"

The gloomy Mikhail sat motionless on the bed, the folds of his dressing gown wrapped tightly about him. His dinner was on the table barely touched, beside it a bottle of wine brought by Feodor, which Mikhail had refused with a fastidious movement of his hand. He was silent, trying to evade the extraordinarily clever and unpleasant eyes of the Director.

"I don't want to listen to you," he said at last. "I realize you are the executor of another's will and I neither blame nor resent you. But that doesn't mean that I feel inclined to talk to you. You say and do only what you are ordered to say and do."

The words stung Feodor. The muscles of his face jerked irritably. "You are right, Mikhail Alexeyevich, only in part," he said hurriedly. "In part, because in this case there is much of a personal nature for me, and I am by no means unbiased. I am interested in knowing everything about you, every detail. I want to satisfy not only my curiosity, but to check my conclusions about you. Who are you? Why did you become what you are? And, particularly, why do I hate you so?"

"You hate me!" exclaimed Mikhail, shocked. He turned, and for the first time looked straight into the Director's eyes.

"Yes, I hate you," replied Feodor.

Feodor spoke the truth. That his feeling toward Mikhail Gorin was in fact hate he no longer doubted. Otherwise why had he stood by yesterday, when Sergeant Polikarpov was beating up Gorin: indiffer-

562

ent, making no move, speaking no word to stop him? He could have prevented the beating: he had authority for that, but he had not used it. Therefore, in his heart, he must wish pain and disgrace for Mikhail Gorin. Feodor suddenly remembered very vividly how he had even felt an inner satisfaction, almost joy, particularly when Mikhail had fallen and the soldiers began to bind him with ropes. Why did the fall of Mikhail Gorin give him such joy? Why? What had roused in him such hatred for this great man?

"Let us leave the question of hate for the future, for dessert, as they say," said Feodor roughly, coming out of his reverie. "That is a personal matter, and has no immediate importance. Right now I have an urgent matter to discuss with you. You know that this confinement was not forced on you because of the need to guard you from an attempt on your life by the enemies of the people. Of course not. You are a shrewd man and have seen through our game perfectly. Actually, you are under arrest. That is obvious. As you see, Mikhail Alexeyevich, I am completely frank with you. Personally I consider your arrest a mistake . . ."

"Thank you very much. I am quite touched," sneered Mikhail.

"It is possible that I don't know the whole significance of this step, possible that it was not a mistake but a clever psychological maneuver, whose hidden meaning I have not yet grasped. But I do know one thing: the Government has been dissatisfied with you recently. It's not that you have committed any crime against the State; nothing like that. It's just that certain remarks of yours have come to the ears of the Government. Or rather, some shades of your remarks—nuances, as it were. For instance, your strange and ambiguous speech at the wedding last week. From the formal point of view one could find no fault with it. But where would our Party be if it considered only the formal point of view? It's the significance of events that interests them, the hidden meaning. Understanding perfectly the meaning of your latest depression, your words, and even your thoughts, the Government considered it necessary to restrict your freedom somewhat. Mind you, they have actually dealt very liberally with you. In comparison with what they would have done with an ordinary mortal in such a case, they have merely stroked your head, scolded you lightly, like a loving parent to a naughty child.

"You sneer, but there is no irony in my words. You must look on the Soviet Government as your parent—stern, but with a kind heart. Don't forget that up to the present it has been very generous with you

563

and sincerely wants to remain so. You are under arrest, yes. But you are in your own house, you are served good food and even wine. This points to one thing, the measures are temporary——"

"Again, I thank you, Comrade Director. There seems to be no limit to your generosity," said Mikhail caustically. He was sitting with closed eyes, as if submerged in sleep, but his hearing was sharpened and he didn't miss a single word of Feodor's.

"Yes, the measures are temporary," continued Feodor, trying to ignore Mikhail's stinging remark. "But everything depends on you—on you alone. I'll explain everything. The Government considers your arrest not as an arrest, but as a term of probation. If you pass the test, everything will be restored to you: your freedom, your family, your friends. The test consists in the Government proposing that you write a series of articles on certain subjects. Shortly after the appearance of *Ivan the Terrible* rumors began to spread in this country and abroad that you were not satisfied with your own work, and were even complaining about your lot. Your silence tends to confirm these rumors. They must be stopped once and for all. Your articles will serve this purpose as nothing else could. The subjects for them are selected with this thought in view—they must confirm indirectly that you have always been, and remain, true to your principles. I have brought the subjects with me.

Feodor took a sheet of paper, folded in four, out of his side pocket. Mikhail opened his eyes and began to follow the movement of his hands with horror. Feodor, not noticing his strange expression, unfolded the paper. "Here is a brief outline of the subjects desired. I'm sure you'll find them very interesting and very pertinent. For instance: 'The upbringing of the Soviet child and the difference in principle between honor, duty, and courage in Soviet and bourgeois society.' . . . Notes, or suggested leads, are given on each subject which will lighten your work."

Feodor spoke sincerely and fervently. He had no doubt whatever that Mikhail would agree to the proposal. His only anxiety was to present it as accurately and clearly as possible, so that Mikhail would not get a wrong impression or misunderstand what was required of him.

"And so, Mikhail Alexeyevich, that is the significance of what has happened. I hope that with my frank and clear explanation I have dispelled all your agitation, your . . . perhaps even fears? You can see that everything depends on you. By writing a series of articles you will regain the trust of the Government and the sooner you do that

564

the better." Feodor extended the paper to the writer. "Here: read it, please."

He had been so carried away while he was speaking that he had not noticed the change that was taking place in Mikhail's face. It had suddenly become as white as a sheet. "G—get out! Get out of here!" gasped Mikhail, recoiling as from a scorpion and shaking with rage.

Feodor, startled, dropped the paper. "You mean that you are turning down the offer of the Government?" he asked incredulously.

"Yes, I refuse. Please, leave me!"

Feodor's heart sank. For an instant he seemed to see the sneering face of Veria. He shook his head, to drive away the awful specter.

"Are you sure you know what you're saying?" he exclaimed with emotion. "You are destroying yourself with your obstinacy—foolish, rash obstinacy, nothing else! You will regret it afterwards, but afterwards will be too late. . . . Wake up! Now! Now, while there's still time. What will it cost you to write these articles? You wrote them before!"

"Before?" Mikhail repeated, looking at him queerly. "Yes, I wrote before, but I wrote of my own free will. But now I am being ordered, threatened: 'Your life or the article!' " Mikhail's voice was suddenly stronger. He drew himself up. "No, I was never a slave, and never shall be!"

In desperation Feodor threw up his hands.

"What are you talking about, Mikhail Alexeyevich? How can you talk platitudes at a time like this? There's nobody here but me. Nobody will hear your noble speeches. And since no one will hear them, what use are they? I assure you that no one will know about your arrest or this conversation. So what difference does it make under what conditions you write your articles, so long as they are profitable to you? When the articles appear in *Pravda* their price will not be on them. Surely you can think of yourself and your family?"

Mikhail got up. His wild outburst of anger had gradually subsided. "Listen, Director, have you heard of such things as honor and conscience?"

"So you refuse?"

"Yes."

"I repeat once more: Do you agree to work for the Party and the Government?"

"No."

Feodor moved a step closer to him.

"Mikhail Alexeyevich, I will be frank to the end. Your refusal places

565

not only you but me in danger. Do you understand that? If you don't think of yourself, at least consider my position. For my sake, I ask you to agree." There was almost open despair in Feodor's voice.

Mikhail turned away disgustedly. "Your fate doesn't interest me."

"All right, Mikhail Alexeyevich, remember this moment well!"

CHAPTER 12

IN THE SILENCE, the room became crowded, filled with the hatred of the two men. Feodor suddenly wanted a glass of wine. He sat down at the table and opened a bottle. "Pardon me, Mikhail Alexeyevich, if I drink your wine," he smiled grimly. "I brought the bottle so that we could celebrate our agreement. Instead I must drown my failure. A sad fate."

Mikhail, continuing to stand with his back toward him, did not move.

Suddenly Feodor asked the writer: "Why did you come back from abroad, Mikhail Alexeyevich?"

Mikhail shuddered.

"What, are you afraid of my question?" jeered Feodor, malicious lights burning in his eyes. "I'll bet you've asked yourself that a hundred times. You must have wrung your hands, ground your teeth. That was your first mistake, Mikhail Alexeyevich. You could have been sitting peacefully on the Island of Capri among the wonders of the Mediterranean, signing manifestoes on behalf of the Soviet, protesting the lynching of Negroes, playing at being a humanist and receiving honors."

"Even a blind dog comes home to die," said Mikhail softly.

"And there they kill it off, because it's blind. . . . No, don't argue. You made a mistake three years ago when you came back to Russia. And do you know what? The Russian people, wishing you well, have killed you. They have killed you with their love. When hundreds of thousands of people gathered on the square in front of the Kursk Station, in the rain, without any coercion—note, without any coercion whatever—to meet you with unprecedented enthusiasm, at that moment it became clear to many keen-sighted people that you were doomed. You see, in Russia, you are supposed to shout 'Hallelujah' to only one man.

"You, of course, didn't know that. Where could you have learned such things? You were flying in the clouds on the white wings of your

566

ideals, you were too busy with dreams of the happiness of humanity to look into such nonsense as the fate of several millions of Russian muzhiks. Yes, the people were mistaken in you. The people believed you were brave, truthful, sincere.

"Do you remember how the woman fell on her knees before you and burst into tears, asking you to intercede on behalf of her son? I heard her words: 'Mikhail Gorin, you are a great man, you have a heart . . .' A kind heart, that is what the people prize more than anything in a man! The Russian people are starving for kindness. They looked on you as on their own conscience. But what a conscience! The whole country around you is writhing in agony, millions are dying in terrible torture, while you see nothing? Who will believe such an absurdity? No, you knew damn well, but you pretended to be naïve. It paid you better to be naïve. It was easier to philosophize that way and play the humanist."

"Why are you talking like this?" asked Mikhail, turning and looking closely into his face. It was angry and forbidding. "What's the matter with you? You're behaving very strangely. I hardly recognize you."

"You'll recognize me yet!" Feodor drank another glass of wine at a gulp. "You will learn a lot if you don't close your eyes. Why don't you ask, for example, where the servants are? After all, they waited on you for three years, fed you, served you with drinks, cleaned up after you—and you don't even think of them! Why don't you ask me where they are?" shouted Feodor with sudden passion and thumped his fist on the table. "Do you know what, Mikhail Alexeyevich? You love humanity, but you hate people. Tell me, isn't that true?"

"Foolishness! Drunken gibberish!"

"Why do you pretend with me? . . . But that isn't important. You have just called me a puppet and naturally you consider me a slave. You look on yourself, on the other hand, as a free man, even now, when you are under arrest. I can imagine how proud you are of yourself: 'I'm arrested, but my spirit is free. Nobody can make me a slave . . .' and a lot more in the same vein. Not being a writer, I haven't the talent to compose a beautiful monologue, but I'll bet that you have. For you it would be the most beautiful music.

"And, of course, you laugh at me: 'There he is, a pathetic little manikin trying to break the spirit of a Hercules, of a moral Titan. A blown-up pygmy vying with a mountain. Of course he disgraces himself, bursts, sits down in a puddle. And while sitting in the puddle, in desperation he begins to beg for his insignificant, useless life. And I turn away from him in contempt.' Isn't that the way of it? A scene made

567

for the theatre: the strong, exalted spirit conquering the world and carnal temptation. Beautiful . . . That is, it would be beautiful, if it actually happened. But in reality, Mikhail Alexeyevich, you have conquered no one. You crooned your monologue in vain, as a dying man comforts himself with charms. Your speech at the wedding reflected better than anything else the condition of your mind. That speech was the outcry of your soul! You howled, because you were in pain, in much greater pain than when the sergeant beat you in the face and tied you up with ropes. Before these ropes bound you, Mikhail Alexeyevich, you were already bound! Ha—ha—ha!" Feodor laughed wildly, looking into the writer's face with half-closed eyes.

Mikhail, pale, barely able to control himself, stood in front of him, his eyes black with anger. But his look merely provoked Feodor. Besides, the bottle was almost empty. "You're drunk," said Mikhail. He placed his broad hand on his forehead, as if to cool himself. "And when you're drunk, you're very tiresome. I hadn't noticed that in you before."

"And *Ivan the Terrible*? Answer me truthfully, how can one value that play?" Feodor continued loudly. "You should be proud of that work, you free artist! The Government didn't reward you for nothing. Of course not! *Ivan the Terrible* was the unfettered creation of a free genius."

"What do you mean by that?" asked Mikhail curtly, sensing the deadly irony in the Director's words. He approached the table. Feodor got up and they stood face to face. "What do you mean by those words?" repeated Mikhail, his voice breaking.

Feodor smirked drunkenly, passed his finger before the writer's eyes. "Tut, tut! So I have touched you on a soft spot! You're all afire! I mean that every word of that beautiful work was written in the fear of God . . . for your own skin. You thought you would regain Stalin's trust, so he would allow you to go abroad. You wanted to correct craftily the mistake which you made three years ago."

"That's a lie! A monstrous lie!" cried Mikhail. He caught Feodor by the collar and shook him. Feodor did not resist. "Why are you lying, you drunken idiot? Why are you lying!" shouted Mikhail, beside himself.

"Ha! You certainly are in a fury—you're even starting to fight!" Feodor suddenly stopped smiling and tore Mikhail's hand away roughly. "It seems that Veria was right when he said that the best argument of an intellectual was the fist. You've gone the limit—that's good! Maybe your conscience will talk in the end, and you won't pre-

568

tend to be an innocent." Feodor began to walk up and down in front of Mikhail and shouted out his words in time to his steps. Behind him on the wall his shadow flitted.

"I've been watching you for a long time, Mikhail Alexeyevich. When you were writing the play, you looked like a gambler, playing for the bank. You were pushed to the very edge of the precipice and your *Ivan the Terrible* was a desperate leap into the unknown. You perceived the depth of the fall: having recovered your sight and stopped deceiving yourself; understanding the whole horror of your country, you still found it possible to whitewash the dictator with your talent. . . . What more is there to say? I have finished. I didn't want to insult you, and I really couldn't—one slave can't taunt another with being a slave. But it's unpleasant to see such a great man as you submitting to coercion so abjectly and trying so helplessly to cover his lack of human dignity. It offends me to see the image of the hero whom I have worshiped from childhood fall to pieces before my eyes. You are no longer my hero. On the contrary, I look down on you, because you lack the courage to admit the bitter truth; you play the hypocrite and still have the gall to question me about honor and dignity. . . .

"So, do what you are ordered to do. Here is paper and ink. Continue your career to the end. You lost your way before, or made out that you had lost your way. Now you will not dare to pretend. You see, I know everything and there's no sense protesting. You have no right to look on me with contempt, and on others like me—to call us puppets. I want you to do your job, knowing that you are a slave, like myself, like all Soviet intellectuals. I want you to do the will of the dictator with open eyes. I want to wash that mask of naïveté and ignorance from your face."

"You're insane!" whispered Mikhail through white lips.

"With you one could go insane! . . . Sit down at the table and write. Now I won't even give you the ideas. Why should I? You are sufficiently experienced. Why explain to a whore——"

Feodor didn't finish. His whole body trembling, Mikhail threw himself at him. Horror froze in his wide-open eyes. He was pitiful and at the same time menacing. Feodor wanted to hit him, but with a last effort of will restrained himself. He merely caught Mikhail around the waist and threw him onto the bed. At that moment he felt the joy of revenge and was not ashamed of it. Breathing heavily, he stood over Mikhail.

"I'm going away, Mikhail Alexeyevich. I have something pressing to attend to . . . a small secret . . . But I'm coming back. By that time you should have weighed every word of mine, and above all, you should appreciate one thing: I have been frank with you."

CHAPTER 13

HAD IT NOT been for this "small" secret, Feodor would hardly have behaved so roughly, so vindictively, and so frankly with Mikhail. By his behavior he had doomed his mission to failure but he had gone recklessly ahead, stopping at nothing. He was going through a terrific inner struggle. He had, he thought, just experienced the wreck of his own character—he was in agony.

After Drozd had murdered Cheprok, Feodor had been in a highly nervous state. He had a feeling that he should be doing something, something very important, but he did not know what. This vagueness drove him to frenzy. When Drozd sent Luba and Nina out of the house, Feodor had sat through the whole procedure unconcerned, saying nothing, merely awaiting the outcome with impatience. Even the fate of the two women had not agitated him as much as this feeling that there was something he must do.

After their departure, Feodor went straight to Cheprok's room. It was locked, but Feodor had the key in his pocket. When Sergeant Polikarpov, on his orders, had searched Cheprok, he had handed Feodor the key along with the old man's clay pipe and tobacco pouch. That was all that they had found on him. Only now, standing before the closed door, Feodor remembered how Cheprok had suddenly started at sight of the key and had looked strangely into his eyes. There was something special, almost menacing in that look, so menacing that Feodor could not stand it and had turned away. At the time Feodor saw no significance in it. But on thinking, he became convinced that the old man's look had some relation, not to the fate of Mikhail Gorin, but to the key. With sudden excitement Feodor opened the door. Before doing so he looked around, for some reason, as if he wanted to be sure that there was nobody around. The corridor was empty.

Cheprok's room was in the right wing of the palace, at the very end, beside the conservatory. It was a small room, simply furnished, clean, with bright wall paper and ocher-stained floors. The narrow iron bedstead stood along the left wall. In front of the single window was a table

570

and a chair; against the right wall stood a very old iron-bound trunk covered with a long narrow carpet, half of which dragged on the floor. This attracted Feodor's attention. He approached the trunk, lifted the lid, and almost cried out: inside, curled up in a ball, sat a boy, not more than ten years old. His whole body shook and at sight of Feodor he sighed weakly and squeezed himself closer to the walls of the trunk. Something burst inside Feodor. The dumb look of the innocent child broke through the crust of his toughened heart. Barely able to keep back his tears, and speaking as softly as possible, Feodor said: "Don't be afraid, son. For God's sake, don't be afraid! I won't do you any harm. But be quiet, don't shout—that's dangerous. Cheprok hid you here, didn't he?"

The boy, still looking at him with fear, was crying silently. But Feodor had guessed everything. Now Cheprok's look and his extraordinary agitation at sight of the key were plain to him. And now Feodor remembered the boy: his father was the gardener, his mother the cook.

"Tell me, son, what's your name?"

"Igor."

"Listen, Igor, don't be afraid of me. Cheprok gave me the key; here it is, you see. He told me—yes, he told me without words, with his eyes only—not to betray you. And I won't betray you, trust me! I'll look after you, take you away from the estate. Only don't be afraid. Sit tight, and don't give yourself away by crying."

"Tell me, have they killed my Mama and Daddy yet?" Igor asked him suddenly. The boy's question shocked Feodor.

"Why do you ask that? Who told you that they were going to kill them?"

"They told me themselves. Mama and Daddy asked Cheprok to take me away from here today. They told me that the soldiers would kill me too if I didn't hide. We were sitting in our room and we heard cries outside, and then we saw through the window how the soldiers beat Mikhail Gorin and tied him up. Daddy got scared! He made the sign of the cross on me and then he and Mama took me to Uncle Cheprok. Cheprok locked me in while he ran to Mikhail. He said he would come back soon. But he hasn't."

"Calm yourself and don't think about anything. Your parents are alive. You'll see them yet. And Cheprok did right to hide you—these times are dangerous. . . . Say, I'll bet you're hungry. When did you eat last?"

"I had breakfast. And I drank a little kvass Cheprok left."

"All right, I'll bring you something to eat. You sit quietly, don't look out of the window, and don't stand in front of the keyhole. Sit here, in the corner. I'll put the chair there for you. Like that. When I come back I'll knock twice, softly, so you'll know it's me——"

"Uncle Cheprok said he would knock three times. When you began to open the door without knocking I was scared and hid in the trunk . . ."

"That's all right. I'll come back quickly. Now don't worry."

CHAPTER 14

LEAVING the room, Feodor was thoughtful. The boy's words brought home to him with extraordinary keenness the fate of the servants. He hadn't believed that Drozd seriously intended to kill them when he ordered the sergeant to lock them in the basement. He had thought that, in a state of high tension, he had become over excited and that Sergeant Polikarpov would simply let his words go in one ear and out the other.

But when Feodor went into the kitchen to get some food for the boy, he saw through the window in the twilight that the soldiers were leading the servants into the yard one by one and lining them up. About twenty of them had gathered in the yard, and among them was Gorin's secretary, Volkov.

Feodor ran out and asked the sergeant where he was taking them. Polikarpov answered that Drozd had ordered them to be taken to the city and "handed over to the authorities." Feodor wanted to question Drozd about this, but it was too late—Drozd had already left for the city.

An hour later he needed no explanation. The sergeant and the soldiers had returned. This was strange: to have gone to the city and back would have taken much longer. But what impressed Feodor most was the look of the soldiers, and especially of the sergeant. They looked like drunks, but there was no smell of wine on them. They talked excitedly in jerky phrases, laughed too loudly, winked at each other. No doubt was left in Feodor's mind as to the fate of the unfortunate people. But to satisfy himself, he went up to one of the more simple-looking soldiers, and, winking at him as casually as possible, asked suddenly: "Where?"

572

"In the woods, of course," replied the soldier, caught off guard, but stopped at once. Frowning, he went quickly away from Feodor.

Before the soldiers returned, Feodor had secretly brought supper for the boy. Igor was terribly upset and didn't touch the food.

"Thank you, Uncle. I'll eat afterwards," and suddenly he fell to the floor and cried bitterly.

"Quiet! Quiet! Igor!" Feodor was scared. He had no doubt now that danger threatened the boy. When the boy had calmed down, Feodor left the room.

That night Feodor hardly slept at all. The thought of the boy wouldn't leave him. Feverishly he turned over in his mind the surest way of saving him. To get him off the estate presented no particular difficulty. But what about afterwards? Leave him to the mercy of fate? That would mean almost certain death. Feodor racked his brains. It would be almost impossible to take the boy away that night. Polikarpov was very drunk and wandering about the house. He had been nagging the soldiers, had thrust himself into Feodor's room to talk; and to top it all had rung the alarm at two o'clock in the morning, lined up the troops, who ran out into the corridor in their underwear, and delivered a long speech on class vigilance, until Feodor forcibly led him away to sleep.

Besides, Feodor was afraid to leave Mikhail Gorin alone in the care of the drunken sergeant. He was sure that something must inevitably happen to the writer, and his immediate presence would be required. This was Mikhail's first night under arrest and Feodor was very nervous.

Feodor had been in a thoughtful and gloomy mood the following day. He had been easily irritated, rough and curt. He had been rude to the foreign journalist who had come in the morning, whereas under a different circumstance he would have been respectful and diplomatic. He had sat sullenly at dinner with Drozd, and Drozd had remarked on it. Finally, Feodor had so behaved with Mikhail Gorin as to destroy any hope of success, if there ever had been any such hope.

On leaving the writer's room, Feodor went at once to the boy. He had definitely decided to take him off the estate that night, and he knew now where he would take him. But first he had to insure the success of the first step: leading the boy through the estate which was swarming with soldiers.

In the corridor Sergeant Polikarpov stopped him. He was tipsy, but not as bad as the previous day. The sergeant looked searchingly at Feodor.

573

"We are having no luck, Comrade Chief," he smirked.

"Luck in what?" Feodor asked him curtly.

"With the patient, of course. Who else—"

"That, Sergeant, is not your business," Feodor cut him off roughly. The sergeant became sulky and wanted to pass. Suddenly a thought occurred to Feodor: "Wait, Sergeant! Maybe you can help me. Tell me, how long does it usually take you to clean your boots? You know, so they shine like a mirror?"

"Half an hour, no more. Why?" The sergeant was surprised.

"Well, now, if you want to help the business to succeed, go at once to the patient and clean your boots in his room—and not for half an hour, but a whole hour. And don't say one word to him. You understand? This is a deep psychological maneuver—a demonstration with a double meaning."

The sergeant grinned. "I fully understand, Comrade Chief. I've got a head on my shoulders—I learned all these niceties long ago. I'll give him such a demonstration that tomorrow he'll lie down in front of you, face down. You'll see."

"That's the idea . . . And in the meantime I'll go and get some fresh air, take a ride on one of the horses, maybe run into town. I hope the horses haven't died yet. Has somebody been feeding them?"

"Damned if I know! There were no orders about that."

"All right, I'll see for myself. And be careful—don't touch the patient. He's at the breaking point now, going through the crisis. Don't let him out of your sight, or before you know it he might do something to himself. In short, use your head, keep your weather eye open," and Feodor winked at the sergeant significantly. Then, as if he had remembered something: "Yes, and another thing. Give me the key to the wine cellar. I want to take a bottle with me on the drive so I won't be lonely."

Laughing, the sergeant gave him the key. "Look out, Comrade Chief, leave some for us."

In the wine cellar Feodor chose one of the larger bottles, tucked it under his arm, and went to the kitchen, where the soldiers off duty had gathered after supper: they were telling yarns, playing cards. Selecting the most knavish-looking soldier Feodor said to him in a casual way, so that they would all hear: "Here's the key to the wine cellar. Give it to the sergeant, only not now. At the moment he's busy with the patient. Wait for an hour or two, or better still, until tomorrow morning. I'm going to town. I won't be back till evening and he'll probably be asleep by that time."

574

Handing the soldier the key, Feodor went slowly to the icebox and selected some things for a snack: a slice of roast beef, bread and salt, which he wrapped in a napkin. Then he took a tumbler, breathed on it, and deliberately wiped it with a towel. The soldiers watched his every movement, holding their breath. They even stopped playing and all turned their shaven heads toward him. Feodor, whistling a brave aria, went out of the kitchen, but in the corridor he hid himself behind the nearest projection of the wall. He had not miscalculated. For a minute there was complete silence in the kitchen, then a racket arose. The soldier to whom Feodor had given the key hissed to the others. The door opened, then closed again, a hurried whispering was heard, then the door opened again quietly and the soldiers tiptoed down the corridor one after another toward the stair to the wine cellar. In front the knavish soldier gamboled like a goat, pressing the key to his breast.

When the last soldier had disappeared down the flight of stairs, Feodor went quickly along the corridor in the opposite direction, toward Cheprok's room. The boy was waiting for him. Feodor gave him the food.

"You eat, and I'll tell you what you must do. The main thing is, don't be afraid and don't panic. You understand? No matter what happens, don't give yourself away by a single sound——"

"Uncle, I know they killed Mama and Daddy," the boy interrupted him suddenly.

"How do you know?" Feodor was astonished.

"I looked out of the window yesterday right after you went away—very carefully, just with one eye, and I saw them being led into the yard. Mama raised her eyes to me, just for a moment. I saw her, I saw her . . . darling Mama . . . But Daddy didn't look once at my window, he looked the other way on purpose, but he was thinking of me. I know that. He was afraid of giving me away with his look. They were killed. What for? Tell me, why did they kill them? And Uncle Nikifor, and Uncle Volkov, all of them! Why?" The boy dropped a piece of meat out of his hand and began to cry. Suddenly he got up and said with passion: "When I grow up big and strong, I'll be fearless like, like . . . like you! And I'll get even with them! I'll get even for Mama, and Daddy, and Uncle Nikifor, and all of them! They'll find out yet!"

CHAPTER 15

WHEN THE BOY was calmed again, Feodor said to him: "Now, let's go, Igor. Keep as close to me as you can in the corridor, so I can cover you in case anything happens. We'll go into the conservatory. From there we'll go into the park, to the pond. But in the park you'll have to crawl from bush to bush, like an Indian, while I walk in plain sight so they'll watch me. When we come to the fence I'll talk to the sentry while you jump over it and hide in the bushes. Then you crawl quietly away as far as you can and wait for me. I'll ride out in a few minutes on horseback and call to you like this: Coo-coo! Can you answer me like that—three times? . . . I'll ride up and pick you up. The main thing is, don't be afraid, do everything in silence. Do you understand?"

"Yes."

"All right, let's go."

Feodor took the bottle with him in case he needed a weapon. They passed through the corridor without mishap—there were only ten paces to the conservatory. At the outside door Feodor looked around him: a sentry with a rifle on his shoulder was walking along the path. When the sentry turned his back to them, Feodor whispered to the boy: "Now, run across the path into the bushes and crawl after me. I'm going openly."

The boy ran out of the conservatory and fell about five paces from the bushes. At the same time Feodor came out onto the path. The sentry, attracted by the noise, turned around abruptly.

"Halt! Who goes there?"

"A friend! Novikov!"

"Give the password!"

"Bolt."

"I thought some son of a bitch was slipping through, but it's you. It was so sudden."

"Yes, I want to check the guard. Everything in order?"

"Everything's quiet, Comrade Chief. May I ask the time, please?"

"A little after nine," replied Feodor. "Listen, Comrade, do me a favor, go and give the horses in the stable some oats and water them. Give the black stallion some extra. After I've made my check I'm going to town and I'll take him."

576

"It's a bit awkward to leave my post, Comrade Chief."

"I'll be handy. And the stable's right by. I'm sorry for the horses; they haven't been fed for two days."

When the sentry ran off to the stable Feodor went along the path toward the fence, beyond which was the steppe. The large fountain wasn't working; the figures of the three graces stood out against the starry sky in dark silhouette. Feodor saw the boy run from bush to bush behind him. In this way they reached the fence. This was the most difficult part. Along the stone fence a sentry paced back and forth. About fifty paces from him was another one. When they met, they exchanged a few words and separated. Feodor waited until they were together, and then approached them.

"Halt! Who goes there?" shouted both sentries in alarmed voices.

"Novikov. I'm checking the posts, to see that no one's asleep."

"The password?"

"Bolt."

"Right. But why isn't the sergeant checking up?" one sentry asked suspiciously. Feodor came up close to him.

"The sergeant is checking up on a bottle," he said, feigning anger.

Both sentries grinned, completely reassured. The one who asked about the sergeant shouldered his rifle in accordance with general orders, turned smartly on his heel and stepped off on his beat, apparently wanting to show the chief his zeal for duty.

Out of the corner of his eye Feodor watched for the shadow of the boy. He was almost invisible. Feodor gripped the bottle firmly, holding it a little behind his back. Suddenly Igor, like a shadow, broke from the bushes; he crawled quickly across the path along the fence, his figure for several seconds clearly visible on the light sand of the path. "If the sentry turns towards him, I'll smash his brains in," thought Feodor. He had firmly decided to kill if necessary. But apparently it was too soon for the sentry to die; he didn't hear a thing. Noiselessly the boy climbed over the wall and only when he jumped to the other side, a twig snapped. The sentry turned around quickly: "What was that?"

"Probably a fox—there are a lot of them here," answered Feodor, breathing with relief. "Well, Comrade, don't go to sleep," and he went toward the house.

The black stallion had been fed. The sentry was very glad that the chief returned so quickly. Feodor saddled the stallion and led him into the yard. He was a Don race horse, Nina Gorin's favorite. After a whole week in the stable, he literally danced.

577

"Some stallion!" exclaimed the sentry delightedly. "A marvelous animal!"

Feodor jumped lightly into the saddle, shouted the password at the gates which were barely open before he flew out onto the steppe. He turned off the road at once. Placing both hands to his mouth, he "coo-cooed" softly twice. Nobody answered. Feodor rode on, called again, and caught a weak "coo-coo," like an echo. The boy was hiding in the bushes about a hundred paces from him. Feodor rode up to him, picked him up and set him behind him on the saddle.

"Now, hold on, tight!"

The stallion tore off at a gallop.

The night was silent. Over the steppe wafted the pungent scent of wormwood. The air was cool and clean, but the steppe, plunged in darkness, was invisible, as if it had merged with the stars. Feodor raised his eyes to the glittering sky. Across it, in a broad river, flowed the Milky Way, all speckled in gold. Glorious and enchanted the world seemed, as if in sweet expectation of some revelation. Feodor's heart beat calmly and evenly. In the noise of the onrushing wind he seemed to hear a song from another world—a song of happiness and brotherly love. Completely absorbed by this unusual uplift of spirit, feeling the rescued child behind him, Feodor could barely keep back the tears of happiness. His heart, exhausted these last days by an unbearable burden, revived. The broad steppe, the starry sky, the mad speed of the stallion, only these could hold the incomprehensible happiness of his soul. His debt had been paid; his depression had ended.

Suddenly Feodor thought with surprise: "Why did I go yesterday to Cheprok's room? I certainly had no definite object when I went there. What prodded me?" He didn't look for an answer. In the very question itself there was something great, inspiring, and, though not understanding the mystery of it, he reveled in this unexpected happiness.

The man he wanted to see first was his brother Nikolai. Yes, he was going to him now. He would take Igor to him, he would hand him over as a precious possession into trusted hands. Now, as never before, Feodor felt that he was worthy of his brother.

CHAPTER 16

FEODOR KNEW that at that moment Nikolai and a group of students should be at a sovkhoz vegetable garden in the suburbs doing their summer work. Before he had moved into the Gorin house Feodor himself had visited his students there. He had seen Nikolai on these visits, but had not spoken to him. At that time they were enemies. Now Feodor looked forward to meeting his brother with pleasure.

At the sovkhoz Feodor left the boy on the road, while he went to look for Nikolai. But he was told that Nikolai had gone to town on important business. Feodor decided to go and look for him there. Things were becoming complicated and he hadn't much time. About half-way to town they overtook Nikolai.

"Nikolai!" exclaimed Feodor, so loudly and happily that his brother stopped, though he would otherwise have continued his journey as if he hadn't noticed him. "How glad I am to find you! . . . Listen, I have something important for you, but first, lift this boy down. . . . Igor, this is my brother Nikolai—jump into his arms; he's a very good man." Feodor got down and let the horse nibble at the grass. "It's quite deserted here, nobody around—that's very good . . ."

Feodor spoke so rapidly and excitedly that Nikolai looked at him in surprise. "Feodor, what's wrong with you? Are you drunk?"

"No, I'm not drunk. Why do you think that? Oh—the bottle! It's just a cover-up and a weapon. But now I don't need it. See, I'll throw it away." With an abrupt movement Feodor pulled the bottle out of his pocket, threw it far into the grass. At this, Nikolai was more surprised than ever, and even a little scared.

"What's the matter with you, Feodor? You're not like yourself at all."

"No, no. I'm quite well. Don't rush off—you'll get to town yet! I'll take only a few minutes, although I'd talk all night with you with pleasure. What a beautiful night! Do you see the stars, Nikolai? You know, I somehow never noticed them before . . ."

Nikolai smiled coldly. "Maybe you're in love?" he asked, and there was open sarcasm in his voice.

"Oh, Nikolai, don't make fun of me. And tell me, where are you hurrying?"

"I'm going to Lida," Nikolai replied reluctantly. "Any day now she will have to go to the hospital."

"To the hospital? What's wrong with her?"

"It doesn't concern you in the least. She is expecting your child, but you're too occupied with stars to think about such details."

"Nikolai, forgive me. I completely forgot about that—my head has been full of a thousand things. I know I wronged Lida. I admit my fault and I only hope that sometime she will forgive me. She wouldn't

579

understand, but believe me, I sincerely wish her happiness. Of course, you won't believe that either. But ask this boy, this good innocent boy. Ask him if I can be a man with a heart. . . . Go on—ask him! . . . Tell him, Igor: Am I a good man?"

"This man is very brave and honest. He's not like the others. He kept his word and rescued me," replied Igor firmly, wondering at the same time why this important man needed his evidence.

"See, Nikolai? . . . He says I'm a good, honest man! . . . Yes, I'm good! I have a heart, like you. A heart!" repeated Feodor in ecstasy, thumping his chest. "But listen: I've brought this boy to you. To you, to nobody else! I trust you completely; I trust you more than myself. Take him; hide him for a time somewhere. Call him your cousin, whatever you like, but bring him up. Make him like you. Do you understand? A man with a heart!"

"Why don't you take him yourself?" asked Nikolai.

"He's an orphan. His parents are martyrs; they are sacred. I can't take him myself. In the first place it would be dangerous for the boy— I'm too prominent; questions would be asked about him. With you it will pass unnoticed. In the second place, and most important, I don't trust myself. It wouldn't be fair to him. You heard me: I ask you to bring him up as a man with a heart. Could I bring him up like that? Me—an unfeeling official? *Right now* I have a heart. That is a miracle. But what about tomorrow, the day after, and later? Can I be sure of my heart? No, I can't. I have been evil, probably I will remain evil for all time. But you, my brother, you will always be a good man. Who knows, maybe fate herself made you like that just so you could rescue and keep this boy!"

"You are talking very grandly," remarked Nikolai. "Tell me, has something happened to you?"

"Yes, something tremendous; I have never experienced anything like it!" exclaimed Feodor. "A miracle! Probably it will pass . . . yes, of course it will pass. But until then—be my brother and do what I ask: take this child."

"Of course I'll take him," said Nikolai. "He can live with Natalia. I'll help them in every way I can. She'll have plenty of worry with Lida's child in any case, but this boy is big enough to help."

"I'll help also," Feodor interjected. "Yes, I'll give you some money right now. Here!" Feodor took his wallet out of his side pocket, pulled out some bills, and gave them to Nikolai. "Take it. It's bad money, but let it serve a good purpose. I'll give you more later, if I can, but I may never see you again."

580

"Why, Feodor? What's happened? Is it Durov?"

"No, not Durov. Everything's finished with him. It's quite different. It's simply that I'm in a blind alley, a terrible blind alley. There's almost no way out." In Feodor's voice there was complete despair. "But I'll think about that tomorrow!" he exclaimed suddenly, again in exaltation. "Today I'm happy because of this boy. I have done my duty." Feodor went up to Igor, put his arm around his shoulder. The boy pressed against him. Feodor turned unexpectedly to his brother. "Tell me, Nikolai, have you ever asked yourself if there is a God?"

"Yes, I have."

"And having asked, of course, you came to the conclusion that there isn't?"

"Yes, I don't believe in God," replied Nikolai.

"It was the same with me. But today I came very near to believing in His existence. It's very strange to hear such words from the Director of a Soviet University—but today, you see, I am simply a human being. I came close to belief in God when I was riding with this boy over the steppe, under the stars. But it wasn't the stars that disclosed this secret to me. They merely made me recall my every step, every act during the past two days. I recalled them and did not recognize myself. You understand, these last two days I have been an entirely different person. Outwardly I remained the same, but my feelings, my actions, my words were completely unfamiliar to me. In you, I wouldn't have been surprised to have seen them. But in me? They were very strange. And I wasn't afraid of them, nor ashamed! On the contrary, they gave me extraordinary joy, an almost creative joy.

"But what really astounded me was that I went to Cheprok's room. . . . You don't know anything about him; perhaps I'll tell you some time. . . . But now understand one thing: there was no need for me to go to that room. But I was moody all day; I felt there was something I *must* do, right up to the time when I went to his room—*his* room, and not some other one, as though someone were leading me by the hand. And there I found this boy! And another surprising thing: I had the key to this room. This key came into my hands quite accidentally. The guard sergeant might have kept it, and I wouldn't have asked for it; I had no need for it. But the sergeant, without thinking, handed me the key with Cheprok's pipe and tobacco. The key came to me, to *me,* the only person who could rescue the boy! Could the sergeant or Drozd have rescued him? Never."

CHAPTER 17

"NEITHER could Cheprok have saved the boy. They killed Cheprok.
. . . Yes, son, they killed him. . . . You see, he's crying, he loved the
old man. . . . But even if they had not, and Cheprok had been able
to bring him out through the guard line, what would he have done with
him afterwards? Where would he have put him? He didn't know anybody in town; all his old friends died long ago. But I have a brother
Nikolai, an exceptional, excellent man, whom I trust. Can all this be
called simply chance, a series of coincidences without any significance?
No, there were too many coincidences, and too definite a pattern in
them. That is why I said that perhaps you were born in order to save
this boy. Who knows, time will pass and it may fall to his lot to save
more than one human being. I repeat, today I came close to acknowl-
edging God."

"But you haven't acknowledged Him yet. To be close still doesn't
mean anything," Nikolai responded.

"You're quite right; to be close means nothing. I will never cross that
border, I know that. Even if I had the opportunity I would stop on
purpose. To my lot has fallen the honor of fulfilling a simple duty; I
have fulfilled it and have been present at a miracle—I was even a part
of it. Its light blinded me and aroused in me the most unusual feelings,
bright and magnificent. By tomorrow I'll probably be as before. I will
recall these two days with astonishment. I will even laugh at myself
. . . No, I won't laugh. Something of today's feeling will remain and
keep me from laughing.

"Do you remember when we fought in my apartment, and I complained to you about my fate? You said nothing, but I read contempt in
your eyes. You didn't believe me. You knew I would turn again, that
it was a mere temporary weakness. You were right. It was merely a
fleeting feeling which your fists beat into me. Now it is different—now
my soul is crying out. But I'll turn back, I'll become hardened again.
That's why I pity myself, but there's no path to faith for me.

"Do you know, Nikolai, I'll tell you frankly, I was quite distressed
when you said that you didn't believe in God. Long ago I thought
about you and decided that you did believe in God. I would not have
laughed at you for that. I was afraid only that sometime they would
catch you. Every time the chief of the Special Branch brought me a

list of students who had been discovered as believers, to discuss expelling them from the University—you would be surprised how many of them there are!—I always opened the list with a tremor, fearing to find your name on it. That's how sure I was. Yes, it always seemed to me that somewhere in a dark corner, all alone, you were praying to God. I often imagined this picture and, do you know, I would smile to myself warmly and joyfully."

If it had not been dark, Feodor would have seen how deeply Nikolai blushed.

"I'm sorry that I haven't justified your image of me," he said in a soft voice. "But I'll tell you this: I believe in the superiority of good over evil. It is my yardstick for everything in life."

"Do you know, Kolya, at this moment you remind me of Alyosha Karamazov?" Feodor said. "You're outwardly quite different in character, upbringing, in the time in which you live. He was a youth with a gentle soul; his actions were gentle, as were his words. You, on the the other hand, wouldn't stop at beating your own brother in the face, if you saw that your words didn't help. Yes, outwardly you are as different as the two poles. But nevertheless there is something in you that resembles him. Maybe it is the same characteristic that made me think you believed in God. This inner quality that distinguishes you from most of our youth makes you a member of the third generation of Alyoshas, his spiritual successor.

"Alyosha lived in a time of general confusion and bewilderment, when everybody was groping for life: at that time people listened to Alyosha, who preached love for one's neighbor, with the same interest as to his brother Ivan, who denied God. Preaching love, Alyosha was deprived of action. He believed in God. You don't believe in God— you live in a kingdom of hate and you do not preach love, but you practice effective, active love; and right now that is more important than anything. You are working in an incomparably difficult time. Dostoyevsky thought that people like Alyosha would become the leaders of Russia; he dreamed that the next epoch would be the epoch of love and justice. Instead of that came the kingdom of hate and terror, unparalleled in the history of mankind; the third generation of Ivan Karamazovs came to power.

"Yes, that is our kingdom. Who are we, indeed, but his successors? We—that means thousands such as Veria, Malenkov, Drozd, and your brother Feodor. We are practicing what Ivan thought in the last century, what we were taught rigidly and forcefully by the representatives of his second generation—Lenin and the other theoreticians and revolutionaries, of whom the spiritual force was our friend Mikhail Gorin. It was they who inherited from Ivan Karamazov his denial of God, his denial of morals, and the alluring idea that everything is permissible."

"You include Mikhail Gorin with the others?" asked Nikolai in amazement.

"Yes, I include him," said Feodor flatly. "You remember how, once, in a moment of desperation, I said to you that if I found the man who made my life accursed, I would choke him with my own hands. Well, I have found that man. It was Gorin who spiritually headed the second generation of Ivan Karamazovs and begat us, the practicing people, the people who have turned into frightful reality the confused thoughts of the rebels of the past century.

"Last week Mikhail Gorin gave an interesting speech. In it he complained about us, his successors. He hinted that we had distorted his beautiful conception, that we had poisoned the clean banner of humanism which he had raised with such pride at the beginning of the century. But he said this to smother his own conscience. No! We learned his lesson well—let him not reproach us. Tomorrow I'll show him that we could not have carried out or translated his thoughts into reality in any other way. Our kingdom could not have been different. Yes, this terrible kingdom. The people would not have evaded it for anything. In Mikhail Gorin's promises, in Lenin's promises, there was too much that was tempting not to test them and try our luck. People had to convince themselves of the worthlessness of an idea; when through their own experience they are convinced that happiness and a just kingdom cannot be built on innocent blood and hate, only then will they throw us off and turn to such people as you, the third generation of Alyoshas —or to the fourth generation, such as I hope this boy will be . . . or even to the fifth—to the son of this boy.

"Do you understand me? It's quite possible that this process of disillusionment in us will take the people several generations—the Russian people are terribly patient—but this process has already begun and, as sure as day follows night, it will come to its decisive end. When it comes, you must be ready. It has fallen to your lot, and to the lot of people like you, to preserve the seed of your generation amid the raging hurricane of hate and terror, to gather them, to foster them so that when the people turn to you for leadership you will already have people capable of leading the nation—leaders who believe in love for their neighbor, people with hearts, people who have not forgotten the will of God.

"I am doomed to unbelief. I am serving hatred and terror and I am unable to stop. I am horrified at myself, but I cannot change. And it may be that I don't want to change. When all's said and done, this is my kingdom and I want to reign to my heart's content—until such time as I reach my moral limits, which I cannot cross. But that, of course, will be my personal weakness, not that of my generation. My generation, on the whole, has no moral limits. Has Veria a moral limit? No. Has Drozd a moral limit? No. But I have. I felt it today when I saved this boy. No one, except yourself, knows about this, but probably I will fall a victim of my own weakness, of my inability to come up to the expectations of my generation. That is characteristic. The fate of our generation is eventual ruin, but for me, personally, this ruin may come tomorrow."

"But what on earth is going to happen tomorrow?" asked Nikolai, unconsciously infected by his brother's agitation.

"Tomorrow my fate will be decided. I am on the verge of catastrophe. Perhaps on that account I am talking as though in a fever. At the most critical moment of my life I must unburden myself of everything."

"Maybe I can help you in some way?" asked Nikolai. "You really do look strange. You're quite ill. Let's go together to town. I'll find a doctor; you must lie down and rest."

"No, I can't go to town. My duty awaits me. My anxiety is not your concern. You go and do what you have begun. Take this boy, look after him, bring him up in your own spirit, make a man with a heart out of him. In our kingdom of hatred such people will be more precious than diamonds. I'll go and serve my devil, the red devil of terror . . . I will decide my own fate. As I told you, I have found an enemy. But don't think that I'm planning murder. No, certainly not. Of course, that thought has entered my head, but I repeat, I won't entertain it on any account. At this solemn moment I swear to you, Kolya, that I will not commit murder. I would rather do away with myself than agree to murder!"

Feodor suddenly came up to Nikolai and embraced him impulsively, kissed his left shoulder. He didn't kiss his cheek because he wanted to hide from his brother the tears that were pouring down his face. "Forgive me, Kolya. Forgive me, and ask Lida to forgive me."

"Feodor, you're all afire—you've got a fever," exclaimed Nikolai, frightened. "Listen, I beg you, seriously: come into town with me. I don't know about your affairs, but no matter what they are, you're sick and not yourself. You might kill yourself."

585

"No, no—I'll cool down by morning; this will pass." Feodor pressed his brother's hand hard again. Then he stroked the boy's head. "Do what my brother tells you, Igor." Bringing up the horse, he jumped into the saddle.

"Feodor, take care of yourself!" Nikolai cautioned him.

"Good-bye, Kolya! Good-bye, Igor! Remember me. You know, Kolya, I would like at this moment to ride full tilt into a stone wall and perish. Perish at full speed."

Feodor rode away a few paces, but stopped suddenly. He shouted from the darkness: "Kolya, do me a favor: Call him Feodor. Call him Feodor!"

"Who? This boy?"

"Of course. Let his new name be Feodor."

"All right. I understand. I'll call him Feodor."

Feodor galloped away. The hoof beats of his horse, racing madly over the steppe, could be heard for a long time. Then everything was still. Nikolai took the boy by the hand and started toward the town, whose lights were reflected over the horizon.

PART NINE

CHAPTER 1

"WELL, THAT beats everything! I never heard the like!" The sergeant choked with laughter. "Comrade Chief, you're killing me. Tell me again."

"Well, as I said before, I was riding along the steppe when suddenly two shadows came toward me. I thought: What's that? Who can be walking on the steppe at night? I rode up closer. I looked. A couple of women——"

"A couple of women! For God's sake!"

"Yes. . . . I looked closer. They were young and fairly plump. I asked them: 'What are you doing here at night?' They were silent, only giggled and nudged each other in the ribs with their elbows. Well, I thought, they're probably drunk. Suddenly one caught my leg and pulled me from the saddle. The other held the horse by the bridle. 'Hey!' I shouted. 'What do you want?' One of them laughed loudly: 'It's you we want, not the stallion.' "

"Ha—ha—ha! The devils!"

"I couldn't make it out. But they had pulled me off the saddle and thrown me onto the grass—and then suddenly I gathered what they were after!"

The sergeant, wrinkling his brow, listened with curious attention. To give him full satisfaction Feodor described in detail the pulled-up skirts, artistically shading their naked thighs with the black velvet of night. The sergeant even began to drool. "Love throbs over the world, man throbs over love," he said with real ecstasy.

"As soon as I found out what they wanted, fear seized me, and I began to fight desperately. The girls, unfortunately, were stronger, and I barely got away from them."

With shy impertinence the sergeant slapped Feodor's shoulder: "Comrade Chief, tell me the truth! You're hiding something."

"Why, no. I really beat them off. They're probably still out on the steppe. If you like we'll go and catch up with them."

"Smart! Together we'd beat them off easier. Ha—ha—ha!" the sergeant laughed.

But Feodor laughed louder and more violently. He laughed until the tears ran, until he choked. He laughed, while with astonishment, almost with fear, he listened to himself, to that inner being who forced him to laugh and said to him with cold hostility: "Go ahead, lie a little more. Play the clown."

Feodor had come to himself sooner than he expected. He came to himself and couldn't understand what had happened to him during the day. Vexation and a callous emptiness enfolded him. The memory of the meeting with his brother on the steppe was the first thing Feodor threw overboard as unnecessary ballast. By the time he had arrived at the estate his eyes were dry.

It was late. He had been delayed on the steppe. But it was not playful women who had kept him there. When he was about five miles back along the road on which he had met Nikolai—galloping, the wind beating against his chest, feeling cramped though wide open space was around him—he saw a small light in the night. Involuntarily he was drawn to it. His whole being balked at going back to the estate. The light turned out to be a campfire, at the edge of the steep bank of the river. Its flames were reflected and scattered in a red gleam in the water. Two people, an old man and a youth, were sitting beside the fire. Without getting up, they met the rider with guarded glances. From Feodor's bare head and broad back a light steam was rising. His overheated stallion was in a lather. They were astonished by his agitated appearance; however, the old man merely asked:

"From the town?"

Feodor didn't reply directly. "I saw the fire, so I rode up. If you've no objection, I'll sit down."

"Why, no. Sit down," said the old man.

Feodor, still trembling from excitement, jumped to the ground. His hands were shaking, his eyes burned feverishly, strong pulses hammered his brain. The old man and the lad looked at him intently, as people look at the mentally sick. "We're kolkhozniks from the Petrov-

588

sky village. Spending the night here, looking after the horses," said the old man. His calm voice and simple face encouraged Feodor. He took his cigarette case out of his pocket, extended it to them. The young man took a cigarette eagerly, but the old fellow declined. "I'm not used to city tobacco. Thank you, all the same." He rolled his own in a piece of newspaper with tobacco from his pouch. Then he quickly lit it from a coal he pulled out of the fire. The young fellow took a small twig from the fire and extended it to Feodor, who lit his cigarette from it and inhaled smoke deeply.

By now Feodor had calmed down somewhat. The appearance of the two kolkhozniks in the flickering light of the fire, especially their faces, was remarkable. The old man had no boots; he wore a pair of old Cossack pants with the red Don stripe, and a print shirt. His face was dour, eyebrows black, but the wise light of his steppe eyes shone merrily. When he looked closely at Feodor, the latter felt suddenly uneasy, even frightened. The young lad's face seemed familiar to Feodor. He had no doubt that he had seen this strong youth with the tousled forelock somewhere. It would be hard to forget a face like that: lean, with an eagle's nose, alert boldness in the deep-set eyes, an irreverent smile on the thin lips. The broad shoulders and slender waist called for a military uniform, and it was strange to see him wearing an ordinary shirt and wrinkled pants. He was seated, but from his long legs Feodor saw that he was tall. Several times he looked intently and strangely, first at Feodor, then at the horse, which was standing close by, outlined by the firelight. He seemed to be trying to remember where he had seen them before. .

It was still, and the river stole into this stillness with an endless babbling, whispers of dreams, some arousing and hurried, some irritating and provoking, others lazy and sleepy. The rustling of birds in the bushes, the lapping of the water against the crumbling bank, the monotonous croaking of frogs, or the barely audible whistle of a distant steamer—these were the only sounds, and over all, like a soft veil, the starry sky.

"Hm—m, this is good tobacco," said the lad, inhaling the cigarette with pleasure. The words were simple, but in the silence of the night they sounded mysterious. From somewhere behind, on the steppe, came the snort of a horse. And again there was silence.

Feodor, half closing his eyes, looked into the fire. A bird flashed over the water, leaving behind a sad, fading cry.

The night, like a distant song, was wonderfully peaceful. It was as if someone were singing and harmonious visions arose—the steppe, hidden in the darkness, the fitful fire, the damp wind from the river, and the heavy fragrance of the grass. Feodor was in despair. A mood of depression seized him; he was filled with fear before the unknown. The whole of the past day flashed before his eyes. The scenes were terrible and poisonous—at times his whole body shook. But, ignoring the dismay of his soul and his agitation, the ancient river was telling its own story, and it seemed to Feodor that as it was now so it had always been—the fire burning on the steppe, the shadows trembling as if alive, and the young lad looking at him with wild eyes. The stern old man with the wise face sat motionless, as if he had stepped out of an old fairy tale.

The two men, by now accustomed to Feodor, continued their conversation, apparently interrupted by his unexpected appearance.

"So, Silich, why are you against Hanka marrying me?" the young man asked, looking into the fire.

"You've spoiled her——"

"All you do is harp—you've spoiled her, you've spoiled her! That's why the world was arranged half and half, so there could be fornication —otherwise we'd all die of boredom. And anyway, I'm to blame."

The old man frowned, cast a searching look at the young fellow from under his eyebrows. "Now—yes. But who are you now, Rudoy? An ordinary kolkhoznik, the same as me. That is, you're as bare as a rolling stone, as the saying goes; you've got no moss."

The young man ground his teeth. "But if I'd been in the cavalry detail, you would have agreed?" he asked and his eyes half closed like a wounded hawk's.

"Probably also no: You run around too much, like a tom-cat. What kind of husband will you be? Of course, Hanka wouldn't have asked me in that case—she'd have hung around your neck herself."

"Then why are you so obstinate now?"

"You've spoiled her . . ." drawled the old man again.

They were silent. Somewhere nearby a bird kept beginning, and never finishing his song.

"Shall we throw in a few potatoes, eh?" asked Rudoy and, without waiting for consent, took half a dozen potatoes and placed them on the coals. Hurrying after him, his shadow did the same. "Hell, it's a long time since I've eaten meat. If I could shoot down a bird or a hare! But we have no gun!" Then, as if he had remembered something, Rudoy said: "The commander of the company's a funny fellow. I came to hand in my uniform and gun, and he said: 'Well, Rudoy, you used to ride a horse; now they'll ride you.'"

590

"True words."

"Well, I won't give in. Nobody has ridden me yet and they won't. I'm going to run away, Silich."

"Where to?"

"To the city."

"And is it any easier there? There they stick men like you up against the wall a lot sooner."

"That's all right. If you fear bad luck, you'll never see good. And in any case, I'm pretty fed up here. I'll run away and take Hanka with me."

"Now, now, go easy."

"And what's it to you? She'll be lying in the chairman's bed in any case."

"Now, now, I said go easy," said Silich sternly, but a minute later spoke more softly: "Now lad, don't rush off to the city on a fool's errand; you may be there sooner than you think. There's a rumor that the chairman wants to put you in a nice little plant as far from here as possible. He can't stand the sight of you. 'My God,' says he, 'have we got to place a guard over our women to protect them from this tatterdemalion of a knight?' "

"That's him worrying over his Mashka," sneered Rudoy. "Am I to blame if she crawls to me? Nearly every night, whenever the chairman is away somewhere, she runs to the threshing shed. I barely close my eyes, am just getting into my first sleep, when there she is—running her hand over my body. 'Rudy, dear, it's me.' Must I drive her away with a pitchfork?"

"It may be that way, but look out he doesn't actually send you off with the first mobilization to the plant. There, brother, is an accursed place. Here at least the air is free, you can breathe it as much as you like."

"And if I refuse to go to the plant?"

"They'll take you by force, like a ewe lamb."

"And how's that?"

"Just like that."

"Pretty smart!" Rudoy got up abruptly. His shadow, as if it were afraid, darted far away over the steppe. "You think I'd stand for that kind of a deal? It's not in my character!"

"They've broken stronger characters than yours. They make it simple: one—two, and you're crowned."

As if it had been lashed by a whip, Rudoy's face twisted. "But not me!" He clenched his fists. "I won't stand it. Each one to his own taste. Some like a yoke, some a whip. I like the free wind. It's right here in me, in my chest. It's raging, it wants to break out. At times I want to turn everything upside down, to let everything fly into the depths of hell!"

"He's a rebel!" thought Feodor, admiring Rudoy's wild look. "There are a lot like that on the steppe . . ."

But the old man said calmly: "Don't shout. Sit down." When Rudoy sat down, the old man said to him: "You're a good lad, but you weren't beaten enough, or kicked around. I'm afraid for you; you're too hot-headed. You should be either a bad drunkard or a big general."

"I don't understand—speak plainer."

"You don't understand, you suckling?" the old man knit his shaggy eyebrows, but his eyes were smiling. "One must know one's own path, that's what."

"I know my own path."

"Oh, you—you're just a puppy," said the old fellow kindly. "There are all kinds of paths, some straight, some crooked."

The old man suddenly noticed Feodor's eyes fixed on him. Indeed, Feodor was looking rather strange, as if he had seen something new in him, as if he wanted to ask him a very important question. In their conversation Feodor sensed something unspoken. With a sort of second hearing he gathered that if he hadn't been there, they would have been talking about quite different things. One could feel it in the very air—something heavy, brutal. Feodor shuddered with his whole body, as in an icy wind.

"What do you want?" asked the old man.

"I'm afraid, Father," replied Feodor in a jumpy whisper, and involuntarily drew closer to him.

The young lad, chewing a potato, snickered: "Afraid of the dark, eh?"

"Leave him alone," said the old man sternly. "Who knows what a man has on his mind? . . . Here, have one!" He took a hot potato out of the coals and handed it to Feodor. Burning his fingers, Feodor hastily broke the baked skin and began to eat the mealy pulp. "It's surely got you, stranger—you're all atremble. You need some vodka with pepper. That's wonderful, biting stuff! It'll turn a copper pan into a sieve. Do you drink? You don't? You will. I see by your face that you will. You've a remarkable face, young man."

"I'm afraid of myself, Father," said Feodor quickly. "I would like to believe, but I must suspect. I want to forgive, but I am forced to

592

exact. Not wicked by nature, I commit savage crimes." Feodor groaned deeply and dropped his head on his knees, as if hiding from shame.

Rudoy stopped chewing, stared at him in surprise.

"What the hell is he? A nut or something?" he asked the old man.

Silich, waving his hand to him to keep quiet, turned to Feodor sympathetically: "Where are you from, Sonny?"

"From the Gorin estate."

It was as though not words but a long whip resounded—swishing, winding itself around them both. Silich and Rudoy froze. For several seconds there was a silence that swallowed all the noises of the night. The old man and the youth exchanged peculiar glances, then munched their potatoes again. A little later Rudoy rose lazily.

"I'll go and look at the horses . . ."

And along with his shadow he vanished into the darkness. The old man didn't move.

Feodor waited for what he would say. But the old man was silent. Thrusting his fingers into his black beard, he looked closely into the fire, and in this silence there seemed to be a rapt thought: the dark steppe itself was thinking. Rudoy returned soon—Feodor heard his footsteps behind him. Then the steps ceased. Feodor was going to turn around, but at that moment somebody grunted savagely as strong hands clutched him from behind, and a belt coiled around his wrists.

There was a wicked laugh, and then Feodor found himself face down on the ground with his hands bound behind his back. Trembling from head to foot, he tore at the rawhide thongs, but only cut his wrists more painfully. Rudoy got up, wiping his hot, sweaty, satisfied face with his sleeve. He didn't sit down at once by the fire, but stood shifting from foot to foot, like a blown horse.

"He's strong, the devil! I didn't expect it, barely managed." Rudoy at last dropped onto the grass, gathered his legs under him, and sat looking at the flickering coals. The fire was dying now. The bound Feodor lay in silence and in silence the calm stars hung above him.

"Once our detail took part in maneuvers on just such a night," began Rudoy. He stretched, yawning, and tensed his muscles. "It was dark as hell. We had to make a crossing under the mock fire of the enemy. Well, you never saw such a mess: artillery, horses, infantry, everything was mixed up. We moved like blind men: you might land in the river with your horse any minute. And if you got lost, no one would notice. But when it grew lighter, everything was shaken down so simply it was even funny."

593

"Yes, night maneuvers are the most difficult."

Feodor's first shock gradually passed. His brain was feverishly trying to understand the meaning of what had happened. Yes, it was he who was lying with his hands bound, it was the fire that was glowing, and it was the same Cossacks who were talking to each other in an everyday voice.

"What's this for? What's the matter?" he asked, and didn't recognize his own voice.

"Shut up," said Rudoy, and turned to the old man: "What'll we do with his horse?"

The old man didn't answer, coolly blew on a potato.

"How's the other one?" he asked the lad about something a little later.

"Poorly."

"What do you want with me?" shouted Feodor. "What have I done to you? Why don't you say something? Have you gone crazy? Or what?"

"What's your hurry? Let us finish the potatoes and then we'll drop you to visit the crabs at the bottom of the river."

The silence fell on Feodor like a stone. As if he were indeed pressed down by a terrible weight, he began to breathe deeply, formed words with difficulty: "If you need the horse, take it. It's not mine."

"Ha—ha!" laughed Rudoy. "And you'll come later and catch us and the horse together."

This wicked laugh at once reminded Feodor where he had seen the young lad. He was the same Cossack who had made a coarse joke about pants when the cavalry detail met Feodor and Nina on the road to the estate, the first night of their love. Yes, of course, the same face—the same poisonous smile, stiff neck, and eyes glittering wolfishly.

"Honestly, I won't come back! . . . Take the horse——"

"We don't need your horse. We're kolkhozniks and a kolkhoznik isn't allowed to have a horse," said the old man.

Again silence. The night stood still in expectation of something terrifying and merciless. Feodor felt this and recalled fearsome stories about how city people were killed on the steppe. They might kill him, or they might let him go, laughing at his joy and relief.

Feodor, holding his breath, watched the old man and the lad. They ate the potatoes, blowing on them in a businesslike way, chewing them slowly, with the serious faces of people engaged in serious business. Feodor realized that they would drown him just as calmly and seri-

594

ously. A strange, magnetic force emanated from them. He looked and looked, unable to take his eyes off them: they sat like steppe idols, silent, bronzed, as if they were clothed in the armor of the fire and the night. Suddenly there rose before him long-forgotten pictures, distant shouts; the long manes of horses stretched out in a race, the rattle of swords, the screech of arrows, night fires on the steppe. The Scythians! A thousand years ago they were like this—mysterious, unpredictable, wild—and so they remained.

Then Russia rose before Feodor. The old man, Rudoy, all Russia rose slowly like a gray phantom: stubborn, with cruel yet kind eyes, steppe and jungle, many-sided Russia, repeatable a thousand times in every drop of his blood. Russia, leaning on his shoulder, rumbled like a bear, rolled the age-old clods in his disturbed brain. Feodor suddenly felt weak, insignificant, a miserable chip of wood in the mighty current of the Don. What accursed hand had cast him here, into disaster? No, it can't be! There is still hope! Of course he would live, of course his ambitious dreams would be realized.

Feodor came to himself with Silich's voice: "I remember, Rudoy, in 1915, at the front, I was still with your father, may his soul rest in peace. I was fighting in the third Don regiment—so we finished off a couple of officers, the whole bunch of us, in broad daylight. We hated them, and there was good reason: some slight mistake—bang, right in the teeth, and then the penal squad. Well, the boys decided to kill them! Our position lay beside a little wood, and beyond the wood was a village. We noticed that as soon as there was a lull they managed to slip away to the village—for girls, of course. We caught them on the road through the wood. We surrounded them and they realized at once that this was their end. What a sight that was! How they screamed! How they cried! Bad people apparently fear death most. They collapsed on the ground. Begged for mercy. But that only made us madder. We cut off the head of one of them right away. And the second one, the second one . . . we . . . we . . ."

Rudoy blew for a long time on a potato, then asked impatiently:
"Well, what then?"

"We bound him by the hands and feet and hung him between two horses. And then we began to tighten him up slowly. He was hanging in the air tight as a fiddle string, howling with a drawn-out wail like oo—oo—oo—oo! And then he began to scream . . . like laughing, but, my God! What terrible laughter! And we laughed too! The man's joints cracked while we, devils, roared almost danced around. Some whipped up the horses; others caught hold of the rope and pulled.

595

And then he stopped screaming. His arms were the first to give way; they were torn off. So the horse bolted between the white birches with two bloody arms. And how the blood flowed! We beat it! . . . Brrr!"

"Aw! Go to the devil!" said Rudoy, and threw away his potato. He got up and went to the terrified Feodor. Turning him around by the hair to face him, he looked right into his eyes. His teeth sparkled with savage joy.

"Still alive? Come on."

"Where to?"

"You'll soon find out."

CHAPTER 2

THE OLD MAN lit a dry twig in the fire; then, lighting the way, went ahead down the steep bank of the gully. The shadows flickered convulsively on the bushes. As in a dream Feodor felt Rudoy lead him, holding him by the shoulders. In front the old man stepped heavily, waddling, crunching the twigs with his bare feet. It was as if not a man but a dangerous animal was making its way through the thicket.

"Surely they're not going to drown me?" Stupefied with horror, Feodor felt the cold perspiration dropping from his face, his heart jumping and beating in his chest. When they stepped onto the sand his legs gave way. Rudoy caught him, dragged him along.

They stood beside a rowboat pulled half way up the river bank. Inside it lay a human figure drawn up as if dead, motionless. In the darkness Feodor could distinguish only a white bandage on the head.

"Show a light, Silich," said Rudoy. The old man brought the brand closer.

"Mitrich, can you see?" the old man asked the prostrate form. The latter moved weakly, groaned.

By the light of the burning brand Feodor saw only the beaten, bloody face; the body was covered with sackcloth, through which dark stains seeped. Inexpressible suffering had frozen on the man's face. His forehead was knotted painfully; his blood-clotted hair stuck out from under the rough bandage. Suddenly Feodor started. In the wounded man he recognized the Gorin gardener, the father of Igor. A sudden sharp pain pierced him. In the awful face of the wounded man Feodor saw his own tomorrow. He recoiled as from a ghost.

"Aha! You know him!" said Rudoy sharply.

"Mitrich, we've brought a visitor for you—do you recognize him?" asked the old man.

The wounded man slowly raised his eyelids, fixed his eyes, dull from suffering, on Feodor—at once his head jerked back, as if from a convulsion.

"Don't be afraid! He's tied up."

Several times the wounded man soundlessly opened his mouth. The old fellow bent over him.

"That's Novikov," whispered the wounded one, barely audible. "He's the main one. How did he land here?"

"He flew in himself. Maybe he was looking for someone."

The wounded man became still, for a long time lay motionless and silent, then slowly opened his eyes and, with a burning hatred that caught at his heart, scorched Feodor—"Murderer! Butcher!" he groaned and tried to raise himself on his elbow. A fine dew of perspiration came out thickly at his temples.

"Oho! So he's an important bird!" said the old man. "At first I took him for one of us. He rode up all in tears, didn't look like a man. 'Aha!' I thought, 'he's hiding from somebody.' But apparently tears are cheap, blown in by the wind." The old fellow wiped away the sweat from the wounded man's face and turned to Feodor: "How'll it be, murderer? Bury you alive in the earth, you crawling snake? Or tear you in two with horses?" Feodor moaned and, as if he had been cut down, fell to the sand. Rudoy didn't pick him up.

"You, Mitrich, how do you feel?" the old man asked the wounded one.

"I'm going to die soon. I won't last till morning. Oh, God! How I'd like to live until the little sun . . ."

"We'll have to tie on a good heavy stone and into the water with him," said Rudoy.

Feodor understood that this was meant for him. His hair stirred on his head.

"Yes, just to live until the sun," repeated the wounded man weakly. Suddenly he squinted at Feodor: "Tell me, where's Cheprok? Don't lie in the face of death! Where is he? In the city?"

"He's dead," replied Feodor.

The wounded man shuddered, groaned. Feodor understood. "Don't worry about your little boy. He's safe."

"How do you know?"

"I took him myself to my brother."

The wounded man stared fixedly into Feodor's face.

"He's not lying," said the old fellow.

"Why did you order us to be shot?" whispered the wounded man. "God! There in the wood they finished us all, to the last one. They had mercy on none. Only through a miracle did I remain alive, and not for long at that—I'll be dead before morning. Why did you kill us? How were we bothering you?"

"I didn't give the order. The sergeant shot you without my knowledge."

"He's not lying," said the old man again.

Rudoy snorted wickedly. "How do you know that he isn't lying? Even a wolf is gentle in a trap, but let him go free . . ."

The old fellow brought the brand to Feodor's face, looked steadily into his eyes: "He's not lying," he repeated firmly.

"Whether he's lying or not—into the water with him anyway," said Rudoy. "We daren't take a risk."

Not answering, the old fellow bent over the wounded man. "Lay me beside all the others there in the woods," the latter whispered to him. "Bury me beside all the others, and remember the place. The time will come when others will remember us."

"That's all right—we'll do that. But don't worry about your son, I know that he's not lying."

"That's not like him."

"That happens. His conscience is rejoicing in him. That happens."

The wounded man beckoned Silich with his eyes, began to speak hurriedly: "Listen, friend, tell me, do you think that there, beyond the borders of living, something good will begin, something we haven't found here?"

The old man tried to comfort him: "Don't think about death, Mitrich. I'll cure you yet . . . I'll put some herbs on your wounds, herbs that will draw up the wound at once . . . There is such an herb; it's a wild herb . . . Valerian, too—that helps a lot . . . If these herbs don't happen to be handy, I can use sage and quitch grass . . ."

The wounded man smiled wanly. "No, no one will cure me now . . . Give me something to drink, friend."

The old man brought him river water in a dipper. "If you want to drink—you'll live," said he kindly. The wounded man took two gulps. "Everything's burning," he groaned. "No, I'm not of the living—towards morning I'll die. Take me into the wood before dawn, otherwise they'll see us here . . ." He again beckoned the old fellow to him, said softly into his ear: "Let him go . . . it may be true—maybe it

598

wasn't his fault the sergeant committed that crime. I remember, he came up to the sergeant, as if alarmed, and the sergeant told him they were taking us into town. Yes, yes, I remember . . . perhaps he really didn't know. . . . And just think, if he saved my son, and you kill him . . . There's no need to take a sin like that on your-self."

In the meantime Rudoy had brought a heavy stone and placed it beside Feodor.

"Must I tear out my own heart to prove the truth of my words?" screamed Feodor. He pronounced the entreating words forcefully, but they sounded insincere. He repented his sins, remembering Lida, Nina, his brother, all his friends and all his enemies; he wanted to forgive them and to ask forgiveness of them, but realized himself that all this was merely animal fear raging within him. His real thoughts were quite different, not at all what he was saying—they were without form, unclean, base. Like vomit, they rose into the throat. At that fate-ful moment he wanted, by the power of will, to lift his thoughts into the clean firmament; and he could not. Other thoughts—cruel and re-vengeful—overcame and dragged them down.

The events of the day followed each other in his mind in fateful sequence, step by step, along their secret paths, leading him to a sense-less end. The talk with Gorin, the rescue of the boy Igor and the sudden spiritual uplift, the meeting with his brother on the steppe, the campfire and the two Cossacks. Suddenly he saw clearly how alien he was to all these people. No matter what he said, what he thought, he was still a stranger to them.

"The people!" he thought bitterly. "There they are, the people. These are the people about whose salvation I spoke so enthusiastically to Nikolai. They see through everything. They can't be bought with sugary speeches. They're not concerned with my spiritual experiences: to them I'm an enemy and they'll destroy me like an enemy, calmly and without mercy. Just as I have had no mercy on them . . ."

Rudoy took a piece of an old net from the boat, wrapped the stone in it, drew it tight.

The old man shook his head.

"Drop it, Rudoy. Instead, untie the man."

"What the hell! Have you gone crazy, Silich? In an hour he'll return with people and grind us into crumbs."

"No, he won't come back."

"I don't understand you, Silich! For the life of me, I don't understand! You believe a man like that. I'll bet the bastard has so many crimes on his conscience that three more deaths would be too little for him."

"You spoke strongly, lad, but you missed the point," replied the old man to Rudoy. "According to you, if the sky is clouded there's no sun? Ridiculous. No matter how thick the clouds, they can't stop the sun. And our souls are like that—let the wind blow stronger, more freshly, and before you know it the clouds are gone, only radiant space is left."

He himself went over to Feodor, untied him. Unable to believe in his freedom, Feodor remained on his knees. The old man, not moving away, fingered the belt in his hand thoughtfully. His wise, steppe face was stern. He raised his eyes, smiled broadly, then said simply: "Remember, little fellow: people are born to good, like the field to grain. Sow good and you will harvest good. But if you sow evil, you will reap only stones. Therein lies our life, our happiness, and our sorrow. And life would be paradise on earth if people were more thoughtful of their neighbors, loved them, as the farmer loves his field. So that's that, friend."

Feodor raised his eyes timidly to the old man. A strong, stocky man. His eyes were not visible in the darkness, but his heavy hand rested paternally on Feodor's left shoulder. Its strength penetrated his whole being, evoking faith in him. Feodor felt that he could neither lie nor pretend before this man. Indeed, this was not a man, but everlasting truth that stood before him, and not a coarse peasant touch, but wise rays, old as life itself, which had reached his heart and conquered him. Feodor's tense nerves couldn't stand it. The light of an unknown power, triumphant and penetrating, illuminated his soul. A quiver of joy and revelation shook his whole being. From sudden tears everything swam before his eyes.

"Old man, Silich, the people," he whispered passionately, "you can, I know you can save yourself, save the country . . . Save us from ourselves! Save us before it's too late!"

"What's he talking about?" asked Rudoy, surprised.

"His conscience, his conscience is triumphing. . . . And, of course, he is happy to have his life returned to him," replied the old man, and turning, said to Feodor softly: "Well, go away, dear friend."

Feodor, hurrying and scrambling, overflowing with the joy of life, climbed up the ravine. Rudoy, evading the old man's glance, was going to go after him. Silich caught him by the sleeve. "Cut it out, Rudoy! He

600

won't come back. He won't dare. Now he has a scar on his heart for the rest of his life. And to kill a man is to kill oneself."

For a long time Feodor was unable to mount into the saddle; his foot slipped from the stirrup; the reins fell out of his shaking hands.

"Farewell, Silich!" he cried hoarsely, when he was finally mounted. "I'll never forget you!" He set off at a gallop.

During the ride Feodor tried to preserve that sudden, exciting feeling that had just overcome him, and noticed with surprise that it disappeared quickly, leaving only an irritating sediment. Again and again he writhed mentally in the agony of death. With painful clarity, more real than life itself, he saw, he even felt his own body on the bottom of the river, with the stone tied to his neck. Anger burst in his heart, a thirst for vengeance—the sweet desire to return with the sergeant and shoot them all. But that would betray his weakness to the sergeant. That thought alone stopped him. Angry at himself, at the Cossacks, and even at the starry night, Feodor didn't understand at first what possessed him. In the end it seemed foolish not to understand, and he understood.

"The lesson is clear—there isn't and must not be a middle course. I softened unforgivably. That can lead to only one thing—disaster. No, no, maybe the old man was right, but his truth is the truth of the people—difficult, torturing, prolonged, not for my generation. We have our own truth—a heart of stone and an adamant faith in force . . ."

Feodor reached the estate about two o'clock in the morning. Lifting his feet heavily, as if wading through thick muck, he entered the house and, not noticing his own breaking voice, ordered the man on duty to waken the sergeant. He washed himself for a long time at the sink in the kitchen, dousing his head in water and puffing loudly.

"Damn foolishness . . . nuisance . . . rot . . ." But his heart was still sunk in fear and his legs were weak.

The sergeant appeared in brightly polished boots. "Ah, at last you've come, Comrade Chief. I just couldn't wait up for you. I wanted to report my success personally: from my demonstration the patient lost his psychological balance and at the moment is in a state of nervous prostration."

Feodor didn't understand at once what he was talking about, but when he did, he waved his hand: "Oh, it doesn't matter."

When the sergeant asked him where he had been delayed so long, Feodor immediately spun the yarn about two women on the steppe.

601

The sergeant laughed, Feodor laughed, laughed, while he thought: "I must have been asleep. That was a dream. And Igor. And his father . . . and the two Cossacks on the steppe . . . and my foolish talk with Nikolai—it's all a dream. But my suit is rumpled and covered with sand. And my wrists hurt from the belt and the marks are there. There they are, red, the skin is bruised."

The memory of the meeting with the Cossacks, the fear he had experienced of almost certain death, sobered him. Death had been near, but not death in full fight, the kind he wanted—rather death with plenty of time for thought, the most ignoble death of all. Feodor stood unnaturally tense, compressing his lips tightly, bringing his feelings and thoughts into order. The sergeant looked closely at him.

Feodor shuddered. "Where's everybody?"

"They're sleeping, the devils! They all got dead drunk in the cellar; we had to drag them out by the legs. How did you come to trust them with the key so carelessly: It's such a pity about the wine—they slopped up half of it."

"Well, that's not so bad. There'll be enough to last us. Come on, let's check. I want a drink."

Together they went into the cellar. It was cool there. A lot of empty bottles were scattered over the floor—remains of the soldiers' orgy. Behind a barrel lay a forgotten soldier. Arms and legs spread wide, mouth open, he snored.

Feodor looked at him with a long, jeering look.

"I envy the blessed soul," he said and reached for a bottle. He broke the neck on a case, began to drink. His teeth chattered against the glass, the wine spilled over his hand, while in his eyes there was no longer laughter, but pain.

"Drink, Sergeant. I'm celebrating my resurrection from the dead."

"They sure put the heat on you."

"Who?" asked Feodor sharply.

"Why, the women——"

"Oh, yes."

Feodor passed his hand over his chest; his panting heart beat unevenly, strongly. Suddenly he brightened up. "Sergeant, give me your revolver."

The sergeant was surprised, but unstrapped the revolver from his belt and handed it to him. Feodor looked at him strangely, straight into his eyes; the revolver was pointed at the sergeant's chest.

"Careful, Comrade Chief! . . . It might go off."

"Afraid?" asked Feodor in a tone that turned the sergeant pale. He

602

took an involuntary step back. His belts creaked pitifully. "Afraid?" Feodor repeated dully and jerked his neck. Suddenly he turned and, without taking aim, fired into a barrel standing by the far wall of the cellar, neatly in the bung. At once a red stream flowed.

The sergeant recoiled, scraping a spur on the stone floor. Feodor laughed: "See that? Right in the heart? See the blood? Ha—ha—ha!"

The sergeant, speechless from fright, nodded his head. "Yes, yes. A marvelous shot. I would never have thought that a professor could shoot like that."

The boom of the shot still hung in the cellar; the powder smoke smelled of rotten eggs. Feodor stopped laughing, absent-mindedly blew through the muzzle of the revolver.

"Tell me, Sergeant, do you believe in the soul?"

The sergeant was offended, but looked guardedly at the revolver in Feodor's hand, then answered diplomatically: "I can't give you a clear answer."

"And if not a clear one?"

The sergeant wrinkled his narrow forehead. "Excuse me, who do you take me for, Comrade Chief? I am sufficiently educated to judge these things. There is a heart, kidneys, bowels, but there's no soul."

"Well, and if you were told that you had a soul and you yourself felt that it was there—that it was hindering your living, what would you do?"

"He's drunk," thought the sergeant anxiously. "What does he want from me?" But aloud he tried to answer cheerfully: "I would go to a doctor and get it cut out. If it's in the way—out it goes!"

"Like an appendix?"

"Yes, yes . . . like a boil."

With an abrupt movement Feodor handed him the revolver. "You and I are brothers, Sergeant, blood brothers! You and I serve one devil! So be it! To hell with the soul! To hell with God-fearing drivelers! We have our own truth—the truth of the conqueror!"

"Why, he's completely tight!" thought the sergeant.

But he was mistaken: Feodor wasn't drunk. He was sober: terribly sober.

CHAPTER 3

FEODOR had a strange dream. Mikhail Gorin stood before him in a white shirt, looked at him kindly and affectionately, as at his own son, and said: "I forgive you, Feodor, I forgive everything. This is how we should all be living, like brothers." His voice sounded unusually soft and his eyes smiled warmly.

A quiet joy overwhelmed Feodor; a sudden feeling of love for this man aroused waves of exultation in him. His eyes were full of tears, his soul enraptured. And Mikhail Gorin, bending slightly, stroked Feodor's hair with his broad hand, and everything around became transparent and joyful, as in childhood. Feodor, unable to take his eyes off the amazingly spiritual face of the writer, wanted to say something inexpressibly warm to him, to thank him, to share with him his own joy—when suddenly Mikhail vanished and there appeared the face of Rudoy, watchful and malicious. "Why should you be forgiven? A stone around your neck, and into the water with you," he said roughly.

Feodor awoke in a cold sweat. He had slept no more than an hour. Beyond the window a pale ribbon not far from the river was growing brighter; morning was beginning.

Suddenly an unexpected thought shocked Feodor: "He has died. Mikhail Gorin has killed himself!" Shaking, Feodor placed his ear to the wall. In Gorin's room it was quiet. Feodor gasped for air. His heart sank from his terrible surmise. Dressing hurriedly, he ran into the corridor. The sentry at the door of Gorin's room was asleep, sitting on his heels, his forehead pressing against his rifle.

"Hey, you! wake up!" Feodor shouted at him, and didn't recognize his own voice.

The sentry jumped up, frightened, confused, while Feodor, restraining his rising dread, wrenched the door open.

Mikhail Gorin sat at his desk, writing.

"You're alive! Nothing happened to you?" cried Feodor involuntarily. But he felt no relief. The unsolvable problem fell on him with renewed weight. He felt again the malice in his heart.

"Were you expecting to find me dead?" asked Mikhail, looking at him with an effort, as if it were painful to see him. "If you want my death, arrange it yourself. I won't help you."

"What are you writing?" asked Feodor in a shaky voice.

Mikhail twisted his lips scornfully. "You needn't rejoice. It's not what you think." His tired look seemed to say: "Are you still hoping that I'll consent?"

So clear was this look that Feodor answered aloud: "No, Mikhail Alexeyevich, I will not try to persuade you any more. I can see myself that it's useless."

604

"Then what do you want from me?"

"What are you writing?"

"I am writing my belated thoughts, which I have never before examined."

"Who's going to read them?"

"Not people like you. These thoughts are not for you."

"Not for me?" Feodor took a step toward the writer. With a quick movement Mikhail snatched the paper off the desk, crumpled it in his hand.

"No, it was not for you I was writing," Mikhail repeated. "This is for those like Andrei Demin. You remember him?"

"I know one like him."

"Who is he?"

"My brother, Nikolai."

Mikhail sneered: "Is that a joke?"

"Why a joke? Is it so difficult for you to believe that I might have a good brother? Do you think that he must be like me, that we must be moral twins?"

"Yes, that's what I thought."

"Well, it isn't so. My brother Nikolai is entirely different. There is a youth with a clean soul! He's simple, like millions of people. In this simplicity lies his strength. A noble heart beats in him." Feodor didn't notice that he had begun to speak about his brother with pride. Mikhail looked at him with surprise. "But wait, wait!" Feodor continued. "Once I told him . . . yes! I said, I have a heart. I had it, but I lost it. But trust me, I will give to him what you have written. . . . Give it to me," Feodor held out his hand, but Mikhail recoiled.

"Never! I don't trust you. I know you and all your deceit!"

Feodor began to feel oppressed. Something had to be removed, broken off, finished one way or another. Sweat broke out on his forehead. His gray eyes burned with a dry metallic glitter. The collar of his shirt was unbuttoned, as if he were suffocating. He sat down on a chair, lit a cigarette. Inhaling deeply, he considered how to bring his talk with Mikhail to a head. He was burning to blurt out the whole terrible truth at once, to shock the writer. Something mysterious and powerful had arisen between them for which there was no name and which could not be overcome. He felt how, breaking his resistance easily, this unknown was drawing him toward the fateful line beyond which his actions, his thoughts, his words—all the intense effort of his will— would be useless. This wasn't death, but the horror of that cold indifference in which death is clothed and which is more frightful than death itself. And Feodor did not realize how softly but clearly his own words would sound in the room:

"No, Mikhail Alexeyevich, you don't know it all yet." He said this, and made a mental note to himself: another step toward the line is taken.

Mikhail Gorin seemed to understand this also. He became noticeably watchful. Uneasily, with an inner trembling, he asked: "What more is hidden from me?"

Feodor's look became heartless and cold.

"You wrote the play because you were prompted by me. Understand? By me!"

"By you!" Mikhail stepped back. "And Nina?"

"Don't speak of Nina! Don't speak of Nina!" Feodor cried out in pain. He got up quickly, moved close to Mikhail and in a gurgling, crazed whisper, said: "Yes, it was at my will that you wrote. . . . I was sent into your house with the coldly calculated purpose of squeezing out of you the word needed by the Government. Recall recent events and you will see that they were all part of one precise plan: to seize your last fortress—your brain, your thoughts. . . . Remember our first meeting, when Glushak introduced us, our game of chess together? At that time you suspected nothing, but it was precisely at that moment that the idea came to me to get the play out of you—not individual articles, as my chiefs had suggested, but the play. The idea justified itself, the result exceeded all my expectations. . . .

"Remember Glushak's agitation—he was shaking for his own hide then and never stopped shaking right up to his own ruin. Remember how he tried to warn your wife Luba? Oh! That cost him an inhuman effort, but neither she nor you understood him. . . . And then at the wedding he confessed to you, exposed me. But it was already too late, and in any case he was unable to expose me completely, because he did not know everything. But even for that he paid with his life. . . . And our talks together! What a devilish game! You frightened me at first by the readiness with which you took up my idea. I didn't know then that you were in the last stage of despair; and your discord with the people surrounding you baffled me. . . . Remember all this, Mikhail Alexeyevich. Remember, understand, curse me! But don't mention Nina—don't mention her!"

The writer suddenly rose, tall, raw-boned, and with unconcealed horror in his face, said: "Tell me . . . is all this true? Is it?"

He asked, but by his painfully twisted face it was evident that he had no longer any doubt. The whole intrigue, the whole fraud became

606

clear to Mikhail. He groaned heavily and sank into a chair. Yes, the revelation of the truth had come—the naked truth in all its shameless-ness, in all its cynical baseness. It became stuffy—there was neither air nor life. He understood that Novikov hated him, but it seemed to him that it was not Novikov who was flaying him with merciless words, but some huge dark spirit bending over him. With a heavy hand it was squeezing his throat and choking him slowly, calmly, mercilessly.

CHAPTER 4

FEODOR began to speak again, laying his words like nooses. "Nina is my wound, bleeding, unhealing. She is fate's revenge for my self-confidence, my cruelty, for the coldness of my heart. A brutal dreadful vengeance. Coming into your house like a disguised enemy I had no feelings except, perhaps, curiosity. I saw her unexpectedly . . . A few words in the park and I realized what a pure and tender being she was. Some power drew me to her. And what happy days we passed then! I—a man besmirched in lies and intrigues—became clean under her influence, felt the hateful shell dropping from me. At times I even forgot why I was in your house. It was no longer important; our amazing love was important . . . Nina, and I. . . . Then sud-denly, when everything seemed so beautiful, Veria said: 'Stop it! A Bolshevik cannot mix business with pleasure.' Veria is a skillful surgeon: he touched the most tender and unprotected spot and then twisted the knife in the wound. With one stroke he reminded me who I was. Harshly, by the roots, I had to wrench this most precious feel-ing out of my heart. I'm not made of stone . . . and my heart is not of steel; it is corroded with rust. . . . They tore me away from Nina; I threw Lida over myself. I can't look my own brother in the eyes. . . . Who am I? A man or a beast?" Pounding his fist on the table, Feodor cried out: "Answer me, Mikhail Alexeyevich—who am I? You and others like you begat us! What for? . . ."

Feodor spoke as if he were obeying somebody's orders, not of his own will. His face was twisted in torment, saturated with hate, and his voice broke: ". . . You promised us heavenly bliss—where is it? We are your despoiled heirs; we hate you. Yes, deprived of love, we can only hate. . . . Evil has become our natural element. Crime is en-couraged by the State. Veria explained the whole alphabet to me per-sonally. He said: 'The State can do anything—deceive, rob, kill—

that is not a crime. Personal passions, desires, the petty seeking after one's own happiness—these are the most serious crimes.' They demand from a person that he throw out enfeebling pity, forget morals, crush all traces of compassion.

"I wanted and attained the highest ideal of the Soviet man—a fact recognized by Stalin himself. By strength of mind I forged for myself a coat of mail of faith. However, no man knows himself to the limit. I, Feodor Novikov, am disillusioned. I am thirty-two years old and my career is my only reason for living, but that is probably an illusion, self-deception. I feel myself a pauper, a man spiritually robbed. I have found only emptiness; I am in a frightful wilderness! Right now I want to cry out to the whole world: 'Give me a reason for living, give me back the soul taken out of me by filthy hands!' I dream of a second birth so that I can find in another's kindness and a new love my lost source of life, strength, and manhood."

"And how do you expect to accomplish this?" whispered Mikhail through pale lips.

"Through the resurrection of the soul!"

Feodor caught Mikhail abruptly by the collar, drew his face close to his own, shouted in a strained voice, his eyes staring frenziedly: "Do you hear, Mikhail Alexeyevich, do you hear the frightful moaning? It's everywhere—it's in us and around us. That's the world writhing in inexpressible pain. They're tearing the soul out of the earth with the bloody forceps of hate. Surely you can see: deprived of love, mankind is becoming hardened like a far-away planet forgotten by the sun. An icy crust of enormous thickness covers the earth layer upon layer: revenge and hate, revenge and hate . . . Who will make amends for the human suffering caused by violence? What cares a child, dying at this very moment somewhere in a hungry village, what there will be later? This accursed happiness won't come in ten years, twenty years— ever!"

"You don't believe it will?"

"No!"

Panic seized Mikhail.

"Why are you speaking so frankly with me?" he asked in a shaking voice. "Aren't you afraid that I will tell your words? Maybe to this sergeant whom you send to torture me?"

"No, Mikhail Alexeyevich, you won't tell. You won't tell because there is nothing left for me but to kill you. Yes, the game is coming to an end. The stage manager has ordered me to drop the curtain.

608

. . . And so I have come . . . yes, I've come! I've come! . . . I've come to kill!" He repeated these words again and again amid jerky, barking laughter, twisting his face, rolling his eyes. Mikhail stared at him in horror. For death he was prepared, and knew that he had enough pride to meet it bravely with open eyes, without asking for mercy. But here! Here it wasn't his pride that was touched, but conscience itself. Through a dark hurricane the Director's face, distorted with hate, appeared dimly, and Gorin's heart sank in agony. It seemed to him that he was falling, falling, and there was no end.

Suddenly, as if some inner light had illuminated his whole life, he became unbearably sorry for Feodor. Not anger, not fear of him, but compassion for this man, maimed by fate, with his spiritual desolation, his sufferings, seized Gorin. And not Novikov alone, but thousands like him, a whole generation of Novikovs stood before him—they shouted, laughed in his face, their furious, arrogant masks hid the monstrous emptiness of their hearts—they stood among a heap of skulls, broken bodies, red pools of acrid-smelling blood. Chilled, shivering as if a wild wind had blown open the door on the black night of their life, Mikhail for an instant sensed their feelings, sensed and shuddered before the icy wilderness. Everything he had borne these three days: the blow, the fall, imminent death and now repentance, all dimmed before the horror of the revelation. "They all could have been good, kind people, with noble feelings, with warm hearts, but they have become monsters. Is it their fault? And if not, then whose?"

As in a delirium the overwrought Feodor saw Mikhail Gorin fall on his knees before him and whisper something heatedly and passionately. His eyes shone with a strange inspiration, sweat came out on his broad forehead, his long hair tossed about like the graying mane of a lion. Speaking confusedly, hurriedly, tensely, as if he were overcoming himself, Mikhail asked Feodor's forgiveness, all the people's forgiveness. In that short minute Gorin was able to say only a few words, but each one was born of the suffering of long years.

But Feodor did not understand him. It was as if a whip had lashed him across the face.

"You . . . you are begging me for mercy? Coward!"

Nostrils distended, eyes mad with fury, he swung and struck Mikhail in the face with his heavy fist. Mikhail fell on his side, his temple striking the radiator, and groaned. From the excruciating pain he lost consciousness for a short time.

When Mikhail came to, Feodor was standing over him, looking

straight into his wide, panic-stricken eyes. Feodor caught him by the head with both hands and bashed the back of it with terrific force against the radiator, feeling with revengeful joy how the bone crunched. Mikhail cried out. There was a rattle in his mouth, blowing out froth. The sharp smell of warm blood struck Feodor's nose; as though drunk, he beat and beat him until Mikhail became silent and his great body received his blows softly, obediently. Then Feodor crawled away—he couldn't get up: a fever shook him, his legs had grown weak. Ten feet away he stopped, staring with a blank look at Mikhail, writhing on the floor.

"So this is the end. Now I must kill myself," the thought rushed through him and left a strange sensation of emptiness in his head and chest.

Suddenly Mikhail groaned. Feodor cast a frightened look at him: Mikhail turned onto his belly, slowly and with difficulty rose on all fours; then, holding to the table leg, he began to get up. Feodor, seized with horror, was unable to move. Mikhail rose. His whole face was covered in blood; bloody bubbles oozed through his mustaches. His half-blinded eyes moved—he was looking for Feodor. He caught sight of him. Feodor shrank, froze. Mikhail, swaying as if in a strong wind, extended his right hand which was squeezed tight. Feodor, looking up at the tall and terrible figure of the writer, began to retreat from him. Mikhail stood in one spot, but it seemed to Feodor that he was pursuing him and about to catch and choke him. He was sure it was not the living Mikhail but his revengeful spirit that was standing over him.

Mikhail's bloody lips moved. With difficulty he said: "Give . . . brother . . ." And suddenly he slumped—noisily, felled like a tremendous tree. His body upset a chair; a heavy mirror crashed from the wall. He lay still, his head at Feodor's very feet. The gaping wound at the back of his head, like a wide-open mouth, cried out something terrible and inexorable. The tightly closed hand slowly relaxed and in the broad palm lay the crumpled letter, all stained in blood—the last thoughts of Mikhail Gorin.

Feodor, whining thinly, took the paper, placed it in his pocket, then rose—and staggering, left the room, which had become the frightful wilderness of death.

CHAPTER 5

THE SENTRY looked at Feodor and cowered—his chief's eyes were dead, blind. Looking around wildly, the sentry ran along the corridor, his heavy boots thudding. Soon an alarm was raised in the house. The sergeant appeared. He hurried after the sentry, buckling on his belts on the run. His look was still bold: his boots shone, the jingle of his spurs marked his steps clearly. He was going to ask Feodor with his usual shallow laugh what the trouble was but, seeing his wild look, held his peace; the little laugh stuck in his throat. Going warily around his chief, he glanced through the open door of Gorin's room, stepped back suddenly, his face pale. For a few seconds he was speechless.

"You'll answer for this! You'll answer!" he cried out at last in a weak, cowardly squeal and ran nervously around Feodor, who was standing motionless and apathetic. "I'll write a report at once . . . here is a witness . . ." The sergeant clutched the sentry by the sleeve. "You sit down and write also . . . What? You can't write? . . . Hell! All the same, you'll be a witness. I didn't know anything, didn't see anything—the instructions didn't say that the patient's skull was to be bashed in. Let him answer for it alone!" Fear for his own skin made the sergeant crazed.

Remembering something, he ran into Feodor's room. As though through a thick layer of water Feodor heard the sergeant talking on the telephone: "Yes, yes . . . this is Polikarpov. . . . The patient has been killed. . . . Of course not, not I . . . the chief. . . . Yes . . . I'll write a report; there's a witness . . ."

In the same room the sergeant began to write his report, breaking pens, splattering ink. Unable to stand it, he rushed out into the corridor every other minute, glanced at Feodor with round eyes: at his hands covered with clots of blood, at his torn shirt covered with red stains. Then he would wave his pen in despair and disappear into the room again.

The soldiers came crowding into the corridor, but on learning what was wrong they dispersed quickly one by one, silently, not looking into each other's eyes, sensing the danger of the moment. Nobody wanted to be a witness—they knew well what happens to witnesses.

The fury, which a few moments ago had possessed Feodor completely, suddenly vanished and was replaced by weakness, dejection, and a loathsome, almost convulsive feeling of fear. His whole future, all his dreams and ambitions, tumbled into a bottomless pit. In the faint-hearted whispering of the soldiers, in the hysterical outcries of the sergeant, he seemed to hear Veria's hellish voice and before his eyes floated the toadlike face, contemptuously distorted.

Stumbling across the floor, he went to his room, sat down on the bed, then fell on his back and shut his eyes tight.

The sergeant, finishing his report, hurled reproaches at him over his shoulder, complained about his own unfortunate fate, cursing bitterly. But Feodor didn't hear him. Out of the ocean of sounds one shout defined itself, grew and drowned out all the others: "Conquerors are not judged! . . . Not judged! . . . Not judged!"

And suddenly the thought that he was not a murderer but a hero lashed his heart like a whip. Before his crushed consciousness flashed, not the wall, not the firing squad, but a keen sense of hope: Yes, of course, I'm not a murderer, but a hero! . . . Committing this monstrous crime, killing the "conscience of the people," surely I did what the Politburo needs more than anything else? Stalin hated Gorin—that's obvious. Now Gorin is lying with a crushed skull in the next room—could there be more pleasant news for the dictator? . . . And Veria? . . . Wasn't he egging me on to murder by leaving me alone with the impossible task? Was that not the reason he ordered Gorin arrested, so that I would have no way out? Thus Feodor thought. But his heart refused to believe his words, writhed in the vise of fear.

An hour passed without Feodor noticing it. Suddenly he saw Drozd in the room. When did he arrive? Drozd wasn't alone. Beside him fussed a small man with the face of a rat, small black eyes, and a tremendous suitcase. The man was twitching his nose, sniffing, just like a rat in a strange place. He looked stubbornly into Feodor's eyes.

Feodor jumped off the bed, stared with horror at the ratty man. Not Drozd, but this stranger, fidgety and meddlesome, frightened him more than anything.

The sergeant drew himself up like a ramrod, handed Drozd a paper.

"What's this? Well?" Drozd demanded, and the sergeant hastened to explain:

"The report about the murder committed, Comrade Commissar of the First Rank. Allow me to report, I didn't know what was going on for the natural reason that I was sound asleep . . ." In giving his explanation the sergeant, with the readiness of a dog, brought his fingers to a nonexistent peak—his cap wasn't on his head—and pranced in one place, unable to stand still.

612

"Fool!" Drozd interrupted him. "Destroy this scrap of paper at once." He turned to Feodor: "Is he all ready?"

Feodor, not understanding what he was talking about, stood silent, swaying like a drunken man. Drozd looked him over with a surprised glance, shook his head: "Comrade Director, what's wrong with you? Your face is swollen, your eyes like a mad dog's, your nerves as unstrung as the reins of a drunken coachman—pull them up or they'll get stepped on! . . . Why are you standing there like that? Go and wash. . . . But wait, show me first."

As in a dream Feodor went with Drozd and the rat-man to Gorin's room. It seemed to him he was being led to his own death. At the threshold he stopped; he hadn't the strength to take another step. The rat-man scurried inside, bent over Gorin's body stretched out on the floor, gave a drawn-out whistle.

Stepping around the body fastidiously, Drozd went over to the window, jerked the curtains open with a tinkle of the rings—there was no reason to be afraid of the light now—stopped at the radiator, glanced at the blood on its sharp edges. He set the overturned chair in its place, pushed the splinters of the mirror under the table with his foot. Returning to Feodor, he said through his teeth: "Not exactly a neat job," and a grimace of contempt passed over his face.

In the meantime the little man had placed his suitcase on the table.

"Leave me alone," he said, and added, casting an annihilating look at Feodor: "As you see, it's a big job, I'll hardly be through by dinner time."

Drozd and Feodor returned to the next room. The confused sergeant was waiting for them. He had just burned his report; the smoke was still rising from the ash tray.

"Sergeant, bring some soap and water," Drozd ordered him. "And give instructions that the guard is not to blabber. That applies to you too," and he added scornfully: "Writer!"

The sergeant vanished. Drozd and Feodor remained alone. Drozd looked the rumpled figure of the Director over again from head to foot, and without parting his lips, laughed through his nose. Then he snickered louder. Still louder. And suddenly, unable to hold himself in longer, he burst into a peal of laughter, began to poke his finger into Feodor's chest. Amid the laughter one could distinguish only: ". . . the mental surgeon, the expert psychologist! And suddenly— the skull against the radiator! . . . Ha! Ha! Ha! . . . 'I believe in the power of the will and not in naked force' and—bang! The back of his head is split! . . . Ha—ha—ha! . . . I congratulate you!"

613

Feodor trembled.

"But remember all the circumstances!" he cried in complete despair.

"As if I had forgotten them," Drozd stopped laughing. "In general, Comrade Novikov, with all respect to you . . ." He didn't finish. The sergeant came in with a kettle and basin. When he had placed them in front of Feodor, Drozd signaled to him with his eyes to get out.

"Wash yourself, Comrade Director, and change your shirt while I call up Veria. We'll have to give him the news as soon as possible."

Feodor leaned forward. He longed to look into his future, to find out, to guess, what the simple movement of Drozd's hand in lifting the telephone receiver threatened him with.

"Give me long distance—Moscow . . ." Drozd waved a hand to Feodor: "Wash, man, wash . . . your hair too . . . Hello? Central—3-7-8-5 . . . Yes, yes . . . Petrov, is that you? . . . Drozd speaking. Connect me with the chief . . . What? . . . I know he's still in bed, but this is very important . . . extraordinary, yes."

Feodor felt that his whole life would be settled in that minute. His forehead began to burn like fire. Splashing water as quietly as possible and holding his breath, he followed every word of Drozd.

"Hello . . . Good morning, Lozo Pavlovich. Forgive me for disturbing you so early, but there's an important matter . . . The weather? . . . It's all right, sunny. I'm afraid our news is not quite sunny. . . . What? . . . Exactly. How did you guess? Amazing! . . . Yes, yes, the patient died. . . . Yes . . . yes—he . . . A heart attack? I understand . . . Exactly . . . The Director? He's all right, only . . . ," Drozd glanced with a sneer at Feodor, ". . . only he's terribly sorry about what has happened. . . . Yes, I'll tell him. Good-bye, Lozo Pavlovich . . . What? . . . Yes, the repair man is working. . . . Yes, we can depend on him. Everything's in order."

Drozd hung up the receiver. He sighed.

"Your luck's good, Director. Veria asked me to congratulate you. But if I were in his place, I'd give it to you in the neck for such a job. A drunk would have done better. . . . Oh, yes, he also asked me to remind you about some green file. What is that?" Drozd, without knowing it, had pronounced the words that left no doubt. He was silent. Feodor raised his head. Everything became different. The sun shone differently. The room was different. Drozd's face was different.

The black blood rushed out of Feodor's heart—fear had vanished.

CHAPTER 6

OVER WIDE and narrow roads to all corners of Russia rolled the news of Gorin's death. The newspaper *Pravda,* bordered in black, announced: "Yesterday at 5 o'clock in the morning, as the result of a heart attack, Mikhail Alexeyevich Gorin died." The newsboys didn't need to rasp their throats: the papers were torn out of their hands, change forgotten.

On the following day Gorin's body was brought to Moscow to the Kursk Station where, three years before, Moscow crowds had met the living Gorin enthusiastically when he arrived from abroad.

Three years . . .

Is that a long time? During their course Gorin experienced the joy of returning to his native country, the growth of hopes, their shattering, and remorse. Now he was dead and people had hurried to lower his lifeless eyelids over his open eyes, in which horror had frozen.

Three years . . .

During that time Gorin had lost his son Pavel, lost his faithful friend Cheprok, lost himself. It wasn't long since the words of the former Bishop of Rostov sounded over Pavel's open coffin:

"The days of your sorrow have ended, that your joy might become eternity." Now, over Moscow, the radio was broadcasting other, lying words: "The Soviet Government, members of the Politburo, bow their heads before the remains of a great son of the Soviet people, an implacable fighter for the cause of the party of Lenin-Stalin . . ."

Over the stone city, holding its noisy breath, passed a solemn procession. On the walls of the houses shadows of black banners fluttered mournfully. The people crowded in the lanes, squeezed along the sidewalks, removed their hats, sighed, crossed themselves. Children stood on tiptoe to see the features of the writer. But Gorin's face, sunk in sumptuous wreaths, was almost invisible.

For two days Gorin lay in state in the luxurious hall of the House of Unions. The rows of marble columns were decorated with flowers, the numerous chandeliers were hung with crepe. In front of the bier, amid mountains of wreaths, stood the guard. Beside the bier was the guard of honor: prominent members of the Party, writers, scientists. In the semidarkness a military orchestra in the choir played Chopin's Funeral March softly.

615

At noon of the first day Feodor Novikov stood at the head of the bier in the guard of honor. He wanted to decline this terrible ordeal, but Veria insisted, said curtly: "You must do it." Beside Novikov stood the writer Sholokhov; opposite them the president of the Academy of Sciences, Komarov, and the actor Cherkasov, who played the role of Ivan the Terrible in Gorin's play. Feodor could not help seeing the face of the writer. Gorin's face was calm and not disfigured by his death sufferings. The rat-man had done an excellent job. To the coarse, broad features of Mikhail Gorin purity had returned; the mysterious light of eternity surrounded his clear forehead.

An endless human stream passed by them—with downcast faces and hands twisting caps and kerchiefs. Above the incessant shuffle of feet, sighs and sobs were frequently heard. Feodor knew that the queue stretched outside along the whole of Sadovaya Street.

Suddenly the stream stopped. Into the deserted hall came Stalin, Molotov, Shcherbakov, and Veria. An officer of the NKVD hurriedly approached those standing guard and said softly: "You will be relieved; please step down."

Stalin went up the two steps to the head of the coffin slowly, stood in Novikov's place. To Feodor there was a strange symbolism in this. "I wonder if Stalin has taken the place of me, the murderer, on purpose," he thought, and a new aspect of Stalin's character appeared. When Stalin passed him, their glances met. Feodor, trying not to change the sad expression of his face, turned his eyes away; but he managed to notice that Stalin's face was impenetrable—only in the very depths of his eyes gleamed satisfaction.

Stalin and his friends stood by the bier no more than ten minutes, time enough for two photographers to take pictures. Then they departed and the stream of people moved again. Only after half an hour did a young student, a representative from Moscow University, relieve Novikov. Next day Feodor saw a large photograph on the front page of *Pravda*: Stalin at the bier of Mikhail Gorin. The face of the dictator exuded deep sorrow and distress.

CHAPTER 7

ON THE SECOND of August Mikhail Gorin was solemnly buried on Red Square. The day of the funeral was clear. The towers of the Kremlin shone in the rays of the sun. Beyond the artistic onion-shaped

616

cupolas of the Cathedral of Vassily the Blessed, the Moscow river was reflected in a blue haze. The square was packed with people and soldiers, standing shoulder to shoulder.

On the left wing of the Lenin Mausoleum stood the members of the Politburo, with Stalin at their head. Veria's small figure stuck out at the end of the solid row, his eyes and protruding ears glowed with a newly acquired happiness.

On the steps to the right of the Mausoleum the delegates from Soviet organizations swarmed. Among them was Feodor Novikov. To the left, in a fairly numerous group, stood the foreign representatives.

Luba, and Nina with her husband, Shcherbakov, could be seen on the elevation in front of the entrance to the Mausoleum.

Facing the important spectators, the regiments of the Moscow division stood drawn up in precise formation. To the left were the cadets of the Kremlin Military School.

The ashes of Mikhail Gorin were immured in the dark red walls of the Kremlin. Stalin himself, under the thunder of the farewell salute (ten salvos from a dozen guns behind the walls of the Kremlin) bore the urn to the niche. The buglers sounded the mournful melody slowly and sorrowfully. Then Molotov made a speech.

Feodor listened attentively. Like all those present, he tried to discover from the tone of the speech to what extent the Government wanted to mark Gorin's death. From the very first words it became evident that there were to be no limits.

"Next to the death of Lenin, Mikhail Gorin's death is the greatest loss to the toiling masses of the whole world . . ." said Molotov. His usually slightly hesitant speech was particularly nervous and sounded like sincere emotion.

Over the square sounded the metallically dry words: ". . . companion in arms, friend of Lenin and Stalin, founder of socialist literature, Gorin was a fiery patriot of the Soviet land, a writer passionately affirming the ideals of our Party. . . . Great and fertile was the friendship of Stalin and Gorin. This was the friendship of two Titans working on the one effort . . ."

They buried a writer, but the funeral was military. Soldiers of the NKVD held back the crowd of thousands. Everywhere were military men, everywhere dry, official, grim faces.

After Molotov's speech the ceremonial march began.

"Atten—tion! Present—arms!"

The commands resounded over the ranks, repeated dozens of times at all points on the square. The ranks of the soldiers moved, in unison

617

presented arms, and froze in their positions. Dully and dreadfully the drums beat. A shiver ran up the backs of the spectators. Under the slow and disturbing roll the regiments of the Moscow division, in steel helmets, with fixed bayonets, banners lowered toward the ground, marched past the Mausoleum with measured tread. They passed with unnaturally tense faces, with eyes bulging from zeal and fear—devoured with their glances the all-powerful group on the Mausoleum. It was obvious that not one of these armed robots was thinking about Gorin.

And the Red Square accepted this masquerade as its due. This was not the first one. Nothing could surprise it. Many events had flowed over it, many lives and deaths. How many hot heads had been raised here to giddy heights, had ruled Russia from here amidst Byzantine luxury, and then fallen in disaster, cursing their fate! Unbelievable happiness had been turned into bloody retribution; dreams of power into prayers for the safety of their lives; boisterous flush of victory and glory into the disgrace of public execution.

Feodor looked toward Luba and Nina, who, overcome with grief, were standing with the almost indecently bold Vassily Shcherbakov. Like all the other attending Party officials, Shcherbakov wore a black mourning band on his left arm. He supported Nina by her elbow. Bending toward her, he whispered something into her ear, assuming a sad expression. But it was clear that he was not adept at the game. Unable to restrain himself, he raised his head proudly every now and then and glanced over the surrounding people with a triumphant look. He took the funeral of his father-in-law as his own celebration.

Luba held herself erect and seemed calm. But her fingers clutched at her necklace as if its thin thread was choking her throat. Nina, dressed in black, attracted the attention of everybody. Her face, pale and thinner, was unusually beautiful and at the same time stern, almost wrathful. Suddenly she turned toward Feodor and her glance, full of fierce hate, hurtled over the crowd, scorched him. Feodor shuddered and turned away. He realized immediately that he had now and would always have a personal enemy—grim, implacable, eagerly awaiting an opportunity to wreak vengeance on him. As if he sought confirmation of his thoughts, he glanced at Nina later, but cautiously, stealthily. She was no longer looking at him. Yes, the same proud, beautiful, terribly pale face. But screening it with an ineffaceable shadow were the lips, drawn together tightly, and her tremendous, sunken eyes in which there was no mercy.

618

CHAPTER 8

BY ORDER of the Government the City of Rostov was renamed Gorin. Gorin's wife, Luba, received a large life pension. Several scholarships were allotted in the name of Gorin at the Moscow and Leningrad Literary Institutes. The main street in Moscow, the Sadovaya, was renamed Gorin Street. Several plants, kolkhozes, steamers, and a large park in Moscow were given the writer's name. The authorities immediately set about organizing a Gorin Museum in Moscow. For a whole week *Pravda* and every other paper in the country came out with black borders—an occurrence unknown since the death of Lenin.

And those who had made it possible for the Government to display such generosity in memory of the writer were not left without recognition. Drozd received the Order of Lenin, Novikov the title of Academician. But the announcement of these awards appeared somewhat later and in such a manner that nobody connected them with Gorin's death. Indeed, those who knew kept their knowledge to themselves.

Luba went to live in Moscow. She was drawn into the work of establishing the Gorin Museum. Nina returned with her husband to Gorin. There could be no talk about a revolt. Against the background of the exceptional recognition given to Gorin's name by the Politburo any outcry would have looked like the cry of lunatics.

CHAPTER 9

VERIA LOOKED long at Novikov before he began to talk. At last, playing with his pince-nez, Veria spoke and, as usual, obliquely.

"Academician Novikov, you and I are old acquaintances. We don't need to play hide and seek with each other. And so, Gorin took ill and died. That, of course, is a great loss. Let us, however, speak just now about the living. You fulfilled an important State mission; that is clear. But Gorin was, as the saying goes, the last of the Mohicans. For you there is no longer a field of action. I have in mind for a man of your caliber . . ."

Feodor became joyfully watchful. "Surely this isn't an end to the secret work! Can it be that at last my cherished dream will be realized and I will now be merely a scholar, not a twin?" A tempting picture of the future grew in his mind's eye: a quiet study, shelves of books, and the appeased Academician Novikov among them.

Veria, in the meantime, got up from the table, and going over to Novikov, took him by the arm.

"The fact is, we want to send you to America, to Washington," he said quietly, but to Feodor his words sounded like deafening peals of thunder. "There you will be First Secretary at our Embassy but, mainly, you will handle the agency work. There you will work not with one man, but the whole country. That, probably, will be a bit more difficult than Gorin. Well, how do you like it?"

Feodor was silent. Two unexpected emotions tore him in half: in the first place he was disappointed. Not only did he remain, as before, a twin, but he was also being deprived of a scholarly career. His heart contracted painfully. On the other hand, the rare opportunity of being abroad (he recalled how he had envied Pavel and Doctor Tsibik) pleased him. He wanted very much to see the other world: strange, unknown, and, he was sure, hostile.

Upset, excited, he could only think to ask: "But I am known as a historian, an Academician. What will the attitude in America be to my appointment in diplomatic work?"

"Their attitude?" repeated Veria. "I would say that they will be flattered. When all's said and done it's not some thin-legged diplomat who is being appointed to them, but a man with a name. That alone will inspire the Americans with faith in you. You see, abroad the word 'scholar' is synonymous with the words 'honest,' and 'open soul.' "

"I begin to understand," Novikov said ironically.

"About the work, our specialists will talk with you. They will tell you also how to conduct yourself abroad. In the meantime I have one piece of advice for you, Feodor Pavlovich: Keep your little mouth tight there. A word is silver, silence golden. Is that clear?"

"It's clear."

Veria still did not take his steady, almost probing eyes off Feodor. "Feodor Pavlovich, remember also that I know some of your failings. Yes, yes, you have them. Don't deny it. Mainly, this leaning toward psychological experiences, this actual love for them. You probably imbibed it with your mother's milk. But I see that you are yourself trying to get rid of it without outside help. That is very praiseworthy. And otherwise I would not have entrusted such work to you. . . . You know, I'll tell you frankly, if I were asked whom I would rather see in America, Drozd or you, I would say Drozd. He has no psychology."

"Then why don't you send him?" Feodor couldn't hold back.

Veria sighed.

"I can't. Unfortunately we need brains there." Veria tapped his round head with a finger. "Brains—and Drozd hasn't got a hell of a lot."

In spite of the obvious compliment Feodor was offended. "Lozo Pavlovich, if you don't trust me fully, you'd better not send me."

"But I do trust you! Of course I do. You don't understand me. I trust you on this work more than Drozd. He would chop so much wood there that one wouldn't be able to cart it away. No, I simply wanted to say that *there will come a time* when we shall send men like Drozd there. And in order to bring that time nearer, we are sending men like you. Do you understand? That time will come, believe me, Feodor Pavlovich. That time will come! Our Drozds will yet bring order there. Ah!" Veria actually clenched his little fist so that the knuckles turned white. His eyes filled with anticipation. "Hmm—yes . . ."

And again, as he often did in the presence of this little man, Feodor felt fear and revulsion. He hurried to change the subject.

"Lozo Pavlovich, I would like to visit Rostov before my departure; I have personal business there."

"Gorin," Veria corrected him and laughed. "You are behind the times, Comrade Academician. For a diplomat to lag behind the times is worse than to lose his pants. . . . Go, by all means; you have plenty of time. Only be careful not to come within sight of Nina—she'll chew you up alive. . . . Hee—hee—hee!"

CHAPTER 10

FEODOR NOVIKOV'S departure for the United States took place six months after his talk with Veria. Feodor spent most of that time in Moscow in intense preparation for his diplomatic and secret work. If previously Feodor had guessed dimly that the Soviet diplomats were engaged in espionage as well as diplomacy, he was now stunned by the extent and depth of this work. His sincere amazement gave pleasure to his instructors. "Of course, our intelligence is the best in the world," the chief of the operative section told him with pride. "The Germans have a good intelligence corps. But look what a narrow base they have: Germans. In England—Germans, in America—Germans, even in Japan—Germans! Suppose there was war tomorrow, all these Germans would be in a concentration camp the first day and the whole of the German intelligence would fly apart in soap bubbles. But with us it's different. Why? Because our base is not limited by nationalities. There is nothing broader than our base, for it is brain, ideology. Anybody can be a Soviet agent, as you have already learned: English, Italians, Eskimos, and even millionaires, the most unpredictable people in the world."

In the middle of April Feodor Novikov left Leningrad for America aboard the steamer *Veria*. He was sure that Veria had arranged that on purpose. "He wants to escort me to the very shores of the new world," he thought.

The day of sailing turned out to be dull. There was a drizzle. The Baltic Sea was all in whitecaps. The ship began to roll heavily and the passengers dispersed to their cabins. Feodor alone remained on deck. Holding onto the rail and not noticing the roll, he looked into the impenetrable shroud of rain. The steamer forged ahead, while his thoughts turned stubbornly backwards. Again and again he relived his last visit to Rostov—Gorin. He was able to escape from Moscow only just before his departure. Holding his breath, he had hurried to see his child. He didn't know even whether it was a son or a daughter. When he saw Nikolai, whom he found in the city park, waiting for somebody, he noticed a change in him at once. Nikolai's face had matured, there was an unfamiliar expression of sternness and grimness in it. Nikolai looked at him strangely, fixedly. Of course, he was thinking of that unexplainable night when Feodor, not himself, had spoken those absurd words about God, about innocent blood, about his burning heart. Feodor felt uncomfortable under his brother's gaze.

"I have something for you," he hastened to say. "A fellow asked me to give you this letter. It is addressed to Andrei Demin, the one you tried to save. But Andrei is dead and now by right, you understand by moral right, this letter belongs to you. The fellow who wrote it has also died——"

"Gorin?" asked Nikolai simply.

"Yes. But you keep that secret. Nobody else knows about the letter."

Nikolai took the letter, opened it, noticed the blood stains, frowned. "And is this blood his too?"

Feodor acknowledged this with a nod of his head and turned his eyes away, fearing that Nikolai would at once ask the most important question. But Nikolai was silent. He carefully folded the letter and put it in a side pocket.

"Well, good-bye, Feodor. I read in the papers that you're an Academician now. Will you live here or in Moscow?"

"No. I'm going abroad."

"Oh! Obviously they trust you a lot. Well, good-bye . . ." Nikolai got up from the bench.

"Wait," Feodor stopped him. "Tell me, how is the boy, Fedya?"

Nikolai answered evasively: "I don't know . . . He doesn't live with us."

Feodor flared up: "But you promised me, Nikolai, that you would take him under your care. What's the matter?"

"We found one of his relatives. Now he's with them."

"I want to see him."

Nikolai sighed. "No, you'd better not, Feodor——"

"What's wrong with you? Don't you trust me?" demanded Feodor.

"It's better not to," repeated Nikolai and added quietly, even a little sadly, "Don't bother, Feodor. You have cooled off; you know that yourself. What happened to you that night was a miracle, and miracles, as you know, don't repeat themselves."

Feodor understood. He frowned painfully.

"All right," he said, hiding his confusion with his voice. "Tell me, how is Lida? How's the baby? A boy or a girl?"

"A son, and a very good boy. Lida has called him Andrei."

"After Andrei Demin?"

"Yes."

Feodor was disturbed. "I want to see him," and, expecting a refusal, he insisted: "Yes! I want to see my child, and nobody's going to stop me."

"Maybe you'll get along without seeing him. You know Lida will hardly be glad to see you."

"Rubbish! . . . Where is she now?"

"She works in the drafting room of a plant. Nina arranged it."

"Where is that? . . . I want to see her and my son before I leave."

"Feodor," said Nikolai abruptly, "Lida and I are married."

Feodor started, lowered his head. After a minute he said hoarsely: "Of course. Why didn't I think of that? . . . I congratulate you, Nikolai."

He got up. "I didn't know, Nikolai . . . I merely wanted to see Andrei. You see, I'm going far away. You never know what may happen." He waved his hand, turned to go, and suddenly saw Lida. She was walking toward their bench with the baby in her arms. So it was for them that Nikolai was waiting here!

Lida, seeing Feodor, at once slowed her step, as if undecided whether to approach or not. She came on, looking a little confused, but no longer surprised at the meeting. Feodor bowed to her with humble reverence. She quickly threw up her head and looked at him with stern, clear eyes.

"How do you do, Feodor?"

She sat down on the bench beside Nikolai. Placing the baby on her knee, she dropped the kerchief from her head onto her shoulders. Her face was calm, but Feodor noticed that her fingers shook.

"Nikolai has already told me the news . . . that you are married. I congratulate you."

"Thank you, Feodor."

Nikolai got up. "I'll leave you together . . . Lida, I'll wait for you up there." Nikolai indicated a terrace in the park with his eyes.

"All right. I'll be with you in a minute."

Feodor and Lida were alone.

Feodor spoke first: "Lida, let me look at Andrei." Lida opened the blanket in which the baby was wrapped lightly. Feodor bent over him. He was small, blond—looked like him; he was sleeping, his lips pursed ludicrously like a little trumpet. His son. Feodor shook. His hands reached for the baby of their own accord. "Let me take him."

Lida handed Andrei to him, but he woke up and began to cry. Hurriedly Lida took him back. She said, as if recollecting an old thought: "Feodor, you're a terrible man. Whatever you touch, you destroy."

"Be merciful," he said in a despairing voice. Without answering she got up and went toward the stairway. Feodor wanted to go after her.

"Lida—a few words."

Lida turned quickly and stumbled. Feodor caught her by the elbow. She freed her arm, shook her head.

"Good-bye, Feodor," and she hurried her step.

The last time Feodor caught sight of her small figure among the trees, she was walking straight ahead, and did not look around. He lowered his head and looked long at the sand of the path where the marks of her slippers were imprinted. From somewhere far away, from the other end of the park, the radio was bringing the voice of a famous singer:

> "Tenderness, dreams of me,
> Love, an embrace.
> Your bundle of letters
> Has gone up in flames."

624

The steamer hooted anxiously. It was audible many miles away; but Feodor, who was standing on the deck, did not notice its hoarse wail.

"Tenderness, love, an embrace," sounded the words of the song in his brain: "dreams of me . . ."

"I have no friends. Never, never in all my life have I had friends, and I never will . . ." And then he thought bitterly: "And Andrei, my son, will be Nikolai's friend, but not mine."

The steamer hooted anxiously, rending the shroud of rain, the distance, the unknown . . .

CHAPTER 11

NIKOLAI, leaning on the railing, waited for Lida. He had just read Gorin's letter—his hands were shaking from agitation, his heart beat loudly. He watched from above as his wife came up the gently sloping stairway. She felt his glance, raised her head, smiled. He looked at her with a strange, surprised look. Coming up to him, she handed him the baby and asked softly: "What is it, Kolya?"

"I've just been thinking," he said with a tremble in his voice, looking straight in front of him. "Around us there is unbelievable cruelty, a terrible hurricane of hatred, icy despair. One wonders if it is worth while living. But no! In this gloom I see a bright light, an eternal star. And this light, this star—is your heart, Lida. As long as you're with me, I live. So——"

"So, we must always be together," Lida finished for him and took his arm. Looking around with shining eyes, she whispered: "What a wonderful spring! How good it is to be alive, Kolya!"

It had rained the day before, a fierce wind had blown, but today it was quiet, except for the water gurgling merrily in the ditches. Green was breaking through between the cobblestones. The earth bathed in the vapor. Steam rose from the pools and in each one floated a whole sun. There was an exultant spring hubbub in the air. From each stone, from each hillock came the cry of birds, as if the earth itself were singing. And the sun shone brightly, pouring warmth and joy over the earth and the people, who wished so much to live.

"Kolya, let's go to the Don. I'll feed Andrei there."

"Is there time? Have you had lunch already?"

"Yes, I had dinner with Mother. Let's go, let's go. For some reason

I want very much to go there now. I'm impatient to breathe the fresh air."

On the way to the river they didn't mention Feodor. Nikolai didn't even ask what his brother had said to her. He was thoughtful. Gorin's letter, lying in the pocket of his shirt, scorched his heart.

Lida was lively, happy, as if she were illumined from within. What a stranger, what an intruder Feodor had seemed to her! The meeting with him had not even upset her. The spring, her nearness to Nikolai, absorbed her completely. They climbed the bank of the river to the highest point. Cut off on three sides by the course of the Don, this hill unfolded a broad panorama. From behind came the noise of the great city with its houses, its tall factory chimneys enveloped in a hazy silver mist. In front the river bank, overgrown with bushes, ran down a steep slope, from where the lapping of waves sounded. The distance beyond the shore was the greenish-blue of spring.

Eagerly Lida absorbed the air, the golden distance, and the widely flooding Don. She was getting warmer. A glow was burning her cheeks.

"What beauty, what happiness! I can't feast my eyes enough. I even feel giddy from the fresh air, as if I were drunk," she said delightedly.

Before spreading his jacket for Lida, Nikolai took a cold meat ball, wrapped in newspaper, out of his pocket. He had got it at the students' mess. It had cost him an effort not to eat it and now he was openly proud of his will power. Lida noticed the expression of pride on his good-natured face.

"Why do you starve yourself?" she asked him reproachfully. She couldn't refuse it, say that she didn't want to eat it. Nikolai would know that wasn't true.

"Take it, take it. You need it more. You have the baby. What's the use of talking?" he protested.

"Thank you, Kolya."

"How are things at the plant?" asked Nikolai. He sat down beside the baby and began to play with him.

"There's plenty of work," sighed Lida. "We're working ten hours a shift now. I'm afraid that soon they'll shorten our lunch hour and I won't be able to come and feed Andrei. I'll have to take him to work with me and put him in the plant nursery. And will they look after him there the way Mother does?"

The boy cried. Lida smiled, rejoicing beforehand that she would have to fuss with him, with his warm little body. Wishing to prolong the pleasure, she took her time, enjoying his every movement. The child stopped crying, was gurgling something of his own, moving his little legs zealously, and stretching his hands toward her eyes, catching at her nose. A wave of tenderness touched Lida's heart, spread over her whole body.

"Look at his beauty! I used to tremble from the thought that he would be born sickly. But look at him—healthy and full of life. And what a fool I was at that time! I lost my head completely. You can beat me for that sometime, Kolya . . . Listen how he purrs. Give me your paw to kiss, little man . . ."

"Hurry and feed him. You've grown soft . . . As they say, a fine cage won't feed the bird," laughed Nikolai, uncertain himself which to admire most, the child or his wife.

Lida quickly pinned the boy up, unbuttoned her blouse, took out her full breast, and gave it to the child. The boy sucked his mother's breast, pinching it lightly with his soft little hands.

Nikolai lay on his back and, placing his hands behind his head, looked at the clouds.

"Kolya," said Lida. "Do you think there will be war soon? That's all they talk about at the plant."

"I don't know. It's hard to say. It might be soon."

"I'm afraid of war," said Lida. "I'm afraid, even though I have suffered much myself. What I dread most is that the good, kind, honest people will be killed in war, and the bad ones will be left. The bad ones are always left. . . ."

"No, Lida, I think otherwise," replied Nikolai thoughtfully. He raised himself on his elbows. His face was serious, so serious that it seemed to Lida there was something new, unfamiliar in it.

"No, I think otherwise," he repeated. "I have great faith in good people."

Nikolai sat facing the river, absorbed by the boundless space. The thoughts passing through his head seemed of such overwhelming importance that he was afraid to express them in words. He sat motionless and gazed, gazed with perplexity and effort, as if it were not the Don he saw before him, but his whole life: himself, his wife Lida, his brother Feodor . . . Was this not a dream? No, it wasn't a dream. There in front of him was the river, and he was trying to perceive his future in the spring distance. He knew that his youth had vanished as in a blue mist. He was now on a new shore, before him breath-taking space, and beyond it severe trials . . .

Holding his breath, Nikolai took Mikhail Gorin's letter out of his pocket and read it again avidly. Yes, yes, this was his path, this was where fate was calling him! Gorin understood this at the last moment of his life. Andrei Demin, whom he was addressing, had been killed. "But we are alive! I'm alive, Lida is alive, the boy Fedya is alive, and our son will live! . . . Mikhail Gorin had time to place in the right hands the truth he had found through terrible suffering." Nikolai slowly lowered the letter onto his knee and stared thoughtfully at the river.

". . . At last I understand, Andrei," the disturbing words of the letter resounded in his head, "that one must not only love the idea born in man's brain. One should and must love the man also. The most simple man is infinitely more precious than the most brilliant idea. . . . And I believe, my friend, that your truth and your happiness will bloom on earth. Violence will become a word whose meaning historians will have to explain, while freedom and justice, having thrown off forever their veil of dream, will become a beautiful reality, guarding with their purity the sacred lives of people and nations."

Nikolai imagined this happy race. The same earth on which he was standing now, but a festive one, beautiful, as it should be. No matter what might happen, it belonged to Nikolai. Yes, he would live and prove his purity, his great love for man, for this earth: for its forests, rivers, sky. Nikolai felt within him a tremendous, inexhaustible strength. In the depths of his heart burned a never-dying fire of hope for this freedom, this transformation of the Russian soil, when the chains of tyranny would no longer bind her. Could one possibly imagine the feeling that would possess the Russian people when at last they were free! The feverish thought beckoned Nikolai toward the future. He saw himself marching in the ranks of millions in the onslaught against monstrous oppression. It seemed to him that the whole world could see and hear him, Nikolai, and that from all over the world thousands, hundreds of thousands of courageous hands were extended toward him. He felt the triumph in his breast, greater than any he had ever known, merge with his dream and his hope, growing and expanding. This was true immortality. He saw himself in the present, in the distant past, and in the unfolding future. The panorama was exciting and clear. Especially precise and clear was the future.

Nikolai was not thinking of himself, nor of his own fate. He was thinking of all simple people, who yearn only for peace and simple happiness; people not without imperfections, with faults which are only redeemed by a simple and kind heart. The assurance of their future happiness he saw in their hearts, where there is and always will be, in spite of whatever trials, that love for man, love for one's neighbor, which is more powerful than all the evil schemes of tyrants. In

628

this lies the greatest strength of the simple man. He will triumph in the end and lead his race out onto the wide, bright road of freedom.

Thus thought Nikolai. But he dared not speak his thoughts aloud, fearing that with unskillful words he would distort the thoughts so precious and close to his heart. Therefore, he merely said: "The good man will remain, he will outlive everything."

Glancing at Lida, he felt suddenly that his fears were vain. Lida understood very well. She sighed.

"I hope it will be like that. Otherwise it would be useless to live."

"How like the Madonna she is," thought Nikolai. He recalled how, in the quiet of a museum, he had seen a beautiful painting: the Madonna with the Radiant Child. "Yes, all mothers are like the Madonna. She is mankind, and the Child in her arms—He is the hope of mankind."

On Lida's dark, calm face was imprinted a quiet inner joy, which shone with everlasting kindness. Nikolai felt suddenly awestruck and charmed. He wanted to say something simple, endearing, warm to Lida: to explain that through his nearness to her he felt cleansed, determined, strong, capable of only the very best . . . But he dared not break the enchantment either with word or gesture. Silently he looked at his wife. Gracefully inclining her head, Lida fed the child.

The thin white clouds parted for an instant high up in the sky. The sun shone—springlike, friendly, long wished for. Its strong caressing rays struck the three people on the hill, burned their outline in gold and fused the river in front of them.

Little Andrei tore himself away from the breast, and turning toward the sun, extended his arms to it. Then he looked into his little palms— had he caught it? Suddenly he laughed gaily.

Nikolai leaned over the child, carefully took his little hand and kissed it very solemnly, saying softly:

"Our hope, the hope of us all . . ."

The broad Don, circling the hill in a majestic curve, flowed calmly toward the ocean of time, toward the future.